THE WAR OF POWERS

THE WAR OF POWERS

Robert E. Vardeman and Victor Milán

NEW ENGLISH LIBRARY

First published in three volumes in the USA in 1980 by
Playboy Paperbacks

First NEL Paperback Edition February 1984
Reprinted May 1984
Reprinted September 1984
Reprinted December 1984

NEL Books are published by
New English Library,
Mill Road, Dunton Green,
Sevenoaks, Kent.
Editorial office: 47 Bedford Square, London WC1B 3DP

Set by P.R.G. Graphics
Printed and bound in Great Britain by
Cox & Wyman Ltd, Reading.

British Library C.I.P.

Vardeman, Robert E.
  The war of powers.
  I. Title   II. Milan, Victor
  813'.54[F]   PS3572.A/

ISBN 0–450–05661–9

—20,000   The reptilian *Zr'gsz* settle the Southern Continent and begin construction of the City in the Sky.

—3,100   Istu sent by the Dark Ones to serve the *Zr'gsz* as a reward for their devotion.

—2,300   Human migration begins.

—2,100   Athalau founded by migrants from the Islands of the Sun.

—1,700   Explorers from the Northern Continent found High Medurim.

—1,000   Tension increases between the *Zr'gsz* and the human settlers.

—31   *Zr'gsz* begin active campaign to exterminate all humans.

—3   Martyrdom of the Five Holy Ones.

0   *The War of Powers*: Unable to wipe out the human invaders, the *Zr'gsz* begin to use the powers of Istu. Most of the Southern Continent is desolated. In Athalau, Felarod raises his Hundred and summons up the World-Spirit. Forces unleashed by the struggle sink continents, tip the world on its axis (bringing Athalau into the polar region), cause a star to fall from the heavens to create the Great Crater. The *Zr'gsz* and Istu are defeated; Istu is cast into a magical sleep and imprisoned in the Sky City's foundations. Conflict costs the life of Felarod and ninety of his Hundred. Survivors exile themselves from Athalau in horror of the destruction they've brought about.

Human Era begins.

100   Trade between humans and *Zr'gsz* grows; increasing population of humans in the Sky City. Medurim begins its conquests.

979   Ensdak Aritku proclaimed first Emperor of High Medurim.

1171   Humans seize power in the Sky City. The *Zr'gsz* are expelled. Riomar shai-Gallri crowns herself queen.

2317   Series of wars between the Empire of Medurim and the City in the Sky.

2912-17	War between the Sky City and Athalau; Athalau victorious. Wars between the City and Athalau continue on and off over the next several centuries.
5143	Julanna Etuul wrests the Beryl Throne from Malva Kryn. She abolishes worship of the Dark Ones within the Sky City, concludes peace with the Empire.
5331	Invaders from the Northern Continent seize Medurim and the Sapphire Throne; barbarian accession signals fresh outbreak of civil wars.
5332	Newly-proclaimed Emperor Churdag declares war on the City in the Sky.
5340	Chafing under the oppression of the Barbarian Empire, the southern half of the Empire revolts. Athalau and the Sky City form an alliance.
5358	Tolviroth Acerte, the City of Bankers, is founded by merchants who fled the disorder in High Medurim.
5676	Collapse of the Barbarian Dynasty. The Sky City officiates over continent-wide peace.
5700	The Golden Age of the City in the Sky begins.
6900	General decline overtakes Southern Continent. The Sky City magic and influence wane. Agriculture breaks down in south and west. Glacier nears Athalau. Tolviroth Acerte rises through trade with Jorea.
7513	Battle of River Marchant, between Quincunx Federation and High Medurim, ends Imperial domination everywhere but in the northwest corner of the continent. The Southern Continent becomes the Sundered Realm.
8614	Erimenes the Ethical born. Population of Athalau in decline.
8722	Erimenes dies at 108.
8736	Birth of Ziore.
8823	Death of Ziore.
9940	Final abandonment of Athalau to encroaching glacier.
10,091	Prince Rann Etuul born to Ekrimsin the Ill-Favored, sister to Queen Derora V.
10,093	Synalon and Moriana born to Derora. As younger twin, Moriana becomes heir apparent.
10,095	Fost Longstrider born in The Teeming, slum district of High Medurim.

10,103	Teom the Decadent ascends the Sapphire Throne. Fost's parents killed in rioting over reduction in dole to cover Imperial festivities.
10,120	Jar containing the spirit of Erimenes the Ethical discovered in brothel in The Sjedd.
	Mount Omizantrim, "Throat of the Dark Ones", from whose lava the *Zr'gsz* mined the skystone for the Sky City foundations, has its worst eruption in millennia.
10,121	Fost Longstrider, now a courier of Tolviroth Acerte, is commissioned to deliver a parcel to the mage Kest-i-Mond.

BOOK ONE
The Sundered Realm

For my grandmother, Frances McEvoy, with love.
-vwm-

For Hazel Slider, who listens and cares. With all my love.
-rev-

CHAPTER ONE

'Up! Up you!'

Growling, the six dogs sorted themselves out of the heap in which they'd spent the night.

'We've a hard day's travel ahead.'

Bleary-eyed from too much wine and too little sleep, Fost Long-strider forgot the caution a courier learns to exercise with the high-strung dogs of his sled team. He kicked out and caught the newest animal, a two-year-old named Ranar, smartly in the ribs. With a snarl of rage, the dog launched itself at Fost's throat.

Fost stepped backwards, tripped on a loose legging-strap, and sat down hard in the kennel yard. Cursing, he fumbled for his dagger. It was trapped beneath him.

The breath exploded from his body as Ranar landed atop him. He threw up his arms to ward off the beast. White fangs flashed inches from his face. Dog-breath stank in his nostrils.

Then the angry dog was no longer between Fost and the overcast morning sky. He heard a heavy thump, followed by low warning growls.

The big man hauled himself to a sitting position. His two lead dogs, Wigma and black and silver Raissa, had bowled over the offending animal and now stood above it, teeth bared.

'Good dogs,' Fost called to them. 'Back Wigma, Raissa. Let him up.'

The dogs backed away from Ranar, still rumbling deep in their throats. Ranar picked himself up, slunk to a stuccoed wall and began to lick himself.

Fost knelt briefly to pat his lead dogs. They both looked sheepish. It was their responsibility to keep order among the team and though

Ranar's outburst had been a result of their master's carelessness, they felt guilty for allowing it. A courier depended on his team, particularly his lead dogs; Wigma and Raissa were two of the best.

The animals allowed themselves to be strapped into their harnesses with no further demonstration. Ranar hesitated but came when Fost called him. Fost made no further attempt to punish the dog. Wigma and Raissa had amply shown what would happen if the newcomer misbehaved again.

Fost checked the rotation of the rollers. Satisfied, he tossed a coin to a pimply-faced kennel boy who emerged from a booth by the gate and urged the dogs out of the yard and onto the road. He pushed the sled a short way to get it moving, then leaped aboard.

Southward bound toward the castle of Kest-i-Mond the Mage, Fost found sleep overtaking him. The bumping of the sled as it labored along the road hardly affected him. He'd long since developed the merchant's ability to sleep upright with his eyes open, letting the dogs shift for themselves. If anything, the rhythmic rocking of the sled brought him closer to nodding off.

Memories of Eliska drifted through his mind. *Such a lovely wench*, he thought dreamily. So passionate and comely and nakedly appreciative of what the rough-hewn courier had to offer.

The question of who had been behind the attack of the night before, in the alleyway in Samadum as he made his way to the waiting Countess Eliska ra-Marll's bedchamber, still troubled him, but he no longer suspected the lusty Eliska or her spouse. The many kingdoms and city-states of the Sundered Realm were jealous and fiercely competitive, and their rivalry often embroiled bystanders. Fost had probably been the victim of mistaken identity in some petty trade dispute.

He found himself eager to deliver his burden to Kest-i-Mond and return to Eliska's embrace. Few women could compare with the superbly endowed countess. Her eyes, her perfumed scent, her full breasts, her willing mouth and hot, probing tongue . . .

'I quite agree,' a voice said, faint and from no apparent direction.

Fost snapped awake. His hand moved to the small blade sheathed at his right hip.

'Who spoke?' he demanded.

Ahead stretched the dusty, deserted road leading off into the everlasting emptiness of the steppes. The dogs pulled steadily, showing no sign of sensing an intruder. Fost frowned. Many times he'd stayed alive only because of the sensitive noses of his lead dogs.

If they scented no one, no one was there.

The terrain on either side was bleak and barren. The rolling landscape was covered with sere, scrubby grasses dotted occasionally with gnarled brush. Ahead and to the right of the road, a copse of trees jostled the horizon. Even had the dogs' noses played them false, there was no place in voice range for a stranger to hide.

Behind, the road to Samadum reached empty. The city's outline shimmered in the heat of late-summer sun. Above drifted idle clouds, slowly burning away in the sunlight.

'I'm imagining things,' Fost said with a shrug. The sound of his own voice reassured him.

'A hazard of your calling, no doubt,' the sourceless voice said, more distinctly this time. 'A product of too many nights alone, I shouldn't wonder.'

Fost's lips drew back from his teeth. He feared no man or beast — nothing he could see. But to be addressed by invisible beings unnerved him.

'Who speaks?' he growled, fingers tightening on the hilt of his broadsword. 'Show yourself.'

'Do not be perturbed, dear boy.' The voice sounded amused. 'I certainly mean you no harm.'

'Halt! You miserable curs, *stop!*' Fost dug his heels into the soft dirt of the road. The dogs stumbled and jerked in the harnesses at the sudden stop. They snarled and snapped at each other until Wigma and his mate restored order with authoritative growls.

'Why do we stop? Is there something intriguing to do or see?'

Raissa and Wigma were regarding their master as if they feared for his sanity, as puzzled as the unseen speaker by the abrupt halt. Fost whipped forth sword and dagger, slicing empty air.

The voice chuckled. 'You're overwrought,' it declared. 'Perhaps because of your exertions with the delightful Eliska. A tasty lass, is she not?'

'Eliska? By the Dark Ones, what do you know of Eliska?'

'Really, Fost, I was there. Do you forget so soon?' The voice gave a very human sigh of pleasure. 'Such a hot-blooded young beauty. And your own performance was truly inspired!'

Fost straightened. A curious calm came over him. He knew now what he faced.

Only one thing in the Sundered Realm and the wide world beyond would speak to him thus from empty air of his nocturnal tryst with Eliska ra-Marll. It was a demon come to issue him the Hell Call. Legend had it that only Melikar the One-Armed had ever defeated a demon giving the Call, but Fost vowed to fight well and go down to damnation as befitted a man of his calling. Only the brave succeeded as couriers of the Sundered Realm, and he was the bravest of the couriers alive.

He steeled himself and waited for death.

'I'm ready, demon,' he said. 'Take me if you can.'

'Demon?' The tone of the voice wavered between pique and pleasure. 'No demon, I. Only the poor shade of one long dead.'

Clammy fingers gripped at Fost's belly. Demons were not the only spirits a man had to fear.

'I call upon the Great Ultimate for protection,' Fost said, too loudly, not really believing it would work. He'd called on the Great Ultimate before, without result. Still, a man never knew, and any ally could prove useful when dealing with the undead. 'Ust the Red Bear, Gormanka, patron of couriers: I beseech your protection against the denizens of the netherworld.'

'Such theatrics,' scoffed the disembodied voice. 'Do you truly believe in those antiquated deities? They do not exist, not a one of them. I am dead, and you can believe me. There is nothing but gray limbo, with here and there a hardier spirit clinging to the last spark of life.'

Fost had quit glaring wildly at the surrounding steppe and looked intently at the clay vessel secured to the frame of his dogsled. It was the same pot that had dangled in his pouch the night before when he fought the killers in the alley – and when he had slipped unseen into the chamber of Eliska. A suspicion formed in his mind.

He sheathed his sword. With the tip of his dagger, he touched the sealed jar. Instinct kept him from doing more. A courier never poked into the contents of things he carried, especially when he served a powerful magician.

He studied the vessel for the first time since taking possession of it. The dark red surface appeared ordinary enough, though he could make out crow-track cuneiforms when he held the jug at the proper angle to the sun. The lid, sealed with pitch within the neck of the jar, was black, slate-like rock. It was a common type of jug, of a sort often used to carry wine or other portables.

Thoughtfully, he tapped the jug with his dagger.

'Stop that!' the voice snapped. 'You've no idea the racket that makes.'

Fost jumped again. Without thinking, he cast the jug away from him with the full strength of his arms and upper back. The clay pot banged against a rock thirty paces distant.

Fost wiped sweat from his forehead. He shuddered at the thought of the breach of duty he'd just committed. Sorcerers weren't noted for their leniency. If he'd damaged that which he was supposed to safeguard, his fate would be grim, indeed. He screwed up his courage and walked across the dead grass to where the jug lay.

Its plug had come out. From the mouth of the jar issued a thick blue vapor, swirling and thickening before Fost's eyes. He blinked. A vagrant breeze scattered the mists momentarily. Then they coalesced into a thin spire rising directly from the jar.

Dancing notes of energy appeared in the center of the vapor column, almost too faint to be seen. Whirling like a miniature tornado, the mist achieved its final form. Before the startled courier stood the likeness of a man, tall and thin and aquiline of feature. It smiled at him benignly, almost beatifically.

'Who . . .?'

'I am Erimenes the Ethical.' The spirit introduced itself with a bow. 'Dead these past one thousand, three hundred ninety-nine years, but still in possession of my awesome mental powers.'

'Erimenes the Ethical?' Fost touched his jaw with a thumb. 'The name strikes a chord in my mind, but . . .'

'Lowborn and ill-educated as you are, you cannot call up the proper referents. But yes, even such as you has heard of me.' The spirit sounded pleased.

'You seem to know who I am, but the only Erimenes I can recall is an old philosopher famed for unpopular beliefs.'

'Yes,' sighed the spirit. 'I espoused a monastic philosophy entailing abstinence and the avoidance of all earthly pleasures.'

'I can see how that would be unpopular.' Some of Fost's courage was returning.

'The centuries spent in that miserable jug convinced me of the error of my tenets. Abstinence, I now feel, should be enjoyed only in moderation. And without excess there can be no moderation.' A zephyr made the figure waver. 'My time as a shade has not been wasted, my brawling young friend. No, it hasn't. You will be pleased to hear that Erimenes the Ethical now preaches nothing but

15

hedonism.'

Nothing remained of Fost's fear. He was confronted by a ghost, true, but a spirit so garrulous hardly proved a menace.

'Isn't it somewhat late to change your views? After all, you've been dead fourteen hundred years.'

'One thousand, three hundred ninety-nine,' the sage corrected. 'But yes, of course, you are right. Without corporeal being, I am nothing. It is regrettably impossible for a vaporous spirit such as myself to enjoy the pleasures of the flesh. Not directly.'

'What do you mean?' Fost asked, frowning.

'I merely point out the obvious. A shade must garner whatever sensations it requires vicariously.'

Fost realized the source of the mysterious comments last night during the height of his passion with Eliska.

'You mean you're no more than a long-dead voyeur?'

'Really, young man, that puts it so crudely.'

'How else would you put it?'

'Let us say I am interested in accumulating experience of the carnal delights in which you revel. Since I sipped not of the sweet wine of youth in life, I may now only look on as others freely quaff.'

'Do you mean,' Fost asked incredulously, 'that you're a virgin? A fourteen-century-old innocent?'

The spirit seemed to blush. 'Really, now . . .'

Fost guffawed. 'A bedroom-peeper and a virgin! A fine ghost you are, Erimenes. Erimenes the Ethical, indeed!'

The spirit sniffed and turned. Fost laughed uproariously, slapping his muscular thighs in mirth. His earlier fears of Erimenes's bodiless voice amused him now. Kest-i-Mond had gotten a bad bargain when he purchased the jar containing the philosopher's soul.

At length the big man's laughter died down and the shade turned back to face him. 'Well,' Erimenes said irritably, 'I certainly cannot expect someone like you to understand the finer points of my philosophy. Still, you are ideal for my purposes. Your undercover talents are considerable. At least, Eliska was favorably impressed. And the way you dispatched those ruffians in the street was exemplary.'

'You saw all that?' asked Fost suspiciously.

' "Saw" isn't precisely the term, but I would not wish to confuse you with the metaphysical details of how I perceive the world of the living. Suffice it to say I was witness to your exploits in battle as well as bed.'

The mist-stuff of the spirit thickened and swirled, and the faint motes of light glowed more brightly. Fost stepped back involuntarily. It took him several seconds to realize the sage was showing his excitement at the thought of killing and wenching.

'I feel we will all be better off when I deliver you to the hand of Kest-i-Mond,' he said a bit unsteadily. The spirit looked surprised and opened its mouth as if to protest. Fost swooped down on the lid of the jar, jamming it tightly back into place. The look of surprise and the pale, ascetic face beneath it faded into nothingness as the wind scattered the remnants of the ghostly body.

From inside the jar came a whining complaint. 'You didn't have to act so precipitously. I mean you no ill. I only wish to taste, to feel, to know through you the pleasures I denied myself when living.'

Ignoring him, Fost walked back to the sled and his patiently waiting dog team. He tossed the jar into the air several times and caught it. A grin spread across his face at the sounds of motion sickness that came from within.

High above, in the bright blue sky, a raven wheeled and cursed Fost Longstrider for a meddling fool. Did the courier somehow suspect the nature of his cargo? But, perhaps, the spirit in the earthenware jar would reveal nothing of its true worth to Kest-i-Mond and the raven's mistress.

The bird quaked at the thought of the sorceress in her high tower. She would not respond well when she learned that Fost knew of the existence of Kest-i-Mond's tame wraith.

Hundreds of feet below, Fost recapped the jar.

Oh, that my hearing were as keen as my sight! the bird lamented. *Then I would know what the long-strider has learned.* It wheeled and headed south.

Its sharp eyes searched the terrain for the small stone cairn that marked the campsite of its mistress's men-at-arms. The ground grew rockier, irregular stands of trees dotting the countryside. The marker was invisible from the ground, but the raven soon picked out the sparkle of the stacked quartz and pyrite stones and began to spiral downward.

With a quick beat of its wings it killed all forward momentum and alighted on the cairn. It cawed loudly. In less than a minute, a soldier appeared from a dense copse a bowshot distant.

'You have information of value?' the man demanded. A long scar ran from the corner of his eye to his jaw.

The raven croaked in irritation. Humans could be so vexing. Why would it come, if it didn't have something to impart?

'The courier is but an hour's ride hence,' it said in its thick-tongued voice. 'He carries the vessel you failed to obtain last night.'

'It was not *our* failure,' rapped the scar-faced officer. 'Those were groundlings hired by our Cloud Mistress. *We* shall not fail.'

The raven flapped its wings. 'You have not seen this man Fost. He is death incarnate to your kind. But I weary of this stilted man-speech. Go now and seize the jar for our mistress.'

The scar became a red line down the man's cheek. 'We do not take our orders from the likes of you,' he said harshly. 'For our *mistress* we shall triumph!'

The bird shook its head, smoothed the feathers of its left wing with its beak, and took to the air. Let the foolish one discover for himself how deadly his quarry could be. The raven only observed. Better to report failure, onerous as that duty was, than be the author of that failure.

The sled rolled smoothly along the road. Since the days of the Empire, upkeep of the Realm Roads had been spotty, but the surface of this highway lay smooth and even. That was one thing that could be said for Count Marll. He attended well to his roads, if not his wife.

The jar in which the spirit of Erimenes the Ethical dwelt was strapped once more to the sled frame. Remembering the way the ghost spied on him the night before, Fost had been tempted to let him bounce around in his jug until he wished he'd never achieved ghostly immortality. The dictates of his profession overrode temptation. Best to deliver his charge to Kest-i-Mond in the best possible condition. An angered enchanter is no one's friend.

He pondered what the departed sage had told him. From his youth in High Medurim he recalled snatches of conversation heard when he stood and begged for bread outside the great seminaries. Erimenes's philosophy of self-denial had enjoyed its popularity – if that was the word – ten centuries ago, but there were still a number of monastic cults devoted to following the master's doctrine.

If only the faithful could see their master now!

Personally, Fost couldn't see the appeal of self-denial. To do without tall flagons of ale and warm, full-bodied wantons to share his bed . . . he shook his head. Life was too soon ended by Hell Call. He

18

could understand the philosophical arguments in favor of abstinence – but look where it had gotten Erimenes. He had life everlasting, true, but it was a pallid thing, lifeless. If that was the cost of immortality, Fost would gladly face the demon of death when the time came and die with a last defiant shout of laughter.

A high-pitched yelp of warning from Wigma made him alert. Instinctively Fost looked over the traces and harnesses, but they were free of fouling. Raissa echoed her mate's cry. Fost looked back along the road.

A cold lump settled in his belly. Dust grew in a spume from the highway perhaps a mile behind: half a dozen men on battle mounts, if Fost read the dust aright. They could not be couriers in such numbers. And travelers rarely ventured so near the Southern Wastes this near the end of the warm season. That left one possibility.

Brigands.

'On! Faster!' Fost cracked his short lash, urging the dogs to greater speed. He had no hope of outracing the long-limbed battle mounts, fierce dogs so huge they could carry an armored man, but he could try to tire them. His sled team had far more endurance than the war-dogs.

The cloud came closer as the minutes raced past. His dogs breathed hard, straining in their harnesses. His pursuers' mounts were fresh, while his animals were wearied from a half-day's travel. His tactic had failed.

He thrust a heavy boot into the dirt and slewed the sled off the road toward a clump of *ofilos* trees. On rough terrain the riding-dogs could still outrun his team, but amid the heavy-limbed trees and tangled brush he'd have a better chance of eluding his enemies.

'What in the name of the Three and Twenty Wise Ones of Agift are you doing?' cried Erimenes from his jug.

'We've got bandits after us. I'm trying to evade them.'

'Bandits?' Erimenes said hopefully. 'Why not stop and fight them? You're a skilled bladesman. That was a splendid display in that alley last night. Such strength and skill, such shedding of blood.'

'Have done. To fight one man or even three, yes, that may be done. But six or more? Sheer madness!'

'But you cannot flee! That would be cowardice.'

'Easy for you to say, who are already dead.'

'I long to experience the death-throes of your enemies, the triumph on your face as you slay them. Do you not feel a special thrill when you spill a foeman's lifeblood? Don't your sexual desires soar?'

Fost tried to ignore the spirit as he guided his sled between the silent trees. Here in the forest the dog riders couldn't all attack him at once. He drove the team at a desperate speed.

The headlong race ended when a dog put a foot down on a small animal's burrow. The impetus of the sled snapped its leg. The dog fell with a howl and instantly entangled the harness.

Cursing, Fost leaped off the runners and bent over the animal. 'You have been a faithful companion, Balf,' he said, stroking the matted fur of the dog's head. 'Now I must do my duty to you.'

A quick slash of his knife sent blood gushing from the dog's throat to soak into the thick carpet of dead leaves. Fost hacked the corpse free of the harness and yelled to the dogs to move on. He jumped onto the sled as it went by, leaving Balf silent and cooling on the ground.

With a gap in the team, Raissa and Wigma redoubled their efforts, and the other dogs followed their example. The sled flew across the slippery, leaf-clad earth. The dogs' panting, the thumping of their paws, the creak and jingle of the harness resounded in Fost's ears.

'Fight!' Erimenes shouted. 'Do you wish the rogues to think you craven? Surely you are able to defend yourself.'

It was no time to explain the realities of mortal combat to the sage.

'Don't you want to be delivered to Kest-i-Mond?' Fost asked, glancing over his shoulder. No pursuers were in sight. 'If you're taken, he'll have to pay a handsome price for your return. He'll be wroth with you.'

'Pah! Kest-i-Mond wants knowledge only I possess. He will pay any amount for me, and little count the cost. And what matters it to me who claims ownership of the pot in which I reside? What is the nature of ownership? Is it purely possession or . . .'

'No philosophizing on my time, you long-winded wraith. I'm racing for my life. Yours is forfeit these fourteen centuries past.'

The sage started to speak. The sled hurtled toward a shaggy-barked tree overhanging the game path the dogs followed. Fost seized the jar and leaped upward to grab a stout limb. With the philosopher's jug in the crook of his arm, he pulled himself up and began climbing the thick, rough trunk.

Green leaves closed about him like a shroud. The footfalls of the war-dogs pounded closer. Fost tried to make himself as small as possible.

'I never believed a man of your abilities would be capable of such a thing,' Erimenes cried. 'Running from a noble fight!'

'Quiet,' Fost snarled. 'What's noble about being sliced to bloody ribbons? Be silent, you fugitive from Hell Call!'

The first of the dog riders passed under the tree in hot pursuit of the unoccupied sled. The rider was small and wiry with a black cloak thrown over his deep purple tunic. No mere bandits, these. Fost's heart hammered as he recognized the curved blades and wicked barbed darts of soldiers of the Sky City, the City of Sorcery.

What could the men of the Soaring World want with him?

The only answer was the spirit in the jar. For all his bloodthirstiness and pomposity, Erimenes possessed some secret of enormous value. And these men, like the unknown assailants of the night before, were ready to kill Fost to get it.

He counted four riders. As the fifth went by Erimenes sang out, 'Here, up in the tree! Dolts. A plague on you, look up!'

Fost hit the pot with the base of his fist. 'What's wrong with you?' he demanded, sotto voce. 'He would have heard, had he been nearer.'

'I'm trying to save you from years of mental anguish. You should fight. If you don't, your honor will be tarnished. You will turn in your bed at night, worrying that you are less a man.'

'In the tree!' came shouts from below. A sixth rider had heard the dead philosopher discoursing. Fost reacted reflexively. He dropped onto the broad back of the battlemount, landing behind its rider and slitting the man's throat with a quick slash of his dagger.

Fost hurled the dying man from the saddle and tried to get his feet into the stirrups. The dog snarled and reared. Fost fell to the ground. He stood up, only to fall flat once more to avoid a sword cut from the fifth rider.

'See?' Erimenes's jug had fallen and rolled against the bole of the tree, where it lay unharmed. 'You *are* capable of heroic feats when properly motivated. You'll thank me for this in the future, mark my words!'

'I'd mark your back with a whip, had you a back,' Fost panted. His sword sang from its sheath to engage the dog rider's blade. Broad paws slapped the ground as the others returned. The need for speed took precedence over chivalry; Fost cut the brindled war-dog's legs from beneath it. It fell, frothing and snapping at its injured limbs, and spilling the rider.

21

Fost gave the soldier Hell Call, then snatched up the dead man's blade and threw it at a charging blue-black dog. It sank to the hilt in the muscular chest. Bloody foam burst from the dog's nostrils. It toppled, pinning its rider's leg.

Fost had no time to finish off the trapped man. The others rushed the courier. He ducked beneath a silver arc of hard-swung steel and drove his left hand upward. The short, broad blade found a sheath in the man's armpit. The dog rider gave a hoarse cry as his mount carried him past, wrenching the dagger from Fost's grip. The dead man tumbled onto the fallen leaves.

'Dismount. Take him afoot.' The scar-faced leader reined in and dropped lithely to the ground. His scimitar twitched in the air like a living thing. 'From the sides.'

If the two Sky City men were dismayed at three of their number dying and another being disabled in such short order, they didn't show it. They advanced on Fost, the officer on the left and the other swinging wide to take him in a pincers' movement. Fost smiled grimly. He was determined to kill one before the other fed a foot of cold steel into his back.

'A superb fight! Blood everywhere. A wonderment!' applauded Erimenes. Fost had a momentary urge to smash the jar before he fell. He didn't know if that would dissipate the ancient philosopher's life-essence and send him at last to Hell, but it would be an interesting experiment.

There was no time for that. The black and purple clad riders pushed him back, trying to herd him away from the spirit's jar. They wanted to insure he couldn't pick it up and flee.

Flight was the last thing on Fost Longstrider's mind. He let his opponents set their pattern of slow, inexorable advance. Then he lunged, flicked a scimitar aside with a forehand stroke, and cut through the right-hand man's throat just below the point of his neatly trimmed beard.

As the rider sank down, drowning in his own blood, the officer closed with a tigerish rush. Fost whirled, throwing up his sword in a blocking motion. The movement came too late. The officer brought his blade down in a slash that laid Fost's back open and sent pain shattering through his spine. Fost gasped and fell forward on his face. He lay, unmoving.

The scar-faced officer raised his hand to slay the injured courier. Then he lowered it and turned away. The discipline of the Sky City

22

was absolute. He had been ordered to return to the Floating Realm with the jar and the spirit it contained without delay, and that was what he would do. Secondary concerns, such as the pleasure of gutting the lowborn scum who had slain four of his men, were luxuries he would not allow himself.

Besides, the courier was as good as dead.

The dog rider walked to the tree and plucked up the jug. 'You, my black-cloaked friend,' Erimenes said brightly, 'are an excellent swordsman. Tell me, do you enjoy a good tumble in the hay with a handsome wench from time to time? If so, we might become fast friends.'

The officer stared down at the jar, perplexed. He had been warned the spirit might prove uncooperative. Nothing had prepared him for Erimenes trying to beg friendship from him.

He was still puzzling over this turn of events when Fost killed him.

The courier came from behind to drive a dagger, taken from a fallen rider, to the crossguard, just below the man's left shoulder blade. The officer gave a small, surprised cough and collapsed bonelessly.

Fost dropped to his knees and shook the jug as hard as he could.

'You double-dealing spirit,' he choked. 'Why did you betray me? If you weren't already dead, I'd kill you. I call on the Great Ultimate to give you life so that I may reave it away from you again!'

He continued shaking the jug until Erimenes began to cry. The sound of such pure sorrow made Fost stop.

'I am so weak,' moaned Erimenes. 'This is why I espoused self-denial. I could never cope with temptation. You – you're so strong. You can live life to the utmost!'

He sniffed, and, even half-dead and dazed, Fost wondered how he accomplished it without benefit of a nose.

'I, however, I have become addicted to sensation since my death. I cannot control myself. I must see blood. I must see carousal. I must. I *must!*'

Fost dropped the jar. Dizziness assailed him. He was torn between disgust and pity for the tormented, treacherous spirit. He tore the Sky City officer's cloak into strips and staunched the flow of blood, then sat weakly with his back to a tree. He was as weak as a day-old pup, but he lived. In spite of the odds, he lived.

A moan of pain came to his ears. He looked around. Not far away lay the last dog rider, still pinned under the corpse of his massive dog.

Now, Fost thought, *we'll learn why Erimenes is so valuable.*

Unable to walk, he crawled on hands and knees. He was not halfway to the pinned man when a raven flapped down from the sky and landed on a black-cloaked shoulder. With a quick peck the bird took out the rider's eye.

A shriek rent the forest. Another peck plucked out the other eye. A final stab of the iron-hard beak penetrated the soldier's brain. He convulsed once and fell back dead.

The raven swiveled its head as only a bird can, and regarded Fost with such malevolence that the courier's nausea turned to fear. It spread its wings and rose skyward. Fost watched it vanish through the canopy of leaves. Then he fainted.

The raven's mood was bleak as it winged westward. The Sky City was its nest, but it was also the lair in which its mistress's wrath crouched like a waiting beast. The sorceress would be infuriated that six more of her men, Sky City troops this time, not mere hirelings, had failed at such a simple task. The raven wished another could deliver this message.

It beat stolidly through the air. No war-eagles soared out to meet it. Evidently the enchantress had given orders none was to hinder her winged messenger. It flew in an arched window. The brass perch felt cold and alien in its talons. It cawed once at the sight of its mistress sitting in stony silence with an indigo cloak wrapped about her, awaiting its report.

'Mistress of the Clouds,' it said, 'I bring bad tidings.'

'Failure.' The word rang coldly, a death sentence.

'Y-yes, Mistress. Fost Longstrider still lives, still possesses the jar you seek.'

'My soldiers.'

'All dead. Exalted One.'

'Just as well. All would have forfeited their lives for permitting this lowborn lout to best them.' She crossed her arms beneath full breasts and began to pace the length of the small room. 'Fools, all of them! fools! So simple a chore, and yet it ends in abject failure.'

'Do not despair, Mistress,' the raven said nervously. 'This Fost is mighty, indeed, and cunning.'

She turned on him, fury brewing in her eyes. 'Enough! How *dare* you suggest this scum can flout the power of the Sky City? *How dare you?* Prince Rann expended forty men learning of that amulet and he who carries the knowledge of it locked in a vaporous brain. I personally conjured for long hours with potent scrying spells to find the jug – and my powers are second to none in the Sundered Realm, including my dear sister. And you *dare* tell me a simple courier is able to thwart my plans? Must I leave the Sky City in this hour of unrest? Must I personally do everything? I dare not leave Rann to deal with such things. So I make plans, simple, easily obeyed plans, and they go awry. *My* plans! How dare you fail!' she screeched.

The raven looked into her cobalt eyes and saw its own death. Wings exploded from its sides as it tried to flee out the open window. The enchantress was quicker. A slim finger pointed. Lambent light shot forth and bathed the creature in flames. It screamed once, piteously, and fell to the floor, a cindered, lifeless ruin.

The stench of burned flesh and feathers filled the chamber. The woman turned and stalked from the room without a glance at the body of her messenger. There were plans to be made for securing the shade of Erimenes the Ethical.

And plans, as well, for the death of the man called Fost.

CHAPTER TWO

A wasp woke Fost by daubing mud in his ear to build its nest. He lay still, too weak to fend off the creature. It soon departed to seek more mud and he rolled over.

Dizziness twisted his senses. He clutched at the moist ground. The spinning died, and Fost struggled to sit up. Agony shot through his back. He reached around to touch the sword cut and regretted it immediately. Pain drew a red curtain before his eyes. 'By the Great Ultimate, I hope never to feel this miserable again,' he groaned.

'It was your own fault,' said Erimenes primly. 'Had you fought like a man from the first, you would have won handily. But no, you had to hide and make them ferret you out. You got what you deserved.'

'Demons rend you and your sanctimonious prattle,' Fost said. 'I only want to sleep.' He curled up once more, savoring the warmth of sunlight on his aching body. He slept more easily this time.

The setting sun roused him. As he pulled himself upright, he found his hunger nearly as sharp as the pain of his wound. He whistled shrilly, then listened. In a moment he heard the creak of leather and the clinking of the sled's harness. Raissa and Wigma trotted from the dense wood to lap eagerly at his face.

'Old friends,' he said shakily, ruffling their fur. 'Thank you for standing by me.'

He dragged himself to his feet and rummaged through the food-stuffs packed in the sled. He drew out cloth-wrapped rations. From the dogs' bloodied muzzles, he knew they'd found food for themselves, and indeed there was meat aplenty, harvested by their master's sword arm. He shrugged and began to eat.

The five surviving sled dogs curled up and went to sleep. Finishing his food and washing it down with a swig of brackish water from his canteen, Fost decided a nap was an excellent idea. He lay down between the two lead dogs. While they couldn't compare with Eliska as bedmates, he was in no shape for the activities he'd engaged in with her.

Erimenes's voice woke him with the dawn. 'Slugabed! Will you sleep away your life? Get up, man, go forth and live. Experience the rich world around you. Fight, love, hate, do something!'

'Demon in a jar,' Fost said deliberately, 'listen well to me. If ever again you speak unbidden, I'll seek out the deepest crevasse on this planet and heave you into it. I don't have to listen to your words. You're an item to be delivered, and nothing more.'

'Nay, I am far more! Locked in my memory is a secret which would cause brother to kill brother, daughter to slay mother. It is – '

'I don't want to hear about it,' Fost said with finality. He stood and flexed his powerful limbs. As the blood flowed back into them, he felt the full burden of his weakness. It'd be days before he regained his former strength. Still, with six foes wormfood at his feet, he felt the headiness of victory. The castle of Kest-i-Mond lay but half a day from here. With luck and a bit of caution, he should make it with no further interference. Once at the keep he'd be free of Erimenes and his endless carping. And perhaps then the men of the Sky City would leave him alone.

He dozed intermittently as his dogs paced out the miles. Occasionally he would stir himself to look for signs of pursuit. None showed in sky or steppe.

The sun had dipped past the zenith when Kest-i-Mond's huge stone and wood pile came into view on the horizon. Fost felt a weight lift from his shoulders.

'Erimenes, old spirit,' he said, feeling almost comradely toward the long-dead philosopher, 'yonder is your new home. Imposing, isn't it?'

'Utilitarian in the extreme, much as I might have advocated in years past. I should much prefer something more appropriate to my new outlook. A brothel, perhaps.'

'I understand Kest-i-Mond lives simply, relishing his privacy. A powerful mage such as he might be able to conjure up something to amuse you.'

'In exchange for the secrets I can divulge, he ought to,' the spirit said sourly.

27

'I don't want to hear about your secrets,' Fost said. 'Only trouble comes to those who learn a sorcerer's dark knowledge.'

'Rubbish! There is no dark knowledge, merely the layout of a city. It lies in the polar regions. My home,' sighed the spirit, 'lost these many centuries. Eaten by a glacier.'

'Come, Erimenes, a city eaten by a glacier? You make sport of me. A glacier is nothing but a mountainous sheet of ice. I've seen many with my own eyes.'

'This is a special glacier,' Erimenes said in conspiratorial tones. 'Within it lies Athalau, once a mighty city but now dead. A great queen entombed in ice.'

'Very poetic.' Fost sniffed the air. '*Faugh*. Something reeks. Don't enchanters lime their cesspools?'

'That's sulfur, from the great volcanic activity in this area. The keep was raised in my time by a wizard who kept frequent commerce with the spirits of the inner earth. Perhaps he built it over a fumarole.'

'How does Kest-i-Mond stomach the stench?'

'Perhaps he's grown accustomed to it. Now, in Athalau . . .'

Fost shut him out. Let the sage reminisce over his lost city. All Fost wanted was to be rid of him and this treacherous assignment. In the future he would accept only simple tasks. Let the daring venture forth to deal with assassins and eye-plucking ravens.

As for him, he'd take Kest-i-Mond's money and idle away the rest of Count Marll's religious retreat with Eliska. His thoughts turned to the hot-blooded countess. He smiled. And the sage droned on.

The walls of the castle loomed so high they seemed about to topple and crush man and sled alike. In height the keep resembled the buildings of High Medurim, where Fost had been born, but it was angular and ungainly, with none of the baroque ornamentation popular in the old imperial capital. The odor of brimstone hung in the air, and that, too, brought back Fost's childhood. The sewers ran uncovered in the poorer parts of Medurim.

'End of the line for you, old spirit,' he said cheerfully. 'I cannot say it's been pleasant knowing you.'

'Nonsense. Without me your honor would have been besmirched beyond redemption.'

'Never in all my days have I known such a tiresome – hey! What's this?' He jerked the sled to a halt.

'What disturbs you now?' the sage enquired peevishly.

28

'The doors are ajar.' Fost bent and picked up Erimenes's jug. 'Strange. I heard Kest-i-Mond was more cautious.'

He walked to the bronze doors and peered inside. Nothing stirred. He rapped his knuckles on the doors. They rang hollowly.

'Fost Longstrider, courier, to see the master of the castle.'

There was no answer. Fost pushed through the doorway, and the foyer beyond echoed his footsteps. He stood and listened. His heartbeat was the only sound he heard.

He was angry with himself. The philosopher's constant goading had unsettled him. He was growing too wary, almost timid, for fear the bloody-minded shade would precipitate him into another catastrophe. It was only reasonable to feel leery of invading a magician's castle. Still, Fost had legitimate business within the walls of Kest-i-Mond's keep. And an enchanter was just a man, after all, his spells no more than peculiarly potent weapons.

'This vestibule is of no interest to me,' Erimenes said. The sound of his dry voice booming in the hallway caused Fost to jump. 'Why don't you move on, there's a good lad.'

'Shut up! You scared me half out of my wits.'

'Little enough to do.'

The corridor veered right. Fost followed it, trying to stifle a growing sense of unease. At least he detected no trace of the unpleasant sulfur stink in here. The mage must have spells to freshen his air.

Fost halted. His hand dropped to his sword hilt.

'You sense danger!' Erimenes cried. 'What is it? Why do you fondle your weapon?'

'Hold your tongue, if you have one.' Fost pointed at the floor in front of them. A dark green marble pedestal lay tumbled on its side, the white bust of a human head in fragments around it. 'That's what troubles me.'

'Debris. What does it signify?'

'Kest-i-Mond has a fetish for order. It's legendary. In Kara-Est a courtier rearranged the mage's personal effects when he was there on a visit, as a jest. Kest-i-Mond was not amused; he turned the man into a pig. Those who'd enjoyed sexual congress with him were likewise transformed. Fifteen ladies and three squires ended their days in the duke's swineyards.'

'A touching story, I'm sure,' Erimenes said, 'but how does this relate to our dawdling in this dreary hallway?'

'The door open, a statue shattered on the floor — these indicate the

29

presence of uninvited guests, do they not?' He drew his sword.

He scanned the passageway. A dark stain on the stone floor caught his eye. He bent over and sniffed it.

'Blood. And not human blood, if I'm any judge. The color's wrong, as well as the smell.'

The purplish pool trailed off into an alcove. Fost stepped cautiously to the archway. His gorge rose.

Had the thing in the alcove been alive Fost would have cried out in fear. But it was very, very dead. It had been a monster with the head and upper torso of a muscular man, slimming to the hips to become the thick, powerful tail of a giant serpent. Its throat was disfigured by huge blue weals like the marks of misshapen fingers. Its head had been pounded to a pulp.

'Intruder? Or guardian of the way?' Sweat beaded on Fost's forehead, though the corridor was cool. 'Either way, someone's been here before us. Finding Kest-i-Mond takes on greater urgency.'

'Why trouble Kest-i-Mond?' Erimenes asked. 'He's obviously lost interest in me, or he would have been at the door to take delivery. Let's return to Kara-Est. It's a seaport; you can guide me through the fleshpots. They should prove quite diverting.'

'Are you never quiet? I accepted the commission to deliver you to Kest-i-Mond. I cannot forsake my duty as a courier, nor am I about to risk an enchanter's wrath merely to satisfy your unnatural tastes. I've been damned near cut in two trying to deliver you, and deliver you I will!'

'I hardly expected to find you so humorless.'

'If I don't find Kest-i-Mond, I don't get paid. I want *some* recompense for getting cut up and having to listen to you. I . . .' He stopped. His ears had sensed a slight rustling, as if a mouse hastened to its hole. He knew no mage would permit mice to run freely in his keep; a simple spell banished vermin. A flicker of movement in another archway snared his gaze.

A reverberating roar filled the corridor. A great, shaggy, reeking form rushed from the arch and blundered into a wall. Bellowing with rage, it turned toward the courier.

Fost backpedaled, keeping his sword at *garde*. Facing him was an immense apelike creature with long fur striped brown and black. The upper half of its face was blackened ruin, as though blasted by a bolt of lightning. Below its blinded eyes and flat, wide-nostriled nose was a loose-lipped mouth filled with vicious yellow fangs.

Blind as it was, Fost knew better than to underestimate it. The monster flexed long-fingered hands and uttered a shrill cry like a cross between a child weeping and a man dying in agony. The stench of the thing put to shame a charnel pit.

'What manner of being is this?' Erimenes asked brightly.

'Blind, you idiot!' hissed Fost. 'Don't let it hear you.'

'Don't be absurd. You can defeat an injured creature. Go on, attack!'

The ape-thing's lips curled into a ghastly semblance of a human smile. Its expression sickened Fost more than its smell or its devastated face. Something in that half-human visage mocked his very existence.

He ducked and dodged as a hairy arm groped for him. The creature grinned and slobbered down its chinless face. It struck out again, and Fost saw gobbets of flesh adhering to its filthy nails.

'Really, Fost, this is ridiculous. At least let me out so I may have a decent view. You jostle me around so!'

Fost refused to be goaded into answering. The spirit wanted him to speak and draw the monster's attention. Instead he lay the jar on the floor and slid it away from him. The creature's head turned to track the sound of the pot skittering across the floor and hitting the wall. It let out a gloating growl and leaped.

Fost side-stepped and jammed his sword into its side. Bone deflected his blade, but the sword bit deep. He twisted it and yanked it free. The creature spun on him with an angry snarl.

He slashed at the arms that reached out to draw him into a crushing embrace. The cuts bled fiercely, but seemed to trouble the monster no more than the huge, flowing wound in its side. Fost found himself driven to the wall.

'Enough of this,' he mumbled. He took a quick step and lunged. His blade sank into the hairy beast.

The beast wrenched the sword from his grasp by turning, the blade half embedded in its chest.

'By the Dark Ones, will nothing stop you?' Fost threw himself to the side. The hallway resounded as the monster slammed into the wall. Had Fost not moved, the bulk would have smashed him.

He whipped dagger from sheath, more out of habit than because he thought it would do any good. The impact of the ape-creature against the wall had driven Fost's sword to the hilt in its chest, yet the monster seemed stronger than ever.

'The being, you will be pleased to know, lacks something of substance from this dimension,' Erimenes said from his jar.

'What are you talking about? "Lacks substance"? It nearly pulverized me!'

'It appears to hail from a reality paralleling our own. The fabric of space has been altered to draw it hence, and the transition is only partially complete.'

Fost shook his head. His outburst had drawn the apparition's attention to him again. It approached slowly, grinning hideously.

He felt no surprise that the beast was not of this world; an earthly being would have died a dozen times from the wounds it had received.

Fost shouted, then dove past the monster and beneath the sweep of its talon-tipped arms. His dagger bit the back of the monster's knee in passing. It staggered.

By the time it recovered, Fost had rolled to his feet and was pounding down the corridor.

'Coward!' Erimenes's voice rang at his heels. 'Stand up and fight like a man!'

Up the hall a door yawned. Fost dashed through, shutting it behind him. A massive key jutted from the lock, and he turned it with a sigh of relief. The door was stout oak and surely enough to withstand even the monster in the corridor.

'Fool!' Erimenes's scornful voice echoed faintly through the wood. 'That won't do you any good. Fight, fight I say!' Fost closed his eyes and leaned wearily against the door.

And almost died. The monster's arm came *through* the wood and dealt him a vicious blow to the side of the head. He sprawled headlong. Stunned, he turned over to see the ape-thing emerging slowly from the heavy door.

'Great Ultimate!' Fost scrambled to his feet. His head reeled from the blow but he had no time to waste. He forced himself into a brain-jarring run even as the monster came fully into the room.

He jerked open another door and fled through it. Blundering and crashing, the monster followed. He led it a nightmare chase through a maze of rooms and corridors. Slammed doors held it up for scant seconds and, though blinded, it trailed the courier with the grim facility of a tracking dog.

The air grew hot. At first Fost thought it was due to his own exertion, but when he leaned against a wall to catch his breath the stone was hot to the touch.

Perhaps I'm near the scullery, he thought. *There may be a way out of this hellhole.*

He came to another door. It refused to open. From behind sounded a clatter as the monster overturned a table in its haste to reach him.

'Let me in!' Fost shouted, hammering frantically on the wood. 'Gods below, open up!' The door stayed shut.

He heard toenails scraping stone. The door shuddered as he threw his weight into it. Long disused, the door had warped until it jammed the frame.

Fost heard the gurgling breath of the monster. He expected at any instant to feel those foul hands close around his neck. He yelled in desperation and lunged full force against the door.

It burst inward in a shower of splinters. Fost lurched into the room beyond. A nose-searing reek of sulfur hit him in the face, and he pulled up short.

It was well that he did so. He looked down. A hand's-breadth beyond the toes of his boots was . . . nothing. A vast black pit gaped before him. Sulfurous fumes issued from it in thin yellow wisps.

He flattened himself against the warm, sulfur-encrusted wall beside the door.

'Come on,' he called. 'Come and take me, you bastard spawn of hell!'

With a roar of triumph, the monster charged the open door. Straight over the brink it ran. For a moment it hung in air, clawing at nothingness. Then it dropped from view.

Fost pushed off from the wall and peered down the hole. The fumes made his eyes water. The ape-thing had been swallowed by unfathomable darkness. The courier heard it bellow once, faintly; then all was silence.

He backed from the room, bent double, gripping his knees and gasping for breath. Gradually his strength returned as the aftermath of fear subsided. When he felt more fully himself he went in search of Erimenes. After his experience with the monster, even the company of the verbose spirit was preferable to being alone.

'I'm bored with searching,' the philosopher said. 'Let's go and find some winsome lass. Perhaps two. Yes, a fine idea, as fine as I've ever had.'

'I'm glad you think so,' Fost said dourly.

33

'Really, Fost, your unimaginative adherence to what you conceive to be your duty astonishes me. If Kest-i-Mond cared whether he got me or not, he wouldn't have left us to wander about this drafty castle all afternoon.'

'Dark Ones! I must find the enchanter, if only to learn why I am beset by brigands, dog riders and devils,' Fost said. 'Besides, how do you know it's drafty? You're in a jar.'

'True. But it looks drafty.'

They came to a stairway. Fost peered up. 'I think I've found something,' he said.

A corpse, charred to a grotesque doll, sprawled on the steps before them.

'This changes things!' Erimenes' voice rang with delight.'Press on, press on. Battle may await us.'.

'Grand.' Despite his own misgivings, Fost mounted the stair. He kicked the burned body from his path. An arm broke off and tumbled down the stairs. He shuddered and started to climb.

A sword lay on the steps. It was short, curved, keen of blade – Sky City workmanship. Fost sighed. He picked up the weapon, tried unsuccessfully to fit it into his straight scabbard, and finally thrust it under his belt. His own sword had gone into the pit with the monster, still embedded in its breast.

He climbed higher up the spiraling stairs. They came upon another body, burned into two pieces. Further up was a corpse with its head and shoulders cindered beyond recognition. The bodies wore the all-too-familiar purple and black of the City in the Sky.

In all, Fost passed seven corpses on the long, tiring climb. Whatever magic Kest-i-Mond had employed had proven effective. He recalled the way the ape-creature's face had been blasted and burned.

But not effective enough, he thought.

Erimenes seemed to read his thoughts. 'Fortunate for you that you came across the fumarole. If Kest-i-Mond's death-bolts did not slay the monster, you would have faired poorly. Still,' he sighed, 'what a fight it would have been.'

A brass-bound door barred their way. Fost kicked it open, his sword held ready. The light of the setting sun streamed in a narrow window to fill the cramped room like melted butter.

'Your purchaser has indeed lost interest in you,' Fost said. 'He has heard the Hell Call.' At his feet lay the body of a frail, ancient man.

34

His head had been turned around on his neck so that his dead face studied the uncaring stone floor of the chamber.

The room had been ransacked. There seemed to have been no purpose to the destruction. Benches were overturned, phials of powder and noxious-looking fluids smashed, a case of scrolls cast down, all at random. Fost surmised that the monster, blinded by the sorcerer's spell, had broken Kest-i-Mond's neck and vented its rage by tearing the room apart.

'*Now* can we repair to some house of ill repute?' Erimenes asked. 'I desperately need some diversion after the dreary miles we've walked today.'

'*I* walked,' Fost corrected. 'You rode.' He examined the relics scattered about the floor. Against one wall lay a tiny ebony bowl chased with silver and covered with a tight-fitting lid. He set the jug down and picked up the bowl.

'Fair workmanship,' he appraised. 'Not much in the way of booty, but it looks to be all the payment I'll get for this ill-starred mission.' Nearby sat a chalice of similar design. He put the bowl in his pouch and picked up the cup. On impulse he pulled off its cover and watched in surprise as it filled with clear liquid. He took a sip, spat it out. 'Water. Tepid water, at that.'

'Kest-i-Mond appears to have had simple tastes,' Erimenes said. 'I prefer being with you. A brawling young buck who knows how to *live*. Yours is the kind of existence I want to observe.'

Fost prodded the corpse with his toe. It rolled onto its side. A scrap of parchment stuck out from under the body. He bent to retrieve it.

'What have we here? A map, a sorcerous one, by the look of it.' His brow wrinkled as he studied it, tracing outlines that glowed with a silvery light of their own. 'Old High Imperial script – this must be a thousand years old! The steppes, Samadum, the Southern Waste and the . . . what's this? Here, south of the Rampart Mountains in the polar lands. What does this circle mean?'

Erimenes did not reply.

Fost eyed the jug suspiciously. 'Speak to me. You've filled the air with words whenever it was least convenient for me. This map is old and valuable. Any artifact with scriptsilver is worth a king's ransom. What does it mean?'

'I know nothing that would be of use to you.'

'You're lying. You started before to tell me of your home in the south. "Eaten by a glacier," you said. There's a glacier marked within this circle. Is this why Kest-i-Mond wanted you?'

'Yes.'

'You're reticent for once. What secret does this city hold? Why do armed men and a netherworld demon invade a mage's castle? Why do minions of the City in the Clouds seek to wrest you from me at every turn?'

'How should I know this? I weary of your tirade. Let's go to Kara-Est or perhaps back to Samadum. Eliska awaits you – and the white circle of her arms . . .'

'Enough! Speak to me of your long lost home. Tell me about Athalau.'

'You remember the name. I commend you.'

'And I'll give you to the Josselit monks if you don't tell me what you would have revealed to Kest-i-Mond.'

'The Josselit monks?' quavered the spirit.

'You know of them, surely? Their philosophy is one you would heartily have approved of – once. Abstinence from the pleasures of the flesh and the company of women. Bread soaked in salt water and a cup of vinegar each day.' Fost grinned hugely. 'Of course, once a year, or so I'm told, they cease their prayers and indulge in a solemn play about the Five Holy Ones. You'll love the Josselits, Erimenes.'

'Your jest is in extremely poor taste.'

'It's no jest. Keep your secret to yourself and soon there will be none but monks to hear it.'

There was a lengthy pause which Fost enjoyed immoderately. He knew the spirit would answer. Nor did Erimenes disappoint him.

'Very well,' sniffed the shade. 'I never realized the streak of cruelty ran so deep in you. In Athalau is the Amulet of Living Flame. Evidently, Kest-i-Mond desired it.'

'Go on. What is this amulet, that so many have died because of it?'

'A mere bagatelle. Clasp it to your breast as you die and you escape Hell Call.'

'You live again?'

'Exactly. The sorcerers of my city know many potent magics. Before the glacier consumed Athalau, the Amulet of Living Flame was considered a mere trinket compared to others, which imparted great wisdom, the power over fickle chance, overwhelming inner peace. Only the sorcerers of the Sky City have ever approached the skill of the Athalar.'

'To cheat death.' The words tasted good.

'Yes, that is what the amulet does, if it hasn't crumbled to dust.'

'What!'

'The power tends to drain from a magical item as the centuries pass,' Erimenes explained. Then, as if in afterthought, he added, 'I doubt this to be the case with the Amulet of Living Flame, though.'

'Why not?' Fost almost shouted.

'Its property of storing the life-energy to restore it to the deceased individual, of course. Some little accrues to the amulet with each usage. Such would tend to preserve it, or so I suspect. These sorcerous matters are outside my province, you understand.'

'To defy the demon of death,' Fost breathed. 'That is a trinket worth fighting for.'

'Indeed,' said Erimenes carefully. 'Many a glorious battle would have to be fought to obtain the amulet. All in vain, of course. Even with the map to guide you, you could never get into the city in the glacier. And if you could, you'd never locate the amulet.' He paused. 'Not unless you took me along to guide you, as Kest-i-Mond intended to do.'

'Done!' cried Fost. He caught up the jar and ran down the stairs, his feet barely touching the cold stone. A treasure more precious than any hoard of gold or jewels beckoned him southward.

The promise of everlasting life.

CHAPTER THREE

A breeze shifted the limbs of the big tree. Fost snorted in his sleep and half-turned. His perch threatened constantly to dump him to the ground fifteen feet below, and the hard, rough limbs could never be mistaken for a sumptuous down mattress. Despite the draft and the discomfort, he slept soundly.

Once, in the forests above Port Zorn, a magician's apprentice had hidden his scent under a sorcerous potion and crept past Fost's dogs to within reach of the courier's bedroll. Fost never knew what sense it was that saved him. Abruptly, his eyes had opened and the apprentice's sickle was a yellow arc of moonlight curving for his throat. He had rolled to the side, the curving blade cutting deep into the soft ground. Fost had slain his attacker with an underhand dagger toss.

Since then he'd learned to sleep with a healthy distance between him and the ground. Raissa and Wigma were incomparable watchdogs, but even they could be fooled.

He moved his shoulders in an unconscious effort to ease the pressure of the wood against his body. He hadn't lashed himself in place, since that tended to cut off circulation. His scimitar hung in easy reach, looped through his belt and dangling from a nearby branch.

As he slept, he smiled. His dreams were pleasant. Eternal life! The very thought that he alone in all the world had the secret of the Amulet of Living Flame's location filled him with a warm, triumphant glow. He'd not been paid gold for his troubles in delivering Erimenes to Kest-i-Mond, but a vastly greater reward seemed just within his reach.

Old Gabric, his employer back in Tolviroth Acerte, would take a dim view of one of his couriers going absent without leave. And

38

whenever delivery of an item was impossible there were explanations to be made and forms to be filled out in bushel-loads. The Dark Ones take Gabric and his forms in triplicate! With the amulet in his hand, Fost would be as far above such concerns as the Sky City was above the plains and mountains of the Quincunx.

Eternal life! He would outlive his enemies, gain new ones, outlive them as well. Sword cuts would heal instantly; disease could gain no hold in his body; he could quaff poison like clear spring water. He would be unkillable.

His ambition did not stop there. Since his days as a starving guttersnipe in High Medurim, he'd had a hunger for knowledge. He'd taught himself to read ancient scripts and spent what time he could poring over books of science, history, philosophy. But the hard life of a courier left little time for such luxury. With the amulet, though, all of time would be his. He could exhaust the Imperial Library at Medurim with its nine million volumes; he could become the most knowledgeable man in creation. With his strong sword arm and his mind filled with a hundred centuries of human wisdom, he might become invincible.

He sighed. A dream fluttered pleasantly across his mind: himself and a voluptuous black-haired woman whiling away eternity in an unending assortment of passionate embraces. He'd drunk the luke-warm water from Kest-i-Mond's magic chalice, and filled his belly with the equally uninspired gruel provided by the covered bowl. Now his sleeping mind turned its attention to other appetites not so recently sated.

Then he was sailing through the air.

For a second he thought his erotic dream had taken flight. The ground slammed him with the impact of a falling building, and his breath exploded from his lungs.

His still-healing body felt as if it had cracked all over like a pot dropped on pavement. He lay still while bright lights danced behind his eyes. He fought to regain his wind. Vivid in his mind was the impression of strong fingers grasping his ankle the instant before he fell.

'What's this?' Fost heard Erimenes ask. The intruder's clothes rasped bark as he slithered down the tree, carrying Fost's pouch with the philosopher inside. 'Most foully done! How can you have a rousing duel with one of the participants stunned?'

The intruder hissed at the spirit to be silent. Fost got his arms under him and pushed his leaden body off the ground, intending to snare the thief's leg as he went by. A footfall thumped the springy earth nearby and lightning split Fost's skull as the thief smashed his sword's pommel down on top of Fost's head.

Fost's face slammed into the dirt, but he didn't lose consciousness. He lay for a moment while his stomach performed remarkable acrobatics, then he raised his head, spat out a mouthful of dead leaves and shouted, 'Up, Wigma, Raissa! Rend him!'

Silence greeted his shout, broken only by the muffled steps receding into the forest. It occurred to him that his sled team had given no warning of the intruder's presence. He climbed to his feet, an effort akin to scaling a sheer cliff with large rocks strapped on his shoulders. For a few ragged breaths he stood propped against the tree, fighting nausea and the blinding ache in his head. Then he dragged himself laboriously up the trunk to retrieve his sword.

The climb almost exhausted him, but he had no intention of going after an armed opponent with no weapon of his own, particularly in this condition. Nor did he intend to allow the sneak-thief to escape with Erimenes. He wouldn't be robbed this easily of eternal life!

He set out in the direction his attacker had taken. He passed his dogs, who lay still, dead or unconscious. That explained why no warning had been given.

It was far too dark and the tumult in his skull too great to allow him to track the thief by sight. But the crack on the head seemed to have sharpened his hearing. Pausing, he heard a faint, familiar voice say, 'Wait. How can you run so cravenly? You're as bad as Fost!'

Despite the agony in his head, he smiled grimly. For once the spirit's garrulity was disrupting someone else's plans. It was high time.

He followed the sound. True to form, Erimenes was berating the thief at the top of his voice, demanding that he turn back immediately and fight like a man. Fost hoped the thief would be distracted by the spirit's chatter. In his condition, he only had one strong sword thrust in him, and he had to make it good.

He all but stumbled across the thief. The cloaked form had stopped in a clearing and stood shaking the pouch with both hands, cursing at Erimenes to be silent. Though his sword felt as if it weighed ten pounds, he swung it with a strength fed by fury.

The scimitar's tip brushed a low-hanging branch. The thief spun away like a cat. A straight, slim length of steel quickly glittered in the

40

starlight between the dark-cloaked form and Fost.

'Pah!' jeered Erimenes. The thief had dropped him to the ground. 'Such a clumsy stroke. My new friend will show you skill!'

Perhaps he would. It was taking most of Fost's strength simply to stay upright. The confident, easy stance of his foe spoke eloquently of skill. Fost couldn't afford to fence with the thief.

The intruder twitched his sword tip in tight patterns in the air, hoping to snare Fost's gaze. The instant that happened the blade would straighten and stab unerringly through the courier's heart. Fost took a deep breath. Roaring, he beat aside the thief's sword and charged like a rogue bull. His body collided with the other as the straight sword cartwheeled away. A shrill, angry squeal burst from his foe's lips and shocked him like a blow.

His opponent was a woman!

They went down in a tangle. 'Ground-born lover of goats,' the woman snarled. 'I'll cut out your liver and make you eat it!'

She eeled out of Fost's arms and tried to get up. His own sword had fallen from his grip. He seized her by a trim calf and brought her crashing down. Erimenes was cheering wildly, but for which of the combatants Fost couldn't tell.

He pulled himself atop the woman, striving to pin her with his greater weight. Her fingers clawed his face and sought his eyes. She brought her knee up hard. He stopped it with his thigh but in turning slipped off the writhing body.

They rolled over and over, grappling, struggling for advantage. Fost was weakened by wounds and his fall, and the woman's muscles seemed wound from steel wire. But Fost had grown up on the hard tenement streets of High Medurim and he knew all there was to know about vicious rough-and-tumble fighting before he reached his teens. After a few panting, cursing minutes, he lay on top of her limp body, trapping her arms at her sides.

For a time he could do no more than lie there. His head reeled and his body cried from a hundred aches. His face was thrust into the juncture of shoulder and slim neck, his cheekbone pressed to hers to keep her from turning to bite him.

Gradually his sickness subsided. He became aware of the scent of her crisp, clean hair. He'd been sleeping with his tunic unlaced, and the garment had been partially torn from him in the fight. Disturbingly, his bare chest touched equally bare feminine skin.

Without moving he swiveled his eyes down. The clasp holding her cloak had opened and ripped a long rent in her jerkin. Her breasts were naked, crushed by his powerful chest, and he realized in amazement that the nipples were poking solidly into his flesh.

He raised himself slowly, ready for the explosion of movement as the thief tried to escape. It didn't come. She lay on her back, eyes closed, lips slightly parted and her full, pale breasts rising and falling with the cadence of her breathing. The nipples were dark as wine, and jutted from coppery aureoles shaped like dainty mushroom caps.

He closed his eyes. Unbidden came the memory of his dream of Eliska. This wench was as lovely as Eliska, and the fullness of her body covered an athletic musculature the pampered countess could never hope to match. It had been long days since Eliska, too long.

His eyes opened. She was looking up at him. The night turned her eyes dark, but they showed green highlights in the shimmer of the stars. Her tongue peeked out to make a slow circuit of her lips.

She squirmed an arm free. He let her. She lifted a long, fine hand and stroked her forefinger down his chest.

'You are strong,' she said. Her voice was husky, but not from exertion or fear.

Erimenes spoke. Fost never heard him. The thunder of blood in his ears drowned out all sound as his arms circled the woman and his face came down to hers. She raised her head and boldly met his kiss. Her tongue slipped into his mouth. His twined around it slowly. He felt the sweet tension build in the luscious body trapped beneath his own. Pain and tiredness ebbed magically from him.

He laid a scarred hand on her breast. Her hands slid down on his hips to tug at his breeches. He tilted his body off hers, squeezing the nipple between his fingers as he did so, and tangled his other hand in her golden hair. He sighed as her cool fingers wrapped around his manhood and tugged it free.

She undulated beneath him as she shed her own breeches. Their mouths were still joined, lip to lip, tongue to tongue, salivas mingling to form a heady wine. Her legs spread in wanton invitation; the sweet perfume of her body enveloped him like an aphrodisiac. He lowered his body slowly, gliding into her.

Her arms twined around his neck. She drew him down into a long, fervent kiss as he thrust into her with a steady pressure. She drew in a breath, tightening herself around him like a noose. His fingers kneaded her back. Fire flared within his loins. He withdrew, meaning to make his lovemaking slow, but her hips began a slow circle and he lost all control.

Her fingers ran up and down his back like tiny animals as he plunged in and out. The thief dug her heels into the carpet of the mulch and gave him back stroke for stroke. Her femininity devoured him as Fost ground his chest against her breast.

Air hissed from the woman's flared nostrils; his breath came in short gasps. Her fingers clawed in frenzy at his back. Pain shot through him as they raked the half-healed sword cut, but then his body yielded to the sweet insistency. The pain went far away as ecstasy washed over his senses.

Passion subsided into gentle langour. Their mutual death grip eased. Fost let himself slip to one side. Her eyes were half-lidded, her breath warm on his lips. She kissed him once, unspeaking, and closed her eyes.

Weariness settled over him like a blanket. He had pushed himself too far, too fast. Though instinct told him he should be shaking the woman roughly awake to demand who she was and why she wanted to steal the spirit in the jug, nature demanded rest. Instead he slept, his arms locking the slender woman tightly to him.

His arms still circled the naked woman when he awoke. The forest was dark, but overhead birds sang to greet the first pink touches of dawn in the eastern sky. The cool air washed his body, which seemed one enormous ache. The lovemaking of the night before had been hot delight, but it hadn't done his physical condition any good.

His stomach grumbled. His mouth felt as if it were stuffed full of cotton. Food and drink seemed in order. He disentangled his arms from the sleeping woman, and winced at the twinge from the slash the Sky City officer had given him across the back a few days ago. She opened her eyes. They were brilliant green in the growing light.

'Good morning,' she said. Her voice was low and lilting, and despite her sleepy muzziness it was as lovely a voice as he'd ever heard. He smiled and brushed black hair from his eyes.

'And to you, thief.'

'Moriana,' she said. 'My name is Moriana.' She sat up and thrust her arms high above her head and stretched like a waking cat. He watched the play of muscles across her belly and up her arms. The sun's first rays turned the thatch between her thighs to fine golden wire. She arched her back, conscious of his attention. Her high breasts flattened against her ribs.

Fost tried to sort out his feelings toward the lovely thief. She'd come within a hair of robbing him of his chance at eternal life – she'd come close to robbing him of life, period. But then it somehow changed, and she had been feigning nothing when she gave herself to him. It was as if each had seen in the other some sign that changed them from adversaries into something he could not yet put a name to.

'Moriana, then,' he said, yawning widely. 'What made you decide to take up thievery?' He fumbled in the satchel containing Erimenes and found the bowl and chalice he'd taken from Kest-i-Mond's study. He casually tossed aside Erimenes's jar, hoping to infuriate the spirit. The shade remained uncharacteristically quiet.

Moriana shrugged. It made her bare breasts wobble enticingly. 'I've little enough choice,' she said sadly. 'I've neither money nor birth. If I want to survive out on the road, I must steal, or . . .' Her words trailed off, but the meaning was clear.

Fost said nothing. The state of his belly occupied his full attention. He drank from the cup, looked across its rim at Moriana, and handed it to her. She sipped as he uncovered the bowl and began to spoon up gruel. The thin porridge was as unappetizing as ever, but it was preferable to the cavernous emptiness in his stomach.

'Thank you,' she said, setting down the cup. She tilted her head and smiled. 'Whomever you may be.'

'Fost Longstrider. I'm a courier.' He spooned up the last of the gruel, made a face at the tasteless stuff as the bowl began to fill again. He proferred it. 'Do you want some? There's plenty, the gods know.'

'It's most courteous of you to try to feed someone who tried to rob you.'

He laughed. 'You did rather more than that. Besides, I'm curious. How did you manage to get past my dogs?'

'A small potion I stole from an enchanter. The dogs sniff it and turn drowsy. It's harmless.' She paused, lowering her eyes. 'I'm sorry.'

'You mean you're sorry I caught you?'

'No.' Her eyes avoided his. 'You're a generous man. You shouldn't be plagued by petty thieves like me.'

He stared at her. She seemed to mean it. She made him strangely uncomfortable. He tried to pass it off with a joke. 'Petty? Pretty, I'd say.' He lifted her chin and smiled.

She reached out, hesitant, and touched his cheek. The slender fingers were supple-skinned and pale. The only trace of marring hardness was the characteristic swordsman's callus on the side of her

44

right index finger.

'You're kind. I knew you were when you didn't kill me last night. Lesser men would have.'

'Lesser men would have missed a beautiful experience.'

'So would I.'

It was his turn to avoid her gaze. 'You still haven't told me how you come to be out cutting purses and drugging defenseless animals. Eat, and give me the story. I'd think one so beautiful would long since have married into lands and wealth beyond the dreams of a poor man like myself.'

Her cheeks flushed slightly. Modesty? Or something else? It was hard to reconcile her almost virginal attitude with her bold wantonness of the night before. And she made no effort to cover her nakedness.

She was a complex creature, this Moriana. He would enjoy unraveling the mysteries surrounding her.

She hesitated, cast away fastidiousness, and dipped Fost's spoon into the replenished gruel before speaking.

'I cannot marry. I've no dowry; my family is dead, all but my poor sister.' She wrinkled her nose at the gruel. 'Awful stuff.'

'But all we have. And anyway, it's free. Go on.'

'It's not a pleasant story. My father was an artisan in Brev, in the Great Quincunx. An evil sorceror lusted after my mother. She spurned him; my father challenged the mage to a duel. The mage slew him. When he came for my mother, she killed herself. So he took my sister, my poor lovely sister, and forced her to be his mistress instead. I was gone from the house, at the market. When I returned . . .' Her voice broke. She dropped the bowl and buried her face against Fost's shoulder, sobbing bitterly. He cradled her, stroking her long hair and murmuring soothing words to her. He found himself once more acutely aware of what an armful she was. His hand dropped to her behind. He snatched it away. This was no time for such things.

She pushed herself away and looked up at him with red-rimmed eyes. 'Help me forget,' she said. 'Help me.'

He reached around her and carefully packed bowl and chalice back into the satchel. The tip of one breast lay against his chest. He felt the ripeness of the nipple prodding him. With a deft flick of his wrist, he dropped Erimenes's jug into the satchel and drew the string tight.

45

Her hands gripped his biceps, shaking. He lay back, pulling her down on top of him. Their bodies twisted demandingly, reliving the passions of the previous night. Afterwards, he slept.

When he awoke, he was alone.

CHAPTER FOUR

Fost rolled over. Pain stabbed through his muscles. He stretched, groaning as joints cracked. Feeling better, he pulled himself to a sitting position and looked around.

The grass around him was crushed, testimony to the passion of the night before. The satchel containing Erimenes, the chalice, and the bowl was gone. Fost lifted a corner of Moriana's cloak, on which he'd lain with the pretty thief. It was fine maroon velvet lined with gold silk. Expensive, plainly – but no compensation for the loss of eternal life.

Fost rose, stood a moment amid the clean, sweet odor of grass, trees and morning, holding the cloak by a corner. He sighed. He leaned down, collected his sword and stuffed it back through his belt, and set off through the woods toward the tree in which he'd begun last night.

A breeze gently sighed through the trees, and a yellow bird sang from a high limb. Retracing the steps that had led him to the clearing was simple. In his fury and urgency, he'd trampled through the undergrowth like a hornbull in rut.

The heavy cloak draped over his shoulder, he came to the tree from which his empty scabbard still dangled. His sled wasn't far away. He saw no sign of his dogs. Putting fingers to lips, he whistled once, twice, three times. In a few minutes, Raissa and Wigma trotted from the brush side by side, followed by the other three surviving animals of his team. The black and silver bitch licked bloody froth from her muzzle. She had been hunting again.

'Do you know that devious witch almost had me believing her?' he asked his dogs as he knelt to strap them into the harness. 'Even after the clumsy way she tried to lie to me.' He shook his head. 'Telling me of the simple life of toil she'd led when her fingers were as soft as a maiden's bottom save for a swordsman's callus. And that fanciful tale about a magician stealing away her sister — ha! An insult to my intelligence.'

Finished, he straightened. His dogs looked up, their ears cocked to listen attentively, as though comprehending their master's words. 'Nor was her accent that of Brev-town; and had she been raised in the streets, she'd have known enough of rough-and-tumble fighting to make me unfit for our later bout of wrestling.' He sighed again. 'Still, she's a rare one. It'll be a pity to wring her devious neck when I've run her down.'

He climbed onto the runners and clucked the dogs into motion. Steering skillfully among the trees, he brought the sled to the clearing where he'd awakened. Halting, he hunkered down by the lead dogs and held the rich cloak to their noses. They sniffed obediently and pulled the sled forward to the patch of flattened grass. Ranar wailed with excitement as he recognized the thief's odor. Wigma snarled savagely at the youngster, then lifted a hurt, puzzled face to his master. The older, wiser dog had already discovered that the scent they were to follow couldn't be detected outside the circle of the crushed grass.

Fost laughed. 'So she covered her personal scent with a canthrip. As I knew she would; that spell's hedge-magic, and I suspect she knows enchantments far more esoteric.' He reached into a pocket of his tunic, produced a mottled handkerchief redolent of soured gruel, and held it down for his dogs to smell.

Raissa yipped, strained a few feet away from the slept-on patch, smelled the ground, and yipped again. Her mate echoed the call. They'd found a trail.

'On!' Fost shouted, jumping back onto the runners. 'Track down that deceitful bitch, and we'll see why she's so eager for Erimenes's company.' Guided by their sensitive noses, the team set off through the forest at a brisk trot.

Life in High Medurim's slums allowed few fools to survive to manhood. Short of killing the lovely thief on the spot, there'd been no way to keep her from stealing the jug from him out there in the woods. Hard as he was, Fost had been unable to bring himself to murder Moriana in cold blood, especially after making love to her. He had, however, jammed the lid of the ever-filled gruel bowl open a hair's-breadth with a small pill of pitch, and then made sure the bowl

48

went into the sack with the philosopher's jug. The gruel would seep out in a slow stream, soak through the satchel, and leave a trail for the dogs to sniff along in pursuit.

Confident that the spell hiding her own smell would keep Fost's dogs from tracking her, she was making no other effort to escape detection. He would catch her soon. He wanted to know how she'd learned of Erimenes's existence – and what she intended to do with the sage. He had a suspicion her motives were different from his straightforward lust for immortality.

Immortality. The word rang in his brain. He would not forsake it, no matter the cause for which Moriana might desire the Amulet of Living Flame. The conviction was growing in him that he'd have to kill the beautiful adventuress to get her to give up the idea of using the amulet for her own ends. The thought troubled him strangely.

Whistling to cover his odd discomfort, he rode the sled northward among rapidly thinning trees.

North of the Southern Steppe, the land began to turn green and undulate into high-grassed prairie. Rivers ran down from the mountains of the Thail, branching into myriad streams and brooks. At the bottom of a shallow depression, one such stream had widened into a clear pool. Moriana sat on her haunches beside it, staring intently into the water.

Her gold hair hung to her shoulders, stirred now and then by a stray breeze wandering down the course of the stream. She was clad in a brown leather jerkin over a long-sleeved orange blouse of light fabric. Her breeches were tan, as were the high-topped riding boots she wore. Her slender fingers caressed her chin.

'Why do we tarry here?' demanded Erimenes peevishly from his jug. The satchel that held his jar was slung from the saddle of a tall, supple-limbed riding dog, which stood lapping from the stream. Moriana had hidden the nervous gray beast on the fringe of the woods when she'd gone after the courier the night before. 'I find little of interest in this stream – unless you plan to disrobe and bathe your lovely limbs, of course.'

Moriana ignored him, frowning. For the third time, her lips formed the scrying spell. Once more the waters turned to milk, bubbling, frothing, swirling in meaningless patterns.

'Istu!' she cursed. The water cleared as she stood. Something was blocking her vision, preventing her from looking into the Sky City.

And that something could only be the magic of her sister Synalon.

The bitch grows more powerful every day, she thought somberly. *How long before she makes her bid for power? While our mother lives, she dares little. But Derora is old, and not even we of the Etuul blood are immortal. If only my powers were stronger!*

But Moriana knew that wishing for the Sky City to augment her magical powers was futile. She needed the forces imprisoned in the solid bedrock of the city to perform her more complicated spells. And even then, her powers were not those of her sister. And they never would be, for she refused to make the dark pacts required to attain such magical stature.

Anxious to feel the power surging through her again, she hurried to the top of a knoll overlooking the pool.

'Ah, how can one so beautiful be in such a foul mood on this fine morn?' Erimenes called after her. 'I'm much in your debt, you know. Your nocturnal sporting filled me with fresh experiences to savor. The glibness of your lies was most illuminating.'

Fost. She thought of the big man's touch, gentle with the gentleness of great power held in check. He was no ignorant swineherd, never. It had hurt her in the soft dawnlight to steal from him his hope of immortality, just as it hurt her that she'd never see him again. He was a big man in more ways than one, hurling himself at life with boundless energy. She could even love such a man, perhaps.

Maybe when the fight is done, and I hold the throne of the Sky City.

No, best not to think of that. There was no knowing whether she'd survive her confrontation with Synalon. Or whether she'd want to. If she failed, she'd certainly be given over to her cousin, Prince Rann. The thought made her shiver despite the growing heat. Not even the spies she had so carefully insinuated into the ranks of Rann's most trusted men could save her.

She brushed her hair back and gazed out over the land. To the north and west rose mountains, blue and indistinct with distance, in which nestled the city of Thailot. East lay many-towered Brev. Between them fell the line of the Quincunx, unmarked save for stone docks for the hot-air balloons that plied between earth and city. Following its age-old random pattern, the Sky City had recently come south from Bilsinx and veered through half of a right angle over Brev, floating ponderously and inexorably toward Thailot. From there it might swerve inwards to Bilsinx again, or head northwest to Wirix near the border of the shrunken Empire. Not even the sorceress who ruled in the city could predict its course.

Moriana looked west. Over the horizon hung a thunderhead, ominous and dark. But no mere water vapor comprised that cloud. It was stone, black stone, the ground-spurning stone of the City in the Sky.

Desperately, Moriana longed to make straight south for the Rampart Mountains and glacier-swallowed Athalau. But she dared not stay away from the city that long. She had to return and shore up her position against the wiles of her sister. She was a few breaths younger than her dark twin, and therefore heir to the throne by law. Yet legalities would matter little if Synalon could seize power and completely crush her sister's backers. If Moriana let that happen by making the long detour to the south, not even the amulet would be of much help. With the full powers of the city to draw on, both sorcerous and military, Synalon would be virtually invulnerable.

Moriana shook her head to clear it. She *had* to have the Amulet of Living Flame. Her spies had reported to her immediately when Rann had learned of its existence. Some had died rather than warn Rann and Synalon that they had spoken. She couldn't betray their memory. And with the amulet, she could conjure and not heed agonizing death spells hurled against her. Moriana smiled grimly. She knew spells not even Synalon could ward against. But time! How those spells took time to cast! The amulet would free her from worry while she cast them.

Immortality, yes, but protection against Synalon's most deadly spells and Rann's elite bird riders rested foremost in Moriana's mind. Synalon's invulnerability would crumble, and the city would be rid of a potential tyrant.

'What?' Erimenes said as she went to her mount. 'You're not going to bathe your magnificent body? Do not your garments cling and chafe with sweat? Come, come, girl, think of your health. A little cool water, a little warm sunlight on your naked, luscious breasts . . .'

'Be silent or I'll stuff your pot with mud.'

'That would do nothing to me,' the spirit grumbled. But he was silent for a long time thereafter.

'Ouch!' shouted the black-and-purple garbed soldier, flapping his hand in the air. 'Istu piss on you, imp. You've bit me!'

From the iron box that held the fire elemental came a popping sound. 'You laugh at me,' the soldier snarled, clutching the wrist of his singed hand. He grabbed a dripping waterskin and brandished it. 'I'll teach you, hell-wight. I'll drench the filthy life from you, Dark Ones eat me if I don't!'

'Rann will eat you if you do,' said one of his comrades. The words fought their way through laughter. 'Fire sprites are expensive. If the dockmaster must send down another balloon to retrieve us, and the palace mages have to conjure a fresh elemental into the bargain, you'll not gain favor in the sky.'

The third soldier tamed his mirth with great effort. 'We'd be lucky if we weren't left for the brigands to slay,' he said, and his eyes grew serious, darting this way and that in his fat, bearded face. 'I hear that all new elementals brought into being are being requisitioned by the Monitors. Orders of the prince himself.'

'Spreading rumors, are you,' said the second man, scowling fiercely. 'You know the penalty for that, don't you, Flyer Tugbat?'

The fat man snapped to attention, quivering so enthusiastically that his jowls shook like bladders.

'Y-yes, corporal.'

Lying among bushes on a low hilltop overlooking the dock Erimenes chirped with glee.

'A disciplinary infraction! Mayhap the corporal will feed the fat one to the salamander, inch by inch.'

'Be quiet, you,' Moriana hissed, savagely swatting at the jug. 'If you give me away, I'll conjure a fire sprite into your jug.'

A gurgling emerged from the clay pot. Moriana doubted that being closeted with a salamander would do the ghost any permanent harm, but the prospect clearly didn't cheer him. She filed the threat away for future use and thought hard about her problem.

These comic worms were common troopers, not bird riders. No bird-riding Guardsman would have been so foolish as to try to feed green wood to the fire elemental. The sprites were capricious enough without being antagonized in such a manner. The soldier had been too lazy to search out fuel that was properly dried, and the elemental had burned him.

It would be easy enough to take them out. One silent rush, a few thrusts of her sword, and three corpses would be cooling on the ground. But that would shout her presence as clearly as if she rode to the very porticos of the palace on a golden sky-barge borne by war-birds with jeweled pinions. Her chances of entering the city unnoticed were sufficiently slim already. She knew a better way.

52

The corporal finished chewing out fat Tugbat. The hapless first soldier had poured water on his injured hand and was waving it around again.

'Behold!' Tugbat roared. 'Risrinc thinks he's become a war-eagle. Flap your wings, O mighty one. Fly up to your aerie.'

Risrinc opened his mouth to reply. His jaw dropped farther than he'd planned. 'Look,' he said, pointing past his fellows.

Moriana had slid down the rear of the hill, slung the satchel over her shoulder, and boldly walked around the flank of the rise.

'Dark Ones suck my soul,' the corporal said, turning. 'This is a welcome sight, indeed.'

'We've earned the favor of the Dark Ones,' Risrinc said, his scorched hand forgotten. He leered as he said, 'Look at the fine gift they've sent up.'

Moriana felt fury boil in her veins. She stood before the men, legs parted slightly, head held high. 'Take me at once to the Sky City,' she demanded.

The soldiers exchanged glances. 'Who do you think you are?' the corporal asked with a sneer. 'To order the troops of the Sky City about like serfs is risky business, wench. And His Excellency Prince Rann has himself decreed that none shall be permitted to ascend without a special pass.' He eyed her with his head tipped to one side and lust plain in his eyes. Her garb was outlandish, and her build taller than was common among those from the Sky City. He obviously mistook her for some slut from the Quincunx cities.

'You need a lesson in manners,' he said, starting toward her. 'You'll not go to the Sky City this day. Instead, you'll go with me beyond yon wall and relieve the tedium of my watch. After that, I'll let my men amuse themselves as well. Please us and we may not cut out your tongue for impertinence.'

Moriana let him draw near, then casually dropped her right hand so that her fingertips touched the hilt of her sword.

'It's you who needs a lesson in manners,' she raged. 'Curs! On your knees before the Princess Moriana, daughter of Queen Derora, scion of the House of Etuul, Mistress of the Clouds!' Fury blazed from her like a hard, clear light.

The soldiers dropped to their knees. 'Your pardon, Sky-born,' gasped the corporal, rubbing his face in the black loam at her feet. 'We did not know!'

'Had you knowingly addressed a princess of the Blood as you did me, you'd find yourself flayed and bathed in brine before the sun touched the Thails.' She walked to the crumbling wall of the dock. The hissing roar of the fire elemental was the only sound disturbing the sudden silence. 'Now,' she continued, 'do as you were commanded. Take me to the city at once.'

The corporal struggled to his feet. He kept his eyes averted. Color seeped up from the collar of his jerkin.

'Speak, man! Why do you not obey me?'

The corporal looked at his men. They looked elsewhere. 'Uh, Your Ascendency, we . . . our orders are very strict. None is permitted up without a warrant signed by Prince Rann himself.'

'Surely you don't think such prohibitions apply to me?'

'The orders were, uh, quite specific. No exceptions.' He looked up at her with doleful eyes. 'Please, Lady, have mercy. We are poor men who do our duty and have no wish to be exiled.'

Moriana held in a sigh. She'd hoped to deal with the soldiers individually, or at least with two first, and then the other. But there was no choice now. It had to be all three at once. She hoped her absence from the city hadn't made her powers wane too much. But the nearness of the Sky City aided her. She reached out and felt the immense power flowing from the bedrock of her sky home. The magical powers mounted, then flowed smoothly, her will directing them easily.

Her eyes became disks of green fire. With a choking gasp, the corporal reeled back. The eyes became green moons, became suns, became glowing infinities engulfing the soldiers' souls.

Feeling magic near, the elemental vented a whistling scream. Moriana fought to keep her concentration. She had the two soldiers, but the corporal fought back more strongly than she would have thought possible. He didn't lightly surrender his soul.

The green, flaming eyes focused on him. His mouth worked spastically. Drool rolled down his chin. He raised trembling hands as if pleading, then jerked violently and let his arms fall limply to his sides.

Sobbing with exertion, Moriana slumped against the wind-and-rain-worn wall. The three soldiers looked at her with dead eyes. The compulsion would last an hour, enough time for the corporal to ferry her to the city that loomed like a dark, oblong moon overhead, then return to his fellows and awaken, like them, with no knowledge of the encounter.

'What's this?' a querulous voice demanded. She jumped. 'Have you enchanted them? Foully done! You could have slain them easily.' The spirit's voice turned sulky. 'You're no better than Fost. Fine behavior for a princess, if you are actually a princess.'

'I am.' Moriana frowned. She had no time to waste on the garrulous spirit. She turned to the corporal. 'Can you hear me?'

'Yes,' the man said in a distant voice.

'Good. Take me to the city, then come back here and forget you saw me. You others will forget all that has happened, also.'

'As you say, Sky-born.'

The wicker gondola bobbed as she climbed in. She felt a momentary surge of indignation. It seemed disgraceful that a princess must ride in such a plebeian manner. Moving stiffly, the corporal loosed the ratchet that held the great, rusted windlass immobile, dragged himself into the gondola and finally moved a ceramic lever that opened vents in the top and bottom of the fire elemental's vessel.

Air rushed in through the bottom and, heated by the sprite, billowed upwards. The red-and-white striped gasbag swelled to gravid tautness. The elemental was contained by symbols etched around the vents. Moriana could feel its fury at being confined. The rage sang along her nerve endings, as discomforting as the heat that washed from the glowing firebox.

Pulleys squealed as the balloon lifted. The ground fell away beneath Moriana's feet. Guy lines of woven silk ran from the windlass at the dock below to one set in the rock of the city. As each ground station was passed, an eagle-riding engineer flew to the next to affix guidelines for the balloons.

Moriana glanced at the corporal. He stood as rigid as death beside her; with no volition of his own, he was incapable of movement except in obedience to her commands. The woman felt triumph at having wrapped three men at once in the soul-numbing compulsion. Granted, that they were Sky City men had simplified the task. Sorcery always worked best against those already touched by magic. Sky Citizens lived intimately with enchantment, from the simple running-trim spells that kept the vast raft of skystone that was the city stable, to the powerful wards that bound Istu, dread demon of the Dark Ones.

One not so imbued with magic would prove more difficult to subdue. She doubted that all her strength and skill would have served to make Fost submissive. The courier's life-force, his will, would extinguish itself into death before permitting another mastery over his soul.

Moriana shook off the image of Fost, wondering that he'd come into her mind again. She looked about her and forgot all but the view. The Sundered Realm spread itself beneath her. Forests and mountains, plains and the distant glimmer of the Gulf of Veluz, her gaze encompassed all. Far off to the north brooded Mount Omizantrim, marked by a horizon-hugging smear of smoke from its crater.

'Poor ground-crawlers,' she sighed as the wind whipped through her hair. 'They know nothing of beauty, who have not seen this spectacle.' The corporal did not respond.

Above, the city grew until it filled the sky.

'Is this the fabled Sky City?' asked Erimenes. His voice was muffled by the heavy, tattered cloak Moriana had wrapped about her to conceal the outland garb. 'I expected somewhat more. Where are the streets paved with gold, the statues of nude maidens with perfumed wine fountaining from their nipples?'

In the crush of bodies that packed the approaches to the Circle of the Skywell, no one noticed the voice had no attendant body.

'You're thinking of High Medurim,' Moriana whispered.

'Even so, I find this tedious. Why not betake yourself to the bird riders' barracks? A woman as lusty as I perceive you to be should have her appetite no more than whetted by that mongrel Fost. But eighty, say, or ninety hot-blooded stalwarts would . . .'

She thumped the hidden jug with the butt of her hand. She'd hidden her glorious, distinctive hair in a kerchief as ragged as the cloak. She'd taken both from a drink-sotted derelict lying stupefied by a warehouse in the wharf district. Her new garments reeked, but they kept the mob from pressing her too closely.

No sooner had she set foot on the ornately carved pier jutting from the rim of the city than she had seen a great fluttering in the sky above the city's center. Something of importance was occurring. Chilled by premonition, she hurried inwards along narrow streets flanked by soaring buildings.

The human torrent carried her out into the openness surrounding the Well of Winds. Moriana gasped as she saw the procession approaching down the Skullway.

From the Palace of the Clouds the parade stretched down the skull-paved avenue that ran broad and straight to the Well. First came captives dressed in greasy prison smocks, moaning and raising bound hands in supplication. Dog riders herded them, hitting out with clubs and jabbing with lances. Next came the band, three hundred strong, lifting a dirge with flute, trumpet, and somber drum. Mages followed, shaven-headed, chanting and swinging fuming censers.

A sky-barge came after. Twelve feet square, an airy, arabesqued framework of silver, it floated inches above the foot-burnished skulls. Chains at its corners hung from the harnesses of war-eagles, their great wings beating in time to the slow roll of the drums. On the barge was spread a cushion, and on it lay an urn of dark jade. A few steps behind, servants carried a smaller silver litter that bore a golden vessel the size of a cooking kettle.

Above all flew the Guards. Sunlight broke from polished helmets and the heads of lances couched in holsters of serpent hide. At the fore flew an eagle black as any raven. A blazing red crest adorned its head. Moriana's head lurched. There was no mistaking the war mount of her cousin Prince Rann, commander of the bird riders.

Tightness gripped her throat. Her eyes stung. She tugged at the sleeve of a stout woman nearby, who was raising her voice to join the lament that wailed from the throng.

'What's happening?' she asked, pitching her voice shrill both to carry and disguise it.

The round face turned toward her was flushed and tear-bright. 'You don't know?' the woman cried. 'Our gracious Queen Derora is dead. She died in her sleep a night ago.'

Erimenes spoke from his jug. Moriana didn't hear him. She swayed dizzily, fighting against panic, against sudden wild grief.

'By rights, Moriana should ascend the throne, and blessed would we be if that could happen. But rumor says she came to misfortune in the wastelands of the south, and I fear . . .'

A mighty shout drowned out her words. As one, the flock of bird riders descended, Raan bringing his mount to rest on the very lip of the Well. Heads turned toward the Palace of the Clouds. Silence blossomed.

Vast black wings reached across the front of the Palace. A splendid war-bird with feathers like midnight flapped slowly along the Skull-way. Hatred burned within Moriana. Here was Nightwind, greatest of all eagles, and the slim feather-cloaked figure on his back was Moriana's sister Synalon.

Moriana's fingers crushed against her palms. It was all she could do not to begin muttering a deathspell. Her sister would sense it before it was half uttered, and a swarm of Guardsmen would fall on her like owls on a mouse. Never had she felt her weakness more. If only she had the amulet now! She could conjure the spells and give Synalon the Hell Call. But the Amulet of Living Flame rested far to the south, locked in the bowels of a glacier. She had to bide her time, as much as she loathed the idea. She was still too weak and Synalon too strong.

Nightwind touched down at the head of the procession. Scarred, handsome features obscured by a sallet, Rann himself helped Synalon to the pavement. Raising her arms like wings, Synalon chanted toward the sun. Rann gestured to the dog riders.

Shouting, they drove their mounts among the captives. Driven by spear, bludgeon, and knout, the prisoners fell forward. They shrieked as they pitched into the Well. They screamed as they fell, fivescore men and women, until the prairie a thousand feet below cut short their cries.

'A sacrifice of a hundred souls!' crowed Erimenes. 'This is more like it.'

Tears gushed from Moriana's eyes. 'Be quiet, you,' she shouted at the spirit. 'Be silent or I'll cast you after them!' In the roar surrounding them, no one noted her outburst.

Singing, Synalon paced to the hovering barge, carried the jade urn to the Well, uncapped it and hurled forth its contents. She returned to the barge. Next she lifted the golden vessel. Forty feet from the Well the skull pavement ended, to reveal the marble beneath. The stately black-haired princess paced solemnly to the end of the ghastly cobblestones, set down the vessel and dropped to her knees to open it. Whiteness gleamed within.

Thus did Derora V, called the Wise, find rest after a long rule, with her bleached skull set among those of her forebears and the ashes of her remains scattered to the winds.

'No, gentlemen,' said Moriana as she emerged from the passageway. 'Don't rise on my behalf. I have small standing in the city these days.'

The man at the head of a long, knife-scarred table shot to his feet, his face the color of the white halo of whiskers that fringed it. The others stayed seated, gaping at the golden-haired apparition who had invaded their den through a panel in what they'd believed a solid wall. A hint of wood smoke hung in the air and through closed doors

58

drifted the sounds of thriving trade being done in the common room of the inn. Dusty sunlight fell in through cracked and fly-specked skylights, providing the room's sole illumination.

The normal crimson hue returned to the standing man's features.

'But how did you find us?' he asked. Moriana regarded him levelly. 'My lady,' he added, after a short pause.

Moriana's lips twisted into a smile of confidence she didn't feel. 'Properly, it's "Your Majesty",' she said, 'but I'm in no position to insist, am I? Do be seated, Councillor. Your secret's safe with me.'

Uriath of the Council of Advisors to the Throne lowered himself heavily into his chair.

'I would still like to know how you found our meeting place, my lady.'

She laughed. 'What sort of fool do you take me for? I've long known what would follow my mother's passing. My sister is not the only one who has spies throughout the city.' At a great cost in lives and effort, her agents had infiltrated Rann's intelligence network. She had known of the amulet hours before Rann and Synalon, even if she hadn't been able to prevent that knowledge from reaching them. Her thoughts turned to Kralfi, ancient but erect of stature, the palace chamberlain and master of Moriana's own intelligence network. She hoped he'd made his own position secure against Derora's death. He was more to her than a trusted servant; he was a friend she'd loved since childhood.

'Don't worry,' she continued, pulling a chair to the head of the table and seating herself next to Uriath. 'Rann's creatures don't know of this rendezvous of yours, or you'd be writhing on a grill this very minute.' Uriath's face lost color again.

Moriana gazed intently at the man to her right, until he passed her a jack of ale. She'd had a long, thirsty day. She drank deeply of the bitter brew.

Synalon obviously did not know that Uriath was head of an underground movement dedicated to preventing her accession to the throne. But she'd be watching him, all the same. He had long been the voice of the loyal opposition in council, standing against Derora in stormy confrontations that often skirted treason. He was too powerful to do away with out of hand, but Synalon would watch him as keenly as any war-bird, waiting the slip that would give grounds for his arrest.

Moriana was proud that her own spies knew more, in this matter at least, than Synalon's. Kralfi, wise as he was, could not easily out-match Prince Rann's cunning. Yet he had found out about the meeting in the back room of the Inn of the Boiled Eel, and the hidden passage that gave access to it. One question he had not answered. Uriath opposed Synalon. But would he back Moriana? It was that which she had come to learn.

Another question burned more urgently within the princess. 'My mother,' she asked, leaning forward. 'How did she die?'

The men eyed each other uncomfortably. 'She'd not been well for some time, Princess,' a man halfway down the table said in a high-pitched voice. 'Skilled chirurgeons attended her but could not restore her strength.' He dropped his eyes uneasily from Moriana's. 'She died night before last. And yesterday she was cremated and her skull purified to take its place upon the Skullway.'

'The Sky City disposed of its queen with unseemly haste. Why wasn't the weeklong vigil before cremation observed, Master Tromyn?'

Tromyn bit his lip. 'The mages of the Palace feared contagion.'

'Do you believe that?' she flared at him. 'My mother was murdered, and her body was burned to conceal evidence of the crime. Isn't that true?'

'We don't know that for a fact, my lady,' Uriath said. 'But it seems likely.' He tipped his head to one side. 'Still, what is there to do about it?'

'What I propose to do about it is claim the throne, as is my right, and bring retribution to the murderers.' Moriana stared at the fleshy man in his rich, feathered robes, her eyes bright as though about to take fire in the compulsion spell. 'Do you back me, Lord Uriath?'

Silence drew taut between them. To the sides, men shifted and murmured uncomfortably. Moriana held the Councillor with her gaze.

Air gusted from him. 'Yes, Lady,' he said. 'We will.'

'Master,' the sooty-faced apprentice cried. 'Master, look at this.'

A half-smile curving his lips, Prince Rann moved to the boy's elbow. 'What do you see, Inkulri?' he asked. His voice was silken.

The youth shivered. The palace mages could be arbitrary, even cruel, but next to the prince they were mild children. Inkulri was scared to the bone at having to work under Rann's direct supervision.

Now eagerness overcame apprehension. 'Look, Master,' he said again, pointing to the fire-filled crystal dome. 'Is that . . . isn't that the Princess Moriana?'

Rann's eyebrows rose. He leaned forward, a small, wiry man dressed in close-fitting clothes of black. His thin, hard face would have been handsome but for the network of tiny white scars that filigreed it from brow to chin.

For a moment, all he saw was the yellow dance of flame. Slowly, his skilled, pale eyes resolved the fires into an image.

'Even so, Inkulri, even so,' he murmured softly. He laid a hand on the apprentice's shoulder. 'You've done your city a great service. It shall not go unrewarded.'

He took the hand away. Inkulri shivered again, violently, despite the heat of the fire elemental trapped scant inches from his face. Somehow Prince Rann's promise of reward was more ominous than the direst threats of a master sorcerer.

The warm, spicy smell of broth filled Moriana's nostrils. Gratefully, she sipped the liquid. Its heat suffused her limbs, easing her weariness. She'd had nothing to eat since – had it been just that morning? – sharing the gruel from Fost's ever-filled bowl.

Her host and hostess sat across the parlor from her. They stared at the princess as though she'd just materialized in a billow of smoke instead of being guided through a labyrinth of alleys to their house by a youthful member of Uriath's underground. They were simple, solid folk, a master stone mason and his wife, and were utterly overwhelmed by the presence of royalty.

'It's good of you to shelter me like this, Freeman Onn,' she said, trying to put the man at ease. 'I hope you and your wife understand the risk involved.'

Onn nodded gravely. His face was as red as Uriath's, and his hair as white. But his cheeks were rounder and he had no beard, only snowy sideburns that wisped outward an improbable distance from the sides of his face.

'No one's safe if Synalon rules,' he said. 'We're glad to help.' His wife Ruda nodded. She was a more or less faithful replica of her husband, though without the sideburns and not balding.

Outside, the sun fell toward the forward edge of the city. The pot of broth bubbled over the hearthfire. The aroma of dove boiled with fennel and spice-lichen lent the air a homelike, comforting aroma.

His jug in its satchel propped against a wall, Erimenes sulked.

61

Moriana had threatened him with dire punishments if he broke silence, first at the gathering of conspirators and now in the mason's house. She had enough sorcerous power to cow him, at least for the time.

A peremptory rapping on the door made Moriana start. Shaking her head, she realized she'd dozed off. The day had taken a greater toll of her endurance than she'd thought.

The knock came again. 'All right, all right,' Onn said peevishly. He padded to the door.

Moriana heard the door open. Onn gave a startled cry that ended in a groan. Cup poised halfway to lips, the woman looked toward the door. The black iron head of a barbed javelin jutted from the center of the mason's back.

Onn folded, leaking blood. A man in the uniform of a Guardsman stood above him, trying to pull the javelin loose. He'd used a short, heavy dart as a thrusting spear, and the barb had caught on his victim's ribs.

Ruda said nothing. She rose and went to the hearth, seemingly calm. Moriana stared from the grisly scene in the doorway to her, too stunned to move. Ruda wrapped a cloth about her hand, hoisted the pot off its rack and hurled the boiling contents into the face of her husband's murderer.

The man shrieked and fell to his knees, clawing at his scalded face. Cursing, a comrade thrust past him. Ruda stood her ground, offering no protest or resistance as he jammed his javelin into her belly, once, twice, three times, forcing her back to stain the wall of her home with blood. He grunted each time his spear point sank in flesh.

Moriana had recovered from her shock. The javelin-butt came back for another jab. A single whistling slash of her sword cut through the back of the man's neck. He twitched, evacuated his bowels and fell. Ruda dropped atop him. She died without uttering another sound.

The burned man was keening horribly. An officer barked orders as more soldiers crowded past the injured one. Moriana's sword flickered restlessly before her, scattering shards of reflected firelight.

Uriath? Had he betrayed her? If so, he'd also betrayed his own secret meeting place and the rest of the underground, as well. Not him, not from what she knew of him. But how? No time to wonder. Five soldiers faced her, poised for the attack.

'Take her alive or you'll go to Rann in her place,' the officer bawled from the doorway.

The Guards closed in. They were at a disadvantage, and knew it. They'd have to grapple with Moriana to capture her, and the straight sword made that risky.

Moriana moved first. A bird rider sank with a gurgling cry, strangling on his own blood, his throat pierced. A Guard seized the woman. She raked nails across his face and kneed his groin, spun to slice open another's belly and danced back from their clutching hands.

She panted, trying to catch her wind. The officer shouted into the street. The man with the burned face lay at his feet, head hacked apart. The officer had cut him down to clear the door.

More soldiers poured in. Shouting with hopeless anger, Moriana threw herself among them, cutting wildly. Her sword bit flesh, spattering the once-neat parlor with blood.

A Guardsman ran in with a saddle-cloth taken from his war-bird outside. Moriana lunged at him. Her sword point pierced the cloth and the soldier's heart. The cloth came down over her head, blinding her.

'Marvelous! What action!' she heard Erimenes applaud. Then the soldiers bore her down.

CHAPTER FIVE

Scarcely breathing, Fost lay on the hilltop. His cheek itched abominably. He was allergic to the oilbush, but he found no other cover on the rise overlooking the lonely balloon dock with its slumped stone walls.

A hundred yards away he'd come upon a large, long-legged dog asleep in the shadow of a cutback along a stream. Nearby lay saddle and tack of exquisite manufacture. The creature rose to its feet, surprise and sadness in its eyes, as Raissa and Wigma ran barking to sniff the riding gear. The leather was obviously ripe with the scent of gruel they'd been tracking since morning. Mount and equipage were Moriana's.

It had long been clear to Fost that the thief was making for the Sky City. Now, with the city like a stone cloud above, he would proceed afoot, as Moriana had, and see if he couldn't find a way of following her aloft.

He never doubted that she'd found a way up. When he'd peered over the top of the knoll, his guess was confirmed.

For ten minutes he'd watched the dock. The three soldiers on duty seemed occupied by some debate. He heard snatches of it – 'Must have been a dream . . .' and 'A sending of the Dark Ones, I tell you!' and 'No, no, some joker laced our rations with dream-powder . . .' – but paid scant attention. He was too occupied trying to form a plan.

He knew he could slaughter the three. Like most Sky City dwellers, they were short, though one was much rounder than the whip-lean norm. That lulled him little, since he'd had ample grief at the hands of small wiry bird riders. But, by their slouching and carelessness, he guessed these three were no elite Guards. As caught up in their argument as they were, he felt sure he could sneak to within a sword's stroke of them unseen.

The problem was the balloon. He knew the principle: the fire elemental heated air, which became lighter and rose, carrying the balloon up with it along the guidelines. However, the courier had no idea how the elemental was controlled. If it was by spell, he was in trouble. He didn't relish the thought of inadvertantly setting the salamander loose.

Time pressed. Its motion all but imperceptible, the Sky City passed ponderously overhead. Fost guessed that before long the sentries would have to ascend or be left behind. He had almost decided to overrun the soldiers and try to catch one alive to operate the damned balloon when something came whizzing down from the city to bounce with a *clank!* against the rusted windlass.

The soldiers jumped at the noise. They clustered around the object, a small cylinder attached to a set of pulley wheels to ride the lines. The one with corporal's insignia opened it and pulled out a message.

His face showed consternation. 'I'm ordered back to the Sky City at once,' he said. 'I wonder what this can mean.'

The others exchanged looks that said they doubted it meant well.

'This reeks of trouble,' the corporal said. 'If the powers above have dreamed up some imaginary misdeed to take me to task for, as the Dark Ones are my witness I'll have one of you slugs along to stick with the blame!' He gazed narrowly from one horrified trooper to the other. 'You're elected, Tugbat. Haul your round, red arse into the gondola and make ready to lift. You'll stay, Risrinc. Give my love to the brigands.'

Horror-struck, Tugbat waddled over and climbed into the wicker basket. The corporal got in next. When Moriana had compelled him to take her to the city, he'd released the windlass, which meant the gasbag had to raise the weight of the guidelines as well as the passengers. Tugbat was more knowledgeable. The gondola was tethered to a runner on the line; the fat man undid the clutch that made the runner grip the guy so that the pulley inside could free-wheel up the strand. The windlass was meant to crank the balloon down.

Fost neither knew this nor cared. He saw his chance to reach the city, if he could act fast enough.

Sword out, he was up and running down the hill even as the elemental began to roar and the balloon began to lift. Risrinc stood

gazing up at his comrades. The sound of a heavy footfall brought him
around. Fost cut him down. He couldn't have the young soldier
seizing his legs as he tried to climb into the gondola.

A leap, a grab, a quick heave of powerful shoulders, and he was in
the basket. His antics made it swing wildly. Tugbat pitched against
him as the corporal shouted contradictory orders.

Fost grappled with the pudgy soldier. Tugbat was far from his
match in strength, but between the soldier's girth and Fost's size, the
three were packed snugly into the tiny gondola. Fost had no room to
maneuver. Air blasted upward through the firebox. In panic, the
corporal had thrown the vents wide.

The balloon shot skyward. Accidentally, Fost glanced over the side
to see the ground receding at a horrible rate. His stomach did a
somersault. Ust and Gormanka had never intended their children to
be so far from earth without solid rock of mountain or rampart
beneath their feet.

Pain seared his side. He gasped. Tugbat had drawn a dirk and was
busily trying to saw him in two at the waist.

'All right, damn you,' Fost bellowed. 'If you're going to do that, get
up and walk!' He raised the squirming trooper above his head and
cast him over the side. Tugbat howled down the several hundred feet
that already separated balloon from ground.

Fost had no time to watch. He turned to face a shining arc of steel.
With Tugbat gone, the corporal had found space to draw his blade.

For a moment they stood, gazes locked. The corporal swayed
easily to allow for the rocking of the gondola. He might be a fool, but
he was more at home in this devilish contraption than was Fost. If Fost
tried to draw steel he'd lose an arm. Either staying put or leaping for
his foe would get him gutted, and he had no wish to follow Tugbat.
That left but one way.

The corporal lunged. Breathing a prayer to his patrons, Fost sprang
up and back. His hands caught shrouds, and his feet found purchase
on the rim of the basket. The corporal slashed. Fost pulled up his feet.
The scimitar whooshed beneath him, severing lines.

Before his opponent could ready another swing, Fost clambered
up onto the rope network containing the gasbag itself. For a moment
he clung like a suckling child to the giant teat that was the balloon. A
juggling in the line told him his foe was climbing after him.

He ripped out his sword and waved it in the corporal's face. With a
squeal of anger and fear, the man dropped back into the gondola.

Fost shut his eyes as the ballon lurched crazily.

The taut fabric of the bag stung his cheek with heat. Curses assailed him from below. He peered down at his adversary, taking care not to let his gaze slip over the side of the gondola. The basket hung at a slight but discernible angle. The cut shroud lines had let one side drop a few inches.

Gripping the gondola's rim, the corporal began to throw his weight from side to side in an attempt to dislodge the courier. Fost gulped and clung tighter. He got a grip in the lines by his waist, timed the pitch of the balloon and bent down in a fast swoop.

The corporal dropped to the bottom of the basket as Fost's sword swung past his head. The stroke wasn't aimed at him. Stays parted with a whisper, causing the basket to tilt further. Fost reeled himself in and pressed against the flank of the balloon.

As the corporal picked himself up, Fost began to edge around the curve of the bag, his booted toes scrabbling for holds in the netting. *If everlasting life is to be filled with adventure of this sort,* he thought, *perhaps I should settle for the usual span.*

Fost ground his teeth as a blade bit into his calf. The corporal had grabbed an intact line and jumped up to slash at him. Steel ripped at Fost's legs again. He didn't try to evade the blows. If he dodged them he'd lose his grip. All he could do was hang on and hope the corporal didn't hamstring him.

Between cuts he swung down and chopped another pair of shrouds. Upright again, he chanced a look up. The Sky City loomed scant yards above the balloon. Its under-surface shone mirror-smooth and bright, and slightly convex. The stone piers of the sky-dock jutted like mandibles from its leading edge.

Fost leaned down and cut the final shrouds.

Balloon and gondola went separate ways. Fost had a last glimpse of the corporal's pale, astonished face. Then the basket screamed away down the guys, and the gasbag, freed from most of its load, rocketed up past the rim of the city.

At once Fost was faced with a new difficulty: the ludicrous chance that he'd miss the Sky City altogether. Freed of the gondola, corporal, firebox, and guiding lines, the balloon rose rapidly, a breeze carrying it over the city proper. Fost wondered how long it would take the heated air in the bag to begin to cool enough for descent. He didn't have long to wait. When it came down to twenty feet above the street, he jumped clear.

Having had some experience leaping out second-story windows a pace or two ahead of sword-swinging husbands, Fost knew how to curl up and roll as he landed. Still, the impact jarred him. He measured his length on the uneven pavement, feeling as if his bones had been jolted loose from their joints.

The balloon soared again, this time freed of all burden. With a squawk and sudden boom of wings, what seemed a thousand ravens boiled from rookeries under the eaves of the high, narrow buildings all around. Cawing raucously, they circled the balloon, tearing at the gaily colored fabric. In seconds the gasbag was shredded, bits of cloth fluttering down like crippled butterflies.

Fost picked himself up, rubbing the back of his head and wondering if the knock on the skull had made him imagine the slashing attack of the ravens. But no, he saw them settling back into their nesting places, croaking in satisfaction as if they'd just repelled a major invasion.

'Ust,' he moaned, 'Gormanka, and the Five Holy Ones, as well.'

'Those names have no power here,' a voice said from behind.

He wheeled, clutching for his sword. Too late he realized he'd dropped it as he jumped. It lay on the stone, far out of reach. Then he looked at the speaker and knew he'd have no need for the weapon.

'You chose a hazardous mode of entering our city,' she said. 'The ravens attack anything that flies above the level of the guard wall, and their talons are poisoned. Who are you, and why do you come here?'

Fost took his time answering. She was young, hardly more than a girl, and slight with a lithe slenderness that gave the illusion of more height. Her short-sleeved green tunic and brief trews left her tanned, shapely limbs mostly bare. Her face was oval, the nose fine, cheeks softly contoured with all framed by square-cut brown hair. Dominating the face were the eyes, as huge and golden as coins.

'I'm Fost Longstrider, and I seek a thief.'

Lips and eyes smiled as she said, 'There are many here.'

'This one's name is Moriana.' He bent to recover his blade.

The girl's eyebrows rose fractionally and her mouth tensed. From somewhere came shouts and the sound of hobnails striking cobblestones.

'Come,' she said. 'The Monitors will be here soon to see what provoked the ravens.' She spun and tried to dart into a nearby alley.

Fost caught her waist. 'Where are you taking me?'

'None is allowed up from the surface since the death of Queen

Derora,' she said. 'Yet you rode up by balloon – alone. Did you kill the soldiers on guard below?'

'Two of them – at least.' Fost grinned wolfishly. 'I'm not sure how the corporal fared.'

'Then I take you to friends.'

'Go, my children,' Synalon purred. 'Go forth and burn the traitors out!' Blinding coruscations of yellow flame capered above the buildings. Indigo smoke, rank with herbs and incense, roiled forth to spiral around the sorceress.

Chittering sounds came from the three salamanders. Their sinuous reptilian shapes flickered this way and that. Synalon clapped her hands three times and gestured at the high-arched window standing open to the dusk. Like three small comets, the elementals leaped from the grill and streaked away.

Synalon strode to the window. Three lines of light arced high and fell upon a spired building several hundred yards away. A white flash made her blink. When her eyes cleared of the pulsing afterimage, she beheld flame beginning to gleam from windows, like a hundred baleful red eyes opening.

'Spectacularly done, O Queen in all but name, but perhaps not too wisely.'

Synalon whirled, her brows arching with fury. Unheard, Prince Rann had entered the room behind her. His spare frame was wrapped in a purple robe trimmed with black fur.

'As softly as you tread, still you might overstep,' the princess said, her voice like poisoned honey. 'Why do you think this wrong, cousin mine?'

Rann went to the window. Already flames reached high from the doomed building. The fire's rushing bellow mingled with the screams of the inhabitants.

'Such displays serve only to incite the populace. There are better ways to deal with dissent.'

'Calamanroth dared speak openly against me. Thus do I demonstrate my power, and the fate awaiting those who do not acknowledge my supremacy.' She gazed narrowly down on him. 'I'd think you'd find this most diverting.

The prince smiled. 'Wholesale destruction interests me but little. My pleasures are more intimate.' He gazed from the window. Outside it was as if the sun rose in the north. Over the crackle of the flames an eerie wailing soared: the triumphant ululation of the salamanders. 'The fire sprites are fickle beasts, mindless and cruel. Have a care they don't get out of hand.'

'I can control them!'

'One hopes so.' The smile never wavered on Rann's lips. This game was not as risky as it seemed. Even in her most frenzied rage, Synalon would not lightly toss away a tool as useful as Rann. Barred by gender from the line of succession, his ambition could never grow to threaten her. Both knew it. So, like a court fool, he could speak as he pleased without fear of retribution. And Synalon knew his sense of duty ran deep. For her, he would do anything. 'Still, there are better uses for them.'

'Such as?' Synalon stood back pettishly ignoring the fiery display she had created. Prince Rann's carping had spoiled the amusement for her.

'Surveillance. Given sufficient sprites, our watchers can attune to any fire lit within the confines of the city. Any business transacted by flamelight, whether of taper, hearth, or furnace, will be revealed to us.'

Synalon frowned. She felt stirrings of interest at the idea, but was too piqued at her cousin to admit it.

'Is there any practical application for this folderol?'

'You may judge for yourself, Princess.' From within his robe he produced a bell. 'Here is a captive taken as a result of our fire scrying. Or perhaps I should say captives.'

He rang the bell. The silver-bound doors of the chamber opened. A squad of bird riders entered, dragging a prisoner with them. They flung the captive forward. She fell to hands and knees with a ringing clatter of heavy chains. She shook back matted hair of gold and raised her head.

Synalon gasped as she looked upon her sister. She recovered quickly.

'How sweet of you,' she said, 'to come in this sad hour to console me over our dear mother's death.'

'Words, words, I'm surfeited by words,' a voice said peevishly. 'When does the torture begin? Or barring that, the debauchery?'

Synalon's sapphire eyes widened. 'What's this?' she demanded of Rann. 'These words that come from thin air. Is it . . .?'

'It is.' The prince bowed low. A soldier handed him a stained satchel of the kind carried by Realm-road couriers. 'My lady, may I present to you Erimenes the Ethical, late of Athalau.'

He opened the bag and took forth a plain earthenware pot. 'My blessing on you, good sir,' the spirit said. 'I was sick nigh unto death of the stench of that gruel leaking all day from Kest-i-Mond's bowl.'

Synalon clapped her hands with delight. 'You may name your reward this night, Prince Rann,' she said. 'In these two you have brought me the means by which I shall restore the lost greatness of the Sky City!'

'My reward is serving you, my queen.' Rann bowed deeply, his mouth curling into a slight sneer to hide other emotions, which he could never sate.

She stroked her sister's cheek. Moriana glared at her. Synalon asked, 'Tell me, Rann, how was this deed done?'

'While I possess no magical powers of my own, others who do were posted to observe. Somehow, your sister made her way undetected into the city. A sprite-watcher noticed her in the household of a traitor. We sent a squad of Guardsmen to fetch her.'

'Were these traitors long nurtured by her?'

'I'm sure she was brought to them by someone else whom she contacted on arrival. I fear organized resistance has sprung up already.'

'No doubt the traitors have been induced to name their cohorts.' The princess returned to the window. The house of Calamanroth slumped into itself and sent livid sparks high into the nighttime sky.

Prince Rann's smile turned feral. 'I fear not, my lady.' Synalon spun and angrily faced him. 'The fool of a captain in charge of the detachment allowed his men to slay all but Moriana. Moreover, he got five men cut up in the capture.'

'I trust he has been . . . chastised.'

'He is chained naked in my aerie, with his belly slit open for Terror to dine upon his entrails,' Rann said. His eyes showed more animation than at any time since entering Synalon's chamber.

'You coddle that bird overmuch,' Synalon said sulkily.

'Oh? And did you not feed your serving maid's eyes to your own Nightwind when you caught her pilfering your jewels?' He chuckled, a sound like coins falling into a silver cup. 'It increases the mettle of a war-eagle to taste man-blood now and then.'

Moriana had floated in a daze since being clubbed senseless by the bird riders. Seeing her sister and cousin had whipped away the mental fog. She sat up straight and fixed her kin with a gaze of fine contempt.

'You two have changed little since last I saw you. You're still wicked children delighting in the torment of small, helpless creatures.' She spat upon the marble floor.

'Is this the courtesy you show us? We, who are your loving family?' Rann towered above her, hands on slim hips.

Moriana's lips curled. 'Speak not of loving, half-man.' Rann went dead white. 'You knew nothing of what it meant even before the mountain people burned off your manhood.'

'You said I might name my reward,' Rann said to Synalon, his face a mask of awful rage. 'I name it now: give me this slut, that I might pleasure her with death lasting long days.'

'You shall not have her, Rann. Choose some other token.' A slim hand raised to check his outburst. 'Stay. I'll not argue now. I would speak with our other guest.'

Synalon sat in an ornate chair carved from a single beryl. Tormented visages looked forth, not wholly human. They seemed compounded subtly of the features of men in anguish and the serpents devouring them. At a languid gesture, a soldier placed a similarly carved stand in front of her, and another set Erimenes's jug upon it.

'Welcome to the Sky City, ancient one,' Synalon greeted.

'You are Princess Synalon? You rule this city?'

Synalon's eyes flicked at her sister like a scorpion's sting. 'I am Synalon, yes. As to the question of my rule, my sister would deny it, though I feel she'll repent her error soon.'

'Not while I live!' shouted Moriana.

'My meaning precisely.'

The golden-haired princess slumped back. The sick certainty of defeat washed over her. *My failure will cost me my life,* she thought bitterly. *But what shall it cost my city?*

'Your sister doubtless knows countless secrets regarding those who conspire against you,' Erimenes said. 'Why not put her to the torture to wrest the information from her?'

Synalon looked at the jug. 'You surprise me, sage. As I recall, the philosophy you taught in life was utter disavowal of worldly considerations. It's not easy to reconcile that outlook with your desire to witness torture.'

'Bright lady, know that on the occasion of my death I foreswore all my foolish theories of abstinence,' Erimenes explained. 'I glory in seeing life, raw life, be it in pleasure or in pain. Bring on the whips,

72

the pincers, the red-hot irons! I've never watched a rousing torture.'

'Shall I do as he suggests, Princess?' Rann tongued his lips in anticipation. Seeing that slight action made Moriana wince.

'No!' Synalon sliced the air with her hand. 'I've other uses for her, uses requiring that her body remain unsullied by your gentle mercies.'

Rann's face paled with anger again. Synalon rose to her feet, glaring down at the prince.

'Do you think I'm being arbitrary?' she demanded. 'Do you think that I wouldn't like to take blade in hand and peel this bitch's hide from her cringing body? Yet that is a pleasure I will forego for a greater reward.'

She strode across the chamber. A breeze stirred the heavy blue and green tapestries that decorated the walls. The murky, somber designs were highlighted by the raging fire across the city. The scent of burning made the wind bitter on Synalon's tongue.

'Long have I planned for this moment,' Synalon said. 'Long have I dreamed, step by careful step, of the torments with which I'd end my sister's life. I would cut her and burn her and flay the skin of her face to make a rag for menials to swab the cesspipes. And I would keep her alive, oh, so long, so very long.'

She stood above Moriana. Her sister stared up at her in untrammeled horror. Smiling, she took Moriana's face gently in her hands.

'Yes, she is beautiful, almost as beautiful as I. Despoiling such beauty is a rare privilege, even for one with my power. There were times when I'd have given up my hope for the throne to behold my sister squirming as the flames gnawed on her tender flesh; such is my hate.

'So do you conceive of what it means to me to forego my vengeance, cousin?' She stood so close that the moon-pale globes of her breasts, scarcely contained by the low-cut velvet gown, touched the prince's chest. Synalon moved closer, her hand brushing quickly, teasingly, over his empty crotch. His jaw set and tawny eyes flickered. The scars shone forth in the intensity of the Prince Rann's emotion, making it appear that a fine gossamer mesh covered his face.

Synalon pirouetted away, leaving him trembling from her taunting nearness. She evoked passions in him that could not be sated. Not directly.

But captives would howl their anguish that night.

'Take my sister to the dungeon, and let no harm befall her. Otherwise you'll answer with what remains of your soul, Rann.'

He clasped hands to breast and bowed.

At a signal, the Guard pulled Moriana to her feet. She didn't resist as they marched her from the chamber. Her last sight before the doors slammed shut was of her sister leaning forward on her throne, in eager conversation with the spirit.

CHAPTER SIX

'If you move the blade a bit farther over to the left you can sever the artery,' Fost said, rolling his eyes down to look at the fist holding the dagger to his throat. 'Is this what passes for friendship in the Sky City?'

His guide stood before him in the dusk, an enigmatic look in her eyes. 'Perhaps so. All depends on your telling the truth – why do you seek the Princess Moriana?'

'Princess? She's no princess. She's a lying, thieving, yellow-haired harlot! She robbed me. I trailed her here.'

The blade tightened at his throat. He felt a sting as skin parted and a trickle of blood oozed forth.

'Let me slit his throat, Luranni,' a brusque young male voice growled from behind Fost's ear. 'He's a foul spy. A creature of Rann's.'

Luranni sucked in her breath and heaved a deep sigh. 'You've said this Moriana is yellow-haired. Is she tall, well-built, carrying a straight sword which she can use as well as any man?'

'By the Holy Ones, yes! She nearly spitted me with that thing last night.'

'That is the princess.'

I knew her tale was a lie, Fost thought. *But a princess!*

'His story's as thin as one of Synalon's gowns, Luranni,' the youth who held him said. 'Why would our princess rob a lowborn scum like him?'

'Doubtless she had her reasons,' Luranni said. 'What is this property you claim to have lost? Is it valuable?'

'It . . .' Fost stopped. He couldn't very well tell the flat truth. A treasure such as Erimenes held the key to would cause a saint to murder his mother. 'In truth, I don't know. I'm a courier. I had a

75

parcel to deliver. She took it. It's not my business to poke into the items I deliver, but it is my business to make sure I deliver them.'

The youth with the knife made a skeptical sound. Fost wondered how his attacker would react if he knew the circumstances under which Moriana had gotten the satchel.

'Look, I know I've not shaved today, but I prefer to tend to such details myself. Kindly call off your budding barber.'

Luranni laughed musically. 'Erlund, release him.'

'Not until we . . .' Before he'd finished, Fost ran a hand up to grip the knife hand, and jabbed his elbow back into the pit of the young man's stomach. Erlund doubled over, gagging. The big man spun out, wrenching the arm so that the knife cartwheeled away, to clink against a wall. His boot lashed out. Erlund grunted and collapsed.

'Erlund should learn to obey orders.' Fost felt his neck, winced and brought away bloodied fingers.

'Think no ill of him. He's upset with himself. Just three hours ago he guided the princess to a house we thought safe from her sister's spies. Not long after, bird riders broke in, slew our folk, and captured Moriana.'

Fost stared at her. He felt ill. Of all the places he might have had to penetrate to retrieve the philosopher's shade, by far the worst was the keep of the rulers of the Sky City. It was just like Erimenes. Fost kicked a wall, hurt his toe, and cursed volubly.

He sensed others approaching. 'A bargain,' he said quickly. 'I'll help you rescue your princess, on condition that the parcel be returned to me, unopened and unharmed.'

'How much help can you offer?' Luranni said skeptically. 'You were led easily into our trap.'

Fost's laugh made her take a step back. 'Led? No, I came of my own free will, eyes open to the danger.'

'Words!' spat Erlund.

'You think so? Listen: two of your friends were on our tails before we'd gotten out of sight of the docks. We acquired two more escorts as we passed the warehouse with the broken windows and the woman-breasted gargoyles. A final four drifted out of doorways in our wake as we turned onto this block.'

The courier turned a malevolent grin on Erlund, who stood slightly stooped, his tow-colored hair dangling in front of eyes that blazed hate.

'Moreover,' Fost continued, directing his words to Luranni, 'your

76

bright young lad's shoes scuffed cobblestones as he came for me. If I hadn't wanted to deal with you, I'd have spitted him like a fowl to be roasted for dinner.'

'That's a lie!' Erlund struggled to get free of the friends who held him upright.

Luranni shook her head. 'No. He's right.' A vee of consternation creased her smooth brow as she regarded Fost in the waning light. 'Very well, Longstrider. You have your bargain. Follow me. We go to meet my father.'

The shadowed shapes of Luranni's comrades faded back into the gloom. Luranni turned to go with them. Realizing Fost was not following, she halted and turned.

'We must hurry,' she said, fluttering impatient fingers.

Fost stood where he was, as dark and unmoving as a basalt statue. 'I don't reject your hospitality,' he explained, 'but I can't help thinking of where it got Moriana.'

One of the youthful conspirators rematerialized from between two buildings close at hand. 'No fault of ours,' he said. 'That damned bitch-slut Synalon has her sorcerers mentally attuned to a horde of fire elementals. The salamanders can see anything lit by flame, and what they see, Rann and his henchmen see as well.' He showed white teeth in a lupine grin. 'That's one thing we gained from this disaster. Seizing the princess so quickly showed they had some special source of information; her whereabouts were known only to a select few, who would not hope to escape Rann's mercies no matter whom they betrayed.'

'The city reeks of fire-magic,' Luranni said. 'It took little time for us to realize what our enemies were doing.'

Fost's stomach iced over again. He'd known from the beginning he dealt with utter amateurs. It was no comfort to have a demonstration of how skillful his enemies were in contrast.

'You mean that so much as lighting a taper would give us away to this Rann?'

Luranni's mouth opened to reply. Blinding white light abruptly washed the storefronts on the far side of the avenue. Fost, Luranni, and several of her cadre ran into the center of the street.

To the east, the soaring Palace of the Clouds dominated the skyline. From the palace's highest tower sprang three lines of flame tipped with incandescence. Fost could feel the stinging, hungry heat beat against his face as the three points of brilliance hung for a moment like new stars in the night sky. They plunged down like meteors, leaving glowing trails. Stone melted before them and wood exploded into fire. Like water thrown up by a falling stone, red flames splashed high into the ebon sky.

'Such is the vengeance of Synalon,' Luranni said at Fost's side. Her fingertips were soft and tremulous on his brawny arm. 'Such is her power.'

The stricken mansion vomited flame like an erupting volcano. Fost had a vision of lovely Moriana held captive by a power and malice that hurled fire elementals against those who opposed it. The thought brought an upwelling of heat within him to match the dragon's-breath that washed over his face.

Cold sobriety quenched the emotional outburst. *Why waste my concern on her?* Fost thought. *She robbed me and tried to deny me eternal life.* Deep within a voice reminded him that she'd done far more than that. He ignored it and let Luranni lead him away.

The limits imposed by the city's circumference meant that space was at a premium. Streets tended toward labyrinthine narrowness. Buildings lofted high and slender, so tall they seemed to lean together at their tops to form an arcade of dizzying height. Yet here and there the elaborately graven stone walls fell away, to let a small fountain play gently in a trim garden, or a statue brood in silence. Fost came to understand this was to keep the inhabitants of the city from losing intimate contact with the sky that was their home.

As they walked, Luranni filled Fost in on recent events in the Sky City. She spoke of the long-standing enmity between the royal twins Synalon and Moriana, of the long illness and abrupt demise of Queen Derora, of Moriana's absence and disastrous return. Her voice was low music, transforming the lilting accent of the city into a liquid concerto.

'How did you come to meet our princess?' Luranni asked.

He craned his neck around, framing his response carefully. The scene was eerie enough to make his distraction convincing. A dancing interplay of shadow and orange hellglare destroyed all perspective. The distorted figures peopling the friezes that clung to the narrow facades seemed to move with a life of their own.

'We fell in with one another on the road from Samadum,' he said, deciding to heed wisdom learned long ago in the slums of High Medurim. *The simplest lie serves best,* the wise old thief to whom he'd been apprenticed had said over and over. 'She showed interest in a parcel I was to deliver in the Southern Steppes. Perhaps she believed it contained property stolen from her; I don't know. I do know she drugged me, and when I awoke my sled-dogs trailed her here.'

'Odd that they were able to,' Luranni said. 'Moriana is a sorceress, as are all of noble birth in the city. I'd have thought she'd possess tricks to throw your beasts off the scent.'

'I have a few tricks of my own,' Fost said, smiling down at her.

A quick pressure on his arm halted him. 'Here,' Luranni said. 'My home.' She gestured to a wood-fronted building three stories tall, sandwiched between structures high enough to snag passing clouds. The fireshot darkness made it impossible to discern details, but Fost had the impression they'd passed into a more genteel district than that fronting the docks.

With a trace of a smile on her lips, she lifted a finger and signaled for silence. Taking his arm, she led him up the short flight of steps to the triple-arched door. Courteously, Fost reached a hand out to open it but found it locked. Luranni gestured and it slowly opened before them.

Inside was blacker than in the street. Fost paused in the door as the girl glided down a short hallway. He expected her to light a candle. She stopped at the foot of a dimly seen stairway and turned back expectantly. He realized there would be no candle within this house while he was there – no fire at all. All flames were Synalon's eyes within the city.

She took his hand and led him up the stairs. Behind them he heard the door swing softly shut. The hairs at the back of his neck lifted slightly. This wasn't called the City of Sorcery for nothing.

His toe slammed into a projection at the second-floor landing. Luranni smiled at his curses. He could see her face in the starlight filtering in through window slits.

She led him to a doorway masked by a bead curtain. She swept it aside and nodded for him to enter. Ducking his head, he entered the chamber. He discovered painfully that he couldn't stand upright. The ceiling was meant to clear the heads of the locals, not someone of his large stature.

The curtain fell back with a tinkle like tiny chimes. Luranni walked by Fost and plucked something off a shelf, untroubled by the darkness.

'Well,' Fost said. 'When does your father arrive?'

Luranni laughed. 'Do you seriously think High Councillor Uriath would welcome being dragged from his dinner to speak with some ragged groundling?' Mention of dinner brought a growl from Fost's stomach. 'We will see him in the morning. Sit and I'll bring food.'

'I'll be forever in your debt.'

He found a fat, silky cushion against a wall and lowered himself onto it. Relaxing, he began to battle drowsiness. He'd had a long and tiring day, and not much sleep the night before.

Luranni returned from another room with food and a jug of wine. She pulled up another cushion and sat facing him, the food between them. In one hand she held the object she'd taken from the shelf. She raised it and shook it briskly.

Light flooded the room. Fost froze with a morsel of spiced meat halfway to his open mouth. His blood cried *betrayal!* and his pulse hammered in his temples.

Luranni set the lamp down and clapped her hands delightedly. 'Oh, but you looked so astonished when the lightfool came on!' she sang.

'You'll look more astonished when five dozen bird riders drop in through the skylight.'

'There's no fire here.' Luranni's eyes were alive with mirth. 'Creatures so minute they cannot be seen individually reside within. When they are disturbed, their bodies give off light, but no heat.' She tapped the clear glass figurine with a fingernail. Waves of greater brightness rippled through it. 'They're North Cape magic, common toys here in the city.' She shook her hair as she filled a bronze goblet with wine. 'I never thought my little fool would prove so useful.'

Chewing on a savory strip of meat, Fost leaned closer to examine the lamp. It had been blown in the shape of a jester at the court of High Medurim, hang-bellied and great-eared, naked but for a breechclout. Cool radiance pulsed from it. Far from being dazzling in its brilliance as he'd thought when its first light shone, the glow was soft and calming to his twisted nerves.

He sat back. Having taken a bite of food, he was overcome with a hunger so great that he felt a mad desire to stuff handfuls of the sweet, hot meat and little pastries into his mouth.

'Tell me of the Sky City,' he said, hoping to eat his fill while she spoke.

Luranni gazed a moment into the fool's glow, sipping wine. 'Very well,' she said. 'Your height is great, your bones massive. You are northern-born, aren't you?'

Fost nodded as he gulped down a mouthful of pastry. 'I was born in the Teeming, the slum district of High Medurim itself.'

Luranni was still. She rocked back and forth, long graceful legs tucked under her, eyes gazing into the light. Just as Fost began to wonder if she were entranced, she spoke again. 'Twelve thousand years ago men came to this land. Your ancestors came from the cold mountains and forests of the Northern Continent; they founded the city-states that later grew into empire. From the Islands of the Sun came my own folk, to make landfall in the southeastern corner of the continent. The Realm was sparsely inhabited. Beings lived here, manlike and yet not men; warm-blooded and shaped like us, but with the scales of reptiles. Their women nursed their young at the pap, but the young were hatched from eggs. Zr'gsz they called themselves, *the people*. Men named them Vridzish, the Hissing Ones, after their manner of speech. At first there was amity. The People were an ancient race and barely noticed the newcomers.'

She paused and moistened her throat from the goblet. Fost found his eyes slipping from her face and moving down the graceful curve of her throat to the shadowed valley between her breasts. Her breasts were not large, but the slice of each, visible where her tunic had come loose, looked tender and inviting. With his hunger beginning to be sated, Fost felt a new appetite asserting itself. He bid his manhood be still and forced his eyes up to hers.

'High Medurim was built by the Northbloods, Athalau by the People of the Sun. Inevitably their domains spread. Cities rose in what is now the Quincunx: Wirix on its island in Lake Wir, Thailot at the head of the pass connecting the lands east of the Thail Mountains with Deepwater on the western shore. From Athalau were settled Kara-Est, at the head of the Gulf of Veluz and Brev, which lay on the trade route between Athalau and Deepwater. Later, Medurim and Athalau joined to build Bilsinx, the central city of the Quincunx, to protect the strategic junction of routes from north to south and east to west.

'The Hissing Ones grew uneasy. They had little use for the surface, save for their skystone mines in the lava beds of Mount Omizantrim, from which they built their skyrafts and the very city itself, launched twenty thousand years before. Most were content to dwell here, depending on trade with the groundli – uh, the surface folk, for food. But they came to fear that Man would try to topple them from their city. The city was not confined to the Quincunx then, but traveled where its owners wished. Whoever controlled the city ultimately controlled the Realm. This was a balmy land in those days, and humankind is covetous. It would not long permit ownership to remain in other hands.'

'Wait,' Fost protested. 'You said this land was balmy, and before that you said the Northern Continent was cold. Living this far south you might think that, but traders plying northward from High Medurim take only light garb with them and need extra stocks of water due to the heat. And where we sit this instant, we're not two hundred miles from the Rampart Mountains, and south of them lie ice fields. You've been sadly misled, Luranni.'

'I said this is how things *were*, outlander. Haven't you heard of the War of Powers?'

'Vaguely.' Fost shrugged and drank some wine. 'Mere legends, no more.'

'Oh? Untrue. Listen: the sorceries of the Hissers were great, beyond even those of Athalau. The People held captive a demon, black Istu, against whom neither might nor magic could avail. They decided to cleanse the Realm of humanity. For a hundred years they systematically slaughtered, laying waste the Quincunx cities and whipping the armies of High Medurim off the battle field like curs to the kennel.' Fost scowled at this description of his forebears but did not interrupt. 'Their skyborne armies usually overwhelmed, but when they didn't, the Demon of the Dark Ones strode forth across the land. The earth itself groaned beneath their might.

'At last only Athalau remained unconquered. All of humankind that survived north of the Ramparts was a few thousand pitiful refugees, too weak to threaten the People. Athalar wisdom was great enough that even with Istu's aid the Hissing Ones didn't wish to go against the folk of that city until they were completely isolated. That time came at last.

'Even then, the Athalar had come to be more of the other world than of this one. One alone in that city, Felarod the Mystic, preached the call to arms against the People. The Athalar did not heed him, scorning him for his materialistic concerns. A few listened, though, and began to work secretly with him.

'In Athalau lived five prophets who had dwelt among men since long before the colonization of the Realm, and who were sacred to the Wise Ones of Agift. These five went to the Sky City to intercede for

Athalau. The Hissing Folk laughed and sacrificed them to Istu, after inflicting terrible tortures.'

'The Five Holy Ones,' Fost said in surprise.

'Just so. The Three and Twenty Wise Ones gave their blessing to Felarod, which enabled him to open the Gate of the Earth-Spirit. The very planet had been outraged by the tread of the star-born demon; its power surged, channeled by Felarod and his hundred acolytes.

'The conflict was fierce beyond imagining. A star fell from the sky and blasted a great crater in the Southern Steppes; in the west the great island Irbalt sank beneath the sea; the very planet tipped on its axis, bringing the Realm almost to the South Pole, and the Northern Continent into the tropics. At last the People were overcome. Nine out of ten died, as did ninety of the Hundred. As great as was the power he guided, Felarod couldn't destroy or banish Istu. He did manage to trap the demon within the foundations of the city, with wards that would last an eternity. All but dead, he summoned up the Ullapag from the guts of Mount Omizantrim to guard the skystone beds and keep the surviving People away from this last resource of their strength. Then he gave himself back to the Earth-Spirit.'

Luranni sighed. Though the evening was cool, sweat beaded her brow. 'Little of the tale remains. The People sued for peace. They renounced all claim to the surface world and restricted the path of the city to the Great Quincunx. The survivors of Felarod's Hundred, appalled at the destruction they'd wreaked, exiled themselves. Later, Athalar came to dwell in the Sky City. Eventually they became strong enough to banish the People and claim the city for themselves.' She sat back, drawing into herself. She had chanted the tale like a priestess reciting a litany. Now that it was done, she seemed as spent as if she'd performed some complex and demanding ritual. 'Beyond that, our story is of rise to glory and eventual decline. I imagine it's as depressing to me as the story of High Medurim's fall from mastery of the Realm to nominal lordship over a handful of squabbling city-states must be to you.'

Fost shrugged. The past glories of High Medurim meant nothing to him; they were too far past, and the gilded and hollow empire was now too plainly a joke. He poured himself more wine and refilled Luranni's cup. All the while, his eyes kept drifting toward the floor.

'Is it true a demon lives beneath our very feet?' he asked at last.

The girl nodded solemnly. 'In earlier times, the rulers could partially awaken it and tap some of its strength, though they couldn't free it, even if they had been fools enough to try. The Rite of Dark Assumption was performed at the accession of each new ruler. It involved the sacrifices of one of the royal blood to Istu.'

For a moment, Fost had trouble swallowing his wine. 'Do they still do that?' The fear in him did not spring solely from self-interest.

Moriana . . .

'No. Not since the Etuul dynasty came to power five thousand years ago. Derora was of that lineage, as is Moriana – and Synalon as well, though you'd hardly know it.'

Vague worries still gnawed at Fost's brain. He realized Luranni was leaning forward, her tunic opened farther, her red lips parted. Her eyes turned to glowing moons.

The fears evaporated, and with them all thoughts of the thieving princess. Fost touched Luranni's cheek. She kissed the rough, scarred fingers, never taking her luminous eyes from his face. The faint, exotic aroma he'd noticed on entering the apartment thickened, became a heady musk, intoxicating and arousing. He recalled her saying that all nobles of the Sky City possessed some sorcerous power, and as a High Councillor, whatever that was, her father was undoubtedly of exalted birth. The great-eyed girl had worked some enchantment on him. The musk grew stronger, caressing his palate with a taste of cinnamon. He recalled a similar taste in the wine. Then he pushed such things from his mind; he took Luranni into his arms.

Her mouth opened. His covered it eagerly. Her tongue danced over the very tip of his. She pressed his hand to her breast. Warm flesh yielded to his touch. Her nipple throbbed its urgent need against his palm.

Their tongues flowed together. His hands, at once rough and gentle, tugged open her tunic with a *snap!* of the lacings. Her own fingers deftly undid the front of his garment, and stroked coolly across his hirsute chest.

His mouth left hers. Her lips glistened moistly in the heatless light. He nibbled down the line of her jaw. His hands kneaded the pliant softness of her breasts as he felt the lustful hammering of her pulse beneath.

His lips brushed down the curve of her throat. There was tension in the fingers that peeled Fost's tunic away, tension and need. The courier kissed the soft, pale ripeness of her left breast. A quiet, 'Oh!' broke from the girl's gleaming lips.

Fost worked the succulent melon with his lips as ravenously as he'd devoured the bread and meat the woman had set before him earlier. Her scent was like the scent of the wine, strong and sweet. Her ivory teeth pinned her lower lip as she sucked in her breath in passionate response. One slim hand trapped the courier's head against her small, firm breast. The other caressed the cabled muscles of his back.

Questing fingers found a long transverse wound. Luranni felt Fost stiffen. 'You've been wounded,' she murmured. She pushed him away reluctantly.

At the girl's silent urging, Fost hoisted himself into a sitting position. Naked from the waist up, Luranni went to a low table, picked up a silver jar and from it began to apply a stinging cream to the swordcut.

Gradually the fire died, and with it the last of the residual ache that had not left Fost's back since the bird rider's blade had laid it open.

'Thanks,' he said, unable to keep a note of grumpiness out of his voice. 'But I can think of other, better things you can do to heal me.'

'You flatter me, Longstrider,' she said. 'But lie back down and I'll do what I can.

Fost obeyed. The cream had dried on contact with his skin. The silky covering of the pillow soothed him further. He vented a throaty sigh of contentment.

Like a vision she appeared before him. She was nude, her lithe limbs shining as though oiled. Dark aureoles covered her breast-tips like palms, and the nipples jutted proudly erect. The fur beneath her flat belly was fine and brown. In the tangled ringlets between her thighs, a drop of moisture threw back the fool's-light like the facets of a reflecting diamond.

Fost's sigh became a growl of lust. He started to lunge for her, his hand reaching outward.

'No, no,' she laughed, tossing back her straight hair. 'Rest. I shall do what is necessary.' With strong, insistent hands she pushed him back down.

Without seeming to move quickly, she had the big man's trousers and rough undergarment off in an instant. His manhood swung upright like a flagpole. Luranni's eyes and mouth smiled in appreciation of what she'd found.

'It's truly spoken that northern men are mighty,' she murmured.

She swung a slender leg across him. His hands caught her about the middle and slowly lowered her down. Rolling her hips in subtle circles, Luranni leaned forward. Fost's hands left her waist to slide up her ribs and grasp the rounded cones of her firm breasts.

She gasped at the rough pressure of his hands. She threw away all restraint and began to drive Fost wild. Time ceased to have meaning. In a vague, detached corner of his mind not blinded with a red fog of lust, Fost thought that Luranni had not lain with a man for some time. But then, he'd coupled passionately with Moriana the night before, and here he was, as ready and randy as if he'd been six weeks on the road with only his dogs for company.

Not even the thought of Moriana could quell his rampaging desire, such was Luranni's magic. Sweating, straining, groaning, they built the sweet electric tension until it burst free in loin and brain and fused their souls with ecstasy.

When the fury was done, Luranni fell forward, laughing her spring-time laugh. For a long time they lay still, with murmurings and small caressings, content with the feel of each other close.

'I see a question building in your eyes,' Luranni said after a while. She raised herself to look at the courier's face. In the soft glow of the fool, his features looked curiously young and vulnerable. 'I haven't the power of thought-scrying, so you'll have to speak it with your lips.'

She broke into giggles as he darted his head up and kissed her on the nose. He patted her upturned rump affectionately, but his face grew serious at once.

'This Rite of Dark Assumption,' he said. 'What did it achieve? The demon cannot be summoned or released, you said. Did the ritual serve just to do away with troublesome rivals to the throne?'

A shudder passed through her naked body. She rolled off him, clinging to his side for comfort. 'No, not that. Or rather, not that alone.' Her golden eyes were grave. 'So great was the magic with which Felarod bound Istu that the demon cannot fully be awakened by any magic men know, though the People could perhaps achieve it — if any of them survive and still remember. But Istu's dreams are filled with power and vengeance. The rulers of the Sky City tapped into them, winning the good will of the slumbering demon with sacrifice.'

She lay unspeaking for so long that Fost thought she had fallen asleep. Just as he was about to stir, she spoke again. 'Even asleep and bound, Istu's strength is vast. With that power augmenting their own sorcerous knowledge, the rulers of the city challenged the empire

86

during its most powerful epoch.'

Fost nodded. He knew of the wars between High Medurim, at the peak of her glory, and the Sky City. Eventually High Medurim had triumphed, with the aid of mages he now guessed to have come from Athalau. But victory had proven costly. Driving the human Sky Citizens back into their floating stronghold hadn't required such cosmos-wrecking magic as had the defeat of the People, but it had sapped the strength of the empire enough so that in a century invading barbarians from the hot Northern Continent had seized the Sapphire Throne and started High Medurim on its own road to decay.

'So they gave up the Rites?' he asked.

'Julianna the Wise, who wrested the crown from Malva Kryn and founded the Etuul line, forbade it as an abomination. The rulers of the city would no longer rule through power gained from the anguish of sacrifice.' Absently, she stroked the great muscles of his chest. 'Our sorcery is still the strongest in the Realm, but not what it once was.'

Her voice rang dim and far away in Fost's ears. Too much exertion and too little sleep had finally worn him down. The thought fluttered through his mind that Synalon, from what he had learned, was formidable enough without the aid of sleeping Istu. The fool's-glow began to dim. Fost slipped into deep sleep with his hand resting on Luranni's silken flank.

'Greetings, cousin.' Moriana looked up from the bottomless well of her misery to see Prince Rann standing in the doorway of the torture chamber.

Like a malevolent spirit he glided across the floor, feet soundless on stone worn smooth by the feet of generations of torturers and their victims. His limbs were cloaked in a robe of dark gray silk that shimmered in the light of the bracketed torches. With his hair slicked back from his ruined, aristocratic face, he looked like an idle noble come to while away the night at some mild diversion.

Which is exactly why he comes to this room, she thought. As another might compose sonnets or contemplate ancient statuary, Rann took his rest and pleasure in the contemplation of pain. For all her physical courage, Moriana shuddered at his touch.

The examination was as thorough and impersonal as any physician's. Few chirurgeons possessed the eunuch prince's knowledge of human anatomy. None could have gained it as he had, by testing living bodies to destruction in a thousand hideous ways, without violating the powerful oaths binding them to the cause of healing.

'You are well, I judge, outside of being helpless from the ward spells Synalon cast on this cell,' he said, rising. 'A few bruises caused by that lout of a captain. I daresay he's sorry. At least he seemed so when Terror ripped out his liver. Your hurts are nothing the blessed queen can lay to me.'

'By what right do you call her queen?' Moriana flared. 'I am the younger by seven minutes. By law I am ruler of the city!'

He smiled. 'Cling to your pride, my dear. It's all you have. Soon enough even that will be torn from you.' His face darkened. He was still bitter at being prevented from torturing his cousin.

He had been scrupulous in following Synalon's orders regarding her sister. Moriana's torn garments had been replaced with a clean but shapeless linen smock, prisoner's garb; the chains that bound her wrists and ankles were carefully padded with silk to prevent chafing. Synalon's instructions hadn't mentioned Moriana's mental well-being, however, so Rann had conveyed her here to what he liked to refer to as his study, where incense and scrubbings with lye had done little to mask the raw stench of death and pain.

The sound of voices made Rann turn. Moriana tried to calm her heart as she looked to the doorway. She felt her sister approaching, and knew that she was about to learn her fate. She was not fool enough to imagine for an instant that Synalon had denied her to Rann out of any mercy.

If Synalon will not allow Rann to torture me, the princess thought, *what horror does she have in mind?*

' . . . but for the really jaded taste, as I perceive Your Majesty's to be,' a voice was saying as the stately Synalon came into view, 'the sensations to be had from sexual congress with the male of the kine kept by the farmers of the city-states, the so-called hornbulls, cannot be matched.'

Looking neither right nor left at the implements of torture, Synalon entered the chamber. She wore a gown of crimson silk, slit to reveal flashes of creamy thigh as she walked. She held Erimenes's jug in the crook of her arm. Her eyebrows were arched in a look of feigned shock.

'Hornbulls? My dear sage, whatever makes you think I'd consider such bestiality?'

'Recall that a beast may carry a greater load than any man, particularly in his loins.'

From the corner of her eye, Moriana saw Rann blush.

'I can't see why you allow this demon to speak so familiarly to you, my queen,' he said stiffly.

Erimenes sputtered.

'He's not a demon, Rann,' Synalon said, laughing. 'He's but a ghost. And I do not mind his speech. In truth, it makes my loins tingle, and I almost wish his spirit were cloaked in flesh. What might a man learn of love after fourteen hundred years?'

'Thirteen hundred and ninety-nine,' the spirit said pedantically. 'Had I a body, O Queen, I doubt even I could teach you. The way you served those soldiers in the barracks, six at one time! Phenomenal. Still,' he went on unctuously, 'I'm sure Prince Rann, wise though he is, cannot fully appreciate such – '

Rann went the color of Synalon's gown. 'Were your spirit clothed in flesh, demon, I'd teach you more about pain than ever Synalon could of rutting! When my cousin is done with you – '

'Enough!' Synalon's voice cracked like a lash. She turned to her sister, who sat listening without interest to the byplay. 'Moriana, beloved sibling, rejoice! I have consulted the stars, and they bode well. Glorious destiny shall be yours.'

'What are you talking about?' she asked, fighting the dread that threatened to fill her mind with madness. *Could she?* she wondered wildly. *No, it cannot be! Not even Synalon would dare such a thing.*

But as soon as her sister parted lips to speak, she knew it was so.

'I speak of the Rite of Dark Assumption, sister dear, left unperformed these past five thousand years,' Synalon said.

'*No!*' Moriana shrieked. The word rang as though all the agony suffered in this room in thirty millennia had condensed inside her. 'No, *no, NO!*'

Synalon's laugh rolled around the chamber. Rann smiled hugely, in admiration and anticipation.

'Say,' Erimenes said, 'will someone have the courtesy to explain the joke?'

'Synalon!' the captive princess screamed. 'You can't mean it! To disturb the demon after so long – do you think you can control it? *Do you?*'

'I have learned much that our weak mother turned from knowing.' From a mask of inhuman exultation, Synalon's face became that of a crusader, stern and righteous. 'Too long has the Sky City hidden its greatness. To think that for five millennia the most that our magic has accomplished has been the summoning of tame salamanders to light the pleasure palaces of fat bankers in Tolviroth Acerte! Our people cry out for a return to the greatness that was ours when we cast the damned reptiles from our city, and the groundlings shrank in terror from the shadows of our warbirds. Only the dark wisdom of Istu can win us back our power.'

Moriana stared at her. Her features were as white and stiff as sunbleached bone. 'What if you can't control it? Humans never truly dominated the spawn of the Dark Ones, and the Rite of Dark Assumption has been lost for generations! How do you know that you won't destroy the city instead of bringing back its greatness?'

'Perhaps I don't.' Synalon smiled. 'What does it matter to you? You'll not know it, sister dear. Your soul will be joined with Istu's in unholy matrimony, after he's worked his will upon your wretched flesh.'

'This sounds interesting,' Erimenes said.

The black-haired princess ignored him. 'Two days,' she said. 'In two days the stars will be right for Istu to receive his bride. Prepare yourself for your groom, sister mine. The nuptial hour approaches.' With Erimenes's jug tucked under her arm, she left.

'My lady.' Rann's voice stopped her in the doorway. 'Two days is a long time. I fear the hours will weigh heavily upon her.'

Synalon scowled impatiently. 'What is it you want, cousin?'

'I can lighten the waiting for her.' He held up his hand to forestall a furious outburst. 'I know ways to, ah, *amuse* Her Highness without working any harm on her body.' He smiled wickedly. 'Trust me.'

'Trust you?' Synalon sniffed derisively. 'Do you take me for a fool?' Rann did not answer. He stood stock still regarding her with his eerie, pale eyes.

Synalon felt that anticipation would be the most exquisite torture her sister could possibly endure. But Rann was more than an able servant, he was the best military mind in the Sky City. Her future plans required his skill and cooperation. She wouldn't get them if she thwarted his desires too often.

'Very well,' she said with a sigh. 'Do as you wish. But I warn you, Rann, do not damage her.' She paused, pursing her lips in thought. 'You are of royal blood, my cousin,' she purred. 'I wonder if Istu would be wroth if you took Moriana's place?'

Rann stared at her, and she had the satisfaction of seeing the flicker of emotion in his eyes that was normally alien to him. It was good to remind him that she could still make him fear.

'It's something to think about,' she said. 'Come, Erimenes. There are no hornbulls in the city, but perhaps a stud from the kennels will serve as well . . .'

In earnest discussion with the dead philosopher, Synalon's voice faded down the corridor until it was lost in its own diminishing echo. Rann's face had recovered its serenity. Rubbing his hands together in a washing motion, he turned to his captive.

High Councillor Uriath was a busy man, and Fost found small cause to complain that he'd been unable to meet with the dignitary the night before – Luranni had produced an astonishing variety of suggestions for activity more diverting. So diverting, in fact, that Fost had no clear memory of the end of the night's festivities. He recalled a sensation of soaring, caused as much by the giddiness of sheer exhaustion as by ecstasy, then a plummet straight into darkness. He remembered nothing of his dreams, but he woke with a vague unease that stayed with him all day. He suspected he'd never sleep untroubled as long as he remained in a city where magic permeated even everyday activities.

Luranni woke long before he did. She looked fresh and unruffled. When he dragged himself to a mirror to shave, he shuddered at the sight. He looked as if he should have been squatting by a campfire in the Thails, with a bone through his nose.

He found water to shave, warm water heated by a captive elemental in the basement of the building. Running water wasn't common in Medurim or Tolviroth, with heated taps available to those who could pay for imported Sky City magic. Such luxury was in short supply on the steppes, however. Fost felt a touch of shame at how much he'd enjoyed it. Like most Realm-road couriers, he professed a disdain for civilized comforts.

'How do you get the water up here?' he asked, rubbing his face with a towel. 'It's heavy to haul up by balloon.'

Luranni only smiled. She had grown accustomed to his outlandish ignorance. From a small kitchen on the other side of a beaded curtain came the sounds and smells of cooking, as a servant prepared breakfast. Fost's belly growled like a hungry sled dog.

'We haul some up from the surface,' the girl said. 'But we are careful about conserving it, and we use our salamanders to distill waste water for use again. Also, we have drains and cisterns to trap rainwater. And, of course, there are the aeroaquifers.'

'Ara-what?'

'Aeroaquifers. There are places in the city where water can be brought from the air, as though from an aquifer on land. There are fountains in many streets – I'll show you some day. We don't know how it's done. Magic of the Fallen Ones, you see. My father says we'd work it out fast enough, though, if our rulers paid more mind to practical matters and less to intrigue.'

'I thought your father was one of the city's rulers.' Fost seated himself on cushions across from Luranni. She wore a shift blazing with color, scarlet, orange, vivid blue. Somehow, the combination did not affront his taste.

'He is an important man, chief of the Council of Advisors. The Council must be consulted on important decisions and is charged with managing the accession of a new monarch when the old one dies – like now. But they cannot make policy.'

The curtain parted with a sound like wind through dry branches. The servant entered with that peculiar walk servants accomplish without seeming to move their feet. The servant was a small, wizened person of indeterminate sex, dressed in a shapeless robe. Luranni and her guest were given bowls of steaming, clove-scented tea.

'I don't imagine that sets well with your father,' said Fost.

'My father is an ambitious man.' Luranni started to sip her tea, halted with the bowl poised beneath her lips. 'But his true concern is the welfare of the city, of course.'

Fost masked his smile behind his own vessel. Luranni's qualification had come a beat too slow. He wondered what Uriath really had in mind. Yet the underground members he'd met so far had seemed devoted to Moriana. He shrugged and tasted his tea. The hot brew scorched his tongue and tickled it at the same time. He found the effect refreshing.

'When do I meet your father?' Fost asked, feeling impatience begin to prod him again.

'This afternoon, surely,' said Luranni.

Fost choked on his tea. 'Great Ultimate!' he gagged. The servant reappeared, leather androgyne face wreathed in steam from plates heaped with food. 'What in the name of Ust's claws am I going to do till then?'

Accepting her plate, Luranni said to him, 'I'm sure we'll think of something.'

92

Luranni proved no less inventive by daylight than by the soft, steady glow of her lightfool. It was a weak-kneed and somewhat befuddled Fost who set out with her several hours after breakfast for the promised tour of the City in the Sky.

Before they left her apartment, she insisted on disguising him. If the corporal in the orphaned gondola had survived his return to the ground via the guidelines, the Monitors might have a description of the man who had gained entry to the city in such an unorthodox fashion. Fost groaned at the inconvenience. He didn't doubt that the authorities might be looking for him, but he had little confidence in Luranni's concept of what constituted a disguise. He didn't fancy wandering through strange and hostile streets wearing a plaster nose and a bright orange wig.

His fears were unfounded. Luranni produced a black eyepatch.

'Only this?' he asked, skeptical.

'Any seeing you will remember only the eyepatch. None will be able to describe what you really look like.' He nodded, remembering his days in Medurim spent as an apprentice cutpurse. His master had insisted that the most effective disguise was also the simplest.

When Fost peered at himself in the mirror, with the patch in place and his cheeks given a gaunt appearance by a shadow drawn below either cheekbone in plain charcoal, he had to admit that no one would mistake the hungry, one-eyed wolf reflected back for Fost Longstrider.

'Raffish,' he muttered, not displeased with his new appearance.

'Handsome,' said Luranni, smiling. She took his arm, and they left the apartment.

As they wended their way through the tangle of the city's streets, Fost's impressions of the night before were confirmed. The lines of architecture took the eye upward along tapering buildings with peaks hundreds of feet above street-level. It took periodic nudges from Luranni's elbow to keep him from gawking like a hayseed. Nothing would attract unwanted attention faster than acting like an obvious newcomer to the city.

Strangely, the Sky City disconcerted Fost even more by daylight than it had at night. Dark had masked the buildings, revealing only hints of intricate stonework. That had been eerie enough, but the daylight heightened the effect. The proportions of the building did not fit themselves to Fost's eye. The balance of space and mass, the flow, the curve, all of it grated. It was wrong only subtly, but still wrong.

His reaction was not mere provincialism. Fost had been in most of the cities of the Realm, seen buildings from the stately colonnades of Medurim to the parti-colored pastel houses scattered among the hills of Kara-Est and the onion-squat domes of Bilsinx and Brev. In the great seaports of the land he had seen embassies and residences built in the fashions of Jorea, the Northern Continent, and even the Far Archipelago in the Antipodes. He'd found some exotic, some amusing, some pleasing, and others not to his taste – but none *disturbing*. Nothing among all the many works of humankind he'd seen affected him in the way the city did.

'The works of humankind,' he repeated aloud. Luranni looked at him sharply. So did a dozen passersby. While he ruminated, they wandered into a bazaar lined with narrow stalls carved into the facades of buildings.

The answer blazed like a comet in his brain. The City in the Sky was not a 'work of humankind'. It had been constructed by an alien race thirty thousand years ago. The idea had seem far-fetched when Luranni had told him the night before. Now it came to him with a force that made him a bit shaky. He had read accounts of the Hissing Ones and the War of Powers and Felarod when he was a youth in High Medurim, and had dismissed them as fantasy. Now, observing the alien architecture of the Sky City, he couldn't deny that some of those fairy tales were true.

'Good day, excellents,' a voice said. 'Would it please you to pamper your palates with such delicacies as I have to offer?'

A ginger-eyed youth with hair like a bonfire stood behind one of the graven stone counters. Its bins overflowed with fruit. Fost looked at him, surprised at how good the offer sounded.

'Would you like some?' asked Luranni.

He nodded. 'I've been on the road for weeks. It's hard to get fresh fruit in the south. But isn't it late in the season for fruit?'

'Yes, quite.' Luranni picked up a three-lobed yellow fruit and held it up for Fost's inspection. Out of the shade of the booth, its surface showed moist mottlings. 'We get them packed in snow, but they don't keep forever. How much for this bedraggled specimen, Herech?'

'For one of your discriminating tastes, Lady Luranni, eleven klenor.' Fost blinked. He was no stranger to haggling, but the price was higher than the central spire of the Palace of the Clouds.

'If this *spinas* wasn't so elderly, it might be worth it,' she said, tossing the fruit back into the bin. 'Come now, Herech, you know better than to toy with me in this fashion. Don't embarrass me before my friend. Give us something worthwhile.'

'For you, then,' the boy said. He turned into the recesses of the stall and came back with a tray half-filled with melting snow. A globe the size of two fists rested in a cone of white snow. It was pale blue in color, with a silvery sheen that made it as iridescent as a butterfly's wing.

'What's this, Herech? It's lovely!' Luranni exclaimed.

'Unique,' the youth said proudly. 'A magical hybrid, raised in the hothouse of a Wirixer horticulture mage.'

Fost raised an eyebrow. Wirix had no arable land, being located on an island in the midst of Lake Wir at the top of the Quincunx. With the peversity for which they were noted, the Wirixers made an obsession of cultivation. Their savants had developed techniques of growing plants without soil; their mages devoted themselves to creating new and ever more wondrous varieties of plants. Wirix decorative plants, whether miniature trees small enough to flourish on tabletops or shrubs that produced blossoms the size of shields, were valued around the world. A new Wirixer fruit would be a treasure, indeed.

'What do you ask for it?' enquired Luranni, her eyes gleaming at the sight of the fruit.

'A mere hundred klenor.'

Fost almost choked at that. A 'mere' hundred klenor was a contradiction in terms. Fost earned that for a month's work as courier, and he was among the highest-paid couriers in the Realm. It would buy the favors for the night of a Tolviroth courtesan of the second class, and perhaps even one of the first class if she were not engaged with a ranking banker or corporate head; or a hauberk of heavy scale armor of the type favored by the cataphracts of the Highgrass Broad. To hear such a princely sum mentioned as the price for a piece of fruit made Fost's head spin.

As he stood open-mouthed, Luranni haggled Herech down to eighty klenor, a price for which Fost could have bribed the Bishop of Thrishnoor to denounce the Doctrine of Imminent Confabulation. Her hand darted into the pouch hung from her belt, emerging to rain a brief shower of gold onto the counter in front of Herech. Almost reverently, the youth picked up the fruit and presented it to her.

She broke it in two, handing a piece to Fost. He stared at it, numbed at the prospect of putting three weeks' wages into his mouth, chewing it, then swallowing it. Luranni bit into her half. The flesh within glowed translucent and pink, with yellow veins prominent.

Fost took a bite. The meat dissolved on his tongue into a flavor of sweetness and smoke with a tart edge that kept it from cloying. Before he knew it, he had devoured the entire piece. Young Herech hadn't lied. The flavor was unique. Never had he known a fruit so luscious.

'Thank you,' he said to Luranni.

'It was worth the price?' she asked needlessly. She turned and started walking up the street. Fost followed her but not before he caught a comradely wink from Herech.

It stopped him in midstride. He realized that Herech thought the highborn, successful, and lovely merchant had imported a strapping groundling barbarian to amuse herself. An initial upwelling of anger gave way to sheepish amusement. It wasn't all that far from the truth, and it was a role Fost had played before.

He winked back and set off at a long, loping pace.

'Our prices are high,' Luranni confessed, waving at the stalls laden with colorful goods of every description. 'But everything must be imported. Raised up from the surface by balloon. In fact, we're going now to the cargo docks on the starboard side of the city.'

'Starboard?'

The city changes direction every time it arrives at a juncture of the Quincunx. To say something is on the north side and something on the west makes little sense when the bearings change every few weeks. Here we have port and starboard, and fore and aft, just as you do on a seafaring ship. In a way, that's what we are, a ship that sails the sky.'

They left the street of merchants, turned a corner and found themselves by one of the compact clear spaces dotted around the city. A fountain in the center arched water from the mouth of a monster with sideways-hinged jaws into a wide, shallow stone basin. Luranni touched Fost's arm and nodded towards the odd fountain.

'An aeroaquifer.'

Fost swallowed hard, uneasy at the sight. It felt as if tiny insects crawled over his flesh, and the cut across his back seemed to pucker and bind. Water springing from thin air disconcerted him. The idea that even the adepts of the City of Sorcery failed to understand how the aeroaquifer worked frightened him even more.

They walked on. Sky Citizens passed them in both directions, going about their business. Watching them, Fost noted that they almost scurried, as if they were afraid it was about to rain. In the sounds of bargaining at the bazaar he'd heard a slightly shrill note; he put the two observations together and realized that the residents of the city, as much as they tried to hide it, were very, very scared.

From what Luranni had told him about the candidate for their next queen, Fost didn't blame them.

Luranni alone seemed unaffected by the fear. He reflected that she probably felt her position as daughter of High Councillor Uriath protected her from harm. All of the underground youths he'd seen the day before looked well-born. They probably all harbored similar feelings. It certainly accounted for the lack of skill at clandestine activity. They didn't – couldn't – take it seriously. It was only a game they played, in which the stakes were no more than embarrassment and inconvenience should they lose.

Fost hoped Luranni wouldn't learn the truth the hard way. It would almost certainly be Prince Rann who would teach her.

CHAPTER SEVEN

'I don't wish to be pessimistic,' High Councillor Uriath intoned, 'but our chances of rescuing the Princess Moriana are slim. Very slim.' He shook his great white-fringed head with ponderous regret.

Seeing Fost's scowl, Luranni squeezed his hand. The courier grunted and glanced across the table. For the first time since he'd entered the wine warehouse, led blindfolded to this rendezvous by Luranni, Fost wasn't the object of Erlund's hate-filled glare. The straw-haired youth frowned at Uriath instead.

Luranni confirmed what Fost had already surmised. Young Erlund was of the city's petty nobility, almost as far below Moriana in rank as was the slum-bred courier. That hadn't kept him from falling in love with her.

Fost welcomed this alliance in urging Moriana's rescue. The meeting in the murky storeroom, surrounded by tar-sealed casks of wine, was composed half of men and women Fost's age and half of men like Uriath, lords and merchants of advanced years. Despite the gap in ages, the mood was almost unanimous; the sour smell of wine and pessimism hung thick in the air.

'You see, young man,' Uriath said, leaning toward Fost, 'the princess has, beyond doubt, been under questioning by Prince Rann for hours. We can only assume that she's told her captors anything they wish to know.'

'That's a lie!' Erlund boiled to his feet, shaking with rage, his face as red as the High Councillor's. 'Moriana wouldn't tell those scum a thing!'

'Don't be a groundling, Erlund,' a voice growled from the dimness that filled the storeroom despite the bright morning outside. 'Rann could make the Vicar of Istu confess to worshipping Felarod. She's

98

sung like a raven in mating time by now, you can bet your last sipan.'

Erlund dropped into his seat as though stunned by a mighty blow. Fost's eyes widened. The name 'Rann' must hold powerful magic if it could quench Erlund so easily.

'Who is this Rann, anyway?' he demanded. 'The mere mention of his name makes everyone goggle as if they're about to birth a whale.'

'You don't know of Rann?' a girl asked, incredulous at such ignorance. Fost shook his head.

'Rann is prince of the city, first cousin to Synalon and Moriana,' Luranni explained, pitching her voice low as if afraid that speaking the prince's name might cause him to appear in a puff of brimstone. 'His mother was Ekrimsin the Ill-Favored, as unlike her sister Derora as Synalon is unlike Moriana. He was always a wild and unmanageable child, but not uncommonly so. He showed an early aptitude for war.

'Then he led an expedition against the tribesmen who plague the passes through the Thail Mountains. An accident crippled his warbird; he landed alone and was captured. His men found him and rescued him. But not before the Thailint had burned away his manhood with a torch.'

Fost shuddered. Rann might be a fiend straight from Hell, but Fost could pity anyone who'd undergone such an ordeal.

'His spirit was warped,' Uriath said. 'Denied more natural outlets for his passion, he vents his lust in torture, to which he brings all the intelligence and imagination of the Etuul line.' He puffed himself up slightly at the mention of the dynasty. Luranni had mentioned to Fost the night before that her line traced descent from an Etuul monarch.

'So not only is it likely that Moriana has revealed everything she knows about your underground, but that . . .' He paused, testing the flavor of possible ways of phrasing it, and liking none. ' . . . that, in her present condition, the princess might not conceive it a favor to be rescued. I fear that all she desires now is the palliative only death can bring.'

The silence grew more dense than the wine-smell. Fost's mind spun. *If Moriana dies, I'll never find Erimenes,* he thought. But worse was another thought, like a spear of ice in his gut: the woman with whom he'd lain beneath the stars might soon be reduced to a shapeless, broken thing that wept blood from eyeless sockets and mewled for death. Sweat cascaded down his forehead, stinging his eyes.

The door swung open. The conspirators gasped as one. By the time the interloper had fully entered the storeroom, Fost stood with curved blade in hand, ready to take out his rage and frustration in hot blood.

But it was another young conspirator, whom Fost recognized from the night before. 'Soldiers,' he said. 'A troop of them just coming down the street.'

Uriath paled. The conspirators all began to talk at once.

'Hold on a moment,' Fost said. The panicky clamor mounted. He slammed the pommel of his sword against the table. '*Hold*, dammit! And keep the noise down, or we're lost for sure.'

The noise subsided. He turned to the frightened messenger. 'Now tell me, are these bird riders or the Monitors everyone fears so?'

'Common soldiers of the watch.'

Fost nodded. 'And would Synalon dispatch such dross to arrest the High Councillor?'

He didn't know if she would or not, but he knew that if the conspirators' fears weren't soothed, they'd bolt into the street like frightened cattle. If, by some chance, the soldiers hadn't already guessed something was amiss, that would give them the idea soon enough.

'You are right, boy,' Uriath said, straightening unconsciously. 'You, Testin, go and watch them. If they approach the warehouse, give the alarm. But be certain.' The youth bobbed his head and disappeared.

If Fost had ever lived longer minutes than the ones which followed, he'd long since forgotten them. Every eye in the dank chamber fixed on him. The wait sparked the certainty that he'd guessed wrong. In spite of Uriath's vanity, the dark princess had sent low-caste troops to bring him to account. In a moment the doors would burst apart, the room would fill with men, and Fost Longstrider, outlander and courier, would shortly learn all he'd care to about Prince Rann's personality quirks.

The door burst open. It was only Testin, carrying a sheet of birdskin parchment in trembling hands.

'They nailed this to the front of the storehouse across the way and went on,' he said. He passed the sheet to Uriath. The High Councillor squinted, held it at arm's length, and scanned it rapidly.

'This changes things,' he said. ''Be it proclaimed: tomorrow at the fifth hour after dawn, the false traitor Moriana is, for the crimes of regicide, matricide, and treason, to be sacrificed to Holy Istu for the good of the city. With this seal confirmed, Synalon, Queen.'' '

'The Rite of Dark Assumption!' Luranni breathed.

'Lies!' Erlund shouted. 'She would not dare!'

Everyone ignored him. Uriath's eyes were as huge as his daughter's. 'We must act,' he said. 'We must free the princess. The Rite must not take place. If Synalon gains the demon's power, we are doomed.'

'I thought it would be no favor to rescue Moriana?' Fost asked.

Uriath shook his head. 'I was wrong. Rann won't have touched her. The Bride of Istu must be unsullied when she goes to the Vicar.'

If that means she has to be a virgin, Moriana is going to disappoint the Vicar, whomever he might be. Fost almost reeled at the impact of returning hope.

'You must help us,' said Uriath.

'Not so fast,' Fost said. 'I've no interest in your civil affairs. All I'm interested in is getting back my parcel.'

Uriath frowned. 'You'll get your parcel back. If you help us free Moriana, you can have any parcel in the city. You can have my whole trade stock if you so desire, wine, salamanders, everything.'

'Salamanders?' Fost asked.

The High Councillor gestured irritably. 'Of course. I own a concession to export small fire elementals under spells of obedience. They're our main item of trade.' Uriath allowed himself a rueful smile. 'The prevalence of the sprites is one reason Rann's found it so easy to use them against us.'

'All I want is the property I'm to deliver,' Fost stated with absolute honesty. 'If you can guarantee me that, I'll help you as best I can.'

'Done.' A hint of suspicion lurked in Uriath's blue eyes. Did he wonder at the courier's determination to risk the wrath of Synalon and Rann merely to regain a parcel? Fost didn't delude himself that the question would fail to occur to the Councillor. He only hoped that the pressures of the crisis kept Uriath's mind from worrying the puzzle too hard.

'One more thing,' Fost said as the meeting began to dissolve. Fost held up his short Sky City scimitar. 'You need me to fight for you, and I'd rather work with the type of blade I'm accustomed to. Have you any broadswords in stock, or do you know where I can get one?'

'Yes,' Uriath responded, his brow creasing as he thought. 'I have one that may suffice. Luranni will see that it reaches you before tomorrow. Go now. My daughter will show you what you must know to plan the rescue. We'll meet tonight to plan further.' He looked at

Luranni for a moment. 'Take good care of him, Luranni.'

'I will, Father,' she said innocently. Turning, the older man missed the look she gave the courier.

The girl screamed as the whip bit her flesh.

Moriana's scream rose with hers, scarcely less agonized, though the princess was untouched. 'Catannia!' she cried. 'Oh, Holy Ones, why is this happening?' The girl whimpered. Moriana didn't know whether the pitiful noise was a response to her cry or just a mindless protest against pain. The brutal caress of the many-thonged whip had changed the lovely, active girl Moriana had played with as a child into a mass of shredded, bloody rags of flesh hung from the ceiling of the dungeon.

His hands clasped behind him, rocking slightly on the balls of his feet, Prince Rann cocked his head toward Moriana. 'You invoke those heretics' gods on the eve of your wedding to Istu? How droll.' A wheeled black brazier smoldered near him, cradling white-hot instruments to await his pleasure. The glow turned his face into a demon's visage. 'If you must know why your friend suffers, it is through your own evil in turning traitor to the Sky City. Treason is contagious, you know. You were raised with this slut and doubtless infected her with your sedition. We must purge this sickness, wipe it out before it spreads.' With a splendidly helpless gesture, he turned to the burly guards who flanked the suspended girl. The whips sang again.

The smell of blood filled Moriana's nostrils like molten copper. Rann's eyes moved restlessly from her to Catannia and back, as the whips made the nude, dangling body rotate slowly. Moriana winced at every stroke.

Had she had room in her mind, she would have marked how her sister's power had solidified. Catannia's father was a minor noble of some influence among the aristocracy of the city. It was a bold stroke to have the daughter seized and subjected to torture for no more than lifelong friendship with the Princess Moriana. Yet it was a clever move, adding weight to the spurious claims of Moriana's treason.

But Moriana's mind was overcrowded with horror. Not even thought of her impending degradation by the Vicar of Istu could force its way past the knowledge that she was responsible for her friend's agony.

Under a new onslaught, Catannia's cries had grown perceptibly weaker. Now, as both whips gouged at what had been her buttocks, the cries ceased altogether. Rann frowned.

'Rouse her,' he commanded, irked that his sport had been interrupted.

The soldiers laid down their whips, fetched buckets of icy water and threw them over the limp figure. Catannia did not stir. The treatment was repeated without success. Then a soldier laid his head to the girl's ribs, beneath the flaccid ruin of her breasts.

'My lord,' he quavered, 'her heart has stopped.'

Rann sneered. 'A weakling. Such creatures are better off dead. There will be no room for weaklings in the new dawn of the city's glory.' He sighed. 'Well, Darman and Krydlach, why are you loitering? Bring in the next traitor to atone for his malfeasance.'

The guards went out, then returned supporting between them what Moriana thought to be a skeleton somehow imbued with a ghastly semblance of life. But though it couldn't stand unaided, its gaunt head was held high. Something in its carriage struck Moriana as familiar.

The head turned toward her. The sockets were empty, running thin streams of blood. The face was disfigured with half-healed burns — but the princess knew it.

'Kralfi,' she said, not loudly but in a shocked whisper, as if speaking the name quietly she could deny the reality facing her. The mouth that had smiled down on her in her crib was a jagged hole rimmed with stumps of teeth. Fingers that had frequently stroked her cheek with paternal affection hung limp as worms, their bones smashed almost to powder. To a princess barred by tradition from ever seeing her father or learning his name, Chamberlain Kralfi had been a beloved substitute.

He had also been the chief of Moriana's personal spy network, her best hope of countering Synalon's ambition. All hope was shattered now, shattered with the loyal old retainer's joints.

Rann smiled at his cousin's expression. 'I regret that we had already entertained the excellent Kralfi for some time before your apprehension. But now that you're here, dear cousin, I've arranged a most suitable . . .'

'Jackal!' The voice that cut through Rann's was garbled by the old man's wrecked mouth, but it cracked with defiance and pride. 'Save your childish torments, half-man. I have failed my lady. That's punishment more dreadful than any your feeble wit can devise.'

'Forgive me, my princess,' the ghastly visage said.

Moriana forced words past an obstruction in her throat. 'I forgive you.' It seemed to her that the torn lips formed a smile. Then the old man pitched, face forward, to the floor and lay unmoving.

Rann knelt by his side. Kralfi was as dead as Catannia. His heart had not been weak, merely old; already he had suffered torture sufficient to kill a man of lesser resolve. Will alone had kept him alive long enough to seek Moriana's absolution.

Rann turned livid. He clenched his fists beside his cheeks and squalled with fury. 'Cheated!' he screamed in shrill tones. 'Twice cheated! But not again!'

He took personal charge of torturing a string of victims like a procession of memories from Moriana's past: her ancient serving-maid, her fencing master, the sages who'd tutored her in arcane lore, other playmates. His hand wielded the scalpel that sliced, the heated pincers that tore, the ladle that dripped molten lead into mouths and eye-sockets and other orifices. In the detached voice he used when most caught up with the elation of pain-giving, he informed the princess that he'd even have tortured her war-bird Ayoka before her eyes, except that the eagle had disappeared from the royal aerie.

'Doubtless he died unnoticed and alone, and fell from the city for the scavengers to gnaw his bones,' the prince said, as he slit open a shrieking serving-maid with surgical exactness.

Through it all, Moriana felt every pang suffered by her friends and loved ones. Synalon had been wrong and Rann horribly right: being made to witness the final agonies of those she held dear was infinitely worse than merely waiting her tryst with the Demon of the Dark Ones.

With a raucous cry and a flurry of wings, a raven entered the small opening near the top of the arched window. It fluttered down to perch on a shelf laden with books. Beside it rested the bust of an ancient poet. The statue seemed to be contemplating the feathered invader of his sanctuary with quizzical interest.

Moriana slumped in a chair. The nightlong ordeal had left her exhausted, physically, spiritually, and emotionally. The raven cocked its head at her, regarding her from small, bright, evil eyes. With a derisive caw, it took off and flew back out the window, unwilling to associate with one already condemned.

After Rann had finished his grisly entertainment, Synalon had ordered her sister to the rooms she had once occupied in the palace. For the moment, the captive had allowed herself a frayed wisp of joy, if not actual hope. Some unacknowledged scrap of decency must exist in Synalon, if she was willing to let Moriana lighten her final hours by a return to the chambers that had been her home for most of her life.

Guards had escorted her into the tower nearer the leading edge of the city, and then pushed open the door. Moriana saw inside and knew she was a fool.

Of all her sister's aberrations, Moriana found few less palatable than Synalon's preoccupation with her poison-taloned ravens. The beasts were a sorry contrast to the lordly war-eagles of the Sky City. Filthy, craven, unmannered things they were, eaters of carrion and the lice that swarmed through their matted ebon feathers. They imitated human speech, but that made them more disgusting to the golden-haired princess. Their clacking, wheezing conversation sounded like crude parody of a consumptive.

Synalon had not allowed Moriana's chambers to rest idle in the months since she had departed the city in her quest for Erimenes and the amulet. Synalon had converted them to a mew for her reeking pets.

The door opened. Moriana looked up listlessly. Synalon stood in the door, clad conservatively in a deep gray and ochre wrap belted firmly against the chill. Her pale skin glowed with its own luminescence in dawn light the color of soured milk.

'Good morrow, sister,' Synalon said softly.

Moriana ignored her. She turned away. Her eyes brushed shelves bowed under the weight of cracked and ancient tomes of history, poetry, sorcerous lore. Shelves and books alike were fouled and streaked with the white excrement of Synalon's ravens. Moriana stared at the bare stone floor and wondered if despair could be more complete than hers.

'No kind words for me, your beloved sister?' Synalon glided in and sat in a chair facing her captive. The door closed quietly. Moriana did not doubt that a score of guards waited outside, poised to lunge through to the rescue at the first sound of trouble. Fit though she was, Synalon lacked her sister's skill at physical combat, armed or otherwise.

Yet Synalon's mere presence was a flaunting of her own superiority. Face to face with her sister, Moriana would not have the least chance to outmatch her in a test of magic. Moriana's skills were great, her powers sharply honed, but interest and temperament had led her to the pursuit of bright magic, healing magic, that magic bringing peace and plenty. Synalon had steeped herself in the lore of the Dark Ones. She glanced death, and gestured with thunderbolts; her destructiveness was as invincible to Moriana as it was alien.

The Amulet of Living Flame would have changed that invincibility. With the Athalar magic to restore her life, she could weather the hellstorm of Synalon's deathbolts. With luck she could draw on the life force within the amulet to add power to her own conjurings.

'You should not have returned,' said Synalon.

Moriana paled, holding in a breath of air tainted by the sharp, stale-sweet stink of the ravens.

'You wished to see our dear mother again, didn't you? You felt concern over her health.' Synalon's lips curled. 'Sentiment was always your weakness, my darling sister.'

'You may be right.'

Laughing, Synalon rose, walked to stand beside her sister. Moriana did not turn. She tensed as Synalon laid hands on her shoulders but made no sound.

'You wish to know of Queen Derora's last hours?' asked Synalon. 'How she died, and if her last thoughts were of you?'

'Of course.'

Synalon began to knead her sister's shoulders. Icy feathers brushed along Moriana's spine.

'Our mother had not been well for quite some time. Her condition was not improved by the way you vanished in the middle of the night without a word for those who loved you. I think she entered her final decline with the news that you'd gone.'

Moriana tried to guard against heeding her sister's words. Yet they touched a guilt that had burdened her since her last departure from the city. She had abandoned her mother in the queen's final illness — abandoned her to the tender attentions of a daughter who hated her.

'She died badly. There was much pain.' Synalon made no attempt to hide the relish she felt mouthing those words. Moriana went bowstring-taut with the sudden impulse to lash out, to strike down her sister.

With a quicksilver peal of laughter, Synalon glided back. 'Transparent as always, sibling,' she said mockingly. 'Will you never learn? You cannot compete with me.'

'What did Derora die of?' asked Moriana. 'She had sickened before I left, but the doctors offered no cause.'

'No mystery there. It was of a poison most subtle.'

Moriana's head snapped around. Synalon giggled with girlish delight at her expression of horror. 'You lie,' Moriana said in a dead voice. 'Not that I doubt your capacity for such vileness. But Derora was wily, more than either of us. She could scent any venom-brew you could concoct before your hand finished conjuring it.'

'Quite true. So my hand never concocted it. It was instead prepared by the hand of an Elder Brother of the Brethren of Assassins, and used to permeate a stole sent by Emperor Teom of High Medurim to mark the anniversary of his conception.'

Dizziness whirled within Moriana. Though she knew her sister must have murdered their mother, still she dreaded admitting it. If even Derora was powerless to stop Synalon, Moriana could hold out little hope for besting her sister.

'She had the Sensitivities,' Moriana said. 'She could have detected any substance in lethal concentrations.'

'In lethal concentration,' Synalon said, nodding. 'But not in a dose nicely tailored to sicken, without being potent enough to kill. Similar dosages pushed her nearer to earshot of Hell Call. It took time, Istu knows; our mother was as cunning as a bitch-fox with a lair of kits. But I'm the bitch's bitch-kit, and am cunning, too.'

'Who gave her the poison? She would never trust you.'

'True, nor Rann or any of my retainers. But she trusted Kralfi.'

Had Moriana eaten she would have vomited. Kralfi, who was tortured to death not seven hours before, had died proclaiming his fealty. She didn't believe Synalon.

Synalon watched her closely, shrugged and spoke. 'You'd divine the truth soon enough, so I shall tell you. He did not know. He thought he was bringing his queen a present of great beauty and value. She stroked over it, the poison insinuated itself through the pores in her skin, and slowly she died.' Synalon laughed. 'Did you say something?'

'Yes,' Moriana said, almost inaudibly. 'I asked, did he know?'

'Of course. Rann told him – later. Watching his reaction gave our cousin the most exquisite pleasure, I'm sure. Dear Rann must have almost recalled what ejaculation feels like.'

Moriana sat unmoving, unspeaking. Sadness for a mother murdered and a loyal servant who died knowing he had helped murder her crowded out all thought of her own impending doom.

'So,' she said at length, 'Derora the Wise succumbed to poison. A shabby end for a great monarch.'

'But she did not die of poison.' Moriana looked up, eyes wide with surprise.

'You said . . .'

'Yes, we weakened her with poison. But, Istu gnaw her entrails, she hung on in spite of all we did. We pushed the quantities of the toxin as high as we could without alerting her. I think she had magics of her own that helped her cling to life so tenaciously.'

'How did my mother die?' demanded Moriana.

'Why, I smothered her with a pillow.'

With an eagle's cry of killing rage, Moriana launched herself from the chair. Synalon's moon-pale skin turned the color of a water-logged corpse. She leaped back, stumbled and struck the floor in a tangle of slender limbs and expensive cloth.

A frantic heave took her out of her sister's path. Then she was on her feet, interposing a writing table between her and Moriana. Moriana wrenched it from her and threw it away with such force that the hardwood broke like glass against the wall. Her fingers sought Synalon's throat.

But Synalon's lips moved rapidly. Moriana heard no words above the roaring of her own pulse. Her nails touched skin. Then a light exploded in the center of her brain.

Strength fled her limbs. She fought to stay on her feet, to keep her arms reaching out for her sister's life. A yellow glow surrounded her like a fog, growing brighter in gradual pulses. Her legs gave way. She dropped to her knees not even feeling the pain as they raked along the floor.

Synalon loomed over her. The black-haired enchantress's shape wavered like an elemental. Moriana blinked. Her stomach surged with nausea.

'Sometimes I despair of you, sister,' said Synalon. 'You never learn.' She turned and walked to the door.

Once there she paused to look back. 'Your strength will return in a short while. My little spell did you no permanent harm. We can't have you ill on your wedding day, can we?'

She danced out through the door. Moriana felt sensation return to her limbs in a many-pointed prickling. The sickness in her stomach subsided slowly.

But even when the paralysis had left her, Moriana did not weep. It was not courage that kept her eyes dry; it was simply that her state transcended tears.

A wind sharp with autumn chill whipped across the Circle of the Skywell, scattering small bits of rubbish. Fost held the bulky cloak close about him, grateful for its warmth as well as its concealment. The air was noticeably cooler here, a thousand feet above the prairie.

Few people stirred. Those whom Fost and Luranni encountered ducked their heads and hurried by without so much as a greeting or a glance. The grip of fear had clamped the city's heart.

Luranni's great golden eyes moved constantly, alert for the purple tabards and black breastplates of the Monitors, the dread police instituted by Rann. Seemingly, they were as much under the spell of tension as ordinary citizens. Luranni and Fost had seen a squad of them a few blocks away, but they had gone on without challenging the pair.

For the hundredth time, Fost dropped his hand to the reassuring feel of his new broadsword in a bird-leather scabbard swinging at his hip. Uriath had done well by him. The new sword was a far better weapon than the one which had gone into the fumarole with the faceless ape-thing in Kest-i-Mond's castle. Broad and wide of blade, the sword was lightened by a wide blood gutter, and tapered to a serviceable point. Its blued-steel basket hilt protected the hand that gripped it without restricting the wrist. The High Councillor's daughter told him he'd have small need for it today. His height made him conspicuous, but the merchant-nobles often employed big outlanders for their personal guard.

Fost could see why. Aside from the elite bird riders and the royal family itself, the Sky Citizens didn't seem a prepossessing lot. The tall courier was only too aware of the limitations of his own co-conspirators. Leaders and followers alike came from the aristocracy, which was comprised of merchant princes such as Uriath and his leisure-loving friends. They might be adroit at convoluted palace intrigues, but they were innocents in the gutter-fighting realities of insurrection. Fost had ample evidence of their clumsiness, and he knew that the reason they were so eager for his aid was that they had no other swordsman of any skill. Fost doubted that the lithe girl walking beside him knew which end of a sword to use. He couldn't help contrasting her with Moriana.

Moriana!

Tomorrow would tell whether he lost her to some awful fate none had yet fully explained to him. With her would go all hope of immortality. His only allies would be dilettantes and amateurs who knew nothing of stealth, security or battle. They'd lost Moriana within a few hours of her arrival; Fost had seen through their clumsy attempt at a trap even as it was being set; and this very morning a knot of soldiers out tacking up Synalon's proclamation had thrown Uriath's underground into desperate panic.

Nervously, he fingered his sword. He almost wished someone would challenge him. Then he could quench his anxieties in the hot rush of action.

Their steps carried them along the cleared circle around the well itself. In ancient days, Luranni informed him, the People had used the vast opening to focus Demon Istu's powers against opponents below. Now the Skywell was mostly used for the purpose of 'exiling' undesirables.

Fost's eyes kept returning to the palace, several hundred yards distant along a wide, white avenue. The structure bulked huge, yet its construction was so airy, spun of arches and flying buttresses, that it gave the impression of weightlessness. Fost wasn't deceived. He knew enough of fortification to see that, for all its baroque appearance, it'd be a formidable citadel to assault.

Something in the way the light struck the avenue running from the palace brought him to a halt. The paving seemed to be large, round rocks set in some black substance. The curious cobbling ended before the avenue joined the circle and was cordoned by almost invisible threads strung between brass posts.

'Magic barrier?' Fost asked. Luranni nodded. 'Why?'

'None but the feet of royalty may walk upon the skulls of past queens,' the girl replied.

'Skulls?'

'Yes. When a ruler of the city dies, her skull becomes another paving stone, set in pitch among the skulls of her mothers.' Luranni spoke with the atonal solemnity she always used when discussing the history and traditions of the city. Fost wondered if she were reciting litanies taught by her father.

He couldn't help shuddering as he looked at the Skullway. The Hissing Folk might have been defeated long ago, but they had left their legacy. Thirty thousand years of grim evil had steeped the very stones of the city.

They walked on, skulls and palace burning in Fost's mind. 'Don't take offense,' he said, 'but your father strikes me as the ambitious type. Why doesn't he forget about saving Moriana and try to seize power himself?'

Luranni laughed. 'None but a woman may hold sovereignty in the city. So it is written. The people wouldn't accept a male ruler, fearing it would rob the city of the magic that makes it float.'

Fost's stomach turned over. He'd managed to forget that he'd spent almost a day on a platform of stone that hung a thousand feet off the ground with no visible means of support. The firmness beneath his feet suddenly seemed to pitch and roll like a ship on storm-tossed waters. The gusting breeze threatened to overturn the vast sky-raft and dash him to destruction. He had meant to ask Luranni why her father didn't try to put her on the throne, but for a few minutes it was all he could do to keep from hurling himself face-down and clutching the street with desperate fingers. When the fear passed, the question had gone with it.

'Tell me about the Rite of Dark Assumption,' he said when he'd mastered himself, looking studiously away from the gold eyes that glinted with amusement. 'What does it involve?'

'With much ceremony and incantation, the prin – , the victim is violated by the Vicar of Istu. When that is done, the demon takes her soul.'

They had gone past where the Skullway met the Circle and around a quarter of the promenade surrounding the Well. Luranni gestured at a point directly across from the mouth of the Way of Skulls.

'There is the altar where the royal victims are bound.'

Fost saw the low, flat slab next to an immense black statue. He pulled on his chin, trying to beat down fear and clear his mind for scheming. 'We'll need a diversion,' he said, keeping his tone light. 'You can't have a rescue without a diversion.'

He thought some more. 'How is it that your father can keep warehouses full of fire elementals without burning out a whole quarter of the city? To say nothing of how he's managed to avoid Rann's spies.'

'I can answer both questions at once. The elementals are small ones, enchanted to obey commands from those unskilled in magic. They're bought for smelters, heating, the kitchens of estates. While they prefer easily burned substances for food, they can burn almost

111

anything at need, and consume it all, with no ash. This makes them in demand among those who can pay our prices.' He caught a note of pride in her voice. She served as negotiator with Quincunx city factors on behalf of Uriath's concern. 'So they're kept in magicked clay vessels. That holds both them and their heat. It also blinds them to what goes on outside the jars. Those vessels are quite handy. They were invented centuries ago, in Athalau. Spirit jugs, I believe they're called. What's the matter?'

Fost had gulped audibly at the mention of Athalau and spirit jugs. It became doubly important that no member of Uriath's underground ever get so much as a glimpse of Erimenes and his pot. He didn't know how widely the existence of Erimenes and the amulet might be spread. But Kest-i-Mond, Moriana, and Synalon knew, at the very least. It seemed a fair guess that Uriath might, too. If he connected the parcel Fost was so desperate to recover with an Athalar spirit jug . . .

'What?' he said, feigning distraction. 'Oh, nothing. I simply felt a moment's trepidation at the thought of the odds we'll be facing tomorrow.' He finished with the most wolfish grin he could muster to let Luranni know he felt no trepidation at all. In fact he did, a great deal, but saw no reason she should know.

She smiled back and squeezed his arm. The contact sent a thrill through his body. He hoped he could formulate a rescue plan soon enough to have a few hours alone with Luranni before meeting again with the underground. Already the rudiments of a scheme came to him.

'I think I see how it'll go,' he said, grave as a field marshal planning his campaign. 'Our larcenous princess is brought forth and bound to the altar. Then this Vicar of Istu has his way with her, right?' The girl nodded. 'So the Vicar – the name conjures up a skinny old codger with yesterday's gruel in his beard, and spectacles perched on his nose like a Tolviroth accounting clerk – so he gives Moriana a dose of his withered old prod. That'll be the best time to make our move, when all eyes are on the, ah, main event. I'll make for the altar with a team of picked men, if we can find any among your comrades who're more of a menace to others than to themselves. At the same time, you'll release a passle of tame salamanders into the crowd, under orders to make things warm for the onlookers. Then . . .

His words dwindled to uneasy silence. He became aware of large golden eyes fixing him with a peculiar look. 'You don't think that'll work?' he asked plaintively. Luranni shook her head. 'Why not?'

She pointed once more. They were forty yards from the altar and the statue looming over it, near enough to make out detail. Short columns held the marble slab of the altar, which formed the shape of a Y. Fost scarcely noticed. The statue was of such uncommon ugliness that it commanded all his attention.

It squatted, clawed hands resting on basalt knees, leering down on humans less than half its height. Its form was manlike, but disproportionately thick of trunk and limb. Teeth filled its awful grin, blunt and bone-crushing save for two curving tusks. Nose and cheeks were wide and flat, eyes slanted beneath great juts of heavy brow. The whole expression was chillingly malevolent. Stubby horns curled outward and upward from either side of its head, an unnatural touch in a land where horn-bearing creatures wore them on nose and forehead. Between its thighs hung an immense, misshapen member of the same dark stone.

'What,' Fost said, knowing that Luranni's objections to his plan were bound up in this monstrosity, 'is that?'

'The Vicar of Istu,' she replied.

CHAPTER EIGHT

Shadows of high clouds fell on Moriana like a weight as her feet paced the uneven yards of the Way of Skulls. A bitter wind whipped her green sacrificial cloak about her legs, causing her to stumble repeatedly.

To either side, the Skullway was lined with jeering multitudes kept at bay by the magic cordon. *Synalon's done her propagandizing well,* the princess thought. Any citizen should have known Moriana was innocent of her mother's murder, the mother whom she admired and Synalon despised. But Moriana's arrival in the city on the heels of Derora's death, and the lies spread by Synalon's agents, had turned the people of the city from sympathy for the blonde princess to rabid hate. Even the repression by Guardsmen and Monitors was laid to Moriana; but for her act of treachery, the rumormongers said, such stern measures wouldn't have been required.

A gob of spittle hit her cheek. She bit back the soul-frying curse that rose to her lips and kept her eyes from moving to her tormentor in the crowd. She might not die a queen, but she would die like one.

Escorted by halberd-bearing Monitors, Moriana reached the Circle and began the slow procession to the altar. From above, the beat of wings rolled down like thunder. Rann, astride red-crested Terror, led the regiments of the Guard in a sardonic escort of honor.

The raw passion surging from the mob pushed her gaze aside into the gape of the Well itself. Below, land slipped by at a mile an hour. A few puffs of cloud drifted between earth and city. The green hills beneath, already changing to autumn yellow, beckoned the princess.

A brief dash, a leap, a blissful float to Hell Call, she thought. *How much better than the degradation and damnation that awaits me.*

But the hope was no more substantial than the clouds below.

Against such an attempt to cheat Istu – and Synalon – the Monitors had been armed with weighted nets.

I'll walk to my fate, and not be carried like some miserable ground-ling, she vowed to herself.

For all her determination to hold her head erect, she couldn't make her eyes rise to behold the leering Vicar. The phalanx of Monitors snapped to a halt. Moriana raised her gaze.

Her sister stood on the far side of the altar. Her hair was caught up in an intricate coiffure, her body wrapped in a pearl-white robe. The blue eyes glinted with triumph. Moriana felt her knees go weak. It was obvious that Synalon intended to carry through with the unholy ceremony.

Until this instant, some corner of the princess's being had cherished the hope that Synalon's threats to invoke Istu had been no more than that. Surely, not even she would dare disturb the demon. She would torture her sister and cast her over the side to clean oblivion.

But Synalon wore the ceremonial vestments of the Rite, which hadn't been donned in five thousand years.

When she saw the realization in her sister's eyes, Synalon turned and lifted her arms to the crowd. The eager susurration died.

'Hear me, O denizens of the clouds,' the sorceress cried. Her words cut across the wind to the city beyond. 'The honor of our domain has been besmirched by an act of treason so vile that my lips hesitate to speak of it.' She swept her hand toward her captive. 'Behold Moriana, who basely contrived the death of her mother, our queen, to seize the throne for herself!'

A moan of animal rage rolled from the crowd. Moriana's soul shrank from its intensity.

'It is judgement, O citizens.' The raven-tressed woman clenched her fists. 'That one of us, my own sister, should perpetrate such a deed, shows how far our city has fallen into decay.

'No mortal suffering would be sufficient to punish the murderess of Derora the Wise. Thus do I consign the traitor Moriana to a fate commensurate with her offense, and at the same time turn our noble city's path from decadence to domination.

'Thus do I give Moriana to Istu, the soul of the city, to be his wedded bride throughout eternity!'

A wail rose from ten thousand throats, compounded of eagerness and dismay, of terror and pure, surging lust. Rough hands gripped

Moriana, stripping the green robe of shame from her. In her nakedness, she still stood proud, despite the bite of the wind, the voices that
cried out to see her ravaged by the demon, the towering nearness of
the Vicar. The Monitors, faceless in their bronze masks, drew her out
on the altar, clamped her legs wide on the branches of the Y-shaped
slab, and tied her wrists above her head.

She saw rather than heard Synalon recite the summoning. She felt
the power rising, as if from the very stones. She smelled incense and a
sudden stink of decay. At last some magnetism drew her eyes to the
basalt ikon that was the Vicar.

Its eyes opened.

In darkness, its bower roofed in tons of stone, a demon slept.

It had slept thus for millennia. Once, though, it had known freedom.
In the youth of the universe it had been created, and in time sent by
the Dark Ones, its creators, to their votaries the *Zr'gsz*, to aid them
and keep them strong in the cause of evil. Those had been the high
days, the days of glory, when the black demon rode his raft of stone
across the sky and visited shrieking death upon the foes of the
Hissers.

Change.

The Pale Folk, the Ones Below who crawled like maggots across
the face of the planet, began to resist. Their efforts were paltry at first,
and with orgiastic glee Istu destroyed them. But they learned.

One rose among the Pale Ones, one whose name rang now and
again through the sleeping demon's brain in a discord of agony:
Felarod.

He had the blessing of the Three and Twenty of Agift, sworn foes
throughout eternity of the Lords of the Elder Dark. And more than
that, the World-Spirit, very soul of the planet itself, had rebelled
against the chaos sown by Istu. War raged that wracked the cosmos.

Istu fell.

Not even Felarod commanded power to unmake Istu, however.
He had bound the demon with chains of spells in the depths of the
Sky City and drawn a curtain of eternal sleep across its brain. The
most furious efforts of the Dark Ones could not free their spawn.
Perhaps in another turning of the galaxy the time would be right for
Istu to gain freedom again, as perhaps it would be right for the
demon's final destruction. The Dark Ones settled back to bide their
time and nurse implacable hatred.

Istu knew none of this. Istu knew only dreams. Dreams of bitterness, of longing for revenge. But occasionally his slumber had been enlivened with strange stirrings and fresh sensations, the sense of venturing once again into the world, of slaking his thirst on pale, soft-skinned victims. Those times were good. Yet in time those ceased as well. No more did the demon's sleeping self hear the chanted summons from far above.

Not for five thousand years.

And then a voice began to tickle the underbelly of the sleeper's mind, drawing part of it out of itself and upward, ever upward. Istu resisted for a moment. Then memories of dark delight poured into his eternal dream. With a growing sense of anticipation, the sleeper responded to the call . . .

Slits of yellow hellfire blazed beneath shelflike brows of stone. A tremor ran through its black form. It lifted a hand, stared at it, and then raised both arms above its head to cast a wordless shout of triumph and defiance towards the clouds above. No sound emerged from the being's mouth, but the roar reverberated in Moriana's mind and drove her close to madness.

The Vicar's yellow eyes swept down and fell upon the recumbent form of its sacrificial bride. The statue's lips spread. A forked tongue flickered over fist-sized teeth. The member between its legs rose like a charmed serpent.

Stone groaned and broke as it lifted one leg free of its pedestal. The other leg followed. A ponderous step sent vibrations through the marble pressed against Moriana's naked flesh. Four-fingered hands reached for her as the Vicar approached. She saw the blunted ram of its maleness lift toward her and felt the unyielding pressure, the tearing awful pain of entrance into her body. A voice that was hers and yet not hers screamed.

Red agony exploded into blackness.

'Wine,' the vendor shouted, his lungs carrying his cry over the rumble of the mob. 'Refresh your palates, honored ones, while you watch the traitor meet her fate. Twenty sipans the half-pint, wine!'

A stout, balding merchant with a teenaged, pock-marked mistress simpering at his elbow bought a pair of purple glass bottles. Fost accepted a handful of small silver oblongs, bobbed his head as if in gratitude, and limped away through the crowd. Slowly he edged

117

toward the altar.

He played the role of a lamed bodyguard earning his keep by hawking his master's wine at the great event. His sword was strapped like a splint to his left leg, and both armed him and augmented his disguise. At the bottom of his leather pouch of bottles rested a round Athalar spirit jug and its volatile cargo.

'Wine!' The disguise worked well, at any rate. No one spared him a second glance. He felt the tingle of lust in the air as the crowd awaited Moriana's denudation.

Despite the day's chill, he sweated vigorously. *This has to be the most crack-brained scheme I've ever heard of,* he thought, not for the first time that day. The fact that he was the author of it from beginning to end didn't comfort him at all.

'Ahhhh!' A sigh rippled through the mob as a Monitor stripped away Moriana's cloak. Fost's heart jumped within his chest. Again he felt the urge to rip loose his sword and lunge to the rescue, as he had wanted to do when he'd entered the Circle and first saw her marching the slow march of the condemned. A glance at the massed ranks of soldiers on the ground between him and the princess, and the squadrons of eagles wheeling overhead, stifled the urge at once. *Lovely wench,* he allowed himself to think. *What a waste if this doesn't succeed.*

A tug at his sleeve brought him 'round to produce two bottles for a lean aristocrat with a jewel in one nostril. The pomaded dandies and the looks they exchanged reminded Fost of High Medurim.

His eyes scanned the crowd. Mingling with the onlookers would be Uriath's men, carrying jugs like the one in his pouch. That part of the original plan remained, to use the fire elementals to draw attention from the altar. At first it had seemed a cold-blooded scheme even to Fost, but the eagerness with which the mob anticipated Moriana's doom robbed him of any compassion for them.

He caught sight of a tow-headed figure making his way through the crush of bodies. In a drab workman's smock, Erlund walked with legs bent under his burden, a pitch-pot resting on a brazier of coals, with handles to insulate his hands and a leather apron protecting his belly. There wasn't a good reason for a worker to be abroad in the Circle with a pot of hot pitch, but nowhere in Fost's experience were folk inclined to question a common laborer who was obviously going about his business. These people didn't disappoint him. They edged away from the heat and stench of the pitch-pot, but otherwise paid

Erlund no heed.

Fost stood near the ranks of soldiers holding back the crowd. A sudden crunching noise grabbed his attention. He looked over the soldiers' heads and gasped. The statue had uprooted itself and strode toward the captive princess.

The nearness of such magic overwhelmed him. For a mad moment all he could think of was flight. Anywhere, anyhow – even straight over the lip of the Well, if this would get him away from the demon.

His instinct for survival saved him from panic. Any Medurimite street urchin knew instinctively when he'd attracted the attention of the authorities. A prickling along his spine warned him something was amiss. He jerked himself into control and back to the problem he faced.

An officer eyed him suspiciously. Gaping at the statue come to life was not unusual. But something in Fost's manner had alerted the man. He limped forward, dragging his stiff leg.

'I grow weary of my burden, lordly one,' he said to the man, dropping his eyes in the deference proper for ground-born when addressing a child of the Sky City. 'Would the colonel and his gallant men partake of my wine, as a gift from my humble self?'

The officer, who was plainly no more than a lieutenant of infantry, grinned acceptance. The last of the squat bottles were dispensed to the troopers. Caught up in the mood of the event, they forgot discipline to the extent of prying open the seals with daggers or simply breaking off the necks on the pavement. Purple wine gurgled down throats and slopped onto black tunics. Fost bobbed his head at them, smiling servilely. Then he saw what the idol was doing and the smile hardened on his lips.

Delight surged through the living stone of the demon's Vicar. Yet sensations lost for millennia awoke only part of the sleeping demon's mind. They stirred an elemental and primitive part, capable of tasting raw sensation and feeling raw emotion. That tiny fragment of the intellect responding to a bribe of carnal pleasure was enough to make the ruler who invoked it the mightiest sorcerer of the Sundered Realm.

Howling like a maddened beast, Erlund threw himself through the crowd. He jostled soldiers aside. One shrieked and fell down flapping as pitch splashed onto his tunic and ignited. Alone on the cleared area of the Circle immediately behind the Vicar, Erlund dropped the brazier and flung the steaming pitch onto the broad back of the statue.

The horrid rhythm of the basalt hips never faltered. As the squad stared at the Vicar, Fost lunged a hand into his pouch and cast the spirit jug at the idol. The pot bounced off a churning dark shoulder and fell to the marble flagging, shattered.

The salamander flashed free. It was a small one, a green shimmer against the day's grayness. For a moment it hung in the air. Then it sensed the fumes, volatile and seductive. It moved.

One instant the Vicar reveled in single-minded joy as it raped the bound woman. The next the sun fell through the clouds and lit upon its back. The violence of its mental shout of pain blasted through the city.

Normal fire would not even have drawn its attention. But the fire of the salamander ate greedily at the clinging pitch and turned the stone molten where it touched. The demon Istu was in no danger; it slept far beneath the streets, as invulnerable as it was immobile. But the spark of its life which animated the Vicar knew dreadful agony. It wheeled, saw a pitiful man-thing crouching at its back, and stared at him. It reached down, caught up the creature by its leather covering, and began to rip off its limbs, like a small boy dismembering a flying insect.

A fresh blaze of agony brought Moriana awake. She no longer felt the piercing pain in her loins. Only a throbbing ache remained. The crowd sounds that washed against her ears had changed from lewdness to terror. Nearby, someone screamed.

A jerk at her right wrist made her open her eyes.

'Just lie still,' Fost said, 'and I'll have you free in a second.' As she lay unbelieving, he quickly cut through the bonds that held her other hand and feet.

'What . . .' she began.

Fost grabbed her waist and flung himself backwards. The hard pavement bruised Moriana's limbs as he rolled atop her. A streak of light flared viciously overhead with a hiss and sizzle as a deathbolt from Synalon drew a charred line across the altar. The sorceress shrieked her fury and prepared another lightning-cast.

The blue flash caught the Vicar's attention. Its pseudo-awareness identified magic fire and the one who cast it with the cause of its pain. It turned, casually tossing the armless, legless husk that had been Erlund into the Well. The stink of fire-magic hung like a fog around the tall woman in white. It went for her, arms outstretched to maim and hurt and kill.

A bird rider swooped on Fost as he dragged Moriana to her feet. The Guardsman misjudged his distance and passed too close to the blazing statue. Eagle and rider erupted in a ball of green flame.

Moriana stood, still babbling questions. Fost looked around frantically. The rescue had gone off as planned – but where was his diversion? No other fire elementals frolicked among the spectators. The crowd had thinned considerably, but the ranks of soldiers Fost had burst through to reach the altar stood with backs unthreatened. All had their pikes leveled. Uriath's promised support hadn't materialized. Fost and Moriana were caught between the anvil of the troops and the hammer-like fists of the raging statue.

Only one course lay open. Gripping Moriana's wrist, Fost turned, took three running steps, and vaulted over the altar straight at Synalon. The black-haired princess gaped at him, hair flying as she swiveled her head from him to the advancing statue and back. Moriana managed to scramble over the still-smoking altar as her sister dropped flat to avoid a roundhouse sweep of the courier's broadsword. The soldiers on that side of the altar had fled the onslaught of the Vicar, leaving their mistress as thoroughly in danger as Fost's allies had left him. Hard on Fost's heels Moriana followed, joining the shrieking tide of humanity streaming away from the demon's wrath. In an instant they were across the Circle and into the safety of the city's twisting streets.

Synalon struggled to rise before the Vicar tore her asunder, as it had killed Erlund. Her plans lay in ruins. She had meant to beguile the demon with pleasure; she had given it searing anguish. Istu would not forget. Despairing, she considered letting the statue wreak its vengeance on her.

But she was no less a princess of the city than her sister. She straightened, a slim, slight figure before the monster's bulk. Her lips shaped the words of dismissal.

And then she realized it was too late.

Wings boomed over her head. A wiry shape dropped to the marble. In astonishment, the Vicar stopped to gaze at this puny thing that dared interpose itself with its pathetic sword and javelin. Doomed but unflinching, Prince Rann Etuul faced the maddened Vicar.

At the end of a street radiating from the Circle of the Skywell, Fost paused to let Moriana catch up. Her hair hung in strings about her face and thin rivulets of blood ran down her thighs, but she seemed in good enough condition. Looking past her, Fost saw Terror fall from the sky to drop Rann between the statue and his cousin. Synalon's voice reached Fost as she shrilled a chant. A vast black arm lashed out and swept Rann like a doll from the Vicar's path.

Moriana's hand sought Fost's. He picked her up in his arms and ran.

Later, sheltered against a building in the palace district, Fost stopped, gasping for breath. When it no longer felt as if spears pierced his lungs each time he breathed, he turned to Moriana.

'I owe you my life and soul,' she whispered, 'and no Etuul shirks her debts. That which you seek is in the penthouse of the north-western tower of the palace. It's doubtless guarded by sorcery, but I think you can seize the philosopher's jug.' She dropped her eyes. 'Words are too small for thanks. Farewell.'

Fost spent several breaths eyeing her appreciatively. For all her ordeals of the past few days, she was still breathtakingly lovely. In her disheveled nakedness, she stood as proud as any queen could hope to.

'Don't talk nonsense, wench,' he told her. He took off his peddlar's cloak and wrapped it around her shoulders. 'Come along. We'd best reach the palace before the Guard collects its wits!'

CHAPTER NINE

Blue lightnings surrounded Synalon's head in a crackling nimbus as she surveyed the wreckage of her sitting chamber. A mage lay spreadeagled on the floor, his chest blasted open by a deathbolt. The wounds that had claimed the lives of three palace guards were obviously of more mundane origin.

'How did he get here?' she screamed. 'The spirit said Moriana robbed him in the night and got away. How did that dirt-spawned dog reach the city?'

A Monitor officer and several magicians stood clumped in the doorway. The officer cleared his throat. 'We assumed that the Princess Moriana hijacked the balloon and killed its crew; it seemed so apparent that was the way she'd gained access to the city that we never troubled to question the ghost about it.' He paled at the look in Synalon's eye, swallowed hard, and continued. 'Now we feel she placed the crewmen under a spell of compulsion, and the barbarian, lacking her knowledge of either sorcery or aeronautics, resorted to force to reach the city.'

'You *assumed*.' Contempt filled her words. 'Your assumption has cost us dearly, Gulaj.' The man cringed. Synalon turned the full heat of her displeasure on the trio of sorcerers. Their shaven heads bobbed up and down. Fearful perspiration had begun to make the cabalistic designs painted on their skulls run down their cheeks. 'And how fares my gracious cousin?'

The eldest mage looked at the next eldest, who pivoted his head to peer expectantly at the youngest. That worthy only just saved himself from looking around for someone else with whom to saddle the unhappy task of answering.

'H-he fares well, O Mistress of the Clouds. His ribs are cracked where the Vicar struck him. He sleeps well under sedation; a few days of rest shall make him whole again.'

Synalon paced to her beryl throne and sat. The silk cushion lay askew. She paid it as little heed as she did the remnants of her headdress hanging in her face or the pink-tipped breast that peeked from her pearl-white robe. Rann had bought her time to conjure the life out of the Vicar and return it to Istu, but the stony fingers had been clutching at her garments when the light went out of the statue's eyes. Dispatching the elemental had taken little more than a gesture. But the struggle with the Vicar had brought her near exhaustion.

'He shall not have days to rest,' Synalon said. 'Go and rouse him. Even now the Guards comb the sky for the fugitives, but I expect the prince will have ample opportunity to redeem his failure by personally bringing the criminals to justice.' After a moment's hesitation, the mages turned and left.

Gulaj started to follow them.

'Colonel.' Synalon's soft voice brought him to a halt just inside the doorway, which was blocked by the massive ironbound door, blasted off its hinges by Moriana's sorcery. 'Did you hear me give you leave to go?'

'Your pardon, Lady. Istu . . .'

A lance of fire from a pointing fingertip cut him off. Blue-white light filled the chamber. The colonel fell forward in a reek of burnt flesh and ozone.

Synalon paid the corpse no mind. It was Rann who deserved to die. But Rann she could not spare. Only the prince, she was sure, had the skill necessary to recover Erimenes and work retribution on those who had stolen him away.

Why did he help her, that miserable groundling of a courier? She robbed him! Sparks popped from her fingertips as fury gripped her. The injustice tied her muscles into knots of frenzied anger. She sat for a hundred heartbeats, clenched and sweating at the deviousness of her twin sister.

The fit passed. She slumped limply in the chair. A shaft of sunlight fell through clouds to waken the green fire in the gemstone arm of her throne. Moodily, she drew herself up and stared out of the window at her bird riders wheeling their mounts about the sky.

'My thanks for saving me from those despicable rogues,' Erimenes said.

'You dare speak of roguery?' Moriana shouted. 'You, who begged to be allowed to watch my torture?'

'I toyed with them, no more,' Erimenes said airily. 'If I seemed sufficiently intent on watching them torture you, I knew they'd never touch you. Psychology, you see. It must have worked. Your flawless skin remains intact.'

Moriana's eyes smoldered. 'They tortured my friends to death before me. I'd rather they'd worked their fiendishness on my body.' She snatched at the jar once more suspended in its pouch slung beneath Fost's arm. The courier fended her warily. 'Psychology, you say! Is that what you call it, to sit talking of exotic perversions with Synalon while my loved ones died, screaming for oblivion?'

'I was only trying to win her confidence,' said Erimenes. 'And I knew those ward spells she'd cast hindered your powers. Rann felt nothing, lacking in any magical skills, and could have physically overwhelmed you. And Synalon, well, she was scarcely in the position of having to use magic while you were chained. So, you see, my behavior was consistent and in your best interests. In fact, I . . .'

'Enough!' Fost bellowed before Moriana could reply. 'For Gormanka's sake, you'll alert the entire district.' His voice reverberated the length of the street and sent foraging rats scurrying for cover.

'Here,' he said in a softer tone, unslinging the pouch and handing it to Moriana. 'Hold on to this blatherer. I'm supposed to meet my contact with the underground, if they haven't botched that as well.' He glimpsed the glow in Moriana's eyes. 'Don't throw him over the edge. It's not likely to do him much harm.'

'Of course not,' Erimenes declared. 'Being immaterial, a fall of a thousand feet would be as a . . .' A vicious shake by the princess shut him up in mid-sentence.

Leaving Moriana to deal with the dead philosopher, Fost moved up the block, around the corner and slipped into an alley. After the rescue, he was to bring Moriana to a certain warehouse near the docks at the edge of the city. He had been told the route to take. He didn't go that way now. Instead he traced a roundabout course, to bring him upon his contact from an unexpected direction. He'd had enough of Uriath's lack of security.

He had no difficulty in sneaking up behind the undergrounder. Fost was in his element now, far more than the dilettantes of the resistance. He paused a moment to make sure that the contact was alone. Then he moved, as swift and silent as light.

A heavy hand muffled the cry that broke from Luranni's lips as a dagger-tip pricked her throat. 'So you came,' he said. 'Was it mere oversight that I was left facing the city's whole army alone?' She shook her head, her eyes glazing with fear.

'Make a noise louder than a whisper and I'll slit your throat,' Fost said before taking his hand away from her mouth.

'No treachery,' she breathed. 'I swear it! I don't know what went wrong. The men with the elementals said they never got the word to act.'

The courier hesitated, still holding the girl immobile, his dagger hovering near her neck. The cinnamon scent and the nearness of her body awoke memories, but they had grown pallid and distant. Finally he shrugged and let her go. Her tale was likely true. He could expect no more from the amateurs in the underground than he had already gotten.

'I suppose you've come to tell me your people failed to find us a way to get to the surface.'

She shook her head, sending a soft cascade of brown hair swirling out around her shoulders. 'No.' Her eyes were bigger and rounder than normal and the word came hesitantly. She obviously thought that the man she had taken to bed a few days earlier was ready to slay her at any moment. 'The way is prepared. But it'll be hazardous. Won't you stay? With me?'

'No. Synalon's men will take this town apart clear to Istu's bedchamber on the chance that we'll remain.' He looked into her eyes. Emotions stirred within him. Her invitation hadn't fallen on deaf ears, and however ill her comrades had done by him, she had tried her best on his behalf. She'd come to mean something to him, as well. He couldn't leave without some explanation.

'Moriana and I have something we must do. If we succeed, our chances of freeing the city will be much improved. I can't say any more.' He knew that Moriana's purpose in seeking the Amulet of Living Flame opposed his own, though the reckoning of who should have it had been put off for the moment.

'You have the parcel that you wanted?' she asked. He nodded. 'And you will deliver it as you intended?'

He hesitated. 'Yes.'

The faint cry of a circling war-bird drifted down from the sky. Luranni gripped his arm. 'We must hurry,' she said. He led her back

126

to where Moriana waited, hoping he didn't disengage his hand from hers too blatantly.

'What have we here?' The words made Fost stop and turn. Moriana stepped from a recessed doorway. Her parted cloak revealed swatches of pale skin. Fost grinned in appreciation. Here was no clumsy amateur. She was almost as skilled as the courier himself.

'Yes, what have we?' Erimenes asked with interest. 'A lovely lass to be sure. Quite lively in bed, too, I don't doubt.'

Luranni gaped at the satchel, her expression turning quickly to keen interest. Fost ground his teeth. She was no more of a fool than her father, except at the game of insurrection. He knew she was quite capable of drawing conclusions he didn't wish made.

'Time to go,' he urged, looking uneasily at the sky.

'You've not introduced us, dear Fost,' Moriana said, hanging back.

Fost groaned. The look that passed between the two, emerald eyes to golden, left no room for secrets.

'This is Luranni, daughter of High Councillor Uriath. Luranni, uh, meet the Princess Moriana.'

'You could fight over him,' Erimenes suggested helpfully.

'We may as well give ourselves up as stand here any longer,' Fost said. Luranni gave him a narrow glance and turned to lead the way.

Moriana let her get a few paces ahead before she asked, 'What does this one mean to you?'

'A way out of this wretched city, nothing more.'

Moriana scrutinized him like a bird sizing up possible prey, then followed the brown-haired girl.

'Faugh! It smells like bird droppings in here. Can't we seek out more wholesome surroundings?' Erimenes's voice rang with lofty disdain.

'If he suggests a trip to a brothel I'll use his jug for a chamber pot,' said Fost. A strangled sound emerged from the jug. Fost peered around the darkened passageway. Luranni led the way, holding aloft a crystal vial shaped like a dove, which cast a heatless illumination like that of the lightfool. 'But he's right. I do smell birds.'

Moriana sniffed the air. 'No common birds,' she said. They rounded a bend in the tunnel. Sunlight fell through a barred aperture and splashed the floor and walls of a chamber cut from the skystone of the City's base. 'It's the scent of war-birds. Luranni, where are we?'

'An ancient aerie, last used during the wars with the surface-dwellers. My family has known about it for generations; our cargo balloons moor near here.'

'Why do we waste time here, then?' asked Erimenes. 'Surely we've better uses for our time than a survey of historic sites. Of what interest is this abandoned . . .'

A rustling noise came from the shadowed recesses of the aerie. Fost's sword hissed free of its bird-leather scabbard.

'Abandoned?' he said quietly. 'I don't think so.'

A figure appeared, dim and monstrous in the gloom. Higher than Fost's head it loomed, approaching with a lurching waddle. The hefty broadsword felt as inadequate as a lady's poniard in the courier's hand.

'What kind of trap is this?' he hissed at Luranni, as he made ready to launch himself at the monstrosity.

'Wait!' Her cloak flapping behind her, Moriana lunged at the creature. Fost shouted a warning. The cry died on his lips as the princess threw her arms about the giant shape and hugged it fiercely. 'Ayoka!' she cried. 'Oh, Ayoka, they told me you were dead!'

Standing in the light, Fost saw a war-eagle of the Sky City, huge and deep of chest, its razor-sharp beak immense. But white cataracts crusted the saucer-shaped eyes, and the once-sleek body shed feathers in a constant molt. The bird was obviously an ancient creature, with few days left him.

'He came to us here, the night Derora died,' said Luranni, standing at the courier's side. The big man was acutely aware of the soft hip pressing into his. 'A watchman heard noises and found him. The eagles lack man-speech, unlike the slit-tongued ravens Synalon favors, and none of us know the war-birds' tongue. I recognized him as Princess Moriana's mount, though, so we fed and watered him, and closed the gate to keep him safe from aerial patrols. My father says he's sound enough to bear you to the ground.'

Fost eyed the creature dubiously. Ayoka had once been a mighty bird indeed. That much was clear. But his prime had long since passed. And for even a young bird to bear the combined weight of Fost and Moriana would be a considerable task. Fost sheathed his sword and shook his head skeptically.

Moriana knelt on the ground, stroking the ragged feathers and sobbing, crooning to the bird in an unfamiliar language. The bird preened her long blonde hair with his beak and made some burbling reply.

'He says that the night the queen died, a palace functionary named

128

Kralfi came to warn him to flee,' said Erimenes. ' "Fly, O winged warrior; we human friends of the princess and true queen are lost, but still may you serve bright Moriana." Very poetic, if you go in for that sort of sticky sentimentality. Not to my taste at all. Give me a bawdy limerick any day. Have you heard this one? "There was a maid of Medurim . . . " '

Fost ignored the spirit. 'Is that actually what he said?' Moriana turned a tearful face to him and nodded. 'Can he carry both of us?' The princess spoke to the bird. The eagle threw back its head and voiced a cry that filled the chamber like a trumpet blast. For all the bird's decrepitude, there was no denying the power in his call.

'He says he can,' Moriana declared, standing. 'And I believe him.' She turned to Luranni and asked, 'Do you have a saddle for him?'

The girl nodded and disappeared into the shadows. She came back dragging a pile of tack and other equipment. Fost stood idly by, fretting at his inability to be of any use, as Moriana selected a double harness and cinched it to Ayoka's back. From the stack of gear, she drew two short recurved bows and two filled quivers.

'No, thank you,' Fost said as she offered him one. 'I couldn't hit the Dowager Empress in the rump at three paces with one of those. A sword is more to my liking.'

'A pity,' Moriana said with a grimace. 'There's little call for sword-play in bird-back combat.' She hoisted herself agilely into the front of the double-seated saddle and threw her legs forward around the eagle's neck. 'Here, climb up behind and strap yourself in. This is a training saddle. You're not likely to fall out of it.'

Gingerly, Fost clambered up onto Ayoka's broad back. The bird grunted at his weight. He winced and fixed a sturdy strap around his middle.

'How about you?' he asked Moriana.

'I was born to the back of an eagle,' she replied haughtily. 'I need nothing to hold me in the saddle. Nor would I ever use a strap. I need my freedom if we're to make it past the patrols.'

Fost blinked. It hadn't occurred to him they might have to fight their way to the surface. The ride down would be harrowing enough without being beset by swarms of bird-riding Guardsmen. He fixed Erimenes's satchel to the harness and loosened his sword in its scabbard, just in case.

Luranni unlatched the circular gate and threw it wide. 'Farewell, my Princess,' she said to Moriana. The bird walked forward, stooped under his double burden. Luranni stood on tiptoe, grabbed Fost and dragged him down for an impassioned kiss. 'And you, my courier,' she said, eyes shining brightly.

'Our thanks, Luranni, daughter of Uriath,' said Moriana. To Fost's surprise she sounded sincere. 'When we return, we shall bring with us the freedom of the city!' She nudged Ayoka. The bird reeled forward and pitched headlong into space.

Fost shouted in dismay as the prairie hurtled up at them. It seemed he had left his stomach behind in the aerie. Nausea and terror fought for control of his senses.

Huge wings burst from Ayoka's sides. Their headlong plummet shallowed into a wide, circling dive. Fost clung to handfuls of feathers, only slowly realizing that their descent was controlled.

Moriana's cloak billowed in his face. He brushed it aside, allowing it to stream over his shoulder. He was rewarded with the sight of her slim, white back and shapely buttocks flattened against the high-cantled saddle. He had forgotten that the Sky City's fugitive princess was still naked beneath the borrowed cloak.

'What a vision of loveliness!' Erimenes caroled. 'Doesn't it stir your manhood, Fost? Why, if the delectable princess were to lean a touch farther forward, perhaps you could plunge your doubtlessly raging manhood — '

Fost thumped the jar. Hard.

Still, he thought, *is it such a bad idea? Moriana does stir my manhood.* The thought of making love a thousand feet in the air on the back of an eagle had a definite appeal. Fost was considering leaning forward to suggest it to Moriana when the princess turned her head and looked straight past him.

'Hold tight,' she ordered. A hand reached behind her for one of the quivers slung across her back.

Fost's head snapped around. A trio of winged shapes drifted down toward them from the rim of the city. He thought he saw a flash of a pale face and arm as Luranni waved from the aerie. Then the gate slammed shut as the girl fell back to avoid drawing the attention of the bird riders who pursued Ayoka.

A raucous cry reached their ears. More birds appeared until half a dozen Guardsmen were swooping down on the fleeing pair. Fost felt his stomach tie itself into a knot.

'A fight! Glorious!' Erimenes was plainly beside himself with glee. 'Oh, what a memorable battle this shall be!'

130

'I hope I'm alive to remember it,' Fost said sourly. With morbid fascination, he kept his head craned around to watch the pursuers approach. The nearer three were armed with javelins and bows. One held a long lance, its head designed to break away from the shaft when it struck, so that it wouldn't drag its wielder to his doom. The Guards wore no armor. They depended on the speed and maneuverability of their mounts for protection. And in both those respects, their birds would hold every advantage over a half-senile eagle who bore three times the weight they did.

Something whined past Fost's ear. The rider on the left dropped his bow and tumbled from his saddle. Silently he spun groundward, arms and legs splayed.

'Marvelously shot!' Erimenes cried. 'As lovely a sight as your own naked limbs, Princess.'

Fost didn't think so. He knew it had been the bird rider's intention to slay him and Moriana, or return them to captivity and torture beyond imagining. Fost had often reveled in the hot rush of a foeman's blood as his blade bit deep, but the lonely suddenness of death in the air bothered him. Nor was he insensible that the bird rider's fate could be his.

The tactician in Fost appraised the peril they faced. He had no experience in aerial warfare, but it was plain to see that with their advantage in height, the pursuers could fall on their quarry whenever they chose. Moriana's arrows might claim more of them. On the other hand, some of their opponents were armed with bows, too.

Fost drew his sword. Moriana cast him an unreadable glance over her shoulder but said nothing. It might do him no good; still, the feel of the leather-wrapped hilt in his fist comforted him.

The world suddenly spun through a quarter circle. A pressure of Moriana's knees had sent the giant war-bird wheeling to one side to avoid the onslaught of the two nearest Guardsmen. A high wailing cry broke from a feathered throat as an arrow buried itself to the fletching in an eagle's chest. The Guard shrieked as his lifeless mount began the last long fall.

But there was no eluding his comrade. The gray-plumed war-bird had flattened its wings to its sides. Its rider lay along its neck, lance couched and aimed for the kill.

Sunlight gleamed on the keen lance head. Moriana strove frantically to nock another arrow. Erimenes gibbered orgiastically in the fulfillment of blood. Neither could change the grim judgment of the

131

steel arrowing at Fost's heart.

His senses dilated until all that existed was the lance point, glittering and hungering for flesh. Fury exploded within him. Bellowing, he swung his sword with all his strength.

The blade bit. The lance head went cartwheeling away, its tip laying open his cheek in passing. The blunted lance struck him full in the chest.

Breath burst from his body. Blackness and vivid stars whirled around his eyes. Instinctively his hand grabbed, felt smooth hardness, closed. An awful wrench sent agony stabbing from his abused shoulder, and he was thrown violently against the restraining strap around his middle.

A howling beat through the haze of agony and breathlessness that wrapped his brain. Colossal wing-tips brushed his face. The war-bird rushed by, riderless. The man who'd sat astride its back a moment before was falling after his two comrades, unseated by the reflex that had made Fost grip the haft of his lance as it struck.

Moriana's head turned. Her lips formed words twisted by the rush of the wind.

'What?' Fost shouted. His voice sounded rusty and as hoarse as if he had been inhaling smoke.

'Are you all right?' she cried. He felt his chest gingerly before nodding his head. He felt as though he'd been hit on the breastbone with a sledgehammer.

'Struck with your typical lack of chivalry,' said Erimenes sourly. 'Not one drop of blood did I see spilled.'

'That's not true,' Fost said, touching his torn cheek. An arrow whirred by not a hand's-breadth from his head. He yelped and twisted in the saddle to look behind, as Moriana drew her bow to return fire.

One of the three remaining pursuers had forged ahead of the rest. His mount squalled battle lust not a hundred feet behind the tip of Ayoka's tailfeathers. Even as Fost watched, the great bird-shape swelled. Moriana shot. Her arrow went wide. The eagle was too close for another shot. She slung her bow and gave all her thought to flying.

Voicing his own harsh battle-cry, Ayoka sideslipped, evading another shot from the Guardsman's bow. Still the archer's mount closed with its prey. Ayoka was laboring now. His breath came in vast, heaving wheezes, and Fost could feel the bird's heart hammering between his thighs. Moriana threw him into defensive turns, first to the right, then to the left. Ayoka's size, immense even for a war-bird, served him poorly now. The smaller eagle behind matched his every maneuver effortlessly, coming nearer and nearer.

The Guardsman held an arrow to his cheek. Fost saw the excitement and triumph glowing from the man's dark, thin features. The courier guessed he was holding fire, hoping to cripple Ayoka and force him down. The reward would be great for presenting Synalon with the corpses of her sister and the outlander who had thwarted her; a thousand times greater would be the reward for whoever presented her with their living bodies.

The wind of the attacking eagle's wings pounded Fost. Their sound grew louder as the thump of Ayoka's pinions ceased. A command from Moriana had made him press wings to his side for a last, desperate dive. It was a futile ploy. The pursuing bird folded its own wings, swooping for the kill.

Fost shook his sword in the Guardsman's grinning face, shouting defiance even as he steeled himself for Hell Call. With a sound like stone striking stone, Ayoka's wings broke from his flanks and seized the air. The giant bird slammed to a stop in mid-dive. Fost's defiance turned to astonishment before he went face-first into Ayoka's feathers.

The pursuing soldier acted too late. His mount threw out its wings in a braking maneuver, but its speed was too great and the span of its pinions too small. The eagle slid beneath Ayoka and stalled. Moriana's bow sang. The Guardsman uttered a choking yell as the broadhead arrow bit through his chest and pinned him to his mount.

Ayoka gave a cry that was half a gasp of pain. Fost snapped his head around to see a javelin sticking through the bird's right wing. Bravely, Ayoka flapped on but he now flew in a tight spiral. Only by some miracle did he keep from giving in to the anguish that filled him. As it was, the dart transfixing his wing interfered with its motion. All he could do was circle down and down.

Shouting hoarse exultation, the bird riders orbited him. The ancient bird had put up an epic fight, but with the dart through his wing he couldn't maneuver properly. The kill had become a certainty.

Moriana loosed arrows as fast as she could, scarcely aiming, to keep their foes at bay.

'Out!' she shouted at Fost. 'You must pull it out, or we fall.'

He started to protest. Undoing his safety strap at this moment seemed suicidal. And the kind of gymnastics it would take to pull the javelin out of Ayoka's wing . . . he felt dizzy at the very thought.

'Ah, such a fight,' Erimenes sighed. 'Too bad that it must end so soon. I'll almost sorrow to see your lifesblood shed, friend Fost. But what must be, must be.'

That did it.

'You've seen all my blood you're going to today, demon in a jug,' the courier growled. Not permitting himself to think, he unfastened the strap that held him in his saddle, sheathed his sword and turned to crawl out along the weakly pumping wing.

Understanding what the man was doing, Ayoka stopped flapping and held his wings straight for a glide. He sensed no updrafts on which to kite. They kept corkscrewing inexorably downward, faster now that his wing-beating had ceased resisting gravity.

The bird's body canted as Fost's weight shifted off-center. Fost clutched the wing, felt the hardness of bone and muscle and probed for the javelin. A glimpse of the ground spinning madly below sent cold fire dancing along his nerves. He shut his eyes and groped.

His fingertips bumped wood. He gripped the javelin's shaft and tugged hard. Ayoka coughed. The eagle's body jerked in response to the pain. Somehow, Fost had gotten tangled with the saddle harness. His body swung momentarily free of the sail-sized pinion, held only by his entangled foot.

'Gormanka!' he grunted, wishing the deity actually could aid him.

Realizing that intervention of a divine power wasn't likely, and that he must rely on his own abilities, Fost reached back and drew his sword. Moriana's harassing fire kept the Guardsmen at a distance, but she had to shoot too rapidly for accuracy. As usual, Erimenes was cheering both sides of the fray impartially.

Fost lunged forward and caught the javelin. He began to hack at its shaft just above the barbed head, trying to keep from jarring it in the wound. He felt the tremors of agony shudder through the mighty wing-muscles.

'Hurry,' came Moriana's voice. 'He cannot hold on much longer!'

The barb came away. A heave threw Fost backward, pulling the javelin out of Ayoka's wing with the same motion that sent the courier sprawling across the eagle's back. Ayoka swung away to the left. Fost would have fallen, but Moriana turned to grab him. Then Ayoka's wings were beating again. Their headlong plummet eased.

134

Frustrated, the Guardsmen charged. With a jarring impact, Ayoka twisted to meet one. Fost managed to grab a convenient strap with his sword hand and almost dropped his weapon. He smelled new rankness. A shadow fell on him. He jerked himself against Ayoka, his cheek pressing into Moriana's bare rump. Talons like heated wires raked his back.

Cursing, he flung the beheaded javelin after the eagle that had clawed him. The spinning shaft struck its tail and knocked free a handful of its stabilizing feathers. The bird pitched forward, righted itself with a wild plunging of its wings, and went fluttering away, fighting to stay airborne as its rider clung helplessly to its back.

Fost heard screaming. Ayoka had plucked the other Guard from his saddle and now held him in his claws while his beak ripped and tore flesh. A few savage strokes caused the man to hang limp and blood-soaked. Contemptuously, Ayoka let the body drop.

'A splendid battle. There was nearly enough blood spilled to satisfy me,' Erimenes said. 'Still, there's the matter of one surviving bird rider. Hadn't we best pursue him and finish him off?'

Miles across the sky, Fost saw the outline of the disabled bird still struggling to stay aloft. 'Break off,' he said wearily. 'We'd best not go looking for trouble; I'm sure we'll find ample quantities of it before we come to Athalau.' He listened a moment to Ayoka's breathing. 'Nor can this bird carry us forever.'

Erimenes said something sulky. Moriana leaned forward, conversing with the bird in its warbling pidgin.

'He says he sees my riding dog. I ordered the beast to keep pace with the city as best he could. It's no great trick. The city moves slowly enough to leave him time to sleep and search for food.' A puzzled frown creased her forehead. 'He also sees several other dogs that seem to be pulling something. He can't be more specific. He doesn't have the concepts.'

Fost laughed delightedly. 'Never mind. That's my own team and sled. I told them to follow your beast, thinking you might have him pace the Sky City. They're good dogs. They know how to forage in harness.' He smiled at her continued look of bewilderment. 'They led me to you.'

'But how? I covered my scent with minor spells.'

'But not the scent of the gruel from Kest-i-Mond's ever-filled bowl.' He explained to her the trick he'd used for tracking and found himself telling the whole story of his flight to the city and his adventure there

– suitably edited.

'But one thing still bothers me,' he finished. 'Why do they call that ugly statue the Vicar of Istu? I thought a vicar was some old dodderer who kept the stocks of incense and sacramental wine in order.'

'The word means *substitute* or *representative*,' Moriana told him.

'Oh.'

The ground flew by below. They came within the weaker human sight of the dogs. Moriana's long-legged mount loped along, with Fost's team dragging his sled on a parallel course some distance away.

With Ayoka gratefully winging his way to a landing, Moriana turned once more to look at Fost. The light in her eyes woke his blood. He put a hand on the nape of her neck and drew her face to his for a lingering kiss.

She screamed.

CHAPTER TEN

Fost jerked back. For a moment he wondered if he'd done something to draw such an outcry. She pointed past him into the sky.

Like smoke, a small black cloud swirled around the fringe of the great dark stone that was the city. As Fost and Moriana looked on, the blackness detached itself and began moving downwards. With a shock, Fost realized the cloud was heading for them.

'My sister dares not disperse the Guardsmen, lest rebellion break out while they hunt us,' said Moriana. 'Doubtless a company or two is being readied for the chase. In the meantime, she sets the ravens on our trail.'

Fost frowned at the cloud. Ravens? The image leaped into his mind. The balloon that had brought him to the city, shorn of its gondola, had been slashed and ripped by a savage attack of the black ravens.

Luranni's voice echoed through his mind: *their talons are poisoned.*

He quickly took stock of their situation. He found little to lift the chill that had settled on his soul. A scant five arrows remained in Moriana's quiver. The bird they rode was exhausted. The dogs could never outrun the swift-winged black killers, and the prairie's grassy swells offered no concealment from the air.

'We may fail,' Moriana said, seeing the bleakness in his eyes, 'but for my part I'd rather die with venom in my blood than spend eternity writhing in Istu's grip. You've won me a decent death, warrior. My thanks for that.'

Fost told himself that this was small recompense for the loss of immortality. Her words warmed him anyway.

Taloned feet touched ground. Ayoka took a few running steps on powerful legs as his wings fought the forward momentum. He came to a halt and sank to the grass. Moriana leaped from his back and ran toward her dog, who turned to meet her with a happy bark. Fost's dogs halted, their pointed ears pricking as they sensed their master's presence once again.

Moriana dug furiously in the pack she retrieved from her dog. 'We'll make a fire. Perhaps we can stand them off with torches.'

'For how long?' Fost asked. When he didn't get an answer, he bent to help her gather clumps of grass. The long strands were beginning to go dry and brittle with the onset of winter. At least starting a fire wouldn't be hard.

The ravens' shrill, evil cries reached them. Fost waited for Moriana to produce flint and steel. He jumped back when a word and a gesture brought the pile of grass into a blaze. It was easy to forget that the woman was a sorceress as well as a princess, thief, and warrior.

He took a handful of burning straw and stood. Already the swarm circled overhead, cackling gleefully among themselves, savoring the fear and consternation of their victims. Moriana stood by his side. She gripped his hand briefly. He returned the pressure without looking at her. His eyes were riveted on the great living cloud roiling above their heads.

A great ringing cry of anger rose from Ayoka's throat. He followed it. Like an immense projectile, he rose straight into the wheeling flock of ravens.

Black birds broke in all directions. Feathers flew and dark shapes fell lifeless to the prairie. Ayoka had risen to his final battle, and his foes had felt his wrath.

'Ayoka!' screamed Moriana. If he heard his mistress, the war-bird gave no sign. His huge form was almost totally obscured by shrieking ravens, but now and again Fost caught the glint of a giant beak slashing.

Dead ravens fell like diseased rain. A straggler, or one remembering his duty, dived on Fost and Moriana. Fost swung his sword. The blade sheared through a wing, causing the bird to drop flopping to the ground. Moriana lopped off its head.

Fost looked into the sky. The late afternoon sun dropped towards the Thails, casting a mellow golden light over a scene of utter horror. Striking beaks had burst Ayoka's eyes. Blood stained the white feathers of his head and ran from a score of lesser wounds. But even the poisons of the Sky City took time to kill a creature as large as Ayoka. He was making each second count.

His beak snapped and struck, shredding ravens like old cloth. His talons clutched, closed on struggling shapes until all movement stopped, and then dropped the carcass to seize another. Even the eagle's wings served him as weapons, buffeting the close-packed ravens and dashing them to the ground, where Fost and Moriana made short work of them.

With a shrilling of outrage and alarm, the ravens broke away from the eagle. He traced a tight circle, a wingtip smashing an incautious foe.

'Enchanted!' a raven croaked.

The survivors took up the panicked call: 'He is enchanted! We cannot harm him!'

Like a single frightened organism, the ravens spun away and fled back up the sky toward home. Ayoka floated serenely, turning his blinded eyes as if watching the rout of his attackers. His crimsoned beak opened and a harsh cry rang across the prairie, defiant and triumphant. Then his wings flowed upward like quicksilver and his body dropped behind a low ridge.

Moriana started to run to him. Fost stopped her. 'He's dead. He gave his life to buy us time. Let's not waste it.' She fought him briefly, then slumped sobbing against his chest.

He gave her a moment with her grief. Before he moved to rouse her, she broke the embrace. 'Let's go,' she said, and her eyes were dry.

Her saddle and pack with her spare clothing and gear lay miles behind. Fost introduced the princess to his dogs, who took to her readily after giving their master a noisy, face-licking greeting. The courier rummaged in his own sparse baggage, and in a short while Moriana was decked out in rough breeches and a tunic of homespun drab.

'I'll miss my sword,' she said, ruefully eyeing the few arrows remaining in her quivers.

After a few more seconds of searching, Fost found a long, heavy-bladed knife, which Moriana thrust through the length of rope she'd knotted around her waist. Fost mounted the runners of his sled. Moriana strode to her mount and swung astride it. The animal whimpered and sidestepped nervously. She leaned low and patted its neck, speaking softly to soothe it.

Not even Erimenes found much to say as they began their long journey south.

'I freely acknowledge my failure, O Mistress of the Clouds.' Prince Rann sat before the beryl throne in Synalon's disordered chamber, his head bowed. 'I implore you for the opportunity to redress my errors.'

The mages hadn't needed to fetch the prince from his sickbed. They had met him in the hallway, already clad in the purple and black of a bird rider. Despite the pain of cracked ribs hastily bound with linen bandages, the small man had walked erect to meet his royal cousin.

Now Synalon presented every appearance of a stern but just queen attempting to find the proper course to take with a trusted subordinate who'd proven derelict in his duties. It was all a sham, as Rann knew well. Synalon had already decided his fate. He knew that, too. He was still alive and free. Had the verdict gone against him, he would even now be straining his muscles against the inexorable pressure of his own rack. Or lying on the floor cindered and dead like the unfortunate Colonel Gulaj, whose body still sprawled near the door.

'I have decided,' she said with a slow, regal nod. 'In view of your past loyalty and service, you shall have the boon you crave. I charge you now to overtake and return to justice the traitor Moriana, her lowborn accomplice and, ah, whatever rightful property of the Crown the miscreants have stolen.' She paused in thought while Rann hid a smile. 'You may take a company of Guardsmen, no more. The city lies in grave danger of insurrection, thanks to the evil influence of my sister.'

'I shall need no more, Your Majesty.' His scars became a white net overlaying his features, as he thought of his own debts to settle with the fugitives. The coin was pain and humiliation. He would take payment in kind, a thousand-fold.

Synalon sat back in her throne. Dismissing the kneeling prince, she turned to the new palace chamberlain, who hovered anxiously at her elbow wringing fish-white hands.

'Tell me, Anacil,' she said, 'how long would it take to procure a hornbull?'

Southward and eastward fled the fugitives, on a line that would take

140

them near the walls of Brev. Like all the cities of that Great Quincunx, Brev teemed with the paid agents of the Sky City. Fost and Moriana would forgo the pleasures of civilized accomodations for a night beneath the stars. They wouldn't thirst or hunger, though. Synalon had left the self-replenishing bowl and goblet Fost had taken from Kest-i-Mond's castle in the satchel with Erimenes's jug. The courier had given in to the spirit's whining pleas and taken out the resin pellets that jammed the bowl's lid open, so that Erimenes no longer had to ride sloshing about in gruel. Not at all to Fost's surprise, the philosopher displayed no gratitude.

Beyond the line of the Quincunx that connected Brev and Thailot, the prairie broke apart in a network of narrow ravines. Whether natural action of erosion had formed them, or as legend said, the very earth had cracked under the stresses of the War of Powers, couldn't be told. Some of the ravines ran with swift torrents of water birthed amid the snows and springs of the Thails. Others lay dry, with no sign of ever having carried streams. So much Fost learned from Moriana's descriptions. By now the sun poised fat and swollen, ready to burst itself on the jagged fangs of the mountains and spill daylight from the sky. Shadows masked the bottoms of the gorges, though from some issued the impatient murmur of running water. As they entered the cracked lands, the autumn-dried grasses of the prairie gave way to a short, coarse heather whose dark green and purple leaves masked prodigious thorns. They tinged the air with a faint, astringent odor. They also slowed down the pair considerably. The dagger-like thorns penetrated even the thick fur of Fost's dogs, forcing him and Moriana to pick their way around the densest growths.

Fost's mood began to lighten. He had faced overwhelming odds and won. He was on his way to adventure, with a woman at his side who possessed both beauty and skill in combat, and at the quest's end lay immortality. The fact that Moriana had ideas of her own about what should be done with the Amulet of Living Flame didn't trouble him now. The time to settle that issue was when it arose.

Now he rode beneath the open sky, and his nostrils gratefully drank in the freshness of the air. The medicinal aroma of the heather came as a relief after the intermingled scents of the Sky City. Thirty thousand years of habitation had imbued the city with a smell that was more an aura, never truly noticed after the first encounter, yet never absent and coloring every perception. It wasn't a bad odor, but Fost was glad to be free of it.

He looked back at the way they'd come and saw bands of glorious color staining the sky. With winter coming the sun's arc had swung far to the north. Directly to the east, the Thail Mountains pulled tighter the cloaks of cold shadows, dotted only occasionally with towering, gold-tipped treetops. At the other end of the sky rose the green moon.

Fost studied the dark shapes moving slowly against the striations of orange and violet and indigo. Then, a dryness in his throat, he called out to Moriana to look. Her first glance confirmed his fears.

'War-birds,' she said.

'At least ten riders against the two of you,' said Erimenes thoughtfully, 'and this time you're groundlings, and in the open. This promises to be interesting.'

'Interesting it may well be,' Moriana said, 'but we won't meet them in the open. That would be suicide – and how much fun would that be to watch?'

For once, Erimenes lacked a reply. Signaling Fost to follow, Moriana rode toward the head of a cut that fell steeply to join the maze of canyons. Sword in hand, Fost steered his team in her wake. They hurtled through the heather, ignoring the thorns that raked them constantly.

Moriana braked to a sudden halt; Fost's sled slid to a stop behind her. She leaped from her mount and slapped the dog. With a yelp, it kept on running. She had her sword out and was hacking at his dog's harnesses.

'What are you doing?' Fost demanded.

'This ravine's only a few feet wide . . . room only for us. Besides, the dogs might throw them off the scent. And we'll need a roof of some kind over our heads to keep us safe from aerial attacks.'

Fost joined her in chopping down the squat, dry brush. 'Why can't you use sorcery against the Guardsmen?'

'The same reason I didn't use magic to free myself back in the city. Synalon's ward-spells protect her from enchantment, and her Guardsmen almost as well. I can't even use a compulsion on them as I did with the guards at the balloon dock.' She swept a lock of hair from her eyes. 'There are limitations.'

Five minutes' work allowed them to bridge the narrow cut with the dense brush over a six-foot length. It was slim cover, but enough to keep off the birds and spoil their rider's aim, and, with the sun setting, the light would be gone in minutes.

Huddled beneath the thorny covert, they heard angry squawks from thwarted eagles. 'Land, men,' came a voice. 'We'll take them afoot.'

Wings booming, five birds touched down in the sandy bottom of the cut. 'Remember the reward if we take them back alive,' rasped the officer. He led, walking bent-legged and wary, twitching his sword before him like a feeler as if testing the air.

Mindful that four Guardsmen were still aloft, Fost didn't advance to meet him. Weapons ready, he and Moriana waited in the makeshift shelter.

The Guardsmen walked noisily through the brush. They walked around the ravine, swords swinging — and kept on walking. Fost stared at the soldiers' backs and looked at Moriana. She shrugged in surprise.

'There she goes!' a Guardsman yelled. He pointed his sword into the distance and his comrades lunged forward into the darkness that now shrouded the cut. Fost heard a clash of blades, then cursing. 'She's gone again, dammit.'

'Listen!' another voice shouted. 'Over there! I hear them over there!'

A crashing through the underbrush told them the soldiers were blindly in pursuit of something that wasn't there. Now that skyriders could no longer see them, Moriana grabbed Fost's hand, and they ran in the opposite direction.

'I thought you said your enchantments wouldn't work against them,' Fost said reproachfully as he gained the top of the rise.

'I did,' said Moriana, 'and they won't.' Taking Fost's hand, she struck out across the fractured lands.

Later they lay side by side, huddled in blankets. With their pursuers afraid to venture after them, Fost had returned to his sled to gather what supplies he could. The dogs were all dead, killed by Guardsmen's arrows. Wigma had still been breathing, though barely. He had raised his head at the human's approach. The reproach in his eyes was all for himself: *I tried, Master, but I could not fight them all.* He licked Fost's hand as the courier threw himself down at his side. His tongue left a bloody track.

The big dog laid his head in Fost's lap and died. The courier groped for words of farewell, but there was a catch in his throat and he wasn't able to speak.

Moriana had led the way through the broken country until she judged they were far enough away from their pursuers. She had hunted these lands as a girl, running down dire-weasels and fleet-footed antelope on Ayoka's sturdy back. She had found a place where the earth of a ravine's bank had fallen away, leaving a flat slab of shale to roof a shallow cave. They made their cold camp here, sharing gruel and lukewarm water.

'If you didn't cast some kind of spell of invisibility over us, who did?' asked Fost, stretching a finger to trace the line of Moriana's jaw.

'I don't know.'

'If either of you had the sense the Three and Twenty Wise Ones gave a dung beetle, you might infer the identity of your savior.' The peevish voice emerged from the satchel propped against the bank. 'Though why I should expect gratitude from the likes of you I'll never know.'

Fost drew himself up on one elbow, peering through the darkness at the spirit's jug. 'You? But how?'

'Moriana didn't. You certainly did not. Whom does that leave?'

'I didn't know you were a magician, spirit. What else have you concealed from us? Remember the Josselits, Erimenes.'

'No magic was involved. A mere trifle of mind control. Why, even when alive I could have accomplished such a feat with ease. My thirteen hundred ninety-nine years of contemplation have only honed the edge of my abilities.'

Moriana's eyes met Fost's in the darkness. 'The savants of Athalau were noted for their mental abilities, apart from sorcery,' she said.

'Which explains how,' the courier said, 'but not why. Why, when you were on the verge of seeing our blood shed as you've so avidly desired before, did you rescue us?'

'Even if I felt called upon to account for my actions to some lout of a courier . . .'

'The Josselits, Erimenes. Remember them.'

' . . . I strongly doubt you have the mental capacity to follow my reasoning,' the spirit said testily. 'As for your incessant caviling about the Josselits, I can only observe that they would be as stimulating company as you've proven this night. Lying beside you is a lovely wench who owes her life and soul to you, and yet you lie there like a pious divinity student without doing a thing about it.'

Erimenes's comment made Fost aware of an urgent tickle below his belt. He gazed at Moriana for a minute. Her expression was unreadable in the starlight.

'No,' he said at last. 'I think not. After what you've been through today . . .'

Moriana kissed him lightly on the lips. 'Thank you, Fost.' With that she rolled over, snuggled herself against him, and went promptly to sleep.

In a short time he too slept, but his dreams teemed with enemies and screaming faces.

CHAPTER ELEVEN

Like damp, rumpled cloth gradually dried and drawn taut over a frame, the land flattened from undulating prairie to a virtually featureless steppe. High gray-green grass, bowing before the ceaseless wind, stretched as far as the eye could see in all directions. Winter and the nearness of the polar zone had dropped a blanket of dreariness on the land. Leaden gray clouds rolled across the sky, building an impenetrable wall above the low, black bulk of the Rampart Mountains. Even the sunlight was robbed of its brilliance and cast a wan radiance. And every step took the fugitives deeper into bone-chilling cold.

Fost and Moriana had spent three days winding through the labyrinth of ravines. Twice flights of war-birds had flown over, but overhanging banks had provided them cover from observation. By the time they emerged from the broken country, not an eagle could be seen through the whole vast dome of the sky.

From there on, they had to traverse open country, which gave no shelter from the keen eyes of Rann's eagles. So they decided to travel mostly at night, halting at the first pallid tint of dawn to dig places to sleep away the daytime. The roots of the steppe grass reached deep. They knew they could cut up great chunks of sod and then pull them back into place to provide camouflage.

For their own reasons, the two felt increasingly eager to reach the city in the glacier and the treasure it concealed. Yet their path did not lead directly toward the Gate of the Mountains, the pass that lay due north of Athalau. The swallowed city lay on a southeastward line running through Thailot to Brev. The traveler's weary legs, however, carried them almost directly south.

Moriana broached the subject the evening they emerged from the ravines. They had just finished the celebration denied them the night of their escape from the City in the Sky. Facing one another, naked, they pressed close with the aftermath of passion.

'If we make straight for the Gate of the Mountains, Rann's men will have us before we go thirty miles,' she said, the words slightly distorted as she lay with her cheek against the courier's chest. 'Their eagles have poor night vision, but on the steppe they don't have to see well to make out moving figures.'

'What can we do about it?' Fost asked as he absently stroked her golden hair.

'I remember hearing of a way through the Ramparts near the Great Crater Lake directly south of here.' She rubbed her smooth cheek across his chest. 'Synalon has some scheme in mind; I don't think she'll let Rann have many men to hunt us. He'll concentrate on the straight path to the Gate. If we make for the Crater Lake we'll have a better chance of eluding him.'

'Hmmm,' Fost rumbled thoughtfully to himself. 'I remember something about a western passage on that map I took from Kest-i-Mond. I don't recall exactly, but I have the impression there was something ominous about the name.'

'The Valley of Crushed Bones, it's called.' Erimenes's tones seemed even more sour than usual. 'If that sounds at all ominous to you.'

'It does. But no name, however awful it sounds, scares me as much as Rann and his bird riders.'

'Nonsense. You've dealt with the Sky Guardsmen before.' Erimenes made a sound as though clicking a vaporous tongue. 'Really, Fost, I cannot fathom your timorousness.'

Fost made a rude noise.

'What became of the map?' Moriana asked him.

He grimaced. 'Obviously Synalon knew its value. I had it in the satchel you stole from me.' He felt her tense at the words and patted her rump affectionately. 'Never mind. That's long gone by now. At any rate, I don't have the map any longer.'

'And Rann does,' Erimenes said. 'He'll know of the westward route. He'll lay a trap for you, mark my words.'

Moriana eased her head around to look at the satchel. 'I have the feeling there's something about the Crater Lake country that our distinguished colleague dislikes. Why don't you want us going to the Great Crater, Erimenes?'

Erimenes mumbled something about them regretting such ill-considered judgments and spoke no more.

'Another mystery,' Moriana said to Fost. 'First he renders us invisible to the Guardsmen despite their protection spells. Now he displays this curious reluctance about the Great Crater Lake. I wonder what it means?'

'Nothing but good, if it shuts him up like that,' Fost replied. He reluctantly pulled away from Moriana's grip and sat up, the cold wind from the steppes whipping around him. But the wind felt good, clean, fresh, and crisp after the blood and death they'd been through. 'Let's be on our way. The night soon will be dark enough to cloak our movements from Rann.'

'I suppose you're right,' sighed Moriana. She straightened and stared southward.

Fost didn't have to be a mindreader to know what she was thinking. On this score, their thoughts were as one. The City in the Glacier. The Amulet of Living Flame. Immortality.

Immortality!

They had endured much at the hands of Synalon and Rann. They had defeated them. Now only reward lay ahead for the courier and his princess in the southlands.

'Come on, let's *move!*' Fost cried, struggling into his clothing. 'The sooner we're off these steppes the better I'll like it.'

'Yes, Fost,' agreed Moriana, dressing as quickly as the courier. Neither could hide the soaring anticipation they felt.

'Why you're so eager to freeze, going in this direction, I'll never know,' sniffed Erimenes. 'There's nothing this way you could possibly want, mark my words.'

But Fost and Moriana ignored him. They strode off onto the night-shrouded steppe with a spring in their walk, hand in hand, knowing the worst lay behind them.

BOOK TWO
The City in the Glacier

For Carrie, who's earned it
— vwm —

For my parents, with love and gratitude
— rev —

CHAPTER ONE

'If Rann's bird-riders don't kill us, this damned wind will. Doesn't it ever stop?' Fost Longstrider shouted over his shoulder. As if to mock his words, the wind died momentarily. A teasing lull, and then it blew full force again, hurling the eternal chill of the antarctic waste beyond the Rampart Mountains into their chapped, reddened faces.

His companion hunched closer, both to hear his words and to share his body's warmth. Numbed hands plucked ceaselessly at her heavy velvet cloak, tightening it against the cold in a gesture long since turned into reflex. The woman's fingers were long and fine, unmarked by labor save for the small, distinctive calluses left by long hours spent wrapped about the hilt of a sword.

'I thought you were used to living in the wind and weather,' Moriana shouted back, blinking as the blast whipped her golden hair painfully into her eyes. 'I thought you couriers spent all your time out on the road.'

'I thought you princesses spent all your time lolling about in jewel-encrusted towers on satin pillows and thinking about how best to gratify your every whim.'

Moriana managed a short laugh. 'I suppose we've still a lot to learn about each other.'

'In the old days,' a third voice said, 'the weather was worse. The wind blew harder and colder, the snow lay deeper when it came, and for months out of the year the sun never rose at all this far south.' The thin, plaintive voice issued forth from a bulky knapsack slung over the courier's back.

'Come, Erimenes,' said Fost. 'You don't expect us to believe such wild stories. '

'It's true,' the voice insisted. 'It was quite some time ago, of course.

Long before my birth, to say nothing of my death. During the War of Powers ten thousand years ago, it was, when Felarod and the Earth-Spirit challenged the might of the Dark Ones. The struggle tipped the world on its axis. It brought these once fair and temperate lands into the icy grasp of the south pole and sealed the fate of lovely Athalau. I would not lie to you.'

'Oh?' said Fost, in mock surprise. 'Has the cold caused such a drastic change in your character?'

'Scoff, lowborn,' sniffed Erimenes. 'I tell you nothing but the truth.'

Fost nodded, inclined to believe the spirit this time, yet unwilling to allow Erimenes the opportunity to gloat. In the vast libraries of High Medurim, Fost had read of a cataclysmic struggle in the distant past. But being born in the worst slums and learning the treacherous ways of the capital of the once-great Empire had turned him into a bitter realist. He had dismissed the tales as fantasy, mere legends concocted by the romantically inclined to add spice to the otherwise dreary march of history. He had forgotten the tales until just a few days past, when the honey-haired daughter of High Councillor Uriath of the Sky City had entertained him with the history of that ancient community.

Now he wondered how much truth was contained in those ancient tomes. Yet his hardheaded approach to reality refused to yield totally in spite of his recent confrontations with fire elementals, ape-monsters that ran through walls like wraiths but whose talons tore flesh like steel hooks, and idols that came to life imbued with the souls of sleeping demons. Abruptly he threw back his head and laughed into the teeth of the wind.

'Are you taken insane?' asked Erimenes hopefully. 'Might I expect some new and diverting escapade from you?'

'It's nothing, old spirit,' said Fost, wiping away a tear before it turned to ice on his cheek. 'It just occurred to me how absurd the universe really is. Here I am tramping across the Southern Steppe beside the sorceress-princess of a city that floats a thousand feet in the air, and riding in the satchel at my hip is the spirit of a philosopher who has died fourteen hundred years before . . .'

'Thirteen hundred and ninety-nine,' corrected Erimenes haughtily. 'Get your facts straight.'

'And,' Fost continued, as though the wraith hadn't interrupted, 'this bizarre trio is bound for a city lost in the bowels of a glacier, in search of a talisman that confers the blessing of eternal life.'

154

'All you ever think about is that amulet,' complained Erimenes. 'One would think there is nothing else in the world.'

'Isn't eternal life a worthy enough goal, Erimenes?' asked Moriana.

'Yes, laugh, ridicule my warning to snatch at all the experience you can now. Mark my words. This fool's errand to retrieve the amulet will only earn you death, not eternal life,' Erimenes said sourly. 'Right now the journey is easy. You'll find it otherwise when Rann catches you and starts winding your guts onto a spool before your eyes.'

'You'd like that,' said Moriana with sudden savagery. 'It would be quite a thrill for you to watch, wouldn't it? I don't doubt you'd stand by and offer helpful suggestions as you did when I was captive and my eunuch cousin forced me to watch him torture to death the friends of my childhood.'

Fost gripped her shoulder. Moriana's face had gone white. Her capture in the Sky City had left scars on her soul that even time might not obliterate. She had returned to the Sky City to find her beloved mother dead and her hated sister usurping the throne. Within hours she was a prisoner, trapped by her cousin Rann's secret police. And at Synalon's command, Prince Rann had refrained from tormenting the prisoner – physically. He had found other ways of torture, ways leaving her body unsullied for her sacrificial marriage to Istu, the Demon of the Dark Ones.

Black Istu slept in the foundations of the Sky City, bound there at the end of the War of Powers by a victorious Felarod. For centuries the humans, who had supplanted the reptilian Fallen Ones responsible for building the City thirty millennia before, had sacrificed select members of the Blood Royal to Istu, in the form of his Vicar, an obscene stone statue that squatted at the City's core. Though Istu slept eternally, his subconscious remained active with a primitive, elemental life. This force could be drawn into the Vicar by the arcane chants of the Rite of Dark Assumption. For a time after the chant, the stone would pulse with unholy life – time enough for the demon to consummate his union with his latest victim.

Five thousand years before, Julanna the Wise had overthrown the necromancer Malva Kryn and founded the Etuul line. Her first act had been to suppress the Rite and all worship of the Dark Ones.

'Rann tortures only mind and body,' continued Moriana bitterly, 'but this is nothing compared with Synalon. My sister strives to serve the Dark Ones again after all these years.'

'Don't let Erimenes goad you into argument,' cautioned Fost. 'He craves excitement. These dreary steppes are boring to him – and they are getting to me as well.' He glanced at the blonde woman and felt a lump forming in his throat.

Fost had rescued Moriana from Synalon and Rann, but it had been no mere altruism that prompted him to take such insane risks. He had followed a beauteous thief who had robbed him in the night, made it memorable with her lovemaking when he caught her, and then stolen away before dawn with the jug containing Erimenes the Ethical. And Erimenes alone, who had dwelt in Athalau before the glacier engulfed it, knew the location of the Amulet of Living Flame.

Fost's first discovery upon entering the City in the Sky was that his nocturnal thief was no less than Princess Moriana Etuul and rightful ruler of the City. His second was that she had been captured by her sister. Fost had already encountered Synalon's men searching for Erimenes and knew how deadly confronting them could be. With Erimenes secreted somewhere in the Palce of the Winds, Fost's only hope of finding him lay in asking Moriana. He had been forced by circumstance to rescue her.

He looked at the woman who strode beside him with steps still long and sure despite the fatigue he knew weighted her limbs. She was tall, nearly as tall as he. Her slimness made her appear almost frail beside his brawny bulk, belying a tigerish strength and swiftness that had almost claimed Fost's life at sword point the night they first met. The exchange of sword thrusts had turned into an exchange of thrusts of a different nature, but Fost had never forgotten the coldness felt when he realized he faced an opponent his equal in skill.

Her eyes, bloodshot now from the wind, were green, brighter and livelier than his own of smoke-grey. She was fair and blonde and lithe; he was burly, tanned and weatherbeaten, with a face framed by an unmanageable growth of black hair. In appearance they were as disparate as their backgrounds.

But even that first night, Fost had sensed something in her, some strand that matched one in the skein of his own existence. When he had trailed her across the steppe, fought his way up to the Sky City and found himself caught between Rann's ruthless efficiency and the equally deadly ineptitude of anti-Synalon rebels, he had told himself over and over that self-interest was his motive. She had robbed him of the key to life everlasting; he had meant to have it back. But he had never been able to hide from himself that his interest in rescuing Moriana ran far deeper.

And after rescuing her and escaping on the back of her aged, faithful war bird, he had learned that she, too, felt a strong link between them.

Moriana sensed his gaze, turned her eyes to his, smiled. He smiled back and looked away. In the green pools of her eyes he had seen the same knowledge that haunted him. Each ever-harder step to the South carried them nearer the decision that could sever forever the bond between them – or end one or the other's life.

Only one could possess the Amulet of Living Flame and the immortality it gave.

Night descended like a dome of black crystal, shutting out both wind and light. The steppe lay still under the cold blaze of constellations. Small soft sounds rustled in the dead grass around them, but none came near. The lesser predators of the steppe had learned that the smell of humans meant danger. The greater stayed clear, kept at bay by Moriana's magic.

Despite the cold the night was beautiful. But with his usual perversity Erimenes chose to wax morbid as Fost and Moriana supped on gruel.

'Rann may concentrate his search farther east, as you say, Princess,' he said, with an obsequious bow in Moriana's direction. When they had stopped for the night, Fost had yielded to Erimenes's pleas and uncorked his jar. Now the spirit rose from the broad mouth of the jug, a thin spire of glowing blue haze that grew and resolved itself into the figure of a man. Except for his complexion Erimenes appeared much as he must have in life: a gaunt man of medium height, high of brow and ascetic of feature, with a lordly prow of a nose that seemed designed expressly for peering down at those of lesser intellectual attainments. The spirit looked exactly what he was, one of the more renowned philosophers of a city famed for its savants. Only a certain gleam in his eyes and a few lines etched around his aristocratic mouth hinted that Erimenes the Ethical had undergone a change since departing corporeal life.

When Moriana did not respond, he turned his attention back to Fost. 'Even so, you must cross the southernmost reaches of the steppe, and then cross the domain of the barbarians who dwell in the shadows of the Ramparts. They are known to be most inhospitable to strangers.'

Fost rubbed his chin, wishing they had a fire. But even if they had possessed fuel for one, a rare commodity on the virtually treeless steppe, they would not have dared light it. An airborne observer could sight even a spark for miles.

'I've heard of them,' he said. 'Nomad warriors, insanely suspicious, feuding among themselves like the clans of the Highgrass Broad. I've never been this far south before – not much call to make deliveries in these parts. But it's said they ride all manner of outlandish creatures, bears and badgers and outsized goats. No fit mounts for civilized folk, not like a good war dog.' He caught the look Moriana shot him. 'Or giant eagles,' he amended. 'But that may be just campfire gossip. You know how couriers are.'

'Don't mention fires,' Moriana said, drawing closer. Fost grinned and put his arm around her.

Erimenes shook his head. 'Never have I seen folk so eager to commit suicide,' he said. 'And two so young! A shame to die, with all your lives before you.'

'You're an old woman, Erimenes,' Moriana said, looking at him wryly. 'I'm not afraid of any skin-clad savages, no matter how unorthodox their mounts. Fost is right; rumour is as fickle as a fire sprite. These nomads of yours are probably starving and as timid as mice.' She shook back her hair defiantly. 'And even if they're not, what of it? I'm a princess of the City in the Sky. What have I to fear from a passel of wretched groundlings? I mean . . .' She blinked, and her skin darkened in the starlight.

Fost laughed at her eagerness to correct herself. The Sky Citizens' disdain for those who dwelt beneath their feet had been obvious to him the instant he entered the City. During his short stay in the City, he'd become acquainted with their favorite derogatory term for their earthbound fellows.

'And what of the storms?' Erimenes asked, returning to his point like a dog to its bone. 'The Ramparts bear the brunt of the antarctic storms, but it is fast becoming winter. How will you find your way when a white wall of snow blocks your vision past the tip of your nose? How will you find food, shelter?'

'We've food a-plenty, Erimenes.' Fost held up the bowl he shared with Moriana. As always when uncovered, it magically brimmed with an infinite load of unappetizing, murky, thin porridge. Ebony filigreed with silver, the bowl had been part of Fost's meagre loot from the keep of Kesti-i-Mond, the mage to whom he'd been sent to deliver Erimenes some weeks before. Moriana wrinkled her nose.

Though nourishing, the gruel lacked anything resembling taste.

'For shelter we can dig in,' Fost continued, 'and I have a tent when the ground gets too hard. By that point the storms will probably be severe enough to ground Rann's bird-riders so we won't have to worry about concealment.'

An idea hit him. 'I know Rann's Sky Guardsmen are proof against your sorceries,' he said to Moriana, 'but do you have any power over weather? If you can whistle us up some nice, low clouds, we'll have nary a worry about running into your cousin.'

'I've some of the weather magic,' she admitted, 'but no vast amount. It is a field all its own, one requiring much study and certain affinities I lack. The best I can do is — how can I say it? — shape and expand existing weather patterns, harness forces already set in motion by nature or the gods. I cannot create a cloud, but if one appears nearby I can influence it. Likewise a storm.'

'Excellent.' Fost brightened. 'There's usually an overcast in the morning. If you get started early . . .'

'I don't think you understand,' Moriana said quietly. 'My control over weather is imperfect. At this time of year, so near the Southern Waste, I wouldn't dare to tamper with a storm. If I tried to make it grow it would probably get away from me. We could wind up in twenty feet of snow.'

'Oh.'

'Doomed,' Erimenes intoned. 'A shame. A sorrow. A waste.'

Moriana put her chin in her hand and stared at him in exasperation.

'You, Princess,' the spirit said. 'So lovely, so fine and noble of limb and face. What a pity such a vision of loveliness should be nipped in the bud.'

'You're mixing metaphors, Erimenes,' Fost said.

'And you, even if you are lowborn and something of a guttersnipe, you're not displeasing to the feminine eye, I should say. Those muscles, while they could be larger, are far from insignificant. Remember the adventures you've known with other ladies. Would you throw all that away? I remember sweet Eliska . . .'

Fost shook the jug hard enough to disintegrate the vaporous being momentarily. Actinic sparks swarmed within the luminous cloud, dancing like agitated insects. Erimenes's face reappeared wearing an expression of supreme indignation. 'That was an ungentlemanly thing to do,' he sniffed. 'Most rude.'

'This is not the time to elaborate on my, uh, adventures,' Fost said. He rested his hand on the jug, lightly but menacingly, to show the spirit that more of the same could be expected if he continued that line of conversation in Moriana's presence.

'Spoilsport,' Erimenes pouted. He turned a sorrowful face to the princess. 'Have pity on a poor, disembodied spirit,' he said. 'Turn back from this mad escapade. Don't leave me stranded to spend eternity on the steppe beside your bleaching bones.'

'So that's why you're so against us going south, Erimenes,' said Moriana. 'You're afraid we'll both be killed and leave you helpless and alone. There wouldn't be any more vicarious excitement then, my nebulous friend, would there?'

'My foremost concern is the welfare of you, my two best friends in all the world,' the spirit said, sincerity ringing from his words.

'I'm sure,' said Fost sarcastically. He eyed the spirit intently. He had the feeling Erimenes's reluctance to venture south depended on more than fear of being marooned.

The spirit looked keenly at him, then at Moriana. 'You're still determined?' They nodded in unison.

He sighed. 'Well,' he said, 'if you are committed to this folly, so be it. But since you have so little of life left, why not make the most of the time at hand?' A knowing leer marred the spirit's distinguished features. Fost sighed. Erimenes was up to his old tricks again.

In life Erimenes the Ethical had preached a turning away from all wordly concerns – and most especially the pleasures of the flesh. So great was the power of his mind, he maintained, and so total his otherworldliness, that on the death of his body his spirit survived to be immured in an Athalar spirit jug. But Erimenes's after-life was blighted by a tragic irony.

Death had brought a revelation to the ascetic philosopher: The only worthy life, he decided after centuries in the jug, was one of utter hedonism, the only goal sheer physical pleasure.

Both of which it was now too late for him to enjoy.

He could, however, watch others live their lives and experience through them the sensations forever denied him. If those around him did not show what he considered a properly hedonistic outlook, he was quick to offer suggestions. At the best of times it made him a nuisance. At the worst, when danger loomed and his bloodlust was aroused, it proved perilous. Erimenes was indispensable to their quest for the Amulet of Living Flame and eternal life, but sometimes both Fost and Moriana wondered if immortality was sufficient recompense for putting up with him.

Something small and warm slipped inside Fost's cloak and into his jerkin. He looked down at Moriana. She smiled slowly and kissed him.

'It's cold out,' she said, nuzzling closer. 'And who knows? Perhaps tomorrow we will hear Hell Call. For once I think our friend's advice is sound.'

'Since you put it that way . . .' Fost began. She stopped his mouth with hers.

And for a time the cold of night was banished.

The tenth day after their flight from the City, they reached the foothills of the Rampart Mountains. The Ramparts blocked off the huge ice-sheets and the bitterest cold of the Southern Waste, but the wind blew southerly, its tendrils seeking out every winding passage through the Ramparts to clutch at the travelers' limbs like frigid, insistent fingers. The night was simply too cold to be walking. Marching during the day had not pleased Fost at first. Should Rann have bird-riders on picket duty along the north face of the Ramparts, the arduous journey could come to a short, ugly end.

'If Rann comes this way he won't patrol this region with less than his full force,' Moriana had assured him. 'The thulyakhashawin lair in these mountains.' The thulyakhashawin were winged foxes, the only flighted creatures in the Realm capable of meeting the eagles of the Sky City on equal terms in the air. Not bats but actually winged vulpine carnivores, the thulyakhashawin hunted in packs and attacked the Sky City birds on sight. This news had alarmed Fost as much as the thought of Rann finding them, and Moriana's assurance that the foxes seldom attacked humans afoot did little to soothe him.

'Well,' he said, looking up, 'we'll not be plagued by eagles or foxes today.' The clouds hung dense and impenetrable, so low it seemed as if he could reach out and touch them. It was as if a fluffy white roof had been laid above the rocky hummocks that had begun to interrupt the steppe.

'Brrr.' Moriana shivered and drew close to him as a gust of wind blasted into their faces. She wore her gold-lined maroon cloak, the one she'd left with Fost in the forest after robbing him of Erimenes. He had taken it from his sled along with the other gear, which now rode in a knapsack slung on his back.

Fost squinted into the wind, tears rolling down his cheeks. 'That damned gruel doesn't do much to warm a body,' he said. The cloud cover took his words and cast them back in a flat, ghostly echo. It was as if they had somehow stumbled into a gigantic hollow chamber.

'You've no one to blame but yourself,' Erimenes said. 'You insisted on coming this way against all my good advice.'

'It's doubtless just as cold to the East,' Fost pointed out. Erimenes lapsed into sulky silence. Fost sucked in his cheeks. At first he had relished Erimenes's lack of verbosity, but of late he'd come to share Moriana's suspicions. The spirit had displayed unexpected abilities at the fight back in the ravine. He was, after all, born in Athalau, though he had lived long after the heyday of that city. It was unlikely Erimenes would tell more of his powers unless it suited him, and Fost could think of no way to compel him. With one hand hugging Moriana close and the other holding his own cloak shut against the gelid wind, Fost put his head down and trudged on into the stiff gale.

They had walked for what seemed an eternity when the blizzard struck. The wall of white rolled over them like an avalanche. At first, blinking at it as the gusts stabbed his eyes like daggers, Fost thought it was the cloud that perpetually hung over the Great Crater Lake. According to Moriana a volcanic vent at the bottom of the lake kept it from freezing even in the deepest cold, and the steam that rose from the warm waters held heat within the crater like a lid covering a bowl.

'Look,' he said, fingers plucking at Moriana's shoulder. 'The cloud – we've made it!' Thoughts of sinking his half-frozen limbs in balmy water drove him forward. He broke into a run, dragging the princess with him.

He saw dancing motes of whiteness, and the snow swept over him like a tide. He cried out in disappointment, wiping the snowflakes from his face and watching them melt slowly on his palm. Moriana glanced up at him but said nothing.

He shook his head violently. The nervous strain and physical exhaustion of the last two weeks were wearing him down. The erosion of his strength and will could be as deadly a foe as the cold or the forces of the Sky City. 'We should stop and try to ride the storm out,' he shouted above the clamor of the wind. 'It's death to keep moving through a blizzard like this.'

Moriana shook her head. 'There's no place to take shelter, and the ground is too frozen to dig in.' She waved a hand to still his protests. 'I know we could sit with our backs to the wind, huddling beneath our

162

cloaks for warmth. But why delay what must be? All that could save us would be a fire, and we don't have any dry fuel. I'd rather meet my fate standing up – and fighting.'

Erimenes spoke. The torrents of wind washed away his words. Fost's arguments died unspoken. *What difference does it make?* he asked himself. *If the storm subsides, we may have a chance. Otherwise we die, sooner or later. What do a few miserable hours matter?* He bent his head and walked on.

The snow mounted until they stumbled through deep drifts, their feet leaden. The cold leeched thought and emotion from their minds as it sucked the heat from their bodies. They moved through a white swirling fog that existed as much inside their skulls as without. Fost tripped over an unseen obstacle and fell. The wet bite of the snow on his numb face revived him for a moment. Moriana apathetically helped him to his feet. A few minutes more and the spark of life that had flared within him died until he was scarcely aware of who he was.

Knives stabbed up his calves at every step. He vaguely welcomed the pain as a sign that some life still lingered. His lungs burned. The force of the wind was like a river at full flood. It took all his dwindling strength to make headway.

The white hours passed, a waking nightmare of featureless, icy, surreal tapestry. A voice cried for him to stop, to sink into the snow and conserve what vitality remained. He ignored the voice within his skull and concentrated on the task of lifting one dead weight that was a foot and heaving it in front of the other.

What does it matter, what does it matter, what does it matter? The question thudded in his brain like slow blows of a mallet. Yet he also heard the words, *Listen to me, fool, I can guide you to safety. Curse you, you thickheaded clod of a courier, I can save you!*

He stopped short. Moriana plodded on a few steps and then sank to her knees. Cascading snow turned her instantly into a white statue.

'Erimenes?' Fost asked dumbly.

'By the bones of Felarod, yes!' The spirit's words rang inside his mind.

Am I imagining this? he wondered.

'Turn forty-five degrees to your right and proceed,' the voice said. 'You'll come to a gentle slope. Go up it until I tell you where to go from there.'

Fost shook his head. He had aged millennia since the storm began.

'Too tired,' he said.

'You mush-brained lout, you'll be more tired soon. Your body temperature is dangerously low. If you lose much more heat, you'll experience eternal rest. And I shall be stuck in the midst of this eternal waste, watching two frozen bodies that instead could be intertwined in acts of fornication.'

Fost blinked. 'I could never imagine a statement like that,' he said, shaking his head hard. From somewhere strength flowed into his limbs like a warm tide. His fingers, toes and nose began to sting as circulation returned. 'Erimenes?'

'Yes, fool, I'm stimulating the flow of your adrenaline. But the effects will soon be gone, and then you'll be beyond my power to help. Get the princess to her feet and *move!*'

Fost struggled forward and shook Moriana's shoulder. Her head swung disconsolately from side to side. 'Lost,' she said. 'We've lost the amulet. What shall become of my City?'

When a second shake produced no further result, Fost stopped, put his hands under her armpits and hauled her upright. She looked at him, green eyes glazed and dull. When he started walking, she went along without protest.

As predicted, the ground soon began to rise in front of him. Slick with snow, it offered little traction to his bootsoles, and he found himself and Moriana floundering along on all fours. When he blinked snow from his eyes to look at the princess, her pale face had set in determined lines. Apparently Erimenes had invigorated her as he had Fost.

The slope went on forever. The fresh vigor ebbed from Fost's brain and limbs, gradually at first, then rapidly draining until he felt as if his life seeped through his bootsoles and into the frigid ground.

Something jarred his knees. It took him a half-dozen heartbeats to realize he'd fallen to his knees on snow-sheathed rock. Even the jagged pain did not tear through the deadness that shrouded his brain.

'Up, up! A few more steps. I beg of you, Fost, stand up and walk!' The note of pleading in Erimenes's words roused Fost to action. Dimly he realized that for the shade to abandon his usual superciliousness was a significant event. He hoisted himself to his feet once more, though it seemed he carried the weight of all the Rampart Mountains on his shoulders.

'Erimenes,' Fost gasped. 'Where are you leading us? Don't toy with us. If there's not safety ahead, let us die here and now!'

'Onward,' the spirit commanded. Fost obeyed. But his limbs were slipping from his control. His senses dimmed. The final weariness set in. Then there was no ground where he put his feet. He fell. And rolled.

A boulder stopped his headlong plunge. He raised his head and screamed as boiling air scalded his face. He covered his face with his hands. Live steam ate the flesh from his fingers. Shrieks of agony ripped from his throat as madness seized his mind.

Slowly the realization came to him. He was not being boiled alive. His nerves were only responding to the sudden onslaught of warmth.

Warmth! He dropped his hands from his eyes. Clouds still billowed around but they caressed with gentle, soothing. , life-restoring heat.

He stood. He was alone. 'Moriana!' he cried, his voice a raven's croak. 'Moriana, we've made it. We've reached the Crater!'

Silence answered him. He peered about in the fog. Where was Moriana?

A slim figure approached through the swirling whiteness. With a happy cry, he slogged toward it. 'Moriana!'

A puff of wind parted the mist that veiled the figure. Fost saw a face of unearthly beauty, of calm and sculptured features. But it wasn't Moriana's. A stranger's face, effeminate but clearly male, regarded him with quiet pity.

Fost toppled into darkness.

He woke with a familiar hand clutching his. 'Moriana?' The name came out in a broken whisper. With prodigious effort he raised his head.

Lying on a pallet next to him, the woman nodded. The skin on her face had turned to parchment, stretched taut across her cheekbones. Yet for all her gauntness she was as beautiful as when first he'd laid eyes on her. More beautiful perhaps. He perceived nuances of feature and form, shadings of beauty in the planes and curves and texture of her face, that he had never before noticed.

He let his head drop back and slept again.

Delicious warmth bathed Fost's tongue. He raised his head, eyes shut, and felt the tingling warmth suffuse his body. The aroma rising from the earthenware bowl satisfied his hunger almost as fully as the rich, thick broth.

He opened his eyes. Moriana sat cross-legged on the other side of a low wooden table. She wore a robe of orange cloth inlaid with intricate whorls of red and silver that lay open in the front, revealing creamy slices of her breasts and a tuft of tawny hair below her belly. The sight filled him with desire, yet of a languid sort, not at all demanding.

Moriana's eyes gleamed like green gemstones. Love and serenity shone from them. Fost and Moriana raised their cups in a silent toast. The broth tasted like hearty meat stew and also like a fine liqueur. Fost found it both nourishing and intoxicating at the same time.

'Good,' he said.

'You are welcome,' said their host, entering the room and seating himself at the table. The man's nostrils dilated delicately to drink in the essence of his own steaming cup. 'We have not seen outsiders here within our lifetimes. We seek to avoid the brutish hurly-burly of the outside world. Yet we are glad that you've come to us. You are an influx of clear, fresh water into a stagnant pond.'

A single taper, which burned without flickering, lit the room. Fost glanced around, noticing that the steady, mellow glow illuminated darkly irregular walls of slag. The rock had been poorly cut and dressed, and chinks had been stuffed with moss the colour of dried blood to keep out the questing fingers of the wind. Still, Fost found the chamber pleasing. He recognized a higher standard of aesthetics than he was accustomed to. He couldn't truly appreciate it but he saw enough to know he was in the presence of beauty.

There was beauty in his host too, though Fost normally didn't spend much time contemplating the perfection of the masculine form. As tall as Fost, though slimmer of build, the man reclined in a robe of the purest white. His hair was the color and texture of spun gold; cobalt eyes looked forth from a perfect face, aquiline and fine. His only ornament dangled on a silver chain around his neck. An oblong inset with a rectangle of jet, its workmanship appeared as crude as that of the stonework Fost had seen. In the contentment brought by the broth and the smoking incense cones set on the table, Fost perceived the inner beauty of it.

'Tell me,' he said, pausing self-consciously, aware how harsh his voice sounded after his host's dulcet, quicksilver tones. 'Who are you people? We had thought none lived here but the barbarian tribes of the steppes.'

Their host smiled gently. 'Perhaps the world has forgotten us,' he

166

murmured. 'Just as well. Ah, would that we could forget.' His eyes met Fost's. 'What we are, and who we are, cannot truly be expressed in words; only abstract concepts that require years to comprehend are meaningful. But you may call us the Ethereals. And I am Selamyl.'

'Ethereals?' Moriana's brow furrowed. She set down her bowl. 'I've heard of you, though I thought the stories were more legend than truth. Aren't you the ones . . .'

Selamyl raised a slender hand. Moriana fell silent at once, a flush creeping up the column of her throat at the awareness that she had said something to perturb the man.

'Do not be embarrassed, sister. The past is immutable, and we cannot change our part in it. Yet we do dislike to hear it spoken of by others.' He set his own mug noiselessly on the table. 'Yes, we are the descendants of the Ten Who Did Not Die, the survivors of Felarod's acolytes who summoned the wrath of the Earth-Spirit.'

He steepled his fingers on his breast, sighing heavily. 'Though the evil our ancestors helped to curb was great indeed, it was only at the cost of further evil that they acted. After the deed was done, they couldn't bear to remain in Athalau surrounded by constant reminders of their guilt. They wandered for years, homeless. Eventually they came here, where a star dragged from heaven by the War of Powers wounded the earth. By that time they had come to realize that they couldn't escape what they had done, and that it was only proper that they should dwell here, reminded forever after of the destruction magic could unleash.'

'You spend your time in contemplation?' asked Fost.

'For the most part we do. Each must take his or her turn doing small tasks around the village, building, repairing, helping glean food from the lake or raising our few summer crops. The barbarian tribes hold the lake taboo and do not trouble us.' For a moment Selamyl sat with eyes turned inward. 'It took years for our forefathers to find a direction that had meaning to them. Then one day fourteen hundred years ago and more, a man came among us whose wisdom reshaped our lives. Of Athalau he was, yet he turned away from the materialism that had infected the city since the War of Powers. With marvelous cogency he set forth the very tenets toward which generations of Ethereals had been groping. Denial – this was the essence of his philosophy; denial of the worldly, its temptations and its baseness.'

'Wait,' Fost said, 'could you be referring to Erimenes? Erimenes called the Ethical?'

Selamyl's eyes glowed. 'It is so!' he cried. 'Ah, that saint of a man who walked among us. He left us, alas, and what became of him later has not been revealed to us, though our deepest thinkers have long theorized that he was bodily assumed into the Paradise that is A Gift, to dwell among the Twenty-three and the Five. For such was his holiness.'

Moriana coughed. She seemed to be choking on her broth. Fost opened his mouth to tell Selamyl that his saint was back among them, but a sudden tightening in his throat squeezed off the words. He glanced at the satchel laying by his pallet. Now he knew why Erimenes balked at passing near the Great Crater Lake. To come among folk who followed his teaching of his earthly years would prove an excruciating embarrassment, to say nothing of a bore.

Selamyl rose. 'Would you care to tour our village?' he asked. 'It's small enough, but adequate for our needs. Our healers inform me you're well enough to be up and around.'

'I've never tasted anything like this,' Moriana said, finishing her broth.

'Nor I,' Fost agreed, rolling the last of his own around on his tongue. 'When we sat down I was famished enough to eat a roast war bird whole, complete with rider. Yet the one cup has filled me.'

'We do not gorge ourselves on vast quantities of food,' the Ethereal said. 'Rather we have learned to prepare dishes that satisfy the appetite in small portions. Long ago we learned that a growling belly served to distract our minds from higher thoughts.'

They followed Selamyl into the daylight. He moved with a gliding walk, his sandaled feet seeming to skim the ground. Looking at him in motion, they felt themselves models of clumsiness.

The cloud-muted sunshine showed them a settlement of two-score huts, all of the same melted rock as the one in which they were housed. The streets were wide, the earth packed by many generations of slowly pacing feet. Ethereals paced them now, men and women of fragile, otherworldly beauty, who discoursed in quiet voices or simply thought. To one side several inhabitants labored inexpertly at restoring a roof that had caved in. The others ignored them, as genteel folk ignore one forced by circumstances to relieve himself in a public place.

The water of the lake caressed a beach on the outskirts of the village. Flat-bottomed boats plied across the water, ghostlike in the omnipresent fog.

'Are they fishing?' asked Moriana.

'But no!' exclaimed Selamyl, his face showing horror. 'We wouldn't feed upon the flesh of any living creature. They gather edible weed that grows in great profusion in the lake. This forms the staple of our diet.'

In the past Fost had always been partial to great steaming joints of dog or hornbull beef, washed down with oceans of black ale. Now the thought of consuming the flesh of a fellow creature stirred uneasiness in his stomach. He found himself pleased that the broth he had consumed contained no meat. He looked at Moriana and knew at a level beyond words that she felt the same.

Her hand gripped his. They smiled at one another. It was as if they were children discovering the vastness of the world. The gentle Ethereals had opened to them vistas of a reality neither of them had imagined existed.

Laughing, they followed Selamyl along the beach.

The first day Fost felt a few vagrant tugs of urgency to continue the journey to Athalau. They quickly diminished to nothing. The Ethereals were expanding his mind to realms beyond the mundane. Time ceased to matter.

He and Moriana joined the routine of the Ethereals' life. They sat in circles with the rest on the floor of the round temple in the center of the village, chanting meaningless monosyllables meant to open their minds to oneness with the universe. They attended a dance in which the dancers stood all but motionless for hours on end and learned slowly to read the infinities of meaning implicit in each minuscule gesture. They listened to music played on a stringed instrument that produced sounds both above and below, as well as within, the normal range of human hearing and came to appreciate the richness inherent in the unheard. They reclined on mats in the evening, breathing subtle essences from tiny phials and groping after truths.

When night came they made love in their hut, but without the wild intensity that marked their earlier couplings. Instead they performed their sex in a detached fashion, almost as if the nearness and joining of the flesh in no way involved them but happened to someone else observed from afar. At times Ethereals watched them, but it didn't trouble them. Their hosts seemed pleased at the progress they made away from material concerns, and that approval warmed them more than any carnal sensations could.

169

Erimenes, of course, did not approve.

'You must understand,' Fost told him one night after making love, when the audience of Ethereals had drifted away to their beds and perfumed dreams. 'They have elevated mere sex to the level of art.'

'Boring art,' the spirit said.

'You fail to appreciate the nuances,' Moriana chided him. 'It's the same as with their dance. The tilt of the head, the gradual alterations of posture — these assume paramount importance. It's all part of divorcing oneself from the material.'

'I don't believe it,' Erimenes wailed. 'A tilt of the head more important than a passionate thrust of the hips? Alteration of posture merits greater enthusiasm than a male organ thrusting into your sex? You're as mad as these whey-faced Ethereals!'

'Erimenes.' Fost shook his head with the same mild reproof Selamyl displayed earlier when he had spoken of leaving the village. 'Try to understand them. They have been kind in sheltering us and in granting us the fine gift of their teachings. You of all people should appreciate their wisdom.'

'I'm not people. I'm a spirit and I tell you they're trying to become as disembodied as I. They venerate death, which I assure you is not all it's cracked up to be. This is boring! *Boring!*'

Fost chuckled sadly. He pitied Erimenes. That the philosopher, once so wise, should himself become blinded by the illusions of the material world struck him as tragic.

'Moriana!' Erimenes appealed to the princess, who sat by fondling one of the small clay figurines the Ethereals devoted so much of their time to sculpting. 'Get us away from here. These people will swathe you in wool and suffocate you. You're a lively wench, you hunger for life and all that it implies. Don't deceive yourself into believing they offer anything but death in the guise of life.'

Moriana didn't listen. She laid the figurine down and took up a glass phial filled with yellowish liquid. She unstoppered the phial, drank of the fumes and passed the container to Fost.

The fragrance tickled his nostrils, as fleeting as a snowflake. His mind struggled to unravel the complexities of that one brief sniff. He reclined on his mat, letting the implications of aroma percolate through his consciousness.

At the back of his brain he felt a prickling. It was familiar somehow, and then he realized he had known a similar sensation as he struggled up the slope of the crater, when Erimenes had stimulated him through some mental trick. Fost was not stimulated now. Instead he ignored the feeling, concentrating on the fragrance until sleep claimed him. He dreamed he walked on clouds of light.

The education of Fost and Moriana continued. They worked at modelling statues of yellow clay and were rewarded by murmurs of praise from the Ethereals, though they knew their efforts were shoddy in comparison. Their turn came at the menial tasks that needed doing. Moriana worked making robes and Fost helped in shoring up a part of the temple wall that had begun to sag. His physical strength, immense by comparison to the Ethereals, enabled him to do more than all the other workers combined. He felt abashed by this, as though his bodily powers were a sign of some gross imperfection.

When the job was done, he went back to his hut. Selamyl, who was the chief instructor of the village, had given him a smooth blue stone and told him to meditate upon it. He sat on his pallet and began to eat a meal of stewed pods taken from the lake.

'It's not too late to see if any slop-jars have been left unemptied,' Erimenes told him.

Fost stared dumbly at the satchel. 'What are you talking about?'

'You seem to eat up the Ethereals' dung with relish. I thought perhaps a dollop might liven up your meal. You're a pig, and you rut with sows.'

'Sows?' Fost blinked.

'What else do you call Moriana? She's got the habits of a pig and the smell also.'

'You mustn't say such things about Moriana.'

'Why not? It's true. In fact she's worse than a sow. She and Synalon were lovers, you know. That's why she feels herself debased when she lies with you. She wouldn't do so at all, but when the urge to rut comes over her, she'll couple with anything that moves and much that doesn't.'

'Moriana,' Fost growled, picking up the satchel. 'You can't insult her – me! – like that. I'll – '

'You'll nothing. You're weak and useless. Moriana thinks you much inferior to Synalon. You only have one advantage over her in bed, and even that's not much to brag about in your case.' The courier snatched Erimenes's jug from the satchel and squeezed it. His fingers tightened like steel bands around the neck of the jar, as though he could throttle the life from the taunting spirit.

171

'Fool! Ineffectual fool! You threaten me as much as you pleasure Moriana.'

Fost reared back, holding the jug high over his head to dash it in fragments against the wall. A wave of dizziness passed over him, followed by nausea. He swayed.

'Well?' demanded Erimenes. 'Are you going to do anything or just stand there looking stupid?'

'What's happening, Erimenes?' Fost asked. 'I feel funny.'

'Not half as funny as you look. But there – did the anger purge you of their spell?'

'Spell?'

Erimenes made a sound of disgust. 'Go back to listening to sounds you can't hear and dining on kelp. You deserve no more, man who buggers pigs.'

Fost fought down a fresh surge of rage and sat heavily upon the pallet. His thoughts felt unnaturally sharp, his vision almost painfully clear. He saw the rough walls, the poorly made table that tilted to one side, the bowl so irregularly formed that it could be no more than half filled without its contents slopping over the side. The pallid pods that lay inside seemed to glisten like toads' eyes, and the scent, which had seemed to him so tantalizing and profound, now reminded him of boiled paper. Even so, their odor was more appetizing than the whiff that reached his nostrils from the open latrine near the edge of the village.

He looked down at himself. The white robe he wore had crooked seams and a hem soiled with human excrement.

'Pig?' Erimenes said tentatively. 'Must I go on? I learned some truly fascinating sexual insults back in the Sky City. Would you like to hear them, or have you come to your senses?'

Fost set the jug down. 'I'd like to hear them some day, Erimenes, but right now tell me what's going on. Did they drug us?'

'That was part of it. And despite their avowed distaste for magic, they've used some mental compulsions against you as well; Moriana might have noticed but she was brought here weakened and un-conscious, and when she awoke she was already meshed in the snares of the Ethereals. But mainly the appeal of a life of indolence proved too much for you. You're basically lazy, Fost, as I noted right from the start. You run when you should fight. You stray from the most enticing women. You – '

'Enough of that, you bottle of flatulence! How long have we been

172

here?'

'A week,' said Erimenes, 'during which time you and Moriana were the most stultifying company imaginable, save for our hosts themselves. Do you think I rescued you from the storm just so I could rusticate till the end of time among these pious humbugs? I wouldn't have guided you to the Crater if there had been any other choice.'

Fost didn't hear him. He was on his feet, pulling his knapsack onto his back, then stooping to gather up the satchel and stuff Erimenes back inside.

'A week!' he shouted. 'Ust and Gormanka, Rann will be here at any moment.'

He strode from the hut. Heads turned to regard him with amazement. He walked purposefully to the tumbledown shack where Moriana worked at sewing alongside other dream-sodden Ethereals.

'On your feet, woman,' he ordered. 'We must get to Athalau.'

The Ethereals recoiled at the name. 'Athalau?' Moriana said. 'But it is so far, so full of sorcery and evil. Sit beside me and think beautiful thoughts. Forget Athalau.'

He slapped her. Fire flared in her eyes, but only for a moment. The listless mantle of uncaring dropped back and she smiled at him, a mother's smile for a wayward child. 'We are wanted, Fost. We belong here.'

'Don't you miss Synalon? Don't you wish you had her to play abed with you? And Rann — how is it with a eunuch, bitch?'

'What are you saying?' Her voice had a definite edge to it.

'Erimenes told me you were a pig who slept with her own sister. I denied it but I think I owe him an apology. He was right. You *are* a pig. In bed you're worse.'

'I'm better than Luranni,' she hissed.

'Don't bet money on it. She knows tricks you're far too stupid ever to learn. Stick to eunuchs from now on.'

'Bastard!' The back of her hand slammed into his cheekbone. He fell backward over a worktable. Ethereals drew back, staring at him with round, uncomprehending eyes.

'Bastard I may be, but that's better than a whore.'

She came for him. No longer the mild, vague acolyte of the Ethereals, she burned with fury and the urge to kill. It already felt as if his jaw were dislocated. The lethal purpose of her movements reminded him just what kind of exquisitely trained killer the princess was. He caught her wrist just before she delivered a chopping blow to

173

his neck.

'I'll rip your worthless lungs out,' she snarled, driving a fist into his short ribs. 'I'll roast your shriveled penis over a pit and fling it to the dogs. I'll . . .'

Abruptly she went still, her free hand frozen in the midst of a two-fingered strike at his eyes. 'Fost?' she said, her voice small and unsure.

'The Ethereals. They're trying to change us.'

'Why?'

'The proselytizing urge,' Erimenes said. 'I can't fathom it now, though once I myself, I shamefully admit, fell prey to it.'

A shudder wrenched through Moriana's body, as if she were throwing off the last gossamer rope that bound her to the Ethereals and their fantasy.

'We must leave,' she said. 'Now.'

They left the Ethereals cowering in the hut. The sound of Erimenes's voice coming from the satchel had thrown them into a panic. The presence of magic was something they'd always been taught to dread.

If only they knew who was in the sack, Fost thought. The idea made him throw back his head and laugh. It occurred to him he'd almost forgotten how. It felt good. Everything felt good again.

Their swords had been cast on the village refuse heap. They quickly reclaimed them. As Fost buckled on his sword belt and Moriana tied a sash around her waist to hold her own blade, a voice hailed them from the village.

'Why do you leave?' Selamyl asked. 'This is paradise.'

'This is a shabby, reeking collection of hovels. A paradise only to those who dream,' Fost said. 'We'll take reality, thank you.'

'But you mustn't go! Don't let yourselves be caught in the webs of illusion you call reality.'

Fost felt the gentle tugging at the corners of his mind. 'It's you who weave webs of illusion, Selamyl, you and the rest of the Ethereals. You've snared yourselves in them.' Ignoring the wordless plea within their minds, he and Moriana turned and marched toward the rim of the Crater.

Behind them an Ethereal wept for the first time in generations.

Light blazed far into the night from a thousand arched windows in the Palace of the Winds. Borne by puffing groundling servitors, ornate sedan chairs made their way along the public paths flanking the Way of Skulls. Inside the conveyances rode desperately frightened men and women. They'd been ordered to an extraordinary meeting of the Council of Advisors of the City in the Sky by Princess Synalon. It was none too certain that any of them would leave the Palace alive.

By ancient tradition the councillors met to advise the ruler of the City in the Council Chamber, tributary to the immense audience hall that filled most of the Palace's ground floor. To the councillors' chagrin the stewards who greeted them at the Palace's main door ushered them directly to Synalon's own room, in which she had installed the Beryl Throne. The stewards were, as always, self-effacing to the point of invisibility. The clanking Monitors in their leather and blackened steel armor, faceless within low-swept sallet helmets, marched several steps behind and were highly visible.

The princess sprawled insouciantly at ease on her ancient jeweled throne. Cosmetics had done much to cover the bruises and scratches left by her brush with death the day before. She wore a gown cut loose, the skirt consisting of ebony strips joined at waist and hem. The way she had arranged herself in the blue-green crystal chair of state revealed strips of gleaming, pale flesh. To appear before the High Council so scandalously attired was as calculated an affront as Synalon's choice of meeting place.

Even before they saw the princess, the councillors recoiled from the harsh glare, the heat and the insistent rushing noise filling the chamber. Ten feet to either side of the throne stood a tall bell jar. The sinuous, semi-reptilian shape of a fire elemental writhed within each. Seeing them, the councillors exchanged fearful glances and moistened their lips with their tongues. Even more than the score of Monitors ranged behind the Beryl Throne, the salamanders represented the fearsome power by which Synalon ruled the City.

A tall man, portly and red-faced, his smooth dome of a skull fringed by a ring of snowy hair, moved deliberately to the front of the knot of councillors. The others gave way to let him pass. As high councillor it was his place to protest the cavalier treatment accorded them by the princess. Synalon watched him, a smile playing on her lips.

'Well, High Councillor Uriath, have you something to say to me?' she asked.

Eyes turned to the high councillor, some expectantly, some with an expression akin to fear. His eyes met the princess's for a moment. Then they fell away.

175

'We are honored to obey Your Highness's summons,' he said, stroking his white beard.

'So,' she said, her smile growing. 'Anacil, have chairs brought for our esteemed advisors.' Her chamberlain gestured to the stewards, who began bringing chairs into the throne room. The score of advisors took their seats before the princess like schoolchildren at the feet of their instructor. Councillor Uriath sat in the direct stream of Synalon's gaze and blessed the years of experience at bartering and intrigue that kept his face from revealing the turmoil that raged within him.

Synalon had reacted to the debacle of her sister's sacrifice in the Rite of Dark Assumption with a response as amazing for its alacrity as for its savagery. Within hours after a fire elemental, launched by members of an underground hostile to Synalon, had attacked the Vicar of Istu and driven it to berserk fury, halberd-armed Monitors were kicking down doors all over the City. Overhead the eagles of Rann's elite Sky Guard still patrolled the streets to quell any sign of resistance. Three score had been slain, twice that many herded to captivity in the Palace dungeons. Synalon's ostensible reason for the mass arrests was a hunt for the traitors who had engineered the attack that had resulted in the escape of her sister, the loss of Erimenes and the estrangement of the Demon of the Dark Ones. Yet with the cunning she had exhibited even as a child, Synalon was quick to use the fiasco as an excuse to round up known enemies who were otherwise too powerful to attack. She still had no clue as to the identities of those behind the assault that freed Moriana. Uriath knew that for a fact.

The high councillor wondered if Synalon might be playing a cat-and-mouse game with him, if she had learned of his involvement and only tortured him now. His stomach turned over at the idea.

Synalon looked from face to face. Her advisors squirmed like worms impaled on a thorn. She found it very hard not to laugh out loud. Guilty ones sat among these twenty, of that she was sure. Sooner or later she would sniff them out and deal with them in a suitably instructive way.

But not this night. She had on her mind a matter more pressing even than ferreting out dissidents among the Council.

'I have called you here to ask that you vote me recognition as queen of the City in the Sky,' she said abruptly.

The councillors sat back as if struck. Uriath blinked rapidly, trying to assess the situation. At his back the others whispered to one another in agitation. Each was trying to avoid asking the question that must be asked. At length a middle-aged woman with grey-shot blonde hair stood at the rear of the assembly.

'Your sister the Princess Moriana still lives, Your Highness,' she said, stressing the honorific applied to a princess. 'As the younger twin, she and she alone is lawful heir to the throne. With respect, how can we confirm you against all law and custom?'

Synalon paled. 'Moriana!' she spat. '*Moriana!* How dare you mention the name of that slut, that traitor, that offal! She who slew our mother in order to hasten her inheritance. She whose escape from just retribution cost the lives of a dozen of my Guardsmen. A bloody-handed murderess many times over!

'The gods alone know what means may efface the stain left on the City's honor by the crimes of regicide, matricide and treason visited by my sister. Would you deepen the taint by placing her on the Beryl Throne?' She stared at the woman and dropped her voice to a husky whisper. 'Do you endorse these crimes, Elura? Would you then see such sins rewarded with mastery over the foremost city of the Realm?'

For a moment the woman stood erect against the force of the princess's baleful gaze. The only sound was the hissing of the salamanders, rising and falling with inhuman cadences. In the shadows behind the throne the salamander light picked out eerie highlights on the breastplates of the Monitors.

Elura's face crumpled into a mask of despair. She knew her death warrant was signed already, no matter what she did or said. But her will broke before Synalon's fury like a dry twig in a storm. She lacked the strength for a final defiance, which would cost her nothing not already forfeited.

'I beg your pardon,' she said unevenly. 'You are correct, Your Majesty.' And Councillor Elura sat down under the triumphant eyes of the woman she had just acknowledged queen.

'I've no wish to rush you into such a momentous decision,' Synalon said, winding a lock of hair carelessly about one finger. 'Feel free to debate this matter among yourselves. Pretend I'm not here.' She smiled again, her face as ingenuous as a child's.

'Uh, I feel that will not be necessary,' said Uriath. He swept his scarlet-sleeved arm in a gesture encompassing his fellow councillors. 'The justice of your argument is undeniable. I am sure none of my distinguished colleagues has any further objection to granting your wishes. Is it agreed?'

No one spoke. Hesitantly a woman on Uriath's left nodded. The others quickly joined, bobbing their heads up and down in unison like a collection of marionettes.

'Very well,' he said, rising to his feet. 'It is unanimously agreed by the Council of Advisors of the most favored City that Princess Synalon shall forthwith be proclaimed Synalon I Etuul, Mistress of the Clouds, Queen of the City in the Sky.' He knelt on the unyielding stone of the chamber floor. 'All hail Her Majesty.'

'All hail Her Majesty,' echoed the other councillors.

'Dark Ones, but the witch is cunning,' the high councillor said above the brim of his goblet. 'We had no alternative to proclaiming her queen. None at all.'

He looked around for confirmation from the others gathered in the sitting room of his manor. Outside the high window the land slid by, dark and silent.

Several of his visitors nodded, more readily than they had nodded acceptance of Synalon's request. Another, one who had not been present at the Council meeting, stood by one wall, staring reproachfully at Uriath out of large golden eyes.

The man saw the look and shook his head. 'Luranni, dearest child, you don't understand,' he said, his voice heavy with paternal concern.

'I understand that you pledged to resist Synalon to the last drop of your life's blood,' she said, scowling furiously at her father. 'Now you've proclaimed her queen and you look remarkably pleased to me.'

Uriath's three fellow councillors began to study intently the carved wood screens hung around the walls. Uriath frowned, then smoothed his face into conciliatory lines.

'Luranni,' he said, 'you are intelligent and perceptive for one so young. Otherwise you would not occupy a position of such responsibility in our family business. But still, there is much to be said for the wisdom only experience and age can bring.'

Luranni folded her arms beneath her breasts.

'She held the whip hand, so to speak, and she made sure we knew it. A roomful of Monitors and a pair of captive salamanders no less! Our beloved sovereign was telling us in no uncertain terms that if we didn't accede immediately to her wishes, none of us would ever see the outside of the Palace again.' He sighed, then drained his cup and held it up over his shoulder. A servant glided forth from a niche in the wall and refilled it.

'It was unsubtle, of course,' Uriath continued, sipping wine. 'Terribly unsubtle. Rann would have handled it differently, mark you. But the princess's – excuse me, the queen's – castrated pet is busy preparing the pursuit of Moriana and her courier.'

'Our rightful queen!' flared Luranni.

Uriath licked his lips. 'Of course. Our rightful queen.' He waved a carefully manicured hand. 'But if Synalon lacked her deadly pet, she had his shadow at her side. Colonel Chalowin of the Sky Guard. He hovered by her elbow like a nervous familiar spirit the whole time. Another manifestation, you see, of the power Synalon wields against us. *Now* do you understand, my child?'

Luranni turned her face away. Lamplight glinted in her hair like a cascade of honey. It was a peculiar, heatless light, emanating from a crystal filled with clear liquid set on the table around which Uriath and the others sat. It was filled with luminous beings, invisibly tiny, which when agitated gave forth the yellow glow. It was a less satisfying illumination than torchlight. But the mages of Rann's security network controlled captive fire elementals, using them to peer into any nook or cranny of the City illuminated by firelight. No flame produced this light, though, and so it was safe.

'We must be circumspect, my child,' said Uriath, allowing a precise measure of exasperation into his voice. 'One misstep and Synalon will destroy us all.'

'One misstep?' His daughter spun to face him. To his surprise he saw the bright trails of tears down her cheeks. 'What about the way your men failed to help Fost Longstrider rescue Princess Moriana? He was almost killed. Wasn't *that* a misstep?'

Uriath started to reply, collected himself visibly. 'Why, ahh, yes, I suppose it was.' He kneaded the doughy flesh of his cheeks. 'Yes, it definitely was a mistake. But accidents can happen, my dear, keep that in mind. All the more reason for caution now.'

Without a word the girl turned and stalked from the room.

Later Uriath sat in the sitting room, his only company a fresh bottle of wine. A soft chime roused him from his contemplation.

'Come in.'

His chief steward opened the door, announcing, 'A visitor.' He seemed unruffled by the lateness of the hour.

Uriath turned to look out the window. A white turmoil danced outside: snow. He gestured for his servant to admit his visitor. A moment later he heard a footfall on the carpet behind him and the quiet closing of the door.

'Chiresko,' he said. 'I am disappointed in you.'

'I am sorry, lord. I make no excuses. Failure cannot be excused.'

Uriath sighed. Fanatics were such a dreary lot. 'I appreciate your honesty. You've no idea how tiring it is listening to people whine about how it isn't their fault they didn't do what they were supposed to. But I'm still deeply interested in discovering what went wrong.'

'I ask for no pardon.'

'Thank you, Chiresko. You may dispense with the protestations. I require only facts.'

He turned around to behold a pale youth with bright, bloodshot eyes and a shock of black hair. His intensity and sallow complexion reminded Uriath of Colonel Chalowin, and Chalowin had always made Uriath nervous. Still, Uriath was a businessman and knew he had to make the most of the resources available to him.

'I do not know, lord,' he said slowly, trying to erase the perplexed look on his face. 'The confusion was all you could have asked for. We waited at the distance you ordered. When the time came to make sure things went properly, there were too many people between us and the Skywell. That groundling was more a man than I thought; he had Princess Moriana away from the altar and into the crowd before anyone could react. And Rann, damn him, bought Synalon the time she needed to dismiss Istu's spirit from his Vicar.' He scratched a boil at the side of his neck. 'What I don't see, lord, is why we were supposed to prevent . . .'

'Enough,' Uriath said sternly, raising his hand in a peremptory gesture. 'It's not for you to see. It's for you to obey. That's how you serve your cause. Or do you doubt the sacredness of our mission?'

Chiresko stiffened. 'Never!'

'It is well.' Uriath folded hands over his paunch and lowered his head in concentration. 'I've bad news for you, Chiresko. Word has reached me that you are wanted for questioning in connection with the rescue of Moriana.'

'They'll never capture me! I'll die before I surrender!' Sweat streamed down the thin face.

'One hopes that will be unnecessary. Still, it would be best for you to remain unseen for a time. Possibly even to go to ground until the situation eases.'

Agony etched Chiresko's face at the prospect of exile to the surface. Uriath turned to the table and ruffled through a sheaf of documents before saying, 'I've arranged a temporary hiding spot for you, Chiresko. It is in the warehouse of Councillor Elura, near the starboard cargo docks.'

For the third time in a week the residents of the City in the Sky thronged its narrow streets for a royal spectacle. The first had been the funeral procession of Queen Derora, culminating with her skull being placed in the pavement of the Skullway among those of other past rulers of the City. Next had been the Rite of Dark Assumption, unperformed for five millennia.

Now Synalon, elder daughter of Derora, was to be crowned queen.

Normally a coronation occasioned great joy. Men and women dressed in their finest clothes, apprentices raced and tumbled through the streets, wild with glee at having been freed from their chores for the day, and even the shaven-headed mages relaxed their professionally dour countenances into smiles. A coronation was a time of spectacle and merriment, a doing of bright magic, and feasting at the expense of the new monarch. Coronation Day was banners and bright streamers and the old songs of glory.

The weather seemed prepared to accommodate the usual spirit of the day. The sun shone, unhindered by clouds, and the rapid approach of winter slowed in deference to the occasion. The wind blew only enough to animate the pennons strung along the four broad thoroughfares of the City, emanating from the Circle of the Skywell.

The bands had turned out with their drums and flutes and wide-mouthed trumpets enameled in a thousand colorful designs. Behind them stood the massed ranks of the Sky City's soldiery.

First was a glittering like a forest of glass spires: the brightly burnished halberds of the Palace Guard. Next the City's infantry with shields, spears and conical helmets awaited the order for the procession to begin. Then the huge hounds of the Sky City cavalry, flown up by balloon from compounds on the surface, bayed at one another, avid to be freed from their riders' constraint. Last were the Monitors, sullen in the anonymity of their helmets. The whole parade coiled like a spring around the open area by the aft docks of the City into which the boulevard that followed the floating metropolis's long axis fed. Above it the City's bird-riders orbited in a carousel of wings, the drafts of their downbeats stirring the Palace Guardsmen's ornamental plumes. Higher still, the small circle of the Sky Guard's eagles slowly rotated.

Crowds framed the four great avenues, held back by Monitors and infantry. Others jostled for position in the penthouses of the City's highest buildings. It was only a matter of time before an incautious spectator, like one of those who formed a living wreath around the spire of the Lyceum in the City's first quadrant, would fall to his death on the hard stone streets.

But though the onlookers crowded each other as vigorously as ever, a sullen stillness overlay the multitude. Anticipation touched the air, but it was not the restive, eager anticipation of some pleasurable event. It was the kind of anticipation that might greet the growth of a gigantic black cloud belched forth from the Throat of the Dark Ones, the volcano Omizantrim.

'*Ah!*' The City's populace sighed with one voice. The skyward-tumbling tracery of the Palace of the Skyborn dominated the horizon; its mightly central tower could be seen from any spot within the guardwall. From its apex a pair of wings unfolded, as black as a necromancer's robe.

The eagle took flight. Its fellows in the air above kept still the raucous cries of greeting or challenge with which one war bird customarily met another. Itself in silence, the jet-black bird flapped slowly around the perimeter of the City. On its back rode a slender figure, black hair streaming behind her.

The eagle circled the City once. Returning to the Palce, it flew past. It climbed in a spiral, passing the ring of common bird-riders, and boldly confronted the living crown that was the Sky Guard. A bird detached itself from the flock and flew to meet her. In appearance it was twin of the one the woman rode; the only difference was a fiery red crest on its head. Its rider was diminutive.

The rider of the crimson-crested bird voiced a challenge. Magic crystal set about the City caught his words and resonated them until it seemed the City itself spoke.

'Who dares intrude within the sky above our sacred City?'

'Your queen,' came back the haughty reply. 'By right of birth and justice.'

182

'Then pass.'

They turned back to join the circling Guard. The woman dropped her mount lower to be met by one from the ring of less exalted sky riders.

'Who dares spread wings among the towers of our blessed City?'

'Your queen, by acclamation of People and Council.'

'Descend.'

The watchers inhaled slowly as the black eagle wheeled down toward the waiting procession, wondering how the third ritual challenge would be answered. A soldier, by custom of the lowest rank, stood forth with halberd held horizontal to bar the way of the rider who grounded before him.

'Who dares set foot upon the streets of our most holy City?' he cried, his young voice shrill with emotion.

For five millennia of their rule, the Etuul had answered, *Your queen, by that peace my mothers brought you.* The raven-haired woman swung off her mount and placed herself in front of the Palace Guardsman.

'Your queen, by the favor of the Dark Ones who rule all!'

A shudder passed through the throng like ripples on a pond. For five thousand years those words had gone unuttered. What did they portend for those on whose ears they fell?

Tears gleamed on the young soldier's cheeks as he knelt in wordless acknowledgment.

Synalon turned. A Palace Guardsman took the reins of her eagle Nightwind and led the fierce giant to stand out of the way of the procession. Erect, taller than most of those over whom she placed herself this day, the princess strode toward the Circle of the Skywell.

With the parade following behind in a thumping of bootheels, clamor of trumpets and snap of banners in the rising breeze, Synalon came to the Circle, paced slowly around the yawning Well of Winds and walked on along the wide way to the forwardmost point of the City. There she knelt alone on the parapet, head bowed, speaking to herself the words of a secret incantation.

She rose, returning slowly to the procession. Musicians and soldiers broke ranks to let her through. Then they silently followed her back to the Circle.

There she turned left and paced to the starboard edge of the City. The process repeated itself, and soon she was back in the esplanade surrounding the Well. There she stood before the Council of

Advisors, who sat upon bleachers carved from black onyx, and recited the oath of allegiance. To the ancient creed she appended the words, 'I swear by the blood my mothers shed upon these stones to return the City to the greatness it once knew.'

Face impassive, Uriath rose, took the winged silver crown from its pillow of state and walked to the princess. She fell to her knees before him. As Councillors Tromym and Elura draped the royal robe of black and purple feathers about Synalon's shoulders, Uriath rested the crown gently about her temples.

'All hail Synalon the First, Queen of the City and the Sky, Scion of the Skyborn, Mistress of the Clouds.' He did not shout, but his voice rose as loud as all the trumpets.

The crowd's answering hail seemed less loud.

Synalon rose. Uriath fell to his knees and abased himself. The other councillors stood up from their seats and did the same. Under the watchful eyes of the Monitors the rest of the City's inhabitants dropped to one knee. The air quivered with the cries of eagles proclaiming the new queen.

Thus far she had deviated only slightly from custom. Now Synalon added an innovation of her own. She raised her arms above her head and voiced a high, discordant cry.

Like noisome spores from a bloated toadstool, ravens with talons dipped in dark poison burst from the eaves of the City in the Sky. Crying their own replies to their mistress's summons, they coalesced into a cloud of blackness above her head. The watchers reacted once more in unison – this time with loathing.

Synalon shed the simple slippers she wore. Barefoot, in deference to her ancestors, Synalon the Queen walked slowly over the skulls of the City's former rulers toward the open portals of her Palace.

Eagles fell from the sky like autumn leaves. Relieved of the awesome burden of ceremony, their riders called to each other across the rapidly filling Circle.

Herded by Monitors with lead-tipped staves, the Sky Citizens poured into the Circle. A banquet awaited them. But the quantity of food and drink weighting down tables set around the Well seemed less than suited to the majesty of the occasion. The festive mood of the throng, none too evident to begin with, faded further as the citizenry discovered the scant repast given them to celebrate the ascension of Synalon I.

Having shed solemnity along with his own feathered robe of ceremony, Uriath permitted himself a sardonic smile. He knew the reason for the niggardliness of the feast. Food and drink were expensive in the City since almost all had to be imported from the surface. The luxurious fare that usually accompanied a coronation cost a fabulous amount. Synalon did not intend to spend such a sum. She was determined upon war, and that demanded austerity in all things of minor import.

Her warlike intentions were supposed to be secret, known only to her innermost circle of advisors. Uriath's smile broadened. Near the center of the web of intrigue spun about the Palace, Uriath prided himself on keeping well informed as to everything happening along its strands.

The jet-black eagle landed nearby with an ear-straining screech of talons on pavement. Uriath nodded politely and looked away, pretending to engage his fellows in conversation. Preoccupied with the hunt for the fugitive princess and her lover and impatient to be off, Rann nodded briskly and strode off toward the Palace.

A second bird, egg-grey with flecks of slate, touched down near the prince's mount, Terror. Its rider swung down and handed the reins to a lackey. He was about to follow Rann when Uriath stepped forward and touched his sleeve.

'Colonel Chalowin,' the red-faced councillor said. 'A word with you.'

The colonel's left cheek twitched almost hard enough to close his eyes. 'What is it?' he snapped. He had no time for courtesies, even to a high councillor.

Uriath studiously ignored the affront. Chalowin was a strange man, tall for a Sky Citizen and agonizingly thin. His brow high beneath dark hair and his cheekbones' wide flanges, he looked more like a Josselit monk than one of the Skyborn. He was the sort of man to hurl himself at a problem and wrestle it down; in conversation his manner was that of an aggressor.

Except when the speaker was Rann. Then Chalowin settled into a curious calm, gazing at his commander with the mixture of fear and adoration common to all bird-riders. Chalowin worshipped the prince like an acolyte paying homage to his god.

Devoted as he was, the acolyte was less deadly perspicacious than his master. Uriath moistened his lips, made a conspiratorial sideways flick of his eyes and leaned closer.

'The queen and I have had our differences, Colonel,' he said, 'but I cannot countenance treason. Or traitors. There, I have something to tell you.'

Chalowin cocked his head. His left eyelid fluttered like the banners that bedecked the City. His fingertips drummed on the lacquered scabbard encasing his sword.

Uriath brought his lips near the other's ear. He smelled the rankness of his breath. Uriath repressed a shudder, thinking how much this man seemed like a hunting bird, even to the stench.

'A plotter?' hissed Chalowin.

Uriath nodded. 'Perhaps one privy to the nefarious scheme that allowed the criminal Moriana to escape her due punishment.'

'Where?'

Uriath whispered briefly. Chalowin's head jerked back. His eye was almost shut. His left nostril pulsated in time with the tic. He shook himself and stalked off toward the Palace with no further word to Uriath.

'What was that about?' a voice called out.

Uriath suppressed a panicky start. He turned, his heart as spastic as the muscle in Chalowin's cheek.

'Nothing, my dear Tromym,' he said. He accepted the vessel of golden wine his friend offered him. He squinted at the pewter mug cynically, then raised it. 'A toast, good Tromym.'

'What to, Uriath?'

The high councillor only smiled.

'Great Ultimate!' shrieked the girl with the short blonde hair. 'They've found us!'

Three men looked up from their game of draughts just as the door crashed inward in a cloud of splinters. A man stepped into the cavernous warehouse, his movements as sharp and sporadic as a lizard's. He wore tunic and trousers of purple and black.

'Him,' he said, pointing with the naked blade in his hand. 'Take him alive. The rest don't matter.'

The girl lunged at him with a heavy knife. His scimitar turned it with contemptuous ease. Steel whispered. The girl looked down in surprise and disbelief at the stream of blood hosing from her throat.

'Shishol!' shrieked one of the youths as she sank lifeless to the sawdust-powdered floor. He charged, hands outstretched like claws, to impale himself on the javelins of the men who stepped in behind

186

the swordsman.

The other conspirators bolted. They dodged for the rear of the warehouse, scrambling in and out among elephantine bales of cloth. The plumper one staggered and fell against a bale. He yipped with fear as a flung javelin grazed his calf. Then he recovered and dashed after his black-haired friend.

The emaciated black-haired youth burst out into an alleyway. To his left rose the four-foot guardwall marking the boundary of the City. Twenty yards in the other direction lay a street swarming with black-and-purple-clad soldiers.

He raced away from them, intent on reaching the short wall. His companion hesitated, uncertain of his friend's intent. A broadheaded arrow nailed him to the door. He died with the shadow of wings across his face.

Chiresko heard the hollow boom of wings stop as the Sky Guardsman dropped into the narrow space between warehouses. The confines of the alley left no room for the bird to flap its wings. With a leap Chiresko gained the top of the guardwall. Tottering on the brink of emptiness, he slumped against the corner of Elura's building.

The eagle shot by him like a living missile, claws stretched to clutch his torso. The bird missed by scant inches and plunged over the wall, its angry cries filling the narrow alley with hideous echoes.

Shouts sounded up the street. Time moved like molasses for him. He saw his pursuers spill into the alley. He saw his friend's dead body sagging against the door, head slumped to the side. He saw his own death approach.

Wings pounded air. The war eagle had recovered from its dive and returned intent on vengeance. As it neared Chiresko, its rider banked in toward the City's wall and grabbed at the black-haired rebel.

To his astonishment the boy leaped gladly to meet him. The bird-rider shouted hoarsely as Chiresko wrapped mad-strong arms about his neck.

A riderless eagle spun skyward, crying like an orphaned child. When the other Guardsmen reached the wall, all that remained was the wisp of Chiresko's laugh, stretching thin into the distance below.

CHAPTER TWO

A small fire crackled fitfully inside the circle of rocks. The sere, scrubby grasses that grew in the shadow of the Ramparts burned smokelessly, so Fost pronounced it safe to build a fire. Fost took great care in making sure no stray spark would set ablaze the surrounding dry vegetation.

A haunch of meat sizzled over the flames. Having spent much of his life on the treeless steppe, Fost carried in his knapsack an iron spit and forked uprights for roasting game. After weeks of tasteless gruel and the stewed weeds of the Ethereals, the smell of cooking antelope produced a hunger in Moriana and Fost that was almost agony. The beast had broken from between two boulders in front of the travelers, a tiny yellow-and-cream buck with a flat, saw-edged horn growing from its snout. Useless for lack of arrows, Moriana's bow had long since been abandoned. But the antelope had popped up close enough for a well-aimed cast of the long knife Fost had given Moriana.

The pair had emerged from the Crater the previous afternoon to discover a landscape totally innocent of snow. The same capriciousness of climate that had brought an early blizzard howling through the Ramparts to threaten them a week ago had sent warm winds from the North to sweep away the snow. A chill still edged the air but it was bearable.

Fost lay full length on the ground, fingers interlaced behind his neck. Half-lidded eyes watched round clouds tumble by idly, but he didn't neglect to scan the horizon now and again for the sweep of great wings.

'If we didn't have Rann breathing down our necks,' he said, 'I'd find this the sheerest pleasure.'

'I'm glad your bucolic tastes are so amply gratified,' said Erimenes sourly.

Moriana looked at the courier with curiosity. 'You like the cold and wind and harshness? Strange. I'd thought you city-bred.'

'City-bred and -born,' Fost said, laughing. 'I first saw the day in the Teeming of High Medurim. A soot-faced, starving urchin of the streets, never resting, trusting no one, never sleeping twice in the same spot.'

'You don't make it sound attractive. I'd always heard great things of the Imperial capital.'

'Oh, Medurim's a city of wonder where every fantasy can be fulfilled – if you've the money. I never did. Born poor, die poor – that's the law the city lives by.' He rolled to one side and prodded the roasting meat with the tip of his dagger to turn it. 'Still, I miss it – in a way. For all its corruption it has a certain decayed grandeur like a noted courtesan grown old. It's still a melting pot for the Sundered Realm, and the port attracts merchantmen from all over the world. Caravels from the Isles of the Sun, barkentines from the Northern Continent, vessels from the Antipodes and the lands beyond the Golden Seas, all come to Medurim. I used to go down and sit by the docks and watch them come in. When I grew older I'd get work unloading them. Sometimes they'd pay me, other times they'd beat me and chase me off.' He laughed. 'Those who treated me shoddily came to regret it. I'd sneak back in the night and steal the choicest item from their cargoes. Ah, Medurim, a lovely, pox-ridden, treacherous bitch of a city. How I longed to be free of her!'

'You were a slave?'

'Only to my belly.' He poked at the fire. 'I was an apprentice for a time. An apprentice thief. Old Fimster was my master and he treated me well enough, beating me only when I deserved it. He raised me from an orphan pup; my parents were killed in a dole riot.'

Moriana sat with her legs drawn up, arms clasped about her knees, chewing ruminatively on her lower lip. A flock of large shapes winged across the sky. Fost tensed only briefly. It seemed that forever wings in the sky had been a sign of mortal peril. He was as yet unaccustomed to the notion that sometimes they were signs of safety. No lone eagle would chance upon them while the thulyakhashawin hunted.

'The life history of a guttersnipe,' the princess said, her words gently scoffing. 'Surely there's more to it than that. You've come by education somehow. How'd you do it?'

'I stole it.'

Moriana stared at him.

'Truly,' Fost said. 'I don't joke about such things. The library of Medurim is as big as a palace. It was once as glorious, but by my time had fallen into disrepair, with soot streaking the marble façades and many arcades collapsed with no attempt at restoration. The place always fascinated me. My friends derided the notion, but I was convinced that some fabulous treasure lay behind that vast columned portal.'

He drew himself into a sitting position, eyes fixed on the leaping, sallow flames. 'I slipped in one afternoon, intending to find that treasure and steal it. But I didn't find any treasure. Just books, shelves and shelves of books, so high a man needed a tall ladder to reach the topmost.' He shook his head. 'I stayed. I still don't know why. I wandered through the dusty shelves, pulling out books at random, opening them and scanning pages without comprehension. It frustrated me not understanding what those volumes contained. It seemed unfair. I tried by dint of effort to pry meaning from the pages. It didn't work.

'The hours passed. I fell asleep unnoticed in some dim recess of the library. In the morning I was shaken awake by a rheumy-eyed oldster wearing the indigo gown of a pedant. It scared me at first. He could have turned me in, you know, and I'd have been enslaved for vagrancy. He asked what I was doing there. Rather foolishly I told him. "I thought there was treasure inside this great building, sire," I said. "I came to steal it." '

Erimenes was making ostentatious sounds of yawning. Fost, knowing full well that the spirit had no need to yawn and only did so to make plain his boredom with the tale, continued without interruption.

'He laughed at this, the old man did. "Well, treasure lies herein," he said, "but not anyone may partake of it." And he took me on as his pupil, taught me to read and reckon and think thoughts beyond the gutter and my next meal.'

'But how did you steal your education?' asked Moriana.

'Ceratith made his living as a tutor, though a meagre living it was, for interest in learning had declined among the monied classes of Medurim. I couldn't pay, of course. Ceratith forever joked that I was robbing him.' Fost's expression darkened. 'It wasn't true. I always meant to pay him, if ever I could get together the money.'

'Why didn't you?'

'I never had the chance. One night, as he wended his way home from the library, a pair of alley-bashers knocked in his skull. All he had on him was a devalued Old Empire klenor and three sipans.' Fost rubbed his jaw. 'A poor bargain for the thieves because I found them and killed them. Not long after that, Fimster died of an ague. I signed on with a collier bearing coal to North Keep to feed the hunchbacks' forges. I was fourteen at the time. That palled eventually, and when I turned seventeen I was working as a courier out of Tolviroth Acerte, the City of Bankers.' He turned and slapped the satchel. 'And that concludes the story of my life, friend Erimenes, so you can cease your show of tedium.'

'No show,' Erimenes said. 'My ennui is perfectly genuine. But why stop now, just as you reach the most interesting parts: the fleshpots of Tolviroth.'

'What do you know of fleshpots, Erimenes?' the courier asked.

'Not as much as I'd like to,' admitted Erimenes. 'That bothersome slug Gabric had no sense of adventure. He stuck me on a shelf and left me to rot until you arrived to take me to Kest-i-Mond.'

'Gabric is a slug,' Fost said. He chuckled. 'He'll flay me alive for failing to report back, if ever I return to Tolviroth Acerte. I doubt I shall. The less time I spend in cities, the happier I am.'

'Faugh,' Erimenes said. 'You're little better than Gabric. To show what a dolt your friend Fost's employer is, Moriana, my morsel, on one occasion a wench lissome and most comely pleaded with him not to foreclose on her. She had breasts like suva melons, but that obese capon ignored the obvious and repossessed her house. I ask you! He had no use for one more insect-ridden hovel and infinite use for a nice, rollicking tumble. But no, he allowed his greed to overwhelm his lust. The pinhead. He probably doesn't even like boys.'

'We couriers have it that he frottages himself with his moneybags,' Fost said. He cocked his head at his companion. 'Why the troubled look, Moriana?'

'This talk of cities,' she said. 'It makes me wonder how my own fares.' She rose and knelt by Fost's pack. 'Do you mind if I borrow the water cask?'

'You didn't ask the first time you took it.' He raised his head as she colored. 'No, I'm sorry. Go ahead, do with it what you will.'

She took the ebony chalice from the satchel and removed its lid.

Instantly the vessel filled with water. She set it on the ground, hunkered down and closed her eyes.

Her lips fluttered. An eerie wail came from her that made hairs rise at the nape of Fost's neck.

'Interesting, isn't it, knowing a sorceress?' Erimenes said conversationally. 'She could turn you into a newt any time she wished.'

'You always look on the bright side of things, don't you?' Fost looked on with a combination of apprehension and interest as Moriana extended her fingers over the chalice. The water turned opaque white. It began to swirl round and round, as though stirred by a spoon.

She opened her eyes. The liquid cleared. But it was plain water no longer. Instead it was like a window overlooking a scene two hundred miles distant.

'Look upon the City in the Sky,' she said.

Crowds thronged the Circle of the Skywell. But this was no mere mob of citizens as had gathered to watch Moriana's sacrifice; these stood in orderly ranks, armored in leather enameled with bright designs, bearing shield, spear and short, curved sword. Others marched before them, clad in plate and chain. Fost recognized the sallets of the Monitors. Squadrons of war eagles wheeled across the sky.

Muttering to herself, Moriana gestured. The picture changed. It showed lines of captives being herded to dungeons and heavily armed Monitors moving from house to house, smashing in doors and dragging unfortunates out to join the miserable procession. Next the docks came into view. Balloons, gigantic bloated sausages many times the size of the round gasbag Fost had ridden to the City, rubbed their flanks against the ramparts like amorous whales as files of slaves unloaded their gondolas.

Moriana shook her head sadly. The image disappeared, leaving behind only a tiny ripple.

'Insurrection?' Fost asked, though the pictures hadn't much looked like it.

'No. Synalon arms the City for war, training fresh troops, crushing all opposition, storing up provisions.' She smoothed her hair back from her face. Sweat stood on her forehead despite the cool air. 'She's confident, damn her. She no longer bothers to block my scrying spell.'

'Who could threaten the City in the Sky?' Erimenes asked.

'None. Only the Fallen People might dare but they are few and lack the material.' Fost raised his eyebrows at this, and made a note to ask her more about the descendants of the City's builders. Luranni's tales had piqued his curiosity. 'No, my sister prepares for a war of conquest.' She clenched her hands into knots of anger. 'She will destroy all the Etuul have built. I must return. I must stop her!'

Fost did not answer. After a moment Moriana glanced at him and looked away. She'd trodden forbidden ground. The issue of who should have the Amulet of Living Flame and what should be done with it once they reached Athalau lay between them like a curtain of ice. By common consent they had avoided it until now.

Mercifully Erimenes broke the silence. 'I'm forced to observe that this is an extravagant waste of a lovely afternoon. And pleasure, once wasted, can never be regained, and who knows better than I? Why don't you engage in a little copulation before the cold returns?'

Fost laughed too loudly. 'Not a bad idea, if there were more time. I've another idea.' He grasped the ceramic handle of the skewer and raised the antelope leg. It was done to perfection. 'Why don't we eat and restore our strength? We start into the mountains tomorrow.'

'If you're wrong, rider, you know what to expect.' Though softly spoken, the words carried clearly across the rush of wind and the rhythmic thunder of wings. The soldier so addressed urged his mount to greater speed.

Prince Rann was in a foul mood. His scouts had caught the fleeing princess and her accomplice within hours of their escape, only to have the fugitives best them in combat and vanish into the tangle of ravines north and west of Brev. The survivors admitted being afraid to press pursuit; they claimed their quarry had enchanted them. Nonsense, of course. Synalon's ward-spells protected them from adverse magics. But the damage was done, and the worst of all was that those responsible couldn't be punished for their cowardice and ineptitude. He had too few men to spend them in that fashion.

From the outset Rann assumed the fugitives would head southeast by the straightest route for the Gate of the Mountains. He'd acknowledged to himself the possibility they could have gone due south instead, to attempt passage through the Valley of Crushed Bones he'd seen marked on the map Synalon had found in the satchel with the spirit jar. Yet he'd had men sufficient only to scout one route and had opted for the one he thought more likely to be right. As a result he and his bird-riders spent two and a half weeks combing empty grassland without result. When they drew near the Ramparts, they ran the risk of encountering the winged foxes. Rann had lost four men to the beasts.

Next a storm blew out of the Cold Wastes beyond the mountains, taking the searchers by surprise and whirling five men to oblivion before the rest found the ground and safety. A man and two birds had frozen to death by the time the blizzard lifted and the sneering gods of chance sent a warm wind out of the North to scour off the new-fallen snow. The search had continued, as fruitlessly as before.

Then yesterday a rider scouting the patrol's back trail had been blown off course by high winds. His bird had seen something suspicious, which turned out to be disturbed earth above a dugout trench large enough to accommodate two people. It lay midway between the ravine country and the Great Crater Lake.

So now with his full strength Rann made for the lake to try to pick up the trail there. He had already promised himself that should this prove another false lead the rider who had reported the dugout would suffer, manpower shortage or not.

The multiple chevron formation of eagles knifed through the sky. Rann's eyes, scarcely less keen than those of his mount, scanned the land below for sign of the fugitives' passing. The bird he rode was not Terror, but a lighter, faster eagle, grey spotted with brown, that was more suited to reconnaissance work. The flight reached the Crater, hidden under its perpetual mound of steam. They made a slow orbit of the immense declivity, finding nothing. Rann's impatience mounted by the second.

At last Odol, the soldier who had reported finding the dugout, grew uneasy under the sidelong scrutiny of those tawny eyes.

'P – perhaps they were caught by the storm and sought shelter in the Crater's warmth. Their tracks wouldn't have outlived the melting of the snow, milord.'

Rann scowled at the man a moment longer, too distracted even to enjoy the other's obvious mental agony. Then, without a word, he banked his eagle and slipped into a spiral descending toward the cloud.

Shortly after, they broke through the clammy fog. Below them they saw a collection of dilapidated slag huts. Briefly Rann wondered what manner of primitives resided in such wretched dwellings. He steered his bird toward a cleared space roughly in the center of the village.

A crowd gaped in silent wonder as the bird-riders touched down before the large circular temple.

'There look to be fewer than a hundred souls living here,' Rann said as he dismounted. 'Captain Tays, take twenty men and round up the lot of them. Kill anyone who offers any resistance whatsoever.' Tays, a swarthy, bandy-legged man even shorter than his prince, grinned, bobbed his head and trotted away, calling together a squad as he went.

Rann drew off his thick gauntlets. Scowling, he looked around. He'd taken the group of villagers standing about in the square to be women initially, but now he saw there were men among them in about equal numbers. The males of the town had a delicate, almost dainty look to them and their features looked little different from the women's. The bodies of both sexes were so willowy as to make it difficult to distinguish between them. Onlookers began turning away with an air of complete indifference.

The prince had known groundlings to react to the arrival of the eagle-riders of the Sky City with various emotions: fear, awe, dismay. He had never known the Guard to be greeted with indifference.

'You there,' he said, striding toward the nearest villager. 'I say, I'm talking to you. *Answer.*' Neither word nor movement gave any sign that the man had heard. Flushing, Rann nodded to a soldier.

A javelin whistled through the air to smack between the villager's shoulder blades. He pitched forward onto his face and lay still. Not a sound had come from him.

Tays's party returned, herding a group of the tall, wispy folk with the points of spears and scimitars. The captain's blade was bloody, but he wore a puzzled expression.

'These are strange folk, my Prince,' he called. 'They don't fear death.' He scowled at the several dozen captives his men had rounded up. 'I think they just came along to humor us.'

Rann's scowl etched itself deeper in his visage. He had an uncomfortable feeling that the captain had just experienced one of his rare glimmerings of insight.

'Then we'll have to teach them, won't we?' he said. 'Slay ten of them, and we'll see how apt our pupils are.'

He turned a smile toward the assembled villagers. Javelins stabbed, sword blades cleaved flesh. Dark blood stained the gowns of the doomed ten. They fell, yet no sound came from their lips as they died.

'They don't even moan,' a bird-rider exclaimed.

Approaching another man, Rann fought the urge to draw his sword and hew him down. What was wrong with these people? Were they mad or imbeciles? With apparent civility he asked, 'Who are you?'

'I am Gedrhus,' he answered. 'We are the Ethereals.'

'I seek a blonde woman and a large man with black hair. Have they been here?'

The Ethereal considered the matter. 'I have seen many blonde women and black-haired men. All of them were here, for I have been to no other place.'

Snarling, Rann ripped free his sword and slashed open the man's stomach. 'Insolent pig!' he snapped. 'You think to make me the butt of your puny joke?'

The Ethereal dropped to his knees. 'I don't understand,' he said, his voice unchanged. 'I feel you are too much of the material. Free yourself from the bonds of ill and . . .' Rann's scimitar split his head, finishing the sentence for him.

Rann snapped orders. Bird-riders hurried to obey them. Trees grew within the Crater. In a short time the soldiers had assembled a pile of wood, both raw lumber and the crude furniture they found in the slumping huts. Rann paced nervously back and forth, his blood singing in anticipation, as an Ethereal was stripped, bound to a pole and suspended above the pyre. At Rann's command the wood was lit.

The prince awaited the first groaning cry of agony as the flames commenced their dance. The Ethereal continued to gaze skyward as if nothing out of the ordinary was happening. His flesh reddened, blistered and began to slough off and blacken. Rann bounced up and down on the balls of his feet. The smell of roasting flesh tickled his nostrils. For once it failed to beguile him.

Flames cloaked the bound man. He made no response.

'What's wrong with you?' Rann shouted. 'Cry, scream, plead, do something!' He went to his own knees beside the fire, so close the fur edging of his cloak began to smolder. 'Beg for release from your torment. No, not even that; ask and I shall set you free. But *speak!*'

The man's hair burned now, surrounding his face with a ghastly wreath of fire. He turned his head toward Rann, and the prince's heart rose as he saw emotion touch the mild brown eyes.

'You interrupted my dance,' the Ethereal said. His head slumped as life fled him.

Almost weeping with frustration, Rann rose and turned away from the charring corpse. 'Bring me another,' he commanded. A woman was tied to a stake driven into the dirt of the square. Drawing a special knife he carried for such occasions, Rann went to work on her with all the consummate artistry of which he was capable. It had no more effect than the roasting of the man. Another captive followed her in a death that would have sent the bravest warrior raging into madness with pain. Another followed, and another. The victims sang or spoke of epistemology and teleology or simply stared, each oblivious to the abuse being wrought upon his or her body.

At last Rann slumped in a chair and regarded his prisoners. They stood before him, calm and contemplative, virtually ignoring him. His mind wrestled with the challenge of how to eke some response from these folk since physical torture had failed. Among his talents Rann numbered the ability to read infallibly the weaknesses of those with whom he came in contact, which made him an accomplished warrior as well as a sadist. A few moments' worth of hard thought produced a new line of attack.

'Hear me,' he said in a deceptively mild voice. 'I'm convinced that the woman Moriana and the man Fost have passed this way. Unless you tell me of them, when they arrived, how long they stayed and where they have gone, I shall cut off the feet of every person in this village. Next I shall cut off the hands. Then I will remove the ears, puncture the drums and pluck forth the eyes from their sockets. Finally, if no one has spoken the words I wish to hear, I shall tear your tongues from their roots and leave you here to die, helpless.'

An uneasy murmur ran through the Ethereals. Rann smiled. He had gauged them right at last. His men, searching the village, had brought him word of the statuary, musical instruments and crystal phials of essence they discovered in abundance. These folk clearly devoted their lives to meditating upon what they held to be various forms of beauty. He thought they wouldn't like to be denied all contact with loveliness, for all their words about scorning the material world.

A man stepped forward. 'I remember ones such as you describe.'

A cry rose from the prisoners. An Ethereal lunged forward, his golden hair in disarray, his ocean-blue eyes wide.

'You mustn't tell them, Itenyim. We must hold true to our beliefs. We cannot betray — unnh!' The head of a javelin sprouted from the right side of his chest. Scarlet doused the front of his white robe.

197

'I am sorry, Selamyl,' said Itenyim. 'I cannot bear the thought of being denied my art.' Selamyl's mouth worked in supplication, his hands reached forth. Blood gushed from his mouth as he fell.

'Well,' said Rann, feeling at ease for the first time in a fortnight, 'come and sit at my side and make yourself comfortable, good Itenyim. We have much to discuss, we two.'

'The magic of Athalau,' Erimenes said in his most resonant tones, 'was, at least in later years, not so much magic per se. True sorcery involves the manipulation of powers external to oneself. Our so-called magic came from within our own minds. We schooled ourselves to seek out and cultivate our latent mental powers, using them exclusively to gain the ends of sorcery. Consequently common protective enchantments have little or no effect on Athalar magic.'

The spectral figure folded blue, glowing hands over its middle. 'Nonetheless, the city of Athalau itself possesses talismanic qualities in relation to our magic, largely by virtue of the place it occupied in many of the mental exercises we employed to discipline our minds.'

'In other words,' said Fost, trying to bite back a yawn, 'the closer you get to Athalau, the stronger your powers become.'

'Such a bald statement oversimplifies questions of the utmost philosophical complexity,' the spirit said, 'but essentially, yes.'

Moriana gazed into the low fire. They had ascended far enough into the Ramparts to think it safe to light one at night. It was unlikely the Sky Guardsmen would chance the treacherous downdrafts of these mountains in the dark on their night-blind birds.

'So you were able to stimulate us when our bodies threatened to give out during the storm by working on our minds,' she said.

'And able to keep me from revealing your continued existence to the Ethereals,' Fost said, leaning against the sheer rock face along which they'd camped.

'But you rendered us invisible to the Guardsmen when we were many miles north of here,' Moriana said. 'What can you do this close to your home?'

'Don't build an exalted conception of my powers,' Erimenes said. 'Recall that I couldn't constantly maintain the illusion of your invisibility. My powers have grown, true, but they are far from infinite. Besides, most of the applications of my abilities, sad to say, lack any practical application in the present instance.'

'Tell me, Erimenes,' Fost said. The spirit turned toward him, a look of benign but thoroughly superior indulgence on his ascetic features. 'Your powers stirred us to renewed exertion during the blizzard. Why couldn't they have roused us from the stupor of the Ethereals?'

Erimenes touched his nose with a fingertip. 'I tried. The grip of those worthless creatures' drugs and spells, and your own desire to slip free of reality, held you too tightly for my mental skills to break you loose. You two had to free yourselves, though I was able to provide a suitable verbal stimulus.'

Fost paced uneasily between the fire and the rock face. He paused and gazed up the narrow crevice that split the masses of the cliff. A long slope, steep but climbable, rose up to where black rock framed a wedge of stars. The instincts of a street urchin kept him from bedding down without having an escape route handy.

Worry nibbled at his mind. Erimenes's explanations were glib and plausible enough. Yet Fost had come to know the spirit well, too well to trust him very far. The whole matter of Erimenes's powers – and why he bent them to aid Fost and Moriana – raised far more questions than had been answered.

'Come, Erimenes, surely someone as wise as yourself has any number of useful skills,' said Moriana. 'What other miracles can you perform?'

Apparently unaware of the sarcasm in her voice, the scholar raised himself to his full height. He pondered for a moment, and his eyes opened wide.

'Just now,' he said pompously, 'I perceive a group of between twenty-five and forty men approaching furtively up the hill. You'd best act quickly. They're almost on top of us.'

Moriana's jaw dropped. Cursing, Fost kicked out the fire. A shower of embers rained down the slope, illuminating the faces and forms of men. The courier reached down, scooped up Erimenes's jar and slammed the cap back into place.

'Take them!' a voice cried in the darkness. A spear bounced off stone with a jagged noise, striking sparks as it went. Fost jammed the jug into his satchel and tossed it to Moriana.

'Run,' he told her. 'Climb up the crack while I stand them off.'

'I can't leave you,' she said. Her sword hissed into her hand.

Dark forms reared all around. Fost parried a sword-cut purely by instinct and riposted, eliciting a cry of agony. Moriana crossed blades with a dimly seen antagonist and sent him rolling down the mountain, spewing blood from a punctured lung.

199

'Go, I tell you,' Fost roared. 'I can stand them off here awhile. Wait for me – use your judgment how long.'

He turned to her. Their gazes briefly locked. Moriana nodded convulsively, spun and was gone, scrambling up the slope, leaving a wake of tumbling pebbles.

Fost heard the voice of Erimenes complaining aggrievedly at having to miss what promised to be an epic fight. Then the Sky Guardsmen charged.

CHAPTER THREE

Moriana stumbled and almost turned back as the sound of battle broke loose behind her. Grinding her jaw against the ache within, she made herself keep clambering up the shifting floor of the rock chute. Her lungs worked like bellows by the time she gained the top, and pain knifed through her ribs at every breath. But she was alive and safe – for the moment.

At the top she rested, panting. From below rose hoarse shouts, the clang of steel, cries of pain as weapons found their mark. Hope glowed briefly in the princess. The fact that the din continued proved that her lover still held his own. Even as slightly built as they were, no more than two bird-riders could charge him at any time as long as he stayed within the mouth of the fissure. His greater strength and size would have a telling effect in such conditions.

Then a new thought staggered her. 'Erimenes!' she hissed, shaking the satchel and climbing unsteadily to her feet. 'We must go back. You can make Fost invisible and we can get away!'

'Restrain your emotions, my dear.' His patronizing intonation enraged her, and she started to dash his jug against a jutting of rock. 'Wait! It would do no good, as Fost realized, and as you would too, if you paused to consider.'

Moriana slumped back to the loose rock. She saw what the spirit meant. Even if Erimenes could befuddle so many bird-riders at once, the fugitives would gain nothing by it. The wily Rann had cordoned them against the cliff before moving in. Even invisible, Fost and Moriana would have had no chance to slip past the attackers. If both had gone at once, with no one to secure the bottom of the crevice, the Sky Guardsmen could have stood below and volleyed arrows up the chute. With such a narrow arc of fire to cover, they couldn't have missed, whether or not their targets could be seen.

All this Fost had known at once and acted accordingly. Moriana reproached herself. She should have seen it too. Her fears for the Sky City were obsessing her, wearing down her mind. She could do nothing to help her people if through worrying she grew careless and was killed.

The ringing of swords no longer drifted up the chimney. Moriana's heart lurched. Had Fost fallen? She heard a rattling, scraping sound like metallic hail, and a voice raised in a bold shout of derision. There was no mistaking Fost's defiant cry. Rann had obviously ordered missile troops to the fore, and Fost had just as obviously weathered their first storm of projectiles.

She jumped up, knowing she shouldn't dawdle. Though to flee smacked of betrayal, she couldn't help the courier. *He gave his life to buy time,* Fost had said when grief for her fallen war bird had threatened to drag her down. *Let's not waste it.* If Fost somehow escaped Rann, she was confident he would catch up to her in time. If he fell . . . well, he wouldn't want his own death wasted either.

Settling the satchel's sling more comfortably over her shoulder, she set off. The twin moons had long since set, an event for which Rann had doubtless waited before ordering his assault. The rock underfoot tended to break beneath her weight and slip away. She fell constantly until her arms and knees were a mass of bruises.

'By the Great Ultimate,' Erimenes complained when they had ascended a torturous five hundred feet, 'must you keep bumping me about so? You're as clumsy as that leadfooted Fost.'

Moriana dropped to a flat rock. A narrow trail stretched behind, curving out of sight around the flank of the mountain. Beyond the path the land dropped away sharply. It was a miracle that one of her many stumblings hadn't carried her over the rim.

She wiped sweat from her forehead, felt a stickiness and held her hand close to her eyes to examine it. Her lacerated palm bled freely. She'd just smeared blood across her face.

'If you don't like traveling with me, I can drop you down a crevice somewhere, so you can enjoy peace and solitude for another fourteen hundred years,' she told the spirit.

'Thirteen hundred and ninety-nine,' Erimenes corrected mechanically. 'You will do no such thing. You need the amulet too badly, if ever you're to have hope of defeating your sister. And you need me to find the amulet.'

202

Moriana nodded wearily. She couldn't deny the truth of what he said. Freeing the City from Synalon's oppression was worth any sacrifice, even enduring Erimenes's endless prattle.

What troubled her was what the spirit needed her for. She had seen ample evidence of the late sage's capacity for treachery. The shade was utterly without loyalty. Yet he had interceded time and again in the last few weeks to save her and Fost from recapture by Rann. *Why?* she asked herself. *Back in the City he seemed to find Synalon and Rann more to his taste than us.*

I know why I need him. But why does he need me?

She sighed and pushed herself erect. She would learn the answer eventually, though she had a premonition she wouldn't care for it very much. Right now the only thing to do was climb.

False dawn had begun lightening the sky when she reached the meadow. The warm north winds had melted the snow. Grass grew green and lush and soft. A streambed, drying now that the runoff was gone, provided Moriana an upward route. The bed rose in a brief cliff, its rock worn smooth by running water. Climbing the dead waterfall took the last of Moriana's strength. At the top she threw herself down on the grass, drinking in icy air in gasps, the grass-smell rich in her nostrils with the lying promise of spring.

'You mustn't tarry like this,' Erimenes chided her.

'Just let me rest a minute.'

'If I do, you might not escape the bird I sense approaching.'

'Bird?' She rolled onto her back, her sword hissing into her hand. *Has Rann sent men on birds after me, despite the darkness?* She scanned the sky intently. No vast cruciform shapes occluded the southern constellations. 'I see nothing,' she said. 'Erimenes, if you're . . .'

A shadow loomed above her. Instinctively she rolled and felt something graze her shoulder. She continued her roll, coming to her feet in a crouch, the scimitar tasting the air in front of her.

A bird stood before her in the darkness but a bird unlike any she'd ever seen before. At least as tall as a Sky City eagle, it lacked a war bird's grace of form and movement. Ungainly, it waddled toward her, swaying on thick legs, powerful clawed toes gripping the ground. It stirred its wings restlessly, a sign only of agitation. The foot-long stumps were plainly vestigial and incapable of raising its considerable weight.

The knobby head slowly swiveled. It lacked eyes. Instead a single strip stretched across its head above the blunt, massive beak, dark but gleaming in the starlight like an insect's carapace. The head turned toward her, then stopped. The bird advanced.

'But it's got no eyes,' she gasped, retreating slowly. 'How can it see me?'

'It doesn't see you, obviously,' Erimenes said. 'It does, however, perceive the heat of your delectable body with some keenness, particularly in this chill.' He made a speculative sound. 'We knew them in my day, of course, but they didn't grow this large then. I wonder if they've changed in other ways.'

Glancing over her shoulder, Moriana backed away. She had to be certain she didn't trip over a rock. If she fell, she had no doubt the monster would be on her in an instant, striking with its heavy beak. This time the beak would do more than simply glance off her shoulder.

The bird made no move to attack as Moriana slowly gave ground.

'It's curious,' Erimenes explained. 'It's never encountered anything like you before and wonders what manner of creature it's about to make a meal of.'

She licked her lips. The legs were long, at least half its height. If she bolted, it would overtake her within five yards. The stony wall of the valley lay twice that distance behind her.

If it just stays curious a few breaths longer . . .

As she turned her head to check the path, the monster charged.

The rustle of talons on grass gave her a heartbeat's warning. She threw herself back and to the side, lashing out blindly with her sword. The blade clattered against hardness, slipped and then bit briefly. At the same instant, agony raked across her ribs. She scrambled away on all fours, panting with the pain in her side.

The bird lifted its hideous, naked head and loosed a squall of rage. Moriana's scimitar had struck its beak and had been deflected down to lay open its shoulder. Blood flew from the tip of its wing as it shook the stumpy limb in wrath.

I've only made it mad, she thought. *My next cut must tell, if it's not to finish me. Gods, it's big!*

Moriana's blood shone on the talons of its left foot. The monster had kicked out, trying to eviscerate her. Moriana drew her long knife and moved to meet the sightless hunter.

Hissing savagely, it attacked with beak and talons simultaneously. The knife blocked the beak, but the axelike blow sent the weapon spinning from Moriana's grip. Her scimitar bit deep into the striking leg, chopping through the bone. With an anguished wail, the bird collapsed.

Moriana ended its life with a sword-cut, dancing back barely in time to escape the final lunge of its beak. Shaking, she went to retrieve her knife.

'A monster, that one,' she said, wiping slimy blood from her blade with a handful of grass.

'Don't grow complacent,' Erimenes said. 'You handled yourself bravely and skillfully. I've no complaints about the quality of the fight. On the other hand you do have a problem.'

'What's that?' the princess asked, sliding her sword back into the improvised belt.

'What do you plan to do about the rest of the pack?'

In their eagerness to be first to get at the courier, the Sky Guardsmen completely forgot their discipline and training. Fost retreated into the crack. Three bird-riders lunged in after him, only to find themselves crowded too tightly together to use their weapons to full effect. Fost's broadsword licked out. The Guardsmen fell. Only one showed sign of life, and that was a feeble groaning.

'Do you want more?' Fost asked them, exultant at this initial victory. He didn't fail to heed the small voice in his skull that reminded him how many more bird-riders the night held. But a wild, fatalistic exhilaration settled on him as his dream of immortality evaporated. It was as though a burden dropped from his shoulders. He had lost all fear; the fight was all that mattered.

I almost wish Erimenes was here to see it, he thought.

He was not so giddy that he missed the curt order, 'Back! Give the archers a shot, you groundborn scum!'

Man-high rocks flanked the entrance of the fissure. With a bound, Fost was behind one. An arrow skimmed his calf, ripping the rough breeches he'd put on after leaving the Ethereals' village. Other missiles bounced from the rocks with an iron clamor. His boulder shielded him completely.

He had his dagger in hand as well as the basket-hilted broadsword. A javelin probed around the rock sheltering him. The dagger slammed against its haft, pinning it to the stone, while Fost stabbed around the obstruction. The bird-rider gasped and carried the sword groundward as he fell. Fost yanked the blade free, roaring in triumph.

Darts and arrows winged up the crack. Close behind the volley came another rush of the Guardsmen. Fost slashed open the chest of the first to cross his vision and leaped out to confront the rest, hacking and thrusting with his broadsword, parrying with the dagger. A scimitar cracked against his hilt, a blow that would have halved his hand but for the protecting steel basket. His riposte went through the soldier's throat.

'Come on,' he shouted at them. 'You're no more men than he who leads you!'

Dead silence stretched down the rocky slope. Torches had been lit to illuminate the mouth of the fissure. Fost watched goblin shadows dance on the stony walls.

'Stand back,' he heard a calm voice say.

Cautiously Fost peered around the side of his boulder, ready to jerk back out of an arrow's path. 'Come and die, half-man,' he cried, spitting on the ground before him.

Rann's face turned the color of sunbleached bone. 'You won't have the lingering death you deserve,' he said, his words still flowing like liquid amber, 'because you force me to come up there and kill you now.' His scimitar lightly gripped in a gloved left hand, he started up the slope.

Awaiting him, Fost held himself poised, alert for treachery. He had no doubt Rann would face him alone; any man who would put himself between the Vicar of Istu and the object of its wrath, armed only with a puny sword, possessed courage to match the prince's cruelty. Besides, his life lay on it. The longer Fost held the gap, the more likely Moriana was to escape. A point would come when Synalon would no longer accept failure, even on the part of her cousin, the prince. But Rann specialized in lethal cunning. Fost would take nothing he did at face value.

At the mouth of the crevice Rann threw himself face first on the ground. Three archers stood behind him, weapons nocked. Instantly they let fly at the courier's broad chest.

He was no longer there. The arrows passed harmlessly on to shatter against the rock wall. Rann's first unusual motion had sent Fost jumping back. Rann bounced up now, his left arm a blur of motion.

Springing up to pounce on his presumably disabled foe, Rann was just in time to catch Fost's dagger inside the joint of his right shoulder.

Rann sagged back. His smile went sickly. Reaching up with his sword hand, he extended two fingers and a thumb from his hilt and plucked the blade from the wound with no further change of expression. Casually he tossed the knife aside.

'Let's end this farce,' he said.

Their blades crossed in a geometry of line and curve. Barely turning a low-line thrust with a twist of his wrist, Fost felt his berserker fever dissolve. A normal man would have been handicapped by the flowing wound in his shoulder, to say nothing of a man who still nursed ribs cracked by a demon's hand. Yet Rann's sword hand moved with sure precision, and his feet made no misstep. His foe would need both skill and luck to walk away from this encounter.

Far from disabling his opponent, his dagger cast had served solely to deprive Fost of his parrying weapon. He felt its need sorely now, with Rann's scimitar insinuating itself past his every defence to lick like a steel tongue at his flesh. The sword's caresses were light still, but each touch spilled more of the big man's blood and weakened him that much further. Nor would his strength serve to best the prince. Fost tried a widely swung powerhouse blow, and in turn received a cut across his belly that made him blink with pain. Had the scimitar bitten the breadth of a finger deeper his guts would have fallen around his knees in loops.

Rann did not go unscathed. A whistling stroke nicked an ear and a sudden lunge drew a bloody line along the side of his neck. But it was obvious the big man was wearing down more rapidly.

The decision came abruptly. Fost blocked a sidewise cut at his middle, only to have Rann turn his wrist unexpectedly. The tip of the scimitar whipped down and sank in the great muscle of Fost's right thigh.

Fost reeled back, hoping desperately the blade hadn't severed the main artery. If it had, he would be dead as soon as the shock wore off and the artery opened. But that could be a blessing; the leg gave way beneath him and he sat down with his back to the wall of the fissure. His resistance was at an end.

Rann whipped his sword through a blood-streaked arabesque and brought the hilt to his lips in a mocking salute.

'I hail you, courier. You've given me a better fight than I've enjoyed in years.' He smiled wickedly. 'Also, I perceive my men can now overpower you. It appears we'll come to know each other better, you and I.'

Fost never knew afterward what moved him to speak the words, whether fear or desperation or something else had made his mind fall back on half-held faith. Fending off the prince with his sword, Fost raised his head and shouted, 'I call upon my patrons, Gormanka of the Couriers and Ust, Red Bear of the East, to aid me now against these devil worshippers.'

The response was all he could have asked for. At once an eerie wailing rose into the night from somewhere down the mountainside. Rann turned, as mystified as Fost, who sat with one hand pressed to his thigh and the other holding his broadsword aimed at the prince.

Again the cry, shrill and despairing. Consternation showed on the soldiers' faces. It was the sound of war birds, not only in pain but in fear – a sound no living ear had ever heard.

A torchbearer flew into the air, snatched up by something that rose behind him as though growing from the rocks themselves. His torch limned a snarling visage, immense jaws opened wide and a furry head with flattened ears and flame-dancing eyes advanced. The jaws clamped shut with a crunching sound. The torch fell.

More huge, misshapen figures loomed out of the blackness. Demons rode them, striking out with long spears and clubs. Grunting and whuffling, their mounts shuffled forward, titanic bears whose paws scattered bird-riders like straw dolls.

Rann ran at them, shouting orders. Arrows and javelins flew; a bear reared screaming and dropped, crushing its rider against a knife-edged outcropping. The bear-riders charged up the slope, led by a giant who swung a six-foot sword in fiery arcs.

The lead bear came among the score of Sky Guardsmen who'd followed Rann's commands. Sword and talons struck, men died. The Sky Guardsmen broke. Running as fleetly as any among them went Rann. It was one thing to interpose himself between his cousin and an animated statue gone amok; it was quite another to face an army of monster-riding fiends who'd swept out of nowhere to take his men in the rear and butcher them as blithely as they themselves had massacred Ethereals. The old campaigner in him took over, and with the demoralized remnants of his troops, he disappeared beyond the boundary of torchlight.

The bear paused for a moment to allow its rider to hurl imprecations after the fleeing Guards. Then it turned and lumbered toward Fost. The courier had just about come to the conclusion that his mind had snapped.

A whiff reached his nostrils, laden with the searing, musky tang of bear. He screwed his face up.

'Ust, what a stench!'

'You're very welcome,' the bear-rider boomed. 'We save you from certain death at the hands of the Sky people, and you thank us with insults. Truly you northern folk have odd notions of courtesy.'

Fost shook his head. 'I'm sorry. I'm not at my best just now. Besides, I didn't think you were real.'

The giant swung off the bear's back and stepped forward. To Fost's astonishment his benefactor was a woman as tall as he and a little lighter, her bare arms bulging with muscle that rippled as she stirred. A tightly-laced leather bodice restrained breasts of surpassing fullness. Over it was thrown a fur vest and a gorget of mail. Black breeches lined inside the thigh with leather and knee-high boots completed her outfit. Though far from beautiful, her face was strikingly handsome, eyes blazing blue from a tanned, high-cheekboned face beneath an upright shock of hair the color of flame.

A smile split the face. 'Ask the bird-lovers how real we are.' She looked off in the direction the Guards had taken. 'Run, you cowards! Run or we'll catch you and take your scrotums for medicine bags!'

'A bit late for that, in Rann's case,' Fost murmured. 'My name is Fost, and I am in your debt for saving my life.'

'Jennas,' she acknowledged, her head dipping curtly. 'You owe me nothing.' She knelt and pried Fost's fingers from his wound. He winced as her fingers probed. 'I confess we tarried overlong in coming to your rescue. We came upon the Sky folk unseen and so witnessed your stand. Well and bravely fought, if stupidly. You should never have let yourself be trapped so.'

She rose and took a roll of linen bandages from a pack fixed to the bear's harness. The beast stood placidly, peering at Fost. Blood dried blackly on its muzzle.

Skillfully Jennas began to bandage his wound. 'We get few strangers in this land. The Sky folk we know, and their name has a foul taste in our mouths. Most others have been spies for those who seek to subdue us. So, as a general rule, we kill all who are unknown to us.' She tested the binding for tightness, nodding in satisfaction at her handiwork.

'Why did you help me?' Fost asked.

'Stupid,' she repeated. 'Or in shock. Do you truly not know?' He shook his head. 'You called for aid upon the Sun Bear. We are his people, the People of Ust.'

CHAPTER FOUR

'Perhaps "pack" isn't the proper word,' Erimenes said as Moriana sprinted into the litter of large rocks covering the valley's slope. Squawking stridently, the file of dark shapes that had been slowly stalking toward her up the valley broke into a long-legged run. 'It may be that "flock" is the correct collective, considering that these beasts, after all, are avian in nature.'

'Why didn't you tell me that they hunted in groups?' Moriana gasped, choking down a groan as she slammed her knee against a stone. Behind her the blind birds, attracted by the heat ebbing from its body, had found their fallen comrade. They set up a shrill keening that flayed Moriana's nerves.

'Why, I was unsure until I sensed the bulk of them stealing up on you,' the philosopher said. 'As I stated before, they have changed in form since my mortal years; I didn't know whether their habits had varied as well. I presume now that they have not.'

'Marvelous.' Crouching behind a boulder, Moriana peered into the meadow. An indeterminate number of the giant birds clustered about the corpse, their heads swiveling on their hairy-feathered necks. One's eyeless face fixed on the princess. Instantly it uttered a shriek and ran straight at her.

'How many are there?' she asked, turning and scrambling up the slope.

'In the olden days they seldom numbered more than a hundred to a pack, if you will stipulate for the moment that it is a suitable term.' Moriana made a noise of exasperation that Erimenes chose to interpret as assent. 'I never knew of a group fewer than twenty. Of course, their numbers may have dwindled as their individual size increased, since it takes more food to support each one.' The shade paused, apparently undisturbed by the jostling of his pack as the princess fled over and around the boulders strewn across the incline. 'One thing appears unchanged. They are intensely social animals and will pursue to the end of their endurance anyone who has slain one of their number.'

Moriana slumped against a leaning menhir, her strength exhausted. The sounds of the chase drew nearer. Realizing that the long legs of the birds made them far faster than she over open ground, she had headed instinctively for the cover of the rocks. But even here the birds held an advantage. Their big claws could grip protrusions and irregularities in the stone better than her hands and feet.

'Observe,' Erimenes began. Moriana silenced him with a swat of her hand to his satchel.

'Be quiet,' she whispered. 'They'll hear you.'

'Oh, rubbish,' said Erimenes loudly. 'They know perfectly well where you are. They can sense the heat of your body rising from behind this wretched rock, and your breath displays your presence like a column of smoke.'

Moriana just had time to digest this intelligence when a bird came scuttling over the top of her boulder. Warned by the scratch of claw on stone, she danced back and threw up her blade to ward off a whirlwind assault of talon and beak. Somehow she blocked the blows with half-instinctive turns of her wrist, the beak clanging from metal like blows of a hammer. The scimitar licked in above reaching claws and the monster went down, gurgling blood from a gash in its throat.

Moriana darted away as a wave of birds broke over her rock. For a time they nattered in confusion. But shortly they caught her heat-signature again and the chase was on. Sightless, the hunters possessed a lethal edge over their quarry. In the dark eyes were all but useless, while their heat-sense told them her exact location.

There must be a way to mask my heat, she thought. An idea came to her. 'Erimenes,' she panted. 'Find me some vegetation, quick — the drier the better.'

'That won't hide you any better than the boulders.'

'Do it!'

With ill grace, the sage's ghost directed the princess to a stand of stunted cedars high up near the crest of the ridge that flanked the grassy valley. Some blight had killed them, yet they stood, bent and twisted like emaciated dwarves. Their limbs snapped with dry cracks as she bore down on them.

A burst of energy born of sheer panic had carried Moriana well in advance of her monstrous pursuers. But their cries rose behind her like the baying of hounds, coming inexorably closer with each passing second. Her lips moved in a half-remembered spell. She'd never been the sorceress her sister was, particularly in this complex and exquisitely perilous branch of the art.

For a heart-stilling instant nothing happened. The birds screamed triumphantly as they burst from the rocks and bore down upon the lifeless grove, their claws kicking up a shower of pebbles. Desperate, Moriana shrieked the final words of the invocation.

A sun blossomed within her. She cried out as intolerable heat traveled up her body to her shoulder and down her arm, casting a lurid white glow as though her flesh itself had become incandescent. The blazing agony reached her fingers, and a fire elemental burst from their tips and shot like a fireball into the scrub.

The desiccated wood took fire at once. Flames leaped high with a popping whoosh and the burbling laughter of the salamander chilled her soul. Rank, cloying smoke clutched at Moriana's throat. Coughing, she staggered out of the young inferno her magic had caused.

The birds went mad. The blaze of flame was like a blinding light flashed into a human's eyes in the dead of night. The creatures never had encountered fire before, particularly not the supernatural heat of the elemental. In their astonishment some of the huge killers flung themselves into the conflagration. Their cries rose in a horrid crescendo as the sprite devoured their flesh.

Weakened by the effort of conjuration, Moriana staggered away. With no fire to draw the salamander, the only heat available was that of Moriana's own body; the possibility had existed that the salamander would remain within her as it attained fiery life and consume her own flesh before breaking free. She had rid herself of the being in time but she had no idea how much harm it might have done her. She could barely manage the power to put one foot in front of the other, but that didn't matter now. The burning grove totally obscured her own bodily heat. The blind predators had no way to follow her.

A hundred yards away she stopped and performed the dismissal. The salamander resisted but was finally forced back to where it had come from. Its final shriek of rage stretched across the night like a banner. Though weariness tried to cement her limbs to the bench of stone where she paused, she drove herself to her feet and onward through the darkness.

When she had left the valley of the sightless birds by climbing another nearly dry waterfall, which Erimenes assured her rose too steeply for the hunters to scale, she dropped to the grass and slept the deathlike sleep of total exhaustion. No dreams animated her repose. The chill mists that arose in the hours before dawn failed to disturb her. Only when the sun finally pushed its way above the peaks that loomed all around did she awaken.

'If the blizzard of a week ago hadn't been followed by unseasonable warmth, you would have frozen to death last night,' Erimenes chided her as she sat up. 'I'll thank you to be more cautious in the future. It wouldn't do for me to be stranded among these tedious valleys.'

'Why the concern over my welfare?' Moriana asked. Erimenes gave the same answer as when she had questioned him before about his new solicitousness: silence. *Maybe he's afraid of being stuck here for generations, with nothing to entertain him but the ponderous circling of the seasons.* But that explanation failed to satisfy her.

'I congratulate you on the resourcefulness with which you handled those abominable birds,' Erimenes said. 'It would have been too degrading to contemplate had one of them swallowed my jar. Imagine spending the rest of the monster's natural life – and in past years they were renowned for their longevity – rolling about inside its gizzard with a lot of common pebbles and the occasional bone. Brrr.'

Her every joint feeling like an unoiled hinge, Moriana rose and went to the stream. Kneeling, she splashed water on her face, gasping as the stinging cold revived her. She shook her head, sending droplets glittering off in the early sun. She finally realized Erimenes was speaking to her.

'Pardon?'

'I said, I've decided I'm not at all dismayed at the present turn of events. You're much more stimulating than that slugabed Fost. For one thing your nicely rounded posterior as you bend over the creek . . .'

'Fost!' Moriana's startled cry interrupted the spirit. 'I must find out what happened to him.' She settled on her knees and began the scrying spell, her hand poised above the stream.

'Are you sure you want to?' Erimenes's words sounded strangely gentle. 'Remember the odds he faced.' He didn't say, *Remember what awaited him if he was captured by Rann,* and Moriana marveled at his restraint. She continued the chant.

The water went murky, roiled and became a window. Sun rays slanted across a high rock face honeycombed with black holes. Huge shaggy shapes lumbered across the steppe in front of a high cliff.

'Look!' Moriana cried. She seized the satchel, dragged it to her and pulled out Erimenes's jug, uncapping it in the throes of her excitement. 'Look, Erimenes. He lives!'

Blue mist arose from the jar. It gyrated briefly, coalesced into the familiar gaunt figure. Erimenes bent forward to peer myopically into the water.

'He does indeed,' the spirit said, as violence suddenly swept the tableau. 'But for how long?'

Moriana could only shake her head, her features a mask of impotent worry.

Fost watched the copper band of sunlight expand across the steppes as the sun rose over the distant Gulf of Veluz. He breathed deeply of the clear, brisk air and felt his body tremble, both from the weakness caused by his wounds and anticipation of what was to come.

'The Sun Bear rolls the Great Globe into the sky,' the shaman intoned. 'The time has come.'

Silently the People of Ust rose from their campfires and went to the hulking, reeking shapes of their mounts tethered by the domelike tents. Following them, Fost nursed doubts as to the truth of what the shaman said. From what he had heard, he didn't think the time would ever come to challenge a sorcerer such as Kleta-atelk of the Hurinzyn.

A shirt of mail weighted down his shoulders, its hem slapping his thighs just above the knees as he walked. A round shield of bearhide rode on his left arm. The unfamiliar hardness of a helmet enclosed his head. For what it was worth, he was well armored. In his experience mere armor seldom had any use against enchantment. His thoughts did not run along optimistic lines.

They turned more morose still when his mount was presented to him. 'This is Grutz,' Jennas said, slapping the blunt red nuzzle companionably. 'His rider, Suss, fell last night with an arrow in her eye. Here, Grutz, behold your new master. Fost is a doughty fighter, if a trifle dim. You'll like him.'

Fost failed to appreciate the introduction but felt the time wrong to protest, particularly since the beast looked malevolently at him and

214

growled deep in its throat.

'There,' Jennas said in satisfaction. 'See? He likes you.'

'As appetizer or entrée?' asked Fost.

Jennas guffawed. 'You've spirit for a northlander,' she said, dealing him a buffet on the shoulder that loosened his teeth. 'Irtans and the others are foolish babblers when they say we should have fed you to the bears or let the birdmen finish you.'

'I am, of course, grateful for your timely arrival last night,' Fost said, 'but you seem to assume I'll aid you in your battle against this sorcerer.'

'And why not?' Jennas asked. 'It is only fitting. We save your thick hide from the birdmen and you aid us. Are we not all children of Ust? Do we not worship the same god? Do we not share the same code of justice given us by the Red Bear of the East?'

'Justice?' Fost croaked weakly, glancing from Jennas to Grutz and back.

'A life for a life. We save you, you must offer your life to the Bear Clan in return. One way or the other.'

Fost looked around. Others of the Bear People gathered, fingering knife hilts and smiling more like wolves than bears. Their lumbering mounts rocked restlessly, talons grating against rock. They could as easily slash through his tender flesh.

'You're saying I *must* aid you in exterminating this sorcerer?'

'Of course you *must!*' boomed Jennas. 'It is your duty. You owe it to us. After this duty to the clan, the obligation is erased.'

'I've had dealings with sorcerers in the past, bad dealings. I want nothing more to do with them.'

'Grutz.'

Fost retreated and stopped short when he felt a knife blade pricking into his back. The huge bear Jennas had called moved forward with ponderous steps. Its mouth opened to reveal fangs that Fost fancied to be the length of his own fingers.

'Mount and ride, Fost Longstrider.'

She didn't have to add, 'Or else Grutz sups early.'

Fost smiled, hoping Jennas would read the tautness in the expression as bravado. He could think of nothing to say, so he put his foot in the stirrup and tried to hoist himself into the saddle on Grutz's high, sloping back. Fost had difficulty until Jennas put a hand under his rump and boosted him up.

Grutz grunted, shifting under the weight. Fost swayed dan-

gerously, blushing with furious embarrassment. The other bear-riders
appeared not to notice how their hetwoman had assisted him. They
adjusted the hang of their weapons, fiddled with medicine bags and
fetishes or simply stared somberly across the brightening steppes. A
group of dispirited helots went about striking the tents and stowing
them for the trail. The nomad raiders took their homes with them and
left nothing to mark their campsites.

Jennas had mounted her beast, immense and brown with claws
like black scythes. She plucked a lance from a rest, waved it above
her head and spurred the bear into an eastward waddle. The bear-
riders followed, forming up in a long column behind. Fost took his
station at the end of the line. Grutz's muscles flowed smoothly under
his fur, but his gait was ragged, lurching Fost about until the courier
felt as though he were riding an earthquake.

Misery rapidly overtook him. Rationally he should have been far
more upset by the desperate eagle ride from the City in the Sky and
the twisting, confused aerial battle that could have sent him plunging
to inevitable death. But then he had been too busy fighting for his life
to indulge in excess emotion. Now, with hours stretching empty
before him, he had ample time to spend convincing himself he was
about to fall off and break his neck.

In a way that might have been preferable. Last night, stumbling
away from the scene of the battle, Fost had heard how the Ust-
alayakits, the People of Ust, had chanced to come to his rescue. They
warred with a neighboring folk, the Hurinzyn, who dwelled in
caves east of the bear-rider's range. The Hurinzyn – badger clan –
were ruled by the sorcerer Kleta-atelk, who delighted in producing
magical monsters. In days past the hunter-herdsmen of the Bear
totem had often warred with the more agriculturally oriented
Badgers. Since the advent of Kleta-atelk the conflict had taken on a
far more bitter character.

'Whether to feed his pets or for some purpose more hideous,'
Jennas had told Fost, 'his men and his monsters have been raiding our
flocks. Of late they have taken children too.' Her voice dropped
beneath its usual deep contralto. 'A week ago my daughter Duri was
taken and my freemate Timrik, her father, was slain defending her.
Half a score other children of Ust were reaved away as well. So now
we ride against the cursed Hurinzyn, to triumph or to die.'

Leaving oldsters, children and noncombatant parents to stay
behind with the flocks, the fighting strength of the People of Ust,

216

some hundred warriors of both sexes, had set out for Hurinzyn territory the day before. As they camped, their scouts reported a body of bird-riders swooping in a landing at the foot of the mountains. Intent on Fost and Moriana, the Sky City troops hadn't noticed the bear-riders stealing up silently to pin them against the sheer rock walls as thoroughly as they had pent up their own quarry. Just as Jennas had been about to attack, the Guardsmen had rushed Fost's camp. Though in the habit of slaying all strangers, the bear-riders had been impressed by the courage of Fost's solitary stand against such numbers. Still, they had been prepared to let the Guardsmen do the work of finishing off this valiant warrior – until he had called on Ust for aid. The sign had been clear: Ust had provided this outlander to aid his folk against Kleta-atelk. They had unhesitatingly gone forward to his rescue.

Fost had been bandaged, fed and housed in a hide tent stretched over the bones of some colossal creature. In the morning he had been given the best of the spare equipment. Under the circumstances he could scarcely refuse to join the bear-folk on their raid. Yet he fretted as he rode across the flat, featureless land in the lee of the Ramparts. Time fled. Would Moriana wait for him or was she at this very instant nearing Athalau, intent on using the Amulet of Living Flame to help depose her sister?

His fatalistic fury of the night before had gone. Now he looked back on his reckless berserker rage with something akin to shame. He wished he knew more of his antecedents that he might learn whether his family had a history of madness. Life now seemed very precious to him; joining in a desperate expedition against a wizard of surpassing might and wickedness struck him as a poor way to hang onto it.

For all their ungainly bulk the bears rolled along at a pace much quicker than a man could walk. Feeling his breakfast of dried meat and sour bear's milk churning in his stomach, Fost groaned. In action he would have a hard enough time just staying aboard his mount. If Ust had indeed contrived to have him join the attack, the doctrine of divine infallibility was in for a drubbing.

They had ridden two hours when a shout roused Fost from the dour reverie into which he had fallen. Looking up, he saw two figures rise from the grass and flee with a peculiar hunching lope: badgers, slightly smaller than the Ust-alayakits' bears, with black on their masks and limbs. Their riders wore peaked fur caps and long, dirty robes. They showed no signs of armor and carried javelins with bone shafts.

The bear-riders jeered at the retreat of their enemies. Even Jennas shouted after them, her stern, handsome features flushed as though she'd just won a battle.

Did they seriously expect a pair to fight a hundred? Fost wondered. He began to understand his new comrades better. The growing enlightenment failed to cheer him.

The village of the Hurinzyn came into view. The mountains here rose abruptly from the steppe in a grey, shiny wall. Artists or nature had pocked the stone face with a myriad caves in which the badger-folk made their homes. Ledges scaled the cliff in terraces, chiseled out of living rock to provide lateral access between the caves. Vertical movement was accomplished by means of ladders. Warned by their pickets, the badger-folk had drawn up the lowest of these. By any means Fost could see, the homes of the Hurinzyn were unreachable to the People of Ust. The courier wondered if Jennas had some scheme he'd been unable to guess at.

One hole at the highest level was larger than the rest and fronted with a wide balcony of stone, a single broad slab that jutted from the cliff. From the hole emerged a lone figure. He was a tall man, or so Fost surmised, for his back was badly hunched. Wild black hair shot with grey fell around his shoulders and a beard of the same combination reached knobby knees left bare by the smock he wore. His garment was a faded black, crudely embroidered with white and lemon pictographs. He supported himself on a staff carved of yellowing bone topped with a gap-eyed and fanged badger's skull. His own eyes were round ebony glints.

'Kleta-atelk,' Jennas said, reining her bear at Fost's side. The bridle applied pressure to the beast's neck to guide it while leaving the jaws free to bite.

'I surmised as much,' Fost said. The badger-shaman raised an arm and began to sing in a high, trembling voice. 'What's he up to?'

'He chants up his creatures,' said Jennas. She cinched her helmet strap tight beneath her jaw.

'Are they otherworldly?'

She shook her head. 'He must keep his song to control them. His pets are mortal beasts, 'tis said, transformed to monsters by his sorcery. The change maddens them. Should his chant falter, they'd fall on the Hurinzyn in an instant – and him as well.'

More figures sprang from the waist-high grass. A line of Hurinzyn

218

on foot confronted the bear-riders. The unarmored footmen cast javelins. Slings whined and loosed buzzing projectiles. A rock glanced off Fost's shield, momentarily numbing his arm. A grey bear to his left was struck by a spear just in front of its rider's leg. The creature gave no sign of noticing. Less vigorously driven than the spears and arrows of the Sky Guardsmen had been, the Hurinzyn javelins failed to pierce the coarse fur and fat that sheathed the bears' vitals.

Jennas whipped her greatsword loose from its sling across her back. 'Forward!' she shouted. Growling, the column of bears spread into a line and charged. The Hurinzyn skirmishers loosed a desultory hail of missiles and took to their heels.

Fost's worries about controlling his beast proved well founded. No matter how he tried to rein in, Grutz put his massive head down and charged along with his fellows, rumbling deep in his throat like a distant thunderstorm.

'Hold on!' Fost bellowed, clinging to the horn of his pitching saddle. 'Stop! Can't you see we're being led into a trap!'

A warrior-woman grinned fiercely at him in passing, whether in contempt at his caution or thinking he gave his battle cry, he couldn't tell. Jennas's big brown ran far in advance of the charge, rolling with all the irresistibility of an avalanche toward the departing badger-folk.

Just as the animal's jaws gaped to seize a Hurinzyn, the disaster Fost feared came crashing down on the People of Ust.

From burrows dug into the clay erupted monsters. Horrid parodies of natural creatures swarmed over the bear-riders. A thing like a badger but covered with slimy skin grabbed a rider from his saddle. The man screamed as the acid seeping from its pores consumed him. An eight-legged dog ran in front of Fost's mount, slavering in mad rage. Something that seemed all eyes and mucus lashed at him with a jointed sting. He warded off the blow with his shield and swept his blade in a bloody line over the gaping orbs. Grutz carried him headlong.

Suddenly the red bear put his rump to the ground and stopped so precipitously that Fost had to brace his hands against the pommel to keep from being emasculated. Falling back into his saddle, he looked ahead to see what had made the animal halt. Then he turned his head and vomited.

At the foot of the cliffs a *thing* waited. Twice as high as a bear, wide

219

as several, a mass of obscenely white and obese flesh, it sat and raised its voice in a lament. Great dugs drooped like sacks across its bulging belly and arms lay in boneless loops tipped with clumps of yard-long tentacles. Its eyes were wide and blue, long-lashed and weeping constant tears down cheeks and shapeless nose. The mouth had been elongated into a trunk, ending in incongruously red lips.

The apparition had unquestionably once been human.

'Taimgring!' The shriek soared above the yammer of battle. 'O Ust, it cannot be!'

Jennas's bear had halted and refused to budge. Anticipating the horror's advance, Jennas reslung her sword and seized her lance. At the despairing cry she twisted in her saddle.

A tawny bear lunged past her, slobbering foam in its panic. On its back rode a woman taller than Jennas, with braided black hair flying from her helmet. She plunged her sword into her animal's rump to goad it into motion. 'No!' The black-haired woman howled, an explosion of agony. *My daughter!*

All action stopped. Even Kleta-atelk's changelings ceased battling to watch the dreadful reunion. The amorphous head turned. The streaming dish-sized eyes saw the demented woman who had lost a child and now found it transformed into the essence of a thousand nightmares. Its arms reached.

Its tentacle-fingers wrapped around its mother and lifted her to its breast. The black-haired woman dropped her weapons and embraced her ghastly child. Then she screamed.

The lips had pressed beneath her breasts as though in a caress of love. They peeled back to reveal sharp, chisellike teeth that cut through mail and skin and ribs with equal ease.

Fost's heels dug into Grutz's side. The red bear coughed and broke into a run. Abashed at having to carry a lowly outlander into battle, Grutz displayed none of his fellows' dread of the once-human monstrosity.

Sucking its mother's entrails into its belly through the tube of its mouth, the behemoth turned its eyes on Fost. A sickening stench wafted from it. Its gelatinous flesh wriggled as it stretched a hand toward the courier.

Grutz roared. Fangs flashed. A squeal of anguish bubbled from the thing. Still feeding on the writhing body of its mother, it tried to wrest its hand from the bear's jaws. Fost's broadsword hacked the arm through. Blood hosed over him.

The monster's keening rose to a petulant crescendo. Fost lunged. His sword tip sundered iron links and struck through the heart of the black-haired woman. Dropping her corpse, the being reached for him. His sword rose high and fell again and again, until the bloated face with its questing, sucking proboscis had been butchered to red ruin. With a final slobbering cry the being flopped to its side, convulsed and died.

The fight had surged to life again as Fost, sick to the depths of his soul, turned Grutz away from the mountain of cooling flesh. Badger-riders had appeared to take the attackers from the flank. With shield and spear the lighter defenders took heavy toll of the bear-mounted People of Ust, whose formation had been ruptured by the onslaught of the monsters.

'Jennas!' Fost shouted at the sight of the Ust-alayakits' leader. Though her greatsword had slashed their riders down, three grunting badgers held her bear by snout and two legs while the warrior-woman fought a caricature of the beast she rode. Covered with squirming pink tendrils instead of fur, the bear-thing obviously held the upper hand.

Again Grutz charged. Fost smashed in the skull of a badger. Jennas's bear whipped the freed paw around and disemboweled the animal that clung to its nose. The bear-riders' chieftain struck at the final badger with her sword as the monster turned its wrath on Fost.

The round shield was pushed far up Fost's arm, enabling his left hand to grip the saddle horn. He wasn't going to chance falling beneath all those stamping, clawed feet. Unable to shield himself, the courier chose attack and drove his sword into the bear-thing's hanging belly.

The blade became bloodied. The thing's own fat armored it as well as any bear's. Blinking, Fost barely had presence of mind to lean back in the saddle to avoid a sweep of its paw. The talons raked the front of his helmet, skirring jaggedly against the metal.

Fost fought for balance. Grutz backed slowly away from the beast, sparring with it, swiping with his paws. Gashes hatched his shoulders. The monster had a longer reach. Fost shook his head to clear it and raised his sword, steeling himself for a last suicidal lunge into those lethal claws.

A brown battering ram smashed into the bear-thing's side. It went down, squalling and snapping at the splintered end of Jennas's lance, which jutted from its side.

'Come on!' the hetwoman shouted.

Her brown bear galloped away from the cliffs. Fost sent Grutz lumbering after.

'Did I save you or you me?' he asked, dazed.

'I don't know,' Jennas flung over her shoulder. 'All I know is that we have lost.' Moisture gleamed on her cheeks. On both sides of them the surviving People of Ust turned their mounts and fled.

Behind the routed bear-riders, Kleta-atelk's chant droned like a dirge.

Feeling as weak as if she had fought at Fost's side, Moriana slumped back onto her heels. 'He lives,' she whispered, wanting to affirm it, hardly daring to belive it.

'Indeed,' said Erimenes judiciously. 'I believe I've judged the boy too harshly. He put on quite an excellent fight, don't you agree? Especially the way he rescued that buxom wench who appears to lead the bear-folk.'

'He could hardly have let the monster kill her!' Moriana snapped. Erimenes smirked. With a weary gesture Moriana dismissed the image.

'What do you intend to do now?' the philosopher asked.

The princess shrugged. 'Await Fost here,' she said. 'I could use the rest, and this valley is fair.' She looked at the spirit with sudden suspicion. 'No heat-seeking birds lie in wait here, do they?'

'No.'

Moriana rose, stretched, felt the wan warmth of the sun on her upturned face. Her duty urged her onward, to forge ahead across the Ramparts and take the amulet for herself. Her need for it was greater than his; all he desired was eternal life for himself, whereas her sole motivation was the welfare of her people.

Now that you know he's alive, you owe him no more, her conscience told her. *Go on.*

She shook the thought away with a toss of her long, blonde hair. She had left Fost once, and guilt had nearly crippled her. She wouldn't do it again.

'I'm surprised to find a valley this lovely in these desolate mountains,' Moriana remarked. 'I wonder if it has a name?'

'It does,' Erimenes said. 'The Valley of Crushed Bones.'

Her head snapped toward him. A spectral arm pointed up the valley. At its head several hundred yards away, the green grass was littered with what appeared to be sticks gleaming whitely in the sun.

CHAPTER FIVE

'Attack without our bears?' the clansman roared. 'Impossible!'

Fost scowled, returning the bear-riders' glares in kind. Overhead the sun shone meekly through a high haze. The wind blew from the South, a chilling caress. The false summer had gone, and winter would soon follow.

The abortive assault on the badger clan had confirmed Fost's earlier suspicion. In matters of cunning the Ust-alayakits were competent enough; their trapping of Rann's Guardsmen demonstrated that. But methodical military planning wasn't part of their makeup. If no simple stratagem suggested itself, their response was a headlong charge, and Istu take the hindmost.

It was a phenomenon Fost had noted among other mounted tribes. Nor did the reluctance of the bear-riders to part with their mounts surprise him. The nomads' bears were the central fact of their lives, of war, the hunt and worship. Going into battle in any other fashion except on the backs of the ferocious beasts was, to them, simply inconceivable.

Yet they had to start conceiving of it soon. Or they would have no hope of defeating the Hurinzyn in their cliff dwellings.

'Listen,' Fost said. 'I ask you again. How do you intend to reach the caves of the badger clan?'

'We can stand on our bears' backs,' a man suggested, rubbing his moustache with the back of his hand. 'That would bring us high enough to get a hand-hold on the ledge.'

'And what will the Hurinzyn be doing while you're climbing up? Jabbing you with pikes and dropping great whacking rocks on your ugly faces, that's what. You can count on it.' Fost waved his hand contemptuously. 'Not that the opportunity would ever arise. You were in that charge as well as I. The Hurinzyn light cavalry and

Kleta-atelk's atrocities would rip you to shreds before you got within javelin-cast of the cliff.'

'Aye, we were in the charge,' a scar-faced blonde woman spat, 'and well we marked who first it was to run from the wizard's beasts. You're no sending of Ust, outlander; a common coward, I call you. We should take you out for the winged foxes to eat.'

'Who was it who gave grace to Iedre, when all else sat and gaped in terror?' Jennas's voice cracked like a whip. She stood aloof from the circle, moodily staring at the distant cliff. The other bear-riders stared at her. None could mistake what was on her mind. The canker of defeat plagued the proud war leader and concern over her daughter's fate wore heavily on her. 'Who came to my aid when I was sorely beset by those monsters?'

The nomads looked at one another, shamefaced.

'We may as well admit mere valor won't save our children,' Jennas said bitterly. 'If the stranger suggests new and troublesome ways to meet our problem, I ask, why else did Ust send him? Perhaps our thinking has become like a bone broken and improperly set. Perhaps we must break our ways that they may knit and grow strong again.'

None opposed her. Those that were too hidebound to accept the suggestions of a foreigner bore too much respect for their het-woman's strong sword arm to contradict her.

'Very well,' said Fost, leaning forward to prop his square chin on the backs of his hands. His elbows lay on his knees, and like the Ust-alayakits, he squatted by a dispirited yellow fire of dried grass and bear droppings. 'I propose to scale the cliffs at that landslip five miles from the Hurinzyn's caves. We'll signal you when we reach the heights above their dwellings. You'll attack, Kleta-atelk will emerge to call forth his pets and find us dropping in on him from above. You've ropes with you, don't you?' Jennas nodded. 'Good,' said Fost, feeling almost pleased at the progress he was making with them.

He stood up gradually, his joints stiff with cold and fatigue. 'So who goes with me?' he asked.

No one spoke. He looked around the circle of warriors, male and female. None met his gaze. He sighed. The little progress he felt he'd made slipped away like sand through his fingers.

None of the bear-riders wished to face the disgrace of fighting on foot like a thrall. The raiders were willing to acknowledge the necessity of it, now that a bear-borne assault had proven fruitless. It was just that no one personally wanted any part of it.

Fost decided not to force the issue. The bear-riders who would go with him would be rebellious and resentful. Unbidden, the image of Moriana flickered through his mind. Irritation tautened his nerves. He realized he couldn't stay here among the bear-folk much longer, playing at their war games. What if Moriana went after the amulet without him? His concern was compounded with worry over Moriana and worry over his own prospects of immortality. In what proportion he couldn't easily decide.

'If that's the way you want it,' he said heavily, 'then I'll look elsewhere for my storming troops.' He turned to Jennas. 'Have somebody bring me the senior among your helots.'

Uttering its hunting cry, a hollow, dismal moan, the vast shape of the winged fox spun across the colorless sky and dropped, wings folding to its side. Teetering on the knife-edge of a hogsback, Fost watched the creature drop into the grey shadows at the bottom of a ravine. Below, a dog-sized shape fled with rapid, agile bounds, dodging and weaving around boulders to throw the hunter off its aim. The flyer descended on its prey, and its wings covered the running beast.

'The thulyakhashawin falls on its prey from above,' said Ixrim from behind Fost. 'We'll do likewise?'

Fost turned back to see the gnarled little helot grinning at him with a set of teeth as incomplete as Prince Rann's morals. The man's hair looked grey beneath the grime that coated him from toes to crown, and one eye watched the world through the milky film of a cataract. A more unprepossessing sight Fost had seldom seen. Yet Ixrim was neither the best nor the worst of the score of thralls he led. He grunted and set off.

The outlander had yet to unravel the relationship between the lordly bear-riders and their helots. The slaves lived in abject misery and filth, subsisting on scraps thrown them by their overlords. Yet the ragged helots were trained by their masters in the use of arms and had been known to fight savagely in defence of the bear-riders' camps. In Fost's experience slaveowners were obsessed with keeping their human chattels unarmed for fear of servile revolt. Somehow the concept of turning against their owners had never dawned on the bear-riders' helots. He had met no resistance from the bear-folk at his suggestion that he take a party of armed slaves for his assault on the Hurinzyn's caves.

225

The slaves had been promised their freedom if their attack succeeded, a prospect they had greeted with apparent apathy. One of
the bear-folk had told Fost the helots were both sons and daughters of
slaves and captives taken in raids. As far as the outlander could tell,
the possibility of becoming a slave was an implicit part of the steppe
nomads' culture, which they accepted with resignation if captured.
He wondered if the strapping, buxom Jennas could ever meekly
consent to being another's property. He doubted it.

'Master.' At the timid voice from behind he turned, missed his
footing on a loose rock and flapped his arms to keep from pitching off
the narrow trail into the depths of either side. His right leg ached
abominably. The stab-wound Rann had dealt him had been super-
ficial, and Jennas's healing magics had done much to mend it overnight. But the climbing and walking hadn't done the injured limb any
good.

'What is it?' he asked, more gruffly than he'd intended. Recovering
his balance, he stooped and began massaging his bandaged thigh.

The speaker was a woman, ageless in her rags and filth, who
carried a hide shield and a hand axe. As with their owners, helots of
both sexes bore arms.

'Kleta-atelk is a sorcerer of great power,' she said, her voice a
monotone, as if the question she asked and the answer she received,
whatever its portent, were of only the mildest interest. 'How shall we
defeat him?'

Fost was none too sure of the details himself, trusting to his own
resources to provide a solution at the appropriate time. Plans too
closely laid tended to go far awry where magicians were concerned,
even mad hunchbacked tribal shamans. His assault along the cliff
tops was simply meant to bring him in striking distance of the
sorcerer.

'I'll say his name backward,' he said, grinning. The woman's
expression remained blank. After a moment his own smile faded and
he limped on. In the depths of the ravine to his right, the winged fox
tore at the body of its prey.

The sun had fallen halfway down the western sky when they
stumbled across the Hurinzyn pickets. Fost had lapsed into blank
reverie, his mind numbed by the herbs Jennas had given him that
morning to soothe his leg. He reacted a fraction of a second too late
when a figure sprang from the rocks ahead and lunged at him with a
bone-tipped javelin.

The javelin caught him full in the chest. He gasped, staggered back and sat down battling for breath. His mail shirt had stopped the point, but the force of the blow stunned him. Flaps of his fur cap flaring, the Hunrinzyn lunged at Fost with his javelin poised for the kill.

Someone hurled past the choking courier. A shield turned the javelin, and an ax licked out to split the badger-clansman's cap and skull. He fell. Other Hurinzyn had emerged from the rocks and struggled with the helots. As Fost got to his feet, he saw his benefactor turn to him and smile. It was the black-haired woman who had spoken to him earlier. A javelin transfixed her throat. Fost stared at her as she collapsed, wondering why she smiled.

The fight was done. A half dozen bandy-legged Hurinzyn lay dead with two of the helots. Shaking his head to rid himself of a feeling of unreality, Fost led the party onward.

They had long since left the treacherous hogsbacks and walked along on the tops of the cliffs into which the badger-people had dug their homes. Glancing over the edge, Fost saw the terraces of the Hurinzyn village not a quarter of a mile ahead. No signs of unusual activity showed. No one had heard the brief combat.

Keeping back from the rim, Fost and his helots moved forward. The clifftop was a shelf of rock a hundred yards across that rose sharply on the far side to merge with the mountain's flank. Boulders the size of the bear-riders' tents littered the broad ledge. Fost led the way into a cluster of rocks he judged nearest to Kleta-atelk's cave. Motioning them to stay in place, he crept forward and peered over the verge. Below and to the right was an outcrop of rock that marked the sorcerer's dwelling-place.

Fost looked around. A number of sizable rocks lay nearby. The first glimmerings of an idea came to him. He smiled.

He returned to the helots, who huddled among the boulders without speaking. They had acquitted themselves well enough against the Hurinzyn sentries, but he was glad there'd been no serious fighting yet. He uprooted a dead shrub, carried it to the edge of the cliff and drew out his flint and steel.

He had just set the bush on fire when a wild scream brought him round. The bush flared amid tan smoke, the signal to the bear-riders to commence their diversionary attack. Fost forgot it as he saw the cause of the desperate cries. The peculiar, fecal reek of one of Kleta-atelk's playmates rolled across Fost's palate. His sword rasped free of its scabbard.

227

One of the boulders had come to life — or so it seemed for an instant. The thing was as big as a boulder but its hue was a shiny, bluish white, the colour of a drowning victim. Obscenely glistening tentacles waved, as fat and pale as maggots and as thick as his thigh. He watched one of the tentacles curl around the waist of a helot and lift him into the air. Great suckers sprouted like concave mushrooms from the back of the moist bulk. The thrashing helot was brought down close to them. The suckers clutched his flesh and clung horribly. The man went stiff in agony.

Stillness fell, shroudlike. Fost and the helots watched, stunned, as the man's face contorted, purpled and seemed to fall in on itself like a collapsing tent. At the same time his body shriveled. With a rippling, smacking sound the tentacles pulled the empty husk from its multiple mouths and tossed it away. Blood drooled from the suckers.

A spear drove into the monster's side. Black ichor jetted out with a reek that contracted Fost's nostrils and caught at the back of his throat. Their apathy gone, the thralls hurled themselves against the horror, hacking at its tentacles and jabbing its bloated side.

Keening, the monster fought back. Its tentacles swooped like serpents, coiling around the helots and dashing them to lifeless rags against the rocks. Fost saw Ixrim seized, his dark face set in lines of determination as he sawed with his sword at the member holding him. The blade cut through rubbery flesh, causing the tip of the tentacle to fall away in a gush of corruption, but other tendrils lashed in to trap the wiry little helot. He was still resisting grimly as the suckers met his belly with a kiss that sucked the vitals from his body.

Down on the plain the bear-riders must be attacking the Hurinzyn again, Fost thought, and it seemed to him that he could hear the drone of Kleta-atelk's chant. The Ust-alayakits could fight the enchanter's monsters for only a short time before they were overwhelmed. He had to act fast to defeat the shaman in time to aid them.

But he had already stood by while slaves sold themselves as dearly as any free folk. He could stand by no longer. He raised his sword and approached the horror.

Tentacles dipped toward him, to fall writhing like snakes as his basket-hilted broadsword cut them through. The monster's cries of agony rose to an intolerable pitch, but still Fost came on, swinging his blade until he waded knee-deep through slimy black foulness.

Then he was beside the pulsating fat body of the thing. He cocked his arm to drive the sword to the hilt. From behind the bulk, like a sun rising, came a Face.

It was a face of unearthly beauty, shining with a golden light. A high-cheeked, full-lipped androgynous face smiled an invitation. Fost looked into its eyes, great orbs of amber. The strength drained from his limbs.

'You are different,' the Face said. 'Unlike these twisted rabbits. Your limbs are strong and straight, your chest broad, your face alive with arrogance.' The lips smiled. They gleamed like moist jewels. 'I would love you, outlander.'

Fost's veins swelled with desire. It was as if the Face existed alone, discrete from the obscene bloated mass that was its body. The Face embodied all that he desired. His manhood burgeoned at his loins.

Tentacles enveloped him, caressing, beguiling. He let them urge him forward. Their tips, facile and as dainty as a maiden's fingers, undid the thongs that sealed his breeches to peel the garment away.

A coral tongue made a lascivious circuit of the lips. 'I would taste your flawless manhood, feel your virility flow into me. Come, come unto me, my love.' Lust and adoration glowed in the eyes.

The lips waited, subtly parted. Desire filled Fost, but a small voice of rebellion spoke within him. *Illusion!* it cried. *Beware!* Yet he couldn't believe it. Within the circle of those red, red lips awaited beauty and satiation.

Then he saw the gleam of sunlight on a tooth like a dagger's blade.

'Come,' urged the Voice. 'Give me your masculinity. Impale me with your hardness!' And Fost obeyed.

The eyes closed ecstatically as his hips moved forward. But his arm moved too, and the eyes shot wide again as the tip of his sword sliced through the perfect lips, cleaved the pink tongue and punched out the back of the creature's neck. Rage blazed in its eyes. Its scream spattered Fost with blood. Then a dying spasm of the maggot-pale tentacles cast him away.

He slammed into the ground, rolled over and lay retching until his stomach knotted spastically on nothing. His sword was still in his hand, the blade smeared with stinking black ichor. He glanced down and saw that his arm, the front of his body and the limp worm of his penis lolling across his thigh were all drenched with the foul stuff. He tried to vomit again but his belly had already emptied itself.

Thirty feet away the monster jerked in its death throes. The head hung to one side and the ruined face was slack. The survivors of the assault group crawled away from the dying thing. Its blood fell on

229

them like black rain.

Gagging, Fost pushed himself to his feet. A monotonous chant penetrated the bleariness of his skull and brought about a sense of urgency. *Kleta-atelk!* He staggered toward the edge of the cliff.

He swayed dizzily on the lip of the precipice. Grinding teeth into lower lip to focus his mind, he looked down. Out on the steppe a battle raged. Hulking shapes, indistinct with distance but obviously unnatural, fought with a pitiful few bear-riders. Gradually the monsters pushed the Ust-alayakits back. Fost saw Jennas, embattled and alone, laying about her with her greatsword. Badger-riders circled her, closing in as monsters tried to drag down her bear. She held her own, but the outcome was inevitable and couldn't long be forestalled.

'*Omnegallillagall, Ulltip, nasripul, zazzigazz ra!*' The flow of syllables, nonsense to Fost, brought his attention to a point only yards under his boots. Kleta-atelk stood on his ledge, hunched against his skull-tipped staff, peering through round lenses of black glass as he sang his song of control. He must have heard the sounds of conflict so near above his head but he ignored them, trusting to the guardian horror he had left on the clifftops to deal with intruders.

Weak as a newborn chid, Fost bent down. His fingers grasped a rock twice the size of his head. Groaning, he swung it high. A twitch of the sorcerer's crooked shoulders showed that he had sensed the presence above him, but he wouldn't be distracted from his song.

And then it was too late. The rock smashed his head into jelly.

An oil lamp burned yellow and wavering inside Jennas's tent. From outside came the sound of merriment as the bear-riders celebrated their victory. A constrained tone underlay their revelry. The price had been high.

Bathed, bandaged and somewhat restored, Fost lay on a bed of furs, drinking freely of heady yellow wine. Across the tent Jennas sat in a folding camp-chair. A child sat on the floor of the tent, slumped against her booted calf. It was a girl-child, not yet blooming into adolescence. She regarded the courier with immense indigo eyes. There was a haunting in those orbs but it faded almost as Fost watched. The girl had seen horror but being young would soon forget. Being not so young, Fost couldn't forget. He gulped down his wine and replenished the emptied goblet from a skin hung from a tentpole.

Her hand lightly stroking the close-cropped plush of the girl's head, Jennas watched him. Golden highlights from the lamp danced in her eyes. On her face showed pity, but also admiration.

'You destroyed Kleta-atelk and freed the land of monstrous evil,' she said, sipping moderately from her own goblet. 'You saved the children of the Ust-alayakits – among them my own Duri.' The girl glanced up gravely at her mother, who smiled in return, not even resembling the bear-riding Amazon who had earlier been sundering Hurinzyn bodies with single sweeps of her greatsword. 'Truly you were sent by Ust.'

Fost grunted. He gazed into the wine, saw images there that made him squeeze his eyes shut and shuddered in revulsion. He felt soiled to the centre of his soul.

For a time Jennas sat, hand on Duri's head, watching Fost. Outside, the celebration waned as exhaustion set in. The bear-riders returned to their own tents or drifted to the cliff dwellings. To the Ust-alayakits' astonishment the Hurinzyn had welcomed them as liberators after the fall of Kleta-atelk. His magic had held them subservient, though he experimented on their living bodies and fed them to the night-mares he created. Their raids against their neighbors, the bear-folk, had arisen from the shaman's grim pronouncement: he would have his victims and cared little how he came by them. The Hurinzyn stole the Ust-alayakits' children to preserve their own. The bear-folk would take indemnity, of course, but having experienced the evil power of Kleta-atelk themselves, they bore the badger-clan surprisingly little malice. Some of the raiders had already paired off with some of the conquered tribes folk, and now retired to conduct further celebration in private.

Eventually Jennas reached for a small brass bell and rang it twice. The hide flap of the tent opened promptly to admit an aged helot woman. 'The little one has had a long day,' Jennas told the servant. 'See her bedded down, Unphaia.' The hetwoman bent to kiss her daughter on the forehead. Then, clucking, the old woman herded the girl out of the tent and off to bed.

Fost sat staring obliviously into his cup, concentrating on keeping his mind white and empty. A touch on his shoulder made him start.

Jennas stood over him. Even in his numbed state, he was aware how splendid and barbaric she looked, the gold circlets around her brawny arms, heavy gold loops dangling from her ears and her shapeless garb of fur and hide not managing to hide the ripeness of her figure. The lamplight turned her skin to bronze.

'If you turn inward, you won't come out, my friend,' she said. Her fingers stroked down his arm.

He raised his hand to hers, meaning to pluck it away, sickened by the very touch. He paused, fingers hovering over the back of her strong hand. *Don't blame her,* a mental voice told him. *She wasn't responsible for the blandishments of Kleta-atelk's guardian — nor the way you responded to them.*

His hand closed on hers in a desperate grip. She knelt. Her breath was warm on his cheek, honeyed by the wine. She kissed his ear. He snatched his head away as though her lips burned him.

She put a hand to his jaw and forced him to face her. The lamp's glow turned her pillow-soft, but she was immensely strong, perhaps as strong as he. Though he tried to resist, he shortly found himself looking into her eyes.

'When our young are taught to ride, sometimes they are thrown and hurt by accident and become afraid,' she said gently. 'We make them mount again promptly and ride, lest their initial fear stay with them always.' She kissed him on the lips. He did not respond, but neither did he draw away. He clung fiercely to her hand, the only anchor he could find in a chaotic world.

'I know what befell you today. The thralls told me.' She took his hand and laid it on her breast.

The flesh was warm and vibrant with life. Her heart beat powerfully and fast beneath his fingers. Slowly she drew his hand down until his fingers slid into her jerkin and touched her nipple. Her other hand slipped from his face and began unlacing his tunic. She kissed him again, and he returned it. Her tongue was strong and carried the taste of wine.

His tunic opened. Jennas turned her attention to her own belt. Then her fingers groped for Fost's crotch. He moaned and tried to draw away. Leaving his hand clutching her breast as fervently as it had earlier clutched her hand, she grabbed the back of his neck and crushed his face to hers. Her other hand worked vigorously up and down.

In spite of himself Fost was becoming aroused. He kneaded the handful of her breast, marveling at its firmness. He squeezed her thumb-thick nipples. She moaned and undulated against him.

Her mouth parted from his. Her head dropped, her short red hair tickling down his stomach. He gasped and arched his back as her lips enfolded the head of his trembling manhood.

Unbidden, the Face appeared behind his eyes, lips parted, teeth agleam. With a strangled shout, he tore himself from Jennas's embrace and rolled off the pile of furs.

Jennas leaped to her feet. The short leather skirt she had donned after the battle fell from her hips, leaving her naked from the waist down. The fur of her sex was a vertical red-orange bar, pointing down between smooth, muscular thighs. One brown-tipped breast protruded from the front of her jerkin, jiggling to the angry rhythm of her breathing. Her eyes blazed.

'Be that way then!' she raged at Fost. 'Be like a timid virgin boy, afraid of your own appetites! Go and become a Josselit, for all I care!'

'Jennas, I . . .'

'Enough of words! You fought like a man today – claim your reward like one now.' Contempt edged her voice. 'Or did Ust send us a eunuch for a champion?'

His head fogged with wine and unwilling passion, Fost got unsteadily to his feet. 'You can't talk to me like that.'

She slapped him. His head rocked and lights flickered inside his skull. He reeled back, blinking and rubbing his cheek.

When his vision cleared, his jaw slumped in amazement. The hetwoman had thrown herself down on all fours on the furs, presenting her naked hindquarters to him. Her buttocks were sculpted hillocks of muscle. The pink lips of her vulva lay open, inner secretions reflecting the light like a jewel. The thick, urgent odor of her excitement filled his nose and set his heart beating even faster.

'Well?' she asked. The word was a challenge. She confronted him with a choice: Take her or become a monk.

She was right, you know, the courier thought. A bestial growl rose from his throat as his brief anger dissolved into passion. He dropped to his knees, laid hands on her buttocks. The flesh was like soft, warm marble. He throbbed with unbearable tension. Shaking with lust, he thrust forward.

Jennas uttered a guttural exclamation of exultation as his manhood filled her.

''I simply cannot see why you waste time mooning about this dreary valley.' Erimenes fluttered spectral hands in exasperation. 'Why trouble yourself over Fost? Forget him. The key to everlasting life lies within your grasp. Take it. You can seize the City in the Sky, and with

233

your beauty and power enjoy an unending succession of far more skilled lovers.'

'I wish you wouldn't go on so,' Moriana said, glancing in irritation at the spirit. 'You're just bored.' She began pacing to and fro by the campfire.

'Indeed I am, as any sensible soul would be in such tediously bucolic surroundings.' He crossed an arm over his chest and laid elbow in palm. He tapped fingers against his chin, an action Moriana found disconcerting, since both fingers and chin lacked substance. Then he brightened. 'The time needn't be a total waste though. You could amuse yourself — and me — by engaging in self-stimulation. There's ample wood about. You could carve yourself a dildo of heroic proportions and . . .'

'Enough!' snapped Moriana. She laid elbow in palm and tapped her own chin in unconscious imitation of the sage. 'I wonder how Fost fares.'

'You know the great oaf lives, at any rate. Why, he positively seems to have covered himself in glory.' A sly look stole across the wispy blue features. 'Forget him, I say. It's for your own good. You saw the way that she-bear of a hetwoman cast covetous eyes on him, and her with mammaries the size of crystal balls! He's reveling this minute my lady, with never a thought for you.'

Moriana rounded on him, hair flying. 'That's not true!'

'Prove me wrong.' Erimenes smirked. 'Employ your scrying spell.'

Moriana chewed her lip for a moment, staring at Erimenes, who assumed a look of such lugubrious and obviously false concern for her welfare that she almost refused. But curiosity nagged at her. What *was* her lover doing? He wasn't the most continent man she'd ever known, and that red-haired hetwoman was definitely handsome in a coarse, emphatic way. Nor was Erimenes — damn his vaporous eyes! — in error about the way she looked at Fost. Moriana paced a minute more, then went to the nearby strem and dropped to her knees.

'I don't doubt they'll adopt him into their clan,' said Erimenes, his voice drifting over her shoulder. 'He'll marry the chieftainess and raise up a brood of squalling, hirsute brats. Each spring he and she will ride off to the raid together, with matching bear skulls adorning their heads. Ahh,' he sighed loudly, 'a charming picture.'

Moriana's ears burned furiously as she hurried through the words of the spell. The water stirred and grew luminous.

'I'll show you, Erimenes,' she flung back at the spirit. 'Fost will not betray my trust. He'll spurn that husky slut . . .'

Her words trailed off as an image coalesced.

'Your definition of "spurn" and mine differ, lady,' Erimenes said judiciously, leaning forward to peer into the water.

It required a moment for the princess's eyes to adjust to the gloom of the picture. It took more time for her mind to make sense of what she saw. A woman on elbow and knees, a man kneeling behind her on his knees . . .

She realized what she was looking at and breath hissed inward.

'She seems to find his spurning most salubrious,' Erimenes said.

In stony silence Moriana plunged her hand into the water, dispelling the image. She stood and looked at the spirit's wavering form. Her eyes were like green metal.

'We leave in the morning,' she said.

CHAPTER SIX

Stretching, Moriana emerged from the tent. It was of light, oiled skins stitched together and could be rolled small enough to fit in Fost's knapsack. Shivering in the chill dawn, Moriana thanked fortune she had it.

A light fall of snow had dusted the valley, draining color and contrast from the landscape. Large flakes fluttered down. She hugged herself, blew fog from her lips and shook out her hair. At least the snow hid the ominous scattering of bones at the head of the long valley.

'Are we ready to move on yet?' Erimenes inquired from within the tent. 'This dismal valley was dull enough to begin with. Now it's cold and damp as well. Let's move.'

Teeth chattering, Moriana glanced at the tent. 'Why should the cold and damp bother you? You're snug in that nice, warm jug. *Brrr.*'

'Snug? I'd call this intolerably cramped.' The scholar's complaints had an unusually bitter tone this morning. 'You cannot conceive how dreary it is within this wretched pot. Would that I had a body again!'

Moriana stooped and reentered the tent to wrap her heavy cloak around her shoulders. 'Do you mean that? You're immortal, Erimenes. Would you truly trade that for corporeal existence – the discomfort, the transience?'

'What good is immortality if one cannot truly *live*? To feel, to love, to experience!'

'I thought you got all those through others.' She sat on her bedroll and brought out the magic gruel bowl and began to eat the bland porridge.

'You think so?' Erimenes asked scornfully. 'What would you rather do, make love to a lusty, well-endowed young buck – or watch

236

another do it?'

Moriana laughed uneasily, her mind darting to what the scrying spell had shown her the night before. Her last spoonful of gruel seemed to curdle in her mouth. She forced it down and made herself think of other things.

The Valley of Crushed Bones was foremost in her mind. The day before, she'd spent fretting about Fost, summoning up scryings in the water and watching until she grew too upset to look any more, pacing like a beast in a pen and then dropping to her knees by the water to make the spell again. She hadn't ventured far up the narrow valley.

Her lack of exploration, she admitted to herself, grew as much from trepidation as concern for Fost — which, she now assured herself, had been misplaced. Those bones, those bleached, broken bones . . . what did they signify?

For all that he had spoken ominously of the Valley before, it seemed Erimenes knew little of it but the name. Perhaps a glacier had come this way and uprooted some ancient burial ground in passing, then retreated, leaving bones strewn about the Valley. Moriana doubted that explanation. She knew how glaciers had advanced across the once-temperate lands that men now called the Southern Waste to swallow ages-old Athalau. She'd never heard of glaciers retreating in the region though. Where the ice once took hold, it clung.

If nothing else, the bonefield was the last serious obstacle between Moriana and Athalau, except for the glacier itself in which the city lay entrapped. The Ramparts didn't soar as high here as they did around the Gate of the Mountains. The walls of the Valley of Crushed Bones rose abruptly to become sheer faces of rock, the flanks of two mighty peaks. At the top of the Valley the walls closed to within twenty yards of each other in a narrow pass. And beyond, the land lay downward, down to the City in the Glacier.

She ate her fill, for she wished to be well nourished in case the solution to the enigma of the Valley proved a continuing danger. Finishing, she stowed the bowl and took down the tent, packing it away as well. Erimenes grumbled all the while, but his comments didn't seem directed at her. She paid him no mind.

At last she was ready to proceed. She stood with the knapsack slung over her shoulder, gazing up the Valley. The snow had stopped. The day lay still and white beneath a low, grey sky. She sighed and started walking.

Guilt nibbled at the edges of her mind. *I'm abandoning Fost again,* she thought, but immediately *He abandoned me!* flashed through her mind. *The way he rutted with that redheaded slut!*

She shook her head. Better to contemplate the nearness of her goal. Reaching the city without Fost would be a boon, for it meant there would exist no question as to who should possess the amulet. Moriana felt something very much like love for the courier – *or at least I did,* she mentally amended – but it couldn't compare to her love for the City that was her home.

Synalon. The name burned like an ember in her mind. Moriana recalled the scenes of brutality and repression she had witnessed in her beloved City, both in person and by means of her spells. Nor would her sister rest content with imposing an iron yoke on the people of the City. She meant to restore the Sky City's dominion over the Sundered Realm.

Could she accomplish it? Moriana didn't doubt she could. Synalon's sorcerous powers were great, even though the aid of Istu was denied her, for that part of the Sleeper's mind she could tap into would react with venomous hatred to the being that had summoned it up only to cause it consummate agony. And the military might of the City, though not large in terms of manpower, was formidable. Without venturing far from their randomly-floating fortress, the Sky Citizens could control the Great Quincunx that covered the very heartland of the Realm. From Lake Wir to the Southern Steppe, from the Gulf of Veluz to the Thails, the City could dominate the vital trade arteries of the continent.

What her sister would do with all the Realm under her command was something Moriana shrank from considering. Synalon had already shown herself willing to dabble in the dark and grisly rites of the ancients. With all the wealth and populace of a continent, who knew what she could do? Send ten thousand highborn virgins to shrieking impalement upon the stony member of the Vicar of Istu to win the demon's aid and forgiveness? Assuredly Synalon was capable of it. Release black Istu from his millennia-long durance and subject the world once again to the foulness of the Demon of the Dark Ones? Moriana shuddered. Her sister wouldn't balk at such a thing. And with the resources of the Realm at her disposal, perhaps she could succeed even in undoing the work of Felarod the Great.

Moriana raised her head to face the icy blast that blew down the Valley. She could go on alone now with no regrets. She had reminded herself of the gravity of her quest; to succeed, no sacrifice was too great.

The Valley rose at a gradually increasing angle. Before long, Moriana found the going difficult. Snow had made the dead grass slippery. Head down, she scrambled upwards, buffeted by the wind until her feet flew from beneath her and she went face first into the snow.

Grabbing wildly for support, her fingers closed around something smooth and hard. Turning over and sitting up, she brought the object up to examine.

'Gods!'

'There you have why this is known as the Valley of *Crushed Bones*,' Erimenes said.

The thing in Moriana's hand was a sunbleached human bone, probably a femur. One end had been splintered by some awful force. Normally anything but squeamish, Moriana was horrified by her prize and flung it far away from her. It rebounded off the looming wall of the canyon with a loud clatter.

Picking herself up, Moriana surveyed the ground ahead. The cliffs were vertical here, save for the huge protrusions of what looked like pink granite humped against the base of either face.

'At least you won't have to wade through the snow for a while,' Erimenes observed. Moriana sucked in her cheeks, staring pensively ahead.

The spirit was correct. For a hundred yards the ground was bare. Not bare merely of snow but of vegetation, large rocks and the bone fragments strewn all around where the princess stood. It was as if the stretch of ground were regularly graded and cleared.

'A puzzle,' said Erimenes. Dubiously Moriana started forward. A skull turned beneath her boot and threw her against a wall. She put her hand up only to snatch it back. Gingerly she reached out to touch the wall again.

'Erimenes, it's warm,' she said. 'The rock is warm.'

'There is much volcanic activity in these mountains,' the philosopher said. 'Doubtless what you feel is the very world's lifeblood running through the veins of the rock.'

Moriana glanced at the satchel. What he said was possible. It would certainly explain the lack of snow in the pass. Though why it gave the appearance of being swept clean was another matter.

'Hist!' called the spirit. 'Something comes!'

From the shallower slopes of the Valley behind broke the hunting cry of a mountain cat. Moriana spun, back to the wall, curved Sky City sword in her hand. Unlike the sightless birds, a big cat was unlikely to attack a human. Unless the onset of winter had made its food scarce . . .

In an explosion of flying snow a creature raced out of the Valley and passed Moriana. A large rodent with huge, triangular ears pressed to its neck bounded on great hind legs. Hot on its trail and squalling its fury came a tufted-eared cat, its sleek white hide dappled with dark brown to match the incomplete snowy carpet of early winter. Fangs the length of a dirk glinted in its maw, but it paid Moriana no need as it lunged past.

Onto the bare earth of the pass it pursued the rodent. A rumble resounded in the narrow gap. A ripple passed over the rough, pink surface of the twin protrusions and they seemed to change color before Moriana's startled eyes. Then with a crushing, rending roar they surged together like giant jaws.

As the rocky juts hurtled inwards, the rodent stopped, frozen with fear. The cat sprayed dirt as it sat on its haunches and tried to reverse its course. For all the feline speed of its reflexes, it acted too late. The pink granitelike masses slammed into one another. The crash of their meeting overwhelmed the cat's last defiant cry.

'Saints of blood and darkness,' Moriana whispered. 'The rock lives!'

'So it would seem,' Erimenes said, unperturbed. 'I had heard hints of such things, side effects of the War of Powers, but had never encountered any at such close range. Fascinating.'

The rock, if rock it truly was, pulsated now, veins of darker colour emanating from the spot where the stone mandibles met. A sudden convulsion of the living stone ejected a scatter of white fragments. Moriana gasped in horror as the crushed bones of the rodent and predator were cast into the snow at her feet.

'Now we know the origin of the crushed bones,' said Erimenes with a certain satisfaction.

Moriana stumbled a few steps down the slope and sat in the snow. Her head whirled. *A few steps more,* she thought, *that's all it would have taken. Then it would be my bones that lie there, crushed and sucked clean.*

Snow began to fall. Moriana sat hugging her knees, paying it no mind. At last a peevish complaint from Erimenes roused her. She rose, dusted white powder from her thighs and regarded the stony jaws. They had slid back into place. They now looked like nothing more than rounded outcroppings of rock, save for the fact that snow melted as soon as it touched them.

Moriana's eyes rose up the rock walls that flanked the pass. The sheer, smooth faces offered no handholds. High up on the right-hand face she saw an irregularity that might have been a ledge, or no more than a trick of the swirling snow. She shook her head. Even if it was a ledge, she had no way of reaching it.

'We're stymied,' she said at last, gathering her cloak more closely around her to ward off the chill. 'This passage through the mountains is blocked; the only other I know of is the Gate, far to the East.' She clenched her fists in angry disappointment. 'I may as well surrender to Rann now as try to reach the Gate of the Mountains across the open steppe.'

'Surely you aren't so easily defeated!' Erimenes cried. 'You are a woman of great resource. Can't you conceive of some way to get past the monster?'

The passion in the spirit's voice took her aback. He seemed as feverish to reach Athalau as she. What motivated him? Was it merely homesickness, a longing to see his birthplace after almost a millennium and a half of separation? Or was it something else?

Whatever his reasons, they can't be as urgent as my own, she thought. Aloud she asked sarcastically, 'What would you have me do? Do you think I can run faster than the rock-leaper or the tufted cat? Do you think I can scale the walls like a spider or would you simply have me sprout wings and fly over this carnivorous canyon to Athalau? Would you . . .' Her voice dwindled into thoughtful silence.

'Well?' demanded Erimenes. 'Have you thought of a spell to turn yourself into a bird?'

'No, you garrulous puff of smog. If such magic was in my power, wouldn't I have used it long ago?' She settled the knapsack more firmly across her shoulders, cinching tightly the strap that held Erimenes's satchel. 'But perhaps I needn't fly to get over this obstacle.'

With that, she ran straight for one of the massive juts. Her momentum carried her several feet up the side of the thing. Her hands and feet scrabbled for purchase, but the monster's rocky hide was slippery. The top of the protrusion was a dozen feet or more above the

241

ground. She had not gotten more than halfway before she began to slip irrevocably backward. A muscular twitch of the animated rock sent her sprawling.

'Are you sure you know no spells of avianthropy?' Erimenes asked.

Ignoring him, Moriana picked herself up and strode purposefully for the outcropping, drawing her sword as she went.

'You don't plan to do battle with the thing?' Erimenes asked in horror.

'What's the matter?' Moriana asked. 'Have you lost your taste for gore? No, nebulous one, I don't intend to fight the beast. I do hope to carve us a pathway though.' The scimitar slashed twice, a blur of speed. The thick hide and stony flesh of the monster resisted, but the Sky City blade, its fine blue steel misted by condensation in the cold, cut through both to form a ragged step. The flesh within the wound was yellow and seeped thick red blood.

Moriana hacked another step a foot above the first, and another above that. The great hump of muscle shook convulsively. Syrupy red blood spattered Moriana's face and cloak.

She put her boot in the lowest step. A wild spasm rocked the monster. Her gloved fingers clutched a step, dug in, held.

Clinging with both feet and one hand, hacking with the other, Moriana inched up the flank of the rock monster. When she'd started cutting, the princess had feared the jut would swing back to crush her against the cliff. But apparently the creature was unable to move in any way but back and forth. It could still try to shake her off though, which it did with ever-increasing violence.

Grimly Moriana fought her way upward. She was smeared with the thick blood, and its reek clogged her nostrils. Erimenes shrilled with terror, fearing that at any second she'd be pitched into the monster's maw and be crushed along with his jug. What the destruction of his jar would do to him, Erimenes had no more knowledge than Moriana, and he felt no eagerness to find out.

Then Moriana's head passed the top of the hump and she saw the far slope receding into white oblivion. The creature shook like a dozen earthquakes until Moriana's joints threatened to give way. She held the sword high, plunged it down into the flesh again and then levered herself forward with a powerful shove of her legs. Like a tumbler she somersaulted over the top of the living hump.

Behind her the jaws rammed together again and again with a roar like thunder, as though the monster gnashed its teeth in frustration.

For a few breaths Moriana lay on her back, letting the fat white flakes land on her face and melt, spots of stinging coolness on her flushed cheeks. She finally rose and stumbled down the far side of the hill. At her back the jaws of the Valley opened and shut in an avalanche of noise.

Clawed feet scrabbling for traction, the bears made their way along the ledge. Fost's heart lurched each time the slip of a paw on icy rock threatened to send him and Grutz over the edge. The trail would have been perilously narrow going for the broad-beamed beasts under the best of conditions. With the rock sheathed in ice and clouds of snow blinding them, it seemed impossible that the mounts had come this far without slipping to their doom.

In front of him the dimly seen shape that was Jennas turned in her saddle. 'Look over the side,' she directed. 'You'll see why I don't think you'll ever see your woman again.'

At her command Fost's stomach turned over. But he made himself crane his neck so he could peer three hundred feet straight down to the valley below. A freak of wind parted the curtain of snow, and he saw clear to the bottom.

He blinked, wondering if the cold played tricks on his eyes. It seemed that the very rock of the cliffs was surging out of both sides of the narrow gorge to slam together in the middle and send a deep rumble shivering up the mountains. It reminded him unpleasantly of giant jaws.

'That's a living creature down there,' Jennas said. 'It senses when something tries to pass between its jaws, and they slam shut, crushing its prey.' She bent dangerously far out of her high-cantled saddle to gaze down. 'I've never heard of the monster being so active. Perhaps the blizzard bothers it.'

Perhaps it's chewing Moriana's lovely body to a bloody pulp, Fost thought, and instantly regretted it. He cursed his too-vivid imagination.

Jennas twisted to face him again. 'Now you've seen what your friend would have had to pass. We know she tried it; I showed you the remnants of her camp back in the Valley of Crushed Bones, and no one else would knowingly enter the vale of the heat-hunters.' Her eyes burned like beacons through the snow. 'Shall we go on? I did promise to guide you wherever you wished.'

Fost's chest expanded within his bearskin cloak as he took a deep,

243

pensive breath. *No,* he thought. *I will not accept that she is dead. Not until I see her corpse.*

The icy air was like razor-sharp knives in his lungs, emotion a dagger in his guts. Was his concern for Moriana alone or for his prospect of recovering the ancient, treacherous shade who alone knew the location of the Amulet of Living Flame? He couldn't answer the question.

The look in his eyes answered Jennas. She set her face into the wind and rode on, leaving the courier to wonder if it was the icy blast that made her eyes water.

Then they were descending to the valley on the far side of the pass. The snow began to thin. Jennas nodded silently as Fost shouted and pointed to a thin spire of smoke corkscrewing into the sky.

They reached the valley floor. Fost booted Grutz to a run, galloping past Jennas's mount and shouting Moriana's name. A slender figure leaped from an overhanging bank and came around the campfire with sword in hand to confront the bear-riders.

'Fost!' Moriana sheathed her sword, and she was running forward too, arms wide. Fost dropped from Grutz's broad back and lunged to meet her. Laughing and shouting with wordless joy, they clung to each other. Moriana babbled the story of her escape from the Valley, running on until Fost stopped her with an embrace.

After an appropriately long kiss, he broke away and turned to Jennas. To his surprise the hetwoman smiled.

'Any woman who can pass through the Valley of Crushed Bones alive is worthy even of a Champion of Ust,' she said. 'I leave you now. The tents of the Ust-alayakits are open to you always.' So saying, she turned her bear and loped back toward the trail through the mountains.

Grutz shuffled forward, rumbling deep in his throat. Moriana raised her sword. The great, shaggy head shoved against Fost's chest and nuzzled him. He ruffled the coarse fur of the bear's neck. Then Grutz wheeled and followed the hetwoman of the People of Ust.

Only a few flakes dropped from the leaden sky. Moriana and Fost stood with joined hands, watching as Jennas mounted the trail and ascended with remarkable speed. As she reached the place where the trail disappeared around the mountain, she paused to wave. Fost and Moriana waved back, and the warrior-woman was gone, Grutz lumbering after her.

Fost turned again to Moriana. He saw the peculiar light in her green eyes and thought with sinking heart of her scrying spell.

'Moriana . . .' he began.

She shook her head, placing a finger to his lips. 'Don't worry,' she said. She glanced at the trail. 'I wish she'd said her name. She's quite a woman, isn't she?'

'Her name is Jennas,' the courier said. 'And yes, she is quite a woman indeed.'

And so are you, he thought.

They trudged on during morning and afternoon. At first they walked strongly. Moriana, pausing to wait for Fost, had enjoyed several days of relative inactivity in which to recuperate from the endless trek south. Fost had gone through a more strenuous time but at least, as he told himself, he hadn't had to walk during most of it.

In a matter of only minutes, though, they were exhausted. The very clothes on their bodies weighted them down like the threat of impending death. Their feet were as hard to lift as if they had taken root. Step after dreary, dragging step all too slowly melted away the miles.

The day passed in leaden silence. After exhaustion stilled the happy conversation that had followed Moriana and Fost's reunion, even Erimenes soon lapsed into silence. He could not endure the empty, lonely way his voice rattled up and down the valleys walled with grey stone and mortared with ice.

The autumn polar day was short, and the sun no sooner gained the pinnacle of the sky than it tumbled to a bloody death on the jagged peaks. The onslaught of darkness brought with it redoubled chill. Fost and Moriana moved almost energetically as they erected Moriana's tent for the night. It was a counterfeit energy, born from their efforts to fight the weariness that urged them to lie on the bare, cold earth and sleep for all eternity.

Fingers half frozen, they found it hard even to wield spoons to spill a few mouthfuls of gruel down their throats. Bland as it was, the magical grey mess stung throats gone raw from breathing saw-edged antarctic air. At last they put away the ebony bowl and unrolled their bedrolls for sleep.

Fost wondered if it could have taken any more effort to climb the loftiest mountain in the Ramparts than it did to work his way down into the cocoon of his bed. Yet once he lay inside it, almost warm for the first time that day, he found sleep eluded him as nimbly as a handful of wind.

He lay a long time, becoming gradually more aware of the aches that assailed his body and of the breathing of the woman beside him. His mind was numb with fatigue, but he could not slip off the mantle of awareness. He realized Moriana's breathing did not come in the steady rhythm of sleep. He wondered what made her wakeful. She had to be as tired as he.

'Fost.'

He rolled onto his back. He inhaled deliberately, thinking that his body would have stunk had not the cold leached odor from the air, or perhaps it was the sense of smell from his nostrils?

'Yes?'

'What happens once we get there?'

He breathed out. Vapor ghosted white above him. 'Let's leave it,' he said. His voice sounded ancient, a once-smooth baritone fractured by senescence. 'We don't even know if we will get there.'

'It's time we spoke of it,' she insisted.

He shifted to his side. Her face was a pale blur in the darkness of the tent. His imagination filled in details: satin skin dried like leather by wind and sun, stretched taut over the frame of aristocratic cheekbones; full lips pressed tight, almost pinched, by the endless hours of forcing her body to go on, always on; her naturally bright eyes gone hard and sharp as emeralds; her golden hair turned to straw. Still, she was beautiful, as beautiful as only one can be whose spirit is strong, enduring and indomitable.

Fost freed his arm and reached out to stroke Moriana's cheek with the backs of his fingers. She turned her face away.

'You're evading the question,' she accused. 'I won't have it.'

'What do you mean you won't have it?' he snapped, irritated by the tone of her voice.

She looked at him. He thought he could see the crystalline hardness in her eyes.

'There is a question that must be answered soon,' Moriana said, the words sounding as if they'd been punched out with a cold chisel. 'Who is to have the Amulet of Living Flame? We both desire it. Who gets it?'

Resentment geysered up inside Fost. He choked it back. Yet he knew it was this question, not the ache in his limbs, that kept sleep at a distance.

'I'm too sleepy to think straight,' he said. 'For Ust's sake, can't we

246

talk about it tomorrow?' He shook his head. 'Why can't we just *share* the damned amulet?'

'That's no answer,' the princess hissed. Her hand shot from her roll and seized his wrist. Its grip reminded him of the grip of a Sky City eagle. 'I want it to free my City. You want it for . . . carousal, so that you can drink and wench your way through the ages like some little boy who's just slipped over the edge into adolescence.'

'To learn,' Fost muttered. 'I want to learn.'

'There might only be limited power stored in the amulet. So it is written in the ancient scrolls Rann's men unearthed in Kolinth. So Erimenes affirms. If either of us uses it even once, it may turn into a useless trinket. *So who is to have it?*'

Fost twisted his hand from hers and rolled onto his back with a noisy exhalation.

Moriana reared up like an angry serpent. 'You can't just turn away. Talk to me, dammit. I command it!'

'You *command* it?' Fost shot upright. 'By what right do you command it?' His voice shook with outrage.

'By right of birth! I am Princess of the City in the Sky. I am *queen.* That's by what right, groundling.'

'Queen? *Queen?* Of what? Of all the rocks and rodents in the Rampart Mountains?' He glared at her, nose hovering inches from hers.

For a long moment they stared at each other. Then Moriana said, 'It looks that way, doesn't it?'

Fost blinked. Moriana snickered. She flopped onto her back and gave a hoot of laughter. His eyebrows rose. He tried to speak, but a laugh bubbled up from inside him and burst out past his words.

'I thought you were fighting.' Erimenes's words cut astringently across their mirth. He sounded accusing.

'No, Erimenes,' Fost gasped, trying to gulp in a lungful of air. 'We're making love.'

'If that's what you think you were doing, it explains why your companionship has been so markedly uninteresting of late. You could give lessons to a pair of mating felines.'

Fost whooped and seized Moriana around the waist. Her fists pummeled his back, but not with the full strength she could put into them.

The courier's mind was clear with a kind of feverish lucidity as they grappled and groped their way toward an activity sure to alleviate the spirit's boredom. They had dissolved into laughter over nothing. Their mirth had been a release from the pressure building between them. In his curious acuteness of mind Fost recognized that for all her apparent determination on settling the question of the Amulet of Living Flame, Moriana had been no less eager than he to delay finding an answer.

Perhaps because there was no answer.

His hand slid into her bedroll, touched the yielding smoothness of bare skin. Her fingers kneaded the great muscle of his thigh. He groaned as his body responded despite the protests of overworked muscles.

Their bodies pressed against each other as if trying to blend into one. Yet the naked dagger of the unanswered question lay between them.

Fost felt a twinge in his back, so sharp he cried out. Moriana's mouth muffled the sound. The cramp faded and then she was on top of him.

CHAPTER SEVEN

Prince Rann watched the snow fall.

The cold wind beat upon the sides of the makeshift pavilion. Tents had been hurriedly stitched together to form the shelter, lances and javelins comprising the uprights and the stark gray rock of the cliff forming the rear wall. It kept the survivors of his party reasonably dry. It seemed to hamper the cold not at all.

The prince shivered as icy tendrils of wind crept up his thigh. His right shoulder, bound tightly with linen, burned as hot as the brazier that provided the pavilion's sole heat. His side still ached from the love pat of Istu's Vicar, and his ribs seemed an ever-tightening band of iron around his chest. He tasted defeat and apprehension.

'Haven't you finished that spell yet?' he snapped at the scrawny youth who squatted near the brazier. The youth looked up, nervously running his fingers through his scraggly yellow beard.

'These things take time, lord,' he whined. 'Just now there is some disturbance in the ether. We aren't far from Athalau, centre of magic inimical to ours.'

'Don't lecture me, goat-whelp,' the prince snapped. 'Just finish your casting and be quick about it.'

With a sniff the journeyman sorcerer turned back to the wide half geode propped on a bronze stand to present its polished face to him. Rann suppressed a snarl. Like political power, sorcerous ability passed mostly along the feminine side of the Etuul clan. Rann had some spells, but numbered neither scrying nor the use of the seeing-stone among them. So he must abide with the sorcerer's impudence if he wished to communicate with the Sky City. He viewed the prospect with a feeling as near dread as he was capable of, but call he must.

He thought of how satisfying it would be to flay the impudent sorcerer. The very notion twisted his nerves and gave him stirrings in useless loins. But he couldn't punish the journeyman mage – he was needed. He must not punish those fools who had let the bear-riders take his elite Sky Guardsmen in the rear and rob him of his vengeance upon Fost Longstrider. If he wished, he could return to the Great Crater Lake and torment a few Ethereals, but they met their sufferings with bland indifference. He might as well be inflicting torment on a brass statue for all the satisfaction it would give him. Tension built unbearably in him, tension of the sort he had ever been wont to ease through the suffering of others. Now it found no outlet.

As they had been erecting this rough shelter against the buffeting winds, a creature had darted from its burrow beneath their boots. Quick as a serpent he had snatched up the small furry thing and snapped its neck with a convulsion of his hands. The killing had given him momentary satisfaction, but only momentary. The death had been too quick, too painless. It offered nothing of catharsis.

Now he sat twining his fingers together with a force that threatened to snap their joints. He prepared himself for abasement before his cousin, for he had failure to report and assistance to beg. It was almost enough to make him start to scream and never stop.

'Lord Prince,' the youthful mage said obsequiously through his snout. 'Our Most Gracious Majesty, Queen Synalon, awaits your pleasure.'

Squinting at the youth in disgust, Rann entertained the thought of seizing him by the scruff of the neck and thrusting his face into the coals. Perhaps he could sear off a few of the pimples scattered like pustulant rubies across his visage. He shook himself and moved to stand in front of the geode.

Its surface glowed with the likeness of Synalon. She lolled on her jeweled throne, fingers idly stroking the feathers of a large raven. Her scarlet gown opened to the navel, baring slices of creamy breast. Rann's tongue danced across his lips. She smiled, knowing the consternation it caused him to see her thus.

'Well, cousin,' she purred, 'we trust you've only triumph to report?'

The very silkiness of her tone indicated that she trusted no such thing. Rann swallowed hard.

'I regret, O Mistress of the Clouds, that my expedition has met with a temporary setback.'

Synalon nodded, her eyes half closed.

The prince cleared his throat. 'I would not trouble Your Majesty, save that I must request you release to me more troops.'

'More troops?' She arched a brow. 'What exigencies might you encounter that a half-company of our finest Guardsmen are insufficient to deal with?'

Rann swallowed gall. 'None, Sky-born,' he said, 'yet I no longer possess half a company. Only twelve men remain, twelve out of fifty.'

'How is this?' Tersely Rann told her of their losses to storm, thulyakhashawin and finally to the bear-riding nomads. 'It distresses us that a handful of barbarians could slaughter our elite with such ease.' She plucked a morsel from a bowl at her elbow and offered it to the raven. The bird gobbled it down, regarding Rann with an unwinking crimson bead of an eye.

Rann fought down a grimace. Her affectation of the royal 'we' irritated him, and he despised her poison-taloned pets.

'They came upon us from behind, Majesty.'

'Indeed.' Her hand ruffled the feathers behind the raven's head. 'The foremost of our chieftains permits himself to be taken in the rear by a passel of savages. Is this the man we trust to bring us victory?'

'My life is yours,' the prince said. He bowed his head.

'You'll not get off that easily,' Synalon sneered. Rann looked up in alarm. 'It is your fate to serve the Throne of the City. Though we need them for our own preparations, we will release to you another fifty Sky Guardsmen.' She stroked the bird's beak. It croaked delight at the attention. 'See that you do not disappoint us again. Bring us the amulet – *and my sister!*'

'Your Majesty,' he almost gasped. 'I assure you . . .' With a wave of her hand, Synalon broke the connection as the words left her cousin's mouth. He sat back, boiling with rage as sweat streamed down his face.

The journeyman magician sat by with folded hands and an unctuous expression. 'Does my lord require anything else?'

'Yes,' Rann snapped. 'The stink of the latrine trench begins to affront my nostrils. Do something about it, Maguerr, or I'll bury you to the neck in it so that you may fully appreciate the savor of the sewage.'

He smiled at the boy's expression of horror. It made him feel somewhat better.

The travelers had tramped so long through a fog compounded of

251

tedium, exhaustion and bone-stabbing cold that it took them some minutes to realize they had come to the other side of the mountains.

The storm had gone its way. The swollen sun squeezed into the eastern sky, turning the far mountains to copper. At the faint caress of winter sunlight on her cheeks, Moriana raised her head.

'Ooooh!' A long syllable of wonder rolled from her lips. She clutched at her companion's arm. 'Fost, look. Look!'

He lifted his head and blinked. Weak as the morning sun was, it dazzled him after the long night. Tinged with pink, the icefields stretched away forever southward: the Southern Waste. And that meant to the east lay . . .

He swiveled his head towards the sunrise.

Moriana turned with him, and her gasp rose with his. High mountains formed a bowl beyond which stretched the Gulf of Veluz like a sheet of beaten bronze. In their amazement they took no note of the distant water. A nearer spectacle claimed their eyes.

The glacier filled the bowl between the mountains. It was no blank whiteness like the icelands beyond but was an enormous swirl of bands of color, dark on light. Brown, white, black, yellow, dull red and green cast back flecks of sunlight here and there so that the whole sparkled and danced in the sun. It reminded Fost of candles he'd seen with different hues of wax poured together in colorful whorls.

'Is that the glacier?' Moriana asked breathlessly. 'I thought it would be dull and white.'

Erimenes answered her. 'It is indeed a glacier, my dear. Its progress scoops up earth and rock from the ground below, which accounts for the bands of differing shade. Additionally other, lesser glaciers flow into it from the surrounding mountains, causing the most remarkable patterns. Observe.'

'Enough,' Fost growled. His heart had begun to hammer his ribs in excitement. Then his gorge rose at a horrible thought. He ripped Erimenes's jug from his satchel and shook it violently.

'Come out of there, you poor excuse for a ghost,' he shrieked. When he unstoppered the bottle, blue mist flowed forth. The fog became a miniature tornado with dancing light-motes like the sparkles out on the ice. But Erimenes was a little bluer than usual, from motion sickness.

'Wh-what's the matter?' asked Moriana, confused at Fost's behavior.

'The city — the force of the glacier must have pulverized it to dust.

We've come all this way for nothing!' Fost raised his arm to smash the jug.

'Wait!' cried Erimenes. His spectral arm swept out from his side. 'Behold,' he said.

One broad band near the center of the bowl glowed pale blue. It was to this the spirit pointed. Fost squinted. He realized the ice was not tinted but lay clear, its blue the blue of the cloudless sky above. *Is it my imagination?* he wondered, *or do I glimpse shapes within, spires and minarets and bulging domes?*

'Behold Athalau,' Erimenes said with pride. 'Behold my home. The magic of Athalau has not diminished. The glacier is hollow inside.'

The ice-locked shapes showed clearer now. The structures of that fragment of Athalau they could see had an airy, almost fragile look, similar to that within the City in the Sky, but without its subtle and disturbing distortion. Yet it must be monumentally strong to have withstood the pressure of countless tons of ice across the years. His respect for the power of the city's builders grew as he stood looking on a tableau literally frozen for eternity.

His limbs began to quiver. Adrenaline excitement buzzed in his ears, and his veins sang impatiently.

'Erimenes! How do we get in?' Weariness fell from him like a dropped cloak.

'Do be patient,' the sage said, turning an airy smirk in his direction. 'I've gone fourteen hundred years not knowing how I might once again return to my home. You can wait a while longer.'

'Untrue!' Fost shouted. 'Merely thirteen hundred ninety-nine. And besides, I know I'll have to wait to enter Athalau – we're a good day's travel away. What I'm asking is, how will we get in once we're there?'

'Now, now.' Erimenes wagged a finger. 'You must trust me.'

'*Trust* you?' Fost bellowed. 'I'd sooner trust a starving wolf.'

The spirit looked hurt. 'After all I've done for you,' he sighed, 'such ingratitude is wormwood indeed. Well then, if we're going to fall to mistrusting one another, how can I trust you? How do I know that, once I impart my knowledge to you, you won't abandon me here to sit alone throughout eternity with no companion save the howling wind?'

'He's right,' Moriana said. 'We can wait to learn how he plans to gain entry to the glacier. He would hardly have brought us this far without knowing how. We have to trust him.'

She didn't add, *as we have to trust each other*. He eyed her measuringly and saw the same calculation in her eyes. She was hearing the call of the Amulet of Living Flame as keenly as he. The reckoning could not long be forestalled. A shadow crossed the day.

She leaned forward, rising on her toes to kiss his lips. 'We've almost made it,' she said. 'Against all odds, we're almost there. They'll sing of us, Fost. The bards will commemorate us for generations.'

The problem of gaining entry to the city in the glacier still worried him, and to his mind no empty strophes sung by weak-wristed poets could match centuries of brawling, lusty life. He couldn't rid himself of the certainty that she intended to have the former rather than the latter. But he shrugged his doubts aside and returned her kiss boldly. Then arm in arm they started down the mountainside.

Nightfall found them within a few miles of the glacier's edge. As a parting gift Jennas had given Fost a pack filled with supplies. From this they took a tent and a bit of firewood, more priceless than jewels in the treeless waste. Fost and Moriana dined on a haunch of meat they found in the pack. When the fire died down, they climbed into a bedroll to share the warmth of their bodies. Their lovemaking was still more fervent than that which, the night before, had marked their reunion. Tomorrow they would enter Athalau — providing Erimenes knew the way in. Tomorrow, or soon after, they would possess the Amulet of Living Flame. And then must be answered the question of who should have it.

So their bodies writhed together with restless urgency, knotting, spasming, resting limp with repletion and then building eagerness, thrusting and receiving, until their strength was gone and they slept, undreaming, too tired to brood that this time might have been their last.

Fost had to tilt his head far back to see the top of the blue ice wall. It hadn't occurred to him it would rise so high. The chill seemed to beat from it in waves.

He turned away to hunker by the fire Moriana had built at the glacier's foot. She toasted the last remnants of their meat on Fost's metal spit. Excited, they had risen with the sun and marched on without breaking fast. Within three hours they had reached the farthest extent of the glacier-swallowing sheet of ice. Now was time for resting, eating and taking counsel.

Moriana passed him a sizzling scrap. He wolfed it down, relishing the meaty flavor and letting the juices roll down his throat. Nearby swayed the figure of Erimenes, beaming down on the pair like a mother hen. Fost looked at him.

'Well, old spirit,' he said expansively. 'The time, as the wise are wont to say, has come. Tell us how to get inside the city.'

'All you need do is ask,' the spirit said.

'I am asking.' Fost's face clouded.

'No, no,' Erimenes said. 'Ask the glacier.'

Fost's head snapped around. He eyed the nebulous visage for signs of levity. 'Ask the . . . glacier?'

Erimenes nodded.

'Treachery!' roared Fost, leaping to his feet. He shook his fist under Erimenes's nose. 'I knew it! I knew this vaporous scoundrel lied when he said he'd get us in!' He swept a burning red brand from the fire and hurled it against the ice.

'Ouch,' said a voice.

Fost turned around. The word rolled past him like a boulder and went booming off across the flats. He eyed his companions. Moriana's face showed surprise and Erimenes's no more than its usual quota of smug superiority.

'Is this a trick of yours, Erimenes?'

'It's rather late in my life for my voice to deepen so,' the spirit said. 'Likewise, I deem it unlikely the lucious Moriana has been magically transformed into a basso profundo.'

'If you didn't speak, who did?'

'I did.' The words came louder than before, striking Fost like a sea wave. He turned towards the cliff of ice, seeking their origin. Superstitious fear prickled his neck-hairs. His sword came into his hand.

'Who is "I"?' he demanded. .

A heavy sigh swept over him. 'Too long has it been since I discoursed with humans,' the voice said. The words fell slowly, like water dripping from the tip of an icicle. Fost felt an urge to prod the speaker to greater speed, but as yet he had no idea who the speaker was. 'I don't seem to recall them as being so blind that they cannot see something before their very eyes. Are you as the heat-hunters, then, humans?'

Erimenes tittered. Fost shot him a poisoned look which hardly stilled the spirit.

'O great-voiced one,' the courier said, 'forgive my slowness. Only please tell me who and where you are.'

'Can you really not see me? If you stretch out your hand you'll touch me. At the point where your party lies, my flank is over a hundred feet high, though I'm far thicker in places.'

Comprehension slowly dawned. 'You mean . . . you're the glacier?' Fost stared.

'Of course,' the voice said.

Fost felt Moriana come up beside him. Her arm encircled his waist. She snuggled against him for warmth, looking up at the glaicer with round eyes.

'You devoured Athalau,' she said.

A groan came from the depths of the ice. 'Not my doing, not my doing,' the glacier said ponderously. 'I go where the slow pull of the planet drags me, where the pressure of falling snow drives me. Athalau was a fair city; fair were its folk and wise above all others.'

The glacier sighed again. The sheer ice wall shuddered. A few hundred yards to the wayfarers' right, a chink of ice broke from the clifftop and came crashing down. Fost and Moriana jumped back, gazing anxiously up the glacier's side.

The glacier did not notice. 'Fair were the Athalar, and foul were the Hissing Ones, and so they waged war. Long they fought the reptiles, and mightily. For all their wisdom the Athalar could not defeat the power of Istu, Demon of the Dark Ones. Not till the Blessed Felarod with his Hundred summoned up the Earth-Spirit did the light prevail. Great things transpired in that War of Powers. Continents sank, a star fell out of heaven, the very Earth tipped on its axis so the ice crept north to cover Athalau.' Its voice was sad. 'The raw power of the Earth-Spirit infused many things – the rocks, the mountains, the very snow. Thus did I come to life. But not to power over my own destiny. No. All willy-nilly I moved onward. Though it tore at my heart, I overran Athalau. It lies entombed within me.'

The recitation took fifteen minutes and was filled with many a dolorous pause. Fost sat on a large rock and drew Moriana close. When at last the glacier finished, he asked, 'Can you make a path for us to Athalau? We have journeyed along and faced much to reach the city. But if you cannot control your, uh, body, we may have come this way for nothing.'

'I can control what my body does within itself, though, I fear, not well,' the glacier answered ponderously. 'But, know you: To atone for the wrong I unwillingly did the Athalar, I made with them a compact. I am to guard Athalau until the end of time, to keep the

256

Fallen People or other agents of the Dark Ones from misusing the mighty secrets locked inside to spread their terror across the globe. You appear harmless enough, and your eyes are poor. But how do I know you are what you claim to be?'

'Do hurry and get this over with,' called Erimenes. 'It makes me cold just looking at this lump of ice.'

The glacier rumbled.

'Don't mind my spiritualistic friend,' Fost said hurriedly. 'He tends to babble. But he is himself an Athalar by birth. You may have heard of him. Erimenes the Ethical.'

'Oromanes,' the glacier mused. 'No, the name is unfamiliar.'

'Erimenes,' the spirit said. 'I was, dare I say it, the last great sage of Athalau. I taught that the material world and all its trappings are but illusion and to be spurned.'

'Ah, yes,' the glacier said. 'I do recall you, Arrimines. Some of your pupils used to come and try to convert me to their views. I found them foolish. I am real. The snow that feeds me, the earth below my belly, the sun that burns fat from my back in the springtime, all these are real.'

Erimenes made a mournful sound. 'You are wise,' he said. 'Would that I had been as well. I grew more and more otherworldly as my life wore on. Then, when my body died, I barely noticed, so tenuous had my connections with it become. My spirit lived on. After my phsyical death, when it was far too late, I realized how wrong I'd been. The world of sensation is like a treasure trove and must be cherished. The path of true wisdom is the pursuit of pleasure.'

'An equally callow view. I have had one hundred centuries to mull, and the middle path seems best to me. I flow between mountains, trying to climb neither one nor the other.'

'Bah. Moderation should be enjoyed in moderation. Life should be lived to the fullest. Each instant should pulse with hot sensation, each beat of the heart should be quick with passion, each . . .'

'No one cares, Erimenes,' Moriana said. 'Tell me, glacier, have you a name?'

The glacier pondered a mere ten minutes. ' "Guardian" will serve, I think. I guard sacred Athalau and its secrets.'

'Very well, Guardian. A former inhabitant of Athalau has returned to his home after long years of separation. Will you let us in?'

'Home.' Shifting sounds came from inside the glacier. 'Often have I wished I could share the comfort you warm ones take from the concept, yet to me it means nothing. No place is my home; I cannot leave where I am. I grow by traveling. Though, did the earth resume its earlier inclination and the sun drive me back south, I would miss the caress of these mountains. Many lesser glaciers have formed within them and flowed to meet me, and so become part of me. Ah, the diversity of feeling I have learned to love! Perhaps you feel so about *home*.'

The humans sat as the words emerged with painful slowness. They understood the glacier's deliberation; what need had it to hurry? But its speech dragged on endlessly till they found themselves nodding and blinking despite the cold and their impatience to reach Athalau. When at last the slow word flow stopped, Moriana nudged Fost in the ribs, breaking off a loud snore.

'Will you let us in?' she asked again.

'I have agreed to let no nonresidents into the city,' the glacier said, 'but nothing was said about those who accompanied an Athalar.'

'Erimenes is confined to his jug,' Moriana said, 'and cannot reach Athalau without us to carry him. And know that in my veins flows the blood of Athalau.' She avoided mentioning that she traced her lineage through the City in the Sky. The two cities had often warred between the downfall of the Fallen Ones and the onset of the ice.

'Ahhhh,' the glacier said. It fell silent in thought.

Fost sat, chin sunk in hand. Moriana paced. Erimenes allowed a gentle breeze to push his vaporous substance into a spiral.

'I'm freezing,' Moriana said finally. 'How long will it take the glacier to decide?'

'Not long, I shouldn't think,' Erimenes said lightly.

'Not long? What's long to a glacier?'

'Perhaps there's another way in,' said Fost.

'Don't even think such thoughts,' Erimenes said, gesticulating nervously. 'The glacier will never admit us if we anger him, as trying to break into Athalau would surely do. Besides, an army could dig for a generation without reaching the city. And once inside, it could be crushed by a mere shrug!' The misty shape hugged itself and shivered. 'To be immured in ice forever, barred from all sensation but undying cold – *brrr!*'

'You can't feel the cold, Erimenes,' Moriana pointed out. 'Besides, your lot would still be no worse than that of anyone else who's dead.'

'I don't care about them,' the spirit said waspishly. 'Though I've no body, to be surrounded for millennia with walls of ice would make

258

me *think* I was cold. It's only psychology.'

'Great Ultimate protect us from it, if it can make the dead suffer,' Fost said. 'Is that how the demons of hell torment their victims, by using this psychology? Ust knows you're the only dead man I've ever known to whom it made a bit of difference what anyone did to him. I've found the dead an apathetic lot, by and large.'

Erimenes threw up his hands at Fost's lack of perception. The courier huddled deeper into his bearskin and grumbled, 'You might be able to feel the cold at that. The damned wind stabs through me like a spear. I wish we had enough wood to make a real fire.'

'We'd have to move away if we did,' said Moriana. 'We don't want to make Guardian uncomfortable.'

'I know,' piped up Erimenes. 'I have a wonderful way you two can keep warm. Cast away your bulky garments and fornicate. The heat of passion and exercise will warm you better than any cloak!'

Moriana didn't deign to answer. She sat down beside Fost and leaned against him. His arm went naturally around her shoulders.

They were sound asleep when two hours later the glacier's answer rumbled forth. 'I do not like to make snap decisions,' Guardian said, 'but I understand the impetuousness of your kind. You seem goodly folk to me, and the arguments in favor of allowing Uromines . . .'

'Erimenes!' the spirit corrected sharply.

' . . . into the city are most persuasive. That Erimanus is a ghost is not to be held against him; Athalau is now a ghost city as well.' The voice stopped, waiting expectantly. 'Ah, well. A joke, but no matter. As I was saying, it seems unjust to deny an Athalar entrance to his native city, and since he requires the aid of his companions to reach the city, I must admit them too. Admittedly the young lady's lineage, deriving as it does from Athalau, was a factor in my deciding. However . . .'

Fost found himself leaning perilously far forward, straining for the glacier's next word. He wanted to beat his fists against the ice to force words from it. Guardian had decided to let them into Athalau, but what were its conditions? The promise of eternal life filled him with wild energy.

Just when he thought he'd go mad if he must wait a second more, the glacier spoke again. 'However, in return for admitting you, I ask a boon.'

'Anything!' Fost shouted. Moriana echoed him.

'I am infested with worms. The pesky things burrow about within

259

me, wiggling and twitching and causing me endless misery.'

Fost frowned. Anything that could cause serious discomfort to something as immense as the glacier was something he would think twice about blithely promising to put an end to.

'It will be dark in a matter of hours,' Erimenes pointed out. 'Do the crusty old ice cube a favor and go after the ice-worms for him so we don't have to spend the night in this abominable wind.'

'We'll do what we can, Guardian,' Moriana said.

'Very well, then,' the glacier said. 'Enter.'

The icy mountain shook. Clutching each other, Fost and Moriana fell against the cliff. At any moment they expected tons of ice and snow to smash down on them from above.

Instead the ice gave with a tremendous groan and split with a cracking like a million thunderbolts. Debris rained down, but nothing struck the travelers but wet clumps of snow.

'Enter,' Guardian said again. 'But be quick, I cannot hold the way open for long.'

Fost and Moriana grabbed their packs, recapping Erimenes's jar and stuffing it into the satchel. Slipping, they ran into the crevice. It was about as wide as Fost was tall. An upward glance told him it didn't reach more than fifty feet up the cliff face.

Errie, glistening dark surrounded them. They moved as rapidly as they could into the glacier, keeping arms outstretched to keep themselves upright. The ice underfoot was incredibly slick.

'We need to get out of this damned crack,' Fost said, then clamped his mouth shut as his own voice exploded in his ears, trapped by walls of ice. More quietly he went on, 'We'll never find a way without light. I wonder if it's safe to light a torch?'

'Guardian,' Moriana called, wincing at the loudness of her voice. 'Can we light a torch here inside you? We must have light to see.'

'If you must, you must.' The glacier spoke with unwonted haste. The strain of holding open the crack ran like a taut thread through its words. Razor-sharp shards of ice fell from the ceiling, and Fost thought the walls lurched inwards an inch. 'But hurry! I can't . . . keep . . . this up . . . much longer.'

Moriana dug in the pack. She found two splinters of pine and thrust them toward the courier. His groping fingers found them in the blackness. From his own pack he drew flint and steel and a tinder-bowl. Here in the bowels of the glacier the air was moist and not good for fire-making. Fumbling with haste, it took Fost several tries to get a

260

spark into the tinder. One fell into the dry lichen, glowed, waned. He blew frantically.

With a small sizzling noise, a flame flared up. Hastily Fost lit the splinters. The resinous wood caught eagerly and burned with a smoky yellow light. The ice walls of the crack threw back the light in eye-stabbing golden spears. Fost blinked away the glare and the party hurried on.

A moan came from the bouncing satchel. 'Oh, make haste, make haste!' Erimenes cried. 'I can feel Guardian weakening. The walls will crush us at any moment, and I shall be entombed in ice forever. Woe!'

'Your home city is ice-entombed, so it's not unfitting you should be too.' Fost panted the words, short of breath from the effort of running along the slick, uneven surface. Despite his flip response he was no less worried than the spirit. He felt the trembling in the walls, as if their muscles were overtired and failing fast.

A sharp report rolled through the crevice. The ice walls shifted. Moriana screamed as they touched her shoulders.

Running ahead of her, Fost gasped as the hardness pressed in on both sides. His shoulders were forced inward, his arms beginning to pop from their sockets. Erimenes keened despair.

The glacier groaned. The walls slid back, though not as far as they'd been before.

'Time is short,' Guardian groaned. The words boomed out around Fost and Moriana, who felt as though they scurried along the inside of a giant drum while it was being beaten by a drummer. 'The next time the walls slip, I can help . . . you . . . no . . . moooore!'

Fost pounded his hand against Erimenes's satchel. In his own frenzy of fear and desperation he could not bear the spirit's wailing. *Is this how it ends?* he thought frantically. *So near to eternal life, to have life crushed from me? I see no end to this crevice. How can we get out before the walls close in?* Claustrophobic fingers clutched at his throat. *O Ust, how can we escape?*

Moriana seized his arm. 'There,' she shouted. 'Up ahead – to the left!' The dark gleam of ice was interrupted by a patch of blackness perfectly round and wider than Fost was tall. Fost put on a burst of speed, racing with Moriana at his side. Halfway, his feet slipped. His legs pumped harder and the last ten yards were crossed in a sort of running fall. He reached the tunnel, twisted to the side and dived in, sliding thirty feet on his belly. Something soft bumped his bootsoles.

He turned.

'Moriana!'

The princess nodded, brushing back blonde hair. Behind her the crack slammed shut with a sound that made their insides quiver.

Moriana and Fost crawled toward each other, reached and clung like babies, shaking with reaction. Had it not been for the tunnel, they would have been pulverized more thoroughly than any denizen of the Valley of Crushed Bones.

The same thought struck both at once. *Why* was the tunnel here? And why hadn't it closed as well?

'I shouldn't tarry here, if I were you two.' The terror was gone from Erimenes's voice, and his usual truculence had taken its place. 'This tunnel was made by the ice-worms, if you haven't guessed, and that's why it hasn't been closed off. If the Guardian could shut them, he would have put an end to the worms long since.' The spirit paused. 'The worms are attracted to vibrations, you know. Best move along lest they put an end to you.'

The pair struggled to their feet. Swords swished into their hands. Fost still wore the long mail vest the bear-folk had given him; he had left behind the helmet and shield, which, while useful, were too burdensome to carry. It seemed pathetically little with which to defend against such beings as his imagination made the worms.

'Erimenes,' he said softly, hoping the vibrations of his voice wouldn't carry to any questing monsters. 'Can you get your bearings? Can you sense how we should proceed?'

'Naturally. If you fare along this tunnel, in a few hundred yards you'll come to a cross-tunnel that should bring you to the outskirts of Athalau. Ah, to see my home again!'

Sounds came through the ice as Fost and Moriana paced along the icy passage. Some were readily identifiable as the sounds of the glacier, settlings and rumblings and deep shifting. Others they couldn't recognize: sounds that had a furtive tone that made the two uneasy. Fost wondered if Erimenes had lied about being able to sense where they were and how to reach the city from there. If he told the truth, it was further evidence that the shade possessed formidable powers. Who knew what he might be able to do as he came even nearer to the city of his birth?

'Erimenes,' Moriana asked, 'is it wise to burn these torches? Won't they eat our air?'

'Tut, tut, my dear, fear not. The ice-worm tunnels have thoroughly honeycombed our friend the Guardian; little wonder he's so annoyed. Some of their tunnels reach the surface. The beasts feed on other dwellers in the glacier and sometimes on each other. But at times they venture out at night to feed on the ice.'

'At night?'

'They loathe the light. Even the antarctic sun, feeble as it is, suffices to kill them.'

The tunnel twisted ahead of them. The two tried to go as quietly as they could, but it proved difficult. Footfalls slap-slap-slapped away from them, seeming to grow in volume as they preceded the travelers. When Moriana tried running her feet along the ice without lifting them, the rasping sound was nearly as loud. They just had to run lightly and fast — and pray.

'Just a few yards more, my children,' Erimenes told them. 'Around this next bend is the crossway I told you about. So I regret to inform you . . .'

Fost rounded the bend and dug in his heels. The ice failed to give purchase. He slid forward, pinwheeling his arms, and fell onto his rump.

' . . . there are the worms,' Erimenes finished unnecessarily.

Scrambling, Fost got to his feet. Moriana stood beside him, her sword a crimson arc in the torchlight. Twenty feet away the ice-worms waited.

Like greatly magnified earthworms, but the color of snow, their segmented bodies tapered to blunt ends, and these were tipped with hard-looking black caps. A knot of them filled the passageway, writhing together so that the horrified pair couldn't tell how many they faced. The creatures came in assorted sizes, from one a foot thick to a giant better than four feet through the middle. How long the things might be neither Fost nor Moriana could guess.

The largest worm moved forward, crowding aside its lesser fellows. Short, stiff cilia in its rear segments gripped the ice while its forepart squeezed toward them, elongating. The travelers drew back, swords warily extended. The monster's anterior segments widened, the bristles bit and it drew its body forward with a gruesome slithering.

The head rose, blind and questing. The black cap opened like a flower. The shiny surface split into four even wedges like pieces of a pie and opened to reveal a broad, slimy throat. Inside were toothed sphincters that pulsated even as the humans watched.

263

They loathe the light went through Fost's brain. He thrust his torch before him like a rapier and lunged. Hissing, the worm drew back.

'Ha!' the courier shouted. 'These worms are not so much. See how it fears the flame? Into the tunnel, Moriana.' Advancing a step at a time, he drove the giant worm back far enough that the princess could slip by and into the side passage. Behind the great worm others thrashed in rage, slamming their heads against the walls and hissing angrily.

'There,' said Fost smugly. 'Nothing to it.'

The ice-worm lunged.

Fost threw himself backward. The vast mouth encircled the torch and the jaws slammed together. The tunnel plunged into absolute darkness.

Fost fell again, propelling himself backward with his legs. He felt rather than saw the bulk of the worm coming after him.

'Erimenes, you threacherous blue fart! You said they hated the light, said it could kill them!'

His eyes accustomed themselves to the gloom. From the side passage Moriana's torch cast a feeble glow. It illuminated the head of the worm, striking this way and that in blind agony.

'Sunlight can kill them,' the spirit's voice floated out. 'They hate light of any sort, but torchlight poses no danger to them. Athalar scientists long theorized that some component found in sunlight but missing from torchlight is what kills them. And, as has just been amply demonstrated, sufficiently keen hunger can overcome their aversion to light weaker than that of the sun.'

'I don't want a lecture. How do I kill the damned things?'

'That,' said the philosopher primly, 'is rather your problem, is it not?'

Distracted, Fost missed the creature's quick, purposeful movement. It had recovered from the frenzy of pain the torch had caused it. Nearly too late, Fost snatched back his hand as the head darted forward. Chitinous jaws clacked shut an inch from his fingertips.

He jabbed with his sword, felt it bite. The head jerked back with a hiss of annoyance. The worm's breath smelled like a mouldering corpse. Fost heard a sound like an axe chopping wood. The head reared back, giving off a thin, whistling scream.

'I'll help you, Fost,' he heard Moriana call. 'I'm attacking the thing. Great Ultimate, but it's slimy!'

Her sword struck again. The worm keened and went for Fost. He hacked, his blade bouncing off a mandible. The head pulled back, swaying. Moriana's blows fell with a regular rhythm, but the worm ignored her now, keeping its attention firmly on the courier. He was on his feet again, crouched low, dagger in one hand and his sword in the other. He tried to match the unpredictable movements of the ghastly head, but the thing was quick. Again and again the worm's head snapped forward. Fost met it as best he could with parries.

The worm shot forward, lurching over the defense of his dagger. The quartet of jaws gouged his left bicep even as the dagger sank into wormflesh. He thrust his sword deep into the fourth ring-segment. The worm withdrew. His blade slipped free covered with foul yellow slime.

'Fost! I've done it!' Moriana cried in triumph. 'I've cut the thing in two!'

'Many thanks, Princess,' he called. Thinking his enemy slain, he started forward.

The worm's head slammed into his breast. The jaws closed with a crunching sound. Mail rings snapped like spun sugar, and Fost gasped as muscles tore. He cut wildly at the gleaming segments, dropping his dagger to push at the rubbery, slick hide.

'Gormanka, won't anything kill this thing?' A frantic wrench freed him. He fell back, feeling his blood gush from the wound in his chest.

'Merely dissecting it will most assuredly not do so,' Erimenes said. 'You must strike the brain to kill it.'

Not seeming to miss its latter half, the worm hunched forward, stalking Fost. It had the taste of his blood now. It hungered for more.

'Where *is* its brain?' Fost shouted.

'In the head, naturally. On top, within the fourth and fifth ring-segments. Can't miss it.' The philosopher indulged in a chuckle. 'At least, you'd *better* not . . .'

Fost heard the other worms feasting on the large one's tail. The flesh tore with a blubbering sound that sickened him. He wondered how his own would sound as the black jaws rent it.

With sudden inspiration he reversed his grip on the sword. The basket made it hard to hold point-downward. He met the worm's sallies with jabs, goading it to fury. It was too quick for him to sink a killing thrust, but he lacerated the flesh around its mouth until the head was smeared with ichor.

At last, frustrated in its attempts to reach the man-thing with its crushing jaws by rearing, the worm dropped its head low and struck serpentlike along the floor. It was what Fost had been awaiting. As it struck he dived, flinging his legs out behind him and stabbing down. The sword point struck between the fourth and fifth segments and sank deep.

The worm's death-throes slammed Fost against the roof of the tunnel. He hung on grimly, but the spasms were too violent and tore loose his hold on the sword. Dashed to the floor, he lay there feeling like a giant bruise until the thing was still.

His hilt protruded from the monster's neck. Its struggles had driven the sword full-length into it so that Fost had to pull with both hands to free the weapon. Then he stood back taking stock of the situation.

The bulk of the dead worm lay between Fost and its fellows, leaving no room to pass. It also lay between Fost and Moriana. He frowned, absently wiping blood and worm gore from his chest.

'Well done, Fost,' congratulated Erimenes.

'You didn't seem any too concerned, spirit in a jug. Did the prospect of riding about in a worm's gut not upset you?' Fost asked.

'Oh, I was confident of Moriana's overcoming the brute, even if you failed.' Erimenes sounded cheerful. 'Besides, I might have been able to make it — ' He bit off the sentence abruptly.

'Make it what?' Fost asked, suspicions blooming within him.

'Make it, uh, well, you see — make it into an enlightening experience?' A rising note made the sentence into a question. Fost shook his head. The spirit was lying, and he didn't like what that implied.

He opened his mouth. Moriana's cry overrode his question.

'Fost! Hurry! The worms are eating their way through the dead one's tail.'

Cursing that he had no time to pursue the matter with Erimenes, Fost cast about for a way of reaching the side tunnel. The worm had drawn its forepart up to anchor itself for the fight with Fost, which meant its segments had spread out to fill most of the tunnel. He couldn't get by on the sides and there wasn't sufficient room to squeeze along its top. The grisly sounds of feasting grew nearer.

'If I may make a suggestion?' Erimenes asked hesitantly. Fost stared at him. 'The ice-worms, like their earth-delving cousins, consist largely of a tube within a tube. This one's alimentary passage, as I'm sure you noted, is more than sufficient to accommodate your girth.'

'Are you suggesting . . .?' Fost swallowed heavily as he eyed the body of the worm.

266

'Do you see any other way?'

Moriana called again for him to hurry. He chewed the inside of his cheek. Nausea and horror squirmed to knot in his belly at what Erimines proposed, but he could see no alternative. He sheathed his sword, unslung the satchel and dropped to his knees. Taking a deep breath, he forced open the ice-worm's jaws and crawled in.

Blackness and stink assailed his senses. The teeth rimming the large sphincters tore at his flesh where it was exposed. He shut his eyes, mouth and nose and began to wiggle forward, glad he didn't have to see where he was going.

The oozing walls of the intestine closed in around him, caressing him with a touch unsettlingly like that of the tentacled, human-faced guardian of Kleta-atelk's cliff. His mouth filled with sour vomit. He made himself swallow it and moved on.

Digestive acids stung his flesh. The open cuts on his arms and chest felt as though coals had been dropped into them. His face stung. Ropes of mucus trailed over his lips and nose and tangled in his hair. He felt madness rising within him. *I'm trapped in here,* he thought irrationally. *Trapped forever in the stench and the filth and the clamminess and the darkness, gods, the darkness . . .*

His hand probed ahead of him and found cool air. Then the other, dragging Erimenes's satchel, broke free of the worm's gut. Finally his head emerged, dripping and fetuslike into the glare of Moriana's torch. The princess dropped to her knees with a glad cry, leaned forward to kiss him. She stopped abruptly.

He shook his head. Droplets of milky digestive fluid flew. He carefully rubbed his eyes clear of it before opening them.

'Fost, I'm so glad you made it,' said Moriana.

He marked how she kept her head held away and smiled. 'If you're so pleased, how about a welcoming kiss?'

She blanched. He laughed, wiggling from the disgusting cocoon of the worm's belly, and stood.

'You can owe it to me,' he said.

'They're after us,' Fost said, ear pressed to the wall of the tunnel.

'I could have told you that,' Erimenes informed him loftily.

Fost shook his head. 'I'm none too sure how far to trust you.'

'That again!' Erimenes's voice quavered with outrage. 'I warned you of the worms before, did I not?'

'For reasons of your own,' Moriana said. 'I wonder if they are ours.

You sold me to Synalon readily enough. What do you call that, if not treachery?'

'Expedience. It's all in the point of view.'

As they talked, Fost and Moriana jogged along the sinuous tunnel. The spirit informed them they were drawing steadily to the limits of Athalau. They didn't know how much stock to put in his words.

'I've helped you both again and again,' Erimenes said. 'I've saved your lives — both of them — on many occasions the last few weeks. Admit it!'

Moriana exchanged a glance with Fost. 'You have,' she said grudgingly. 'But somehow your solicitousness troubles me more than your earlier eagerness to involve everybody around you in wholesale slaughter.'

Erimenes sniffed. The fleeing pair passed another tunnel entryway. Many passages crossed the one they followed. Erimenes had counseled them to ignore these. The tunnel they were in would bring them to where they wished to be.

'Fost?' Erimenes asked.

'Pipe down, you noisome old bottle of wind.' The courier had had enough of the spirit's weasel-words for now.

Then he and Moriana rounded a new bend. The worms were waiting. The huge slimy creatures shrank away from the light.

'How did they get in front of us?' Moriana asked. 'You said this was the straightest route!'

'So I did, child. But you aren't thinking clearly. These are not at all the same worms you encountered before. It's an entirely new . . . pack? Flock? Dear me, what *is* the proper collective for ice-worms?'

'Why didn't you warn us?' demanded Fost, drawing his sword.

'I tried to. I was told to pipe down,' the spirit said. 'Ahem. A wiggle of worms? No, no, that's still not right. Incidentally you'd best make short work of these worms. The others are just a few minutes behind.'

Fost looked uneasily over his shoulder. This group of worms seemed to number more than a half-dozen, though with the worms twining together and swaying in the uncertain light it was hard to tell. None was as large as the patriarch Fost had slain, so perhaps he and Moriana had a chance. But if the other worms came upon them from behind while they were engaged, their quest for eternal life would end here, fruitlessly.

The worms had recovered from the shock of meeting light and advanced with their strange bulging-squeezing movement. Their cilia glided like skates along the ice. Moriana moved to meet them, scimitar in hand. Fost followed.

'Hold,' Erimenes said. 'Let me out first. How can I truly enjoy the shedding of blood – even rank, yellow blood – all cooped up in this wretched flower pot? Release me.'

Fost did. Time sped away, inevitable death hunched nearer with each second and fear and battle lust filled Fost with manic energy that could find release only in combat. Yet he paused to draw Erimenes's jug from his knapsack, unstop the vessel and stuff it back into the bag as the blue vapor swirled forth.

Erimenes materialized at Fost's elbow as the courier came to stand beside Moriana. Materialize was the word, too, Fost thought. When he'd first seen the philosopher's shade out on the lonely steppe-road south of Samadum, Erimenes was only a pallid wraith, virtually invisible at times. Now he seemed more substantial, almost solid. Had he not known better, Fost would have believed the man beside him as corporeal as he or Moriana, albeit blue.

'Why'd you let him out? I dislike having him leering over my shoulder as I fight. It makes me feel unclean.' Moriana scowled past Fost at the spirit.

Fost shrugged. The worms came at them, and there was no time for words.

One lunged for Moriana's throat. Her long knife caught it beneath the clacking jaws, the Sky City blade chopped down and the ugly head split open. Fost caught a glimpse of blue-shot yellow ganglia exposed by the wound. A worm attacked him then, and he had to concentrate on staying alive.

Side by side they fought, exiled princess and slum-bred courier. Each swing of their swords sent droplets of gore spattering over the walls, the worms, their own fronts and faces. Fost's wounds, hastily bandaged, began to bleed anew. Both he and Moriana bore fresh raw marks where the worms' jaws had found them by the time the last monster was struck down.

But struck down they all were. Fost leaned against a wall, sword hanging limply, feeling sick and exhausted to the depths of his soul. He glanced at Moriana. Her lovely face was haggard and drawn beneath a viscous film of worm blood.

Erimenes crowed like a rutting cock at the sight of so much blood. Fost regarded him from sunken eyes. The inhuman gloating on the philosopher's ascetic face nauseated him as thoroughly as the reek-

269

ing corpses of the worms.

From behind came a scrabbling noise, echoing starkly in the ice tunnel. The pair spun to see the first pursuing worm's head poke around the bend, shrink away from the light and then come on purposefully. Fost tapped Moriana's arm.

'Away,' he said, hoarse with the reaction of blood-letting. 'With any luck they'll stay awhile devouring their luckless comrades.'

The hisses of the worms cut across the slapping of their bootsoles on ice. Then came the now-familiar tearing sound, and Fost turned his head back briefly to see the worms feeding with cannibalistic fervor. As he watched, two heads reared up and thrust at one another. The beasts were fighting over the choicer remains of their kindred.

'That ought to hold them for a while,' Fost said before a curve took them out of sight.

'A pity it won't delay them long enough,' Erimenes sighed.

'Long enough for what?' demanded Moriana. Without breaking stride, she had pulled a rag from her knapsack and was vigorously scouring the filth from her face.

'I sense that battle has brought your sexual appetites to un- paralleled keenness. What a pity you haven't time to shed your clothes and sate the hunger within your loins. What a striving that would be!'

Moriana snarled something at the spirit, who floated effortlessly alongside them. But her green eyes brushed Fost's grey ones, and she knew that for both of them the sage's words hit uncomfortably close to the truth.

They flew inward through the glacier. Erimenes glowed with a light to rival that of the torches, and the gold sparks that danced within him blazed like newborn suns. Moriana had passed Fost her pine splinter at the onset of the fight, and yellow flames streaked out behind him like a banner.

Abruptly the torch flared high. At the same instant Fost felt a breath of coolness wash over his face, not cool with the chill of the glacier's bowels but fresh and crisp, invigorating.

The tunnel bent and brought them face to face with beauty. It was a beauty so tangible that they stopped and blinked with wonder. Fost and Moriana gripped each other but didn't share a look. They couldn't take their eyes from the spectacle before them. Their lips worked, but it was Erimenes who gave name to the vision.

'Athalau,' he said.

CHAPTER EIGHT

Prince Rann's mount shrilled raucous response to the scouting bird in the sky ahead. His gaze scarcely less keen than the eagle's, Rann strained to see through the dying polar night. There, there it was. At the very foot of the ice sheet was the black smudge of a dead campfire.

The fugitives had made no attempt to cover their tracks after leaving the shelter of the mountains. Conceivably they thought no one pursued them any longer. Rann laughed at the thought.

To all intents and purposes the fugitives had simply marched up to the foot of the glacier and disappeared. Their tracks led to the looming ice cliff, blending into a muddle as though the two had spent hours pacing before the glacier. No tracks led away.

Rann circled his bird into a landing. Around him threescore bird-riders brought their mounts to frozen earth. The promised reinforcements had arrived promptly. The treacherous air currents had dashed two of the newcomers to bloody jam against the peaks and a sudden onslaught of thulyakhashawin had accounted for three more Sky Guardsmen. Rann suspected he'd feel their loss keenly during these next few hours.

A party of scouts clustered at the foot of the sheer, shiny cliff, weapons ready. They peered at the fire's remains, at the rocks the pair had sat upon, at the snow trampled by their feet, at the hundred-foot face of the glacier. Their worried looks told Rann they were as baffled as he.

He seated himself on a rock while more Guardsmen came to search. His tawny eyes stared out blankly across the Waste. The sun fell toward the waiting arms of the Ramparts to the west, spilling its blood on the ice. Rann smiled a little within. Bloodstained beauty he could appreciate.

'Milord.' A lieutenant crunched through snow to bend the knee before him. Bandy-legged Captain Tays had fallen at the fight in the mountains, his face crunched in the jaws of a huge black bear. Newly arrived Lieutenant Odon was now the prince's second-in-command.

'What have you to report?' Rann asked without looking at the man.

'Nothing, lord.' The pale eyes fixed him like spears. 'Nothing I could make sense of. Just that fissure.'

'What about it?' Rann rose.

'I'll show you, lord.' Odon led him to the glacier. Rann felt the chill emanating from it and felt thankful for the fur-trimmed cloaks the reinforcements had brought from the Sky City. He examined the crack indicated by the officer.

A rock was trapped at the base of the fissure. It didn't seem to have been overrun by the glacier's stately advance. The ice was splintered to either side of the rock as though the crack had opened briefly and slammed shut on it.

'Interesting.' Rann nodded, fingering his chin. 'Somehow the glacier opened to them, and they passed within, accidentally kicking this rock into the opening. I've wondered how Moriana hoped to reach the ice-locked city. Obviously she has some sorcery we know nothing of that enabled her to open this way.'

Gloved fists beat his thighs. 'Synalon has grown too complacent. She underestimates her sibling. Moriana has gained much power.'

'Have we no spells to follow them, lord?'

'None.' He spat the word out as if it tasted bitter. 'We must dig our way inside, Lieutenant. Burrow after them like moles.' He shook his head. 'It will take too long. *Too long.*'

'But, lord,' the officer protested, 'all we have to dig with are our weapons. Working the ice will blunt their edges.'

Rann turned toward him. In his eyes dwelled a chill deeper than the ice. 'Then you will dig until they break. Then you will burrow with your fingernails until they break too, and then with your fingers till they wear to bloody nubs. After that you can chew the ice with your teeth. But dig you will, until we reach Athalau. Do I make myself clear?'

'Y-yes, lord.'

Rann nodded curtly and turned away as the troopers attacked the ice with sword and spear. Steel bit with brittle sound, sending splinters and flakes flying like bits of diamond.

'Who pecks at me?' a voice drawled.

The digging stopped. The men backed from the glacier, weapons dropping from fear-numbed hands. Startled, Rann looked at the glacier. Unquestionably the words had issued from the very ice. He'd heard tales of inanimate things, rock and ice, given life in the confrontation between the Earth-Spirit and the demon. Always he had attributed the stories to too-strong ale rather than the War of Powers. He had been wrong. He had little trouble adjusting to the fact; he wasn't a man to let preconceptions hold sway over solid evidence.

'You, glacier,' he said. 'You guard the city of Athalau?'

'I am Guardian.'

'I beg your leave to enter with my men.'

The waiting seconds pulled Rann's nerves ever tauter. He envisioned Moriana and her leman nearing their goal. If they gained it, it would bring disaster upon Synalon's plans – and what befell her befell him. He wanted to scream at the glacier to hurry. He knew it would do no good.

'A millennium passes without human feet ever venturing this way,' the glacier said at length. 'Now in a single blink of the sun's eye I encounter many. Why?'

'I seek my cousin. Her tracks lead here and stop. Did you admit her and her companion?'

'I admitted her with companions.' The booming voice emphasized the plural. 'She had a dark-haired man with the air of Northern heat and haste about him and the shade of one who dwelled here within the city long ago. I felt it unkind to deny entry to an Athalar, and the lady was of that kindred, also.' It paused endlessly. 'You say you are her cousin. The blood of Athalau blesses your veins too, does it not?'

'Why, yes, yes indeed. I seek to aid her in her quest.'

'I wondered why your party was so large.' The glacier mused another thirteen minutes. 'Hmmm. Such a force could slay many ice-worms.'

'What?'

'Ice worms. The vermin infest me. They itch most abominably. I allowed your cousin and her friends inside on condition they slay as many of the pests as possible. But there were only two who could fight, the third being incorporeal, and the worms are strong and wily beasts. I doubt they can account for many.'

'We will account for scores of ice-worms, my men and I!'

'And you will wreak no harm in sacred Athalau?'

Rann laughed. 'I will do nothing Moriana herself would not.'

'Very well,' the glacier said. Again it opened with an earthshattering noise. Rann called Maguerr to him. Loath though he was to rely on the pimpled journeyman, he needed to maintain a link with the outside world. Quickly he instructed the youth to stay behind with five men to tend the war birds, and, every hour, look in on the prince by means of the seeing stone. At this short range the fledgling mage could communicate via the geode without Rann requiring one of his own. That done, the prince drew blade and led his men into the yawning crack.

The bird-riders looked uneasily at the sides of the crevice. It was as if immense jaws swallowed them, jaws that could snap shut at any instant. As if to emphasize the fact, the walls shook, dropping jagged ice fragments from above on the hurrying file of men.

'Ahead of you lies an ice-worm tunnel,' came the glacier's voice from all around the Sky City men. 'That way went your friends. You must reach it soon. I cannot hold the passageway open much longer.'

Rann shouted his troops into a run. The trembling of the walls was becoming more pronounced, and the last of the bird-riders had only just entered the glacier. He set the pace and quickly found he must take short, mincing steps to avoid going down on his back due to the slippery surface. Shouts and curses from behind told him others were making the same discovery.

The walls slid inward. Men screamed. But the looming faces of the crevice did not slam together. Sweating, Rann gained the ice-worm tunnel and dashed into it. Behind him came the Guardsmen in a mad scramble.

A grating sound crunched from the walls. Ice shook beneath Rann's feet. The crack closed with such force that the bird-riders were thrown to the tunnel floor. Shrieks rose, suddenly wild, to be cut off by the doomsday slam of the walls coming together.

Rann hauled himself up. Sweat froze on his face. 'Count off!' he bawled. At his side, Lieutenant Odon echoed his cry.

Struggling to their feet, the men obeyed. Rann listened stonily in the darkness that had descended as the numbers rolled back in the now-sealed mouth of the tunnel. The counting went to twenty-nine.

And stopped.

Rann ground his teeth together. He had lost half of his men at a single stroke.

'Glacier,' he called, 'may we light torches?'

At the reluctant affirmative, lights flared in the passageway. Rann glanced at the bluish ice that had shut off the entrance of the worm path. A red ooze trickled to the floor of the tunnel.

'Move out,' he grated.

Grumbles rose at his back. 'He spends our lives like sipans!' a trooper muttered.

Rann turned back, his grin a death's-head. 'Aye, and what of it? What will your lives – and mine – be worth if Moriana escapes with the amulet?' The looks on the bird-riders' faces told him he'd made his point. They knew nothing of what the amulet did, for that wasn't knowledge to be entrusted to a common soldier. But they knew their queen desired it, and they knew how Synalon served those whose failure thwarted her desires. Shaken and pale, they readied their weapons and followed their leader.

The eunuch-prince strode as rapidly as he dared. He felt the men's gazes burning into his back. Their hatred for him crackled in the air like lightning about to strike. It didn't worry him. Men might claim to love a commander who treated them well and never spent their lives when he could avoid it but they never truly respected him. Rann didn't care for their love but he commanded their fear. Nor did their welfare concern him; he was troubled by the loss of over thirty men but only because he feared he might need their numbers soon. The survivors loathed him for his callousness, but they followed him closely. They had marched into the depths of a cold, living hell. Only a resolute, utterly ruthless man like Rann stood any chance of leading them out again.

Odon walked a pace behind his leader. Rann felt him hovering and looked back with eyebrow raised.

'The ice-worms, lord,' Odon said. His voice shook, and his skin shone faintly green in the light of the torches. Apparently the thought of a score and a half of his comrades being squashed to paste bothered him.

'What about them?'

'Should we be looking for them, lord? We promised Guardian, after all.'

Rann eyed him boldly. He wondered how this pup had ever come by a commission in the Sky Guard. He was too soft for the *corps d'élite*.

'We hunt Moriana, Fost Longstrider and the spirit. Nothing else. If we encounter ice-worms, then we'll deal with them. We'll waste no time seeking them out.'

Odon seemed ready to protest tricking Guardian. The look on Rann's scarred face silenced him. He swallowed his objections, finally saying, 'How will we follow the fugitives, lord?'

Rann pointed ahead. 'We'll find some sign up there, I believe.'

Odon's gaze followed the finger. Yellow blood and fragments of rubbery flesh were all that remained of some unidentifiable creature. The stench made even Rann's head swim. Something had died violently and been devoured here at the junction of two ice-worm tunnels. Rann went into the cross-passage, stooped and smiled with satisfaction.

'Indeed, indeed,' he said to himself. He rose to follow a trail of red drops into the heart of the living glacier.

'I've never seen anything like it,' Moriana said.

'Of course you haven't,' Erimenes said. 'For this is Athalau, and there is none to compare with her.' His voice rang with genuine pride.

Looking at the City in the Glacier, Fost couldn't feel that that pride was misplaced. Athalau was indeed incomparable. Neither Tolviroth Acerte nor the Sky City possessed anything near the simple elegance of Athalau, and deep inside Fost felt sure that even High Medurim in her prime was a slum compared to this.

There were none of the gauds and bangles his imagination had come to expect: no streets paved with gold, no jewel-encrusted façades on the buildings. But each and every structure in the great city was a work of art, each possessing its own essence and its own charm, yet all blended into a harmonious whole. Towers rose dizzyingly higher than any Fost had ever seen, and thin spires beside them buttressed them with a spiderweb of finely wrought stone or metal. Colonnades marched solemnly along the avenues between domes whose very curves were poetry. Off in the middle distance a minaret loomed high above the rest, and here at least was evidence of the city's fabulous wealth, for it was carved from a single ruby. The city glowed with a light of its own, shifting, sourceless, containing all the colors of the rainbow and implying a myriad more.

Not all was perfection, as the courier and the princess saw when the first rush of awe subsided. The ice of the glacier formed a high dome above the city, as though Athalau lay in a gigantic stomach. At one time even the regal Ruby Tower had been well clear of the icy roof. But over the years icicles like stalactites had flowed down from the vault of the glacier and stalagmites of frozen water grew to meet them. Some of the structures in sight were cased in rippling sheaths of ice. Elsewhere great chunks of ice had fallen, crushing masonry.

Moriana was the first to shake free of the spell. 'We must hurry,' she said. 'I feel danger all around.'

'Some people simply aren't cut out to be travelers,' Erimenes said severely. 'You merely suffer a foreigner's distaste for the unfamiliar.'

Fost looked around warily. The tunnel had given way to a ledge of ice that sloped gently until it reached the outermost buildings of Athalau. A hundred yards away on their left lay a fallen stalactite of ice a hundred feet long and twenty feet thick at the large end. It had broken into neat segments as though split by a gargantuan wood-cutter's axe.

'Having eighty tons of ice land on my head would be unfamiliar, spirit, and I confess I'd find the experience shattering.'

Erimenes lifted his nose. He looked more and more like a real, living being. 'That shaft fell centuries ago,' he said disdainfully.

'Perhaps another's overdue,' said Fost.

'Hist.' Moriana raised her hand, her face suddenly taut and distant. 'I hear something.'

Fost closed his eyes and concentrated, screening out the sounds of their breathing. He heard it too, a rumbling of different timbre than the internal groanings of the glacier, an intermittent clicking sound and, rising and falling at their hair's-breadth of perception, the babble of voices.

'I hear them too.' Moriana frowned, her hand falling to rest on the hilt of her sword.

'Rann?' asked Fost.

'Who else?'

'But how did he get in?'

Erimenes stood with one hand cupped theatrically to his ear. 'It is Rann in truth, with more than a score of men,' he said. 'As to how he gained entrance, I fear Guardian is less, uh, perceptive than one might wish.'

'In other words Rann talked his way in the same as we did.' Fost scowled. 'A fine set of circumstances.'

'Come,' Moriana said. 'Let's get down to the city. We should be able to reach the Amulet of Living Flame before they arrive.'

Fost bit his lip at the name. That final question still lay between him and Moriana: Whose should the amulet be? She still seemed willing to defer finding an answer. So would he – for now.

'How to proceed?' he asked.

'We haven't much choice, unless you can climb these icy inclines.' Erimenes gestured. The slope ahead of them was hollowed out into a sort of run that reached down to the city. Steep walls curved up to either side.

'What made it that way?' asked Moriana. 'It looks worn down. Could worms have done it sliding down into Athalau from the tunnel?'

'Of course not!' Erimenes's face showed outrage. 'Even such as they realize what a desecration that would be. They remain in their burrows, devouring one another.'

Fost looked dubious. But Erimenes was right, at least in that they had little choice of how to go. They started gingerly down the slope. Fost took three steps and then lost his balance, his legs flying out from under him. His tailbone hit with an impact that brought tears to his eyes. Immediately he was whizzing down the hill toward Athalau.

He heard Moriana's alarmed shout behind him turn instantly to a laugh of pure glee. She zipped past him, likewise seated with her knees drawn to her chin, stroking at the ice to go even faster.

'Unfair!' shouted Fost. Laughing, he pushed himself in pursuit. As they reached bottom, he caught up with her, seized her around the waist and sent them both sprawling in a laughing tangle on the street.

'My rump is glowing hot!' Moriana cried, rumpling Fost's black hair.

He kissed her soundly. 'I'll agree to that,' he said, reaching and squeezing. 'Perhaps some fresh air will cool it off.' He tugged at her breeches.

'Ahem.' Erimenes's lordly throat-clearing drew their attention. 'Might I suggest you postpone your recreation to a more suitable time and place? Prince Rann approaches.'

Fost and Moriana grinned at each other, disentangled themselves and stood. They knew that their momentary distraction had arisen from the strain they were under. They couldn't afford another such lapse. Nonetheless they were still grinning when Fost took Moriana's hand and they set off up the street.

The boulevards of Athalau were paved with some mysterious smooth substance, hard like stone but which flowed continuously, showing no telltale seams between blocks. To Fost's mind this was nearly as wondrous as streets of gold would have been.

The smile faded from his face. Erimenes had urged them to forget their loveplay and get on with the business at hand – Erimenes! The lecherous, long-dead virgin who would propose they fornicate in the middle of a hornbull stampede. Fost shook his head. There was something very wrong here.

They entered a new block and halted. Sinuous shapes glided out of buildings into the street. A familiar hissing filled the air.

'So they won't desecrate holy Athalau,' Fost said bitterly, glaring at Erimenes. 'What are those – heretics?'

Erimenes's eyes bulged at the worms. A half a hundred had poured from the lovely ruins like maggots from a gilded skull. 'I must – that is – this is certainly an unforeseen circumstance.'

Deliberately Fost slid his sword from its sheath. 'I've a mind to lob your jug to them, Erimenes. A worm's gizzard is a fitting resting place for such as you.'

Erimenes gibbered in terror. Moriana laid a hand on her lover's arm.

'Not yet. Erimenes, can you affect the ice-worms' minds?'

'They haven't minds enough!'

'But you can still work your invisibility trick on Rann's men?'

'Yes,' Erimenes said. 'But it's not merely a trick. It is mental manipulation of the most sophisticated . . .'

'Enough, Erimenes. Fost, can you delay the worms a few minutes?' Fost looked at her, nodded slowly. 'Good. Hold them here. I'm going to have a talk with Rann.'

'You're going to parley with that eunuch-bastard?' he grated angrily.

'Not exactly.' She started away, then paused. 'The satchel. You wouldn't . . .'

'If you mean, would I go on without you to find the amulet, I would not even if the worms let me.' He flicked his eyes toward the approaching worms. Fifty yards still separated them from the humans. 'As to whether I'll let you take the satchel, the answer is likewise no.'

She looked hard at him, nodded and was off, running back the way they had come. He watched her, wondering whether she wasn't hoping to work some deal with her cousin. He shook his head. *I grow too distrustful. The thought's unworthy of me.* He faced the worms.

Moriana heard harsh voices echoing in the huge dome that enclosed the city. She came out at the foot of the street that led to the ice run. A group of men stood clustered around the tunnel mouth. The soft glow of the city looked strange reflected from their naked weapons. Their garb was black and purple, but even without that she would have known the slim, erect figure that stood to one side, surveying the city.

'Rann!' she called. The figure looked at her and went deathly still. 'Half-man, coward, traitorous offal. Come and get me, if you have the courage!'

Even at this distance she could feel his rage. Her voice echoed, amplified by the vastness of the chamber. Somewhere vibrations broke loose a giant icicle and it came crashing down. Ignoring it, Rann broke into a run toward her, bellowing to his men to follow. Moriana stood a moment longer, waiting. Rann managed to keep his feet to the bottom of the run, though none of his men did. Moriana spun and fled like a deer.

Arrows whistled in pursuit. None came near. Making sure she was in sight of the Guardsmen, she led them straight toward the block where Fost faced the ice-worms.

She rounded the corner. Fost looked back at the sound of her footsteps. A worm lay dead before him, his now useless torch buried in its brain. Another writhed in its death-throes nearby.

'Fost!' Moriana shouted. 'This way!'

He turned, saw her and raced for her. Sensing victory, the ice-worms slid in pursuit, their hissing more chilling than the glacier's cold. By dint of furious leg-work Fost gained twenty yards on them by the time he reached the waiting princess.

'Erimenes, make us invisible. Use your mind trick, now!' Moriana cried.

'Certainly,' the spirit said. 'But I must insist . . .'

'And in the name of the Five Holy Ones Who Died for Athalau, be quiet!'

The baying voices of the Guardsmen came nearer. Fost and Moriana hugged each other, not daring to breathe. Would Erimenes's spell work? Or would he betray them to a terrible death?'

A youth, long-legged for a bird-rider and wearing an officer's silver gorget, pelted around the corner an arm's length from the fugitives. At the sight of the worms he halted. Then the rest swept onto the street, and their momentum bore him and them straight into the tangle of worms.

Men cried out in pain and fear. Ice-worms blew their foul breath. The Guardsmen fought savagely, but the ice-worms outnumbered

280

them. Man-blood and worm-blood ran in rivers, blending into a ghastly puree that sizzled and steamed in the cold.

Unseen and all but forgotten, Fost and Moriana slipped from the doorway. They had no cause to feel compassion for the bird-riders, but still the scene appalled them. The worms were tearing the soldiers apart. Black jaws severed arms at a bite, legs thrashed air as toothed maws shredded half-swallowed men. The battle could have but one outcome.

Only Erimenes's no longer spectral face showed triumph as they made their way around the corner and away.

CHAPTER NINE

Hand in hand Fost and Moriana walked through glory. A glory tarnished by time, to a certain extent, with scars showing where ice-worms had laired in buildings or ice had plummeted from above, but glory nonetheless.

Erimenes floated beside them. He was a small, slender man with a long head, receding hair and a blade of a nose above thin lips. Fost wondered if he put his hand out whether or not it would pass through the spirit or meet the resistance of solid flesh. Beyond the specks of gold light that swirled through him, the only evidence of Erimenes's nature was his feet – or the lack of them. His skinny legs ended in a swirl of dense blue fog from which an indigo umbilicus extended to the pot, which rode at Fost's hip.

'Now you must do the service you promised us, Erimenes,' said Fost. 'Only you know the resting place of the Amulet of Living Flame.' Moriana's hand squeezed convulsively in his at the mention of the name. He felt a hot flush creep up his neck.

Erimenes nodded, smiling. 'That I do. It hangs in the nave of the Palace of Esoteric Wisdom, foremost structure in all of Athalau.'

They hurried along broad thoroughfares toward the center of the swallowed city. The shifting light suffused them with a sense of well-being but it couldn't overcome their urgency to reach the end of their quest.

'How much farther is it?' Moriana asked.

'The world unravels itself around you, and you have thought for nothing save yourselves.' Erimenes shook his head. 'Great were the Athalar but they are done, dust. I alone remain to appreciate the splendor of what once was.'

Fost growled warningly.

'Very well,' the philosopher said. 'Another turning of the way and you shall behold the Palace with your own eyes.'

Unconsciously the pair quickened their pace. The pavement underfoot was solid enough but seemed to lend spring to their steps. Hearts hammering, they turned the final corner.

A broad square stretched before them. In its center rested a fountain, its tongue of waters long stilled, an abstract of silent tiers. At the far end of the plaza the tower of ruby flowed upward, the fineness of its lines giving it the illusion of movement and flight.

'The Palace of Esoteric Wisdom,' Fost breathed in awe.

To his astonishment, Erimenes shook his head. 'You are deceived. Poor are you in wisdom. This way, to your left. I shall guide you, never fear.' Chuckling to himself, the spirit led the way.

Puzzled, the two followed. The carved gem tower was the most impressive work of architecture either had ever seen. How could it be other than the 'foremost structure in Athalau'?

Erimenes signed them to a halt. 'Here, children. Here lies the Palace. Within its sacred precincts awaits eternal life. And more, aye, ever so much more.' He chortled as if enjoying some private jest.

Fost stared at the building. He blinked slowly. The structure stayed the same.

'How can this be?' he demanded. Far from the soaring wonder he had anticipated, the Palace of Esoteric Wisdom was a simple basilica of snowy marble, fronted with a portico upheld by columns as devoid of decoration as the rest of the edifice. Its doorway was a single pointed arch, as were the windows of the clerestory. Silver light danced in the windows. 'It's a handsome building, without elaborations or fripperies as you'd find in decadent Medurim. But to call this the foremost?' He shook his head in disgust.

Erimenes looked severe. 'I wonder why you seek everlasting life so assiduously. You lack the discrimination truly to enjoy it. Hear wisdom, child, though scant is my hope that you'll heed it: That which is of the most worth is not necessarily the gaudiest to behold.'

Fost sneered, but Moriana touched his arm and said, 'He may be right. I myself enjoy ornateness, but something in the cleanness of this place's lines beguiles the eye.'

'If you find it so pleasing,' a voice said from behind them, 'by all means fill your eyes with it, for it is the last sight they shall behold.'

'Rann!' The name broke from Moriana in a choked cry.

'The same. My gratitude, cousin, for leading me to the Amulet of

Living Flame.'

Fost and Moriana drew their blades. The bird-riders spread out into a semicircle to hem them against the edifice, five to either side of the prince.

'How did you escape the worms, half-man?' Moriana asked.

'I left half the men to deal with the worms.' Rann's lips tensed into a grin. 'My men had informed me of the invisibility trick you used to elude them in the ravines. When you lured us into the worms and slipped away, I guessed what you were doing. I managed to extricate these men and come after you. I had a feeling our mutual goal would be somewhere in the very heart of Athalau. So we hid and waited for you.'

'You're a coward as well as a gelding,' Fost spat. 'To desert your own men!'

'They gave their lives for the Sky City and its queen. It was an honor I gave them.' The soldiers approached slowly, tightening the net. Rann had pulled out none too soon by the looks of them. Hardly a man didn't bear the marks of the black-gleaming chitin jaws. But their faces were hard with determination, and madness glinted behind their eyes.

They charged. Fost met an upward thrust with a stop-thrust to the forearm. The bird-rider dropped his blade, cursing. Even as he staggered back, Fost's blade swept around him and streaked to the heart of a second attacker.

Moriana stood exchanging deft wrist cuts with a brown-haired trooper whose left arm was missing below the elbow. A ragged, bloodstained bandage wrapped the stump. Moriana flicked her sword at his temple. His blade winked up to parry. Moriana's arm pivoted and brought her sword down to *chunk!* into the man's unarmored side. With a blood-frothing moan he sank to his knees. Moriana sprang past him to engage another.

Fost found himself facing Rann. The prince showed his teeth in a smile.

'You are brave and strong,' Rann grunted, easily turning back Fost's powerful attacks. 'We could amuse each other many a long hour, you and I. I am sorry that you must quickly . . . *die!*'

Like a serpent the scimitar flashed past Fost's guard, striking for his heart. He swung his right side forward and groaned as the point took him in the shoulder. He leaped away. Crimson gleamed on the blade as it slid out. Rann lunged again. The thrust lacked strength; Fost's mail stopped it, though it bruised his breastbone. He hacked with the strength of pain-born fury. Rann's sword warded off the blow, but it laid open the prince's cheek and sent him reeling back.

A sword whistled by Moriana's ear, so near it snipped a lock of golden hair. She bled from cuts in her thigh and arm. She danced back as her enemy drove at her, howling with fury.

He stopped, eyes black circles of amazement in his skull-white face. Moriana stared back, mind staggered by the hammerblow of recognition. 'Odon!' she gasped. 'My friend in my youth, what are you doing here?'

'Lady,' he said, his mouth working like a fish's. 'Oh, lady, I am sorry . . .' His hand came up, sword aimed as duty overcame sentiment. She read his intent. Her sword ripped out his throat like the claw of a beast. He died with his eyes fixed on her. Tears fogged her own as two more men engaged her.

By unspoken agreement the bird-riders let their leader have the big Northland courier to himself. Fost hadn't fared so well the last time he'd crossed swords with Rann and he wasn't eager to face the prince again. Though healed by Jennas's poultices, the wound in his thigh began to throb as if recalling the last encounter.

Fost had the advantage of strength and reach over the small Sky City noble and he wore the mail vest the bear-folk had given him, while Rann had no protection beyond his heavy cloak. On his side the prince had speed, lesser size and — much as Fost hated to admit it — greater skill. They came together again, blades splashing the soft glow of the city in streaks across their sweating faces, singing the mating song of steel.

Back and back the prince forced Fost. Occasionally a massive blow by Fost made the eunuch give way instead, but the great overpowering sweep left Fost's body exposed. After a lightning riposte laid open his hauberk and the belly beneath, Fost let well enough alone and concentrated on fighting a delaying action.

He tried to break for the door of the Palace. A grinning trio of Sky Guardsmen blocked him. His flowing wounds had sapped him of strength. He lacked the power for the berserk charge that would have bowled them over and let him through.

'Kill!' a voice cried. Fost's eyes snapped to his side. Forgotten, Erimenes stood by, clapping spectral hands in glee. 'Oh, the blood. Never has Athalau known such a spectacle!'

285

'Erimenes, make us invisible,' Fost cried. Taking advantage of the distraction, Rann lunged — and pulled up short, a puzzled look on his face.

Then comprehension glowed in his eyes. His sword licked out. Fost gasped as it sliced at his left biceps.

'Your blood,' the prince said, 'falls to the pavement and reveals your presence. A moment now and we'll let the rest out.'

Undaunted by his foe's invisibility, he came in, his sword a sighing whirlwind of death. Beyond him Fost saw Moriana likewise being driven to the wall by a jeering half-ring of foes. Though he could see her, they could not. Like Rann they traced her by the drops of blood she shed.

Five Sky City men were out of the fight, but the odds remained three to one against Fost and Moriana. Weakened as they were, they couldn't hold out much longer.

'Erimenes,' Fost shouted in desperation. 'Aid us! Have you no other powers that can help?'

Standing beside him, not changing his gleeful expression when an occasional sword-cut slashed through his torso, Erimenes nodded. 'Many are my powers,' he said. 'Watch.'

At the very apex of the ice dome, half a thousand feet overhead, the glacier was latticed with deep cracks. The shifting and endless motion of the glacier had weakened the ice over the years. Now a great block hung barely suspended, ready to break away at any instant.

The pull of mental power from below was slight. But it sufficed.

A rumbling brought Fost's eyes up. 'Back!' he screamed to Moriana. 'Against the wall!' He drove at Rann with all his strength. Taken by surprise, Rann was caught high in the left breast. He stumbled back, sword slipping from his hands. His gaze followed Fost's.

He bellowed in rage and pain as thirty tons of ice engulfed him and his men.

For a moment Fost could do no more than stand with his forehead resting in his palm. Then Moriana was beside him, clutching him, kissing him.

'We won,' she said, eyes disbelieving.

'With Erimenes's help. Did you bring the ice down, spirit?'

'Oh yes, yes, I did indeed. Of course it was almost ready to fall, else I should not have been able to budge it. But yes, my powers brought the ice block crashing down upon our foes.' A sudden thought brightened his countenance. 'Say, that means I killed them, didn't I? I, a spirit, shed the blood of living mortals. Oh, this is a great day!'

Fost gnawed his lip. Myriad red streams trickled out from under the ice, scarlet threads weaving a tapestry on the pavement. He saw little to gloat over in the spirit's loss of innocence.

'My thanks, spirit, for what they're worth.'

He and Moriana supported each other up the steps into the Palace. It was a scramble at first. The falling block had shorn off the front of the portico and obstructed the foot of the steps, so the travelers had to climb up the side to gain the entrance. Still unimpressed by the Palace, Fost had to admit the Athalar had built well. Except where the ice had hit, the portico was undamaged. The pillars weren't even cracked. Painfully the two mounted the steps and pushed at the single copper door.

It swung open easily. They stepped inside. At first their eyes were dazzled by the quicksilver coruscations that met them. Then vision cleared.

'The amulet,' Fost said, scarcely able to move his lips.

The nave of the Palace was fifty yards long, yet the altar seemed only the length of an arm away. A pendant hung from a black marble stand by a silver chain, a great gem set in a silver sunburst. The silver glow pulsed from the white jewel.

White? Fost thought. *Was it not black as midnight a heartbeat ago?* Almost invisible in the shine of the radiant gem, a second amulet hung beside it, a poor thing hardly more than a polished grey stone knotted to a leather thong. Fost was amazed to see such dross so near such magnificence.

Moriana started forward as if in a trance, fingers stretching toward the brilliant, half-black, half-white gem. Fost caught her arm with iron fingers. She turned on him, eyes hot and angry.

'Let me go!' she spat. 'I must have the amulet. My people groan beneath my sister's heel.'

'No!' Fost dragged her face to his. 'I have suffered, bled and almost died on your behalf. How would you have fared if I'd left you to the Vicar of Istu?'

Rage was shaken from her by a tremor of revulsion. The green balefire died from her eyes. She slumped in the big man's grip. 'Ill,' she admitted, dropping her gaze. 'Even now I'd be trapped in the mind of the sleeping Demon, prey to his every horrid fantasy, and damnation would seem the purest of blessings.'

He let her go. He felt ashamed. *But life, life everlasting! I cannot let that go!*

'I'll take the amulet,' he said quietly. 'It's mine. It is only right, don't you see?' The woman nodded convulsively. Tears shone on her cheeks. 'There, I'm sorry. I . . . I'll help you fight your sister. How's that? I'll aid you in overthrowing Synalon. Everything will work out, don't you see? But, but I must have the amulet.' He finished with his hands cupping the air in front of him, spreading them in a lame gesture.

'I understand,' she whispered. 'I . . . I'll say no more about it.'

He nodded briskly. A little spirit seeped back into him. It's difficult for gloom to keep a grasp on a man with immortality within his reach.

He walked to the altar. Erimenes and Moriana followed like shadows in that shadowless place. Not even the pillars flanking the nave cast shadows into the walk-ways beyond. The floor, blocks of black marble interspersed with white, thumped like a drum under their boots.

Visions filled his head as he neared the mostly-white jewel. A lifetime – many lifetimes – to spend or squander as he would. Drinking, wenching, fighting his way through rollicking centuries. And more than that. He would make a fortune, a dozen fortunes, return to Medurim as equal to the wealthy to whom he'd once been less than filth. He would devote the span of a dozen natural lives to gleaning the untold wealth from the libraries of the ancient city, wealth he but glimpsed before. All knowledge lay open to his questing hand. He could be the world's wisest man, as well as its doughtiest warrior.

So caught up was he in his imaginings that he didn't notice how his steps slowed until they stopped completely.

'What's this?' he asked aloud. His jaw moved slowly, as though dipped in glue. He tried to raise his foot. It felt rooted to the marble. 'Moriana, what treachery is this?' The words came as slowly as Guardian's speech.

'None of mine, I swear it,' the princess said, her voice a slow roll of molasses.

Fost's head weighed tons, but he forced it round to bear on Erimenes. A whirlwind of suns shone from his blue body.

'Spirit,' Fost said thickly. 'This is your doing.'

'Naturally.' Erimenes beamed.

288

Fost's lips formed the word *why?*

'How can you ask?' The aquiline face twisted with fury. 'You stupid, selfish, senseless clod! I would have what you so blithely take for granted, what you so obdurately fail to appreciate. I would have life – true life! Yes, you understand, I read it in your eyes!

'The amulet gives the blessing of life. It will return me to my body. No more being dependent upon the whim of other, lesser beings for my sensation. I will take life in my own two hands and wring it until its sweet juices pour down my throat.' He raised his hands before him, shaking with passion. 'I will still live forever, with the amulet's aid. But I shall have a body that sees and smells and feels – aye, and lusts.' He laughed a sad laugh. 'Oh, dear Fost, dear Moriana, how could you be so foolish to believe I'd let you have the Amulet of Living Flame?'

'What happens to us?' Moriana asked. It was a struggle even to utter the words. 'I feel the cold entering my bones. Soon we will freeze.'

'No, you won't. You're young and strong, resilient. I shall take the amulet and restore my body. Then I'll tie you, though not so well that you can't in time escape, and leave you to your own devices. There's a good deal of treasure about, of a more mundane variety. Content yourselves with that.' He turned toward the altar, busily rubbing his hands together. 'Now, Fost, my good man, reach out and bring the amulet to my jar.'

The man's arm did not lift of its own accord. It stretched toward the amulets hanging from the altar. His eyes followed its progress. Then his gaze slid past it to the blazing gem.

Amulet of Living Flame, he thought. *It's mine. Mine.* MINE!

His hand stopped. 'What's this?' Erimenes demanded. 'Are you trying to resist me? Come, come, my man. It can't be done. I am at the center of my power. Give in and save yourself the effort.'

Fost frowned. The jewel burned like a sun within his brain. The black eclipsed the white. He ground his jaws together. He recalled the way Erimenes had controlled his limbs near the city of the Ethereals and the softly insidious ways the Ethereals trapped his mind. He recalled the helpless horror the way the tentacled thing, hideous and lovely, had wrapped him in the chains of temptation. And he remembered what had saved him then, starting with a spark within, growing, expanding, eating at his limbs, his rage like a spreading conflagration . . .

Anger!

It drove the creeping cold from his limbs, the lethargy that settled on his brain. *Come, rage, consume me and give me strength!* he thought. His eyes were fixed on the jewel. The fury built, and did the white push away the black?

He saw Erimenes's face twisted in anguish. He saw Moriana's lovely features slack with awe. But before all he saw the jewel, its silver fire feeding his rage, the blackness, yes, the blackness giving way like the shadow of the moon after an eclipse.

His hands backed from the amulet. Erimenes's fingers flew to his temples and clung like spiders. Slowly Fost fought his hand down toward his waist, the satchel, the jug. *Eternal life. He tries to cheat you. Remember!*

His fingers touched the basalt plug. Erimenes shrieked like one damned. The jewel blazed blinding white within Fost's brain. With a muscle-cracking heave he thrust the plug into the mouth of the spirit jar.

'Noooooooooo!' the spirit screamed as he faded from sight. 'Fost! Don't do this to me! I must touch the amulet, I must! I am so weak, so weak!' His voice died to a sobbing lament.

Air gusted from Fost's lungs. He seemed to deflate, falling to his knees on the cold stone. Still the sun-stone burned in his mind. *Life, life, life everlasting!* Did he say the words or merely think them?

It took all his strength, but he made it to his feet. His hand stretched out, and this time it was of his own desire.

Agony exploded in his heart.

His hand jerked closed spasmodically. His fingers brushed past the radiant jewel to clamp around the rude stone pendant. He turned, feeling his legs dissolve beneath him.

Moriana stood, and Fost saw his own heart's blood dripping from the knife in her hand.

'Fost, I love you – but I must have the amulet. Tell me you understand. Oh please, my darling, *tell me you understand.*' Her words came from far away, an infinity away, across a chasm of endless dark.

The dark encompassed him, drew tight like a noose and narrowed his vision to a single point: Moriana's face, beautiful, grieving, lost.

Then Fost Longstrider died.

CHAPTER TEN

Fost sprawled in the gracelessness of death before the altar of the Palace of Esoteric Wisdom. The stone amulet rested like an offering in the center of his chest. His eyes gaped at the ceiling, framing the last of all questions.

Moriana fell weeping to her knees. She covered her face with her hands. The courier's blood had drenched them, and they turned her features to a crimson mask.

'Oh, Fost. Oh, my only love.'

'Hypocritical bitch,' came weakly from the jug.

'Be silent!' she shrieked, beating gory hands on the satchel.

'Why? Haven't I ample reason for complaint? I have lost my chance to live again. Oh, ashes, ashes!'

'I have lost my love.' She sat back, wiping tears from her eyes. The first frenzy of remorse had calmed, leaving emptiness and aching.

'Love.' Erimenes snorted. 'A deadly way you have of showing it. More like a spider than a woman. What happens now? Do you eat the body?'

The princess rose. 'I'll have no more of you, spirit.' She went to the altar, picked up the glowing amulet and looped the chain around her neck. She held the gem in her palm. An electric tingle passed through her body. The jewel shone black like a dark sun. She sighed and let it drop between her breasts. Its touch chilled her.

She turned to kneel by Fost's body. Foolish hope brought fingertips to his throat, seeking any faint thread of pulse. There was none. She gently closed his eyelids and crossed his hands over his chest and the grey stone that rested there.

Tears spattered the lifeless face as she bent to kiss him. 'Farewell, beloved,' she said, her voice cracking like clay in the hot sun. 'I

291

promise you shall not have died in vain. When I have freed my City, and sent my sister shrieking to hell to join her eunuch lackey Rann, I will return and erect a shrine here to your memory.'

'I'm sure that will bring him solace,' Erimenes said acidly.

Moriana rose and turned her back. 'I hope you will enjoy his company here until the sun itself receives Hell Call.' Fighting to hold in her sobs, she began to walk away.

'Wait,' Erimenes called. 'Don't go! You can't leave me here!'

'Fost deserves better company than yours, faithless one,' she said. 'Still, here you will stay to guard over his body until my return. And ever after as well, accursed spirit.'

'Don't be hasty.' The philosopher's voice turned to honey. 'I know something yet that could be of advantage to you . . .'

Moriana paused, then fled, the tears streaming down her cheeks, the amulet beating like a second heart between her breasts. Erimenes called after her, voice rising in desperation. Only the echoing silence of Athalau answered him.

Silence settled in the chamber. Hours made soft transition from future to past. Then, dimly, sound encroached upon the stillness. It started as a rustling, grew to a dry crackling, became at last a rushing roar. A blue glow oozed between Fost's fingers. It seeped out to cover him, leaping ceilingward in a sudden wild dance.

Fost opened his eyes to flames. *Am I in hell?* he thought. Fire wrapped him in pain. A shuddering inhalation filled his lungs with flame. An incandescent point seared the flesh of his chest and ate into his palm. He snatched away the hand and sat up beating at the flames.

They were gone. He looked down at his chest. The mail had been burned away in a perfect circle. Yet the flesh beneath was not charred. An angry round red mark glowed there, but the skin was intact. To the side the rent left by the ice-worm's teeth exposed unmarked skin.

He blinked and shook his head to clear it. Gradually memories seeped into his skull. His eyes widened in astonishment.

'I . . . live,' he mumbled. 'I live!'

'A brilliant observation,' a voice said at his elbow. 'I didn't think you had it in you.'

'Erimenes?'

'Who else? Certainly not that backstabbing slut of yours. She took

292

the other amulet and left you for dead.'

'Other amulet?' echoed Fost.

'The Destiny Stone, which hung next to the Amulet of Living Flame.'

'Which hung beside . . .' his words trailed off. He stared stupidly at the satchel.

'Yes, fool. Your beloved princess stabbed you straight through the heart. You died, and in dying seized the amulet. Moriana took what you both assumed to be the Amulet of Living Flame.'

Fost felt his back gingerly. There it was, the tear in the mail her dagger had made on its way to his heart. He felt a twinge of admiration for her. It took a strong hand and a sure one to drive a knife through linked rings of steel.

He stood. His knees felt like springs. He swayed, then steadied himself against the altar with one hand while the other brushed fine grey powder off his chest.

'Where is the amulet then, if she didn't take it?'

'You're brushing it off your chest,' Erimenes said sourly.

Fost stared down at himself. The round burn on his chest ached, and it seemed to him to have the throb of permanence. On the black marble stone by his foot lay a leather thong charred in two.

'As I mentioned before, the Amulet of Living Flame had a finite amount of mystical energy stored in it. I feared it was near exhaustion, and I was right. You used the last of it in being restored to life.' The spirit sniffed, as though he were about to cry. 'The last! It could have gone to giving me that which I have longed for so long, so long. And you took it, you great, stupid, selfish lout!'

'It was hardly my doing,' Fost said defensively. Erimenes began to weep violently. The sound was so forlorn, Fost almost wished he had the amulet back so he could give it to the desolate shade.

Almost.

'Now, now, old ghost, cheer up. This hoodoo stone of yours has healed my lesser wounds as well as the greater. I'm ready to leave this worm-infested city. Will you come along?'

'Whatever would I wish to stay for?'

'This is your home. And of course your powers are greater here.'

Erimenes made a rude noise. 'Much good they did me. And what use are powers such as mine when they cannot serve to free me from this miserable jar? No, I'll come with you.' His voice cheered noticeably. 'I look forward to adventuring with you again, Fost, do you know? What do you intend now? To fare north through the Gate of the Mountains and sample the fleshpots of Kara-Est?'

'I fare north all right,' Fost said. 'But not to Kara-Est. Unless Moriana's trail leads me there.'

'You follow the bitch to kill her?' Eagerness pulsed in the spirit's words.

Fost shook his head. 'No. Not at all.' He laughed a puzzled laugh. 'I should hate her for what she did, Erimenes, and yet I don't. She murdered me but she thought she did the right thing.' He laughed again, more loudly. 'Maybe I don't feel bitter about it because it isn't permanent.'

'Maybe she'll do a better job next time,' Erimenes grumbled.

'Now, now, none of that.' Fost sobered. 'I want to warn her, Erimenes. She thinks she's got the Amulet of Living Flame and if she goes up against Synalon . . .' Fost paused, thinking. Finally he asked, 'What does this Destiny Stone do anyway?'

'A mere trifle,' Erimenes said. 'Now let me tell you of the rich treasure troves that lie all around you.'

'Think, Erimenes,' Fost said. 'Think how marvelous it would be. All the centuries of peace and quiet down here alone in the middle of this glacier, with nothing to disturb your meditations . . .'

'Very well,' Erimenes said with ill grace. 'It alters the luck of whoever wears it. Sometimes it works ill, sometimes good.'

'It alternates, then?'

'No. There is no predicting the sequence, though many have tried. So it was that the Destiny Stone, though in ways immeasurably more powerful than the Amulet of Living Flame, was reckoned far less valuable.'

'I see.' Fost pondered what he'd learned. The Destiny Stone could enable Moriana to best Synalon at a stroke – or betray her to her sister's unimaginable revenge. There was no way to guess which.

Great Ultimate, I have to warn her! he thought. *Why?* asked a voice in his head. *She tried to kill you. She did kill you. Why do you care what becomes of her? When it comes to that, why not join with Synalon and gain your vengeance?*

'Because I love her,' he said aloud.

'The more fool you,' said Erimenes.

'Yes,' he said. 'The more fool I.' He hitched the strap of Erimenes's satchel over his shoulder. 'Now, my nebulous friend, what's this you say about plunder? I'll do better pursuing our wayward princess if I've

294

gold in my purse than if I go blundering about in my usual poverty-stricken manner.'

Blood seeped into the ancient streets of Athalau. Blood congealed, blood froze. But somewhere beneath the ice blood still ran to the pumping of a heart.

When the ice block had fallen from above, a corner had struck the portico of the Palace. The ice did not lie flat on the street, nor had it entirely crushed the life from one who lay near the portico.

Like a wounded, pale animal, a hand emerged from beneath the upraised corner of the ice. Behind it dragged an arm. A second hand appeared, crushed and bloody. Between them the arms drew forth a body. Many bones were broken and much of its blood had seeped out to mingle with that of a half score of men, but that blood was the Blood Royal of the City in the Sky, and those of Etuul breed did not gracefully heed the Hell Call.

Prince Rann lived.

BOOK THREE
The Destiny Stone

For good friends
Steve,
Fred,
and Roger,
with appreciation
— vwm & rev —

CHAPTER ONE

Princess Moriana Etuul paused on the steps just outside the massive copper doors. The city's glow enveloped her. She breathed deeply, tasting chill and the mustiness of age, letting the polychromatic pulse of athalau soothe her. Her breathing slowed. The Princess let her head sink down, almost forgetting for an instant her grief, her remorse, her self-hatred . . .

An ominous crack from overhead brought her head up. Not twenty minutes before, she and Fost had fought side-by-side against the bird riders from the City in the Sky. The bird riders' numbers and her cousin Rann's lethal sword had seemed certain to overwhelm the pair. But Erimenes was in his home and at the center of his power. With his psychic abilities magnified in this glacier-surrounded city, he had dislodged an immense block of ice from above. It had smashed down, crushing the end of the marble portico fronting the palace — and Prince Rann and his men. The ceiling of the bubble that arched over Athalau was now veined with cracks, the ice rotten with age. The falling block had loosened others and the ponderous groaning from above warned of more icefalls. With a last heart-wrenching glance into the darkness of the palace, now the tomb of her love, Moriana dropped from the broken steps and lightly ran up the street.

The deserted edifices gazed down upon her, calm and empty, serene with the wisdom of millennia. The peculiar street paving gave slightly beneath her boot soles, adding energy to her stride. She found it almost impossible to remain depressed when she was surrounded by the glory and beauty of Athalau.

Almost impossible.

Impulse turned her from the street to climb a few steps and enter a tall, narrow building. Its face shimmered in the constantly shifting light. As she neared the door, she saw the façade was of some pale yellow metal scored with a billion shallow scratches cunningly placed to cast back light in all directions. Even in her dark gloom, Moriana marveled at the blend of diversity and harmony the Athalar had achieved in the building of their city.

Still unsure why she did so, she explored the inside of the building. The princess came to a foyer flanked by closed doors. She tried one. Locked. Humming a half-forgotten song of her childhood, she proceeded into the hallway, checking the doors as she went.

It occurred to her that she might find something of use in one of these long-untenanted rooms. Erimenes had spoken of great wealth stored within the city. Mere gauds and gold meant nothing to her. She was a princess of the City in the Sky, born to riches. Besides, she could not carry much on the difficult and dangerous journey out of the glacier – provided that a way *out* of the glacier existed.

She remembered the ever-filled water flask and gruel bowl Fost had found in the castle of Kest-i-Mond the mage, where he had first learned of the Amulet of Living Flame and the gift of immortality it bestowed. She had no provisions; she couldn't bear to ransack the body of her lover for the flask and bowl. Perhaps some similar objects were hidden away in this building. Or magical artifacts that could prove useful in other ways. She shook her head, blonde hair cascading around her pale face and masking her sea-green eyes. She had no real purpose to her search. She just had to keep moving until the great, raw, throbbing pain inside her eased and she felt ready to try escaping from the glacier's guts.

A door opened. Instinctively, her hand touched the wire-wound hilt of her scimitar. She dropped her hand and laughed nervously. In a city buried within a glacier for a thousand years, it was unlikely any menace awaited her behind a closed door.

The room proved bare. No furniture on the floor, no decoration on the walls. Perhaps an ascetic's cell, she thought, recalling Erimenes's philosophy of self-denial, long ago shed with his corporeal being. The princess reconsidered. Perhaps the room had been left unused or had been stripped of its furnishings when the Athalar escaped the ponderous advance of the glacier. She shut the door and tried another.

This one revealed a desk and four-legged stool. An irregular lump of dark green crystal lay on the desk. Lights flickered randomly within it, chasing one another like berserk fireflies, then winking out of existence. She closed the door on still another mystery in Athalau. It would take as many lifetimes as the amulet could give her to begin to comprehend the city and the people who had constructed it. She thought of Fost's childlike lust for knowledge, nurtured since his childhood in the slums of High Medurim, and strained again against tears.

Two more doors failed to open. As Moriana reached for the latch of the third, a wave of panic swept over her. She froze. Her throat constricted with the impact of the almost palpable dread. There was no smell, no sound, no sight of anything dangerous. But black dread pounded inside her skull and a frantic voice cried *no!*

Her fingers slipped toward the latch. Fear grew to almost intolerable intensity, but her determination to find what lay behind the blank wooden door also mounted. Her fingers found the latch and twisted it convulsively. She yanked open the door.

Death rushed her with a clacking of black jaws.

Reflexes honed in battle saved her. She threw herself aside as the ice worm hurtled past. With a splintering sound, it struck the door on the far side of the corridor. Giving a sinuous wiggle, it doubled back on itself, hissing in rage. Its putrid breath turned her stomach as the sword in her hand swept forth and struck.

The hideous head recoiled. A great gash opened in the translucent, corpse-white flesh. Foul yellow gore defiled the floor. In wounding the ice worm, Moriana had gained the initiative. She didn't waste that advantage.

Another sword slash parted rubbery flesh. The worm screamed. The head darted forward as Moriana swung her sword again. The ceramic-hard jaws had not yet opened. They slammed like a battering ram below her ribs.

She sat down heavily, gasping for breath. The room spun around her, knocked loose from its moorings by her dizziness and nausea. She tried to raise the sword and strike but she failed. It was a struggle even to keep the hilt in her numbed fingers.

The monster reared above her. The four jaws parted, the toothed sphincters above the maw pulsing in expectant spasms. Moriana looked into that mouth and saw more than her own death. If she died, the hope she held out for defeating Synalon died also. Her beloved Sky City would perish.

She waited for the head to descend, the black jaws to slice through her flesh. Oddly, the worm did not move. The sickness slowly ebbed.

301

Moriana edged away, watching the beast warily, certain that her movement would bring it out of its inexplicable lethargy. The thick annular segments that comprised its body rippled in exertion, but the monster remained still, as if held by some compulsion.

Moriana rose. A sudden uncoiling of well-trained muscles sent her sword whistling through the air to land with a blubbery *thunk*. The blunt head of the ice worm slumped forward, half-severed by the face of her blow. Rage exploded inside the princess. She swung the sword again and again, taking out the fear of death and failure on the unresisting worm, purging herself of the unbearable emotions that had wracked her since she'd murdered Fost. When only a goulash of severed flesh and stinking blood and fractured jaws remained, she fell back against the wall. The poison emotions she harbored within her had been worked out.

Then Moriana remembered the amulet around her neck. It granted her immortality. She'd really had little to fear from the ice worm — except that the beast could devour and digest her before the amulet effected her return to the living. Immortality would then have resided in the ice worm's belly along with the Amulet of Living Flame. The nearness of her escape made her shudder — she realized that even the possession of a magical device giving immortality did not make her invulnerable.

When she'd regained her breath and controlled the quivering of her limbs, she started off again. Purpose moved her now. She was still dazed by the closeness of death and her unexplained salvation. All she could do was wonder wanly as her feet led her through a maze of twisting corridors.

She came to a door no different from any of the others, but she knew this was *the door*. It opened readily. Her sword still in hand and her normal instinct for self-preservation returned, she stepped inside.

Well met, my child, a voice echoed in her head.

Moriana tensed. Her eyes swept the room. The walls were lined with shelves that at one time had been lined with clay pots. Some past disturbance had shaken those pots down, and they had shattered on the dark onyx floor.

For a moment, the princess was mystified. Only slowly did she comprehend what she saw. The fractured pots were simple enough, round-bodied vessels of wheel-worked clay. But they weren't common jugs.

Each one was identical to the one that held the soul of Erimenes the

Ethical.

I cannot clearly read your thoughts, child. The words flowed into her mind like soothing balm. *Yet I perceive that you walk near the truth.*

Some unseen force drawing her, Moriana turned to a corner of the small chamber. An unbroken pot leaned against the juncture of walls.

'Is someone there?' Moriana said hesitantly.

'I am,' the voice said aloud. There could be no question the words issued forth from the jug. 'I guided you here. Aye, and tried to save your life: I sorrow that I couldn't stop you from opening that door.'

Moriana stared. Realization dawned on her. Erimenes had thought himself the sole survivor of old Athalau. More likely, he had only been the first; others had followed his path, finding immortality bounded by clay walls.

This spirit, unlike Erimenes, had shown her kindness in trying to warn her of the ice worm. Erimenes would have done everything in his power to make Moriana fight to the death – and then would have cheered both sides impartially.

Weakness surged inside the princess. The floor seemed to bow and buckle under her. She'd thought herself alone in the city, except for ice worms, corpses loved and corpses hated, and the treacherous spirit of Erimenes. Now she'd found another presence. It flowed into her now, as beautiful and serene as Athalau itself.

Moriana sank to the floor, covered her face with her hands, and wept.

'Aye, child, weep. Let your feelings flow freely. If you dam them up inside, they soon will swamp your soul.' Moriana did as she was told. She cried until the blood-soaked and grimy sleeves of her tunic were sodden with tears. When Moriana raised her hand, the crying stopped, she felt calm. The momentary catharsis of butchering the ice worm had been replaced by a more stable emotion. While not a feeling of well-being, it was less jagged and wracking than what had filled her before.

Her sword had fallen from her hand and lay beside her. Ignoring it, she leaned forward to pick up the single intact jug. It felt precisely like Erimenes'. She examined the lid. Like the one capping the philosopher's jar, it was a disk of dark basalt forced into the mouth of the jug. It resisted her attempt to pull it free, then abruptly came loose.

'Ahhh!' came the satisfied cry. A red vapor curled from the jar in a

303

long unsweeping plume. Motes of energy danced through the pinkish cloud as it swirled, formed, and congealed into an astonishingly solid figure.

The rose-colored figure of a woman stood before the princess. What Moriana had sensed from her communication with the spirit was confirmed by its appearance: this survivor of Athalau was the opposite of Erimenes in every detail. Where Erimenes was stooped and scrawny, the woman was tall and robust. Her face was lined by the passage of many years of mortal life, but it retained a calm and dignified beauty. Erimenes' face was hatchet-lean and shrewd, dominated by the blade of his nose and etched by years of repression of every worldly desire, though his newly profesed hedonism kept his lips curled into a perpetual half-leer. The female ghost's hair hung unbound down her back like a pale misty waterfall. Erimenes' smooth dome of a skull was decorated by a fringe of scraggled hair. The shade reached out to touch Moriana's cheek. Feeling a spiderweb tenuous contact, the princess yelped and jerked away. The woman smiled at her.

'Do not be afraid. In the middle of Athalau, I can almost regain the solidity I knew in life. Outside the city, far across the mountains, it would be different, I think.' She frowned and added, 'But my years of solitude have left me sadly lacking in courtesy. My thanks, many and eternal, for releasing me from a durance lasting thirteen hundred years.'

'It . . . it was little enough to do for someone who'd saved my life. You made the ice worm pause before striking, didn't you?'

'The beast's emotions were simple and blunt, and it took me a moment to find one to manipulate that would keep it from slaying you. They are feral creatures, those worms. Their lives consist solely of seeking and slaying.' Her face creased with concern. 'My lack of swiftness nearly cost your life. Accept my apologies.'

'Apologies?' Moriana said in confusion. 'But you tried to keep me from entering the worm's chamber and then kept it from killing me when it had the better of me. I owe *you* my life.'

'It was my mental touch that guided you into this building. You were far away, and I failed to mesh my thoughts with yours at such a distance. But closer, I found it easy to deal with your emotions. I manipulated you, I fear. But your will is strong, child. When you wished to enter the room into which the worm had laired, I couldn't dissuade you.' She watched Moriana intently. When the princess smiled, the spirit also smiled. With a start, Moriana realized the wraith was practising facial expressions, unsure of herself after thirteen centuries.

'But come,' the ghost said, 'I am less than courteous. I am Ziore. What name are you known by, child?'

'Moriana Etuul.'

'Etuul? I remember such a name, though we knew little of the outside world in my convent. Are you related to the ruling house in the City in the Sky?'

'I am of that blood,' came the proud reply.

'A princess!' the spirit cried. Moriana blinked, a headache blurring her vision. 'Forgive me, child. I pried into your thoughts again. But a princess!' The spirit smiled more broadly. 'High company for one who was a lowly nun in life.'

'A nun? I didn't know the Athalar practised that form of devotion.'

'We didn't.' The spirit sighed gustily. 'It was my misfortune to fall under the influence of a philosophy propounded by one who died fourteen years before my birth.'

Moriana stared at her, a premonition dawning. 'And who was this philosopher?'

'A foolish man,' Ziore said with a frown, an expression out of place on her serene countenance. 'And a bad one, I think. Erimenes the Ethical. I am sure you've never heard of him.'

'But I have, Ziore! And your assessment of him is perfect. I came to Athalau with him. It was because we accompanied him that the Guardian – the glacier – let us in.'

'But how is this?' cried Ziore, dumbfounded. 'He died!'

'Just as you did. He survived, in spirit, much the same way.'

'Tell me of it.'

Moriana looked around. The remnants of shattered jugs about her feet gritted like dried bones under her boot soles. Her every impulse was to flee this forlorn graveyard of ghosts, to escape Athalau, to put distance between her and the city in which she had slain her lover.

Ziore's eyes went round.

'I know little of these matters,' she said quietly. 'We Sisters of Denial kept ourselves apart from the world and its ways. But I know this, child. The pain within you will fester and grow if you hold it in. It will destroy you as surely as the cancer that took my life.'

Moriana sighed. The spirit's presence soothed her, though she realized she was responding to a deliberate effort on Ziore's part. She

305

sensed truth in what Ziore said. She sat on a low bench and told her story.

It took an hour.

The words began in a trickle. Then the dam burst, and they flowed forth in a torrent that Moriana later thought she would have been unable to stem, even if she'd wanted to do so.

She told of her life in the City in the Sky. She was one of Queen Derora's twin daughters; as the younger, she was heir to the Beryl Throne. But her sister, the lovely, black-haired Synalon, had been a strange and sullen child. Moriana had been bright, compassionate, effervescent. Synalon had been the antithesis. Resentment sprouted within the elder twin and flourished with the years. In time, dark Synalon had recognized the seedling and actively nurtured it.

Moriana matured into an intelligent, responsible woman. She studied history, statecraft, trade, and arts magical and military. She was an apt pupil. Her mother the queen doted on Moriana.

During this time, Synalon drew ever more into herself. Her interest in external matters manifested itself in a growing entanglement in palace intrigue. She studied the darker branches of sorcery, which were of particular horror to the people of the City, who lived with the knowledge that a demon slept beneath their feet. Derora had looked on in distress but had done nothing to curb Synalon's dangerous magical leanings.

Two factions had gradually emerged in the Palace of the Skyborn: one favoring Moriana and the other Synalon. Moriana at first refused to take part in the unpleasant vagaries of palace intrigue. A series of near-fatal accidents in which her sister's complicity could never be quite proven had changed her attitude.

Life in the City had slipped further and further from the happy simplicity Moriana knew as a child. It was further complicated by the tragedy that befell their cousin when he was eighteen. Two years older than the royal twins, and barred by gender from ever ruling the matrilineal City, Prince Rann Etuul had shown every sign of growing into a strong and capable leader who would be an invaluable adjunct to Moriana's rule. He was a remote boy given to strange moods and fits of emotion; like his cousin Synalon, he dabbled in the black arts. His mother, Derora's sister Ekrimsin the Ill-Favored, had been similarly involved. Palace rumor had it that her death after the prince's birth had been caused by her summoning an entity she couldn't control.

306

But Rann, to his humiliation, discovered that he lacked any trace of magical ability. He threw himself completely and wholeheartedly into military matters, a pursuit for which he soon showed surprising aptitude.

As a young cadet in the elite bird riders, he was forced down as he escorted a trade caravan through the Thail Mountains. He had been captured and tortured by the mountain savages. They disfigured his face with an obsidian knife, leaving behind a network of razor-thin scars. Not content with this simple torture, they robbed him of his manhood with repeated applications of flambeaux.

Rann returned to the City. After recovering, he threw himself into military affairs more vigorously than ever before. And he emerged on Synalon's side in the growing struggle for power.

The situation between the sisters had deteriorated almost to the point of civil war. When Rann's spies on the surface learned of a jar containing the spirit of Erimenes the Ethical of glacier-swallowed Athalau, even further rivalry was touched off. If the rumors were true, he would know not only the location of the lost city but might well find out where within it rested the Amulet of Living Flame.

'The Amulet of Living Flame,' mused Ziore. 'I've heard of it. There were a number of magical items in the Palace of Esoteric Wisdom, but by my time their use had been forgotten. Athalau grew senescent in its final years, even as people do.'

Moriana bit her lip. She sensed trouble ahead. Yet her story impelled her onward of its own momentum.

She had left the City and her ailing mother in search of Erimenes. Synalon was much stronger than she in magical application, and the dark princess made a speciality of the sorceries of destruction and devastation. A magical struggle between them would be no contest at all – unless Moriana possessed the Amulet of Living Flame. With its life-restoring property, it could revive her even if Synalon's death spells struck her down. Her own magic required lengthy preparation, time Synalon would never give her in a real contest of wills. With the Amulet of Living Flame providing the needed time to weave spells not even her sister could counter, she would emerge victorious. Perhaps she might even be able to use the energies stored within the amulet to fuel her own magic. If she seized the amulet and returned to the Sky City, she had a fighting chance of overcoming her sister.

The jar containing Erimenes had turned up in the possession of a Realm courier named Fost Longstrider. She had tried to steal it from him in the middle of the night, but she was caught. She fought with him sword to sword. He had grappled her, and their wrestling bout had turned from struggle to ardor. Without quite understanding how it all came about, the pair had made love.

For all her confused and confusing feelings toward Fost, she still had her mission. As he slept, she had again taken the jug and slipped away. Then, driven by concern over her mother's welfare, she returned to the City in the Sky.

It had been a mistake. She learned that her beloved mother had just died. Before she had time to properly mourn, she was arrested by Rann and charged with Derora's murder. Convicted of regicide and matricide, she found Synalon usurping the Beryl Throne.

Moriana was sentenced to die – and the manner of her execution still caused her to shake uncontrollably at the thought of it. Death by torture was mild in comparison. She was to be given as bride to the Vicar of Istu in the Rite of Dark Assumption. During the early millennia of human rule in the City, that Rite had cemented the loyalty of the sleeping Demon of the Dark Ones to the humans. It involved summoning a part of the sleeping demon's subconscious and using it to animate a hideous statue at the City's center. The effigy accepted only those of the Royal Blood as victims. Suitably bribed by the ravishment, it would lend its power to the City's ruler. Even bound and eternally asleep due to the magic of Felarod and the Earth-Spirit after their triumph in the War of Powers, Istu remained a potent force.

Fost had rescued Moriana. He had followed her into the Sky City by hijacking a military balloon and made contact with an underground force opposing Synalon. Though the members of the underground ineptly failed to aid Fost, he had succeeded in freeing the princess.

Fost had learned of the amulet from Erimenes himself and claimed he had rescued the princess only to reclaim what was rightfully his. But there had been a more complex reason for the rescue. When Fost left the City with Erimenes back in his possession, he had taken Moriana with him. Moriana's skills in flying and aerial combat had assured his escape.

Together, they had trudged southward across miles of peril from cold, hostile nomads and Rann's Sky Guardsmen. They had finally passed through the Rampart Mountains and to the very glacier enveloping Athalau. The glacier possessed a rudimentary intelligence granted it by energies released during the War of Powers ten thousand years before. They had a final confrontation with Rann that ended with the eunuch prince's death and a last desperate struggle in which Erimenes tried to seize the amulet to restore himself to physical being. The bottled spirit had developed a taste for the carnal pleasures he'd eschewed in life. His desire to remedy the lacks of his prior existence had almost cost Moriana the amulet.

During their journey, Moriana had come to love Fost. He returned her love even though a barrier lay between them. Fost had a lust for knowledge that bordered on obsession; he had a lust for life, also, which delighted Erimenes when they first came together. The lecherous spirit couldn't have found a better companion through whom to pursue vicarious sensation. Fost intended to use the Amulet of Living Flame in learning all he could, drinking all there was to be drunk, and sleeping with all the women there were to be slept with. Moriana wanted – needed – the amulet to save the Sky City from Synalon and her insane ambitions to conquer all the Sundered Realm and reunite it under her iron rule. Neither Fost nor Moriana budged from desire for the amulet.

The dispute was settled once and for all in the Palace of Esoteric Wisdom when Moriana thrust her knife through Fost's back.

Finishing her tale, Moriana surrendered immediately to tears. She saw the truth in Ziore's warning of a festering emotional tumor inside her. The telling had sliced out much of the cancer.

Ziore let her weep, then calmed her with a gentle mind-touch.

'I do not know that I can approve of your actions,' the spirit said, 'but it was a terrible decision confronting you. Perhaps you chose wisely. I am no judge of such things. In spite of killing Fost, you are good. You have been touched by the powers of the Elder Dark, but it has left no taint upon your soul.'

Moriana raised her eyebrows skeptically.

'Do not mistake scars for taints, child,' the spirit said.

Moriana nodded, understanding. She leaned back against the wall, cool and firm against her body. The chill of the glacier seemed to seep into her bones. She felt adrift as if all the cause for her urgency had vanished. She suspected this was Ziore's doing, too. But Moriana felt her strength returning and did not resist.

'What happened here?' she asked, gesturing around the room littered with broken pottery. It felt good to change the subject from her own sorrows.

'Some centuries ago – I've lost count now – ice fell from the roof of the glacier. Only a small chunk, but it struck this building a powerful blow. The spirit jars were knocked from their shelves. From within our jugs we cannot influence material objects, though from what you tell me of Erimenes, once released our powers appear to be considerable.' Ziore looked in sorrow at the broken jugs, emotion rippling through her form. 'But when this happened, we were helpless.'

'I felt them die. They were kin to me. I felt their agony, their fear — and for a few, their exaltation. Life within the jugs had become wearisome, and it seemed a blessing to be released. But still, the shock of their final passing unsettled me for centuries.' Sadness radiated from her face, a desolation and loneliness that made Moriana's troubles dwindle into insignificance. 'But pain remembered pales quicker than other, more pleasant memories. I recovered. But, ah, so long have I endured loneliness!'

'You're not alone now,' said Moriana. 'I'll take you with me.'

'You will?' Ziore exulted. She clapped vaporous hands together in silent glee. 'I hardly dared hope!'

'That is . . . if you can guide us out of here.'

'I can sense the ice-worm tunnels, even from here. For all their unthinking voracity, I find beauty in their works. Many paths lead to the outer world. And once there it's a short journey to the Gate of the Mountains and lands beyond!'

'It can be an impossible journey without food.'

'Don't worry, child. Traveler's fare has been stored in the buildings nearby.'

The thought of eating centuries-old food appealed to the princess as much as eating the reeking, rubbery flesh of the ice worms.

'It's been so long,' she protested. 'You need no food in your state. I need something more than handfuls of ancient powder.'

Ziore laughed.

'We knew how to use our magic to keep food from spoiling. An especially potent spell was used on food intended for travelers. I think you'll find it as palatable after a millennium as the day it was laid down.' Ziore chuckled, looking like a small girl caught in a prank as she added, 'Not that it was very palatable when fresh. From what I remember, the stuff tastes like plaster. But it will nourish.'

'I've eaten worse than plaster,' said Moriana, thinking of Fost's gruel bowl and its tasteless contents.

'In fact,' continued Ziore, hand under her chin in thought, 'there are numerous items not far from here that might be of considerable

310

worth in the outer world. I see no harm in helping yourself to them. The original owners can lodge no protest.'

She drew up her arms and laughed, more like a happy, innocent child than the ghost of an elderly woman.

'Oh, to be free, to know companionship!'

Moriana smiled wryly. She wondered if the spirit would feel otherwise after she had renewed her acquaintances with humanity. Or perhaps her knowledge had never been that great, stultified as it was by Erimenes' arid doctrines. Still, the spirit's joy diminished Moriana's own pain for the moment.

'But what of Erimenes? He was your spiritual master, I suppose. Do you want to bring him out, too?'

'No.' The expression on the pale, rose-colored face surprised Moriana. In her brief acquaintance with Ziore, she had come to think of her as a creature of gentleness and loving strength, not of the bitter anger appearing now at the mention of Erimenes' name. 'His teachings led many to waste their lives as I did in contemplation of empty wisdom, empty because it denied experience and served no human end. And from what you tell me, he has caused hardship enough in the years since his death. How many of history's evil men weave such an enduring net of duplicity? I waste no sympathy on him. Leave him.'

Moriana shrugged as she picked up the jar. She made her way out of the room of smashed jugs, wondering what became of the ghosts of ghosts.

They paused to rest near the wrinkled, shiny inner skin of the glacier. This had once been the highway to the Gate of the Mountains. The road had long since been blocked by millions of tons of ice, but up to the glacier itself the road was still the most convenient path to travel. Moriana sat down on a bench of unfamiliar substance. It yielded beneath her form, molding itself to her body's contours. It was marvelously restful, and she wondered at the skill of those whose magic remained potent after so many years.

It was here the question she dreaded most was asked.

Ziore floated free of her jar in a fashion familiar to Moriana after her travels with Erimenes. The spirit now looked diffident as she asked, 'The amulet – might I look at it?'

Color rushed to Moriana's cheeks. Her impulse was to shout *no!* and pull back. Yet she didn't do it. She didn't wish to hurt the spirit's feelings. She owed her life to Ziore.

Moriana hooked her finger into the silver chain from which the amulet hung. Slowly, she drew forth the jewel. Ziore stared. The stone glowed white with only a thin crescent of black around the edge.

'It's beautiful,' exclaimed Ziore, 'but . . .'

'But what?' Moriana asked sharply.

'Nothing. Only . . . I thought it would look different.'

Moriana shrugged. Looking like a child marveling at an intricate toy, Ziore stretched insubstantial fingers out to touch the amulet. Moriana tensed. Her heart almost stopped beating. Erimenes had believed he could make the Amulet of Living Flame restore him to life by 'touching' it, even though he lacked physical substance. Would it restore Ziore to her mortal shape if she brushed fingers over it? And would that exhaust its stored power and render all her torment for naught?

Ziore sensed the tension in Moriana and looked deeply into the princess's eyes. Moriana recalled the great hunger for life Ziore had displayed in the chamber of broken spirit jars. Was it less fierce than Erimenes'? Yet slowly, grudgingly, she felt the mistrust leave her.

Ziore nodded, withdrawing her vaporous hand.

'You need not fear me, child,' she said gently. 'I would give much to live again, but not at your expense. I will not redeem the folly of·my life at the expense of your dreams.'

Moriana dropped the amulet. It still burned like a white beacon. She smiled gratitude, eyes misting with tears. She envied Ziore her strength of character.

Thunder made her look back at the city. The lofty buildings enthralled the eye, subtle and magnificent, as ethereal as spun sunlight. But the slimmest spires seemed to waver slightly. Disturbed by the fall of the block of ice that had killed Rann, the ice overhead shifted, settling back into its ancient equilibrium.

Moriana stood silently for a moment, staring toward the distant Palace of Esoteric Wisdom. Then, with Ziore's jar under her arm, she started climbing for the black cavern of the nearest ice-worm tunnel.

CHAPTER TWO

Blood seeped into the ancient streets of Athalau. Blood congealed, blood froze, blood streamed from fingertips scraped raw on the pavement.

Inch by tortured inch, Prince Rann Etuul dragged himself from beneath the block of ice partially pinning him. In falling, the ice had struck the marble steps of the Palace of Esoteric Wisdom, saving him from instant death.

Though he delighted in the pain of others, he was not immune from feeling his own. Many of his bones were broken; he didn't know if even the surgical arts of the Sky City would mend him. The vicious pain shooting up his legs every time he moved at least assured him his spine was intact.

A rumble from above hastened his strugglings. The ice dome overhead had been fractured by slow shiftings and pressures within the glacier. With one ice block fallen, the others would soon follow. A fist-sized piece ricocheted off the larger block in a spray of glass-sharp shards and went whistling off down the street. He fought harder to escape.

With a last convulsive heave, Rann pulled his legs free. He was hardly the picture of a Sky City prince. The black and purple of his uniform had been stained the color of dried blood. The clothing had dried stiff. He felt as if the pressure of the ice had squeezed the blood from his very pores.

He coughed, spat, then eyed his injuries critically. He saw no blood; internal bleeding could finish him before any possible rescue. He knew better than most physicians of the Sundered Realm how much abuse a human body could take. He had pushed others screaming past those limits often enough.

Exhaustion darkened his vision. The smell of age and blood and death clotted in his nostrils. He wondered if he wanted to live. The savage Thail tribesmen had already robbed him of that pleasure most men reckoned indispensable. The tortures were a surrogate, as was driving his small, hard body through ceaseless exercise with sword and bow. If his injuries could not be healed, still more of his feeble pleasures would be torn from him. Would life be worth much then?

The thought formed calmly in his mind: *Yes*. Those of Etuul blood did not yield easily, even to death.

He must report to Synalon and assure her he had not failed her once again. He and his men had been about to best Moriana and her consort when the world had fallen on top of them. He assumed the princess and courier had been mashed as thoroughly as his own men. He knew that the Amulet of Living Flame lay somewhere within the Palace of Esoteric Wisdom, even if he was in no shape to recover it personally. At the moment, his main concern was getting out of the path of more falling ice cubes.

Haven awaited him in a doorway on the left side of the street, flanked by decorative glass bricks running to street level. Like a broken-backed snake, Rann painfully hunched over to it. The world dipped and whirled about him when a groping finger touched smooth hardness. It was impossible to tell the difference between his own pulse and the creaking of overstressed ice. He forced his eyes open, blinked away the sweat that filled them, and forced his mind to focus on a face.

Magical power as well as political passed through the female side of the Etuul clan. But Rann was not without some basic sorcerous lore. He struggled to contact the one who was trying to contact him.

'My lord.' For a moment, Rann looked without comprehension at the face appearing in the milky glass before him. 'My lord prince, is it you?'

He sighed with mingled relief and disgust. He recognized the nasal, whining tone of the apprentice magician, Maguerr. The youth kept watch from outside the glacier by means of a magic seeing stone, looking in every hour to note the progress of the prince and his party. The rest of the time he was to maintain a loose rapport with the stone. By concentrating on Maguerr's thin and pimply face, Rann had drawn his attention.

The boy tugged his sandy beard in dismay.

'Milord, it's been the *longest* time since I've heard from you. Why, it's almost daylight!'

'Enough!' Somehow Rann found the strength to bark out the word. 'I'm hurt. Send for help.' Each syllable produced a spear thrust through his broken chest.

'I already did, milord,' Maguerr said, his head bobbing. 'When I no longer found you with my geode, I called the Sky City for aid. They are sending bird riders. They should be here soon after dawn.'

'Bird riders!' Rann spat in disgust. 'What can they do to get me out? Chisel a way through the glacier with their eagles' beaks?'

'They bring powerful elementals with them, lord.'

'My cousin's idea, I take it?'

'Yes, lord. The queen herself commanded that the sprites be sent.' A shadow crossed the pimply visage. 'She desired that you report immediately on making contact with me, most noble one.'

'I . . . can't talk now,' Rann said, exaggerating the difficulty of speech. 'Damn block of ice fell on me. Later.'

Maguerr blanched.

'But, lord, I . . . but . . .' He was caught between conflicting commands. Rann savored the consternation radiating from the sorcerer's face. At last Maguerr came to the prudent conclusion that Rann, being closer, commanded temporary priority. He swallowed his gibbered protests and said, 'Very well, O lord, to hear is to obey. But I must communicate with Her Majesty. What shall I tell her?' Maguerr's expression made it clear that he wanted to report success.

Rann smiled mirthlessly at the young sorcerer's understanding of the situation. Synalon was indiscriminate with her wrath. If Rann failed, Maguerr, not being high-born, would suffer no less – and possibly more.

'We overtook Moriana and her accomplice. We fought; they died.'

Maguerr's throat worked like a frog's. His eyes bulged. If an insect had flown by, Rann would have expected to see a long forked tongue dart out of the boy's mouth and snare it.

'And the amulet, lord?' Maguerr stammered. 'Do you have it?'

A vast, flat boom cracked across the city as Rann started to reply. The prince looked up. An irregular piece of ice detached itself from the arched vault of Athalau. The ponderous ice spear moved as if it were dipped in clear molasses, then gained speed, smashing into the ground barely a hundred feet distant. The shock wave stunned Rann momentarily.

'My lord,' called Maguerr. 'Are you there? Do you have the

amulet?'

With a sardonic smile, Rann regarded the huge block of ice that had landed next to its icy brother. The front half of the Palace of Esoteric Wisdom lay crushed now. Getting inside would require exhausting work; he dare not damage the amulet by allowing a fire elemental to approach too closely.

'Not exactly,' he said.

The long drum roll of the ice falling brought Fost's head up abruptly, a spoonful of tasteless gruel halfway to his mouth. The sound rolled like thunder splashing off the frigid walls. The taller buildings swayed to the beat of the massive impact.

'Glad I wasn't under that,' commented Fost, swallowing the gruel. He plunged his spoon into the ebony bowl again and scooped up more, which was dutifully replenished by the spell that animated the bowl. The courier almost savored the slop. He'd never felt this ravenous in his life. Being raised from the dead did wonders for a man's appetite.

'You almost were,' was Erimenes' dour comment. He peered into the city, blue brow furrowed. 'That landed smack atop the Palace of Esoteric Wisdom, I see.'

Something seemed to stick in Fost's throat.

'Desecration,' Erimenes sighed. His thin shoulders moved with such exaggerated despair that Fost laughed aloud. Erimenes looked daggers in his direction. 'Laugh if you will, barbarian. But this was once my city – the greatest on earth!'

'No offense meant, spirit,' Fost said, waving his spoon placatingly. 'But don't look so at me. If it weren't for you yanking that chunk of ice off the ceiling, I doubt the new block would've fallen.'

'And if I hadn't, you wouldn't be here to carry on so witlessly.'

'Well taken.' Fost forced down another mouthful of gruel. 'At any rate, I wasn't laughing at the damage done to your precious city; I was laughing at you. The thought of such beauty laid to waste depresses me, too.'

Erimenes did not look appeased. He folded thin arms, elevated his nose, and in a lordly fashion gazed out over Athalau. Ignoring him, Fost turned back to his gruel. But food would cure only part of the hollow ache he felt inside.

'Man Fost.'

The words rolled forth in a thunderous bass. Fost jumped off the bench spilling Erimenes in one direction and his gruel in another. The spirit turned into an agitated blue tornado as he tried to resume his form. Fost looked about him, hands on sword and dagger.

'You humans are an excitable lot,' the voice rumbled. It came from all around at the same pitch and volume as the falling ice. 'I had forgotten that, along with your poor eyesight.'

'It wasn't poor eyesight, dammit!' Fost shouted. 'And I'm not excitable. It was – is – I'm not used to being addressed by glaciers.'

The pause fell as heavy as the glacier's voice. It took Fost a few moments to realize he'd hurt the glacier's feelings.

He sighed. It wasn't enough to be saddled with a treacherous, lecherous, hypocritical spirit and a beautiful but idealistic princess; he had to cope with a temperamental glacier as well.

His bowl lay tilted against the end of the bench, disgorging a steady stream of fluid that ran down the ice-sheathed road in a stream the color of dirty wool. He wondered whether it would keep issuing gruel until the whole bubble enveloping Athalau was filled with the stuff. He was appalled with the idea of the timeless beauty of the city being drowned in murky, colorless, salty glop. He capped the bowl, still needing it.

'I'm sorry, Guardian,' he said. He looked around for a way to clean the bowl. He finally broke up some ice and rinsed off the bowl with it. Erimenes re-formed and stood by, watching with his usual expression of disdain.

'I didn't mean to insult you, Guardian,' Fost went on. Several minutes had elapsed between the first part of his apology and the second. He was beginning to adopt the glacier's speech habits. 'I was taken by surprise when you spoke.'

'I see.'

An ominous crack echoed above as the words rolled around the bubble over Athalau. Fost looked up uneasily. At its highest point several hundred feet up, the hollow containing the city must come within a few score feet of the glacier's exterior. It wouldn't take much to bring the entire roof hurtling down.

'I thought you might be glad to know that the other two members of your party passed this way not long ago.'

Fost's heart soared. Moriana took the road out of the city leading northeast to the Gate of the Mountains! With luck, he might catch up with the princess in a few days. How surprised Moriana would be, that lovely, golden-haired bitch . . .

Slowly, the courier realized that Erimenes looked at him strangely. At the same instant, his subconscious reran the glacier's words.

'Wait a minute! You said, "the other *two*". What other two?'

'Why, the yellow-haired one who claimed Athalar descent . . .'

'Go on,' Fost demanded, his boot tapping impatiently on the ice.

'And the other was, why excuse me, Ureminus, I'd thought it to be you who accompanied the princess.'

Erimenes jaw dropped. The news was scarcely less surprising to Fost.

'Impossible!' raged the spirit. 'There's only one of me! I and only I, Erimenes the Ethical, last survivor of Athalau! Accept no substitutes!'

'But there was another such as you,' the glacier said. Erimenes turned the color of squid's ink. He beat impotent fists against the air. If he'd been alive, Fost would have thought he was seized by a demon.

'An impostor!' Erimenes roared, his form shifting with passion. 'O gods, O Five Holy Ones and the Three and Twenty of Agift, witness now how I am wronged!'

'You said you didn't believe in any of those,' pointed out Fost. Erimenes ignored him.

'Hmmm, yes, ah, I was wrong. My apologies, Irreminas.'

Erimenes pulled together rapidly, so mollified by the glacier's retraction that he forgot to take exception to the mangling of his name.

'I remember now that this shade was pink and feminine in gender.' The Guardian sighed, rattling Athalau's foundations. 'I have *such* a hard time differentiating between you humans. You're so minute.'

Erimenes puffed up like a lizard in rut, preparing to flirt with the netherworld's approximation of apoplexy again. Fost hastily jammed the lid back into the spirit jar. The outraged philosopher faded from view. A wail emerged from the jug.

'Let me out! This instant, Fost, let me out! I must tell that oversized icicle a thing or two!'

Fost heartily thumped the jar with his fist. Erimenes gulped and quieted. Inside the jug, he was susceptible to motion sickness.

Stuffing Erimenes' jar back into its satchel, Fost set off at a rapid pace into a tunnel the spirit had adjudged to be the way out. A mere twenty paces shut off the light of Athalau. Blackness as thick and heavy as velvet engulfed him. He tried a few experimental steps, bumped his nose into a wall, cursed, and stopped. Even with Erimenes guiding him through this maze of ice-worm tunnels, he might encounter one of the builders. Memory of hard black jaws stayed him.

'Erimenes? If I let you out, will you promise not to squabble with the Guardian?'

'Why should I promise you anything?'

Fost sighed. A century of life and fourteen of death and Erimenes still acted like a spoiled child.

'Because I can't see where I'm going.'

'Ahh,' said Erimenes cagily. 'You need my glow to illuminate your way. And Moriana has your torches. *You* need *me*. Not the other way around.'

'Tell me,' said Fost, 'how many centuries would it take before an ice worm decided to see if a discarded clay pot was tasty?'

'A pot like mine? Oh, very well. But I won't forget this, Fost. You're brutal. *Brutal*.'

Fost opened the satchel and allowed Erimenes to waver into being beside him. Fost smiled broadly and got a scornful sniff in return. The light cast wasn't bright, but it did prevent him from colliding with tunnel walls.

Fost walked rapidly, avoiding the cold walls until a slab of ice slammed sideways into the courier and knocked him off his feet.

Erimenes shrieked in terror as his jug flew into the air. The satchel cushioned it enough to prevent it from shattering. Another tremor rocked the passageway. Erimenes swirled like a tornado, jittery blue lightning crackling through his being. He squealed like an orphaned shoat.

'Guardian,' Fost bellowed. 'What's going on?'

'In-intruders, O man.' Agony etched the voice. 'They come from above like the ones who came after you professing to be your friends.' The words came as quickly as any human's. Something caused the Guardian incredible anguish.

A lull in the quaking gave Fost opportunity to recover Erimenes' satchel and lash it securely to his hip. The philosopher still vibrated.

'Negligence! Criminal negligence! You, a Realm courier, allow your valuable cargo to be endangered by carelessness. I shall complain to your employer, sir!'

To think of his employer Gabric – fat, black-moustached and oily – made Fost grin. Gabric had enough grievances with his star courier already. Making off with the property of a sorcerer and failing to report back in were definite violations of the rules.

319

'Pain,' moaned the glacier, shuddering. 'Such agony!'

Fost felt tons of ice poised over his head. Guardian was shaking himself apart. The courier crawled along as fast as he could.

'What's hurting you, Guardian? Tell me!'

'The bird folk. They brought with them some demon of northern witchery. Ohhh! It burns. It burns into my bowels!'

'A fire elemental,' said Erimenes, voice jittering to the tempo of the quakes rocking the tunnel. 'The Sky City men are burning inward.'

'Yes!' The glacier's voice was the sound of tortured yielding metal. 'Their leader, the lying manling, still lives. They rescue him with the fire fiend. O Felarod, O Athalau, I have failed you!'

Ice shards erupted from ahead as the tunnel collapsed.

Face cut and bleeding from the icy knives, Fost dropped to his knees and crawled. Over the roaring of new ice falling, he heard Erimenes shouting, ' . . . other way . . . back up . . . yards . . . tunnel to north!'

The din deafening him, Fost raced for the cross-tunnel, death nipping at his heels as he went.

Steam geysered from the hole in the ice. The bird riders huddled around, filling their lungs with the astringent steam and feeling the war between the heat that bathed their fronts and the chill that lashed against their backs. The glacier shifted under them like a beast gone mad.

Shapeless in his heavy cloak, Maguerr hunched over his geode.

'The elemental is almost through, noble prince,' he said. 'Do you see it yet?'

Rann rolled onto his back. The city moved around and beneath him in constant randomness. The view above was obscured by debris, flecks and chunks of ice falling to shatter in the streets. All around him, soaring buildings had been hammered to rubble by plummeting blocks.

'Yes!' he shouted. His hand clawed at the glass brick as though actually clutching the young mage's sleeve. 'A yellow glow – red now – I see it! Water's beginning to drip down this side.'

Maguerr fought to keep the fire elemental in check. They were fickle, tricky beings, as were the nobles of the Sky City in their own way. A single wavering of purpose, of concentration, and they would all be screaming torches. The salamanders loved to dine on human flesh.

The bird riders kept well away from the sorcerer. They knew the risks of distracting him at a crucial moment since ice was not a normal diet for fire sprites. Only the strongest spells of obedience known to the Sky City mages forced the fire elementals into contact with water.

To bore a rescue tunnel down to the injured Prince Rann, the salamander needed fuel, vast amounts of it, to maintain its existence. And it needed to be bribed, as well.

The bird riders around the steaming hole in the Guardian's back cast glances at their tethered birds, shrilling and thumping wings nervously at the nearness of such potent savagery. Not one of the men could make himself forget that there were now three more birds than riders. No extra mounts had been brought.

Service to their City in the Sky could be costly.

Under their boots, the salamander bored ever deeper into living ice.

Fost barely noticed the cessation of the tremors. The impossible crashing, like all the world's forges in one, dinned on within his brain. His bruised, weary limbs still felt the glacier's shaking. Had the whole mass of the Guardian's bulk fallen on him he couldn't have ached more.

He lurched along, sometimes erect, sometimes swaying, sometimes dragging himself on hands that had become senseless clubs of meat. He was conscious of Erimenes hovering at his side like a nervous guardian angel. The philosopher's lips moved ceaselessly, but Fost heard nothing.

Blinding glare caused him to recoil. Fear clutched at him. Wondering if he had become turned around, he confronted the elemental impaling the helpless Guardian. He blinked, forcing his eyes to confront the hellishly intense light.

It was the sun. The pale, distant, antarctic sun.

He was out, safe, free. The journey through the bowels of a nightmare had ended. He'd lost precious hours in his pursuit of the woman he loved and was far away from the Gate of the Mountains, but the noise and pain battering his head had ceased. And the fear, too, the soul-rotting fear that filled the mouth with bile and the mind with white howling had subsided. He couldn't be trapped in a closed-in space now.

He pulled himself along the stony, snowy ground. A slope fell away before him. He rolled down, listless, limbs flailing helplessly. At last he hit bottom. The sun dripped warmth into his chilled soul. His eyes closed. He slept and dreamed of . . . *nothing* . . .

He awoke. The sun had fallen low and was about to douse its fires in the distant Gulf of Veluz. Dying light stained the world orange.

Fost was conscious of separation. *Shadow*. He was somehow shaded and exempted from the dying umber sunset. He raised his head in pain.

A great, misshapen figure loomed over him, blotting out the sun.

CHAPTER THREE

A round swell of petulance drifted up through the Sleeper's mind. Black in blackness, the creature stirred. Its mind and body were bound in eternal darkness. Yet the dreaming mind, the mind beneath, refused to be still.

Tenuous dream memory fragments of color, feeling, smell, floated through a mind that had not known these alien intruders for ten thousand years. Yet it had known these sensations recently.

Hadn't it?

Colors, pale, pinkish blurs – faces. Thousands of faces, faces of the soft folk, the folk of the ancient foe, turned toward it in fear and awe and – expectation. One face in particular contorted in a fear so intense that the Sleeper's mind experienced a thrill like freedom, like the destruction of suns, like a boiling in stone loins. The soft one was bound and helpless; its nude form awakened desires buried deep in the mind of the demon. Nostrils newly returned (how? why?) had drunk in the sweet smell of fear and excitement and the harsh musk of anticipation, not from the shape upon the altar but from the thronging multitudes. They awaited the captive's degradation like the blessing of a god. In its dream the Sleeper felt soft flesh yielding to it, enfolding it, causing hot pleasure to blast in pulses up its spine.

And then pain. *PAIN!*

The dream dissolved in a crimson wash of rage. Betrayed! The Sleeper had been betrayed again! Drawn forth from senselessness with the promise of pleasure, it met only the reality of pain.

Betrayed!

The word burst forth and shrieked through the stony corridors of its mind. It was ever this way. From the freedom of the gaps between suns it had been drawn to this insignificant ball of offal. It had been

323

promised consummation of all desires left unsated in the void by those who granted it life. It had reveled for a time in the nearness of benchmarks, by which it measured the immensity of its power. But that had begun to pall. It had come to see it was being used, bound by the strength of its makers to serve beings inferior to itself.

And then the great struggle with the ancient foes, the time of triumph and ultimate loss. Its lords assured it that it could not be defeated by the pale ones. They had lied. It was brought low, cast down, immurred in stone. The black soul that had known the freedom of galaxies now knew only the inescapable confines of a tiny womb of rock and magic. Worse than this, its intelligence had been forced inward and down into this endless slumber. Awareness came in fleeting fragments, yet it knew it had been more.

It suffered.

Betrayed! Always betrayed. It had served its makers well, and they had abandoned it to this prison. In blackness a black shape twisted in wrath and impotence. Black limbs thrashed at invisible binding walls. The ancient stone remained impervious even to fists capable of smashing mountains. Black waves of hate flowed from the sleeping mind like flaming gas from the explosion of a star.

In the City above, thousands of other sleepers stirred uneasily. Unlike the Sleeper below, they slumbered only from the labors of the day. Most slept on and soon forgot the formless dread that had for a brief instant invaded their dreams. Others, more sensitive, lay wakeful. Some rose and looked out at the gelid winter stars above with a new uneasy familiarity. After a time they, too, shuddered and returned to bed. Perhaps some sensed the nature of that which roused them, but if they did, they kept their minds carefully averted. Some things are too hideous to confront directly.

Like a great stone cloud, the City in the Sky floated northeastward. Below, the jagged Thail Mountains began to ease and flow into foothills that would become the central plain. A thousand feet below, Thail tribesmen in reeking furs shook fetish sticks at the City.

The City would continue on its path whether or not the Thailint mystics danced and gibbered. No one, not even the powerful mages who inhabited it, could swerve the Sky City from its slow but unpredictable course around the Great Quincunx of cities. It had followed the Quincunx since the War of Powers had stripped its original owners, the lizardlike folk now called the Fallen Ones, of their dark sorceries and confined them to the City. Humans had seized the Sky City by treachery and cast out the Fallen Ones, who had then shut themselves in a castle in the heights of the Mystic Mountains. They had played no further role in the affairs of the Sundered Realm except as occasional villains in tales told to frighten small children into obedience. The City in the Sky now followed its own whim switching course at the cities forming the sides of the Quincunx – Wirix, Kara-Est, Brev, and Thailot, and Bilsinx at the center. Following no known or knowable scheme, it proceeded a mile every hour of every day.

Vast wings reached into the sky. Eagles rose from the battlements bearing small, wiry men on their backs. A score, two score, then fifty of the warbirds took wing, orbited the City once and flew off to the south. Thailint watchers cowering in the rocks far below marked the grim manner of the troop. Not even the wild cry of an eagle floated down the wind as the Sky Guardsmen beat their way into the teeth of an icy wind.

A hundred miles to the south, just beyond the lower reaches of the Thails, they encountered another smaller party flying out of the snow-sheathed Southern Steppes. Now the eagles throated strident cries to greet their kin. The men saluted one another with weapons but did not speak. The party coming from the south brought a slight, still form strapped amid heavy furs on an improvised pallet. The newcomers swung about and took up stations surrounding the three eagles that bore the burden. Though every man was ceaselessly alert, eyes roving the horizon for sign of danger, none expected trouble. The City ruled the skies over the Sundered Realm. But it was not for protection that the men had flown to meet the stretcher bearers.

Gravely wounded, Prince Rann Etuul, commander of the elite Sky Guard, was being borne home to the City. His men had come unbidden as a guard of honor.

The Sky Guardsmen did not love their prince. They feared him. But despite his personal taste for inflicting pain, his discipline was severe but fair; enemies of the Sky City and its capricious, lovely ruler provided partners enough for the only sort of lovemaking the eunuch prince was able to partake of. A slacker could expect no mercy at his hands, but those who did their duty well had nothing to fear. Prince Rann did not have his men's love but he had from them respect bordering on worship.

High-piled clouds paced the City as it floated toward Wirix. With the wind at their backs, the returning bird riders made good time. They returned home just as dusk began to tint the sky scarlet. The unconscious Rann was removed from the stretcher and taken to his chambers in the royal palace. Nervous mages, their shaven skulls painted with cabalistic symbols, hovered like a cloud of gnats. Synalon had convinced them that Rann's life was more precious than their own.

For three days Rann hovered in the gray no-man's-land between life and death. His injuries should have killed him outright. Yet Rann had retained consciousness until the rescue party had finished strapping him to the makeshift sling. He only vaguely remembered the eagles lifting from the street up through the steaming hole far above. After that, all was black.

His own natural resilience joined forces with the sorcery of the City. By the third morning after his return, the crisis had passed. At midday his eyes opened, and he asked for refreshment. The mages on duty exchanged looks of almost unbearable relief and went flapping into the hall to spread the good news.

He was sipping boiled poultry broth when his cousin swept in. Synalon Etuul was a woman in her early twenties, soft-voiced and self-assured to the point of arrogance. Her sorcery and skill in intrigue had accomplished the death of her mother and the seizure of the throne that was, by tradition and law, her sister's. She was the greatest enchantress of her age, and she was determined to restore the City in the Sky to its former glory.

'Your Majesty,' said Rann, looking sardonically over the rim of his pewter mug. 'I'd abase myself, but my physicians forbid me to leave my sickbed.'

Synalon bowed her head in reply. Her jet-black hair was unbound and fell in gleaming coils past the shoulders of a gown the same color. Her creamy skin glowed in vivid contrast.

'It is we who should abase ourselves to you, Prince Rann,' she said, clasping her hands on her breast. 'You are the hero of the hour.'

Rann raised a skeptical eyebrow.

'You have brought the traitor Moriana to justice. The hearts of our people are lifted to you in gratitude. Moreover, you have secured for us the Amulet of Living Flame, a guarantee that we will be able to spread the benefits of our reign over this noble City for all time to come.'

'I haven't exactly secured the amulet for Your Majesty.' It took a

326

conscious effort to keep from saying 'Your Majesties'. He found Synalon's affectations amusing — amusing and lethal. 'The amulet lies buried under tons of ice. I must, in all honesty, point out that the ice fall might have smashed it to powder. Magical artifacts of such antiquity are notoriously fragile.'

'No matter,' said Synalon, dismissing the possibility with a wave of her hand. 'My prime concern was that Moriana be denied the use of the amulet. I desired it for my own immortality, of course, but no matter. When the Sundered Realm lies conquered at my feet, then will be the time to experiment and increase my sorcerous lore. Perhaps I can make peace with Istu. With the resources of a continent at my disposal, I can find some way to break damned Felarod's restraints and free the Soul of the City. Then nothing would be beyond my power! Nay, cousin, this is but a setback. It is not to diminish the glory of your achievement.'

Rann shut his eyes and lay back. He stifled a moan. A few weeks before, Synalon had been frantic to get the Amulet of Living Flame. Now she dismissed it as a mere trinket. For all her power and wiles, the self-proclaimed ruler was little more than a spoiled child. She could focus her interest on one thing only so long; then her desire skipped gaily to some new toy.

He opened his eyes. Hers burned like blue suns. He was slow to recognize that there might be shrewd calculation behind her apparent fickleness. With Moriana out of the way, the major threat to Synalon's power had been removed. Now the usurper could put her grand schemes into motion.

For that she would need her cousin.

Recuperation was a slow process for the prince. Not even the magic of the Sky City could heal wounds such as his overnight. And his iron will could demand only so much of broken limbs and battered muscles.

Still, the next weeks were a time of activity for the prince. He observed, considered, and planned. Within four days of his return to the floating city, he had himself carried to a great-windowed chamber where he looked out on the Sky Guardsmen drilling on their mounts. Shortly after that, he supervised the drill personally. He could not sit on an eagle, but a sedan slung between slow cargo eagles allowed him to fly among his troops, to watch, criticize, refine.

Militarily, the Sky City possessed both advantages and disadvantages. The troops of the City had a base that was virtually proof against assault, or even against attempts at assault. Several times in her wars with Athalau and the Empire, the City had been assailed by balloon attacks, but such clumsy transports proved bloody jokes when confronting the superbly trained and equipped bird riders.

But as far as the City was concerned, targets for bombings with rocks had to be directly below – and the Sky Citizens had no more control over the movement of their floating home than did their enemies. The only cities vulnerable to attack from above were the five cities of the Great Quincunx. And the attacks brought courted reprisals of the most devastating form.

The Sky City's existence depended on trade. No raw materials were produced within the City. All food had to be purchased or produced on plantations owned and run by the City's agents and then lifted thousands of feet upward to feed the small but well-fed populace. Over half of the water had to be raised by balloon; rigorous water discipline, collection of rainwater, and use of the Fallen Ones' 'magic fountains' – the aeroaquifers – alleviated the problem but did not solve it. Military material especially strained the supply system. Even rocks to be dropped on enemies far below had to be lifted laboriously by the great dirigibles.

If the Sky City wished conquest – and Synalon did – it had to begin by conquering the Quincunx. Fortunately, there was no difficulty in reaching the targets. Sooner or later the City passed over all its earthbound trading partners. And the land dominated by the Quincunx lay in the middle of the Sundered Realm, giving the territory definite strategic value in terms of further expansion. But the City's war with the Quincunx had to be fast and it had to be successful. A cessation of trade would starve the aerial city quickly.

Further complicating Rann's task as commander in chief was the lack of knowledge as to which target the city would attack first. They'd just departed Thailot on the savannah west of the Thail Mountains and were bound for Wirix, fifty miles southwest of mighty Mount Omizantrim. Wirix, surrounded by twenty-mile-long Lake Wir, was dependent on water trade. If the Sky City captured Wirix, that city could easily be cut off. On the other hand, since the City had never been known to double back on its course, from Wirix there were only two possible destinations: Kara-Est at the head of the Gulf of Veluz, and Bilsinx, central city of the Quincunx. Of the two, Rann thought Bilsinx the easier target. The Estil had domesticated huge jellyfishlike creatures from the swamps west of the city which produced lighter-than-air gas within their bodies sufficient to raise themselves and considerable loads. Though still inferior to the eagles of the City, the *ludintip* of Kara-Est gave the Estil the best aerial defense of any of the cities.

The wind blew sharp and evil a fortnight after Rann's return. The night before, it had brought clouds from the south to plaster a blinding white stucco of snow across the land. For all its brilliance, the sun above lacked warmth. And the very air sucked heat from unsuspecting bodies until Rann felt as if he'd been slashed with a hundred knives.

His body was still one throb of pain. The cold was torture this morning as it magnified every ache. Later he would welcome numbness as a blessing, but now he forced himself to continue with his task in spite of the discomfort.

A cup of medicinal tea gave the illusion of warmth. Rann sipped it as he shifted his bandaged body on the divan, trying to find the best view out of the balloon's wicker gondola. Beside him, looking like a small freak of a bear in his furry coat and hood, stood the balloon operator. And huddled against the curving wall of the basket like a fur-bearing crane was Maguerr, hugging his geode and breathing mist on his blue fingers to keep them warm. He was Rann's communications officer. In the past few days, the prince had grown almost resigned to the journeyman mage's presence as punishment for the muddle he'd made of the quest for Moriana and the amulet.

It had been a pity to lose Moriana, he thought. Sighing inwardly, he peered over the gondola's rim to watch the workers laying out strips of dark cloth several hundred feet below. Soon those dark patches would be real enemy troops and not practice targets. Still, better to have his mind on war than on the loving touches he could have given Moriana.

He sipped at his tea, so lost in thought that he hardly noticed its bitterness. Maguerr muttered his grievances endlessly to himself. Rann idly turned his attention to the mage. He hadn't yet caught the words of the youth's aggrieved litany, but from its rhythms he guessed Maguerr repeated himself too much to leave room for inventiveness in cursing.

It had been a pity to lose Fost as well. With the collapse of the Empire centuries before, the Realm had lost all central authority. Its roads and byways were constantly alive with brigands ranging from skulking cutpurses to young armies of cutthroats that occasionally grew bold enough to ransack unwary towns. Those brigands were the reason for the City's large numbers of highly trained troops. The trade arterials had to be kept free. Sky City bird and dog riders guarded caravans, its spearmen held innumerable outposts along the major routes into and through the Quincunx, and its patrols attacked known bands of highwaymen from the air.

Because of the prevailing anarchy of the Realm, the men serving as couriers had to be very special, tough, smart, and resourceful. Fost Longstrider had been no exception. Rann could recall no single outlander who'd given the Skyborn such difficulty. Even before teaming with Moriana, he'd bested several patrols of dog riders sent to take Erimenes from him. To add further insult to his crimes, he'd infiltrated the Sky City and stolen away Moriana. That and the pursuit leading up to his injury inside Athalau made Rann view the courier with a mixture of admiration and hatred.

He could use men like Fost. Mulling over the prospect, an idea came to the prince. Why not recruit as many Realm couriers as possible to use as rangers and raiders? Because of the Sky City's lack of population, tactical doctrine depended on small, well-trained units. For serious conquest once the Quincunx cities had been subdued, Synalon would hire mercenaries to flush out her ground forces. Even here, the couriers could be of use. They would know the best places to recruit such men.

Spun downstream by the wind like flotsam, the notes of a trumpet reached Rann. He craned his neck. A company of eagles rose from the City, formed an echelon, and winged toward his tethered balloon. Another company followed and then another.

Overhead, just out of the reach of missile fire from the ground, the bird riders formed a wide circle. These weren't Sky Guardsmen. Their eagles didn't maintain the awful, foreboding silence until the moment of attack. Their voices rang down fierce and wild, full of challenge.

From a fold in the land appeared a body of dog-riding cavalry. The bird riders broke formation and streamed in a raucous, squalling line to take up a new orbit above the heads of the ground troops. The wind whipped the dark cloth laid out to represent the enemy army. The cloth cracked with a splitting sound, crisp and harsh in the morning chill.

The first company of bird riders drove on the 'enemy'. They held

330

until their front ranks were twenty yards from the flapping cloth. Then a hailstorm of arrows broke from their flyers. The projectiles fell like deadly rain onto the cloth, pinning it to the ground in half a hundred places. The second company followed with the third close behind. When they finished the attack, they circled again, pouring down missiles. The ground-borne skirmishers came whirling forward, casting their own darts and arrows. The cloth strip lay still like a great beast freshly slain.

Rann nodded. This was his drill for attacking formed troops: soften the front ranks with an arrow storm from the air, further disorganize the foe with the skirmishers while the eagles continued to harry from above, and finally drive in with lancers for the killing stroke. Variations would be used as the battle required. His troops had performed well, but his keen eyes saw flaws.

'Get me Captain Sunda,' he growled at Maguerr. 'That first volley was as ragged as a molting eagle's tail. Maguerr bobbed his head and waved spidery fingers over his geode. Rann sat back, at ease in spite of the cold and agony enveloping him.

The Sky City's great conquest was soon to begin.

'You are sad, child,' came the gentle, clear voice through the moaning of the wind. 'Tell me of it. A burden is lighter when shared.'

Moriana sighed and let the amulet drop from her fingers. She had been contemplating it for some time, oblivious to the chill rush of the wind and the acrid stink of the small campfire. The amulet's color divided now between light and dark, but it was never still. The balance shifted from one moment to the next so that she was barely able to perceive the subtle flux. Neither shade predominated. Whatever the interplay of black and white meant, it was in equilibrium for the present.

The wind brushed fluffy snow in soft sibilance across the top of the makeshift shelter. Drawn back to her surroundings by Ziore's words, Moriana tried and failed to keep down a shiver. The lean-to provided poor shielding against the relentless storm sweeping down from the northwest. But it was better than no shield at all.

It had been sheer luck to stumble upon the herd of grazers. It had been greater luck still to find an aged cow, her white winter pelt yellow and dingy with age, resting amid tall, dead grass at the perimeter of the herd. With the wind blowing out of the Ramparts at her back, Moriana had stalked within striking distance of the beast without alerting any in the herd. A bellow of fear turned to pain as she slashed her scimitar across hamstrings and then across the softness of throat skin. The hailstone of hooves as the herd took flight had faded into silence.

She stripped the skin from the dead animal, cut off as much meat as she could carry, and continued on her way. The Sky City beckoned. She had unsettled business with her twin sister.

The single-horned ruminant's flesh was stringy but a welcome relief from the monotony of the Athalar rations. But the important item was the hide. The wind marched ceaselessly across the steppe this time of year, as frigid and merciless as a horde of army ants. The hide offered some protection. This southeastern corner of the Southern Steppes was crisscrossed by streambeds running down out of the Ramparts toward the Gulf of Veluz. In spring they'd froth with the runoff of melting snow, but now they were dead and dry. The long roots of the steppes' grass held the topsoil firm, forming almost perpendicular banks. An hour's labor with her knife gave a snug cubbyhole that could be roofed with the grazer hide. With dried grazer dung for fuel, Moriana indulged herself with a campfire, though only a tiny one so she wouldn't smoke herself out.

She sighed again. Rolling idle reminiscences through her mind was merely a way to put off answering Ziore. On the endless loneliness of the steppe, any human companionship was welcome, even a ghost's. And Ziore provided more than mere companionship. Her affection and concern sometimes seemed to cover Moriana like a warm, soft blanket. Yet even such snug comfort grew cloying at times.

'I'm afraid,' she said flatly. 'My sister knows more sorcery than I. With the amulet, I stand more chance against her. If I can find some place secure against her minions, I can engage her in a battle of magics. When her deathspells strike me down, I'll rise again to challenge her anew. Sooner or later, I will exhaust her.' Moriana fingered the glassy facets of the stone as she added, 'I hope.'

'And for this you must be physically within the City?' asked Ziore. Moriana nodded. 'What if you cannot gain entry into the Sky City?'

'I will gain entry,' the princess said, letting go of the amulet to draw figures in the yellow dirt. 'If stealth doesn't serve, I'll raise an army and force my way in.' She laughed abruptly, bitterly. 'I'm being grandiose today, aren't I? To speak of forcing entry to the City in the Sky when I sit huddled over a reeking manure fire in the middle of a blizzard with nothing but sore feet to carry me across hundreds of miles of barrenness. The way I talk, you'd think I was a princess and not a wretched refugee.'

They sat in silence. The fire burned low. Moriana dug into her pouch for a dried dung chip and threw it into the embers.

A feathery touch caressed her cheek. She started, her eyes darting. Ziore hung beside her. The aged and beautiful face showed concern.

'I believe,' the spirit said at length, 'though I cannot know, for foretelling what will come to pass is a talent never granted me, that you will find some way to reach this reckoning with your sister.' Ziore's eyes were sad. 'I also know that's far from all that troubles you.'

Moriana nodded, acknowledging the pain, grateful there was no need to put a name to it.

'Did I do right?' she asked.

'Don't be foolish, girl,' said Ziore, her tone brisk. 'You know quite well that only you can answer that.'

'I have to feel I did right.' She felt warm tears fill her eyes. 'I feel the anguish of my people as Synalon's tyranny grinds them down. And I feel there's more at stake than even the welfare of my City. Synalon is quite insane. She's in tune with the power of the Dark Ones, more so than any of the City since the ancient time of Queen Malva Kryn. I dread her ambition, not so much for what she might achieve herself but for what she might unleash in her mad striving after power.'

A wave of sickness, starting in the depth of her loins and washing outward, passed through her. She hugged herself and clenched her teeth against a mindless scream. Tears rolled down her cheeks, and blackness yammered at the fringes of her mind. She had been close, so close to that black maelstrom. The Vicar of Istu, animated by the sleeping demon's life, had held her in its stone embrace. The formless dark that swirled behind the statue's yellow eyes as they burned into hers had left its imprint on her soul.

More than anyone else alive, she understood the nature of the forces with which her sister so blithely toyed.

Another feathery caress touched her arm. To feel purposeful contact out in this friendless, icy waste sent a ripple of eeriness down her spine. The feeling passed quickly, and in its place came a strange serenity.

Moriana turned her head. Ziore paused, slim fingers on the princess's arm. The heavy maroon fabric of Moriana's cloak dimpled as though to the touch of solid fingertips. Moriana looked at the spirit in surprise.

'An illusion,' said Ziore, her voice a whisper in the strong wind. 'Another trick I learned as a nun in Erimenes' cult. Not all the master's gifts proved worthless.'

Bitterness tinged the words. After the ghost woman's initial vehemence at the mention of the sage's name, Moriana had been little inclined to press for an explanation. But those few words on Ziore's part said it all.

The princess reached out, taking one of Ziore's hands. The not-flesh seemed warm and dry in her fingers. She drew a ragged breath.

'Oh, daughter, daughter,' the spirit said. She stroked Moriana's cheek. 'You have need. Great need.'

Her fingers slid down Moriana's face, over the rounded jawline and down her slender throat. Moriana felt a stirring in the depths of her belly. She shied away from it, from the strangeness of it. Again she felt the touch of Ziore's mind on hers, gentle and sweet as the illusory touch of her fingers.

'Don't hold yourself apart from what you know you need. You must have surcease from your worries, or they will consume you.'

Moriana knew the truth of what the long-dead woman said. Fear of the future, dread of the present, remorse of the past, these were cancers eating at her from within. She let down her barriers and felt her soul fill with Ziore's warmth.

The makeshift shelter filled with a rich red glow banishing cold and reeking smoke. Moriana felt fingers slip over her clavicle and down the sloped plain of her breastbone. Despite herself she tensed in disbelief. She wore a tunic and thick cloak yet felt the touch with her bare flesh.

'Fear not,' soothed Ziore. 'Do not disbelieve. Erimenes' vile, life-spurning doctrines robbed me of much while I lived. Yet when my life was over I learned many things before the glacier drove the living from Athalau and before the ice fall robbed me of my unliving kin.' Her fingers cupped a breast. Moriana gasped with unexpected pleasure.

She reached out her arms. What they enfolded seemed no less real than Fost the last time they had embraced.

But no, she thought, I must not think of him. Now of all times . . .

She let herself slip into the sweet vortex of ecstasy. Outside, the wind keened, unheeded.

CHAPTER FOUR

Breath rattled in Fost's chest. He felt as if he inhaled sharp-edged pebbles. He tried to rise, but it felt as if the glacier had rolled forward and lay crushing his battered back.

He knew he had to rise. The shape outlined against the setting sun couldn't be human.

He groped for his sword. The motion sent pain lancing up his arm and stabbing through his chest. He gasped. His hand found the pommel and tried vainly to close. His fingers were stone clubs, unbending.

A moan answered his. A guttural, unearthly sound, it rasped like a potsherd along his spine. Trying to blink down the dazzle of the sun, he looked up desperately at the looming bulk.

The image swam in the dying glare. It finally resolved into two figures, still vague, still inhuman.

'I don't know why I came,' a voice said.

Fost blinked harder. Sweat burned his eyes. He shook his head savagely in defiance of the pain it caused. His eyes finally focused.

Tall in the saddle of her great brown bear, Jennas, hetwoman of the Ust-alayakits, somberly regarded Fost. Resting on his haunches beside her mount was a riderless bear, his red fur touched with gold by the setting sun.

'I should have left you,' the hetwoman said. She looked at a point somewhere over and beyond the courier. 'You made your choice and chose to follow your northern woman on her quest. Why should I care what befalls you? Answer me that.'

Fost tried to speak and couldn't, his throat filled with gravel.

'Ust came to me in a dream last night and said that I would find you as he rolled the sun-ball down behind the world.' She sighed, her sad brown eyes sinking to Fost's. Moisture glittered at the corners of her eyes. 'Your destiny is still tied to that of the People of Ust, it seems.' She added, in a hoarse whisper, 'And to mine.'

Fost sat up. With his limbs numb from chill and the beating he'd taken, he felt like he was pulling several hundredweight of sandbags along with him. Bright lights orbiting inside his skull were his reward for the effort.

The red bear lumbered forward. Its tongue lolled over deadly teeth. Confronted with those ivory pikes, Fost recoiled. The jaws widened. As it licked, the tongue hit him in the face like a heavy, wet towel.

He fell backward, squawking. The bear was all over him in a flash, as nimble as a racing hound, plying the courier's face with vast swipes of rough tongue.

'Grutz is glad to see you,' said Jennas, 'though you abandoned him.'

Fost struggled under the bear's loving attack and stifled the impulse to hit the immense, shaggy head. No matter how glad Grutz was to be reunited with his former master, the bear might lose his temper if batted around the ears by accident. Finger-length fangs inches from Fost's face kept the courier quiet. He managed to bury his fists in the fur on either side of Grutz's muzzle and pushed the bear's face to one side. He gulped a frigid breath. Air recycled through a bear's lungs wasn't the sweetest in the world.

He stood, using Grutz's fur for handholds. The polar waste wheeled crazily. He leaned against the bear's flank and finally fell forward, draping himself across the creature's back. He managed to straddle the beast, then lay like a limp rag. Without a word, Jennas turned her own mount and started off at a rolling gait for the mountains. Grutz followed. Fost hung on precariously, never having been much of a rider. And riding one of the Ust-alayakit's bears was like trying to keep astride an avalanche.

'I take it you know this rustic person, friend Fost,' a voice complained peevishly. 'I can't say much for her choice of pets, but wherever they are taking us must be a substantial improvement over this miserable wasteland.'

Grutz snapped upright, snarling in alarm. Arms and legs feebly wheeling, Fost arced through the air and landed hard on frozen ground. Grutz swayed back and forth, growling low, hunched to spring on the unseen intruder.

'Declare yourself, apparition,' demanded Jennas, whipping her longsword from its sling across her back. 'Are you demon or magic of the Sky City?'

'Neither one,' a voice from behind said. 'Merely the shade of a great but unfortunately demised philosopher. Since my loutish companion has neglected to do so, I shall introduce myself. I am Erimenes the Ethical, madam, late — if I may allow myself the clever turn of phrase — of the glorious city of Athalau.' The ghost chuckled at his own wit.

With great effort, Fost turned his head. His satchel had fallen a few feet from him, dislodging the lid of Erimenes' jar. A thin umbilicus of blue vapor wisped from under the satchel's flap. Fost was pulling himself to his feet when an ominous rumbling echoed down the mountain. Erimenes turned the color of winter sky.

Seeing a strange blue being appear from nowhere confused Grutz. He was bright — for a bear — but in his mind he held many of the insular attitudes of the Bear Tribe. It didn't take much for him to form the basic equation: unknown = danger. He attacked with a deep-throated roar.

Erimenes barely had time to bug his eyes and utter a strange squawk before Grutz lashed out with a forepaw. The huge scythe-clawed paw swept through the philosopher's midsection.

Fost yelled in surprise. The ghost poised above the satchel, a gap the width of the bear's arm separating his top from his bottom. Then he collapsed into himself in a swirl of blue vapors.

Fost regained his feet. Concern for the philosopher filled him with urgent energy. Erimenes had been a trial for him, but they were comrades. It would be bitter only for the sage to have survived his own body's death, the fall of his city, and the many strange perils of the quest to Athalau only to be destroyed by a startled bear.

Grutz loomed over the satchel, his wet nose sniffing. An outraged cry caused him to jerk back.

'Awk!' cried Erimenes. 'Outrage! Indignity! To be manhandled so by such a noisome brute — arrgh!'

Fost watched the blue vapor boil out of the satchel, shot through with blue-white sparks of anger. Relief gave way to amusement. Fost had never seen Erimenes reduced to such spluttering, wordless rage.

The philosopher wasn't mollified when Grutz scooped up the satchel with his paw and hoisted it off the ground. When Grutz swatted a foe, it stayed swatted. He shook the bag until finally curiosity won out over fear of the unknown. The bear stuck his nose into Erimenes' jar.

Erimenes howled. He winked into being above the bear and drummed the flat, shaggy head with immaterial fists.

'Oaf! Monster! *Get your snout out of my jug!*'

Jennas's sword drooped in her hands. She gaped as she tried to assimilate the spectacle of a war beast beset by an infuriated ghost. As Grutz took the jug in both paws and shook it, Erimenes' complaints soared an octave. Fost did the only thing he could. He fell down, laughing.

Strain, danger and exhaustion took their toll. Fost's laughter quickly turned to shrill hysteria. Alarmed by the sound of his friend's voice, Grutz tossed the jar away, provoking a fresh outcry from Erimenes, and came to stand over Fost. He licked the courier's livid face.

The danger of being drowned by the bear's sloppy goodwill brought Fost a measure of sobriety. He only giggled now as he pushed the bear away. From off in the rocks, Erimenes vented language unlike any Fost had heard since his days on the docks in High Medurim. Fost wiped bear slobber from his face.

Jennas stared at him. The only sounds now were the wind whispering through the Ramparts, Grutz's stertorous breathing, and Erimenes' chanson of profanity. The nomad woman shook her head in wonder.

'It is truly said,' she sighed, 'that those touched by the gods are touched with madness.' Reslinging her sword, Jennas turned her bear around and again set off for the mountains.

It took three days to cross the mountains and a fourth to reach the winter camp of the Ust-alayakits. During most of the journey, Erimenes kept still, sulking over his ill treatment by the bear. Fost enjoyed the respite.

Explaining the spirit had been hard enough. The People of Ust, ingrained by long years of war with their neighbors, the Badger Clan, had an instinctive dread of magic. The semi-nomadic Hurinzyn had been under the sway of their shaman Kleta-atelk, whose obscene magical experiments transformed animals and humans into monsters. His depredations of the Ust-alayakits had proven too much even for the valor and skill of the Bear Tribe. They had just embarked on a final, all-out suicidal raid on Kleta-atelk when they happened upon Fost. Rescuing him from the bird riders, they had extracted the promise of his aid against the Badger Clan sorcerer. The Ust-alayakits custom of killing all strangers in their realm helped wrest this promise from him.

All had worked out for the best. Fost had led an attack and had come upon the Badger clansmen from above. Kleta-atelk had been directing his horrors in the destruction of the Ust-alayakits when Fost dropped a twenty-pound stone on him. Her people released from the threat of further sorcery, Jennas had agreed to guide Fost through the treacherous Rampart Mountains, though she had pleaded with him to remain and become a member of the Bear Tribe.

The fear of sorcery remained even after Kleta-atelk's death. Jennas suggested dropping Erimenes into the next abyss.

Erimenes talked her out of it. His continued survival, he explained, was due to his tremendous intellect and strength of character which had allowed him to live on incorporeally after his body died. Athalar magic was a misnomer; the Athalar used their mental powers, not spells and captive spirits to work their wonders. Jennas hadn't been fully convinced, but like Fost, she came to the conclusion that a being so utterly garrulous posed no threat, unless it was death by boredom. But that night Fost found himself agreeable to Jennas's suggestion of tossing the philosopher down a crevasse.

They had pitched a tent in the lee of a snow-burdened tree and had eaten supper by the smoky yellow light of a brazier fueled by resin pellets. Chewing the tough, jerked meat, Fost told the story of his foray into Athalau with Moriana and Erimenes. Jennas nodded knowingly at the account of the princess's backstabbing and expressed satisfaction at the thought that Moriana had the wrong amulet.

'If it is capable of wreaking great misfortune on its bearer,' she said, 'perhaps it will bring fitting retribution for her crime. To stab a comrade in the back . . . honor knows no fouler breach.'

'She did what she thought was best,' said Fost, staring into the tiny flames. 'I want to catch up with her and warn her of her mistake.'

Jennas only shook her head.

They soon crawled into their bedrolls. Fost wasn't surprised when a warm and naked Jennas wriggled into his bag with him. Her mouth covered his, tongue probing deep, hand searching for the sudden hardness between his legs. Lust burst like a bomb inside him. Later he would reflect that he had needed the reaffirmation of life provided by lovemaking, that his need sprang from soul as well as loins. He had no such thoughts now. His mind filled with his need for her as his hand fumbled with the thatch between her smoothly muscled thighs. She rolled atop him.

'If you'd remove yourselves from that ridiculous gunny sack,' Erimenes said with marked asperity, 'you'd not only be more comfortable, you'd also be affording me a better view of the proceedings.'

Jennas jerked herself off Fost as though his manhood had blazed white-hot inside her. They thrashed like drowning kittens in a bag, then she stood over Fost, shivering, bare skin sheened with the sweat of desire and goosefleshed with chill.

'You make sport of me?' she raged, dividing her rage impartially between Fost and Erimenes. 'You think me nothing but a plaything for your dirty games?' She burrowed back into the depths of her own bedroll.

In the library at High Medurim while he was under the tutelage of the pedagogue Ceratith, Fost had read a text on ethnology prepared by the Imperial University. The treatise had said that nomads tended toward sexual conservatism and even prudishness. The teenaged gutter urchin had stuffed this morsel of knowledge into his voracious mind and read on, digesting it as thoughtlessly as he did the food given him by Ceratith.

He had thought his earlier experiences with Jennas had given the lie to that Imperial text; she had led Fost through a series of erotic combinations that would have been the envy of a Kara-Est courtesan. Now he learned a new truth about the bear-riding people of the Southern Steppes: what they did in privacy was one thing, public exhibitionism was another. Erimenes being dead, it hadn't occurred to Jennas that he might prove an avid voyeur. The spirit's suggestions filled her with a righteous indignation that included Fost. In her outrage, the chieftainess assumed Fost wanted his vaporous companion to witness their passion.

Fost had been too exhausted in mind and too aroused in body to give any thought to Erimenes, Jennas's powerful body writhing against his, her musk heady in his nostrils, had driven all else from his awareness. His attempts to tell her this elicited only stony silence from the woman. Fost finally gave up and rolled onto his back. He stirred himself to reach over and give Erimenes' jug a hearty thwack when the sage complained at the sudden cessation of the evening's entertainment. The courier eventually went to sleep, feeling robbed and angry.

Fost assumed sourly that his physical liason with Jennas was done.

The woman felt her honor besmirched. She wouldn't forgive him. Or so he thought until the small hours of the morning when Jennas emerged from her bedroll, heaved a protesting Erimenes out the front flap of the tent, and rejoined Fost in his sleeping bag. She uttered no word but her mouth spoke eloquently.

In the morning, Erimenes brooded upon the injustice of his summary eviction as well as the mistreatment at the paws of Grutz. Crushed by the weight of indignities heaped upon him, Erimenes fell into a sullen silence all the way to the bear-rider's camp in the foothills north of the Ramparts.

Somehow, Fost didn't miss the philosopher's repartee, especially in the dead of the night when he and Jennas fought the cold in their own very special way.

'You're determined to go on, then?' the fat woman asked. Fost nodded, distracted by his effort to keep his gorge from rising due to the aroma wafting up from his earthen cup.

'Good!' the woman cried, a hearty backslap knocking the breath from his body. He slopped the hot, stinging brew into his lap. 'Small is the soul craving no adventure. Jennas may sit there looking baleful, but mind you, boy, she'd have it no other way.'

Vancha Broad-Ax took a healthy swig of her own tea and beamed at Fost as though she'd just finished sculpting him from clay. Fost, feeling the tea corroding his crotch, managed a grin in response. The subchief of the Ust-alayakits was a vast, coarse woman, outstandingly ugly with a squashed nose spread across a visage reddened by wind and drink. Her hair was a faded reddish-orange tangle. Her eyes gleamed like emeralds inset in the fatty rolls of her face. She wore a leather harness studded with bronze, and bronzen torques as thick as two of Fost's fingers encircled arms as big as the courier's thighs. Vancha was loud, exuberant, mercurial, and apparently seldom sober.

Fost liked her immensely.

He felt the pressure of Jennas's hip against his. A warm tingle stirred his crotch, only partially dampened by the now-cooling tea. He took a sip from his cup and shuddered. The four of them in Jennas's tent were drinking *amasinj,* the favored drink of the Ust-alayakits. He didn't mind the astringent herb tea; it was the distilled *ofilos*-tree sap liquor the bear people added to it in liberal quantities to give it strength that watered his eyes and crisped his nose hairs.

Vancha poured the stuff down her throat in torrents until Fost expected smoke to pour from her bangled ears. Jennas downed it with a will, too, though not with the relish of her second chief.

As always, Fost felt time pressing him onward. Yet now he had stayed with the People of Ust for a week. His hurts needed healing, but the luxury of relaxing among friends uncovered deeper wounds. Sometimes in the night he clung to Jennas and whimpered like a whipped puppy. She held him, comforted him, and thought no less of him. The Ust-alayakits did not believe in hiding their emotions. And any who could answer the Hell Call and return sane needed no further proof of strength and courage.

But the time had come for leaving. Tomorrow Fost would go north in pursuit of Moriana. Tonight he, Jennas, Vancha and Vancha's young consort Rinzi — and Erimenes — had gathered for a quiet celebration.

'Care well for my people when I am gone, Vancha,' said Jennas smiling. But her expression wasn't reflected in her eyes. Vancha laughed uproariously.

'I shall be a mother to them all,' she declared. 'But it hurts me to be left behind. Put Lurnum or Vixo in charge and let me accompany you. Little Sister is vexed at having missed the bloodletting at the caves of the Hurinzyn.' Little Sister lay on a pillow on the other side of Vancha's bulk from the slender Rinzi. Vancha patted her affectionately. Little Sister shifted, sending shafts of reflected firelight dancing from her blue steel blade.

The ax was of the same monumental proportions as its owner. A three-foot shaft of black hardwood from the Tanzul Forest, as rare as valuable silver on the treeless steppe, was affixed to a broad, spike-backed head weighing fully five pounds. The weapon filled Fost with awe. Despite the exploits of the brawny heroes of Medurimite romance, five pounds' total weight was usually the maximum. Vancha could wield Little Sister with one meaty hand while she held a beaten-brass buckler in the other.

He had always assumed the barbarians of the Southern Steppe chose their leaders by combat. Vancha was easily the strongest of all the several hundred Ust-alayakits. She outweighed Fost and Jennas combined and could break either like a reed in the wind. Yet Jennas seemed to feel no compunction about naming her subchief guardian of her daughter Duri and going off with Fost, leaving Vancha to rule in her absence.

'I fear your Little Sister will drink her fill all too soon,' said Jennas, staring moodily into the flames.

'What's that, girl?' Vancha demanded. 'Have you had a vision?' Jennas nodded.

'What are you talking about?' asked Erimenes. 'Is there a nice, bloody war in the offing? If so, I may stay here and let Fost wend his weary way north without me. I shouldn't like my jar to get cracked by some ignorant ruffian.'

'Ust should so favor me,' Fost said dourly.

Jennas's glance was sharp.

'You, of all people, shouldn't use Ust's name so lightly.' Fost dropped his eyes from hers, feeling warmth touch his cheeks. The hetwoman gripped his arm in an iron band. 'I go north with you because you have done the Ust-alayakits greater service than we can ever hope to repay – and because I want to be with you, though your heart is with that northerner wench. But these things aren't enough to make me leave my people, even in Vancha's capable hands.'

Fost looked up at her, the question in his eyes.

'No,' she said with a bitter laugh. 'I'm no young girl to go mooning off after you like a pet goat. You're a man like no other I've known, Fost Longstrider, but not even you can take me from my people, not even if you gave me all your love and forswore this princess.' She shook her head. 'Not unless the welfare of my people lay in my going with you.'

Fost stared at her. Her proud, high-cheekboned face was set into grim lines. He looked at the others. Erimenes looked bored, Ranzi diffident. A hard glint showed in Vancha's eyes.

'What do you mean?' he asked.

'Danger is building in the world like a storm gathering thunderheads,' Vancha said. 'Our hetwoman fares north to assess the danger. She fears the wind may soon blow foul for the People of Ust.'

'I don't know what you're talking about. There's peril, to be sure, but that lies on the path before *me*. It doesn't have anything to do with your folk.'

'But it does,' said Jennas. 'I feel it. Ust sends me dreams. There is a power – and malice – in the north. They grow. They shall soon break free, and their fury will not spare the people of the steppes.'

'Do you mean the Sky City? They plan for war, true enough. They might conquer the Quincunx Cities, but they can't harm you here. Their city won't leave its travel pattern, and the bird riders have too much trouble with the winged foxes in the Ramparts to carry on a campaign against you.'

'It's not their soldiers we fear,' Vancha said, 'but their sorcery.'

A chill wind blew along Fost's spine. He recalled the ape-thing that had pursued him through the keep of Kest-i-Mond the mage. And unbidden came the memory of the yellow hellfire glowing in the Vicar of Istu's eyes as it lustfully raped Moriana.

'But they're hundreds of miles to the north. And Synalon can't come here to work her magic against you. She's tied to the City itself. She derives her power from it . . .'

'From the Child of the Dark Ones,' whispered Jennas. 'From That Which Sleeps in the foundations of their accursed city. Whom Felarod bound in the War of Powers . . .'

' . . . for all time,' Fost finished.

Vancha leaned forward. Joviality slipped from her as if it were a cowl. Her face glinted like brass in the flamelight.

'We live here beneath sky and wind, outlander. From them we've learned *nothing lasts forever*.'

'But Felarod had the aid of the Three and Twenty Wise Ones. The World-Spirit itself helped him bind Istu. That's a power not easily overcome.'

'Not *easily*,' Vancha agreed. 'But the Dark Ones have had ten millennia in which to work. In that time, a tiny rivulet can wear a deep cleft through the hardest stone. *They* are no tiny dribbling. Their evil is a rushing torrent.'

He looked from one to the other. He accepted the existence of beings beyond his plane of existence. Fire elementals, the occasional demon, even Erimenes, were more or less part of everyday existence. The gods, though, whether the Wise or the Dark, were distant beings aloof from the affairs of men. Fost didn't entirely believe in them for all that Jennas claimed he was a sending from Ust. And if they did exist, it seemed to him they ought to keep a decent distance from the mortal world. That they might again take more of a hand in earthly events . . .

'I think you go too far. You're talking about a Second War of Powers.' He shook himself as a wet dog sheds water.

'I am,' Jennas said flatly.

Uneasy quiet filled the tent. Fost gulped his *amasinj*, welcoming now the acrid taste. It distracted him from the foreboding that grew in his guts. A War of Powers! But that was ancient history so far in the past that it had slipped into legend. Something so distant, so immense could not belong to the present day. The cosmic disruption, the deadly struggle of powers that tipped the very world on its axis couldn't intrude on the life of Fost Longstrider.

Could it?

Vancha sighed, belched, and drained her cup.

'Ahhh,' she said, smacking her lips in satisfaction. 'We're in deadly danger of becoming serious. Let us drink, my friends. Drink to Fost and Jennas and their epic journey to the wild and unknown lands of the North!' She caught up the *amasinj* pot from the brazier and filled their cups to the brim. A robust infusion of the beverage brought gaiety back. But it was strained, fragile, as if the revelers sensed an intruding monstrous presence lurking in the shadows of the tent.

When the evening was done, when the two moons had come down from heaven and Vancha had gone reeling off to her own tent with one arm wrapped around Rinzi, Fost and Jennas turned blindly to each other. They strove furiously, savagely, bodies guided by the dying light. When their passion and energy had been spent, they fell into a troubled sleep.

Fost would always try to convince himself that he did not dream that night. But in later days he often wondered if that were true.

Moriana scarcely believed her good fortune. The blizzard that had blown for two days out of the Thail Mountains to the northwest had left most of its snow on the prairies of the Quincunx, with only flurries and biting winds to lash at the steppe. She need fear no further snowbanks, but still she was almost out of her mind with worry thinking of what her sister planned – accomplished – while she plodded endlessly beneath the lifeless gray sky. Neither Ziore's soothing touch on her mind nor the nimble erotic tricks that left Moriana gasping with passion could ease the princess's fear.

But now chance gave her a gift so great she scarcely believed the testimony of her eyes.

She huddled in an arroyo beneath the husk of a ground-hugging bush, peering over the lip of the cut-bank. Not fifteen yards away sat a man. He was small, and the tunic sleeve on the arm appearing from within the folds of his cloak was purple edged in black. Near him stood an eagle, almost twelve feet tall at the crest of his skull, wings spread over a tiny fire for warmth.

The bird was a lean, wide-winged scout and not a deep-chested warbird like Moriana's lost Ayoka. But it was a riding bird of the City. The storm winds from the north and west had brought snow, but they had brought this hapless bird and its rider, blowing them miles from Sky City-patrolled terrain.

The princess rolled her amulet between her fingers as she pondered. The many-faceted gem showed only a thin fingernail of black along one edge. Otherwise, it was as white as the snow left behind by the blizzard. Ziore had given her warning that they approached another human. Moriana had ducked into the gully until the spirit told her they were near the presence she sensed. By good fortune, the stranded bird rider had his back to the gully.

The eagle shook its wings and gave a racking cough. This wet, frigid weather didn't agree with him. The cold didn't agree with the bird rider either. His form trembled beneath his cloak. Now and then he shook his head, muttering curses to himself. The wind died to sporadic blustering. It wouldn't be long before he took to the sky again and began the long flight to the blessed warmth of barracks and aerie.

Moriana consulted with Ziore. She had no wish to kill this unfortunate soldier because of her need to remain anonymous. Synalon thought her dead, and she must remain that way until she confronted her sister.

Fortunately, she didn't have to kill him. She had only to walk up to the soldier and ask him for his mount. He would be only too happy to oblige, never caring that it would put him afoot in the middle of the Southern Steppe. Such was Ziore's power to mold emotions. Moriana would leave him enough of her Athalar rations to keep him alive for several weeks. He could walk out on his own, or maybe if – *when*, she amended mentally – she overcame Synalon and recovered the Beryl Throne she could send out search parties to bring him in.

She drew the edges of her capacious hood forward to hide her face and distinctive hair and boosted herself up over the bank.

The sighing wind covered the sounds of her approach until she was within a few feet of the bird rider. The eagle raised its head, saw her, and shrilled alarm. The man rose smoothly, sword poised before him. His jaw dropped at the sight of the tall, cowled figure who had stolen upon him out of nowhere.

'I require the use of your mount, my good man,' she said from the shadows of the cowl. 'I will leave you rations. You will come to no

346

harm.'

The trooper opened his mouth to scorn this impertinent offer.

'Yes, my lady,' he said, confused that he mouthed those words. And yet . . . yet he couldn't refuse. He had been offered rations. It was a fair exchange. He was only too happy to oblige the wishes of this mysterious apparition with the glowing black-and-white pendant.

Or was it a black pendant?

A gust of wind struck Moriana in the face. Before she could react, it peeled the hood from her head. Golden hair spilled forth.

'Princess!' the soldier cried, his eyes widening in recognition. 'But they said you were dead!'

Moriana cried in despair as her fingers found the hilt of her sword. Steel glinted dully in the leaden light. The eagle drummed its wings and screamed at the copper smell of blood.

Moriana's secret remained intact – at the cost of a human life.

CHAPTER FIVE

Prince Rann stood at the window watching the ground slowly slide by.

The Sky City was an immense stone raft two thousand feet long and eleven hundred at its broadest point. At the fore and aft ends of the great ellipse, stone piers jutted like the mandibles of some giant insect. Between these piers and the ground moved the hot-air balloons supplying the City with foodstuffs and other necessary supplies.

A broad avenue ran the length of the City from pier to pier. In the center of the City it was bisected by another artery running from port to starboard. At their juncture, the Circle of the Skywell ringed the great Well of Winds, through which malefactors were 'exiled' to the ground five thousand feet below. The avenue running to port from the Well had a peculiar, bumpy, off-white appearance due to the materials used in the paving stones: the skulls of past rulers of the City in the Sky. At the end of the Skullway rose the Palace of the Winds, sharply arched, fluted, attenuated, looming high above even the tall buildings.

The far side of the Palace lay flush with the guard wall ringing the City. Standing now at the narrow arch of a window partly opened to admit a chill blast of air, Rann had an incomparable view of the Sundered Realm.

At the moment, port meant northwest. Looking straight out from the City, Rann saw the Thail Mountains reaching their northernmost extent and dwindling into the high hills of Kubil and the Black March, duchies that gave nominal allegiance to the much-shrunken Empire of High Medurim. To the left, the Thails rose to become a wall blocking all sight of Thailot, westernmost of the Quincunx Cities. To the right, if Rann put his head out into the rush of the wind, he could see the sheen of Lake Wir glinting like a sheet of beaten silver in the early morning sun. Beyond that a pall of thick black smoke gripped the horizon like an iron band. Omizantrim breathed today.

Throat of the Dark Ones, the name meant in the harsh speech of the Fallen Ones who had built the City millennia before human feet trod the soil of the Realm. The alien, humanoid, reptilian folk had hewn the foundations of the City whole from the lava flows of the twenty-five-thousand-foot volcano. They had made smaller rafts from the skystone the Throat belched up from the bowels of the earth, but by what arts no man living could say. Rann doubted if even the degenerate remnants of the Fallen Ones still possessed the knowledge to fly the skyrafts. The City itself was the sole surviving artifact of that era.

He sighed and drew his head back inside. It was unhealthy to brood over the Fallen People. They'd been gone from the City for thousands of years, but still, deep down, every inhabitant of the floating citadel had the unvoiced conviction that some day they would attempt to reclaim their creation.

He looked down again. The land below teemed with movement. Minuscule toy wagons pulled by insects crept across the snowy plains. Around them milled ants, dark against the snow. They were really vast freight wagons drawn by dray dogs and hornbulls broken to harness dwarfed by distance. Northeast, in the path of the City, bloated gray finger-shapes lifted from the ground, the block-long balloons raised on air heated by captive salamanders. The wind brought him the cries of birds and men as one of the gigantic sausages was steered to its mooring on the forward pier by harnessed eagles.

Day and night now the cargo balloons moved between City and earth. The enormous legless, sightless ruby spiders in the catacombs of the City were being forced to turn out ever more of the silk from which the skycraft were made. And still there were too few balloons. Even the mightiest could only hoist a few tons to the skydocks. The City armed for war. Its appetite had become voracious.

The prince shook his head. He was responsible for the success of that initial stroke in the coming war.

The Quincunx Cities had become nervous due to the City's recent feverish trade activity. It was widely known that rule in the City had changed hands. Expansion of the City's trade was given as a reason for the sudden influx of material, with the concomitant increase of military reserve to keep surface trade routes secure. In the past, such a move had always pleased the Quincunx Cities, who otherwise bore the expense themselves. Unofficially, the rumor also went forth that internal unrest had followed Synalon's succession to the throne. While nothing serious, the new ruler felt it necessary to import large quantities of arms from the foundries of Port Zorn and North Keep.

Rann had authored both stories, official and otherwise. Each contained a germ of truth. Civil disturbance had followed Derora's death, and the City was definitely planning to increase the scope of its dealings with the surface.

How long the Quincunx would accept the stories remained an unanswerable question. Spies reported uneasiness in Wirix. In three days, the Sky City would be above the island city. When the City passed by and committed no aggression against Wirix, the fears of the other Quincunx Cities would ease.

And after the transit of Wirix . . .

The City would change direction over Wirix and head for one of two destinations, Bilsinx or the great seaport of Kara-Est at the head of the Gulf of Veluz. Whichever city the floating fortress crossed, there the first blow would fall. With surprise, the Sky City bird riders had a chance of subduing either. To be certain of success — and Rann could afford no less — required allies on the ground.

Small garrisons of Sky City dog riders bivouacked in both Bilsinx and Kara-Est to escort caravans across the brigand-plagued prairie. Neither was large enough for Rann's purposes, and he dared not augment them without exciting suspicion. He needed a dependable, discreet, competent ally whose presence wouldn't be connected with the Sky City's approach.

The unwieldy balloon now rising to meet the City carried a man Rann hoped would be that ally.

The breeze blowing in the window began to make his wounds ache. While no longer bandaged like a corpse in its shroud, the prince was still far from fully recovered. He shut the window and went to a table on which a large map of the Quincunx had been spread. He began to study and plan.

Moriana's mount failed her as the Sky City came into view.

It had been a tense flight. It should have taken less than two days to arrive at her destination. She'd been in the air for three. When her stolen mount touched ground the day before, the princess hadn't

350

known whether or not she'd ever get the bird airborne again.

She had spent half the night awake, caring for the bird. When the wind stilled, Moriana had gathered dried dung, built a roaring fire, and moved the stricken eagle as close to the flames as possible without singeing feathers. He coughed incessantly, a racking, convulsive sound. A hint of bloody froth touched the hinges of his beak. Moriana had massaged him, trying to soothe tortured muscles. Her fingers were expert. She had known the secrets of an eagle's anatomy before she learned the mysteries of her own.

She found no proper herbs for healing. Moriana had strained herself to call up the strongest healing magics she knew – in this branch of magic she was far superior to her sister. Peversely, the healing spells took the same soul-wrenching exertion as spells of harm. The princess had reached down inside herself and had drawn out the essence of her soul, even daring contact with the black blight left there by the Vicar of Istu. She wove the spell to restore the eagle's strength. The royalty of the Sky City had an ages-old obligation to their eagles, an obligation not even Synalon would think of denying.

So she worked, struggled, wept. Despite the midwinter cold, sweat rolled off her in rivers. Exhaustion permeated her body and poisoned her muscles, bones, mind. A cloud of stink rose to assault her: the acrid reek of the dung-fed fire, her own body long unwashed and overworked, the stench of terminal sickness gushing from the eagle with every heave of his chest. It had required all her determination to keep working until she'd done what she could. Only Ziore's masterful calming and soothing and encouragement enabled her to finish her task. And when the princess had at last collapsed into a deathlike sleep, she knew all she'd gained was a pitiful few hours flying time.

The new day dawned cold and bleak. The wind blasted in from the west, quartering her line of flight. It was as if fate had decreed that she would not gain entry to her City for the final confrontation with Synalon. Her amulet, her secret weapon, shone mostly black like a sun partially eclipsed, and she played with it as she flew. A croak from the eagle drew her from the fog of tension. She looked up, alarmed. Did the bird sense danger? Or was it calling above to its comrades on patrol?

The eagle cried again. This time she heard the glad note in its voice. A low, humped darkness appeared on the horizon, an anomalous isolated storm cloud. But it was no ordinary cloud. The City in the Sky floated heedless of the wind. The tempo of the wingbeats picked up. Her mount strained to the utmost, striving to reach home and die.

But this last exertion proved too much. The City grew in Moriana's vision until she made out details, picked out the steep roofs of homes and businesses, the tracery of the palace on the far side. She even saw movement on the walls. Monitors patroling. The bustle of activity on the ground and the cargo balloons sprouting from the strange, prairielike fungi didn't surprise her. Using a scrying spell, she had scanned the City. The palace was denied to her vision because of routine magical precautions, but she saw that the City girded itself for war.

For conquest.

She had just noted the exceptional number of bird riders in the air when her mount coughed and shuddered mightily.

Her attention instantly focused on the bird's dying cough. A sigh from Ziore touched her mind. The spirit sensed it, too. The bird had made it all this way only to fall short by less than a mile, almost near enough to touch the skystone of the City itself.

The wings fluttered, losing strength perceptibly. The City canted and veered away as the bird banked into a descending spiral. War eagles were trained to land when they felt their strength failing them. Moriana felt the bitterness in the creature; it longed with all its fading being to die, if it must, in a last desperate effort to get its claws on the rock of home. But duty lay in protecting its rider. The ancient compact between rider and eagle bound both equally.

The bird straightened its wings. Gliding down, it conserved strength for landing. The irregular ground hurtled upwards at a dizzying rate. An incautious landing would kill Moriana as surely as if the bird's heart had burst a mile up.

Moriana tensed. Thoughts chased one another through her mind with terrifying speed. Her plan had been to fly openly into the City. Citizens didn't question bird riders, and if she rode in purposefully enough, no Guardsman would question her, either. But that scheme lay shattered now because of her bird's fading life-force.

'Say-y-y! Ho there, a rescue!' came the cry from above. Five birds had detached themselves from the unusual number that flocked around the City. Five powerful pairs of wings propelled bodies and riders through the air toward her with purposeful speed.

She had time to appreciate the irony of this rescue. The Sky Guardsmen did not for an instant suspect they were on the verge of apprehending the fugitive Princess Moriana, presumed dead. They saw only a bird rider in distress, and the only bird riders in the Sundered Realm were soldiers of the Sky City. They thought they flew to the rescue of a comrade in trouble.

Moriana knew they'd realize their mistake soon enough. Then the ground came spinning up to meet her.

'I take it for granted, my lord count,' said Rann, toying with the skull he had been using to hold down a corner of the map, 'that you appreciate the need for utmost discretion in this matter.'

'Certainly, Your Highness,' said the count, his manner courteous but clipped, verging on impatience. The edge in his voice would have thrown Synalon into a homicidal fury at his impertinence. It only reassured the prince. The man refused to waste time. Rann needed such a man.

He gingerly put down the skull. He had stripped the flesh from it while its still-living owner thrashed and howled in exquisite agony. The whole experience had been so rewarding that Rann had desired a momento.

He studied his guest carefully. A small man, scarcely three inches taller than his diminutive host, but as stockily built as Rann was spare. He stood in his severely cut, blue tunic and loose trousers with black riding boots rolled down to his calves. He wore a sword hung from a black baldric, a rare privilege for an outsider permitted into the presence of Sky City royalty.

It was deliberate. Rann let the man know how utterly he trusted him. The look in the visitor's watery blue eyes showed his understanding of the situation.

Rann picked up a goblet of hot spiced wine and sipped. The drink spread soothing warmth through his body, erasing the effect of the chill wind, and soothing him while he bided his time. His visitor stood waiting, but not patiently. Though not a muscle of body or face moved, he gave the impression of vibrating with ill-suppressed energy. Even the tips of his prematurely white, waxed moustache stood quivering at attention.

The goblet clanked to the tabletop with sudden decision.

'You will need to arrive in the target city well before we do, with, of course, some ostensible business not at all associated with the Sky City.' The count's only reply was a curt nod. 'That's why it is necessary to meet now before our transit of Wirix. Preparations must begin immediately.'

'It shall be done as you command, Highness.' The visitor smoothed an imaginary wrinkle from the front of his tunic.

'Our friends below are nervous. But they are also complacent. Years of peace have turned them soft. They doubt anyone would dare attack them. The Sky City has made no overtly hostile move toward them since the humans conquered it. As a result, for all their apprehension at our recent activity, they cannot bring themselves to believe that we will attack. *But . . .'* He drained his drink and set the goblet down with a thump of finality. 'But should they receive intelligence – reliable intelligence – of our designs, even the most lethargic bourgeois would be goaded to action. Properly forewarned, they might even successfully fend us off. It is a matter of concern to Her Majesty and myself.'

His tawny eyes moved sidelong to study his visitor's reaction. The man's face betrayed no emotion, but his manner clearly said he was irritated. He grasped the obvious as readily as any other man.

'Well, then,' said Rann, smiling, nodding his head as if to change the subject. 'If my lord will excuse me, I've an appointment in the palace dungeons. My Monitors caught a spy trying to sneak in. The slut rode up in a cargo balloon. I anticipate a most diverting afternoon.' He turned a bland countenance on his guest. 'Unless my lord wishes to come and watch . . . ?'

'Thank you, Highness,' the man said with a courtly half-bow, 'but I fear I must return to the surface at your earliest convenience. There is much to set in motion.' His toneless, staccato voice did not waver. But his florid face had gone pale at the suggestion that he share in Rann's 'diversion'. Rann felt a delicious tingle of amusement. Inflicting emotional upset was, in its own way, as gratifying as dealing out physical pain.

The stone's color shifted to black. Moriana kept it tucked into her tunic while flying, but the eagle's whirling descent steepened as the bird lost control and pitched it free. It seemed incongruous to the princess that the stone's color mirrored her own fortune. Then the tip of the bird's lower wing caught on a tree limb and the eagle spun in.

At the northern edge of the central plains, the occasional trees sometimes banded together into woods. As her mount had started his final descent, Moriana had steered him for the nearest large cluster of trees. It was dangerous landing among trees. But to land in the open was fatal.

A limb laden with snow hit Moriana in the face as her mount cartwheeled down through the trees. A blow to her ribs knocked the breath from her. She saw clear, snowy ground below and threw herself from the saddle.

She hit and rolled expertly, coming to rest against the bole of a tree. The eagle floundered on, smashing through the bare limbs in a flurry of white powder. The snow muted the sound of its passage so that it sounded distant, unreal. The noise of wings cracking branches ceased abruptly. A heartbeat later, Moriana heard a sickening thump. A cloud of snow marked her mount's final resting place.

She raised her head, shaking it to clear snow from her eyes. A lump hung tenaciously to her forehead like a cold, wet hand.

She silently saluted her fallen eagle, then began moving. The ache in her ribs jabbed into pain with every step. Possibly she'd broken a rib, but this wasn't the time to check. She had to find cover before the bird riders descended.

She knew what to expect from those above. Seeking cover, the princess found a spot where interlocked branches had formed a framework roofed over with snow, bent low, and scurried beneath it. For all her care, she brushed the limb. It dumped snow down the back of her cloak.

Ignoring the snow turning to water on her back, she examined herself. Her ribs hurt, but after a few experimental breaths she decided she hadn't cracked any. An ankle throbbed painfully; she'd twisted it and hadn't noticed till now. Her face was scratched, her lips swollen from the limb that had swept across her face. But she was relatively healthy.

She remembered Ziore's jug. Guiltily, she reached around and felt her backpack. The jug seemed intact.

I'm here, she heard the nun's voice say inside her head. *Don't fear for me, child. I'm not harmed.*

Moriana sighed in relief. Overhead, the bird riders swept by.

Instinctively, she hunched down. The eagles flapped by, their wings making the sound of sails flapping in a stiff breeze.

'Look,' came a man's voice. 'That's where he went down.'

Through gaps in the trees Moriana saw the five birds circling over her fallen mount. She held perfectly still. The slightest motion would betray her. She tried to ignore the discomfort of her cramped position as her mind raced.

Moriana knew she was finished if they landed. She considered shooting at the Sky Guardsmen with the bow she'd taken from the lost scout. She dismissed the idea at once. She could bring one down, but with the trees in the way that would end her life then and there. The only way she could escape was to bring down all five at once.

Ziore? she thought. *Can you help me?*

She felt the spirit's negative response. She thought fleetingly of her own sorceries, but these were Sky Guardsmen, warded against anything she could do on such short notice. Her hand slipped to the reassuring firmness of her sword hilt. Her heart hammered in her ears. She waited. It was all she could do.

'I don't see the rider,' called one of the orbiting Guardsmen. 'He may have been thrown free.'

'Ho!' another shouted. 'Ho, down there! Can you hear me? If you can't answer, make some sign. We can't see you!'

The minutes moved as ponderously as the glacier guarding Athalau.

'He's in no shape to respond,' a third voice declared. 'Let's go down and look for him.'

'No!' a fourth voice rapped.

'But flight corporal,' the second said. 'We can't just leave him.'

'We're under orders not to land.' A bird shrilled irritably. The mounts disliked the wing-cramping circle they flew.

'Corporal, he's one of ours!' the second complained.

Hardness pressed into the palm of Moriana's left hand. She realized she clutched furiously at the Amulet of Living Flame. She stared at it.

Its surface was glowing mostly white.

Irrationally, her heart beat faster. She had no reason to think this meant her luck had changed, but . . .

'I'm sure Prince Rann will be impressed with your spirit of comradeship,' the corporal said ironically, 'when we're strapped to the torture frames in his playroom. He commanded that no one land under any circumstances. Rescues are to be left to the dog humpers. Our place is aloft, flyer, and aloft is where we're going to stay.'

No grumbling greeted the corporal's words. The prince's name acted like a potent spell. One of the Sky Guardsmen shouted down, 'Sorry, but we can't land. We'll have the dog boys out with stretchers as soon as we can.'

Then the sound of wingbeats diminished.

'Ziore, did you have anything to do with that?' Moriana trembled with the nervous release of tension.

'No,' the spirit said aloud, sounding puzzled. 'As soon as the corporal spoke, I probed his mind to harden him to the idea of flying off if he started to weaken. But he didn't. In fact, I don't think I could have *made* him land.'

Moriana emerged from the shelter, stood up, and stretched. Hours in the saddle coaxing her eagle along had left her muscles wound into knots.

'These bird riders are afraid of this Rann,' said Ziore. 'I thought you said he was dead.'

'I thought he was.' Moriana shook her head. This was a bad turn.

She looked to the northwest. A balloon grew like a tumor from the forward edge of the City, distended, broke away, and then began to descend as the flyers vented air from the bag. A feeling of despair washed up like bile from her belly. The City was near – and infinitely far away.

'Why, child?' Moriana started. She constantly forgot that Ziore read her thoughts. The nun was better at it than Erimenes ever had been. 'You've gotten this far on a stolen bird. Can't you steal another, or ride up in one of those unsafe looking contrivances?'

'No. If Rann died under the ice as I'd thought, it would be worth trying. But if Rann lives, no. He's suspicious of his own shadow. The City's sewn up like a balloon; trust in it.'

'What will you do now?'

The words played over and over in her mind, clanking like lumps of rusted iron. *What will you do now?*

Her choices were few. But she wouldn't give up. There had to be a way someone as resourceful and daring as she could sneak into the City.

Somewhere, a snow clump dropped to the forest floor. Moriana shook herself. When the groundling rescue party failed to turn up a downed flyer, they would report back to the Sky City. Suspicion would be roused. A full-scale hunt would be fielded.

The disappointment of her failure to reach the City was swept away by a swell of emotion. Rage, hatred, determination flared.

'What will I do now?' she asked harshly. 'I'm going to show my sister that two can play the game of conquest.

'I'm going to invade the City in the Sky.'

CHAPTER SIX

Shadows writhed and capered among the vaults of the ceiling. Shadows pursued each other along the walls, ducking into alcoves, flashing up the piers of the pointed arches that supported the roof. Shadows held court in the throne room of the City in the Sky.

Shadows wrapped Synalon like silk. Clad only in their dark substance, the Queen of the City knelt in a chalk circle scribed carefully on the dark stone of the floor.

Within the seven-foot circle was a triangle, its apexes touching the circle. At its three points burned fires—one yellow, one blue, and the last red. A different scent rose from each: sandalwood, cinnamon, gall.

Thus protected by her magics, Synalon addressed herself to the spirits held captive before her.

She rose and shook back midnight hair. Shadows caressed her thighs, her belly, the palely glowing moons of her breasts, the shadows moving like lover's hands. She inhaled sharply as though she felt the touch.

'As Stone worked with Fire becomes Metal,' she intoned, her hair rising of its own accord like a deadly black halo, 'as Stone mixed with Water becomes Mortar, as both are shaped by the hand of Man, I shape you as I have bound you. You must serve my ends, or Wood shall be your pain!'

The creature she addressed stood splay-footed within its crystal prison, its arms crossed over the round jut of its belly. Bat ears flanked a domed, wrinkled skull. Its skin was rough, knobbed, and pitted like pumice. Its obsidian eyes gleamed forth with white-hot fire.

'You have drawn me into being, mistress,' it rasped with ill grace. 'Say what you would have of me and be done with it.' It spoke slowly,

358

with obvious effort, its tone hovering near inaudibility at the lower end of the scale.

'Hear me. This is my pleasure. Convey my submission to the Lords of Darkness. They have but to render me their bidding, and I shall do it. The greatness of the City shall be as it was, and the glory of the City was ever the glory of the Dark Ones.'

'No.' A stony head lowered to a stony breast.

Synalon's head snapped up. Her hair crackled with furious energy.

'The stone I called on you to animate was gathered from the flows of Omizantrim, manikin. Speak thus, with the Throat of the Dark Ones. Bear me their bidding.' The last words rushed out in a sensuous whisper. She bent forward at the waist, body sheened with sweat. Her nipples stood erect, casting shadows on her breasts.

'Stone is Stone, from wherever drawn,' the stone spirit said. 'I am touched with darkness, perhaps. But not with madness. I will have naught to do with the Lords of Infinite Night.'

'Then you must suffer.' Synalon hissed the words, face contorted with rage.

'Better your punishment than to draw the notice of the Dark Ones,' the spirit replied.

She pressed palms together before her belly. Slowly, she raised her hands. A green shoot sprouted from the floor of the chamber within the domed cylinder that imprisoned the spirit. It grew, touched one ankle of the lavalike homunculus and began to twine up the leg. The spirit stood immobile.

The queen raised her hands higher. The shoot climbed with them, swelling and hardening, green turning to brown along its length. The leafed tendril at the tip of the shoot touched the juncture of the stone man's thighs. It pressed upward with the inexorable pressure of growing plants.

The bat-winged visage lifted. Its lips stretched in a grin of growing agony, but still the spirit uttered no sound. Synalon's arms pressed before her breasts, her throat, her face. The stone head arched up and back, as though drawn by an invisible cord. Muscles stood out on its arms in stark relief.

Synalon began to spread her fingers. A ripple passed through the spirit's body. A shoot burst through stony skin at the juncture of neck and shoulder, curled coyly, green, and seemingly tender. Other sprouts broke from the creature's chest, its sides and belly, thickening into the branches of the tree that grew within the spirit, impaling it as it stood.

Remorselessly, Synalon's hands rose. The growing green and brown cancer rose up in the stone figure. Synalon raised hands above her head and pulled them apart. Stony fragments fell to the floor as fresh branches broke from the cheeks and ears of the spirit. One obsidian eye was pushed from its socket. It rolled down the floor like a black teardrop and shattered on the floor. At last the spirit opened its mouth to scream. Instead of sound, a shoot emerged, thick and leafy, reaching for the ceiling of the crystal cylinder. A shudder wracked the body. The fire died in its remaining eye.

Synalon dropped her hands to her sides. The ineluctable, unnatural growing ceased. It was now a stunted tree and nothing more.

The sorceress stood panting, a sense of frustration suffusing her. She had been so near the consummation she sought. And she had been denied. Her body trembled with rage and thwarted yearning.

Stone had been the likeliest choice as intermediary with the Dark Ones. Darkness was the great Sixth Principle. The other five acted upon each other, Fire consuming Wood, Water stilling Fire, Air dispersing Water, Stone negating Air, and finally Wood sundering Stone. Darkness was aloof, inviolate, the First Principle from which the rest derived. Light, that waste product of Fire, produced the illusion of dispelling Dark; but Dark remained, ever-present, hiding just beyond sight, biding in shadow until the Light vanished.

Dark alone was eternal.

She turned to the captive sylph. The water sprite oozed within its crystal pen.

'You,' Synalon said, her hair waving as if it were caught in a breeze, 'you shall serve me. Great will be your reward, O child of the oceans. Bear my message to the Dark Ones. This I ask and no more.'

The sylph's voice was pleasing, fluid, and as elusive as quicksilver. But it, too, refused the sorceress's command. Quivering with fury, Synalon waved her hands before her in a whirlwind gesture. The sylph's body became agitated and was drawn up in a whirlpool around the insides of its prison. The spirit squealed, an aching, candescent sound. Synalon gestured. Vents at the bottom of the cylinder opened. The dying sylph puffed outward, mist. It filled the chamber for a moment and then was gone.

Synalon rounded the third cylinder. It contained the dryad, a lovely naked maiden whose toes were root and whose fingers were supple branches, her hair a green rustling of leaves. She sang with a voice like wind in spring-sweet branches, but her answer was the same. She dared not contact the Dark Ones.

She screamed lingeringly in her very human voice as a fire consumed her loveliness. It left behind only ashes.

Sparks flickered in Synalon's hair, popping and snapping electrically. Ozone was rank in her nostrils. And fear began to seep in around the edges of her determination. Her voice was edged as she addressed the shimmer that was the spirit of the upper air.

It defied her in the tones of chimes.

Dark crystals appeared on the inside of the vessel. They rapidly obscured Synalon's view of the sprite as they grew together and inward. The spirit taunted Synalon with its tinkling laughter even as the hardness crushed out its life.

Blue radiance bathed her body. Lightning traveled her limbs in a violet corona discharge. Her hair floated in a glowing spark-shot nimbus around her head. There remained only one captive elemental: Fire.

Fire, the elemental best understood and controlled by the mages of the City; Fire, the elemental most inimical to Darkness. It had been the humans who brought salamander lore to the City. The builders had venerated Dark alone.

Fire was the best choice and the worst. And if Fire defied her, too? The thought threatened to melt her resolve. She needed the power granted by the Dark Ones, she *needed* it, if her world-girdling ambitions were ever to be realized. And after Fire there remained no elementals to try to bend to her will. There were no lesser spirits of Darkness. The closest thing to a Darkness elemental was Istu, sleeping in chains of power in the depths of the City. Synalon knew too well what would befall her if she dared stir the Sleeper. The last time she had roused a fragment of his sleeping mind and animated the Vicar of Istu for the Rite of Dark Assumption, the demon had been given pain such as he'd never known before. He would not forget the sorceress who summoned him to anguish.

'Salamander,' she said, fighting to keep the quaver from her words. 'Strength of my City, ally of my folk. I command you and beseech you to bear my message to the Dark Ones.' She stood straight, flames spilling from her outstretched, supplicant hands.

The salamander's vessel exploded.

Flying shards of glass scored Synalon's stomach, thighs and breasts. One glittering fragment laid open her right cheek. She flinched but held her ground. The salamander was loose. The fire sprites were fickle, vicious beasts and never predictable – and never entirely controlled. Something had gone horribly wrong. The enchanted vessel should have held any power less strong than Istu himself.

The flame creature danced in the middle of the throne room. The stone floor ran and puddled like water beneath it. Synalon threw up her hands to shield her eyes from the yellow incandescence.

In a few trip-hammer beats of her heart, she sensed that the blinding radiance had dimmed. Carefully, she lowered her hands. And gasped.

The thing was no normal salamander. They were usually shifting, indistinct beasts. Their only form appeared vaguely reptilian and sinuous. The horror confronting her was like a goat, an ape, a grossly misshapen human. It had a bulky body with ever-changing outlines, and yet its lineaments didn't change with the quicksilver speed and smoothness of an elemental. The thing had hooves on its four feet – two? more? – clawed hands, and bizarre paired horns sprouting from both sides of its head. With a start, Synalon recognized what she had conjured.

'Aye, little one, you guess the truth,' the apparition said. The words came not in a salamander's familiar sibilance but in a dry sound that made her think of dead leaves and blighted lands. 'The Lords of Darkness have taken note of your petition. They have sent me to bear their tidings to you.'

Joy exploded in Synalon's heart, a joy magnified by the frantic fear clutching her. Would they favor her or cast her to shrieking damnation?

She dropped to her knees, throwing her arms wide.

'O harbinger of Darkness, accept my subservience. Take me, Lords! Make me the instrument of your revenge for the wrong done you by accursed Felarod!'

'The Dark Lords hear your voice, little one. They bid me tell you this: their time is almost come. But . . . ' A wave of a tentaclelike member cut off her glad cry. 'But they are as yet undecided as to whether you are the proper tool by which they shall accomplish their vengeance – and their return.'

'Tell me,' she cried, wringing her hands. 'I beseech thee, tell me how I may prove myself!'

The creature's smile was unmistakable in spite of its slowly changing features.

'Your chance arrives soon.' And it vanished. But not entirely. The torches in their brackets on the walls blazed to life. Blinking back the spots swimming in her eyes, she saw only darkness beyond.

Dazed, she rose and walked from the circle and triangle. She noted that the three ward fires had been extinguished. She didn't doubt that the emissary of the Dark Ones had put them out to show how ineffective her spells were against their minions. She slumped into the Beryl Throne.

The stone chilled her buttocks and thighs, reviving her. She brushed sweat-lank hair from her eyes and tried to think.

Synalon tried to tell herself she had nothing to fear. The Dark Ones had been banished for millennia, and few outside the City dared even think of them. They needed an ally on this plane, a powerful one with the skills and ruthlessness to carry out their designs. She was unquestioned ruler of the City in the Sky, the City of Sorcerers. Her winged legions would soon spread out to cover the Sundered Realm. Who would they find better suited to their ends?

Yet she couldn't shake the feeling that the Dark Ones only toyed with her, that she'd been found wanting and they had chosen their earthly instrument – and she was not their choice.

Synalon reached for the golden bell by the throne and rang. She needed wine and restoratives and, after that, the attentions of one of her many lovers. Or perhaps more than one. Perhaps even the trained hornbull.

She did not want to sleep and dream this night.

Tolviroth Acerte had no army. Contrary to popular belief, war is *not* good business. And the Tolviroth were consummate businessmen.

The City of Bankers was not without its defenses. Twenty-five miles of sea separated it from the nearest mainland. The seamen and marines of the Tolviroth Maritime Guaranty Corporation, largest insurance firm on the island, were famed well beyond the Realm for their fighting and naval skills. But that was merely good business. Pirates, with or without letters of marque, interrupted trade. *That* was intolerable. The merchants of Tolviroth paid and paid well to see that their vessels were safeguarded. And the Maritime Guaranty, with a half-dozen competitors only too ready to claim its market share, made certain its customers got their money's worth. Not even the Imperial Navy in its heyday centuries before would have undertaken to protect the wallowing bottoms of an invasion fleet against the lethal black ships of the TMG.

Moriana had spent eight hours in the forest near the City in the Sky as patrols of dog cavalry scoured the woods for the missing bird rider. Her senses, turned animal-sharp, had gotten her through the cordon. One of the searchers had strayed too far from his comrades, and Moriana was soon bound southeast for Kara-Est, a stolen black-and-white war dog bunching and straining between her legs.

Weeks passed as she made her way to Kara-Est and from there by sea to Tolviroth Acerte, paying for her passage with the klenors gained by selling her stolen dog. And after reaching Tolviroth Acerte, she headed directly for the House of Omsgib-Bir, the bank that held the accounts for the Sky City.

They'd given her no satisfaction. She'd established her identity without difficulty. She'd been to Tolviroth Acerte twice before and knew the passwords and countersigns that proved she had legitimate access to the accounts. Or at least the records of the accounts. Tulmen Omsgib, chancellor of the bank, had politely but relentlessly refused her request to release the money to her.

'Your bona fides are not questioned, Highness,' the syndic had said unctuously, stroking his beard. 'Yet we can only disburse funds to the government of the City in the Sky, or its rightful representative.'

'But I'm the rightful heir to the throne!'

'I can appreciate that,' he said with spurious compassion in his sad, round eyes. 'By the laws of ultimogeniture followed in your City, you are the rightful successor to Derora, may the Great Ultimate bring her soul repose.' He sat back and pressed his palms together as if in prayer. 'But you are not in the City. You are here before me in my office, an honored guest, to be sure, but a guest without official standing.'

He held off her protest with upraised hand.

'No, I am most sorry, Highness. But it is not the custom in Tolviroth Acerte, or in the House of Omsgib-Bir, to deal with what might be, or even what ought to be.' He reached down and took a jellied sweet from a salver at his elbow and popped it right down his throat. 'Your title is clear by right, but it is your sister who rules the City. It is she, therefore, whom we must recognize and deal with as the lawful government.'

He tilted his head back and regarded her down his crooked nose. The look in his eye was unmistakable. Moriana's garb was rough and functional and not precisely what one expected of the rightful queen of the City of Sorcerers. It did nothing to hide the curves of her body. Omsgib's oily tongue slipped from the cavern of his mouth and slowly circled his lips.

'Has Your Highness made arrangements for accommodation? If you are in difficulty, please allow me to offer the hospitality of my own humble villa.'

She got up and walked out in the middle of his offer.

She didn't even bother to ask him for a loan. He would be as smooth and slippery as a slug's track, saying nothing to offend, but he would not give it to her. It didn't matter that she was an 'honored guest', or that she'd dealt with him personally before. She was the bitter, deadly enemy of the person who controlled one of his bank's largest accounts. She'd get nothing from him financially, and she wanted no part of what he was obviously only too willing to give her.

She left Omsgib and went to the second largest bank in Tolviroth Acerte. And then the third, the fourth, and on down until she ended up in the boardroom of Iola Trust, the eighth bank she'd visited that day.

The seven members of the Board of Directors regarded her from behind veils of professional politeness. She looked away from the ascetic face of the man who'd just refused her request. She saw no sympathy anywhere. Of the four male directors, at least two would obviously be willing to offer the same 'accommodation' Omsgib had hinted at. But not even they showed the slightest inclination to advance her the money to raise a mercenary army.

'Look,' she said, eyes flicking from face to face. 'I'm not asking you to involve yourself in the affairs of the Sky City. I am applying for a loan. Isn't my credit good?'

A look of pain passed over the face of a female director named Bovre Coudis. A person's credit rating was all but sacred to a Tolvirot, and Synalon had good credit. Refusing a loan to someone with good credit moved perilously close to blasphemy. But obviously that did not extend to Synalon's renegade sister.

'I know the Sky City as well as any person living. Do any among you doubt that? I know the military doctrines of the City, I know the caliber and training of its troops, I know its commanders. If I'm given the proper backing – *if* – I can conquer the City. And then you, gentlefolk of this board, will see a handsome return on your investment.'

'War's bad business,' grumbled one. Another twitched an impatient finger to silence the speaker.

'So you say,' said the man introduced as Kolwyl, dabbing languidly at his lips with a scented handkerchief. Moriana pegged him as totally uninterested in 'accommodations' of any sort with her. 'But no one has ever invaded the City before. For any loan, we must have a reasonable assurance the money will not be frittered away. Success must loom large or it is a poor loan. What makes you think you can succeed in this mad venture?'

She met his gaze levelly, unspeaking. After a moment, he turned his eyes away and coughed delicately into his handkerchief.

'The City *has* been invaded successfully before,' she said. 'My ancestors wrested it from the Fallen Ones.'

'They used treachery,' replied Kolwyl sharply.

'They succeeded. Your obligation to my proposal seems to be that it can't succeed. What does it matter to you how it comes about as long as you realize your profit?'

Kolwyl looked about him for support. Anathas, a small mousy man wearing a thick fur collar despite the heat within the chamber, shifted in his seat with a rustle of expensive cloth.

'You know,' he said nasally, 'it is not impossible that we are being unfair to Princess Moriana. She is, after all, rightful Queen of the Sky City. Surely, she has some popular support among the, uh, the masses.'

'That may be,' said Bovre Coudis, leaning forward so far that her jowls swung like a bulldog's. 'But her sister controls the secret police. And from our intelligence in this matter, the masses would be well advised to keep their place.'

Moriana scarcely heard her. She stared at Anathas, who huddled down inside his fur-lined robe, uncomfortable beneath her gaze. She tried to fathom his sudden reversal. He had seemed against her at first.

Sunlight filtered through the windows, casting a yellow-brown light on the vast oaken table. Servants passed through the room, ignoring the conversation and being ignored, refilling wineglasses and replenishing the trays of dainties. Moriana had the impression that if she touched one of them, she'd find it as insubstantial as Ziore.

'We have a great deal of venture capital at our discretion,' said Anathas, looking everywhere but at the princess. 'Surely, there's no doubting her Highness's resourcefulness. Recall, gentles, how many years we've tried to wrest the City's account from that lascivious hound, Omsgib.'

The decorous tone of the meeting lapsed for the first time. Everyone spoke at once, clamoring for attention. With sinking spirit, Moriana realized the others were unanimous in their opposition to Anathas.

The gaunt man uttered the first refusal and restored order by rapping bony knuckles on the table.

'Gentles, gentles, please! Is this any way to conduct *business?*'

That quieted them.

'Now,' he said, nodding. 'Now, Anathas, it pains me to say this but you seem to be suffering from a lapse of good judgment. This young lady comes to us with a harebrained scheme to conquer the City in the Sky, a City never taken by conquest. It has been taken, as our lovely guest so thoughtfully pointed out, but not by battle. The gradual infiltration of human traders into the City originally made it possible to expel the Fallen People. No outside intervention was used. While military matters are somewhat beyond my province, I must say that the Sky City seems to be impregnable. Even if I am wrong, it is not the place of this bank to become involved in such a risky undertaking as a war. And not just any war, but a *civil* war, as it were.'

He turned to Moriana.

'I might also point out that we've no way of knowing if this woman is who she claims to be.' Moriana stiffened. Her hand dropped to her side, clutching empty air. She'd left her sword in the anteroom according to standard banking practice. Her fingers brushed the rough cloth of her knapsack.

She blinked twice rapidly. She hadn't been asked to surrender the knapsack before being ushered into the august corporate presence of the board as she had at every other institution she'd visited that day. A sudden intuition into Anathas's change of mind made her smile. Her spirits rose in spite of the firm hold she kept on her expectations.

' . . . further enjoy the services of Prince Rann Etuul, cousin to the queen, and widely acknowledged to be one of the most astute military minds of our day,' the gaunt man was saying. He turned to Moriana and attempted to smile benignly. It made him look as if he'd just bitten into a spoiled sweetmeat and was trying to pretend he hadn't.

'I trust Your Highness will forgive my bluntness,' he said. 'It isn't that I personally doubt your assurances that you are who you claim to be. Nor do I doubt your competence as a leader and planner in a venture such as you've outlined. But you must understand that my decision is based on more than my own preference. The investors in this bank had given their trust – and their money – to the Board of Directors to safeguard. Before we venture any of *their* hard-won capital, we must entertain no doubts whatsoever about the feasibility of the project under consideration. I – and I think I speak for my colleagues as well – would like nothing so much as to grant your request.' He shook his head sadly. 'But we do not believe, to speak frankly, that aligning ourselves against the Sky City's current regime is in the best interests of our bank or its investors.'

Kolwyl turned and said to Anathas, 'Really, old man, I'm surprised at you. Falling for a piece of fluff like this. She's pretty enough, I suppose, if you like the type, but is she worth the risk of impecuniation?'

Anathas turned white. Moriana's spirit was crashing back to earth. 'Impecuniation' was the Tolvirot euphemism for the severest of civil penalties, the confiscation of all properties and assets. A true merchant of the City of Bankers would rather be flayed alive in public than suffer impecuniousness.

The other directors glared reproachfully at Kolwyl for his rudeness – and in front of Moriana. But the damage was done. Anathas shrank so far into his cloak that only the tip of his nose showed. Whatever the reason for his support, it had evaporated like mist under the morning sun.

'Thank you for your time, gentlefolk,' said Moriana, rising. Her voice was clear and firm, though inside she felt as if she were melting. 'I apologize for any inconvenience I may have caused you. In return for your indulgence, I'd like to offer some advice.' She looked from director to director, her gaze sharp and fierce. Even pugnacious Coudis cringed away from it.

'If you think to gain advantage by dealing with Synalon, or by doing nothing which might offend her, you are doing your investors small service. My sister's ambitions encompass much more than the City and the Quincunx. There's little room for the likes of you in her grand design, no matter how much you try to ingratiate or appease. You prattle on about her power; do you think she will sit by and *not* use it?'

She took a deep breath. Silence held sway. Even the servants stared at her.

'And if my sister fails,' she said, 'give thought, gentles, who will rule the City in her place.'

She left, panicked mutterings following her out the door.

CHAPTER SEVEN

'I am sorry, Moriana,' said Ziore mounfully. 'I failed you.'

'You tried,' the princess said, patting the knapsack.

'It is with me as you said it was for that pious fraud Erimenes. The farther I go from Athalau, the more my powers wane. I was lucky to influence that mousy Anathas for as long as I did. Strong convictions or passion negates my talent for controlling emotions. My best couldn't override Anathas's fear of – what did they call it? – impecuniousness.'

Moriana crossed her arms under her breasts. A landau rolled past, drawn by four black dogs, each with an identical white patch over its left eye. The carriage body was white painted wood with gold trim in severe lines. The vehicle couldn't be described as ornate, yet neither was it strictly functional. The gilt added a touch of garishness. It epitomized all Moriana had seen in Tolviroth Acerte. The citizens wished to appear reserved but at the same time they hinted at extravagance.

'Why don't you go to the Quincunx Cities and warn them of your sister's intentions?' suggested Ziore.

'The burghers of the Quincunx could give the Tolvirot lessons in smug complacency. They'll not believe themselves threatened until the Sky Guardsmen drop from their skies. And then it will be too late.' She smiled humorlessly. 'And once the first Quincunx city falls to my sister, it will be my life if I set foot in any of the others. They'll not trust any of the City's royal family.'

Approaching darkness sent its tentacles creeping up the block. Across the hewn stone street the most distinguished of Tolviroth Acerte's banking houses stood as stately as spinsters and, for Moriana, as impenetrable. At her back a fountain played, complete with water-spewing fish and naked little boys with urns and gilded bottoms.

'If you can't hire a mercenary army,' Ziore said, 'why not try to raise a popular one? Surely, not all the folk of the Sundered Realm are as phlegmatic as the Quincunxers? In my day, folk feared the City's might, and that was long past the fall of its builders. Can't you awaken the countryside to the dangers of your sister's ambition?'

Moriana gave the unseen spirit a pitying smile. Ziore was wise in some ways, but life in the cloister hadn't prepared her for the harsh reality of the world.

'You're right,' she said, 'about the folk of the Realm dreading the Sky City. Long ago we treated them with contempt – even we Etuul. "Groundlings" we call them. We sneer at them for never rising above the dirt into the freedom of the sky. They fear us, even hate us. The common people will believe Synalon threatens them, but they will also suspect that I wish to entangle them in a war for my own ends.'

'But what of justice? The throne belongs to you!'

'I think it's safe to wager that not a single citizen of the Realm loses so much as a minute's sleep worrying about the fortunes of the City.'

'You are cynical, child. It is your hurt that makes you speak thus.'

'It's reality, Ziore, reality.'

They sat in silence. Darkness deepened and with it the gloom enfolding Moriana. Perhaps, she thought, I should return to the City. Could Rann's peverted amusements be so much worse than the agony of helplessness?

'Don't!' cried Ziore. 'Never think that, child, never! Such thinking is always a trap, a pit without bottom. Once you fall into it, you can never . . .'

The sound of a footfall nearby cut her off. Moriana looked around. She expected to see one of the constabulary come to collect the tariff for sitting on the bench and enjoying the view of the rich statuary. Her hand went instinctively to her sword hilt.

A man stood there, a tall silhouette against the fading sun.

'*Fost!*' she gasped.

'I fear not my lady,' came the warm but unfamiliar voice. 'Just a plain passerby whose heart is torn to see one so lovely in distress. Can I be of service? A kind word? A sword to fight beside you?'

Moriana blinked. The words, coming soft in the accents of the City States, should have repelled her as mere puffery. Yet sincerity flowed through them like a warm, rich current. Something made her want to believe the offer was real.

'I am grateful, sir,' she said, gesturing for him to sit. 'But my troubles are larger than the two of us.'

'That may be so, and may be not,' he said, smiling. She studied him as he took a place – not too close, but not far either. She saw why, with the sun at his back, he had made her think of her lost lover. He had the same big-boned build, and he was well muscled and lithe. He moved with the assurance of the competent.

But up close he was quite different. His hair, she now saw, was brown touched with gray instead of Fost's night-black. The stranger had known far more than the courier had – or ever would. The stranger's eyes were brown and set in a network of fine laugh lines. His clothing was patched and travel-worn, but it was plainly of high quality. As was his manner, as well. He was no guttersnipe but a man of birth and breeding.

'If you'll pardon the impertinence of self-introduction, lady, I am Darl Rhadaman, Count-Duke of Harmis.'

'Lord Rhadaman,' she gasped. Darl Rhadaman, swordsman, strategist, orator, crusader ever in search of some new cause to champion, was no less than a legend. He'd fared around the world in his way, yet his finest hour had come in freeing his hereditary fiefdom of a wizard bent on subjugation.

A kiss on her hand brought her from her daze.

'And you, my lady? To whom have I the honor of offering my service?'

'Moriana Etuul, Heir to the City in the Sky.'

'So,' he said. 'Your pardon, Highness, for my unseeming familiarity.'

'Don't be ridiculous,' she said, pulling at his sleeve to prevent him from dropping a knee in obeisance. 'How do you know I'm not lying, anyway? I could tell you anything.'

'I have seen you, Highness, and heard of your sister's . . . assumption of the Beryl Throne.'

'Seen me? Where?' she asked, surprised.

'In this very city, Highness, not three years ago. The Festival of Debentures was underway and you were pointed out to me. I am appalled I could see you now and not remember your stunning beauty.'

'I-remember!' Moriana cried, clapping her hands. 'I had come to discuss the City's accounts with . . .' She couldn't give name to the banker who'd so recently denied her the means of conquering the City. 'Yes,' she said shortly, 'I was here. If I'd only known a man such as yourself was nearby!'

'I have a confession, Highness. I'm no longer Count-Duke of Harmis.'

'I didn't mean . . .'

'No offense taken, milady. I suppose I am still count-duke, when all is said and done. But I've renounced claim to my homeland.'

'Why?' Such a question would normally have been discourteous, but something in the man's manner told Moriana he wouldn't regard it as such.

'Peace,' Darl said, 'is a wonderful thing, a blessing for the people. The borders of Harmis are secured against foes within and without, and since I helped the people of my country find their pride again, few will issue a real challenge.'

He looked at her and said in a lower voice, 'Peace is a marvelous thing. And it's also boring as hell.'

Moriana's laugh startled her. It sounded strange, alien. It had been long since she'd laughed.

'So now my life story is yours. What of you, bright princess? I know some of the affairs of your City; the Realm lost a great leader in your mother. Tell me why Synalon sits on the Beryl Throne while you are desolate and alone on a bench in Tolviroth Acerte.'

Moriana started to speak, then halted herself. Could she trust this man? He had come to her precipitously, out of the night, a coincidence. Was he a spy for Rann? She cast that notion from her fatigued mind; Rann still did not know she lived. And she would have been whisked away to a dungeon by now. Rann's perverted sense of torture didn't extend to assignations like this.

Ziore, she spoke with her mind. *Ziore, can I trust this man?*

The pause drew her muscles taut. Darl looked at her expectantly with his kind brown eyes. In a moment expectation would turn to impatience. She couldn't afford to irritate him if he could help her. Had Ziore caught her thought?

I have scanned his soul with care, child, Ziore's thought poured smoothly into her mind. *His heart is good. Trust him.*

Moriana tried to speak, but her words were drowned in tears.

The day had been warm for winter, but as dusk deepened into night the bench became uncomfortable. They drifted to a restaurant

373

specializing in Port Zorn cuisine. Island cooking proved dull, but Tolviroth Acerte had an excellent assortment of foreign eating establishments. Moriana told the balance of her story over a meal of sea-grass salad with spiced, boiled crab, a main course of fillet of yellowharp boiled in butter and sweet wine.

Afterward, they walked along the palisades overlooking the harbor to the north. The wind blew off the Jorea, but the highlands of the island absorbed much of its fury. Still, a winter chill gave a steel edge to the wind. In the penetrating cold, it seemed only natural for Darl's strong arm to slip around her shoulders.

'You have done many fantastic things,' he told her, 'but Erimenes is perhaps the rarest treat of all. To have lived in Athalau of old! How I envy you that meeting.'

'Perhaps I should introduce myself,' Ziore said shyly from the depths of her jug. Darl stepped back a half pace, then slowly smiled, accepting. Then he laughed at his own reaction.

'I have indeed led a sheltered life,' he said. 'Never before have I met a jug of spirits quite like you!' He paused, shivered, and drew Moriana closer, saying, 'I could do with other spirits. Milady?'

It seemed only natural for Moriana to accompany the nobleman back to the small but snug room he had engaged at a nearby inn.

Darl poured her wine.

'I am in awe of you, Princess,' he said, seating himself on the bed. 'You've braved incredible hardships and survived unearthly peril. Take no offense, but without the amulet and an Athalar to confirm your tale, I'd find it impossible to credit you. But one thing I'm unclear on.' He sipped his wine. Light danced in his eyes and reflected the image of a single tallow candle. 'What actually happened to this comrade of yours, this Fost? I'd be honored to meet him.'

'I'm . . . that's impossible,' Moriana said, her eyes dropping to her lap where her hands intertwined helplessly. Her throat knotted up with tension as she realized she must tell Darl the truth.

'Fost is dead,' she said in a small, cracked voice. 'I killed him myself.'

Darl said nothing. She looked up and into Darl's eyes, seeking some sign of reproach or repulsion. She read nothing. Only . . . a waiting for explanation.

'Fost wanted the amulet for his own,' she said, the words beginning to tumble out in a carthartic rush. 'But I needed it to help overthrow my sister. It's not just for me but for my City! It's for the entire Sundered Realm that I must destroy Synalon. He couldn't see that.'

She covered her face with her hands. Uncontrollable weeping seized her. She knew she'd done right. She also knew she'd never be done reproaching herself.

Then Darl was beside her, holding her, soothing her. She turned her face to his chest and soaked his shirt with hot, bitter tears.

Though neither seemed to will it, they rose and went to the bed. Her face lifted, seeking his. Their clothes fell without conscious effort as their hands explored each other's body. Moriana's loss and pain crystallized into sudden flaring passion. She needed to open her soul and let her grief pour out.

She lay back. He smiled down at her, gentle, compassionate. And suddenly she remembered Ziore.

What did the spirit think? They'd shared love through many a bleak night in secret ways Ziore knew. Now, how would the shade of a long-dead nun react to sharing her lover with another?

Do not be foolish, child. Your pleasure is mine, however you may come by it.

Darl hovered above her. He had sensed her tension and held back. Her arms went around his neck and drew him down.

Then he was inside her. She moved passionately against him, almost fighting, and lost herself in a frenzy of release that was only in a small way physical. A flurry of motion and the barriers burst. He moved back and forth quickly lighting a fire that burned like the sun. They both lost identity in the blaze of ecstasy. And gradually they cooled, sighing and relaxing, fingers stroking, learning all that their initial urgency had given them no leisure to discover.

The candle flickered near the end of its life when Moriana awoke. She lay on her stomach becoming slowly and deliciously aware of Darl's hand caressing her back. He kissed her when he saw her eyes open.

'I can muster support among the City States,' Darl said musingly. 'Folk may not care much who rules the Sky City, but there are those who will follow wherever I lead. Still, we'll need funds.'

She raised herself on her elbows. Her breasts swung gently, brushing her nipples along the sheets, giving her an exquisite sensation. The amulet around her neck burned like a white star.

'You mean you're willing to help me? After I told you what happened to the last man who aided me?'

'You forget, Highness. I'm a man in search of a cause. In truth, it doesn't matter what cause. I thrive on action. I see justice in your cause; that's why I feel bound to help. A just cause requires sacrifice.'

'It wasn't Fost's cause.'

'I spoke of your sacrifice.'

Moriana reached out and ran a finger down the firm line of his jaw. She couldn't forgive what she'd done. But to know that another understood was comforting. Darl turned his face to kiss her palm.

'So,' he said, 'what about money? – before I become too distracted by your beauty.'

'I hate to disturb you,' said Ziore. 'I fear I can control only this one.'

'What? What do you mean?' demanded Moriana. 'What are you talking about, Ziore?'

Someone giggled.

Moriana realized with an icy shock that the giggle she heard came not from Ziore but from outside the room. Her eyes turned to the door.

A man stood there, short sword clutched loosely in his fingers.

'Hello,' he said, tittering. 'I was supposed to kill you. Isn't that absurd? You're friends!'

'Assassins,' hissed Darl.

The door flew open all the way and a second assassin rushed in.

Moriana and Darl rolled off the bed, groping for swords in the gloom. Moriana reached hers first. The blade hissed free and swung in a moaning arc to strike away a thrust at Darl's unguarded side. The second assassin danced back as Darl got his sword out and cut at him backhand.

The first assassin giggled insanely. His comrade shot him a furious look, drew a long, thin poniard with his left hand, and backed toward the wall waving both weapons menacingly.

Naked, the pair advanced. Without conscious thought, Moriana's hand moved.

The dagger blocked her thrust with a sliding clang. At the same instant, Darl's sword darted for the assassin's groin. The shortsword swept down – too far. Before the killer could react, the broadsword's point raised and sheathed itself in his guts.

His partner laughed himself into a fit of hiccuping.

Moriana teetered back to the bed and sat. Strength flowed from her. Her sword tip fell to the floorboards and stained them with dark, rich blood. She felt sick. She glanced down at the familiar cool

376

hardness of the amulet between her breasts. The blackness that had predominated was giving way to equilibrium.

'You hurt?' asked Darl. His voice was rough. Danger and death so soon after love had jarred his composure. Moriana shook her head. 'Well, then, let's see what Chuckles has to say about whoever hired the Brethren of Assassins to come for us.'

'Ask me anything,' the assassin said. 'Dear friends, how can I refuse you?'

Imin Dun Bacir knew opportunity when he saw it.

For fifteen years he'd held the coveted post of Chief Trade Factor for the Sky City in Tolviroth Acerte. In that time he had absorbed the true Tolvirot's appreciation for *opportunity*. And today fortune had granted him the most delectable opportunity of his career.

He had seized it.

When Derora V had died and Synalon assumed the Beryl Throne, Bacir had considered dropping everything and leaving. Synalon was utterly mad. He had never taken much interest in politics, but he knew that anything less than active support for Synalon would be construed as opposition. He had accumulated enough money as chief factor to make any Tolvirot proud. He could have gathered his treasure, bought passage on a fast ship, and spent his retirement in a villa in Jorea.

To do so, however, would have been to pass up a fabulous opportunity.

It had called just as he was sitting down to dinner in his Medurim-style mansion in the suburbs of Tolviroth Acerte.

'Tulmen Omsgib to see you, Notable,' Trune, his majordomo, announced. Bacir looked longingly at the steaming spread before him. He could not delay speaking with the banker. To defer business until after a meal would gain him a reputation for frivolity. To a Tolviroth the pursuit of gain was not like a sacrament, it *was* a sacrament. He arranged an expression of heartiness on his ample features and followed Trune to see what Omsgib had to say.

Imin Dun Bacir heard from Tulmen Omsgib how the Princess Moriana had come begging for money and how her request had been turned down on the grounds of not wishing to alienate his bank's best customer. Bacir solemnly thanked the banker for the interest in the Sky City, but his brain shifted into high gear as he figured ways of turning this tidbit to his own interest.

Omsgib gave him a clue by mentioning that he had assigned agents to watch the princess surreptitiously. Bacir quickly assured the banker that the Sky City's own men would assume these tedious duties.

Synalon would be lavish to whoever informed her that her sister still lived. And to the person who finally rid her of the threat Moriana posed, her generosity would know no bounds. Bacir considered capturing Moriana, then regretfully discarded the idea. Part of success in business was not to allow greed to overcome good sense. If Rann had been unable to eliminate Moriana, Bacir was not eager to risk capturing her alive.

The Brethren of Assassins was notified of a task as soon as Omsgib left. Bacir then turned back to his long-awaited meal. He scarcely noticed the food was cold. He wolfed it down, barely tasting it, then retired to his leisure rooms to inhale narcotic fumes and soothe his jangled nerves listening to a quartet of naked female musicians play archaic Medurimin chamber music.

Naked girls and archaic chamber music were his twin passions, after the accumulation of wealth. But not even they kept him diverted. After an hour, he dismissed them with an irritable wave of his hand. He turned to pacing grooves in his plush rug, waiting for word that the Brethren had fulfilled their commission.

The water clock had just dripped the eleventh hour when Trune appeared at the door of the leisure room.

'The assassins?' Bacir demanded harshly. Seeing his majordomo nod, he said, 'Well, don't stand there. Send them in at once.'

He quivered with tension and felt as if fat blue sparks would leap from his fingers like static electricity. He bounced up and down on the balls of his feet, chins jiggling, until he heard Trune's subtle footsteps padding down the corridor.

'G-good evening, Notable,' the assassin said. He laughed a squealing laugh through his nose. Bacir wondered if he'd been sniffing vapors, too. It hardly seemed appropriate for an assassin to indulge in such vices while on business.

Another, much larger man came in behind the first. Bacir sensed a third presence in the corridor. He frowned. Three assassins? The Brethren evidently considered Moriana formidable.

'Did you kill the princess?' he demanded, using the word 'kill' in spite of the Brethren's touchiness about its use. Bacir was in no mood to humor the hired help.

'Why, no, Notable. I've done much better than that.' He interrupted himself with a giggle. 'I've brought the princess to you.'

The third member of the small party came into the room. Her hair was spun gold, her eyes green balefires.

'Princess!' gasped Bacir. Trune started to move for a bell rope hanging by the wall. Darl's sword materialized and touched its tip to Trune's neck. The majordomo grew very still.

'That's right, cur,' said Moriana. 'Grovel. Grovel for your worthless life. You've earned a traitor's death, Bacir. I may not be as cruel as my sister, but do not mistake my motives. Give me one reason why you shouldn't pay for the attempted murder of your rightful sovereign.'

'Mercy,' sobbed Bacir. Tears rolled down his round cheeks onto the rings on his fingers, now clutched beseechingly before his face.

'There is a way, foul one,' she said, her voice low and menacing, 'for you to redeem yourself. You can aid me, dropping off a carrion-eater. To do so is no more than your sworn duty, but if you perform your task well, I shall be magnanimous. I will allow you to continue your wretched existence.'

'Mercy, bright one! Have mercy on me, O Mistress of the Clouds!' He rolled a tear-sheened eye at Moriana. She remained unmoved by his use of the title reserved for the Queen of the Sky City. 'I dare not help! Synalon will have my life for it!'

'That may be, but Synalon is far away. I am here.'

Baric stopped snuffling and peered at her from beneath quivering brows. It might have been a trick of the light, but at that moment Moriana bore a startling resemblance to her cousin Rann.

Squalling seabirds rode on the morning wind. Captain Uin Ragalla lounged at ease on his poop. He puffed great clouds of blue smoke from his pipe and contemplated the day's sailing. The wind blew northerly and the sky was blue. He could ask for nothing more. The *Black Flame* could warp out of harbor, run south with the wind through the Karhon Channel till it cleared the southern tip of the island, and be well on the way to Jorea by the noon bell.

A hail from the dock roused him from his reverie.

'What's that?' he demanded, looking up at the annoyance.

'Hail the ship.' The man calling to him was short and so fat as to be almost globular. The roundness of his face was accentuated by a black fringe of beard clinging to the uppermost of his myriad chins.

'What would ye?' Ragalla asked. His grasp of the Imperial Tongue spoken throughout the Realm was good for a Jorean.

'I would take passage to Jorea,' the man said, clutching a ragged cloak about him as the wind whipped up.

'And what'll ye pay with, then?'

'I have no money.'

Ragalla spat.

'Some chance. Nothin' for nothin' — that's what you Tolvirot always say, innit? Well, then.' He nodded and sucked aggressively at his pipe. Blue clouds rose from the bowl.

'But I'm not a Tolviroth,' the fat man protested.

'Nooo,' he said, studying the man. 'I suppose ye ain't. Fact be, I suppose you're that Factor fellow from the Floating City, then? Hey?'

The fat man nodded.

'Well, fancy that. The high-and-mighty trade fellow from that Sky City a'beggin' passage 'cross the sea without two sipans to clink together.'

'I've fallen on misfortune,' the man said with a certain dignity.

'So? May happen I'll fall and get misfortune all over my face one day, then.' He motioned to the man. 'Come aboard. I can always use another cabin boy, hey?'

Imin Dun Bacir took ship for Jorea as he had long planned. He left without the fortune he had spent so long accumulating. But he went with his life, and where he went not even Synalon's wrath could reach.

Imin Dun Bacir knew an opportunity when he saw one.

The Sleeper sensed a Presence.

The demon's subconscious groped for that nearness, a response born of loneliness. The first outpouring of joy crusted over with bitter resentment.

Words formed in its mind: *Why turn away?*

Blank refusal met the query. Again the Presence probed, gently, insistently. *Why turn your face from those who love you?*

Asleep, the demon could shape no coherent thought. Yet the emotion wrenched from it was as unmistakable as it was inchoate.

Betrayed!

The Presence read the outpouring of agony, the loneliness and helpless cruel confinement.

Help me! silently shrieked the demon. You could have helped me!

The Presence recoiled from the plaintive violence of the last

380

emotion. It poured forth its own thoughts like balm into the tortured Sleeper's mind.

I have not the power to help you. Not even those I serve — whom you serve — can free you unaided. But I bring tidings of joy. Soon, your time may come. You must prepare yourself to again serve.

NO! The Sleeper's denial was an eruption of negation. The Presence rode the blast like a free-floating leaf making no attempt to oppose its strength with the Sleeper's. Even asleep, the Demon of the Dark Ones possessed power of cosmic scope.

But freedom, the Presence promised. *You may soon stretch your limbs to the skies again. Is that not worth much? All?*

The Sleeper felt anger. Betrayal had come ingrained in its view of the universe. It knew the Presence lied. The emotion dropped low and sullen. It knew it would receive no help. It was alone, doomed, betrayed!

The Presence stifled its own surge of annoyance lest it anger the Sleeper more. The sleeping demon's mind only functioned in the most basic fashion, considering only appetite and the simplest of feelings. In its hurt anger the demon would spurn any offer of help hoping to wreak infantile vengeance on those who had betrayed it.

The Presence bided its time. It felt Istu's hatred. Reason would never pierce the shell of truculence.

Yet time grew short. The Aspects neared a critical conjunction. And the Lords of Infinite Dark had to know that their sole begotten child would be obedient to their wishes were he released.

A child cannot be reasoned with, the Presence thought to itself. *Yet a child can be bribed.* It turned from the sleeping, imprisoned giant and fled through the corridors of night. A plan formed in its mind.

CHAPTER EIGHT

'I have been betrayed before,' Synalon raged at Rann. 'I have been spurned by my own family, I have been schemed against, lied to, abused, and made to suffer for the failings of others. But never have I been subjected to a more humiliating failure. *Never!*'

Rann's guts trembled before his cousin's fury. If he got away with only being skinned alive, his luck would be extraordinary.

It was impossible for anyone else to have survived the ice fall. It had been only the wildest chance that an edge of the block had struck the portico of the Palace of Esoteric Wisdom and thus failed to crush all life from Rann; for all his resilience and the sorceries of the palace mages he had still not healed. None of the others could possibly have gotten out alive. Not Moriana, not Fost. Even the demon Erimenes should have had his jar pulverized.

Yet not an hour ago a messenger had arrived from Tolviroth Acerte with the stunning message: *Princess Moriana lived.*

Bringing the word to his royal cousin had been the hardest task the warrior-prince had ever faced.

Synalon stalked paving stones that carried the scars of her last foray into demonomancy. Not even Rann knew what the queen had done that night, though he had a few shrewd guesses. The next morning five mages of the palace had been found dead in their beds with expressions of horror twisted into their features. Whatever Synalon had done was potent.

It had also left her in a state of nerves that had sent eight of her lovers and three advisers into exile through the Well of Winds. Whatever else Synalon's ensorcellments had granted her, she had not been given peace of mind.

'You have my life, Your Majesty,' the prince said, eyes locked on the floor. 'You should have taken it before when I allowed your sister to escape.'

She gazed at him narrowly. Today she wore a gown of rich purple, almost indigo, which clung to her like mist. The fanciful condiment of feathers adorning her head fell in wild disarray.

'You – ' she began, but her lips trembled so badly she had to start over. 'You *dare* accuse me of misjudgment in leaving you with your foul life? Oh, you wretch, you rogue, you *groundling!*' Along with the epithet Synalon hurled a bolt of lightning that shattered a five-thousand-year-old statue. Guards and attendants scattered in all directions.

'Dark Ones!' she shrieked. Her hair began to crackle. 'Witness my mortification! I am served by dolts!'

She hauled a quivering Anacil from under the Beryl Throne by one skinny white ankle.

'Must I cast all my advisers down the Skywell? Come out of there, you miserable old fool!'

'Majesty,' he quavered. 'Y-your headdress, O Mistress of the Clouds. It's on fire!'

Synalon raised a hand to cinder her chamberlain. The hand stopped in the region of her right temple. With it frozen there, the queen cocked her head and sniffed. Then she snatched her bonnet, now billowing smoke, and hurled it into the arms of a guard.

'Throw that out the window, worm!'

The man trotted to obey.

'Very well,' Synalon said at length, struggling to control her rage. 'We are on the verge of taking the first step on our road to conquest. I know the penalty of failure as well as any. I cannot dispose of you, my cousin, if for no other reason than that your Sky Guardsmen will follow only you. But be warned. I will tolerate no further failure from you. The invasion will succeed or you will know my *full* wrath.'

Rann's mouth went dry. He remained kneeling, unable to believe what he'd heard. His cousin allowed him to live.

'Do not fear, Majesty,' he cried, springing to his feet. 'I will lead our troops to victory!'

He bowed and turned to go.

'One moment.' Synalon stopped him with that smoothly seductive, bitchy voice she used when she had something particularly vicious in mind. He swung slowly to face her. 'Those captives we took, spies trying to get into the City. How many still live?'

'Twelve, Majesty.'

'And they are in your safekeeping?'

'Certainly, Your Majesty. I plan to attend to their disposal personally.'

'How thoughtful.' She touched a finger to her chin and smiled wickedly. 'You have so much to do with the preparations for the coming invasion. I cannot ask you to sacrifice your time on such pursuits. Captain Tro!' The commander of her personal guard stepped forward. 'Send a party for my cousin's prisoners. Convey them to my dungeons. I shall see that they receive due punishment.'

The queen favored all in the room with a special look, seductive and promising. Rann's groin was empty but the nerves remembered. Too well, they remembered.

'See what a gracious sovereign you're blessed with,' she declared.

Rann tightened his face into an impassive mask. Twelve prisoners, twelve! And she robbed him of them. The torments he'd planned, the sweet expectation he had been nurturing, carefully allowing it to grow so that his ecstasy would be complete – all wasted.

'Your Majesty is too generous,' he said. 'I only hope to repay you in kind someday.' He left quickly before his queen spoke again.

The rulers of Bilsinx officially scoffed at the notion that their town had anything to fear from the Sky City. The townsfolk were in an uproar and weren't calmed when a score of rumormongers were flogged in the Central Square. The rumors stopped totally when Mayor Irb had five housewives dismembered by dray hornbulls.

Despite his official posture, the good lord mayor was plagued by a private uneasiness as he revealed to a distinguished visitor on the eve of the City's arrival.

'We are honored by your presence in our fair city, Count Ultur,' he said, slopping rakshak into his visitor's cup. 'Quite honored.'

'I thank you, my lord mayor,' said the Count Ultur V'Duuyek as he sipped at his potent liquor.

The mayor plunked his mug down on the arm of his chair. The green velvet upholstery was a mass of circles matching the underside of his mug. Irb was a man who liked his rakshak.

'Well? You're bound for the Sjedd, is it? Help them put down those beastly Thail savages?' He looked closely at the count and framed his eyes with what he thought to be a look of perspicuity. Dissolute shrewdness was all he managed.

384

'My dog riders are versatile and up to the task, I'm sure,' said the count. 'Besides, the Thails are quite low at their southern end, and the Sjedd is mostly savannah. A shaman has identified some of the southern tribes as those who've seized Sjedd territory. I will retake the country, then proceed into the foothills to chastise the tribesmen.'

The mayor nodded his understanding in the manner of those who don't really understand. He had heard of the disturbances in the Sjedd. Quite alarming. The Sjedd lay across the end of the Thails along the side of the Quincunx running between Brev and Thailot. Upheavals there always had a deleterious effect on trade. The military ramifications were beyond him.

He knew little of military matters, but he did know that the count's twelve hundred, heavily armored dog riders from the Highgrass Broad constituted considerable force.

'The Sky City goes overhead tomorrow,' he said slowly. 'You've doubtless heard the rumors, milord, that they plan to attack us. I've squelched such talk, to be sure, but still the rumors persist.'

When the count said nothing, Irb persisted.

'Do you think there's anything to it?'

'If they were to try it without substantial ground support, they would be foolish, indeed,' V'Duuyek said, his manner scornful.

The mayor sat back, nodding with satisfaction. The Bilsinx militia wasn't large, but it was kept in reasonable practice battling brigands and occasional nomads drifting in from the steppes. The token Sky City garrison of two hundred dog riders and a score of flyers could be dealt with easily.

'If the Sky City were to attack us, ridiculous as that seems – but *if* they did – your people would not idly sit by?'

'My lord mayor,' V'Duuyek said, smiling thinly and smoothing one horn of his meticulously waxed moustache, 'should fighting break out, I quite honestly doubt I could keep my people out of it.'

This satisfied the mayor, who bellowed out for more rakshak. With the problems of defense all solved, it was time for serious drinking.

For once, Erimenes found nothing to carp about in Fost's choice of a destination. Even the spirit's obsessive appetite for sensation was almost glutted by the brawling, splendid bazaar that was Kara-Est.

From its vantage point at the tip of the Gulf of Veluz, Kara-Est laid claim to being one of the great cities of the day. Younger and more vibrant than Medurim, earthier than the City in the Sky, possessed of an exuberance foreign to the staid merchants of Tolviroth Acerte, and vastly more cosmopolitan than her sister cities of the Quincunx, Kara-Est dinned her self-image into a visitor like an unceasing clangor of cymbals. Built on a cluster of hills that rose steadily as they marched inland, bounded to the northeast by swampland, and giving way to the steppes in the southwest, the seaport looked anything but prepossessing. Boxy homes clumped like hives on the hills. Each painted a different hue, they caught the morning sunlight and presented a chaotic impression. But after the initial shock wore off, the garish splashings of color assumed a curious harmony of their own.

Like giant balloons, the ludintip of the Mires swamps floated lazily above the city, propelling themselves by venting gas through sphincters in their air bladders. The beasts had long been domesticated by the Estil. The Estil alone of all the Realm's inhabitants shared the dominion of the sky with the Floating City. The occasional contrivances of hoops and rings and cross-braced frames on the higher rooftops were engines for defense against attack from the air.

Fost and Jennas rode in from the steppe side by side. With his usual lack of grace, Erimenes jounced along in his jug. A Northern stranger and a barbaric warrior woman from the south mounted on immense and fearsome bears would attract attention enough without a pale blue spirit hovering beside them like a friendly cloud.

The sentries on the New Wall gaped at the newcomers as the bears rolled through the city gates. The guardsmen fingered crossbows. The barbarians from the steppes seldom penetrated to Kara-Est, but when they did they seldom came for peaceful reasons. Nonetheless, this pair seemed well enough behaved.

To Erimenes' immense glee, Fost set a course for the waterfront district.

'At last!' crowed the spirit. 'To visit the fabled fleshpots of Kara-Est! From anecdotes I've heard, the cultural demonstrations to be seen at Madam Tinng's, particularly those involving Highgrass Broad warrior-girls and their dogs, are most educational.' He chortled. 'I'm sure healthy, hot-blooded youngsters such as yourselves will require no schooling from me in the full appreciation of Kara-Est's fabled vices.'

Fost sighed. The philosopher, after giving up his ascetic principles on death, had settled into a perpetual adolescence. Since he lacked the physical equipment to sate his newly acknowledged drives, they grew constantly sharper all the time. Jennas eyed the satchel with more pronounced distaste than usual. Erimenes' mention of the fanciful displays put on by the warrior-maidens had touched a raw nerve. From the morning they'd set out, Erimenes had been suggesting a novel manner for Jennas to improve rapport with her bear. While the Ust-alayakits lived on terms of intimacy with their beasts, the kind of intimacy espoused by Erimenes was regarded by the nomads with acute horror. Jennas in turn had taken to proposing new and colorful ways in which Fost might dispose of his all-too-familiar spirit.

'I thought you'd been to Kara-Est before, Erimenes,' said Fost, as they jogged down a cobbled street accompanied by the stares of the townsfolk.

'Not so. I am always receptive to experience, even repeated experience. In my wisdom I've learned to eschew the young's insistence on novelty.' He sighed. 'Besides, when I came through here before I was in the charge of an acolyte mage from Duth. He'd taken some silly vow of celibacy and wouldn't sway from it. Were it not for your sterling example, Fost, I would sorely fear for the manhood of those from the north.'

'I hate to damage your high opinion of me,' Fost said sarcastically, 'but we aren't going to be exploring the dives. We haven't time. And don't protest,' he continued over Erimenes' outraged cry, 'or I may reconsider Jennas's suggestion that we sell you to a merchant captain for a chamberpot.'

The spirit shut up. Fost smiled. The verbal infighting helped take his mind off the three weeks he'd spent in the saddle – and Moriana.

They climbed a hill, the bears' strong claws giving purchase on the ice-slicked cobblestones. Jennas gasped as the harbor came into view. They paused to take in the impressive sight, then rode down into the city's heart.

For Jennas it was almost too much. She'd been briefly in small trading towns south along the Gulf of Veluz; Kara-Est was a hundred times larger than the greatest of those. Even Fost, raised in the Teemings, the stench-ridden and overcrowded slums of High Medurim, couldn't help being impressed.

Bars and brothels, houses of gambling and houses of worship, government offices, warehouses, theaters, dwellings rich and dwellings shabby, all jostled each other around the wide sweep of the bay. Hundreds of ships rode at anchor in the largest harbor of the Realm. And with the ships came sailors from around the world: surly, shaggy traders from the Northern Continent; blond savages from the Isles of the Sun who powdered themselves with gold dust and were followed by gaggles of mute, drugged slaves; wide-eyed scholars of the Far Archipelago, their wan otherworldliness reminding Fost of the Ethereals of the Great Crater Lake; black merchant captains from hot Jorea forced by the coming antarctic winter to supplement their usual garb of kilts and sandals with heavy fur cloaks.

They tethered the bears to a hitching post in front of an establishment whose sign proclaimed it the *Storm-Wrack Inn.* Riding dogs whined and cringed away from the gigantic newcomers. A stout townsman started to protest. Jennas glared at him and hitched at the strap of her greatsword. He gulped, unhitched his mount, and rode off looking nervously over his shoulder.

They went inside. Fost made his way to a hardwood bar with a gleaming rail of juggernaut fish ivory, ordered sack for himself, and with a shudder, *amasinj* for Jennas. The barkeep, a tall man with a glazed eye, took the order without comment. He didn't even comment when Erimenes demanded loudly to know when the indecent displays began. In a cosmopolitan town such as Kara-Est, not even disembodied voices emerging from jugs excited comment.

Fost elbowed his way back to Jennas in time to be nearly bowled over by a sudden commotion. Yelping bar patrons shoved by him. In the space they left vacant, he saw Jennas pitching a bearded docker out the door. She turned away, dusted off her hands with an air of satisfaction, and resumed her seat.

'What was that all about?' he asked, handing over her mug.

'The lout wished me to kiss him,' she said, downing a slug of her drink that would have stretched Fost on the floor. 'I refused. When he persisted, I put him out.' Fost nodded. He'd never doubted the hetwoman was capable of taking care of herself.

He sipped his own drink more conservatively. They hadn't come to the tavern to indulge Erimenes, who was now suggesting that a redheaded serving girl at a table nearby give into the importunings of a Northlander with checkered trousers and one hand on her rump. Fost was looking for information. He was certain Moriana headed for the Sky City. What he didn't know was its exact location.

Jennas tensed at his side. He glanced at her, following her gaze. Across the table from them stood a tall, dark-skinned woman with the brassard of a Jorean sea captain encircling one arm. She was a handsome, robust woman with gray strands mingling with midnight curls. Her cloak dangled from her shoulders, revealing bare breasts, big and firm and gleaming like polished ebony. She stared with frankly sexual interest – at Jennas.

'Ho there, missy,' she said, saluting the startled Jennas with a foaming jack of ale. 'You're quite a sight, and that's for certain. What say you you ditch this jocko and come with me? I've never seen a lass the likes of you.'

Jennas's eyes went round. Clearly, she was uncertain she'd heard the mariner clearly – which Fost thought for the best. If she had, her next move would have been for the wire-wound hilt of the great-sword leaning against the stuccoed wall. The Jorean was no more the sheltered type than Jennas. She was as tall as the tribeswoman and carried the cutlass familiarly at her hip. Except for the fact she was bare-breasted while Jennas wore her mail, they looked well matched.

She leaned forward, smiling widely.

'Well? What say you? I've a string of pearls on board my *Wave-strider* that'd ride right lovely around your throat.'

'No, thank you,' Jennas said a bit unsteadily. 'Your offer is kind, but I'm happy where I am.'

Fost looked at her in surprise. The mores of the Ust-alayakits being what they were, he'd expected Jennas to carve up the other woman for suggesting such a liaison. Later, he learned that such relation-ships, between two males or two females, were not unknown among the southern tribes; like other sexual matters, they were regarded as the private concerns of the participants.

The captain shrugged and turned away, looking sad.

'Just a moment, captain,' said Fost. 'Have a seat and drink with us. We're new in town and would hear the latest news.'

'You're a good sport, friend,' said the Jorean, cocking her head to one side. 'I'll say that for you.' She sat on a stool across from the pair. 'It would do me poor credit to spurn such generosity. Never let it be known that Captain Karlaya, mistress of the cog *Wavestrider*, ever turned down the invitation to drink.'

'I'm Jennas, hetwoman of the People of Ust. My companion is Fost Longstrider. He's a Realm-road courier. We're pleased to make your acquaintance.'

'A nomad chieftain and a road-rider, eh? I can pick 'em, that's for sure. Good for me neither of you took offense. Damn mainlanders squall so when a simple proposition is laid on 'em.' She eyed Fost more carefully. 'Aye, a good thing you took no offense. I know enough of this Realm of yours to know what a handful you can be.'

'You might have introduced me,' piped up Erimenes peevishly. 'But then again, I can't expect reasonable behavior from you, Jennas. You proved that by turning down the captain's gracious offer. I'm sure she'd be much more stimulating company than this sluggard Fost.'

'You wouldn't need a new slop jar, would you?' Fost asked the captain, who stared wide-eyed at the satchel.

Fost explained Erimenes' clay-prisoned existence, there no longer being reason to keep his existence secret. Karlaya was fascinated by Erimenes and offered to buy him on the spot. For reasons he didn't fully understand, Fost turned down the generous offer. Erimenes did not seem upset at remaining with Fost. He might have been afraid the captain would put his jar to the use Fost had proposed.

Fost bought another round of drinks. Eyeing the serving maid, Karlaya ordered *amasinj*. When it came, she tasted it, pronounced it unfit to drink, drained her mug, and ordered another. As she worked on the second mug, she related some rumors she'd heard.

Mostly it was standard gossip, incomprehensible to Jennas and useless to Fost. Port Zorn was raising its harbor fees; the Emperor in High Medurim had decreed a new pleasure dome, the fourth of his brief reign; sundry border skirmishes occurred. When the captain mentioned the Sky City's unusual activity the courier pricked up his ears.

'Is there any word of Princess Moriana?' he demanded.

'Surely, there is.' Karlaya mulled over a mouthful of drink as Fost fumed. She swallowed, studying the two. 'You look to know how to swing those swords of yours, so maybe this will interest you. You are looking for employment?'

'What do you mean?'

'The Princess What's-her-name, she's in league with Darl Rhada-man of Harmis. They're recruiting mercenaries up in Tolviroth Acerte.'

Snow drifted from a low-hung sky. An appearance of business as usual prevailed in Bilsinx as the City in the Sky floated in from the north. Mayor Irb stood on a balcony of his palace at the exact center of the Great Quincunx, the point over which mystic forces steered the City to a new destination.

390

Despite his official insistence that nothing was to be feared, Irb had mobilized his city's militia. Afraid that an obvious show of force might provoke an unfortunate response, in the air or on the ground, he had ordered many of his troops to remain under cover in the government buildings around the center of the town. The rest mingled with the crowds – merchants, dockers, casual shoppers, and the curious who thronged the cruciform Quincunx Avenues that followed the possible lines of the City's flight.

Titanic fungus-shaped balloons sprouted from the City even before it passed the northernmost walls of Bilsinx. Irb nodded, reassured. He had dreaded the possible explosion of eagle's wings from the Sky City's battlements. The appearance of the familiar, harmless, cumbersome cargo craft was anticlimactic.

The wind streamer dropped from the City's forward piers, a weight dragging a long orange banner behind to tell the Sky Citizens how the wind lay so they could guide their balloons with the least difficulty.

Messengers materialized at Irb's elbow. The barracks of the Sky City garrison had been discreetly surrounded. If anything was tried, the birdsmen would have no support from the ground. And word came from the camp of the Highgrass Broad mercenaries east of town that they were saddling and arming. In case of real trouble, Irb could expect rapid reinforcement from a well-trained cavalry.

The wicker gondola of the lowest balloon bumped cobblestones. The waiting crowd surged forward, handlers reaching for line to dog the balloon to earth. The gondola's side fell away.

Someone screamed shrilly. An instant later, a barrage of arrows burst from the knot of men standing beneath the balloon. The crowd stood stunned. Another volley and frightened townspeople began to run.

Irb gestured frantically. A company of dog cavalry issued forth from the gate of the Palace of Just and Perfect Governance and headed for the outbreak. Elsewhere along the north-south axis of the city, balloons touched down, disgorging their lethal cargo.

And now the dreaded wings of the Sky Guardsmen gripped the sky. Like malevolent spores, the birds dropped from the City, streaking down to preselected Bilsinx targets. Irb shrieked orders to his personal bodyguard. A hundred eagles dived straight for the ramparts of the palace itself!

In the Sky City, commands were shouted to waiting work gangs. Muscle was applied to levers, and heavy stones that had been hauled up from the surface were jacked over the side. Trajectories calculated by City mathematicians, the missiles fell in advance of the landing parties, smashing against pavement to send lethal shrapnel whistling in all directions. Fleeing citizens were shredded by the fragments. Another rock landed on the lead elements of the column riding from the palace. The commander was killed instantly and the remaining dog troopers scattered.

Wounded dogs wailed. Women shrieked. Men fell gurgling with arrows through their throats. The bird riders swept low, shooting indiscriminately into the panicked mass below. The soldiers Irb had ordered interspersed with the mob died where they stood, unable to form any effective fighting force.

But resistance did gather in the Central Square. Footmen with shields and short spears poured from nearby buildings. Dog riders loped to join them, their mounts baying bloodlust. The Bilsinx cavalry were mainly unarmed bowmen equipped to meet the threat of mounted brigands. Their bows sang and arrows arced skyward. Infantry bowmen guarded by their comrades' shields added their missiles to the defensive barrage.

The leading Sky City men died screaming. Shots from the ground did not need to reach riders. Transfixed, eagles plummeted like giant snowflakes, their riders cast helplessly down to smear the cobbles with their lifeblood. A wounded eagle fluttered near the cube-shaped palace as though trying to land on the roof. Two-score arrows feathered its rider as he cast a javelin in pitiful defiance.

Southward floated the City, silent and still deadly. The battle roared and howled and clashed below. Sky City arrows and javelins slaughtered defenders in the Central Square. But officers of initiative were countering the aerial threat. On their orders, troops dragged tables and other furniture from surrounding buildings to erect lean-to shelters to protect the archers while they shot. Others barricaded the avenues leading to the square.

Outside the square there was little organized resistance. But the problem the Sky City strategists had foreseen – and dreaded – had arisen. Their balloon-landed assault teams lacked strength to storm the square and were taking casualties from the archers sent scurrying from the central strongpoint. Given time, the bird riders would wear down the defenders, clear out the square, and then land soldiers to finish the battle. Wherever resistance cropped up, bird riders could harry from above and drop troops to take the defenders in the rear.

Already, flight after flight of eagles dove down on the palace, raking its roof with storms of arrows. They would land on its roof very soon.

But only at a fearful cost in lives of men and birds, lives the City in the Sky could not afford.

This was of academic interest to Irb. He nodded in irritation when the Captain of the Palace Guard informed him of the fact; what did it matter that the might of the Sky City was broken when *his* city was captive? He was about to snarl a rebuke to his commander when the skirl of trumpets drew his attention to the east.

The Highgrass cavalry of Ultur V'Duuyek rode to action under bright swallowtail pennons.

'There,' said Irb with satisfaction. '*Now* we shall see results.'

The scale armor of the dog riders shone dully in the gray morning light. The leader, a compact rider with blue and green ribbons fluttering from the spired top of his helm, raised his sword above his head and dropped it with a chopping motion. Arrows rose from the ranks.

And fell among the startled defenders of the Central Square.

The mobs that had clogged the streets leading to the center of Bilsinx had evaporated, leaving behind only still, dark forms. Nothing hindered the dog riders as they charged down the broad avenue, loosing flights of arrows at the defenders. Militiamen fell among carts and tables and crates in unfinished barricades. Archers returned the mercenaries' barrage. Steel scales clanked like the wings of a billion locust-encased men and dogs alike. The Bilsinxt arrows had no more effect than the gentle falling snow.

Bilsinxt dog riders charged to meet the new threat. Their arrows finally took a toll among the Highgrass Broad riders. The mercenaries slung bows across armored backs, unclamped lances from brackets set alongside their saddles, couched, and charged. Heavy riders met a light wall. The Bilsinxt countercharge melted like a sandcastle struck by a sea wave.

Irb had time to call down the curse of the Dark Ones on the treacherous Count Ultur. Then a five-ton rock from above smashed into the north face of the palace, obliterating Irb and the balcony on which he stood.

Weakened, the battlemented edge of the roof slumped, falling into the street in a stately, horrid silence. The City's savants had reckoned well. As planned, a picked commando unit of six-score Sky Guards-men swooped in the wake of the giant stone. Their eagles' claws scraped to landings on the roof, even as the defenders tried to grasp the horrifying fact that fully a quarter of their number had been dashed to ruins by the huge rock.

First to touch down was a huge black eagle, head crowned by a crest the color of blood. The bird named Terror voiced its bulging war cry as its rider leaped lithely from its back, scimitar and hornbull-hide buckler in hand. Though not fully recovered from his wounds, Prince Rann Etuul led the attack. He had to be there when the stricken city received its deathstroke. With a deft blow, he laid open a spearman from clavicle to hip. Then he was running for a stairway, his Guardsmen shouting triumphantly at his back.

The Grasslanders drove like a lance into the Central Square. Raked bloody from above, ridden down by iron riders from behind, the defenders broke. The lucky ones made it into nearby buildings. The rest were shot down by flying archers. Other bird riders dropped their mounts onto the backs of fleeing militiamen. The defenders' cries rang hideous and defeated as the warbirds disemboweled them.

Prince Rann's men spread throughout the palace like a black and purple plague. Rann cut his way through a shouting rabble to the courtyard, swept the last defenders from the gates, and swung the portals open to clasp his leather glove in Count Ultur V'Duuyek's bloodstained steel gauntlet.

The City in the Sky had won the vital first battle in its campaign of conquest. It had taken forty-three minutes.

Snow fell softly, laying a white shroud over the dead.

CHAPTER NINE

Torchlight splashed orange and ominous down the snowy flanks of the hills to strain the listeners' faces.

'Free men of the North,' Darl said loudly, 'hear me!'

They heard. Standing in the snow with their breath coming in white plumes, the men of the Black March listened to Darl Rhadaman's words. Chores would be neglected that night, beds unoccupied until late. When Rhadaman spoke, men attended.

'Long has the City in the Sky held itself aloof from the affairs of the surface,' he went on, voice deep and clear. 'Even contemptuous, aye. But always apart, alone, trading its magic for the goods we produced. They are sharp traders; so are the Tolvirot. In all, we and they profited.

'Now they are discontented. They want to rule the surface as they command the air above. They have treacherously attacked the Five Cities. They came sowing death from the air and Bilsinx fell. So shall it be until every city in the Quincunx is theirs. But will they be content to stop then? No!'

He swept his gaze around the throng of onlookers. The night was as still as a cathedral.

'With the wealth of the Quincunx they will buy mercenaries as they bought the dogs of the Highgrass to bay after their foes and drag them down. They will spread their dominion like a creeping sickness – no! – like a fever, raging, spreading, until all the Realm is infected with their evil.'

'We must act. The time is now when their schemes are aborning, when their treacherous grip on the ground is tenuous. Now they are vulnerable. Soon they will build momentum and power. And then your steads and crops will be theirs, your wives and children sacrificed screaming to the Dark Ones whose worship the usurper has revived. Will you have that? *Will you?*'

'*NO!*'

The sound boomed forth like the roar of Omizantrim in full eruption. Darl stood erect in the full force of their rage and fury. His expression was transfixed, transported, ecstatic. He was in his element. He lived for moments of power like this.

The incoherent burst of hatred resolved into words.

'Lead us, Darl!' the mob howled. 'Lead us! We'll claw the City down from the sky!'

Standing just beyond the full glare of the torches, Moriana shuddered. She felt the blood-hunger gripping the crowd. If they realized a Sky City noble was practically in their midst, they'd turn on her and rend her like enraged war dogs.

'You wish to destroy the City, then, brothers?' Darl called. He fixed a tall, vigorous onlooker with his gaze.

Singled out, the man waved his cap in the air and cried, 'Yes!' The fever of destruction on him, he added, 'Will you lead us, Darl?'

'No.'

The word dropped like a stone among them. Exuberance left the throng. They stared at the speaker. Hostility began to replace adoration.

'You do not wish to destroy the City in the Sky. Who among you does not benefit from their magics? The metalworker whose captive elemental increases his production tenfold and more? The herdsman whose flocks are kept free of pestilence by Sky City wards and potions? No, my friends. To destroy the Sky City would be to destroy yourselves.'

'But, Lord Darl,' said the man he'd singled out as spokesman for the crowd, 'what do you want of us?' He scratched behind prominent ears. 'One minute you issue the call to arms, and now you'd have us swear eternal friendship with the City. How can we do both?'

'Your quarrel is not with the City, brother,' said Darl, 'nor yet with its people. It is with those who rule the City: Synalon, the evil sorceress who calls on the Dark Ones. She and her minions would make you bend your necks to the yoke of slavery.

'You fear the Sky City, and rightfully so. Yet you cannot exist without it. So you ask, what are you to do?'

He looked around, eyes boring into the innermost recesses of each man's mind.

'You can serve yourselves and at the same time serve a higher justice as well. You can right the wrong Synalon did in seizing the Beryl Throne for herself. For you all know that Synalon is not the true and proper ruler of the City. Her sister, who would be friend to all the peoples of the Sundered Realm, desires only peace and prosperity. Her cause is just. Her cause is *yours*.

'You ask what you can do? I say to you, swear yourselves to Moriana's cause as I have done myself!' And he nodded to Moriana, who stepped forward into the circle of torchlight.

The acclamation washed over her like the ocean's tide.

They had gained over five million klenor from Imin Dun Bacir in Tolviroth Acerte, the sum total of his personal fortune. As Moriana told him, his life was a bargain at any price.

Moriana had thought they had all the money they needed. To her chagrin, Darl corrected her. They had nowhere near the requisite amount to mount a campaign – or a single battle – against the Sky City.

Moriana and Darl remained another week in Tolviroth Acerte winnowing the mercenaries who thronged to the island in search of employment. They looked for leaders of proven skill and experience to command, and a few especially battle-hardened warriors to act as cadre for the volunteer armies Darl promised to raise. With the majority of Bacir's money remaining, the pair *then* started putting together an army.

Even after the news of the fall of Bilsinx reached the North, Moriana got no support from the surviving Quincunx Cities. Each had plans of its own for meeting this new menace, plans in which the pretender to the Beryl Throne didn't fit.

They continued from Wirix northwest to the River Merchant, which bordered that conglomeration of feuding states still called the Empire. Here Darl enjoyed his greatest renown. Here it was that he hoped to garner the bulk of the army to press Moriana's claim to the throne.

The princess still couldn't believe her good fortune in meeting the count-duke. Who else in all the Realm would swear to aid her to victory or follow her to defeat on their first encounter? Mere infatuation was unlikely to motivate anyone of intellect and talent to be of service to her.

But Darl's attraction for her was not the reason he joined her. The reason was simply as he'd stated it: he needed a cause. Without some crusade, some quest, his life lacked meaning. Challenging the City promised the adventure of a lifetime.

Moriana only marveled at the coincidence that brought him and her to Tolviroth Acerte at the same time. It was part and parcel of the bewildering luck she'd been experiencing. One minute she was given great good fortune, the next it was snatched away. It was as if some mad god toyed with her destiny.

But it was no mad god. It was the Destiny Stone.

She still believed she possessed the Amulet of Living Flame. She had marked the fluctuations in color, dark to light, light to dark, in the amulet's great jewel. She had even connected the shifts in hue with her own fortunes. But it never occurred to her that the talisman caused the twists in destiny. She merely thought the amulet had a subsidiary property of measuring a person's good fortune at any given instant. She credited it to the wisdom of the Athalar and thought no more about it.

Again Moriana marveled at her luck in finding Darl. He possessed the means of effectively accomplishing her ends. And he was a magician whose skills rivaled Synalon's.

Sorcery had nothing to do with his talent. His magic was in his tongue and the skill with which he plied it.

His speech was like a torch. It set afire the souls of those who heard it. When she thought about the things Darl had said, it seemed to Moriana there was little remarkable about them. But something in his manner of speaking, his presence, lifted men up and out of themselves. This was the greatest gift he brought to Moriana.

The chorus of approval roared on and on. Moriana faced the crowd, her head held high, trying to look noble and resolute. They would get a hundred volunteers from this gathering, perhaps more, and this was only a small meeting. Success rode on the air like a banner.

And yet she irrationally felt uneasiness dogging her at every turn.

Prince Rann stalked the vaulted corridor that led to the queen's throne chamber. His steel-rimmed bootheels rapped authoritatively, echoes diminishing behind him like the wake of a ship. He wore new boots in the fashion of the Highgrass Broad riders. Unlike the light, soft, knee-high moccasins worn by the Sky City flyers, these were of heavy grazer leather and came to mid-thigh when unrolled. Now the tops were folded rakishly below the prince's knees. He had been given them as a gift from Destirin Luhacs, V'Duuyek's second-in-command, in commemoration of Bilsinx. They were too heavy to wear astride a warbird, but it pleased Rann to wear them about the palace.

He contemplated the coming interview with his cousin with great satisfaction. In the flush of conquest, she had forgotten all about the Athalau affair.

From Bilsinx, the Sky City had proceeded southward passing over Brev and then veering toward Thailot. Of all the Quincunx Cities, Brev was the weakest, and the Hereditary Council governing her knew it. As the City approached, they held hurried consultation, then sent word that the Sky City was as welcome as always to trade there. The City did not answer. Yet when its vast oblong filled Brev's sky, the cargo balloons drifting down held only magic artifacts and other trade goods.

The Sky City had bigger game in mind.

The three remaining Quincunx Cities followed Rann's expectations. Thailot couched its submission in terms of caring little what befell those on the other side of the Thails, but submitted nonetheless. Not so with Wirix and Kara-Est. The Jewel of Wir interned all Sky Citizens on the island and sent its defiance to Synalon. Kara-Est contemptuously expelled the Sky-Born and sent no other message to their aerie.

After Bilsinx was secured and Sky City agents had informed Rann by means of communicator crystals that the news had reached the seaport city, he dispatched a squad of Sky Guardsmen to make an aerial reconnaissance of Kara-Est. Intelligence reports indicated that the Estil were devoting their whole attention to shoring up their defenses.

Observers' riding baskets slung from Iudintip spotted the patrols' wings far off. No other living gasbags rose to challenge the bird riders. The Sky City commander gloated until the ballistae mounted on revolving platforms on Kara-Est's rooftops engaged his patrol. A steel missile pierced a rider's leg, pinning it to his mount's chest. A frantic midair rescue attempt failed. He plunged to death with his mount on the steep streets below. Another eagle was grazed by a bolt before the patrol winged out of range.

Rann had been furious at the news. But the setback was only temporary. Fate – or perhaps the Dark Ones – had gained the City time to prepare for its duel with Kara-Est. Rann knew how to make use of time. When the Sky City passed over the seaport, the groundlings would be amply repaid for their presumption.

Far more serious had been the tidings that Moriana had formed a liaison with Darl Rhadaman. The possibility existed, as much as Rann hated to admit it, that the slippery bitch and her new consort would be able to scrape together enough second sons, criminals, and others in the degenerate North to harry the City's lines of communication. If that happened, he would have to divert precious manpower to avert the threat.

Amazingly, Synalon had taken even that news with equanimity. Rann had expected that more than antique statuary would fall victim to her lightning bolts. But his royal cousin had merely nodded distractedly when he gave her the word and had gone back to feeding gobbets of raw meat to one of her loathsome talking ravens.

Now he was on his way to report that the palace mages met with greater success than anticipated in generating new fire elementals. The salamanders had a special role in the upcoming battle.

'Highness?'

The familiar nasal voice stopped him in his tracks. He wheeled to face Maguerr the mage.

'What is it?' Rann asked. The network of scars covering his face whitened at the strain of keeping his tones polite.

Maguerr was a pissant; what affronted the prince most was that Maguerr was an indispensable pissant. No other sorcerer in the City had his skill in the magics of communications crystals. Though Maguerr's manner with Rann was as unctuous as ever, Rann had to be polite — and he hated it. The rumor had even started that Synalon toyed with the idea of inviting Maguerr to her chambers for nocturnal consultations.

'Word comes from our agents in Kara-Est, lord.' Maguerr fingered sandy wisps of beard. The gray and maroon robes of his recently earned mastery had not lent him dignity. He looked like a scrawny waif who had pilfered a Master Mage's wardrobe.

'Well, what is it?' demanded Rann impatiently.

Maguerr's head bobbed up and down as though on a string.

'Two strangers of a most peculiar variety, lord. They came from the south out of the Southern Steppes, and they rode giant bears.'

Rann stared at him, eyes suddenly without color.

'One of them,' Maguerr continued through his nose, 'was no less

400

than the hetwoman of a clan of bear-riding savages. The other . . .' and he preeened like a warbird, ' . . . the other was a Medurimite courier, Fost Longstrider by name.'

Rann felt fingernails digging into his palms. He was glad his sleeves hid his hands. He didn't want Maguerr to guess the intensity of his reaction.

'So the Long-strider lives,' he mused, almost glad. In his bumbling way, the courier had been a formidable opponent. 'And the chieftain of the bear riders accompanies him. What can this mean, I wonder?' His mouth stretched into a taut grimace. He had not forgotten the Ust-alayakits, how they came from the night to take his Sky Guardsmen in the rear and slaughter them like children when he had the Long-strider at swords' points and Moriana not much farther away. Not since that terrible day in the Thails had he suffered such humiliation.

'Glad tidings you bring me, Maguerr, glad tidings indeed.' He patted the adolescent on the shoulder. 'I must confer with Her Majesty now. But await me in my chambers. We must discuss how best to use this intelligence of yours.'

Without knowing why, Synalon came instantly awake.

She lay for a moment in her bed, straining to hear that which made no sound. She slowly identified those she could hear. From without came the noises caused by the wind in its ceaseless dance past the high windows. The low creakings and settling sounds of the floating City seemed to rumble up through her mattress and naked body. Steam from salamander-heated boilers whispered through a coil of brass pipes across the chamber from her great bed. The radiated heat kept away the worst of the night chill, but it was cold outside and the heavy quilted comforters felt good.

Yet the silken sheets matted to her profusely sweating body. Her well-honed instincts sensed a deadly danger lurking. She summoned up the mental clarity needed to cast firebolts before she scanned the darkened, sparsely appointed bedchamber.

One advantage to the austerity was that it left few places for an intruder to hide. The queen lay motionless, flickering her gaze along the walls: nothing. Lids low and feigning sleep, she rolled onto her back to search the other half of the chamber. The delightful, skin-prickling caress of the Wirix silk sheets on her nipples went unnoticed.

Still, the subliminal message of danger gnawed at her brain. Menace was near. She knew it. Finally, reluctantly, she looked toward the last direction from which a person in a raven-guarded citadel a mile above the earth would expect attack.

As she turned her attention to it, the window exploded inward.

She lay stunned as the doubled arch of glass and metal bowed inward and burst in a blizzard of glittering fragments. The carnage occurred in absolute silence. And for all its violence, it happened with awful deliberation, as if time had grown tired of its endless race and had slowed to catch its breath.

A galaxy of shards cascaded to the floor. Her years of probing the dark corners of the mystic had inured her to both wonder and horror. Yet this was so strange, so unnatural, that all she could do was lie and watch as the glass became a diamond pool of granules on the floor.

She looked up. A figure stood on the sill.

'Guard!' she shouted, even as she reached for the sheathed dagger under her mattress.

The door slammed open. She winced at the abrupt loudness. Two Palace Guards stood with swords clutched in trembling hands.

Her coverlet had fallen away, baring breasts that shone blue-white in the light of the lesser moon. Making no move to cover herself, the queen gestured at the black dwarf crouching on the sill. The guardsmen charged.

The figure shook its head. Synalon discerned no features in the darkness, nothing about the intruder save that its proportions were those of a human dwarf with head large, torso small, and arms and legs stumpy and short. It reared up, however, to the height of a tall man. She caught a glimpse of blunt projections from either side of the long skull, and then the thing turned to face the onrushing guards.

The being laughed. Its chuckle gusted forth like a desert wind. Synalon saw it emerge as a mist of darkness that blew toward her attacking soldiers.

The breath-cloud roiled about the leading guard. He stopped, dropped his sword, and clapped hands to his face. The chamber rang with the sound of his shrill scream. Behind him, his companion stopped. He raised his weapon. The cloud enveloped him. He began to quiver and a gibbering sound, half laughter and half sobbing, bubbled from his lips.

The first guard dropped to his knees. His fingers turned mottled and dark. Synalon watched as the flesh dropped away, leaving the bones as naked as dead twigs. The flesh of his face blackened, too. His eyes met hers, immense orbs goggling from pits of bone, in a look of agony and supplication. Then he fell forward. Seconds later the other guard joined him in death. Through the rippling of mail on mail the queen distinctly heard the soft squashing of putrid flesh.

She moved quickly from the bed, the chill of the flagstones against her soles. With a conscious effort, she forced down the nausea she felt. She raised a silvery arm and aimed her hand at the apparition, palm foremost, fingers wide.

Power raged within her, fueled by fear and hatred and hot anger. The coverlet, bunched and fallen against one smooth thigh, began to smolder. Her hair lifted in a crackling cloud.

White fire blasted from her palm. Her eyes glowed like beacons as heat waves shimmered up from her pale, naked body. Never had she called up such power. The lightning bolt should have spattered the black apparition all over the room. It should have fused the very frame of the window into a vitreous lump.

It should have, it didn't. The lance of stark, raw energy lashed fully into the being's chest, then disappeared.

Synalon reeled. The stink of charred feathers from her coverlet seared her nostrils. She squinted at the glowing suns orbiting in front of her eyes. Beyond them, solid and black and impervious, stood the dwarf.

The thing chuckled again. The harsh and lifeless sound seemed more familiar to her now. Synalon poised for rapid action, but no cloud of corruption accompanied the laugh.

'Poor child,' the creature said. It stepped from the sill. The huge, ungainly figure seemed to float to the floor as if being lowered gently from a balloon.

Synalon let her head slump. Her hair hung in midnight swirls down the slope of her breastbone. Her arms hung limp at her sides. The intruder chuckled again in approval of her apparent submission.

But it was only feigned. As the black soles noiselessly touched stone, a wild cry ripped the night and a bird streaked in through the gaping window. The raven darted in for the kill.

With venom-gleaming claws inches from its broad black shoulders, the intruder raised a finger. The raven's wings shot from its sides. It veered in the air and hurtled toward its mistress, who had mentally summoned it to her defense.

So astonished was Synalon by the raven's perfidy, she could do no more than stand and stare. Talons reached to rip tender flesh. The intruder laughed again, gesturing.

The raven vanished. A black rose fell to the floor at Synalon's feet. She raised wide, stark eyes to meet the intruder's ebony gaze.

'Have you not guessed the truth, little sister?' the apparition asked. 'Or is this the way you greet the answering of your most fervent prayers?'

Then she knew. She had heard this voice before when the messenger of the Dark Ones had assumed the place of the fire elemental. At the realization, the being's form became familiar. With the stubs of horns jutting from its head, it was like a dwarfed cousin of the Vicar of Istu that stood in the Circle of the Skywell.

She fell to her knees. Exultation filled her. But it was exultation tinged with dread.

'Pardon, O messenger of the Great Lords,' she said. 'I could not know . . .'

The being shook its head cutting off her protestations.

'No harm done, except to your unfortunate bodyguards. It is what they are paid for, however.' It chuckled again. 'Besides, your precipitate action provided a useful lesson in the futility of opposing your will to even the lowliest servitor of the Dark Ones.'

The queen slowly stood. Her limbs had turned weak and fluttery. She knew something was amiss. The sense of danger heightened.

'How may I serve you, Lord?'

'No lord I,' the creature said, shaking its head. 'And it is not my will you serve but that of my masters.'

'Convey their commands, I beg you.' Such humility was as alien to her lips as the taste of spoiled food. Yet it wasn't hard to muster deference in the face of such power.

'No commands — now,' the messenger said, placing blunt fingertips together. 'I am merely to tell you that the Aspects are almost right. Soon will come the time.'

'Soon?' Synalon cried, her heart lurching within her breast. 'And will I be the instrument of the Dark Ones' will?'

'It is as I have said,' the apparition said. 'But you must reaffirm your obedience to my masters.'

'How?' Synalon asked, breathless with eagerness.

The creature smiled. Its teeth sent back curved glints of moonlight like twin rows of dusky pearls. It dropped gnarled hands down past its belly. Something dark grew from the juncture at its squatty legs.

404

Synalon watched in fascination as it stretched toward her like a snake. The blunt head glistened like a dome of obsidian.

The Queen of the City in the Sky dropped again to her knees before the dwarf. Her hands, as hesitant as a virgin's, reached up to enfold the black member. She felt the pulsing of the great veins, as hot and fervent as any man's. Yet the skin was dry and leathery, a perfect match with the being's voice.

She opened her mouth to receive the benediction of the Dark Ones.

In the womb of night a dream of hate turned to one of pleasure.

Istu moaned in eternal sleep. The sleeping portion tensed for new disappointment. The last time it had known this peculiar excitement, this tingling delight in stony loins, it had been cruelly jerked away by rending agony. The demon slept, but it remembered.

But this pleasure was no ephemeral delight. It lingered. It grew. It crept like a vine up the imprisoned demon's spine. Softness, moistness, supplication, filled the sleeping mind with lusty sensation.

Images swarmed before the sleeping demon: a white body spread-eagled on a stone altar, with golden hair strewn in wild disarray; a silvery pale body bathed in moonlight, kneeling, faced a whiteness glimpsed through jet hair. The images expanded. The Sleeper felt the brush of thighs on hips taut with fear and horror; willing lips caressed its stony pillar. Hot tightness and futile struggle for escape drew the Sleeper's soul into a knot of delectable tension. Wet pressure, slipping, sliding, moving faster and faster. No longer chained to the altar. But still helpless. The demon's excitement soared.

And the familiar black hair, the pallid skin, the musk scent of excitement reached the Dreamer's nostrils. The one who had summoned him before only to tantalize and torture moved before him with deliberate actions. Certainty pervaded the sleeping demon that it would not be denied again. The black-haired one would make good the pain she'd caused him before.

Hands reached to grip her. Black hands, thick-fingered and familiar, yet alien felt and caused the Sleeper to feel. They gripped, twisted, pulled. Blue eyes flicked up, wide with anxiety. Istu felt himself sinking into a bottomless pit of ecstasy.

Vicarious ears heard the squeal of pain and fear. The Sleeper felt acquiescence enfolding it and gave itself up to pleasure.

A rushing dragged the Sleeper onward filling it with tautness, and the pressure exploded outward in a blaze of dark light. Squeals mounting like steps came to its ears like a song of joy. Blind delight pounded in its loins.

In time the fury ebbed. The Sleeper's mind sank into a soothed and peaceful slumber. The bribe had been accepted.

Sleeping, the demon was little more than a child. It might not be reasoned with, but it could be bought with pleasure.

The Dark Ones would have Istu's obedience when released from bondage, even if his mind remained locked in the torpor imposed by Felarod. And far above the stone bubble still ringing with the bellows of a demon's ecstasy, the messenger of the Dark Ones reflected that a job well done brought more rewards than one.

'Aren't you worried that Gabric will find you, Fost?' asked Erimenes.

'That eunuch' said Fost, making a face in his ale. 'He'd be too busy counting his klenor to notice his own building burning down around his ears.'

The tavern bustled around them. Locations might change, Fost mused as he sipped his brew, but taverns, never. The alehouses of Kara-Est differed little from those of Medurim; those here in Tolviroth Acerte weren't distinguishable from any others. Perhaps inland taverns had a different milieu, but seaport taverns were all the same.

In his current state, this insight represented profound thinking on Fost's part. He had drunk too much. At his side Jennas, who had been induced to try the local dark ale instead of her *amasinj*, matched him mug for mug and showed no effects. He displayed a tendency to rock gently from side to side as though he stood on the slickened deck of a sea-tossed ship.

It might have been newly acquired habit, though. The pair had just spent twenty-three days beating up the choppy Karhon Channel in Captain Karlaya's *Wavestrider* en route to Tolviroth Acerte. It had been a trying voyage. Two days running they had to stand in along the coast while a gale blew down the channel. Winter weather wasn't too extreme due to the slight axial tilt, and the considerable extent of the polar caps owed mainly to the smallness and coolness of the sun. However, the world also orbited near the primary, giving moderately short seasons. Midwinter had come and gone while the *Wavestrider* worked her dogged way toward Tolviroth Acerte.

Karlaya's predominately female crew inspired Erimenes to new heights of inventiveness. Sailors the world over being what they are, the spirit's imaginative lechery was greeted with much amusement by the crew.

Fost had a vague suspicion that some of his companion's more outrageous proposals had been carried out. The equinox celebration had occasioned much merriment and consumption of potent Jorean rum among Karlaya's crew. The Jorean mariners kept on good terms with Somdag Squid-face, God and Protector of Realm seamen. But he was not their deity. Instead, the Joreans worshipped Gormanka of the Wind-Wheel, like Ust the Bear, a patron of the Realm couriers. But so they would slight no one, they saluted all the deities, singing and dancing, during which the revelers became progressively less clad. Naked bodies, black and white, goosefleshed and sweat-polished, writhed passionately under the yellow light of the torches. And after that, in Karlaya's snug cabin in the sterncastle . . .

He didn't really remember more than the gaiety on deck. But the next day Jennas seemed more subdued than called for due to the aftereffects of the rum, and Fost had overheard her informing Erimenes in a low, lethally serious voice that if he ever so much as alluded to the activities of the night before, she'd heave him into the channel.

Now Fost did his level best to recapture the state he was in for the equinoctial festivities aboard the *Wavestrider*. He had arrived in Tolviroth Acerte to find that Moriana, Darl, and their carefully screened cadre had departed eight days before for the Continent. Jennas could hardly hide her satisfaction at the news.

Fost's reaction to his latest failure to catch the princess was to get stinking drunk.

'And whom are you calling a eunuch?' a voice bellowed from the tavern door.

Fost pulled his snout out of the earthenware flagon. The rude, grating voice hailing him sounded familiar, though in his befuddlement he couldn't quite place it. Nonetheless, his guts tensed in anticipation of trouble.

Broad shoulders blocked the tavern door. Below them the shape gave way to an equally broad chest and still broader belly, strong legs firmly planted. Above, the outline rose to something of a point without the apparent intervention of a neck.

The image snapped Fost's brain into focus. He raised mug to lips, sipped insolently.

'Well met, Merchant Gabric,' he said. 'How's business?'

'As good as may be expected when my top courier takes unauthorized leave.' Gabric stepped into the room, arms laid like hawsers across his chest.

'If I'm your top courier, you should pay me top money.' He took a measured draft. 'But that's academic now. I don't work for you any longer. You can consider my resignation retroactive to the beginning of my last assignment. That way, you needn't worry about severance pay.'

'It's not that easy, you rogue,' Gabric shouted, his jowls turning ruddy. 'You have commitments to me! You've taken my coin. You can't just say, "I quit," and have done with it.'

Fost shrugged. He turned away, feigning disinterest.

'Fost's right, you know,' a voice commented at the courier's crooked elbow. 'You are a eunuch, Gabric. In fact, has anyone informed you that you bear the most striking resemblance to a gelded hornbull?'

Gabric's face slowly went from the hue of a cherry to a beet to a ripe eggplant. Worn-thick blood vessels throbbed at his bald temples as he leaned forward, blinking in the gloom at the thin, translucent figure wavering beside Fost.

'Aha!' the merchant roared in a voice that made his earlier outbursts sound like whispers. 'You're not just a contract breaker, you low cur. You're a thief, as well!'

Some inches taller than Fost, he drew himself up to his full height and pointed accusingly at the black-haired courier.

'I hereby charge you with commercial malfeasance. To wit, that you did willfully and without authorization take leave of your duties in violation of your contract with Gabric Exports, Inc., and did furthermore misappropriate to your own use property paid for and duly consigned to one Kest-i-Mond, mage, county of Samadum.' He lumbered forward with heavy menace, looking like some shaved cousin of Grutz or Chubchuk. 'I take you into custody, as called for by the Tolvirot Commercial Code, Section Forty-six, Sub-paragraph A.'

Fost leaned back against the bar. He had no contract with Gabric, and there was no wrongdoing in his having Erimenes. Kest-i-Mond had been dead before the courier delivered the wayward spirit to him. The courier started to explain this to Gabric. He had forgotten, however, the full extent of Erimenes' waywardness.

'You and what army, blubber-belly?' taunted Erimenes cheerfully.

'Great Ultimate,' Fost moaned. Gabric had no claim against him. But if a scuffle broke out thanks to Erimenes' vicarious bloodlust, Fost could wind up in serious trouble. The Tolvirot authorities would not look kindly on anyone damaging a merchant as prosperous as Gabric.

Jennas hissed beside him. He looked toward the door and tensed.

'Fortunate you asked us along, good Gabric,' said a whip-thin voice. 'This ruffian seems of a mind to give you trouble.'

The owner sauntered through the door, gauntleted thumbs thrust through his sword belt. He was a small man, his wiry frame clad in an impeccable livery of black and purple. The sword at his waist was curved as were the sidearms of the five men following him into the tavern.

'Aye, that he is,' smirked Gabric.

'When did you expand into the novelty pet line, Gabric?' asked Fost, eyeing the sextet of Sky City bird riders.

Gabric's pig eyes rolled from the soldiers to Fost. Beads of perspiration gleamed on his brow.

'I knew you might prove difficult since you've always been inclined toward fiscal instability and might prove unwilling to retire your debts. I asked these gentlemen to accompany me. They are the new Sky City trade delegation.'

'Trade delegation,' snorted Fost. If any of these bird riders had ever been involved in any exchange other than sword thrusts, he'd eat Grutz, hair and all.

A sinking sickness settled into Fost's belly. The soldiers' presence meant Rann had found out he still lived. At this stage in their conquest, the City in the Sky did not want to risk murdering a man in Tolviroth Acerte who was nominally a citizen of the City of Bankers. But if its agents accompanied someone with a commercial grievance against the courier in the expectation he might prove obstinate . . .

'Do what you want to the courier,' said the leader of the bird riders. 'But we get the barbarian girl. *Remember*.' His voice snapped at Gabric like a lash. The merchant bobbed his head.

The crowd pressed back. Gabric closed in and a sliver of steel sprouted from one hand, incongruously slim in the vast paw gripping its hilt. Behind Gabric the bird riders drew swords.

'You've got an insolent tongue, Longstrider,' growled Gabric. 'I think I'll cut it out.'

Fost swept his arm around in a blur, his half-filled mug slamming into Gabric's face. The merchant dropped like a bag of wheat. Seeing this, the bird riders lunged in. A whining arc of steel sent them leaping back as Jennas whirled her greatsword. The leader spat a command. They spread out. Inn patrons vanished like quicksilver. Gabric moaned and tried to rise, fingers groping for his gilded dagger. Fost kicked him hard in the belly.

'Bravo!' cheered Erimenes.

Fost feinted at a bird rider, spun, and hacked at another who'd closed in quickly believing the courier's back exposed. A frantic move interposed the smaller man's scimitar between broadsword and his flesh. The bird rider fell, stunned by the force of the blow. As he tumbled backward, he carried the others with him.

Fost couldn't fight well in the cramped interior. He motioned Jennas outside. She lunged for the door, then paused to look back at him. The courier waved her forward again. She ran out into the street with Fost close behind while the Sky City men tried to reorganize.

A staggering patron stumbled in Fost's way. The courier considered the cries from behind him, the drunkard and the impossibility of escaping quickly through the door. So he tucked Erimenes' satchel safely behind him and hurled himself through the large leaded-glass window fronting the tavern.

Glass exploded into the street. Riding dogs barked in surprise. Jennas had already mounted Chubchuk, waving her sword in the faces of a fresh trio of the men in Sky City colors.

Fost threw himself over Grutz's broad back and clung. Pursuers boiled from the door of the tavern, trampling the drunk. As Fost hauled himself to a sitting position, Jennas kicked Chubchuk into a shambling lope up the brick street.

Finally astride, Fost set off after Jennas. Grutz rumbled smugly to himself as he ran with surprising speed. From the other end of the block came a new commotion. The watchmen from Peacekeepers, Inc., had arrived on the scene.

Tarinvar the Steersman sat by the rail of the lugger *Gallinule* scrimshawing a piece of juggernaut fish ivory none too skillfully when he heard a frightful thrashing in the water.

He raised his head. The carving fell from numbed fingers. Clambering up the far rail was a demon twice the size of a man and dripping with water and weeds. Tarinvar's eyes tried to pop from their sockets. The demon returned his stare with a red-rimmed scowl.

410

'Grrr,' said the demon.

Tarinvar leaped over the side, not waiting to hear more.

The bosun emerged from the midship's cabin and came running aft. The first thing he saw was the inexpert idol of Somdag Squid-face which Tarinvar had left behind. The second thing he saw was the monster. Dark and malignant, it hunched near the stern, swiveling its misshapen head. Its gaze came to rest on the bosun.

Heart threatening to explode from fear, the bosun leaped to the railing, then pressed the back of one of his hands to his lips, wagged his fingers in imitation of Papa Squid's squiggly visage to invoke the deity's protection, and dived overboard.

'Monsters!' the cry came from the rigging above. A seaman dived past. He fell in the greasy water of Tolviroth Harbor with a prodigious splash, just as a second intruder clambered over the gunwales.

Blinking saltwater from his eyes, Fost cleared his vision in time to see another dozen men in seamen's garb erupt from a hatch, dash to the railing, and jump overboard in a formation that would have done credit to a squad of Sky Guardsmen. Every one piously wiggled fingers in front of his face before diving. The cry, 'Demons' came floating up from the water like a seabird's call.

Fost looked around in surprise. He had thought the skirmish in the tavern had sobered him up. A few feet away, Grutz pawed irritably at the seaweed wound around his head. Water had soaked his fur, matting the hair into flat, scaly wedges.

Chubchuk hoisted himself up through a gap in the rail, a thoroughly sodden Jennas still clinging to his back. She shook limp auburn hair from her eyes.

'Where is everybody?' she demanded.

'I may be insane,' Fost said, the eerie silence making him shiver, 'but I swear the crew jumped over the rail as I came aboard.'

A splashing by the hull drew their attention. They leaned over the rail in time to see a flotilla of bobbing heads round the *Gallinule's* stern and strike out for the wharf a hundred yards away.

'Demons,' they heard one call. 'Blessed Samdag deliver us from the dreadlings of the deep!'

Fost and Jennas stood for a moment, looked at Grutz, then broke out laughing. A damp, seaweed-festooned bear emerging from the sea had to qualify as startling.

'When you collect your feeble wits,' said Erimenes acidly, 'you might find out if there's someone aboard who knows how to steer this

411

contraption. And you'd best be prompt about it. Your oaf of a former employer has just arrived at the wharf with his associates.'

Fost glanced shoreward. A crowd gathered on the dock. A number were plainly onlookers, but among the mob Fost spotted a knot of Sky City soldiers.

'You're right, Erimenes,' said Fost. 'Time to depart.'

'Before you rush off,' said Erimenes, 'would you please empty this damned water from my jug?. I shipped a gallon of the foul stuff. It sloshes unmercifully. I just know I'll become seasick if you don't do something quickly.'

Laughing, Fost emptied a brown stream from the jar. Then he turned away in search of anyone who remained of the Gallinule's crew.

A breeze quested through tufts of dry, dead grass. Tiny hints of green could be glimpsed at the bases of the tufts where new shoots pushed up through the earth. Snow lay in clumps; more would fall before the season ended. But the hardy growth of the Sundered Realm began its annual struggle for supremacy quite soon after the days began to lengthen and grew imperceptibly warmer.

Moriana walked along a bluff with the stiff grasses brushing her legs. The grass clutched at the skirt of her pale beige gown. She nodded absently to herself, marking the feel of the cloth swaying against her skin. After so long in tunic, boots, and breeches, it was strange to be clad in this fashion.

A strap crossed one shoulder. From it hung the Athalar spirit jar, its lid open. Ziore hovered at Moriana's side like a benevolent pink cloud.

The princess sat, gathering her cloak about her. From her vantage point, she saw the camp marching before her: orderly rows of tents, columns marching and countermarching in a fallow field, soldiers at practice with sword and spear, shooting arrows at targets, the cordoned kennels for the cavalry mounts, the bawling herd of one-horned ruminants penned beyond to serve as provender for men and mounts alike. Banners sprouted from flagpoles of tents like exotic blossoms. Paramount flew Moriana's own device, an eagle's claw clutching a scarlet flower against a field of pale blue.

'I should be happy, Ziore, shouldn't I?' she asked, watching the banners dance in the wind.

'You make it sound like a duty,' the spirit said.

412

Moriana shrugged. She had picked a bare spot of earth to sit on. Her forefinger drew random shapes in the dirt.

'Look, Ziore,' she said, sweeping her hand in a gesture encompassing the camp. 'Almost eight thousand men gathered at my feet. If Darl is right, we'll have ten thousand men by the time we march south. Ten thousand men, Ziore – the whole population of the City is less than three times that. It's power, more than I ever thought I could muster against my sister.'

Ziore poised, waiting. The wind sighed through the bottomland of the tributaries of the great River Marchant. The main flow ran northeast a quarter mile away; on the far bank lay the Empire. Eastward, Omizantrim squatted like a stone effigy. A thin spire of vapor rose from its maw and was lost in the high haze drifting overhead. Ominous as the mountain was, it had laid a blessing on this land. The vomitus cast up over eons from the entrails of the earth was rich in minerals. Crops grew lush to the very brink of the badlands kept desolate by lava and poison vapors from the volcano.

Somewhere to the south floated the City in the Sky. In the weeks since Moriana and Darl had left Tolviroth Acerte, it had passed over Thailot where trade proceeded as if nothing untoward had come to pass. Wirix met the City's passage with sullen defiance – it was almost certainly the last the Sky City would assault. Brev and Thailot were easier targets, Kara-Est immeasurably more valuable. A few days before, the chance that guided the Floating City had turned it southward to pass over its new dominion of Bilsinx.

Ziore's patience had a relentless quality to it that Moriana could never outmatch. She inhaled, held it, then let it out slowly.

'I'm grateful to Darl,' she said. 'No one would – no one could – do for me what he's doing. And yet . . . yet it begins to feel wrong somehow. Events move past my control. And how can I complain? He's doing me a favor.'

A many-throated shout caught her attention. She turned to see Darl riding in from the wooded hills on his tall war mount. He raised a hand. Instantly, a mob surrounded him. Idlers, officers, soldiers at their soldierly tasks, all gathered around crying out their devotion and their love. He raised a salute now, turning his head this way and that. Moriana knew he grinned that grin of his, a look she had come to know well in the last few weeks, a look she thought turned to love.

Ziore laid a hand on her shoulder. She reached up to stroke it though she knew the warmth was no more than a comforting illusion

413.

produced by the spirit.

'Such devotion,' the nun's ghost said. 'It borders on adoration. These men had never before laid eyes on Darl Rhadaman six weeks ago, and now they would lay their lives at the feet of his war dog.' Moriana looked up at her. She looked deep into the living woman's eyes.

'I know little of this world, child, but it seems to me such loyalty is a potent force, as potent in its way as force of arms or numbers.'

'Loyalty, aye,' she all but spat, her face hardening involuntarily into bitter planes. 'Loyalty to *him*.'

'And this troubles you? You resent that their loyalty is given to him but not to you?'

'No.' But she turned her eyes away.

'It can be no other way.' Ziore smiled sadly. 'You admitted that your resources were inadequate to muster support among the northerners. Not even among the people of the Quincunx could you raise an army. Thanks to Darl's persuasion the emissaries of Kara-Est and Wirix have promised to help provision your armies en route.' She touched Moriana's cheek. 'I know it is hard on you. But you cannot evade the knowledge that without him you'd be unable to challenge Synalon.'

Moriana tried to hold in the tears that stung her eyes, tears of anger, of frustration, of the self-disgust that had grown to be an inextricable part of her soul in the weeks since that terrible day in the glacier when she'd had to murder the man she loved for the sake of her City. Her fingers groped blindly for the amulet hanging about her neck. She clung to it as if she could find strength in it.

'There's more to it than that,' she said.

'That, too, cannot be changed,' Ziore said. 'This is the North. Customs differ here.'

There was another reason Darl had become the focal point of the crusade against the City, and Moriana drew even farther from it. In the southern lands of the Sundered Realm, women and men existed in general parity. Armies frequently consisted of both sexes in the same proportion of the population. The second-in-command of the mercenary band Rann had hired as ground troops was a woman. Women had equal say in governments as well, from the chief deputy of Kara-Est to warrior-chieftainesses of the steppes like Jennas. In the Sky City women ruled by law and custom; though the rank and file of its military was male, Moriana had first been blooded while com-

414

manding troops in the war five years before with the Golden Bar-barians who had invaded the savannah west of the Thails and terro-rized the country between Deepwater and the Sjedd.

In the northern half of the Realm it was different.

, Darl's triumphant procession reached the pavilion he shared with Moriana. He dismounted, handing the reins to a soldier eager to do his least bidding. Then, as was his custom, he turned and knelt, abasing himself before Moriana's banner.

Moriana didn't need to turn back to Ziore to know what the spirit felt. The words ran through her mind: *his loyalty is to you*. She shook her head.

Darl's loyalty was unquestioned. And he reaffirmed over and over that he followed Moriana's flag, turning the suspicion of the earth-bound toward her into a kind of reverence. Yet that very reverence passed *through* Darl, just as (according to pagan priests of the Far Archipelago) divine essence passed through them to the faithful.

'I'm a figurehead,' Moriana said quietly. 'A symbol, a living emblem. Not a shaper, not a leader of all the forces gathered in my name.'

That's unworthy of you, Ziore mentally rebuked her.

Moriana's hands clenched the amulet as if to crush it. Yes, the thought was unworthy. She knew it and despised it. She loathed herself for the ingratitude that made her resent her greatest bene-factor.

But deep inside her mind festered a suspicion that more lay behind her concern than childish petulance, that the channel along which she felt her crusade being diverted might dash everything to ruin. The thought tingled and stung like a pulled muscle. She suppressed it. It was rationalization, nothing more.

Within her hands, darkness slipped across the face of the Destiny Stone.

CHAPTER TEN

Tapers burned low, flickering in figured sconces. Gargoyle faces graven into the stone of the chamber by some long-dead, inhuman hand winked at Prince Rann from shadowed walls. He pored over his plans to meet the threat of Moriana's ragtag army.

A knock on the chamber door broke his concentration.

'Her Majesty would speak with you, Highness,' a voice came tentatively. 'She awaits your pleasure in her chambers.'

'I come,' said Rann, draining his goblet. He rose, paused to take a fur-trimmed cloak from the outstretched talon of a fiend on which it hung, and draped it around his shoulders. Synalon's latest fancy was to keep the windows of her throne room wide, day and night. Spring was still weeks distant.

He followed the servant down the corridor to a steeply pitched flight of stairs. Two palace guards stood erect in their sculptured breastplates and greaves. They thumped their weapons' butts ceremoniously on the floor as Rann walked between them without acknowledging their presence.

Clad in a filmy gown the color of her hair, Synalon lounged by an open window. The landscape spread before her, yellow and white, patched over with shadows of drifting clouds. Off in the east, past where the land fell away from the central massif and rolled gently to the sea, Kara-Est readied itself for war.

'Greetings, cousin,' said Synalon without turning. The way she draped herself against the window's frame made her seem part of the design, a sinuous and erotic embellishment. The gossamer material of her gown clung to her limbs like lover's fingers.

'What is your pleasure, Majesty?' asked Rann, bowing deeply.

'Are you ready to crush the upstarts challenging me in the name of

416

that slut Moriana?' she demanded.

'Quite, dear cousin. V'Duuyek will ride north with nine hundred of his men leaving the other three hundred to garrison Bilsinx in case the Estil try to be clever. We've five hundred of our own dog riders accompanying him and eleven hundred infantry. Additionally, we have a thousand Bilsinxt light-dog bowmen for scouting and skirmishing.' Synalon raised an eyebrow at this. Rann smiled with a touch of impudence. The thousand Bilsinxt mounted archers represented a victory for him.

Rann did not possess the preternatural gift of oratory that animated Darl Rhadaman. Yet he was a skillful enough speaker and he knew well the ways and weaknesses of humankind. He had called the citizenry of Bilsinx before him in the Central Square the day after the assault. It wasn't subjugation the Sky City offered, he'd told them. Partnership, rather, in a glorious enterprise that would make the City the foremost power in the Sundered Realm. Mere aggrandizement at the expense of the Quincunx had not been the City's goal. Instead, the City's ruler, the bold and brilliant Queen Synalon, wished to streamline the inefficient process of trade among the Cities and the City and meld the Quincunx and the Sky into one powerful, smoothly functioning entity to stand against an envious world.

He reminded Bilsinx of the 'merciful' character of the conquest. There had been no fires, no looting, no widespread slaughter or property destruction. The only ones who had been harmed were those offering resistance. He had told the populace he regretted even those deaths. The shedding of Bilsinxt blood, the martyrdom of so many brave soldiers fighting nobly – if misguidedly – in defense of their homes, would not have been necessary but for the obstinate unreason of Irb and his sycophants. The wicked mayor had been punished; Bilsinx and the Sky City were now one. It remained only to put hard feelings behind and forge a bond of eternal friendship between two great peoples.

A wave of restrained approval met his words. Irb had not been popular among his subjects. But the Bilsinxt had heard tales of dark and bloody retribution meted out by Synalon and Rann. This avowal of friendship and the chance to share in the Sky City's greatness were unexpected. The cheers had been sporadic at first, then turned into a wave of acclamation.

The Sky City need have no fear of rebellion in Bilsinx.

'We can't spare many flyers,' Rann went on. 'I believe that a squadron of two hundred fifty common bird riders will suffice. Moriana notwithstanding, the Northerners have no experience fighting bird riders.'

Synalon turned. One leg was cocked, the foot resting insouciantly on the windowsill. The other dangled downward to the floor. She nodded slowly.

'And who commands? Not Count Ultur, surely?'

'I will, Majesty.' Rann frowned.

'Really?' said Synalon, feigning surprise. 'You intend to desert the City at the crucial moment of our preparations to conquer Kara-Est? You disappoint me, cousin.'

He could scarcely believe what Synalon was saying. He had to lead the expedition against Moriana. Their best intelligence – and it was good – indicated that her army outnumbered the City's forces two to one. In spite of this, Rann felt confident of success. Had he not led the combined armies of the City, Thailot, Deepwater, and the other cities of the west, outnumbered and disorganized as they were, to victory over the nerveless slave-warriors of the Golden Barbarians?

'Majesty,' he said, voice rasping with sudden dryness. 'Surely you don't expect me to stay!'

'Oh, but I do.' Her voice was like the caress of a silken whip, soft and yet deeply cutting. 'You are needed here, cousin mine. At such a juncture I cannot chance the loss of your cogent brain.' She allowed her lips a subtle curl.

'But I have to lead the expedition! However much you value my . . . cogency, we cannot have Moriana's rabble rampaging through our supply lines. With all due modesty, Majesty, only *I* can guarantee that they will be stopped before they endanger our hold on the ground.'

'Your post is here!' rapped Synalon. Then the harshness flowed from her features and she smiled with mocking gentleness. 'Besides, good cousin, you don't think any Northblood savages can defeat our armies, do you?'

He stood without responding, feeling his limbs turn leaden, feeling the tightening in his bowels, the stinging at the backs of his eyes. For some reason, he was reminded of the frustration of his youth when his best efforts had failed him in learning even the simplest magical lore.

Synalon watched him. Her head tipped forward, slim brows sweeping up like wings, her mouth curved into a coquettish smile.

Yet her eyes were mad lamps. She inflicted her insane whim on him, punishing him for his failure to make an end to Moriana Athalau. That her petulance could make her dreams crumble like a dead, dried leaf did not stay her. Perhaps she didn't realize the danger of holding Rann back now. Perhaps she did.

With bile burning his throat, he bowed, turned, and was gone.

Synalon's laughter followed him like the chime of a tarnished silver bell.

An arrow thumped sod an arm's length from Grutz's churning haunch. Fost turned in his saddle and flung back a defiant curse at his pursuers. It was all he had to hurl at them.

'Curs! Cowards!' shrilled Erimenes, his vaporous being shaking with rage. 'Stand. Turn and fight the rogues. Oh, the dishonor of it all!'

'Is he always like that?' called Jennas from Chubchuk's broad back.

'He's worse at times,' Fost said.

The two bears loped across the undulating hills of the Highgrass Broad. The tall grasses that gave the land its name whipped their flanks, urging them to greater speed. Erimenes hovered at Fost's elbow, occasionally blurring and dissipating in the breeze but always re-forming to heap further curses on the fleeing pair. Looking back in exasperation, Fost saw that the score of dog-mounted archers was gradually falling behind. Relief flowed through him like liquor. Not even Jennas, ferocious as she was, favored giving battle when they'd been ambushed. All the courage in the world wouldn't prevent the lethal steel broadheads from finding their marks.

As if to reaffirm the fact, an arrow sped past Fost's ear.

'On!' he shouted at Grutz, drumming his heels into the bear's ribs. Armored in fat and fur, the beast never felt him. But he heard the nasty whine of arrows and the baying of twenty hounds. Even a war bear of the steppes knew when not to buck the odds.

'You call yourselves heroes!' cried Erimenes disdainfully. 'Yet you turn your backs and flee like rabbits at the first sign of danger. Oh, that my poor eyes must witness such craven, fainthearted cowardice!'

'When did we ever call ourselves heroes, you blue flatulence?' shouted Fost. 'If you want to fight the dog riders, go back and do it yourself!' Jerking savagely at Grutz's reins, he wheeled the bear around to face the onrushing riders. Howling like their dogs, the men rushed forward.

419

Fost snatched at the satchel strap and began whirling it around his head like a sling.

'What are you doing?' Erimenes wailed.

'Giving you a chance to taste the joys of battle firsthand.'

'My jug!' moaned the spirit. 'You'll break my jug! Oh, how can you be so heartless?'

'If I don't throw you at them, will you, by the Great Ultimate, *shut up?*'

'Y-yes!'

Jennas was a hundred yards away and moving fast. 'Come on, you Ust-forgotten fool!' she shouted.

Fost turned Grutz around and booted him. A flight of arrows moaned by and were lost in the weeds.

'For this I gave up being a courier,' muttered Fost. Then he was galloping full tilt down a hill to catch up with Jennas.

The Red Bear rolled the sun down the sky. The pursuers gradually fell back as the land became more uneven. Finally, they became lost in the settling evening gloom.

Fost and Jennas camped on a bank above a stream. The crisp, cold water made a sound like sipans clinging in a beggar's cup as it tumbled its endless way toward the Wirin River. The bears drank greedily, splashing and snorting, their muzzles black with water. Most of the year, water was scarce on the Southern Steppe. It had turned warm early in the north this year, all but a fringe of ice at the edge of the stream had melted. Grutz and Chubchuk fished. Their long talons swept a half-dozen fish wriggling onto the shore where Fost dispatched them by slamming their heads against a rock.

Jennas squatted on the bank, face bronzed by the maiden glow of the fire she was building. Snow had already given way to rain here at the northwestern edge of the Highgrass country, but many peasants had stored more firewood than they needed last autumn and were willing to sell the fuel. Grutz and Chubchuk sat haunch to furry haunch attacking shrubs growing above the water. Fost grimaced. Snowberries had a powerful purgative effect on humans, as he'd discovered to his acute embarrassment early in his career as a courier. Apparently the tiny blue-green berries didn't have the same effect on bears. They had been eating them all the way across the broad without showing any ill effects.

'Ah,' said Erimenes, swaying slightly in the breeze. 'Nothing like a fine fire on a cold winter's evening.' Fost scowled at him but said nothing. Whether in affectation or simply by habit (what with surviving fourteen hundred years of afterlife), he held his spectral blue hands over the fire as if to warm them.

Fost dropped the fish on the grass at Jennas's side. The bears continued noisily consuming their berries. They would catch their own fish later on. Their talent for fishing had been an unexpected benefit of their presence. Since neither Fost nor Jennas had the slightest skill with missile weapons, hunting meat posed a problem, and not even Fost's dwindling supply of gemstones looted from Athalau would survive the prices the peasants charged for livestock, a precious commodity in this war-torn land.

Fost cut a branch from a bush stripped by the bears and whittled it to a point. The fire blazed up eagerly, as if anticipating the roasting fish.

Fost impaled a fish on a sharpened twig and handed it to Jennas. He stuck another on the branch he'd sharpened for himself. The nomad woman stuck her fish into the upper reaches of the flame where it soon began to crack lustily. A succulent odor drifted from the fire.

As his own fish browned, Fost eyed his companion. Her face was as impassive as ever, even in the orange firelight. But he could tell she was troubled.

'We'll reach Moriana's army tomorrow,' he said. He watched the woman closely. A muscle tightened at the corner of her jaw. 'Why did you come, Jennas? I know you . . . you care for me. This has to be painful for you.'

She said something he didn't catch. He asked her to repeat it.

'I didn't come for your sake,' she said softly.

'I'm glad of that,' he said in a neutral tone.

She looked at him sharply.

'You don't believe me?' He didn't reply. 'I could say you flatter yourself, but that's not so. I like the nearness of you. I'd make you my mate if I could, and it's a sorrow to me that you stay set on this Sky City wench who stabbed you once already. But it is not for your sake that I left the steppe. It is for my people.'

He said nothing. One of the bears licked noisily at a paw smeared with sweet juices and ambled down to the stream. A moment later the other joined him. There soon came a splat-splash! of their broad paws slapping fish from the water.

'I have dreamed again,' she said. 'Ust warns me that time is short. He has not told me so, but I feel this coming battle will be crucial. That somehow its outcome may lead to a release of powers once thought chained forever.'

Fost felt a prickling at the back of his neck. The only powers he knew that were 'chained forever' were those of the demon Istu, offspring of the Dark Ones, who slumbered beneath the streets of the City in the Sky. Having encountered a fragment of the demon's subconscious, Fost found it disconcerting to face the prospect of the demon actually being loosed.

'Maybe you read too much into these dreams, Jennas. I've never had a god appear to me, but I've read accounts of those who have. The gods seem fond of generalities. I'm sure if you looked at whatever it was that Ust told you, you'd find it to be no more than the customary calls for charity, pious thoughts, and good hygiene.'

'Do not mock me.'

'I don't. I'm serious, even if I'm too flippant in the way I put things. But I can't credit all this talk of a War of Powers. The old one, yes, I'm willing to admit it happened as legends say. But that was ten thousand years ago, Jennas, a hundred centuries. Most of the magic's gone out of the world. The gods have grown tired with it. They've gone on to other playthings.'

Jennas stared at him, her expression one of wonder.

'But you are the Chosen of Ust. You owe your life to his intercession. Don't you believe in him? Can't you feel his nearness, here, now, in this place at this moment?'

A bear snorted behind Fost. He jumped, turned around. Grutz grunted to him and contined shoving a fish into his mouth.

'You're ready enough to acknowledge the existence of evil beings,' Jennas said, reproach in her voice. 'You can't deny the reality that is the Demon of the Dark Ones, can you? Why do you turn from the Wise Ones, then?'

Gingerly, he plucked his fish from the spit and broke it apart. The meat inside was still steaming. He took a mouthful, chewed it thoughtfully, and swallowed before answering.

'I can't deny the truth of what you say,' he conceded. 'I do find it easier to admit the existence of personified evil than of good. It fits in better with the way the world seems to be.' He broke off another chunk of flesh and tucked it into his mouth. 'And my experience,' he added wryly, 'shows more evil than good all around.'

'I think,' said Erimenes, 'that the real question is what motivates you on this fool's errand, Fost.'

'What?'

'You may not have the Amulet of Living Flame but you have its gift. Or have you forgotten? You lay dead, stabbed by the Princess Moriana about whose welfare you wax so solicitous. And the amulet returned your worthless life to you.' He spoke bitterly. He had desired the amulet to restore his own life, to permit the worldly pleasures he had denied himself so long ago.

'You have your life. You are young, strong, presentable. You have a pocketful of gold. And what do you do with these precious gifts, these things for which I would have given even my immortality? You spurn them. Instead of enjoying them to the fullest, you go rambling off across the countryside in pursuit of the very golden-haired witch who killed you, not to wring from her your just revenge but to warn her of the peril of the Destiny Stone!' He shook his head. His long, ascetic nose was pinched in distaste. 'You are indeed a fool, O Fost.'

'So I'm a fool,' said Fost angrily. 'What of it?'

'It is time to consider your motivations, as I said. I think you know what drives you to this foolishness.'

'Pray enlighten me,' Fost said sarcastically. He felt his anger smoldering. What right did this treacherous, lecherous old wraith have to speak like this?

'When you were a child,' said Erimenes, 'did not your parents die? Were you not left an orphan?'

'Yes,' Fost said, puzzled. 'They were killed in a riot. It was the day young Teom assumed the Imperial yellow. Word had reached the Teemings that the food dole was being cut back. Rumor had it that the reason was the high cost of his coronation. The populace rose.' He rubbed his chin. 'I never found out who killed them, civil guard or rioters. Makes no difference, I suppose. They were dead.'

'And they left you, the parents you loved, alone on the streets in a slum. Is that not so?' Hesitantly, Fost nodded. 'And in all your life, you've never known lasting affection.'

When Fost only scowled at Erimenes, the spirit went on. 'Old Fimster, the thief who took you in, died of fever, did he not? And Ceratith the pedant, who opened to you the doors of human knowledge, he was murdered by alley bashers.' He shook his head. 'It is indeed small wonder.'

'What is small wonder?' snapped Fost. His fists were tightly clenched.

'That you cling to any slight scrap of affection offered you. You became enamored of Moriana and thought she felt the same way about you. So now you pursue her the length of the continent to protect her from her own greedy folly. You are as loyal – and pathetic – as a foundling pup. You follow anyone showing attention, even someone kicking you in the ribs.'

'That's ridiculous,' said Fost. His cheeks felt as if he'd held them too near the flames. 'It doesn't make sense, dammit!'

'Then why are you shouting?'

Fost became acutely aware of Jennas's eyes fixed on him across the dance of fire.

'Because it's untrue! It's absurd. It's not a matter of some fixation on my part but of saving Moriana's life.'

'Why?' the spirit asked with malicious inflection. 'She took yours.'

Fost jumped to his feet. He raised his fists menacingly at Erimenes, who stood calmly by with his arms folded across his insubstantial breast. Slowly, Fost lowered his arms.

'I don't know why,' he whispered. 'But I must.'

He sat by the fire, his face averted. Desolation seeped like a blight into his soul.

He felt Jennas beside him. He tensed, unwilling to face her. She didn't speak. She simply put her strong, smooth arms around him and held him close.

After a time, he turned to her.

Uncertainty about the coming battle formed a lump of lead in Moriana's stomach. She felt the age-old worries of a commander. Would she win? Would Synalon triumph and be free to loose the evil of the Dark Ones on the Realm once again? Either way, win or lose, many would die.

'At times such as this, I don't resent my cloistering,' Ziore said somberly.

'What do you mean?' asked Moriana, distracted momentarily from her worries.

'The dilemma you face, child. If you act, you condemn thousands of men and women to death or disfigurement. Yet if you don't act . . .' She made a helpless gesture with her hands. 'Your sister will return the Dark Ones to the world and there is no Felarod this time.' She shook her head. The folds at the outer corners of her eyes deepened with sorrow as though her face was still flesh. 'We knew no such brutal questions in my convent.'

'Perhaps that's reason enough to forgive poor Erimenes,' said Moriana. Ziore's mouth hardened, and she turned away.

Moriana looked out across the valley. To the north stood a conical hill crowned with a gay pavilion, the one she shared with Darl Rhadaman. Her banner snapped from its staff in the crisp evening breeze. She pulled her gaze from it, unable to bear the thoughts welling up inside again.

Her gaze swept back across the shallow, broad valley. A small stream, tributary of Chanobit Creek flowing on the far side of her army's camp, crossed it and nourished the still-brown grasses. To her right, a long bluff hid the enemy camp from view. Riders shuttled ceaselessly along it, keeping watch. The day's overcast had broken and light from Omizantrim turned the day to splendor.

'My lady,' came a voice from behind her. 'Is it safe for you so close to the enemy?'

She turned to see Darl standing ten yards away. Something in the way he held his head told her he'd been there unnoticed for some time, simply watching her. She felt strangely touched.

'I'm not alone,' she said. 'Ziore is with me.'

'She won't be much help if the Highgrass riders come upon you.'

'I can take care of myself.' The words came out more sharply than she intended.

'You shouldn't wander off,' Darl said, a half stubborn and half indulgent look on his face. She was almost disappointed now that her words hadn't cut deeper.

'The morrow weighs heavily on me,' said Ziore, swirling about her jug. 'I need to meditate. Will you please reseal my jug, Moriana?' The princess looked at her spirit companion in surprise. Ziore had never expressed an urge to meditate before.

Then Moriana realized the spirit's motives. With a grateful smile she replaced the carved stone lid of the pot. The nun's figure wavered and became a formless pink cloud dissipating in the afternoon light. Moriana put the jug in her knapsack on the ground beside her.

Darl stood close by. She felt his eyes on her. His gaze had become a burden she couldn't explain.

'How are you this evening?' he asked quietly. Moriana almost laughed at the seriousness and formality of his words. A look at his face kept her from it. He was very solemn. And very vulnerable.

She had an urge to reach up and stroke his cheek, but something caused her to hold back. After a moment, he stretched out his hands and she took them in hers. His skin was cool and dry.

They simply stood there. The early evening sounds came slowly to fill the silence. The buzz of voices peaking sporadically into shouts, the bleating of livestock, hammers ringing off breastplates and blades at a dozen forges all provided reason enough not to speak.

Darl released her hands. He turned away, walked to the lip of the hill, and drew a deep lungful of the brisk air.

'When I was young,' he said, 'I saw my mother and father killed. It was on a day similar to this one, seemingly peaceful but actually seething with death and forces beyond human control. The Earl of Jav Nihen coveted Harmis – don't ask why. There's nothing there but mountains. At any rate, he invited my family to his summer palace for a revel. So we went, my mother and father, my uncle and I. I was only five then. We ate and I drank watered wine sweetened with honey. It was a great outdoor festival with pavilions by the score and huge bonfires roaring. We watched the players, mimes, acrobats. In many ways it was the finest night of my life.

'The Earl's men circulated through the crowds. Finally, when I stood yawning and ready for bed, Earl Maunrish rose from his chair of state and bade my parents rise. He lifted a great, golden goblet – how it gleamed in the firelight! – and drank to their health. They raised their goblets to return the honor.

'It was a signal. As they drank, they were seized from behind and cut down.'

He turned to Moriana. She stared at him, speechless. She knew the story. Like the rest of his life, it had passed into legend, but she didn't know the details – or his reason for recounting them now.

'I was seized, too. I was too horrified to cry out or even to struggle. Seeing my mother and father hacked apart made me feel as if I'd died with them.

'My uncle Luu saved me. He used a stool to break the man's skull holding me. Seeing me free, he drew his sword and rallied our people. Then he cast a firebrand into the nearest pavilion.'

Darl paced now, hands locked behind his back. She saw the veins standing out on the forearms below the sleeve of his green and silver tunic.

'We escaped, my uncle and I, with me slung across the saddle of his war dog. Harmis-town fell shortly, betrayed. My uncle had to flee to the mountains with those remaining loyal. I was deemed too young for such a life. I suppose I was. I must have been in their way constantly. But how I protested when I was bundled off to Duth!'

The sky turned to bands of slate and indigo while he spoke. A few rumpled clouds remained, dark above and dull red below. Darl clasped his big hands in front of him, each massaging the other as he stared up into the evening sky.

'The treachery of that summer's night I never forgot. Nor was I blind to the evil in Duth. The lords of that city are harsh and proud and suffer no insolence, real or imagined, from their peasants. I saw wrongs done — fathers cut down for failing to doff their caps when some petty lordling rode by, daughters taken for failing to hide their loveliness from some baron. I came to feel each injustice as my own.

'The end came quickly for Earl Maunrish. His mistress refused to be cast aside for a serving lad and poisoned the earl. The people of Harmis rose in revolt, and my uncle drove the invaders back across the border when I was thirteen. Within a fortnight of his triumph, Uncle Luu died of a cancer. Before I could lay claim to the throne, Harmis fell to a civil war. Kubil and Thrishnor invaded Jav Nihen and Duth pledged itself to Harmis's security against invasion from outside. Yet none would intervene to restore order or grant me my birthright. I was too young to muster men to my cause. I ran away and went a'wandering.'

He stopped and stood, head down, unspeaking. Moriana came and touched his shoulder. The watch on the enemy-held ridge was changing, riders in leather jerkins and the black and purple tunics of the Sky City replacing the mercenaries amid blaring trumpets and clanging of weapons. Moriana watched as she laid her head on Darl's shoulder.

'That's how I came to be as I am, bright lady,' he said. 'I eventually returned to Harmis, put down the bandits who festered like pus pockets in the mountains and reunited my land. But I found myself different, my attachment no longer to my country but to an ideal. I couldn't bear the knowledge that ill is done, that evil prospers. Battle pulls me like a magnet draws iron; it is my excuse to war on the side of the oppressed. It will kill me one day. I'll fall in a ditch by the wayside and be forgotten before my corpse grows cold. Evil will march on like a procession of skeletons as if I'd never been.'

'Poor Darl,' she said lamely, unable to find the words to comfort him.

'It's what I've chosen. Don't pity me.'

'I . . . I hate to think that the cause you fall in may be mine.'

His hand gripped hers painfully hard. She made no attempt to draw away.

'My lady,' he said hoarsely, 'this time I've something to fight for beyond an abstraction. You are a cause for me, my lady. Were you a bloody-handed murderess, a lover of the Dark Ones, were you more vile than even Synalon, still I'd follow your banner.'

'I do not ask this of you,' she said in a small voice.

'You need not ask. I give it freely.'

Premonition made her step forward, grasp his face in her hands, and kiss him hard. He kissed her back eagerly. Moriana felt nothing now, nothing but sorrow and self-hatred for using this man.

Still, when they broke apart, he said the words she had tried to dam up. 'I love you, Moriana.'

It was so easy to say and yet those were not the words she wanted to hear from him. Her eyes turned bleak and bright with tears.

'Thank you for your loyalty, Lord Harmis,' she said, turning away. She walked away forcing her spine to stay straight, her shoulders braced and her sobs unvoiced. She hadn't felt this way since her dagger drove through the mail on Fost Longstrider's back on its way to his heart.

She picked up her knapsack and ran down the hill heedless of falling in the dark. She felt Darl's despair following her like a shout and knew that even a brief look back would ease his torment. But she couldn't make herself look back.

It was a long time before he followed her down the hill.

Count Ultur V'Duuyek rode along the ridgeline overlooking his camp. At his side rode Destirin Luhacs, her heavy face grim, her hair swirled into a pale yellow helmet atop her head. Sentries hailed them. The count acknowledged the challenge with a nod and rode on. The sentries were only Bilsinxt rabble.

The count was troubled. He had agreed to this expedition because he thought Moriana would be leading only a mob of criminals, misfits and fools who thought war a glorious adventure. With the admitted genius of Rann to guide it, the smaller army should have had little trouble routing the larger.

But Rann wasn't leading the army. And command hadn't gone to V'Duuyek. Rann had sent his second-in-command, a thin neurotic man named Chalowin. Perhaps, as Rann believed, the colonel was the best possible replacement. Nonetheless, he had not been a happy choice.

V'Duuyek saw his army fracturing, turning to dust. Rann would have been acceptable as commander to V'Duuyek's nine hundred heavy riders simply because of his renown. Chalowin was unknown, an alien speaking in abrupt, disjointed bursts. V'Duuyek had accepted this commission and taken the City's coin. He wouldn't criticize his employers. But his second-in-command felt no constraints. Twice he'd cautioned Luhacs and her tirades against both Chalowin and the Sky City had a poor effect on morale. That in itself bothered him. Luhacs lacked his reserve, but she seldom required such chastisement.

A small animal broke from the bush under the forefeet of V'Duuyek's mount. The dog gave an excited bark and sat on its haunches. Luhacs's red set off in pursuit. The hare fled with all the strength in its powerful hind legs. Cursing and shouting, Luhacs finally controlled her mount. Without a word, she turned its head to camp and rode down the face of the ridge. Even in the evening dimness, V'Duuyek saw that her neck burned with anger.

Another man would have sighed. Perhaps this was an omen. A Grassland soldier's mount was supposed to be better trained. Not even the lowliest trooper's dog should have bolted in pursuit of a rabbit.

Count Ultur felt more apprehensive than he had before his first battle as a boy of thirteen. The enemy was camped only two miles away on the south side of Chanobit Creek. Tomorrow would see battle. And Count Ultur feared the result.

He did not fear for his own life. The stories telling of his ice-hard courage did not lie. He was afraid for the one thing that mattered to him, the thing he had created twenty years ago and nursed as lovingly as a gardener.

He feared that the regiment to which he had dedicated his existence might not survive.

A cold wind blew, carrying the thick smell of rain. The count allowed himself a grimace of irritation. It had rained the last seven days out of ten, and on such days the Sky City eagles could not fly. They rode in cages wrapped in oiled cloth, swaying in the beds of wagons, their yellow eyes glaring from the darkness in accusation. That was an inconvenience. If it rained again tomorrow, it would be disaster.

Damn Rann! Chalowin went with the army because political considerations demanded that a Sky Citizen lead it. But his function was to see that the plan of battle conceived by Rann back in the City was faithfully executed.

V'Duuyek had little enough faith in running a battle from a hundred miles away. But what would Chalowin do if rain made the plan unworkable?

There was nothing to be done now. The morrow would bring what it would bring. Pausing to smooth his moustache back into symmetrical spikes, he nudged his own mount's ribs and cantered down to camp.

'It won't work!' Moriana insisted, slamming her fists down onto the map spread across the table commandeered from a peasant's cottage. 'I'm telling you, it's what Chalowin wants you to do. His bird riders will tear you apart.'

She stared at the faces ranged around her, reading expressions by the light of the lanterns and candles set about Darl Rhadaman's pavilion. Iatic Stormcloud, his face that of a dissolute angel, regarded her with the same smile he'd shown her since he had been recruited as Darl's co-commander in Tolviroth Acerte. The count-duke's other assistants looked at her with a mixture of impatience and something she thought with increasing anger looked like condescension. Darl was looking off at the wall of the tent, a light, pained expression on his face.

'Come now, Your Majesty,' quavered an ancient voice. 'These are battle-seasoned knights. Surely . . . surely they can withstand the assault of – uh – of birdmen.'

Moriana stared at the oldster, schooling herself to patience. Darl had been elated when the Three Notable Knights of the March had volunteered to follow Moriana's claw-and-flower flag. And they were notable knights whose deeds resounded as loudly as Darl's. Unfortunately, the days of their great deeds belonged to an earlier generation. The youngest of the three was a fussy and precise gray-haired man of seventy-six. The eldest was a remarkable one hundred and twenty-three. He spoke slowly, looking at her with his great, sad hound's eyes.

'No one doubts the mettle of your knights, Sir Rinalvus. But mettle is small protection against arrows falling as thick as hail from above,'

430

she said quietly.

'Arrows.' Sir Tharvus spoke the word distastefully as though he had said 'offal'. He sniffed. 'We are not the sort to be afraid of such child's toys, Your Majesty.'

In exasperation, Moriana looked to Darl.

'Can't you explain to them? Bunching together like this is asking to be slaughtered by the bird riders. It's exactly the formation our – the Sky City's – war college regards as ideal for attack.'

Before Darl could speak, the third brother put in smoothly, 'But my dear, our knights fight best when used as a solid mass. If they lose cohesion they lose much of their effectiveness.'

The speaker favored Moriana with a kindly smile. The middle of the brothers in age, he was still a handsome man and powerful of frame despite his ninety years. Moriana heard a voice within her begin to yammer in panic, but she answered him as reasonably as she could.

'Sir Ottovus, your men will be perfect targets. How much effectiveness will they have when they're dead?'

Ottovus only smiled. Lip twitching, Tharvus turned to Darl.

'Is all this discussion necessary? This is speech for men, my lord.'

Moriana colored.

'Now, sir,' Iatic said in his golden voice, 'we are pledged to serve the princess's cause. She has a right to join our councils.'

'As I – um – understand it,' said Rinalvus, 'the good princess – or queen, I suppose I should say since we're trying to restore you to your throne, and begging Your Majesty's pardon – I thought she was going to explain to us how her magic will aid us tomorrow.'

'Yes,' said Tharvus, 'I'm certain *that* is a subject Her Majesty is amply qualified to discuss at length.'

'I have told you before, lord, my magic is not of a sort to be used in battle,' said Moriana.

'But what is this?' Rinalvus asked. 'I . . . I thought magicians threw fireballs and lightning bolts, that sort of thing. Should be quite useful. Yes, indeed.'

'My sister would be able to oblige you with ease,' snapped Moriana. She tried to keep the edge from her words because she admired the aged knight. It was merely that he, and all of them, failed to understand that her participation in the battle was vital for success. They seemed slave to so many misconceptions about the nature of war waged by the Sky City that she had to try to correct them. 'It

431

requires far more involvement with powers best left unnamed to become that facile in destruction.'

'What can your talents accomplish then?'

'Healing the injured. Scrying – you've seen me look into the enemy's camp often enough. Manipulating the weather.'

'That'll be fine,' nodded Ottovus. 'You can stay atop the hill out of harm's way and tend to the wounded. And if you can whistle up a few clouds to keep the bird riders out of the fight, so much the better!'

He beamed at her. It dawned on the princess that he thought he was doing her a favor, that he offered a way to stay out of the fight where no woman would wish to be. But Moriana wanted to be in the thick of it, dealing blows in what was her cause.

She sagged, the table's edge pressing against her thighs. She felt more frustration and sick fear than anger. It was as if she exchanged words with a charlatan's puppets. They spoke to her and she to them, but she no more communicated with them than she could with effigies of wood or ivory. She wished for Ziore. She desperately needed the spirit's calm strength. But Darl had said it would make the others uncomfortable. And Moriana, always aware of the immeasurable service he did her, had given in. As she had done so frequently of late.

'Hear me, lords,' she said, leaning forward on anger-stiffened arms. 'You have agreed to help shoulder my burden, and my gratitude to you is profound. But the burden is mine, and I mean to bear as much as I can.'

'Well, to be sure . . .' began Ottovus.

'I do not mean to languish on a hilltop while my fate and that of my City is decided by others. I have led troops in battle and have been victorious. I have led Sky City troops; I trained throughout my early years as a bird rider. I know my folk. And I fight as well as any of them.'

She glared at them defiantly. Slowly, her defiance softened and melted away like the wax in the burning candles scattered around the pavilion. The others' eyes showed condescension quite openly now. It came to her that they thought her martial experience to be like that of the Emperors of Medurim and other idle aristocrats of the North, that like them she 'trained' by dressing in gilded armor and reviewing the troops once a month.

'Come, this is absurd,' said Tharvus. 'A woman going into battle. Indeed!'

Moriana snapped her lips shut on the challenge that rose to them. Her furious impulse had been to offer a challenge to single combat. That would have only reinforced the other's notion of her as an impetuous creature, ruled by emotion and not to be trusted with the serious business of war. She turned a despairing look to Darl.

The Count-Duke of Harmis stood blinking rapidly. For some reason, Moriana was reminded of a small boy whose fellows will not play nice and who is on the verge of tears because the game goes other than his way.

She knew she was being unfair. He'd done much for her and was only trying to do what he thought right.

'I think your Majesty misunderstands,' spoke Ottovus in round, comforting tones. 'It is only that the idea of exposing yourself to harm is unacceptable to us. We would be remiss in our duty if we failed to protect you.'

Darl moved to her side. He took her hand and fell to his knees.

'Trust us, Your Majesty. We have proved ourselves in war. We know how best to serve your cause.'

And I don't? she thought savagely, without voicing the words.

He kissed her hand fervently. The others nodded benign approval. Even Tharvus was smiling at her now.

'Trouble yourself no more, my queen!' Darl cried, leaping to his feet. 'Leave this to us and we shall give you victory tomorrow!'

The others joined in.

'Victory! Moriana and victory!'

The tension was swamped in the sudden wave of loyalty and passion. The waves of exuberance broke over Moriana. She felt herself eroding bit by bit like a castle built of sand.

CHAPTER ELEVEN

The new day appeared much like the gemstone set in the talisman Moriana wore around her neck: mostly white.

'See?' said Ziore to her as the guards Darl had assigned escorted them to the crest of a hill overlooking the battlefield. 'I knew things wouldn't turn out as badly as you feared.'

Moriana surveyed the scene. Normally, the hill provided a vantage above the broad valley where her army and Synalon's would clash today. But a thick fog cloaked it, making the landscape appear as if it were layers of wool. She couldn't see farther than a few feet. Ripples in the mist now and then exposed shapes, shadowy and indistinct, of men preparing for the day.

Under the blanket of damp, clinging mist, Chalowin's eagles would be grounded. Unless the weather changed, the Sky City's chief weapon would be rendered impotent.

Moriana clutched her amulet. Pale light glowed between her fingers.

'Your amulet has not been wrong yet,' said Ziore. 'See how its color foretells good fortune?'

Moriana looked at it ruefully. She wondered if it was worth the sacrifice.

From below came a shout. It was followed by a strange clanging sound like a cook banging with an iron spoon. Moriana's breath caught in her throat.

The Battle of Chanobit Creek had begun.

'My birds cannot fly,' Colonel Chalowin stated flatly. 'There will be no battle today.'

V'Duuyek's gaze was steady from beneath the rim of his helmet.

He had foreseen such an objection.

'We fight, with or without your eagles. Our army is in place.'

Tension turned Chalowin's usual facial tic into myriad twitching, writhing components. Now the Sky City colonel looked like some insect in his nervousness.

'The prince's plan requires the eagles,' he said. 'They cannot fly. We wait for better weather.'

V'Duuyek smoothed his moustache. He boiled inside. Knowing that Chalowin might try to forestall action, he had taken steps to prevent it. If those steps were discovered . . .

'We must prevent Moriana's army from bypassing us. If they succeed, they can cut the City's lifeline at Bilsinx. Is this what Prince Rann commanded?'

'We have the greater mobility,' said Chalowin doggedly. 'We can catch them.'

'As long as this foul weather holds,' said V'Duuyek, speaking with his usual precision, 'we have little mobility at all. Our army moves at the pace of the wagons carrying your war eagles. If Moriana's army gets past us, we may never catch them.'

They stood on a bluff across the valley from the invisible hilltop where the enemy had erected their command post. V'Duuyek gazed into the formless fog, his blue eyes bright, as if by straining he could pierce the dirty fleece clouds and see their foe. In fact, he strained his ears to catch a certain sound that would tell him his mercenary force stood a fighting chance of survival.

Chalowin glared at him. His left eye pulsed closed with an arhythmic beat so disconcerting to V'Duuyek that he turned away. He felt no concern that this would make the colonel suspect. Chalowin, unlike Rann, was not overly perceptive.

'Our enemy has the initiative,' he said. 'If we hold back, they will attack us with every advantage of momentum. It isn't an advantage I'd advise we give the knights of the City States.'

'We will withdraw then.' Chalowin slapped himself on the chest without being aware that he did so.

'In that case, any offensive move on their part will catch us unprepared and in disorder. We can expect to be overwhelmed. They have a considerable advantage in numbers, colonel.'

Chalowin's pallor grew more marked as the mercenary spoke. When V'Duuyek finished, it took the Sky City officer half a minute to control his angry twitching sufficiently to speak.

'The prince has given us the plan,' he said, raising his voice. Wraithlike figures stopped to turn and stare at the men. 'We must not deviate from it! Order the withdrawal now, my lord. When we make our attack, it will be as Prince Rann decreed.'

V'Duuyek stared at him. He felt sick to his stomach. He knew why Rann had placed a man of such unswerving devotion in command: another might decide on his own to alter Rann's plan. With the Sky Citizen's disdain for groundlings, he might even neglect to inform a subordinate V'Duuyek of any change. Such lack of coordination brought only disaster. And in V'Duuyek's learned opinion, Rann's plan was an excellent one. Chalowin could be relied on to follow it exactly, as if its every detail were graved on his brain. But, as the count had feared all along, events precluded its use. And Chalowin could not conceive of an attack that differed from the original.

V'Duuyek made a production of removing his gauntlets, his left one heavy and backed in steel, his right of dog's hide, thin and pliant so his fingers could grip the string of his bow. He listened for the sounds he counted on so heavily. But he heard nothing. Tucking his gloves into his baldric, he turned to face Chalowin.

From below came a cry, the deep, fierce barking of a dog yelping in pain. The count paused, smiled and took his gauntlets from his baldric, and began putting them on again.

'We are already engaged, colonel,' he said. Even in his triumph, he kept his tones even, his words trimmed neatly to fit. 'We've no choice now but to give battle. Unless the men of the Sky City are inclined to flee from a battle already joined . . .'

Chalowin's jaw worked open and shut. V'Duuyek saw the anguish on his face. Rann wouldn't hesitate to back away from battle if his keen mind told him that was the shrewdest move. But Chalowin was no more capable of bringing down what he saw as dishonor on the City's forces than he was of defying Rann.

Almost choking, he said, 'Give the order to attack.'

'The curs have left their kennel!' cried Darl from the back of his great white war dog. 'To me, O men of the North. Let's whip them back to whence they came!' He brandished his broadsword above his head. Even in the mirk, it flashed with a deadly light.

A roar of approval rose from the hilltop and the valley below. Though most of the troop couldn't see their commander, they heard the ringing clamor of his voice. That was all they needed. The men drawn up in ranks felt their blood take fire with excitement and the nearness of battle.

Moriana heard her voice joining the rest. Though she was condemned to wait out the day on this hillside, she couldn't help sharing the exhilaration of these men who would struggle and die for her.

Darl rode over and jerked back on his reins. The huge dog reared back with a snarl, pawing at the air. Darl caught at a lance thrust into the soil. From its tip fluttered the arms of the princess. He waved it high over his head.

'Moriana!' he cried. 'Moriana and victory!' Then he wheeled his mount and loped off into the fog.

Moriana heard his laugh, high and full of boyish excitement. Then a thousand throats took up the battle cry. The men of the Northland who had come by the thousands to offer service to an alien princess swept forward to attack.

After all Moriana's warnings, the army had been drawn up in a conventional formation. In the center stood a mass of infantry, almost six thousand strong. They were farmers, mercenaries, vassals of lordlings who had offered their swords to Moriana, armed with the short spears and shields of Realm footmen. Flanking them were thirteen hundred archers split roughly in half between the left wing and the right. They were men of proven temper, mostly foresters from the Great Nevrym Forest or deserters from the Imperial Border Watch risking Imperial displeasure for a chance to strike a blow at the forces of the Dark Ones. Moriana was glad of such men, but she feared they would prove inadequate. Although the army they faced was small, it boasted twice as many missile troops. There were ominous numbers of Bilsinxt riders, V'Duuyek dog riders, and several hundred infantry skirmishers with bows and javelins.

But the knights of the City States scorned arrows, as Sir Tharvus had been at such pains to make clear the night before. It was on those knights that Darl depended most. Seven hundred of them poised on the left flank, their dogs snarling at each other, keyed to a frenzy by the excitement charging the air. At their head rode two of the Notable Knights, Tharvus and Ottovus, the first in his armor of gold and the second in crimson. On the right were the seven hundred under Darl's personal command. Almost half of the knights and men-at-arms came from his home county of Harmis. Backing them were twenty-five-hundred light lancers, their armor mail instead of the glittering enameled plate of the knights.

A heavy guard ringed Moriana's hilltop. She was not alone, at least. Two other figures impatiently paced the perimeter, casting covetous glances into the fog, eager to take part in the battle even now beyond their eyes' reach. Young Iatic Stormcloud, his hair a golden wreath and the fine lines of his face slightly blurred by dissipation, paced with the scabbard of his longsword clacking at his thigh. And ancient Sir Rinalvus, visor raised to allow his rheumy old eyes to peer into the mist, stood leaning on the haft of a massive ax backed with a hook. The angelic young mercenary commanded a reserve of a hundred knights and two hundred lesser cavalry. Sir Rinalvus was supposed to oversee the battle and keep his fellow commanders apprised of any new developments – if the fog thinned enough for him to see them. Moriana suspected that the oldster, wearing the same suit of polished blue plate in which he had accompanied so many exploits over the course of more than a century's adventuring, had also been set to watch over her and and make sure she neither meddled nor came to harm. He didn't pace and glare like a caged falcon as did Iatic. But looking at him, pitifully shrunken within armor built to encase one more robust, Moriana felt her heart go out to him. Though he didn't accept her as an equal on the field of war, it pained him not to be able to strike a blow on her behalf.

'This is . . . most impressive,' said Ziore, her voice intruding on the princess's thoughts. 'In my days as a nun, we were taught war was a horrible thing, brutish and distasteful. Yet the air is filled with hot vibrations, energies. I find this . . . stimulating.'

Could the spirit, cloistered throughout her life, be turning into another Erimenes?

'No, child,' Ziore laughed. 'I am unlike the evil man whose false teachings blighted my life. I can take no joy in the pain of others. But I can feel the eagerness pulsing through a million veins. It flows like lightning along my nerves.'

Moriana started to reply to the pale pink figure. A sudden blaring cry of triumph made her turn and look out across the valley. She saw figures surging and striving together. The knights of Harmis, with Darl at their head, rushed down. Her blue, red, and gold banner snaked behind. Among them were others in long linen surcoats. Their armor overlapped like a lizard's scales; their helms were high, worked into curious knobbed spires. From them flew streamers of a dozen bright colors. Dogs snapped at one another, tearing at exposed throats. The foreigners' dogs were bulkier than Darl's. Unlike the knights, who

438

armored only the chests and heads of their war dogs, these riders covered their beasts' bodies with scale armor like their own.

Moriana had no difficulty recognizing the famed dog riders of the Highgrass Broad. Yet she was puzzled. Some of them, trying to avoid Darl's knights, loosed arrows tipped with broad steel heads. Even as Moriana watched, one struck the breastplate of Darl's armor. It hit at an angle and bounced off amid fat blue sparks. The princess was uncomfortably aware that she had screamed aloud in horror.

But although the dog riders were risking the tension of their strings and the glue that held their bows together to the treacherous damp, none seemed to carry the long lances traditionally used. A number of men lay still on the ground, their blood a red cloth spread on the wet grass. For all their steel, they had suffered terribly at the first shock. They turned and fled before the knights of the North.

The bulk of Darl's army advanced at a slow walk. They cheered frantically at the apparent rout of their vaunted enemy. Darl's knights started to follow up their advantage and spur their mounts into the mist. Darl's voice halted them. He had charged with only a few score of his knights. He was not reckless enough to take his whole force when attacking an unseen enemy.

He saw what Moriana had seen as soon as the melee separated itself into sides, one fleeing, one victorious. He had just beaten a mere handful of cavalry. Darl held his followers back to wait for the other knights to catch up with them. They sat impatiently, tugging at their reins to prevent their mounts from licking up the spilled blood.

Moriana let out her pent-up breath. She admitted she had underestimated Darl. She had known with ugly certainty that he would follow the fleeing troops with his small band right into the concentrated arrow flights of two thousand archers. But Darl had reacted as coolly and precisely as might Rann, under whose command Moriana had fought the Golden Barbarians half a decade before. She reached to the bodice of her gown to feel the hardness of the amulet. Perhaps its augury was true. Perhaps success would be theirs this day.

Then she gasped. The fog, the vital fog that kept the lethal bird riders helpless, was beginning to lift.

She turned to the brazier that sent a wistful spiral of smoke to blend with the fog. A stand with herbs and other substances had been placed next to the iron tripod holding the brazier. A pair of boys in the crimson, blue, and gold livery of the Brother Knights stood a few

paces away, alternately punching each other and giggling, staring at
the battle and eyeing the princess at whose beck and call they'd been
placed. Ignoring the adolescent lust glowing in their eyes, she walked
to the brazier and gestured for them to attend.

'Look lively,' she snapped. 'I must keep these damned clouds in
place.'

Ultur V'Duuyek steeled himself. Torn, broken bodies flowed by. He
had sent two scores of his men to probe the enemy position. Only
fifteen dogs returned with riders still aboard.

They had known the nature of their mission, every man and
woman of them. They were to be risked – sacrificed – so that
Chalowin could be forced into battle. V'Duuyek and his officers
knew full well that Darl and Moriana, who cared little enough for
what Rann decreed, would not merely permit their foes to decline
combat until better weather arrived. And for the Sky City army to be
caught at any sort of disadvantage by their horde of foes would be
catastrophic. To save his regiment, V'Duuyek had no choice but to
send the forty on their suicide mission. He had been like a loving
father forced to choose which of his children are to be sacrificed so
that the others may survive.

And his favorite of all had been one of the volunteers. Though his
face remained impassive, his eyes searched for the familiar red war
dog with the heavy jaw.

A moment later he saw the dog. His lips pressed into a thin line. No
rider occupied the saddle of Destirin Luhacs's mount.

Wounded men rode double with their comrades – risky business
because one rider and its own armor brought even a Highgrass
charger near the limits of the burden it could carry. Others had
improvised stretchers from cloaks and the coils of rope they carried
by their saddle bows.

Two dogs trotted straight for the commander. V'Duuyek scarcely
dared glance at the figure slung between them. Its spired helmet had
fallen off. The hair coiled about the head was matted pink with drying
blood.

'Destirin . . .'

The figure stirred. The head lifted. The face was a horrid mask of
blood, a black slash across the forehead. Yet the apparition grinned,
teeth shockingly white against the fog-dulled red.

'I live, Count Ultur,' said Destirin Luhacs, 'but I fear I'll have to go easy on the rum for a while. My head spins even without it.'

Count Ultur V'Duuyek did not smile, but between him and his second-in-command passed a look of perfect understanding. With a nod, he gestured Luhacs's rescuers to bear her to the ridgetop where Sky City mages might attend to her wounds.

Calmly, surely, he drew the oiled case of his bow from over his shoulder. Clamped firmly in place, his lance jutted from its stirrup. He undrapped the bow, felt the string for tautness and nodded. Chalowin was at the rear, behind the long ridge on which the command post had been erected. Foiled of his chance to carry out Rann's strategy, Chalowin had given over conduct of the battle to the mercenary.

V'Duuyek looked right and left. Messengers sat on quivering, long-legged dispatch dogs waiting to carry his commands.

'We go,' he said quietly.

Following Rann's concepts, the Sky City army had been deployed in a way to maximize its strengths. Its fifteen hundred spear-and-shield infantry, in black iron helmets and tunics and breeches of purple and black, were ranged in three blocks of four hundred, with a reserve of three hundred backing up the army. In the left gap waited a thousand Sky City dog riders, heavily armed with bow, lance, and black-painted shield. In the right gap stood the Highgrass Broad riders. Before them, the seven hundred foot skirmishers provided a living screen. These were the half-breeds born of groundling women and of Sky Citizens on garrison duty. Their morale was not as high as that of their pureblooded comrades, but it wasn't their function to stand and fight. They harassed and delayed the foe, keeping them from seeing exactly how the army behind was set forth.

The thousand Bilsinxt auxiliaries swarmed in nervous clouds at either side. At V'Duuyek's order to advance, they galloped forward, drawing bowstrings to ears. Like the half-caste foot skirmishers, they had no armor save for the green tabards they wore over yellow tunics. The mercenary expected no great performances from them, but they were meant only to annoy the enemy and then fall back.

Like a curtain being raised, the mist ascended to a height of twenty feet. The top of Moriana's hill was in the clear. The ridge around which the City's men were arrayed remained cloaked in fog. Behind it, the eagles uttered dispirited cries. The unbroken blanket of fog screened the enemy from arrows fired from above; the lancers could not strike without flying along the ground itself, a role more suited to V'Duuyek's dog riders in their shiny, surcoated carapaces. A bird rider wore no armor but a conical cap of thin steel and a hornbull-leather buckler faced with metal.

Darl rode at the head of the other army, lance held upright, Moriana's banner streaming behind him. Men and dogs growled at his back as the Bilsinxt poured around the infantry in twin streams and rode toward them. They felt their skins crawling with the need to be at their foe. But Darl did not intend to waste the momentum of his knights on mere light cavalry. The Northern army, the army of the Bright Princess as Darl had dubbed it in a poetic mood, moved forward at a stately pace, its gay colors muted by the fog.

If the Bilsinxt swarmed like bees, they had their stingers as well. Arrows buzzed up to fall among the Northerners. Shelled in steel, the knights and their dogs were almost impervious to the missiles. A few dogs yelped as hindquarters were grazed, but none fell and no riders were injured.

Among the lightly armored men, it was a different story. Men of Harmis, men of Thrishnor and Duth and Samazant in the Empire, men who had come from Port Zorn to fight for the beautiful Princess Moriana, from Wirix to fight Synalon, from Kolnith and Deepwater and the Sjedd to champion the cause of the Wiser Ones – men who had come from all over the Sundered Realm to find adventure, booty, or fulfillment of some pious vow, found death instead.

Moriana's archers loosed before a second volley came from the Bilsinxt. Riders screamed and fell from saddles to be dragged across the ground by dogs maddened by pain and the bright stench of blood. The Northern infantry had only light armor and shields. The riders of Bilsinx had no protection but the speed of their swift dogs. For many, it was not enough.

For once, Count Ultur had misjudged. Far from breaking at the first taste of death, the Bilsinxt wheeled their dogs and swept across the front of the hostile ranks for a second pass. Closer they came. Their bows were less powerful than those of a bird rider, but now the lesser range told.

An arrow socketed itself in the gap between the brassard and breast of Sir Ottovus's armor. He smiled and pulled it free. Yet those nearby noted that its tip came out bloody. The man riding at Darl's right uttered a sharp cry and fell with a shaft jutting through the slit in his visor. Darl looked back once, face white beneath the raised visor of his own helm. Then he turned resolutely to the foe.

With a courage as fanatical as it was unexpected, the Bilsinxt circled again and again and again inside the narrowing gap between the armies. More and more of the steel-plated war dogs fell out of the ranks to stand snarling over fallen masters.

Glancing up from her brazier, Moriana groaned as she saw the left-hand array of knights break from the ranks and charge their antagonists. Like men freed from a geas, the Bilsinxt broke off their death ride and raced for the rear.

The Sky City dog riders lunged to meet the knights. They hurtled forward and then broke to their right, spitting arrows into the faces of the onrushing knights. Driven by stouter bows, these arrows punched through the plate armor. Dogs began to fall, spilling their riders in the path of those behind. Confusion blunted the force of the charge.

Darl's hand was forced. A quick sally or a blizzard of arrows might shatter Tharvus's men completely. The Count-Duke of Harmis slammed down his visor, dropped the tip of his lance, and charged.

Sound boiled from the valley floor as the armies collided. Steel glanced from steel with sonorous bell notes. Arrows moaned like spirits of the dead. The soft thump-thump of dog's feet gave way to barks and snarls. The screams of the wounded floated over all like carrion birds.

'I don't like it,' said Moriana, glancing from brazier to battlefield, then at Sir Rinalvus and back to the brazier again. The knight watched Ziore in fascination. He held one hand above his eyes as if shading them from the sun.

'What do you mislike, princess?' he asked.

Moriana frowned at her brazier. With senses not those of the flesh, she felt the sun pour its heat down from the sky, trying to melt away the snowy bank of cloud overhead. Since nature had provided the clouds, she would work them, keep them in a soft ceiling, a lid to trap the eagles against the earth. But it took constant effort.

'The dog riders. It doesn't look as if there are nine hundred.'

'I know little of these things,' said Ziore, 'but wouldn't they leave some back to take the place of wounded or plug gaps in their line?'

'Yes, but fully half their number? I'd swear there are only four hundred there, five at the most.' She squinted into the rising smoke. She felt control slipping. She took a pinch of maroon powder, scattered it on the tiny flames, and recoiled when gray smoke rolled up into her face.

'They probably have some hidden beyond the ridge.' Ziore sounded doubtful. Moriana realized the spirit was trying to bolster her courage and ease her fears. She felt the touch of Ziore's mind on hers, as light as down and twice as soothing.

No! she thought so violently that Ziore winced. *Stay out!*

She glanced up and saw the hurt look on Ziore's face.

'I'm sorry,' she said aloud. 'But I don't dare let you soothe me. I can't let you into my mind at all. It blunts my powers.' The spirit lowered her head.

BOOM!

With a rolling crash like thunder, V'Duuyek's dog riders met Darl's knights. Lance broke against shield or armored breast. Men and women were hurled down, mortally wounded. Dogs lunged at each other, toppled riders, and tore at them until fierce lance thrusts dropped them where they stood.

Like waves, the armored riders smashed into each other and then fell back. For all Darl's prowess, the knights of the City States couldn't break through the wall of iron they faced. Time and again both groups withdrew, only to re-form and surge in again. The tide slowly turned. More dogs from the Empire bayed lament over fallen masters than those reared in the tall grass country of the east. But numbers told.

Blood streamed down Count Ultur's face. His helmet had been torn just above his right eye by a lance. The wound wasn't serious but it bled profusely. He nocked an arrow, drew, sighted across the few yards of corpse-strewn grass separating the riders. He cursed. He was denied a clear shot at Darl.

The count loosed his arrow. A man stiffened, struck dead as his head was turned. The man dropped. Darl saw how close he had come to hearing the Hell Call, waved the hand that still held Moriana's banner, and urged his forces on.

The armies splashed against each other again.

Moriana scarcely dared to look. Her army was winning; somehow that was harder to watch than when the outcome was in doubt. Old Rinalvus thumped on the butt of his ax and yelled himself hoarse. Iatic Stormcloud paced and scowled, angry at missing a fight that came closer to victory every minute.

'Lord Iatic!' a voice cried. Moriana's head whipped up. 'Sir Rinalvus! Your Highness!' A man rode up the hill from the woods along the right flank. Moriana recognized him as a squire with the reserves. Iatic stared at him, holding one hand upraised and cupping the elbow with the other like a messenger of a Wise One about to deliver Law.

'What is it, boy?' Rinalvus demanded.

The youth looked from face to face as if unsure whom to address. Finally, he blurted out to everyone in general, 'We were riding through the woods, lords – uh, and lady – and we saw riders coming this way. They had streamers on their helmets.'

'A flank attack!' Moriana cried. Without a word, Iatic spun and ran to his own mount. Shouting for his reserves to follow, he pelted down the hill. He was too canny to rush into the woods where his knights would be at a disadvantage. Instead, he readied his men at the foot of the hill where they'd be in position to strike the mercenaries as they emerged from the woods.

'Stay clear of the fire, boy,' Moriana told the squire. 'And keep your dog away. The magic may scare him.'

Something popped in the heart of the fire. The dog jumped, slipped on wet grass, and fell onto its side. The squire left the saddle and fell on top of Moriana. She yelped as hot metal seared the back of her hand.

The squire bounded up as though Moriana were a mattress.

'Oh, Your Highness, forgive me! I didn't mean! O Gods, I wouldn't dare to . . .'

Moriana didn't hear him. She was on hands and knees trying to steady herself against the waves of horror breaking over her. In her tumble she'd upset the brazier. The magic holding the cloud cover intact had broken.

And her amulet had slipped from her gown. Moriana stared at it numbly.

It gleamed dully on its silver chain, as black as a lump of coal.

V'Duuyek's men were pushed back for what the count knew to be the final time. His gamble had failed; the troops he sent through the twisting valleys to come upon both flanks of the enemy had not arrived. His beloved regiment was being chopped to shreds before his eyes.

Then a trumpet call drew his eyes outward. An involuntary shout escaped his lips. From first one side of the valley and then the other broke his men, streaming from the woods and a gully. The shouts of consternation among his enemies were sweet music to him.

445

Darl's knights turned to meet the Grasslanders. On the far side of the field, the knights under the command of Sir Tharvus and Sir Ottovus readied for their charge. V'Duuyek sat, his short, heavy sword in hand, prepared for the final charge.

Something made him glance up.

'Great Ultimate!' he·cried. His soldiers tipped back their heads. In a moment, the knights did so, too, pausing and milling as they did.

Breaks appeared in the cover above, revealing patches of blue. The battlefield lapsed into silence as the clouds dissipated with eldritch swiftness. Those below felt a chill, but there was no wind.

Behind the ridge, Chalowin shrieked, 'The Dark Ones have delivered victory to us!' Like bolts shot from twelve-score catapults, the eagles surged into the naked sky.

They fell into the roles assigned them in the master plan. Like a new fog, a hundred eagles spilled over the ridgetop and passed with a drumming of wings. Their riders raked the ranks below with arrows. The riders' aim was good. Most of their arrows found homes in Northern flesh.

Moriana caught sight of Sir Ottovus sitting tall in his saddle, sword raised in defiance. Slowly, like a collapsing tower, he toppled to one side. Moriana saw the ugly black butt of a lance protruding from his neck.

Beside her, Rinalvus sobbed and covered his face with his hands.

A flight of bird riders made straight for the hill. Moriana felt her arms gripped. Two spearmen had stepped up and hustled her toward the pavilion she shared with Darl. They had been ordered to keep her from joining the fight.

She recognized the emaciated figure astride the lead war bird. He shouted a command. Arrows sliced down, striking half a dozen spearmen.

Moriana's guards let her go at the tent flap and ran to join the handful of their number who still survived. Eagles landed, their riders leaping off with javelins and short curved swords in hand.

'Here, old one,' one said to Rinalvus, 'give over that chopper and we'll not hurt you. Don't do anything rash and you'll be in your dotard's bed by nightfall.'

Rinalvus's answer was a deft ax-blow. The man gurgled, teeth spilling from his head like pale seeds. He died.

Shouting their anger, his fellows closed in. Rinalvus moved with fantastic speed. He knocked a sword from a gloved hand, spun his ax

446

to split a javelin, and lopped the arm off another who leaned in to thrust.

'Come down, damn you!' he yelled at the sky. He looked neither frail nor wasted now. 'Come down from the sky and meet the avenger of Ottovus the Golden!'

Chalowin screeched fury. He drew his bow and shot. The arrow glanced off Rinalvus's breastplate. The old man staggered back a step, then straightened, strong gnarled hands resolutely gripping his ax haft.

The bird riders circled him. They shot again and again at the lonely figure on the hilltop. Rinalvus's armor, redoubtable though it was, could not withstand them.

Moriana screamed as one sank into his chest. Another punctured his thigh. Still he stood his ground. His throat was pierced, his upper arm, his cheek. The indomitable old man stood as though the arrows were no more than insect bites.

Moriana rushed inside the tent, picked up a bow and quiver, and stepped back outside. The bird riders still circled Rinalvus like vultures waiting for a wounded beast to drop. But Rinalvus did not stop. He stood watching them defiantly, a dozen arrows in his body.

He turned and looked at Moriana with his sad eyes.

'My lady,' he said, though the words were scarcely recognizable. 'Forgive my failing . . .'

He fell.

Cold as the water that now ran red in the stream below, Moriana nocked an arrow, pulled, aimed. Chalowin caught sight of her.

'There!' he shrieked, face twisted in ecstasy. 'The slut who plots the fall of Queen Synalon! Take her alive, my . . .'

He never finished.

The arrow struck him in the left eye. He gave a maniacal shriek as he backflipped out of his saddle and fell to the ground, as limp as a bundle of rags. He fell beside the body of the ancient hero he had shot down so ruthlessly. Their blood ran together.

Before he landed, another arrow arched upward. A bird rider screamed more fearfully than Chalowin as the missile split his groin and drove deep into his bird's neck. A third rider turned his eagle toward the princess and dived. She stepped forward and calmly loosed again. The arrow went through the eagle's neck and plunged into the rider's belly. They swooshed overhead to collide with the top of the tent.

The remaining rider lost his nerve. Seeing the Sky Guard officer who commanded the army brought down, he fled.

But instead of a straightaway climb, trying to gain as much altitude and distance as possible, he turned his bird in a wing-pumping spiral. Moriana watched him climb almost vertically, a cruel smile wracking her mouth. Had he been a Sky Guardsman, he wouldn't have made such an error. He might even have survived.

Moriana let him get two hundred feet in the air. She raised her arm, slid back the string, aimed, and released.

The eagle jerked, squawked, began to tumble. Its rider came free, arms and legs wheeling wildly. The princess savored his scream until the ground cut it short. Then she walked over to Ziore.

Ziore's face was desolate.

'How can such things be?' she whispered. 'How can the Wise Ones permit such horror?'

Moriana felt deathly tired.

'Perhaps they have no choice.' She threw her bow away. 'Or perhaps it's a game to them and we're merely pawns to be moved at random.'

'You are wrong, child. Oh, Great Ultimate, you *must* be!'

'I fear,' said Moriana slowly, 'that all too soon we shall find out whether or not I'm right.'

The battle reversed itself with stunning swiftness. Darl's amy melted like snow beneath a warm rain as the arrows streaked down from above. Within five minutes, the army that had been within sword's reach of victory was a fleeing, fear-drunken mob.

The man who had done as much as any to bring this turnabout victory was not content to let the bird riders win it themselves. Count Ultur V'Duuyek led a charge head-on into Darl's knights. This time it was the wiry count who cut through foes like a scythe through weeds.

Finally he and Darl faced each other above raised swords. Darl's shield was gone, smashed to ruin by a hundred blows. It was blade against blade, man against man.

Sparks flew in all directions as the blades caressed each other. Snake swift, V'Duuyek laid open the armor coating Darl's thigh and drew a bright line of blood along the leg. Darl winced, grinned, and made a quick cut at his opponent's head.

The count's blade flashed up. Darl pivoted and thrust. With a crunching sound like shellfish dropped on a rock by a hungry seagull,

Darl's point broke.

Through armor.

Through ribs.

Through heart.

Count Ultur V'Duuyek sat bolt upright in the saddle. His foe's blade slid free with a grating sound. Feeling nothing, the count swung around and came to rest with his head in a clump of grass.

'The Count is fallen!' A woman's voice rose to heights of despair. 'Avenge him!' And crying *vengeance*, his men burst forward and swept the surviving knights away in a torrent of madness.

Count V'Duuyek's last sight was that of his regiment charging to its last and greatest victory.

He died content.

CHAPTER TWELVE

When V'Duuyek fell, Darl wanted to stand his ground and die beside the body of his foe. His surviving men wouldn't allow it. They gathered around him, fending off the howling dog riders. A young knight caught the reins of the commander's mount. Darl was led off the field weeping like a small child.

If Moriana had not been allowed to participate in winning victory, there was none to stop her from saving what she could from defeat. She had no hope of ever gathering another army such as this. It was not hope of using survivors of this field to form the core of yet another attempt on the Sky City that motivated her. But these men had left their homes and their loved ones hundreds of miles away to fight for her, though her cause was not theirs. She felt it her duty to save as many as possible.

It was difficult to recognize the refined and beautiful princess in whose cause the battle had been fought. She had become a green-eyed fury, straightsword in hand, elegant dress hacked off above the knee to keep it from tangling her legs. Yet the battered remnants of defeat who drifted her way did as they were bid. She ordered them away through the woods where the eagles could not get them and in parties large enough to make it hard for the enemy to pick them off piecemeal. With her training in command and assistance from Ziore, Moriana put together a successful defense when a band of dog riders swooped down on her little group.

Ziore was still appalled at what had occurred and wanted no further part of fighting. Moriana had pointed out that this was a fight to save lives – the enraged Grasslanders were killing all Northerners they could find. Ziore acquiesced with the sad observation that it was such compromise that led decent people to butcher each other in the first place.

Chanobit Creek ran behind the hilltop holding the Northern command post. And when time permitted, Moriana felt a certain bitterness that the battle had, in fact, been waged by a Northern army and not *her* army. In the trees on its north bank, Moriana worked at organizing the survivors and sending them on their way. She was careful not to let too many group at one time for fear of attracting attention that would be fatal. Fortunately, the death of the two supreme commanders had left the enemy disorganized.

Shortly before night lowered the curtain on this bloody day, a party of knights rode up, leading Darl. The Count-Duke of Harmis seemed stunned, unable to conceive of the disaster that had come to pass. Moriana came out of the thicket to meet them. Her face was grave with more than the concerns of the moment.

'Your Highness, Your Highness,' one said, tears streaming down cheeks barely touched with downy beard. 'We've brought you failure and disgrace. How can we restore to you what our worthlessness has lost?'

She shook her head sadly.

'You cannot.' The boy looked stricken. She wondered how old he was. 'The way you can best serve me now is to live.'

He brightened.

'Will you permit us to fight for you again?'

'If you wish, perhaps you shall. Some day.' She held back tears of her own. 'But that's not what I mean. I mean survive. Live out this day and many more so that I'll not have your death on my conscience, too.'

He blinked in bewilderment. Moriana turned to Darl. He looked at her through strange, old eyes.

'I'm . . . sorry,' he whispered.

Something blocked her throat. She reached up to take his hand. She pressed it against her cheek.

'You tried.'

'What will you do now?' Darl voiced the question listlessly, as though he was reading lines in a boring play.

'I can do two things,' she said. 'I can quit — which I shall never do as long as I draw breath. Or I can go elsewhere for assistance.'

He shook his head, a distant expression on his face.

'Where will you go? I have used up my stock with the folk of the North. Where will you find the men?'

'I will not use *men*,' she said. 'Or at least, not humans.'

'I don't understand.'

'The builders of the City, the Hissers — *Zr'gsz*, as they call themselves. They live at Thendrun in the Mystic Mountains.'

A gasp burst from the listeners. They milled about, shuffling their feet and not looking her in the eye.

'It is a matter of personal interest to the rulers of the City in the Sky to know how things are with them.'

'What can you offer them?' Darl asked. 'You can't offer them the City.'

'By the Five Holy Ones, no! But there are things, artifacts, sacred relics, which they would be overjoyed to recover. Without human aid, they have no chance of regaining them. And I think those trinkets are a small price to pay for my City.'

'But what of your soul?' asked another youthful knight. 'They are evil — they are the soul of evil. How can you bargain with them?'

'They are not the *soul* of evil, friend. You know little of the Dark Ones if you think any earthly evil can surpass theirs.' The intensity of her feeling sent a shudder through her. 'I hate the Dark Ones and fear them more than you know. More than you can know. But I would sell myself to them . . .' Her listeners gasped and drew back. 'Yes, I would do that if it would free my City from Synalon. She seeks to return the City to the Dark Ones, then give them the entire world. Do you think my soul's too great a price to save your wives and friends and children from that?'

The young knight looked away. She swayed, suddenly weary to the point of collapse. She put one hand to the blood-flecked flank of Darl's dog. The other went, almost by instinct, to clutch the amulet within her bodice.

She felt a sudden impulse to tear it off and throw it into the clear, cold waters of the creek. It had brought nothing but doom and death. Then she recalled the high price she'd paid for the talisman and took her hand away.

'We must go,' she said.

A knight gave her a spare dog he'd caught fleeing the field. She mounted, casting a look at the sky. Its hue deepened inexorably to azure night.

They skirted the fringe of the wood when the bird rider squad swept over them like a glowing cloud from the guts of Omizantrim. The young knight who had led Darl to safety fell with an arrow through his back. Only Darl and Moriana made the shelter of the trees alive.

Moriana looked back. The Sky City troopers hadn't recognized them in the gloom. They passed once more over the bodies of their victims looking for signs of life. One figure stirred, trying to raise himself from the mud of the streambank. A sheaf of arrows drove him down face first.

Moriana clutched a fist and ground it against her forehead. Darl looked on, shaking his head numbly.

Turning their backs on the slaughter, they rode into the north. North to the Mystic Mountains and the last stronghold of the ancient enemies of humankind.

The Sleeper dreamed of battle. Armored figures on dogs fought across a valley bisected by a stream, shooting arrows, jabbing with lances, falling bloody and torn and dead. The battle surged, then great winged shapes appeared in the sky. One army broke and fled.

Istu felt pleased. It made his sleeping mind happy to think of the pale ones butchering each other. And in some dim corner of his subconscious he sensed that what he saw had meaning for him. It boded well.

The image changed. The blue and green banners fluttering from lances faded and were gone. In their place the demon dreamed of a gem, a huge, brilliant diamond. And black. Though it hung suspended in darkness as complete as that which enveloped him, it glowed with blackness more intense. The Sleeper sensed that this gem, too, was imprisoned not within walls of cold, solid stone but in a stone that flowed like liquid from heat.

He sensed the stone's pulsations. Even under intense heat and pressure it remained solid, its facets sharp and smooth. But he felt the rhythmic emanations of power and was soothed. The emanations pulsed in tempo with his own heart.

And a voice came to the demon in a dream, a voice unheard for a hundred centuries, a voice that wakened in the sleeping mind whatever a demon can feel of . . . love.

Soon, child it crooned. *Soon, beloved, soon.*

Content, the demon slept.

'We're too late,' said Fost, slumping in Grutz's saddle. The bear grunted in sympathy with his master's despair. 'The battle is already lost.'

Jennas made a bitter sound.

'No, 'tis won,' she said pointing. 'For them.' Her outstretched finger indicated the carrion crows gathered like mourners around the bodies. Fost smiled in grim appreciation. One side, the other side, human, dog, eagle – it was all the same to the vultures. Whatever misfortune befell others, they fed.

They rested their tired bears in a copse of trees beyond what had been the right flank of the Sky City army. The field lay deserted now, save for the dead – and the vultures.

They finally rode through the eerie stillness of dusk. Fost couldn't rid himself of the sensation that the limp bodies strewn so recklessly about would rise up at any instant with a friendly greeting or out-stretched hand of friendship. He was no stranger to death; he'd dealt it himself on occasion. But he had little experience with – and no stomach for – such wholesale slaughter.

He had been horrified at the carnage at the battles of the cliffs when he'd helped the Ust-alayakits defeat the Badger Clan and slay their evil shaman. That had been nothing compared to this. Together in a heap lay more men and women than lived in either Bear or Badger tribe. Fost shuddered. He wanted to throw up.

Though they kept careful watch, they saw no eagles. The bird riders were off chivvying the defeated, butchering the stragglers and the wounded. The wind babbled to itself of the sights it had witnessed that day, stirring fallen banners and mocking the dead.

Fost hoisted Erimenes' satchel high.

'See, old smoke,' he said. 'This is what your passion for bloodshed leads to. Shed blood, what else? Don't your nonexistent nerves pulse with excitement at the sight?'

Erimenes sniffed.

'What could I possibly find to excite me here? This is rubbish.'

Furious at the spirit's callousness, Fost swung the satchel up to dash the jug to pieces on the ground.

'No,' said Jennas. 'Let him be.'

Humbly, a little ashamed, Fost put the strap back over his shoulder and let the satchel fall back into its riding place.

Following the path the routed army and its pursuers had taken, they passed the hill with its crumpled pavilion and heard the sound of running water.

'I'm thirsty,' said Fost, 'and there were too many corpses in that stream back there for even the bears to touch the water. Let's see if this one is less clogged with dead.'

Jennas agreed. They rode toward the sound, at the same time angling toward a stand of trees well beyond the hill. Though none of the bird riders had shown themselves so far, neither felt like taking chances.

They were almost to the water when they heard the moan.

Without thinking, Fost booted Grutz's sides. The big bear rolled over the bank and into the water without breaking stride. The icy water numbed Fost's legs. He barely noticed it in his urgency.

Another sad knot of bodies lay in front of the trees. Dogs and men in the distinctive armor of the City States had been struck down by the equally distinctive arrows of the Sky City. The missiles protruded at angles that told they had come from above.

Fost pulled Grutz to a stop beside a young man who stirred feebly. His fingers raked furrows in the dirt. An arrow had penetrated his backplate and jutted with a horrible jauntiness from the center of his back, as if that was where in all the broad earth it belonged.

The knight had been trying to reach the stream. His first words to Fost confirmed this.

'Water. Need . . . need water.'

Fost sat on his haunches, considering. A stream of bloody spittle ran from the corner of the young man's mouth. Of the boy's mouth. He doubted if the youth was twenty.

'You're in a bad way,' said Fost, trying to remember his healing lore. 'I don't know if you should have water.'

'You don't honestly think it matters, do you, you dolt?' Erimenes said acerbicly from his jug.

Fost shrugged. The shade was right, though it surprised Fost that Erimenes had spoken. Compassion was not a trait he normally associated with the philosopher.

The young man drank greedily from Fost's water bottle. The courier held the man's head cradled in his lap as he drank. Jennas had arrived by this time and stood over them.

The young man coughed. The fit came on so violently that he jerked himself free of Fost's arms. Then to Fost's horror he fell backward onto the arrow still in him. His weight drove it deep and snapped off. He stiffened, coughed up bloody spittle, then sank back with a sigh, as though sliding into a warm and soothing bath.

Fost bit his lip. The young man's chest rose and fell raggedly.

'The princess,' he asked, hating himself for troubling the dying man. 'Do you know who I mean? The Princess Moriana.'

'Princess,' the boy nodded. He frowned then. 'Failed her. Failed her . . .'

Fost felt a cold black hand clamp shut his throat.

'She didn't . . . she's alive, isn't she?' he demanded. To his relief, the boy nodded. Then the youth grimaced as if the movement caused him pain. 'Where did she go?' The boy did not respond. By dint of effort, Fost kept himself from shaking the boy. 'Where did she go?' he asked again.

'The . . . three of them,' he said.

Fost frowned up at Jennas. 'Three?'

'Ah – aye. Princess, Lord Darl and . . . Great Ultimate, is it getting dark so soon? And the spirit . . . the woman in the jug . . .'

'Woman in a jug?' asked Jennas, as confused as Fost.

'It must be the spirit Guardian told us about,' said Fost, trying to remember more of what the glacier had said. Seeing Jennas' baffled look, he added, 'The glacier's name is Guardian. When we left Athalau, the glacier told us Moriana had a spirit jar with her. He said something about the spirit inside, but other matters pressed me then. Guardian had mistaken the other spirit for Erimenes. It put him into a fine rage.' Fost glanced at the blue form wavering by his elbow. Erimenes' face acquired a faraway look.

'A woman,' the spirit said musingly. 'As I live and breathe, a woman! This has interesting aspects I had not considered. Imagine, another such as I!'

'By Ust's snout,' muttered Jennas, 'one of you is more than enough. And you do *not* live and breathe.'

'A *woman!*' cried the philosopher. 'I can at last vindicate my teachings! What the two of us can do together . . .' The shade's substance glittered with dancing motes similar to those Fost had observed in Athalau. But the substance of his body didn't thicken. He took it for extreme agitation on Erimenes' part.

'Be quiet, you,' snapped Fost. 'This man is dying, and you rant on about another ghost.'

'Not just any other ghost, friend Fost,' crowed Erimenes. 'A female! I wonder if it might be possible that we . . .' His face glowed with a lechery so luminous it astonished even Fost.

'The boy, Fost, the boy is dying.'

Fost swallowed and turned back to the dying knight. He felt shame that Erimenes could carry on so. And he was no closer to finding what had happened to Moriana. He leaned close to the youth.

'Where did she go?' The boy did not respond. Fost dribbled water across the parched lips and asked again, 'Where-did-she-go?'

The young knight tried. In his fading mind he was glad that with his dying breath he could help his princess, the bright princess whom he and his friends had let down so badly.

'She went to . . .' His mind struggled to focus. 'Went to . . .'

Another coughing spell shook him. He sprayed bloody foam all over the front of Fost's tunic. Fost held his shoulders, trying to steady him.

The boy tried to say, 'To see the ones who built the City in the Sky,' but the coughing hit him again.

'To . . . City . . . Sky,' was all Fost Longstrider heard in the instant before the boy's head lolled back on lifeless muscles.

Gently he lowered the boy. He rose and looked at Jennas.

'The fool,' he moaned. 'She went back to the damned City.'

'And you will follow her.'

'And I'll follow,' said Fost. 'I'll follow.'

**Give them
the pleasure of choosing**

Book Tokens can be bought
and exchanged at most
bookshops in Great Britain
and Ireland.

DIRECT DESCENT
Frank Herbert

Earth was the archive of all learning, its small population dedicated to the endless task of finding and preserving new information, new truths. An isolated, sheltered haven, Earth was bound by Galactic charter to broadcast and make available freely to the entire galaxy the greatest resource of all – knowledge.

But then the warships came.

What good was truth against the guns of the military, the megalomania of the dictator, the crude violence of the ignorant? Trapped, defenceless, the archivists' only strategy was complete obedience to the oppressors. It seemed they could only save themselves by becoming slaves.

NEW ENGLISH LIBRARY

PZYCHE
Amanda Hemingway

On a desolate planet at the furthest rim of the galaxy lived Pzyche, brought up quite alone by her eccentric father Professor Corazin. Who preferred to carry on his lifelong research into the workings of the human mind quite unhindered by the disturbing presence of actual people.

Pzyche had learned much: history and legend, theory and practice. Her tutor and her sole occupation – father apart – was a computer. Which had taught her well, completely and correctly. She was happy and full of knowledge.

Until the day when quite unexpectedly, her younger sister arrived and Pzyche began to realise that, most disturbingly, knowledge is not the same as understanding. Until the day that she and her newly discovered sister realised that their quiet planet was now the target of a motley collection of cosmic adventurers, prospectors and villainous entrepreneurs.

In danger of losing her sanity, her virginity and even her life, Pzyche had to come to terms with the strange, oddly changeable, teasingly unpredictable habits and natures of humankind.

'this astonishingly assured first novel meshes with the mind long after first engagement . . . Miss Hemingway is a force to be reckoned with, not least in the art of fable-turning.' *The Times*.

NEW ENGLISH LIBRARY

The Best Short Stories of Fredric Brown	Fredric Brown	£1.75
The Song of Phaid the Gambler	Mick Farren	£1.95
Dragon's Egg	Robert L. Forward	£1.50
Dune	Frank Herbert	£2.50
Dune Messiah	Frank Herbert	£1.95
Children of Dune	Frank Herbert	£1.95
God Emperor of Dune	Frank Herbert	£2.50
Direct Descent	Frank Herbert	£2.25
Dragon in the Sea	Frank Herbert	£1.25
The Eyes of Heisenberg	Frank Herbert	£1.50
The Godmakers	Frank Herbert	£1.00
The Green Brain	Frank Herbert	£1.50
The Heaven Makers	Frank Herbert	£1.25
Santaroga Barrier	Frank Herbert	£1.25
Whipping Star	Frank Herbert	£1.25
The White Plague	Frank Herbert	£2.50
Pzyche	Amanda Hemingway	£2.50
Windhaven	George R.R. Martin & Lisa Tuttle	£1.50
The Brothel in Rosenstrasse	Michael Moorcock	£2.50
City of the Beast	Michael Moorcock	£1.25
Lord of the Spiders	Michael Moorcock	£1.50
Masters of the Pit	Michael Moorcock	£0.75
The War Hound And The World's Pain	Michael Moorcock	£2.50

NEL P.O. BOX 11, Falmouth TR10 9EN, CORNWALL

Postage Charge:
U.K. Customers 55p for the first book plus 22p for the second book and 14p for each additional book ordered to a maximum charge of £1.75.

B.F.P.O. & EIRE Customers 55p for the first book plus 22p for the second book and 14p for the next 7 books; thereafter 8p per book.

Overseas Customers £1.00 for the first book and 25p per copy for each additional book.

Please send cheque or postal order (no currency).

Name ....

Address..

....

Title ....

While every effort is made to keep prices steady, it is sometimes necessary to increase prices at short notice. New English Library reserve the right to show on covers and charge new retail prices which may differ from those advertised in the text or elsewhere.